2009
PUSHCART PRIZE XXXIII BEST OF THE SMALL PRESSES

EDITED BY BILL HENDERSON
WITH THE PUSHCART PRIZE EDITORS

Note: nominations for this series are invited from any small, independent, literary book press or magazine in the world, print or online. Up to six nominations—tear sheets or copies, selected from work published, or about to be published, in the calendar year—are accepted by our December 1 deadline each year. Write to Pushcart Press, P.O. Box 380, Wainscott, N.Y. 11975 for more information or consult our websites www.push-cartprize.com. or pushcartpress.org.

Acknowledgments

Selections for The Pushcart Prize are reprinted with the permission of authors and presses cited. Copyright reverts to authors and presses immediately after publication.

Distributed by W. W. Norton & Co.
500 Fifth Ave., New York, N.Y. 10110

Library of Congress Card Number: 76–58675
ISBN (hardcover): 978-1-888889-50-5
ISBN (paperback): 978-1-888889-51-2
ISSN: 0149–7863

For Raymond J. Smith (1930–2008)

INTRODUCTION

Every year our Pushcart Prize celebration breaks some sort of record—new national recognition, new presses, new writers, more pages. This year we broke the record for Contributing Editors: 227 of them (and consequently hundreds of new nominations) up from 26 editors in 1976. Back then Paul Bowles, Anaïs Nin, Ralph Ellison, Joyce Carol Oates and others became our first founding/contributing editors. Over the years hundreds more distinguished editors have made nominations, making Pushcart's prize the largest literary commune in contemporary history. I use "commune" in the 60's and 70's sense—nobody gets paid much and all work is for the common good.

It's the sort of selfless ideal that cutthroat media capitalism abhors. What possible good can emerge from a shaggy cooperative association? Well it turns out that the cutthroats are wrong. Take last year's lead story "Cartagena" by Nam Le from *A Public Space*, a new journal and a new writer. Nam Le, age 29, recently arrived in this country from Vietnam via Australia. "Cartagena" was one of Nam Le's first published stories. It's included in a collection, *The Boat*, just out from Knopf. (This year we feature another new writer, Katie Chase, for our lead story, from *The Missouri Review*. It's her first published fiction).

In interviewing Nam Le, the *New York Times* quoted him at length on the reasons and methods behind his acclaimed art. "I do believe that you can never know yourself, let alone the person next to you, let alone the person half way across the world. Yet at the same time, I believe there is nothing like fiction to fully thrust you into someone else's consciousness . . . the very attempt of stretching beyond one's own limited experience to me is a heroic thing and an incredibly hopeful thing."

Indeed! That's it! I said to myself. After 33 years of editing the Pushcart Prize I can think of no better summary for what we all try to do—reach out to other lives, and our own, not only in our fiction but also in our essays and poetry. It's a bit like compassion, like grace. And that to me is why all of this is so important in an often brutal and thoughtless world. As *Booklist*'s Donna Seaman put it in her review of last year's Pushcart: "intelligence, compassion and artistry are alive and well in America".

This edition of our Prize is dedicated to Raymond J. Smith, editor and publisher of *The Ontario Review* and Ontario Review Press, who died February 18, 2008 in Princeton at age 77.

Ray was one of those selfless people that keep small presses alive and give countless authors hope. He was a friend, mostly by mail and telephone in recent years, but in the 80's we raised a glass together on faculty nights out at a Chinese restaurant in a Princeton shopping mall. I was then a humble adjunct teacher surrounded by some of the heavyweights of the Princeton faculty. I remember how welcoming were Ray and his wife Joyce Carol Oates to the new kid at the mall.

I owe Ray big time in other ways and I told him so. Back in the fall of 1974, Ray published one of my early stories, "Pop", in the first issue of *Ontario Review*. For me this was huge. My stuff had been mostly rejected for over a decade (my favorite rejection was penned by *Esquire*'s Gordon Lish, "Sorry no!" barked Gordon). Ray's publication of "Pop" gave me a bit of faith in myself and when Martha Foley honored it as worthy of special notice in her *Best American Short Stories* I was finally lifted from a decade of discouragement. The next year I actually had the nerve to suggest to a roster of literary icons that we start something called the Pushcart Prize—all of this because Ray Smith gave me an excuse to hope by publishing my story. That's what small press editors do constantly every year and what I've never forgotten as an inspiration for this 33-year series.

Ray started *Ontario Review* in Windsor, Ontario in 1974 to feature 20th century Canadian and American writers "particularly those who have not received much critical attention". Later the *Review* moved to Princeton when Joyce joined the Princeton faculty (they were married for 47 years).

Ray worked mostly alone, unsung and preferring it that way. Among his authors: John Updike, Nadine Gordimer, Edmund White, Margaret Atwood, Annie Dillard, Donald Hall, C. K. Williams and

Russell Banks plus many others at the start of their writing lives. *Ontario Review* authors have won dozens of Pushcart recognitions over the years.

As I reported in this space last year, New York's Symphony Space and National Public Radio sponsored a terrific event in March for the Pushcart Prize—a reading by Alec Baldwin, Chris Lewin and James Naughton from three decades of PP fiction. It was heartening to learn that two of the three authors picked by Symphony Space (Andrew Porter and Stuart Dybek) were from *Ontario Review*. Ray learned of the selection only days before his death. A packed house listened to what Ray had originally discovered and the evening unfolded as a tribute to him.

Richard Burgin, editor of *Boulevard* and an *Ontario Review* author, said: "Ray Smith was one of the nicest, kindest, gentlest and wisest persons I've met. He was a wonderful and very modest man. How very much we need people like Ray in publishing and in the world."

Over the years Pushcart has been honored by the labors of over 50 poetry co-editors. New editors serve for each edition (their names are listed in "The People Who Helped" section). For last year's PPXXXII my friend Phil Schultz took on the impossible task with Ray Gonzalez. Phil, a neighbor, had published a few titles with Viking, Harcourt and State Street Press. Among them, *Like Wings, The Holy Worm of Praise, Living In the Past* and, in 2008, *Failure*, none of which earned back their slim advances, according to Phil. He garnered a Guggenheim, a Lamont and a Pushcart Prize. But this didn't prepare him for what transpired one morning at the Springs, Long Island dog park where we both walk our dogs and sometimes meet for strolls and chatter.

A long, rutted dirt road leads to the park. Phil and his border collie mutt Penelope were just setting forth when Phil saw his wife Monica and son Augie speeding down the road toward him in a dust cloud. "Somebody died," thought Phil. Augie bounded through the gate up to his Dad with a rehearsed tease. "Do you know who just won the Pulitzer Prize for fiction?" "No," said Phil. "Junot Diaz. Do you know who won the Pulitzer Prize for poetry?" asked Augie. "I haven't a clue," said Phil. "You did!" crowed the exuberant 8 year old. For the next few nights Phil didn't sleep much.

Phil shared the Pulitzer with Robert Hass, (poetry co-editor with

Jorie Graham of PPXII). The now much-decorated Phil, I might mention, is a very humble guy and very funny one—in fact, his next career should be as a stand up comic. In the meantime, we continue to walk our dogs with the expectation that even on gloomy days out of nowhere startling news can arrive in a dust cloud and the questions of a child.

The worth of prizes and honors is often debated. But prizes win readers. And prizes state unequivocally just what it is we value. And they change lives. Martha Foley showed me that.

Every year the Pushcart Prize receives from 7000–8000 nominations, about half of that poetry, and every year our new poetry editors tackle the job of narrowing that down to 30 poems for reprint and another 30 or so for special mention. This is a hard, heartbreaking job. (The same for prose.) Every year we need double the space for all that is worthy in poetry and prose.

Attempting the impossible this year were poetry co-editors Phillis Levin and Thomas Lux.

Tom Lux directed the MFA Poetry Program at Sarah Lawrence College for many years and is currently Bourne Professor of Poetry at Georgia Institute of Technology. He is the author of eleven volumes of poetry including two selected editions. His most recent titles are: *God Particles* (2008) and *The Cradle Place* (2004). He describes himself as "a born and bred New England Yankee, a citizen of Red Sox nation."

Phillis Levin is the author of four poetry collections—most recently *May Day* (Penguin, 2008). She's editor of *The Penguin Book of the Sonnet* and her poems have appeared in *Grand Street, Kenyon Review, Agni, The Nation, Poetry, Ploughshares, Paris Review, The New Yorker* and many anthologies. Her honors include: Fulbright and Guggenheim Fellowships and a NEA Grant. She teaches at Hofstra University and the graduate writing program at New York University.

So—reader—welcome to the 33rd Pushcart Prize. Welcome also to the new writers here (most of them still to be nationally hailed) and to our new presses—*Blueline, Ecotone, Epiphany, In Character*, and Wave Books. I am tempted to exclaim about every story, poem, memoir and essay that follows but such exclamations would require another book.

I am deeply and profoundly in debt to all of our nominating editors, the donors to our endowment (see page 577), and to you, astute reader. We do not lack for would-be writers today. We suffer from a hoard of print-on-demand vanity press authors and even more online effluvia—an abundance of would-be scribes in a big hurry to be noticed (speed is fatal to a serious writer). What we need today are dedicated, careful readers with compassion and a taste for the new. That's you, and I thank you.

BILL HENDERSON

THE PEOPLE WHO HELPED

FOUNDING EDITORS—Anaïs Nin (1903–1977), Buckminster Fuller (1895–1983), Charles Newman (1938–2006), Daniel Halpern, Gordon Lish, Harry Smith, Hugh Fox, Ishmael Reed, Joyce Carol Oates, Len Fulton, Leonard Randolph, Leslie Fiedler (1917–2003), Nona Balakian (1918–1991), Paul Bowles (1910–1999), Paul Engle (1908–1991), Ralph Ellison (1914–1994), Reynolds Price, Rhoda Schwartz, Richard Morris, Ted Wilentz (1915–2001), Tom Montag, William Phillips (1907–2002). Poetry editor: H. L. Van Brunt

CONTRIBUTING EDITORS FOR THIS EDITION—*Kim Addonizio, Carolyn Alessio, Dick Allen, Paul Allen, John Allman, Ralph Angel, Philip Appleman, Talvikki Ansel, Antler, Tony Ardizzone, Renee Ashley, David Baker, Jim Barnes, Kim Barnes, Tony Barnstone, Ellen Bass, Claire Bateman, Charles Baxter, Bruce Beasley, Marvin Bell, Pinckney Benedict, Molly Bendall, Linda Bierds, Diann Blakely, Robert Bly, Marianne Boruch, Laure-Anne Bosselaar, Michael Bowden, John Bradley, Rosellen Brown, Michael Dennis Browne, Jane Brox, Christopher Buckley, Andrea Hollander Budy, E. S. Bumas, Richard Burgin, Kathy Callaway, Bonnie Jo Campbell, Henry Carlile, Siv Cedering, Dan Chaon, Marianna Cherry, Kim Chinquee, Genie Chipps, Suzanne Cleary, Michael Collier, Billy Collins, Martha Collins, Joan Connor, Robert Cording, Stephen Corey, Michael Czyzniejewski, Philip Dacey, Claire Davis, Chard deNiord, Ted Deppe, Sharon Dilworth, Stuart Dischell, Steve Dixon, Rita Dove, Jack Driscoll, John Drury, Karl Elder, Angie Estes, Kathy Fagan, Ed Falco, Beth Ann Fennelly, Tom Filer, Gary Fincke, Ben Fountain,*

H.E. Francis, John Fulton, Kenneth Gangemi, Richard Garcia, Timothy Geiger, Reginald Gibbons, Gary Gildner, Ray Gonzalez, Linda Gregerson, Eamon Grennan, Marilyn Hacker, Rachel Hadas, Susan Hahn, Mark Halliday, Jeffrey Hammond, James Harms, Jana Harris, Jeffrey Harrison Michael Heffernan, Robin Hemley, Daniel Henry, DeWitt Henry, Bob Hicok, Kathleen Hill, Jane Hirshfield, Daniel Hoffman, Virginia Holmes, Helen H. Houghton, Christopher Howell, Andrew Hudgins, Joe Hurka, Colette Inez, Mark Irwin, Erica Keiko Iseri, Richard Jackson, David Jauss, Jeff P. Jones, Laura Kasischke, Deborah Keenan, George Keithley, Brigit Kelly, Thomas E. Kennedy, Kristen King, David Kirby, Joan Kistner, Judith Kitchen, Richard Kostelanetz, Maxine Kumin, Wally Lamb, Caroline Langston, Dorianne Laux, Nam Le, Sydney Lea, Fred Leebron, Dana Levin, Philip Levine, Daniel S. Libman, Gerry Locklin, Rachel Loden, Margaret Luongo, Paul Maliszewski, Clancy Martin, Sage Marsters, Michael Martone, Nicola Mason, Dan Masterson, Khaled Mattawa, Alice Mattison, Tracy Mayor, Robert McBrearty, Nancy McCabe, Rebecca McClanahan, Erin McGraw, Elizabeth McKenzie, Wesley McNair, Nadine Meyer, Jim Moore, Joan Murray, Kent Nelson, Kirk Nesset, Josip Novakovich, Joyce Carol Oates, Risteard O'Keitinn, Lance Olson, Dzvinia Orlowsky, Daniel Orozco, Pamela Painter, Alan Michael Parker, Benjamin Percy, Lucia Perillo, Donald Platt, Andrew Porter, Joe Ashby Porter, C. E. Poverman, Kevin Prufer, Lia Purpura, James Reiss, Nancy Richard, Atsuro Riley, David Rivard, Katrina Roberts, Jessica Roeder, Gibbons Ruark, Mary Ruefle, Vern Rutsala, Kay Ryan, Mary Ann Samyn, David St. John, Maureen Seaton, Alice Schell, Grace Schulman, Philip Schultz, David Schuman, Lloyd Schwartz, Salvatore Scibona, Gerald Shapiro, Reginald Shepherd, Floyd Skloot, Arthur Smith, R.T. Smith, Anna Solomon, Debra Spark, Elizabeth Spires, Maura Stanton, Maureen P. Stanton, Patricia Staton, Gerald Stern, Pamela Stewart, Teresa Svoboda, Joan Swift, Ron Tanner, Katherine Taylor, Susan Terris, Robert Thomas, Jean Thompson, Melanie Rae Thon, Pauls Toutonghi, Natasha Trethewey, Deb Olin Unferth, Lee Upton, Dennis Vannatta, Nance Van Winckel, G.C. Waldrep, B.J. Ward, Rosanna Warren, Sylvia Watanabe, Mary Yukari Waters, Michael Waters, Charles H. Webb, Roger Weingarten, William Wenthe, Philip White, Dara Wier, Eleanor Wilner, S.L. Wisenberg, Mark Wisniewski, David Wojahn, Robert Wrigley, Tiphanie Yanique, Matt Yurdana, Christina Zawadiwsky, Paul Zimmer

CONTENTS

13

MAN AND WIFE

fiction by KATIE CHASE

from THE MISSOURI REVIEW

THEY SAY every girl remembers that special day when everything starts to change.

I was lying under the tree in my parents' backyard, an oak old enough to give shade but too young to be climbed, when Dad's car pulled into the garage. All afternoon I'd been riding bikes with Stacie, but we had a fight when she proposed we play in my basement—it *was* getting too hot out, but I was convinced she was only using me for my Barbies. This was eight years ago. I was nine and a half years old.

Dad came out and stood in the driveway, briefcase in hand, watching me pull up grass. "Mary Ellen!"

I yanked one final clump, root and dirt dangling from my hands, and sat up.

"Come inside. I have wonderful news."

In the kitchen Dad was embracing my mother, his arms around her small, apron-knotted waist. "I can't believe it went through," she was saying. She turned to me with shiny eyes, cleared her throat, and said in her sharp voice, "Mary, go get down the good glasses."

I pushed a chair to the cupboards and climbed onto the countertop. Two glass flutes for my parents, and for myself a plastic version I'd salvaged from last New Year's, the first time I'd been allowed, and encouraged, to stay up past midnight and seen how close the early hours of the next day were to night.

Dad took down the last leftover bottle of champagne and popped it open, showering the kitchen floor. My mother laughed and wiped her hands on her polka-dotted apron, as if she'd gotten wet.

"Hold up your glass, Mary Ell," said Dad. He filled it halfway, and theirs to the rim. When in the past I'd been curious about alcohol, my parents had frowned, taken a drink, and feigned expressions of disgust. On New Year's, for instance, my cup had held plain orange juice, and the next morning, while my parents still slept, I'd had orange juice in it again.

"A toast." My mother held up her glass and waited.

I waited, too. The champagne fizzed, bubbles rising.

"To Mary," said Dad, and then he stopped, choked up.

"Our own little girl, to be a woman," my mother said. "Bottoms up."

They clinked their glasses together, and mine met theirs dully, with a tap that brought an end to the pleasant ringing they'd created. I brought the champagne to my lips. I found that, if ingested in small sips, it was quite drinkable, no worse than my mother's Diet Coke, and it had the welcome effect of making me feel I was floating away.

"Don't you want to hear what the big news is?" said Dad. My mother turned her back on us to the cutting board, where she was chopping a fresh salad.

In a small voice I said, "Yes." I tried to smile, but that feeling was in my stomach, made more fluttery by drink. I recognize the feeling now as a kind of knowledge.

"Well, do you remember Mr. Middleton? From Mommy and Daddy's New Year's party?"

At the party I'd been positioned, in scratchy lace tights and a crinoline-skirted dress, at the punch bowl to ladle mimosas for their guests. Many of their friends introduced themselves to me that night: Mr. Baker, Mr. Silverstein, Mr. Weir. Some bent to my height and shook my hand. Mr. Woodward scolded me for insufficiently filling his cup, and his young wife, Esmerelda, my former babysitter, led him away.

"Mr. Middleton—that nice man with the moustache? You talked together for quite some time."

Then I remembered. As I served other guests, he'd lingered with a glass of sweating ice water, talking about his business. He directed his words to the entire room, looking out over it rather than at me, but he spoke quietly, so only I could hear. He offered figures: annual revenue, percentages, the number of loyal clients. And then: "My business is everything. It is my whole life." I looked up at him curiously, and his face reddened; his moustache twitched. When he fi-

18

nally left, patting my shoulder and thanking me for indulging him, I was relieved. I'd had little to say in return—no adult had ever spoken to me that way—and I'd felt the whole time, on the tip of my tongue, the remark that might have satisfied and gotten rid of him sooner.

"That's the good news," Dad said. "He's gone ahead and asked for your hand. And we've agreed to it."

My mother put down the knife and finished off her champagne. I wanted no more of mine.

"Well, don't be so excited," said Dad. "Do you understand what I'm saying? You're going to be a wife. You're going to live with Mr. Middleton, and he's going to take care of you, for the rest of your life. And, one day, when we're very old, he'll help out your mother and me, too."

"Yep." He smiled. "It's all settled. Just signed the contract this afternoon. You'll really like him, I think. Nice man. You seemed to like him at the party, anyhow."

"He was okay," I managed. It was as I'd feared, somewhere, all along: the toast, the party, everything. But now he had a face, and a name. Now it was real: my future was just the same as any other girl's. Yet none of my friends had become wives yet, and it didn't seem fair that I should be the first taken. For one thing, I was too skinny. They say men first look for strength in a wife. Next they look for beauty, and even with braces and glasses yet to come, I was a homely little girl. It's last that men look for brains. You may notice that I skipped over wealth. While rumors of sex spread freely at school, it wasn't clear to me then just how money fit in. It was discussed only in negotiations, when lawyers were present and we were not. It was best that way for our parents, who tried to keep such things separate.

At dinner I pushed the food around on my plate, clearing a fork-wide path and uncovering the blue-and-white pattern of little people kneeling in rice fields and pushing carts. My mother was on her third glass of champagne—she wouldn't last through *Jeopardy!*—and she was laughing at everything Dad said about his anxious day at the office.

A timer buzzed, and my mother rose from the table to pull out her raspberry pie. She approached me with the dish clasped in her oven mitts.

"Take a good look at that pie, Mary."

The crust was golden brown, its edges pressed with the evenly spaced marks of a fork prong. Sweet red berries seeped through the three slits of a knife.

"It's perfect," she said, with her usual ferocity.

The next morning Stacie acted like our fight hadn't happened, and I wanted to play along. We went to ride bikes while my mother showered. Dad's car had left already for work, and he'd dragged the garbage out to the curb. The champagne bottle poked from the recycling bin, ready to be taken away. It was another summer day.

"We had a celebration last night," I told Stacie. "Dad let me have booze."

"Oh, yeah? What for?" She pedaled ahead and moved onto the street, which her parents, and mine, forbade.

I had to shout, she was so far ahead. "Someone named Mr. Middleton wants to take me."

Stacie slammed on her brakes and turned her bike to face me. Once caught up, I kept going.

"When?" she demanded, appearing alongside. "You know he can't take you yet."

"Why not?" I said, but I assumed, as did Stacie, that there'd be a long period of engagement. In the fall we were to start the fifth grade, and it was rare for a girl still in elementary to be taken.

"He must really like you," Stacie said, in awe. We pedaled slowly, pensively. "But you're so skinny."

Mrs. Calderón, in her silken robe, was out watering her rose bushes. She waved.

"We'd better get on the sidewalk," I said.

When we reached Maple Court, we laid our bikes on the island and sprawled in the warm grass, making daisy chains from the flowering weeds. Stacie put her hand on my arm. It was rare for us to touch.

"Whatever happens," she said, "don't dump me."

"What do you mean?"

"I mean, ever since my sister went to live with Mr. Gordon, she never plays with me anymore. When she comes over she just sits in the kitchen with my mom drinking tea." She rolled her eyes. "They talk about recipes, and my mom gives her a frozen casserole that she pretends to Mr. Gordon she made by herself."

"Okay," I said. "I promise."

She held up her pinkie, and I joined it with mine.

20

"I promise, when I live with Mr. Middleton, you can still come over and play Barbies."

"Not just Barbies," she said. "We'll still play everything. We'll still be best friends."

I hadn't even been sure we were best friends, since during school she spent her time with ratty-haired Cassandra and I, in protest, with the studious Chan twins. But I remained solemn. Maybe she wasn't using me. Besides, although I couldn't really imagine what it would be like to be a wife, I knew I wouldn't want to be stuck with Mr. Middleton all the time. I began to laugh.

"What?"

"He has the stupidest moustache!" I drew a thin line above my mouth with my finger, sweeping up at the edges, to indicate the way it curled.

"Probably, you can make him shave it off. My sister makes Mr. Gordon wear socks all the time, so she doesn't have to see his feet."

Stacie picked apart her chain and let the flowered weeds fall—she had a theory they could again take root. I wore mine around my wrist but lost it during the ride back. My mother was still in the bathroom, the mingled scent of her products floating out beneath the door.

After serving us tuna-and-pickle sandwiches, my mother sent Stacie home.

"But why?"

"Shhh," she said. "I need to talk to you."

I folded my arms across my chest and glared at her.

"Don't," she said. "Just don't. Come here with me."

In the living room, she sat and patted the couch beside her. The television wasn't on, which made the room feel too still and too quiet, like nothing happened in it when we weren't around.

"Now, I know Daddy explained that you're going to be a wife. But do you know what that means?"

I refused to look at her, though I could feel her eyes on my face. "Yeah. I'll go live with Mr. Middleton. I'll have to make him dinner."

"Yes," she said. "But you'll have to do more than that."

"Can I still play Barbies with Stacie? I promised her."

"You did, did you."

I nodded. I told my mother everything that Stacie had said. It made me proud that she was jealous, and I thought it would make my mother proud, too.

"I'm sorry to say, it's really up to Mr. Middleton when, and if, you can play with your friends. And he may not appreciate you, still just a little girl, telling him to shave off his moustache. He's had that thing for years." She halted a creeping smile. "What I'm trying to say is, you'll belong to him. You'll have to be very obedient—not that you haven't always been a good girl. Your father and I are very proud of you. You get such good grades and stay out of trouble."

She paused, frowning. "I don't think you realize just how lucky you are that Mr. Middleton has offered to take you. He's a very successful man, and he's made quite a generous offer, for little in return." She patted my leg. "I don't mean you, of course. Any man would be lucky to have you. But to be honest, I'm not sure why he's so eager to settle it."

I stared at the black television screen. "Can I go to Stacie's now?"

"Wait. We're not through." She stood and approached the bookshelf. On days when I stayed home sick, I'd lie on the couch and stare at that bookshelf. Each book's spine, its title and design, suggested something of its story, and their order and arrangement seemed fixed, like the sequencing of photographs along the hallway wall: from my parents' wedding—my mother thirteen and Dad twenty-seven—to the day of my birth to my fourth-grade class picture. But as my mother took out the Bible and a few romance paperbacks, I saw that behind them were more books, a whole hidden row; the shelf was deeper than I'd realized. She removed from hiding a slim volume called *Your Womanly Body*, its cover decorated in butterflies and soft-colored cut flowers blooming in vases.

"This will tell you *some* of what you need to know about being a wife. I imagine Mr. Middleton won't expect much from you at first. After all, you're still very young."

I began to turn the pages: there were cartoons of short and tall and skinny and fat women, their breasts different sizes and weights, with varying colors and masses of hair between their legs. The pictures weren't a shock to me. I'd seen my mother naked before, and Stacie had confirmed that her own looked much the same. Once I'd even seen Dad, when I surprised him by waiting outside the bathroom door for a Dixie cup of water late one night.

"You'll have a child someday, of course. But most people like to wait until they're older and know each other better. I, for instance, had you when I was eighteen. By today's standards, that's still a little young."

"It can be scary, at first." My mother's voice had turned soft, and she was staring out the window at the tree. "The important thing to remember is, even though he's in charge, you can have some control. Pay close attention: what he wants the most may be very small, and you can wait out the rest."

I already knew there were ways to put off sex: some girls "sucked" their husbands "off," others cried until left alone. And if a girl did become pregnant too soon, if it would be unseemly for her to keep the baby, I knew there were ways to get rid of it. But still, I'd rather not think about all that before I had to face it.

My mother was saying, "A man's life is spent waiting and preparing for the right girl. It can be very lonely. In a way, girls have it easy—"

"Mommy, when will I go live with Mr. Middleton?"

"I was getting to that, Mary. You can be so impatient." She lifted the book from my hands and turned to put it away. "You'll be going to him in the fall."

"Oh." I stared down at my bare summer feet, callused, tan and dirty. "After school starts?"

"Mary. There'll be no school for you this fall. You'll have a house to take over."

The feeling was back in my stomach, more of an ache now, and all I wanted was to curl up on the couch while my mother brought Jell-O and chicken-noodle soup. On sick days you could escape the movement of the world. It was always difficult to get back into it, to catch up on schoolwork and eat real food again, but this time I wasn't sure I ever wanted to rejoin the world.

Yet the books were different now. I wouldn't be able to not think about that.

"Of course, he'll probably let you go back soon. He'll want you to. That's what Mr. Middleton told us—that he admired your mind. He said he could tell you're a very bright girl."

"I should be so lucky," she added darkly. "Your father only saw my strength."

It became routine for Mr. Middleton to spend Sunday afternoons with us. At dawn my mother yanked open all the blinds, and the acrid smells of house-cleaning began to fill the rooms. Even Dad was kept from sleeping in and given chores to do. I was ushered straight into the kitchen: "Do me one little favor," she said.

"Knead this dough. No, like this. Punch it, like you're pissed off."

23

"Check the stove. Has it reached the preheated temperature? Well, is it hot?"

"Okay, now we'll let that marinate. You know what's in this marinade? Just smell it—what does it smell like?"

Once I had completed my mother's "favor" ("Umm, it smells sweet." "Good! That's the honey."), I snuck out while her back was turned.

I was to be scrubbed "my pinkest" in the shower. She showed me how to use Q-tips to clean out my ears, to rub lotion over my skin, and to pluck the little hairs I hadn't noticed before from between my eyebrows. She swore under her breath when she nicked me with the pink disposable razor—my legs slathered in a thick gel that smelled like baby powder. "Here," she said. "You finish."

I slid the blade along my leg, pressing as lightly as possible.

I was to wear "one of my prettiest dresses," which meant that I rotated between the three in my closet. Their straps dug into my shoulders, their crinoline scratched my bare legs. The first Sunday my mother threw onto my bed a package from Sears. Inside were three training bras. I didn't have anything resembling breasts, and when I finally did, years into my marriage, they were so small that I continued to wear the trainers for some time. My husband didn't seem to care or know the difference.

Every Sunday had the feel of a holiday—the boredom of waiting for the guest to arrive and the impatience of waiting for him to leave. Mr. Middleton always brought a bouquet of flowers, at the sight of which I was to feign surprise and gratitude. Every week, the same grocery-store assortment of wildflowers that smelled rank and bitter, like weeds. Mr. Middleton sat with my father in the living room while I trimmed and arranged the flowers in my mother's crystal vase. She had me stir something or taste it for salt before nudging me back out to join them.

Mr. Middleton would wear a full suit and tie, despite the fact that our house had no air conditioning. As the afternoon wore on, he would take off the suit jacket, loosen and remove the tie, roll up the sleeves of the dress shirt and, lastly, undo the shirt's top button, revealing a tuft of dark, curly hair. The hair on his head was straight, and he'd run a hand through it, slicking it back with his sweat. Dad, in a short-sleeved polo shirt and khaki shorts, would watch, smiling to himself. My shaven skin felt cool and smooth. I had to stop myself from running my hands along my legs as I sat listening to them talk "business." Their tone was cordial, but they seemed to eye each other warily. I didn't consider it then, but Dad was likely sensitive to the fact that while he had to report to a boss, Mr. Middleton was his own.

"How's business?"

"Business is good. You?"

"Business is good. Clients?"

"Clients are good. Got to treat them right, keep them happy," Dad said.

"Of course."

In and out of the room bustled my mother. She refilled the pitcher of lemonade, replenished the dish of melting ice cubes, brought out bowls of mixed nuts and pretzels and onion dip. Before long, this became my job. I'd stand before Mr. Middleton with a tray of pickles and olives.

"Hmm, let's see." He'd mull over the choices, select a pimento-stuffed green olive. I'd turn to offer the tray to Dad, who had a penchant for sweet pickles, but then: "Please, wait just a moment— perhaps another. Hmm, let's see." And he'd choose a kalamata. The metal tray was heavy, but my arms grew stronger, and I learned to balance it on my shoulder.

Mr. Middleton rarely addressed me directly. Which is not to say he wasn't speaking to me. "Profit margins" and "quarterly analyses" were discussed with glances and smiles in my direction. But he never asked what I thought, how I was doing, how I had spent my week. Adults, I knew, just liked to humor children, and ordinarily those questions tired me, causing me to clam up on the pretense of feeling shy. But in this situation it was disconcerting. After all, wasn't Mr. Middleton supposed to like me? What were we going to say to each other when we were, one day, inevitably, alone? I knew I would be expected to say something; wives, especially as they grew up, didn't have to be invited to speak. They scolded their husbands for things they were doing wrong, or weren't doing at all. They had stories to tell, of what had happened that day at the market, of the rude cashier and the unmarked price of the fresh loaf of bread.

For then, I followed my mother's advice the best I could. I wouldn't speak unless spoken to. I sat up straight in the chair, didn't complain if the food at dinner was strange, didn't ask to turn on the television. I paid close attention to Mr. Middleton; I focused on his moustache, the way it moved with his mouth, studied the shine of his gold watch, viewed the gradual stripping of clothing, the sweat gathering on his forehead and alongside his nose, where his glasses slid. I suppose I may have already been following my mother's advice, but I don't remember thinking so. I never liked to admit I was doing as she suggested. I preferred to credit my own volition.

Mr. Middleton seemed to me older than my father, though he was almost a decade younger. Dad was strict, but he could be silly, wasn't afraid to be lazy, and had been known to watch cartoons that even I found stupid. Mr. Middleton was too polite and too proper. He was boring in the way a robot would be: never leaving to go to the bathroom, never saying anything Dad disagreed with or found ridiculous. They would have had much to argue about—they do now—their strategies in business so different: Dad doting on his clients, trying to keep them pleased each step of the way, Mr. Middleton acting with cool aggression against their wishes, with the long run in mind, the biggest possible profit. I suppose we were all on our best behavior.

By dinnertime the business talk had faltered, and the men punctuated their silence with compliments for the meal—something Dad never did when it was just the three of us. This was when my mother took over. "Thank you," she might say. "Mary Ellen helped prepare that."

"Did she? It's quite good," said Mr. Middleton.

"Oh, she's learning. Believe it or not, just a month ago even something this simple would have been beyond her."

Mr. Middleton smiled politely and chewed, his moustache moving up and down, a piece of couscous caught in the right-side curl.

"There is still so much for her to learn, I'm afraid. You mustn't—you mustn't expect too much, from the start."

"But of course Donna will get her up to speed," said Dad. "Won't you, honey?"

"Of course," my mother said. "All I meant was, Mary is such a fast learner. Why, just the other day the sauce was starting to stick, and instead of letting it burn or calling me, she just turned down the burner and gave it a stir. How about that?"

The heat from the kitchen was creeping into the dining room, and a bead of sweat slipped down Mr. Middleton's forehead. His top button, at that point, remained done. He offered nothing but another polite smile. Maliciously, I wanted, in front of everyone, to call attention to the couscous still in his moustache. "Right there," I'd interrupt, pointing to a spot above my own lip. This was something a wife

26

could do, scold or embarrass her husband for his own good. But I knew I hadn't earned it yet, and it would take years of waiting, quietly noting.

Mr. Middleton seemed oblivious to my parents' fears and cover-ups, but I've come to see that he was not, nor was he too polite to lead the conversation elsewhere. I can look back now with some sympathy. I can see myself in him: he was determined to behave in the way that was expected, in the belief, often false but sometimes accurate, that this gave him some autonomy. And after all, he was getting what he wanted.

One Saturday afternoon Mr. Middleton showed up while my parents were out. They were leaving me home alone more often in preparation for the days when I'd be keeping house, with Mr. Middleton off at work. Usually I found myself frozen, unable to act as I would if my parents were around. I had a great fear of doing something wrong, either accidentally (opening the door to a dangerous stranger or coming upon some matches, which would inadvertently scratch against something and become lit, igniting a raging fire) or purposely, overcome by the thrill of risk. The only way to ensure this wouldn't happen was to remain on the couch until they came back.

At the sound of a knock at the door, I lifted a slat of blind and peered out at Mr. Middleton: no flowers in hand, no suit and tie. He wore blue jeans and sports sandals, a polo shirt like those Dad owned. His arms were covered in those dark, curly hairs. Through the peephole his nose was made long by the curved glass, and his moustache twitched nervously. It gave me a small thrill, making him wait. Just as he began to back away, I did as I should and opened the door.

"Mary Ellen. What a pleasant surprise."

"Hello," I said politely. "Would you like to come in?"

He looked down the block, both ways. It was quiet for a Saturday. Only Mrs. Calderón was out, pruning her blooming roses. She'd recently explained to me that she had to cut them back so they could grow. Mr. Middleton smiled in her direction and entered the house.

"I'm home alone," I said. It seemed best if I made that clear right away.

"I won't stay long. You see, I was just in the neighborhood and thought I'd drop by."

That was reasonable to me, but it seemed out of character for Mr.

Middleton, who operated purely, I thought, on formality and routine. "Would you like a glass of iced tea with lemon?" I asked.

"No, thank you."

He wasn't sitting, so I didn't sit, unaware that I might have offered him a seat. The expression on his face was, as always, neutral, and he didn't return my stare. I felt I was doing something grossly wrong—I was still unfit to be a wife, unable to handle company on my own. My mother would scold me if she knew I'd received him in a T-shirt from last year's spelling bee and purple shorts stained with Kool-Aid.

I tried again. "How's business?"

He smiled and lowered himself to my height, his hands coming to rest on his knees. "Very well, thank you," he said. "But today, you see, I was thinking of you. I thought you might like to show me your Barbies."

No adult had ever asked to see them, and, to my knowledge, they'd never been mentioned in his presence. My mother allowed no visitors, other than my friends, into the basement. She had warned me that the Barbies would have to go when I went to Mr. Middleton. To head off my tears, Dad had added quietly that perhaps, for a while, they could leave them set up in the basement for when I came to visit.

I watched for some sign in Mr. Middleton that he was joking or only humoring me, but he reached out a hairy arm and took my hand. His wasn't sweaty, though the day was muggy and humid, and his skin was surprisingly soft. On the narrow stairway he didn't let go; my arm strained and pulled behind me as I led him into the basement. His knees cracked as he took the stairs.

The basement was unfinished, just hard tiles, exposed beams and many-legged insects. Stacie complained about the centipedes, but they appeared less often than the spiders. Strips of sunlight came in through the windows along the driveway, where you could see feet pass on their way to the side door.

Mr. Middleton dropped my hand and approached the Barbies' houses slowly, as if in awe. The toys sprawled from one corner of the room to the other, threatening to take over even the laundry area; the foldout couch, which I maintained took up valuable space, some-times served as a mountain to which the Barbies took the camper. There was one real Barbie house, pink and plastic; it had come with an elevator that would stick in the shaft, so I had converted the ele-vator to a bed. The other Barbie home was made of boxes and old bathroom rugs meant to designate rooms and divisions; this was the one Stacie used for her family. The objects in the houses were a mixture of real Barbie toys and other adapted items: small beads served as food, my mother's discarded tampon applicators were the legs of a cardboard table. On a Kleenex box my Barbie slept sideways, facing Ken's back; both were shirtless, her plastic breasts against him.

Mr. Middleton asked about the construction and decoration of the rooms. He said he admired my reuse of materials. "A creative way to cut costs," he noted.

I shrugged. "Mom and Dad won't buy me anything else."

He nodded thoughtfully. "You work well within limits."

"I guess," I said, but I was pleased. He was admiring my mind.

"Well, you have quite a talent for design—I've seen professional blueprints more flawed." He suggested that in the future we might have a home built, one I could help plan.

Then he leaned down and stroked Barbie's back with his index finger. "Do they always sleep this way?" he asked.

I blushed and only shook my head. Sometimes they lay entirely naked, as my parents slept. Sometimes Barbie slept on top of Ken, or vice versa.

"Can you show me another way they might sleep?" he asked.

I hesitated, then picked up the dolls and put their arms around each other's bodies in a rigid hug. I tilted Barbie's head and pressed her face against Ken's, as if they were kissing, and laid them back atop the Kleenex box. Mr. Middleton watched with his detached interest.

"Your Barbies must love each other very much," he observed.

I'd never really thought about it that way. They were just doing what my parents and people on television did because they were married. But sometimes, when I was alone, it gave me that fluttery, almost sick feeling deep in my stomach, and I took the dolls apart.

Mr. Middleton stood and turned away. He held up his wrist to the sun strip, examining his watch, for what seemed a long time. "Well, thank you for sharing them with me. But I should be on my way."

I nodded, then recovered my manners. "Can I walk you to the door?"

"No, thank you, Mary Ellen. I'll show myself out."

On Sundays he'd shake my parents' hands before he left, and now I wondered if I should offer mine. But instead he reached out and patted me on the head, once, twice, then the last time just smoothing my hair, as my mother would to fix a stray strand, but much gentler.

When I heard the front door close, I knelt in front of the Barbie house. It was difficult, as my Ken's arms were straight, not bent like some, but I moved his arm so that it stroked Barbie's back. I startled when my mother called from the top of the stairs. I hadn't seen feet in the windows or heard a key in the door.

I didn't tell them that Mr. Middleton had been over, and the next day when he came for Sunday dinner he didn't mention it either. It didn't occur to me until years later that the whole thing might have been prearranged. I could find out now; Mr. Middleton tells me anything I ask. He may tease, but he knows when to stop. It's quite possible he's even learned to fear me. For all his skill in the world of business, I think he understands less about the world without than I do.

That September, with Stacie back at school, my days were spent alone with my mother. She was nervous about the upcoming ceremony and would sit with me at the kitchen table for hours with catalogues of flowers and dresses.

"Do you like these roses? Or something more unique—orchids? But so expensive."

I would shrug. "It doesn't matter."

Depending on her mood, she would either become angry ("If it doesn't matter to you, who does it matter to? Pick out some flowers!") or take my reticence as deference to what she thought was best ("The orchids are lovely, but we'd best be practical, hmm?").

Once, paging together through pictures of dresses, she became so frustrated with me that she disappeared into the bathroom for almost an hour. Finally I knocked on the door. "Mommy? I left it open to the one I like." I heard water running, and when she came out she caught me around the shoulders and held me against her, my face nuzzling her stomach. "That's my good girl," she whispered above my head.

One afternoon was spent sewing, another polishing silver. The cooking lessons took on new vigor, and she had me reducing wine-based sauces, braising meats, and chopping fresh herbs for most of the day. Dad would come home, see everything that had been set out on the table and everything that still simmered on the stove and roasted in the oven, throw his hands up in the air and say, "I don't know how you expect us to consume all this, Donna. Maybe you could lay off her a bit." But then he'd sit down and attack the food with an appetite that had the air of duty, sighing and unbuttoning his pants for dessert.

Stacie came over after school a couple of times a week, but she brought Cassandra; the Chan twins had forsaken me, believing my imminent wifehood to have changed me already. With only two Barbie houses, Stacie, Cassandra, and I couldn't play together fairly. Besides, I didn't want Cassandra and her ratty hair anywhere near them. Instead we sat on the porch eating gingersnaps—just talking and not playing anything. Other girls who'd been promised spent their time in this way.

Cassandra wanted to hear about Mr. Middleton. She believed her parents to be sealing up a deal with a Mr. Crowley from the neighboring town. I recounted Mr. Middleton's afternoon visit to sate her interest and swore them to secrecy. They didn't seem particularly impressed or unnerved. I yearned for either response, to anchor my own.

"Well, is he cute?" Cassandra asked, twirling a dishwater-blond lock.

I didn't know how to answer her. Unlike Stacie and me, Cassandra had always liked boys—but husbands were not like boys. I didn't know how to make her understand what it was really like, but I also had the feeling that Cassandra would handle things much differently when it was her turn. I was thankful when Stacie changed the subject to school, with stories of pencils stolen from the teacher's desk and guest story-readers, even though they made me both wistful and angry, and Stacie knew it.

The night before the ceremony, my parents entertained their friends with chilled rosé wine and a CD of lulling, smooth jazz on repeat. My mother dusted my cheekbones with her dark blush and checked my back to make sure I wore a trainer. I was to greet guests at the door until everyone had arrived, and then Stacie and I could retreat to the basement to play Barbies together one last time. According to tradition, Mr. Middleton was not invited; it was to be his last bachelor night alone. But Mr. Woodward and Esmerelda came, and Mr. Silverstein, and Stacie's and Cassandra's parents, eager to know how it had all been pulled off. Mr. Baker said, as if surprised, "You look very pretty tonight, Mary Ellen," and then he and Mr. Weir stood together in the corner, shaking their heads. The Calderóns arrived last. Mr. Calderón was so old his eyes constantly watered, and he could barely speak or hear anything. Mrs. Calderón was a young grandmother, her braided hair still long and black. She bent to me and whispered, "You're not getting cold feet now, are you dear?"

"Cold feet?" I asked. I peered down at my slipper socks, embarrassed I'd removed the Mary Janes.

"I tried to run away from this one." She winked at her husband, but his expression didn't change. "But then, I always misbehaved."

Mr. Calderón held tight to her arm, and she guided him patiently toward the drinks. She kissed his shaking hand, then placed a glass of water in it.

In the basement, adult feet shifting above us, I understood that Mrs. Calderón had been saying that she knew me and that she understood. From tomorrow on, that would be me upstairs, like Esmerelda and even my mother, laughing a stupid laugh and making frequent trips to the bathroom, with an eye on my husband and his eye on me. Mrs. Calderón had issued me a playful dare and made no promises; but if it was the last childlike thing I did, I would take her up on it.

"Stacie, I need your help."

She stopped pushing her Barbie car, a convertible she'd acquired from me in a trade, and said with suspicion, "You do?"

As I explained what I wanted to do, Stacie's eyes began to gleam. At one point she took my hand. I felt close to her, until she said, "You won't be married first after all!" But still she was my confidante, my partner with her own stake.

What we came up with wasn't much of a plan, but we did identify the basic elements required in running away: a note, a lightly packed suitcase, and utter secrecy. My mother had already packed most of my clothes into a luggage set embroidered with my new initials, M. M. I removed the lightest bag from the pile by the side door and had Stacie sneak it back home with her. After slipping away, having deposited the note in a spot both clandestine and sure to be eventually discovered, I would call Stacie from a pay phone and have her meet me with the suitcase. For this purpose, I used my new skills to sew a quarter into the hem of my dress, which hung, long and white, like a ghost, outside my closet door.

Beneath the covers with a flashlight that night, I composed the note to Mr. Middleton. I could not tell him, as they did in fantasy romance movies, that I had met someone else. What I wrote was this:

32

Dear Mr. Middleton,

I am sorry to leave you at the alter. You seem very nice but I can not be a wife. Please do not try to find me and please try to go on with your life.

Mary Ellen

I thought it sounded quite grown-up and made running away on cold feet seem a serious and viable act. I wasn't worried that we had-n't decided where I would go. I didn't consider then that I knew of no woman who was not a wife, that anyone I might turn to would turn me in, that breach of contract was serious business and punish-able by law. I believed two things: that getting away would be the hardest part of the game, and that you could only plan as far as you could see. I don't know if I believed that I would make it, but I be-lieved that I would try.

I might have left that very night, cutting Stacie's ties to my ven-ture, but I had a romantic notion of wearing that dress. I pictured kicking off the white patent-leather shoes to run faster, and the small train flailing behind me. I pictured that the dress would dirty as I ran; it would rip and tear, and then I would know I was free.

When we arrived at the chapel, I spied Mr. Middleton's car in the parking lot. During a covert trip to the "potty," I slipped the note be-neath its windshield wipers. It had always made me laugh that my parents never noticed an advertisement attached in this way until they were driving.

In the bride's room, Dad, his eyes shiny and red-rimmed, was smoothing out the fold from the contract, to which my signature was to be added. "Why don't you go sit down, Frank?" my mother sug-gested, but she stayed with me, adjusting my dress and hairspraying my hot-roller curls, until the final moments. She hovered in the door-way. "You are wearing, aren't you, all the things we talked about? You remember how it goes? Something old, something new, something borrowed, something blue, and a silver sixpence for your shoe?"

"I remembered," I said, thinking of the sewn quarter. If I wasn't careful to keep my skirt held as I walked, the coin hit the floor with the barest knock. "Mommy, can I have a few minutes alone? This is a very big day for me."

She looked surprised, but her face softened. "Boy, kid, you really have grown up." She kissed my cheek, then rubbed it furiously to remove any trace of lipstick. I felt sad, at that moment, to think that I would never see her again, and wondered if she would privately count me lucky or only be disappointed.

The air outside smelled like a fall barbecue, charring corn and sausages. In the bright blue sky flew a V of birds. Just as I took a breath to run, I spotted Mr. Middleton across the lot next to his car. The collar of his tuxedo was misaligned; he had skipped a buttonhole and set the whole thing off. Facing the sun, he held one hand to his face—to shield his eyes?—and in the other was my note. His shoulders seemed to be shaking with laughter. Had he been about to run away himself when he came upon my note? This possibility, however remote, might have been what led me to walk straight toward him, slowly, steadily, wholly of my own volition. I hate to believe, especially now, that it was as simple as holding to my nature; that I was just a good girl who did always as she was told, without hope and without design.

"Mary Ellen?" he said. "You're still here." I saw as I came closer that he'd actually been crying, not laughing; a tear dropped from the left-side curl of his moustache. I thought of something Dad often said, when, much younger, I'd get caught up in venturesome play with inevitable consequence: "It's all fun and games, isn't it, until someone gets hurt."

"I'm still here," I said. I raised my arms to indicate I should be lifted and let Mr. Middleton cradle me against his chest. I felt his wildly beating heart, and he began to stroke my hair as if I needed calming down. But my stomach felt only the faintest rumble of hunger, an emptiness. I knew that I had done the right thing, the only thing I could, but still, I felt foolish. If I were really as smart as everyone believed, I would never have found myself in this situation, with a ridiculous man I was obligated to care for. My escape would have been better planned and better executed. He would never have taken an interest in the first place.

"Mary," he said, "you do know that I—"

"What?" I struggled to sit up in his arms, impatient suddenly, and restless. I wanted to go inside, where everyone was waiting, and get it over with.

He set me down on the hood of his car and began again. "I think you'll be very pleased with the life I want to give you."

I stared through his windshield at the tan leather seats, sculpted to hug a body as the vehicle took the curves. I saw where the top would fold down. This car would take me to my new home.

"You do understand, don't you, that the deal is irrevocable? If you were to run off, your parents would owe me a great deal of money. They could never hope to come out of debt."

I knew that was a threat, and thought less of him for it. But then he said something I look back on now as the beginning of my new understanding of my life. "I'm yours, Mary Ellen, and if you stay, all that is mine will be yours, too."

In answer, I rebuttoned his shirt.

As I signed the contract, my eyes slid down the page, its tiny print in a formal, inscrutable language. The sum my parents had provided to Mr. Middleton seemed enormous, though I know it now to be less than the cost of my childhood home and much less than the worth of Mr. Middleton's company. Men who'd planned poorly would seek a much larger dowry and might suffer for it in their choice of wives. But it was our parents, always looking toward the future, who put money first. The dowry, like a child that would grow, was ultimately an investment.

I handed over the paper for the minister to stamp, and he pronounced us man and wife.

Mr. Middleton has kept my note folded in his sock drawer, and for years he has teased me for having misspelled "altar." Putting away his clean laundry, I look at it sometimes, not with wistfulness or shame, but because I want to remember. The contract itself is in a safety-deposit box; I'll receive a key for my eighteenth birthday, a day now close in sight. The Barbies, of course, are long gone. Dad succeeded in overriding my mother, and the toys stayed in the basement a year into my marriage. But I rarely played with them—they seemed to have lost their allure, and I never knew what they wanted to do or say or wear. Stacie still hadn't been promised, and I offered them to her, but she pretended not to be interested. She and Cassandra were thick as thieves then. "Save them for your kids," she said, and we couldn't help but dissolve into panicked laughter. By the time she was taken, at age fourteen, she was serious about having children. It is her husband who insists they wait. If we see each other now at the market, grocery baskets in hand, we merely nod in greeting. We have so little in common.

Mr. Middleton has made me apprentice to his business, which he says one day when he is dead, I will take over. Even if—and the decision to have children is entirely up to me, he says—one day we have a son. This is highly unusual and very progressive, Dad has told me. He patted my head and told me he was proud. I looked for something like greed or jealousy in his eyes, but found only love. My mother admitted, over afternoon tea, that she wishes Dad had done something similar for her. As far as I can see, he long ago reached his height on the ladder. What could he have done for her?

"I have good business sense, a ruthless mind," she insisted, and gestured to the piles of butterscotch-chip scones she'd baked for a block sale. "But I suppose I'm lucky, in that we fell in love."

I nodded in agreement, though I knew what would provoke her: *But isn't it easier if we don't think of love?*

Visiting is difficult because, although they think they act differently, my parents still treat me like a child, a newlywed bride. They don't recognize what I've become, but they won't argue when the time comes to face it, when Dad retires and I, with Mr. Middleton's money, am in charge of them. Their investment in me will have its rewards. I want the best for them, as they've managed for me.

After a morning spent at home with my private tutor, Ms. Dundee—whose husband succumbed when she was much younger and much prettier (she says) to a condition she won't speak of—I change into a navy skirt and Peter Pan–collared blouse, hop on my bike and head to the office. Mr. Middleton has given me a fine car, of course, but I normally prefer the exercise. So far I just prepare after-lunch coffee and bring it in on a tray, each cup made to the preference of each board member. Mr. Middleton sits at the head of the table. His moustache, after all these years, remains; he would shave it if I asked, but I suspect that issuing that demand would expose me somehow. Once situated beside him, I'm encouraged to listen in and, if so inclined, take notes. But it's the quiet power struggle that interests me, the way his inferiors look at him and how they cover their desires with neutral jargon, loyal reports. He takes for granted, I think, the way things are now.

"You've learned a lot so far from just watching and listening," he says to me, winking, as I take out my pad of paper. I turn away and roll my eyes: he believes we're always in on some joke. This one is meant to be in reference to the nights I join him in his bedroom, on the floor above mine. Mostly I just lie there while he touches my hair or my back, as he once demonstrated with the doll. He has mentioned in those moments love, and a feeling of fulfillment. For him they may be the same thing. Yet even with me around, taking care of things, I sense he's still a lonely man. I feel guilty sometimes, offering so little reimbursement for his attentions, though he receives more pleasure from them than I do, and I've made attempts to do for him what other girls and young wives have described. Now I believe that the hardest part of the game is staying in it, holding on to your stake. And that you can't plan too far into the future. I've taken this down in my notes: *The benefits mature with time.* I've begun to appreciate just how much work parents invest in their children, and wives in their husbands; it's only fair for the investor to become a beneficiary.

Nominated by The Missouri Review

BLESSING OF THE ANIMALS

by BRENDA MILLER

from THE SUN

> *You touch*
> *the right one and a whole half of the universe*
> *wakes up, a new half.*
>   —*William Stafford, "Choosing a Dog"*

HERE'S THE FIRST THING you should know:

When I sit next to my dog, Abbe, right before she falls asleep, and I stroke her fine-boned head, she turns just enough that her nose nuzzles between my wrist and my sleeve. I keep my hand very still on the top of her head as she breathes in my scent and sighs. The whole house goes quiet then, everything in it just breathing: the cat and the couch, the tulips and the vase, the mirror and the broom. All of us under the spell of a dog—a puppy, really—who has known nothing so far in life but canine grace.

That's the first thing you should know.

A mile from my house in Bellingham, Washington, there's a Unitarian church with white siding and the requisite signboard out front, with fine, literary sayings posted on massive sheets of paper. I have a postcard of one of those signs pinned to my bulletin board: "You are constantly invited to be what you are.—Emerson." For some reason it's a message I need to hear often, this permission to be myself. I've passed by the Unitarian church many times and attended a few secular events there, but I've never gone to a service.

The other day I read a notice in the paper about the annual "blessing of the animals" ceremony this Sunday at the church. And because

Abbe is six months old and full of vast enthusiasm for any enterprise that involves new people and dogs, and because I'm still in that eager new-dog-owner phase where I'm delighted for any opportunity to show off my puppy, I decide to take her. On Sunday morning I gather her collar and leash, her treats and poop bags, her water bottle and bowl; I give her a quick brush-down as she turns in tight circles, trying to grab the brush's handle in her mouth. "We have to look nice for church," I say in that motherly tone I've taken to so easily, too easily, my voice a little hoarse from being elevated to such a high, unfamiliar pitch.

At the last minute I remember my cat, Madrona. Since it would not be a blessing to cart her to church, I quickly print out my favorite picture of her: resting on my improvised altar, paws tucked beneath her chest, a tiny brass Buddha in the foreground—just Madrona being her prickly bodhisattva self. She often strolls into that room when I'm sitting in meditation, brushes against the curve of my crossed legs until I pet her, then settles down on the altar, assuming her place as a deity to be worshiped. No one has to invite her to be what she is. My cat knows she's bigger than the Buddha, that she could kick Buddha's ass if it came down to it, and I've often entered this room to find that serene little statue knocked on its side, its tiny hands still forming a perfect mudra of peace.

Here's another thing you should know:

I've had only one other dog in my life, a Great Dane named Sheba. She was tall, of course, with a smooth, brindled coat. I remember her primarily from photographs: Here's Sheba, a puppy still, in the barren backyard of my parents' new home in the nascent suburbs of the San Fernando Valley, circa 1960. Eventually there will be tall eucalyptus trees in the yard, and a swimming pool, and a jungle gym that will start to rust the moment it's assembled, but for now there's just this big, skinny dog, a newly planted lawn, and some saplings lined up by the fence.

I can't yet talk, can't yet walk. In the photos I'm just a blob with big eyes and a spit curl quivering on top of my bulbous head. After my father has drunk his Ovaltine and Tang and gone off to work, it's just me and my mother and my three-year-old brother and this big, lanky dog stuck in a clean, new house, wondering what to do with ourselves.

The dog doesn't wonder too long. She knows her job is to protect us from whatever dangers present themselves. She follows my mother from kitchen to bathroom to bedroom to yard, barks at the sedans cruising up and down our cul-de-sac, cocks her head with suspicion when the phone rings. She nudges the little baby in my mother's arms when it cries.

That baby eventually begins to leave her mother's arms and get down on the floor to crawl, to walk, to run. This puts her at eye level with the dog, who herds her around the green shag carpet and away from the screen door to the patio. Sheba is just the right height for a toddler to pat her on the head with a fist, or walk under the archway of those enormous legs. Eventually the girl will haul herself onto Sheba's back and squeal, 'Giddyap!" and the dog will comply, moving slowly, swaying like a camel. When the girl is ill with a fever, she'll recline into Sheba's belly, sweating and licking salt off her upper lip.

When I'm eight years old, my family will go on a long car trip to a place like Carlsbad Caverns or SeaWorld or Sequoia National Park. Sheba is too big to go, so we leave her at a kennel. I remember watching the closed gray doors of that kennel from the back of the station wagon as we pull away.

I remember, too, that Sheba dies while we're gone. I remember driving up to the kennel, the heat rippling up from the black asphalt; I remember waiting in the car as our father strides through those gray doors and stays gone longer than seems necessary. My brothers and I roll down the windows and whine for ice cream; my mother fans herself with a map. My father finally reappears, sans dog, his face white, his mouth set in a grim line of displeasure. He walks slowly, too slowly, back to the suddenly silent car.

But now I know this whole scene is a figment of memory. My mother tells me it happened at home: Alone in the house with Sheba, who was vomiting bile, my mother wrestled the 130-pound dog into the car by herself, sobbing and telling her it would be all right. She took the dog to the vet, who called later in the day to say Sheba had died from a twisted colon, a common ailment among big breeds. I must have come home from school—where I'd recently been admonished *not* to sing "The Star-Spangled Banner" with my classmates because my voice was off-key; where my only solace was quiet reading time; where even the games at recess had become dangerous, the heavy rubber ball bouncing at me with more force than necessary. I must have come home wanting to bend my whole body over Sheba's back and lie there like a rag doll, allowing the memory of school to

40

subside, and instead I saw my mother's red face, her eyes rimmed with smudged mascara. She told me, in the way you tell a child such things, that Sheba had been "put to sleep."

Put to sleep. It's such a kind phrase. After all, I was put to sleep every night of my childhood with kisses and hugs and promises of a good day tomorrow. And every morning Sheba lifted her ponderous head and turned her caramel gaze on me as I woke. For those few moments—before the world rushed in to let me know my place—I existed as nothing more than an object of her adoration, a body to be loved.

Let's return to church, or not even the church yet, but the parking lot, where already there's a certain giddiness in the air: *dogs in church!* For the short ride in the car Abbe has curled herself onto the Navajo blanket and gone to sleep. (She hates car rides and has learned simply to pretend they're not happening, a skill I've come to use in my own life as well.) But as soon as the car stops, she's up and wiggling in the back seat. Have I described her yet? She is a short-haired Havanese, a toy breed, with an apricot coat and a narrow, black-tipped snout. She looks, my vet says, like "a dachshund in a golden-retriever suit," with her short, slightly out-turned legs, her triangular ears that flop over or stick straight up depending on her mood. Her eyes are dark and big and shaped like Spanish almonds.

As I clip on her leash and pull her from the car, I watch out for other dogs—the border collies and huskies and golden retrievers trotting up the sidewalk, pulling at their leashes. Everyone who sees me smiles, even those not tethered to an animal. One woman says, "It's so nice to see who's coming to church today." I'm not sure whether she means me or my dog, but it doesn't really matter—we're one unit for now. Abbe has her nose to the ground, sniffing away. She knows something's up, something that involves dogs and more dogs, and she really couldn't care less about me on the other end of this leash. When we get to the front steps, I pick her up and carry her inside.

I'm shy, and when I arrive at new places, I usually avert my gaze until I know what I'm supposed to do. But with Abbe in my arms, I don't have to worry; people look at her first. She nudges them with her nose, sniffs deeply, and finds everyone extremely worthy. In the vestibule, church volunteers with name tags exclaim over Abbe, saying how cute she is, what a good dog. All I have to do is agree. Nothing else is required. It's as if I were holding in my arms some small, furry portion of myself, a micro-me who knows exactly who she is and where she belongs. This self radiates *confidence*—a word that means, in its purest form, simply to go with faith.

You should know, too, that for a long time, without quite realizing it, I blamed my parents for Sheba's death. For years I kept that erroneous memory of the kennel in my head and, using kid logic, even suspected that they had brought Sheba there to die. I thought they'd grown tired of her; that there had been some kind of *arrangement* made, a notion I'd probably picked up from daytime television programs. It was not a suspicion I ever voiced, or even was aware I carried. My parents were gentle, loving people who would never do such a thing. But all I knew was that we never got another dog. Shortly after Sheba died, we kids were trundled into the doctor's office and given allergy tests that came up positive for canines, cats, horses, ragweed, and dust. We became a household without a dog, the backyard empty save for the pool, the jungle gym, and the now-plush grass that rippled against the eucalyptus.

There must have been other dogs on our street, but I have no memory of them; in my mind, after Sheba died, our block became strangely dogless—as quiet and barren as a scene from *The Twilight Zone*. To fill the void, our parents got us a family of gerbils, one of whom bit the palm of my hand and hung there for several seconds while I screamed. Another ate her babies right in front of me. Then there were the turtles and the hamsters and the goldfish, none of whom lasted long enough for me to form any attachment.

And then there was the duck. Why we had a white duck in our backyard is still a mystery to me, but there he is, swimming in the pool, waddling beneath the walnut tree, bright orange beak clacking open and closed, webbed feet slapping the wet pavement. And always quacking, quacking, quacking, as a duck is wont to do. I kind of loved him. We named him, not very imaginatively, "Daffy the Duck." His feathers were sleek and slightly oily, and he stretched out his neck and flapped his wings like an ungainly hummingbird when he saw me coming. I'd slide open the screen door, and there he'd be, lifting himself out of a metal washbasin, waddling as fast as he could to greet me, the curve of his bill a duck's version of a smile. He was no Sheba, but the quality and consistency of his greeting won me over and made the walk home from school more bearable.

Naturally the neighbors complained: All that quacking! And at 5 A.M.! So one day we hoisted Daffy into the station wagon and brought him to the pond at Reseda Park. I'm sure I cried, because all the way there my father wove tales about how much *fun* Daffy would have with his brethren, how he would make new friends *in no time at all*, how he would fly to *fabulous, exotic places* in the wintertime. My mother nodded in agreement, but reached an arm over the front seat to pat me on the head, as if in secret commiseration.

In the back of the station wagon, the duck fluttered and quacked and drew stares from passing motorists. He seemed quite happy, actually, to be on an outing, and kept poking his cool, heavy bill over the seat to say hello to me. When we reached the park, we opened the tailgate, and Daffy jumped out on his own, ruffled his feathers like an old lady straightening her bonnet, and immediately waddled toward the edge of the water, where dozens of nondescript ducks milled about on the shore. We had brought a loaf of Wonder bread and, like innocent park-goers, threw bits of bread to the assembled waterfowl. Our duck poked at the waterline, and we watched carefully to see when he would take off swimming.

Once Daffy seemed happily occupied in his new home, we made our escape, strolling with exaggerated nonchalance to our car. "Don't look back," my father said—that ancient edict. But of course I looked; I couldn't help myself. And there he was, *our* duck, waddling after us as fast as he could, head up high, wings splayed. He didn't look particularly distressed, no sense of *Hey, where are you going?* His bill still looked as though he were smiling.

"He's following us!" I yelled, and I stopped in my tracks. "Just keep walking," my father said, resolutely facing forward. I knew now he hated this, that we were probably doing something vaguely illegal, and that leaving an animal behind, no matter how misguided the impulse to keep him had been in the first place, was anathema to him. But he was a father who needed to take care of a complicated situation in full view of his children. And he worked as an engineer, and like all good engineers he had come up with a plan, and we needed to see it through.

I hesitated, stuck between an awkward love for this white-feathered creature and my love for my father, my fervent wish to ease his discomfort, to make everything OK. I was stuck between the imperative to move forward into the future, where a duck in the backyard no longer existed, and my desire to stay a little bit longer in the past, where a duck had feathered that empty yard and made me feel cherished. I was a child, with a child's distorted sense of obligation, so I did both. I took a quick run back in the duck's direction, flapping my arms and shouting, "Shoo, shoo, shoo!" Daffy appeared truly startled. He looked up at me with his bill open, wings frozen in midflap, and I knew he understood that things between us had changed. He sidled down to the pond, his waddle a little slower, and glided onto the skin of the water. I ran to my father, took his hand, and didn't look back.

And now we're finally inside the church, with its long, polished pews, its chalice on a raised dais, its tall windows that filter the light. Abbe and I find a seat near the back and on the aisle, to facilitate a quick escape if necessary. I'm already regretting having brought her to church. She's such an excitable and sociable dog; it's torture for her to be bound by her leash while so much activity swirls around her. I put her in my lap, but she won't stay there, so I place her on the floor, where she practically flattens herself sideways to say hello to the husky mix in the pew two rows back. The aisles are filled with roaming packs of kids—*dogs in church!*—who track down huggable dogs, and mine, of course, qualifies. One boy of about ten bends down to pet Abbe with such grown-up control and purity of intention that he seems much wiser than his years. He looks her in the eye and pets her ears, and she gazes adoringly back.

Gangs of girls hoist Abbe clumsily in their arms and pummel her with many hands at once. And although Abbe doesn't seem to mind—in fact, she loves it—I feel a pang of juvenile possessiveness. *My dog!* I want to say and snatch her back. But I let them maul her awhile before I gently extract her, saying, "She's a little wiggly today. Let's give her some room."

I see many familiar faces: A former student waves to me from the back row, her dog sitting docilely at her feet. A colleague a few rows over clutches pictures of her cats. Others look familiar because I've seen them at the co-op, or the independent movie theater, or the waterfront park. Bellingham is a small town. Last year I took some classes to meet new people and wound up seeing the same five women everywhere I went. At first I found it depressing, but now there's something reassuring about being part of this small community.

The minister finally calls the assembly to order, or to whatever semblance of order can be achieved with dozens of dogs in church. He says that, for obvious reasons, they'll keep the service rolling right along today—no sermon. One dog howls, and everyone laughs, including the minister, who responds, "Exactly!" There's so much movement and noise, no one pays much attention to the announcements about the pledge drive and a church member's upcoming service trip to Kenya. We stand for the lighting of the chalice, and the young woman on my right shares her hymnal with me for the first song; my hands are full with Abbe. Ever since my grade-school quarrel with "The Star-Spangled Banner," I've been shy about singing in public, but I do know it feels good to be standing with an armload of dog amid this human-and-animal cacophony. So I hum.

Here's the last thing you should know:

Abbe is the first dog I've owned in the forty years since Sheba died; I knew she was *my* dog from the minute I saw a thumbnail photo of her on the Internet. And when I brought her home, my father was in the hospital. It was January 3, a Wednesday, and he'd been there since New Year's Eve, when a guest at their party had said to him, "You don't look so hot." They'd taken him to the emergency room, where he'd turned out to have a blood infection.

So, while my father had antibiotics pumped into his veins—drugs that didn't seem to work, and then they did—I focused on this new creature in my house: Eight pounds of fur and bone and eyes and heart. A dog who immediately took to sliding full tilt across the linoleum, then standing stock-still in the middle of the kitchen floor, tongue out, as if to ask what we were going to do next. A dog who slept all night in her crate but kept me up anyway just by her presence. A dog who never barked, who didn't need to, because I was looking at her every minute. My gaze was so full of Abbe that when I left her for one hour to go to a yoga class, she appeared as an afterimage every time I closed my eyes.

I called the hospital each day to get a progress report from my father. We'd talk for just a few minutes about his condition: he'd either describe his body's insurrection with a chuckle or take the role of the engineer, explaining the mechanics of what had happened to him. And then we'd immediately slide into dog talk. Once all their so-called allergic kids had left home, my parents reverted back to being the dog people they'd always been, and they'd had at least one dog in the house for the previous twenty years. They now owned two dogs:

a stolid corgi mix—a rather odd-looking animal—rescued from a shelter, and a hyper toy poodle who'd proven to be too much for my younger brother's family.

As my parents sat together in the sterile light of the hospital and waited for my father's blood to come clean, we chatted with an ease and camaraderie that had never quite been available to us before. Our thoughts detoured toward Abbe, this animal we could exclaim over and love together simply and fully, without complication, and in so doing, feel that love reflected back onto each other. We talked about all those things no one else could stand: poop and pee, kibble and bones, leashes and halters and the little doggie raincoats I'd never thought I would buy. We talked about my pets' rivalry (Madrona had yowled and swatted Abbe within five minutes of my bringing her home) and the more numinous aspects of pet ownership that can't really be articulated, such as the feel of a dog's paw, how you can run your hand over the pads of her feet for close to an hour. The texture of her belly and the weight of her as she falls asleep in the crook of your arm. The smell of her fur, a little like pears.

We talked about all these things so we didn't have to talk about what might happen next for my father. That Friday the news was not good: The doctors had checked my father's heart as a matter of routine and found several blockages, unrelated to the blood infection. They recommended triple-bypass surgery, and soon. It seemed as though my father's body had known something was amiss and developed the infection to get his attention, put him in the hospital where he belonged.

Over the weekend I fretted over whether I should fly to Arizona and be there on Monday for the surgery. It was quite impractical, but what if? My mother said I didn't have to come. My father said I didn't have to come. But my brother said, in an ambiguous tone, "Make your own choice." I thought about a trip I'd taken with my parents to France the previous June. We'd roamed all over Paris in a heat wave, my pace invariably quicker than theirs. I'd vowed to be a good, compassionate, patient daughter on the trip, but sometimes I couldn't help it; I just strode ahead without them. Now one image flashed in my mind: my father panting to keep up, sweat on his brow, asking me in a plaintive voice, "Can we slow down for just a minute?"

On Saturday I went to my yoga class and started crying during corpse pose. (My body's never been one to pretend.) Everyone kept saying how easy a heart bypass is these days, a quick mechanical fix, but I'd never heard my father sound scared before. He questioned whether he should have the surgery at all; there were risks either way. He was a diabetic. Anything could happen. He was upset that he wouldn't have the chance to get his financial papers in order for my mother, just in case. He missed their dogs and wanted to go home. He and I kept changing the subject to my puppy whenever we had the chance.

And Abbe just kept being a puppy. Her tail seemed to grow an inch every day. Her ears twisted every which way, and all my friends came by to get acquainted and talk about how wonderful she was, which in turn made me feel wonderful, idiotic with joy. It was an odd state to be in: filled with happiness and beset by terror at the same time. I commented to my Buddhist friends, only half joking, that perhaps this was what is meant by the "middle way," because even as I swerved between tears and laughter, I felt wholly present and calm.

On Monday, the day of the surgery, I talked on the phone to my father in pre-op, and also to my mother and my two brothers and my sister-in-law, all of whom asked about the dog and seemed eager to talk about her, though their voices were strained. They asked how Madrona was faring with the new addition. They asked how housetraining was going. I told them of the baby teeth I'd found on the floor, like blood-specked pebbles. We spoke of small matters because the big mattered too much. And perhaps because the moment seemed so portentous, or maybe because there was another creature in my life to be the focus of our attention, they seemed to love me a little more easily, to forget whatever hurt or distance there'd been between us in the past.

My father, as it turned out, would come through the surgery just fine, and even a day later would sound healthier than he had in years, speaking with more clarity, the oxygen flowing unimpeded through his heart. But for now we couldn't know this. Abbe lay next to me on the couch, and I stroked her belly with my knuckles as I talked with my family; the cellphone passed from hand to hand in that faraway pre-op room. I thought carefully about what words to say to my father, because no words would be enough. Then there was the one word I didn't want to say: *goodbye*. I touched the puckered scar where Abbe had been spayed, a small ridge that disrupted the expanse of her shaved mauve underbelly. The dog, of course, was oblivious; she had no idea of herself as a lifeline. For her it was just another day, another good day.

And now we're back in church, Abbe and I. You can find us in the third pew from the rear, Abbe standing with her front paws on the back of the bench in front of us to get the best view possible: *Dogs in church! Dogs in church!* The minister begins making his way up the center aisle, hitching up his robes and kneeling as he arrives at each parishioner with a pet. I can't hear what he's saying, but I can tell by the way he leans close to each animal that this is a private moment, not meant to be shared. The kids have taken this opportunity once again to visit as many dogs as possible, darting up and down the aisles but somehow maintaining a bubble of calm around the minister.

When I decided to come here today, I didn't really understand how the blessing itself would be administered: this one-to-one, head-to-head communion. I'd envisioned more of a parade of animals, with each of us leading our pet toward the altar, the blessings dispensed like rain, falling on everyone at once. But this will do.

As the minister draws near, I fumble with one hand in my purse for the picture of Madrona while trying to get Abbe to lie still on my lap; she stretches out full length, getting as close to the floor as possible, where the dogs and children mingle. Even the adults in the congregation have caught the fever and begun to roam a bit, greeting friends, leaning over the pews to talk. A few rows ahead of me a teenage girl holds a tiny puppy wrapped in a blanket against her shoulder; the dog can't be more than eight weeks old—too young, I think, to be amid such frenzy.

And then, looming over us, is the minister, a tall man with a whiskered face, his red and white robes fluttering in the breeze created whenever the children run past him. He kneels and asks, "Who do we have here?" The din in the church seems to recede, and I tell him this is Abbe, and I also hold out Madrona's picture and tell him her name. "Good," he says, "we'll keep Madrona in our thoughts as we pray."

And then he lays his right hand on Abbe's head, which has gone still, and she looks up at the minister with the same calm gaze she gave to the young boy: tongue at rest in her mouth, eyes half closed, as if in pleasure. He says to her, in a voice low and kind, "May you live a long life of love and peace," and some other words I can't quite catch, because my eyes have begun to fill—I didn't expect this—and I try to concentrate, but it's difficult, because in this moment I know how much I really do love this dog, and this love startles me. It's as if

48

the minister has reached in and laid his meaty palm right on the muscle of my own heart: every animal part of me that longs to feel blessed has risen to the surface, like koi in an algae-filled pond. Sheba's there, and that daffy duck waddling toward me, and my father's heart still pumping . . . *and may we pray in love, amen*, and I croak out an *amen*, and a *thank you*, and then he's gone, and a pack of children and worshippers rush into the eddy he leaves behind. A woman asks cheerfully, "What kind of dog is this?" while fondling Abbe's ears, oblivious to the tears I'm wiping away with the flat of my hand.

I mumble an answer, feeling a little foolish that I'm so shaken—but what can I say, there are *dogs in church!*—and I gather up Abbe and her leash and her treats, and we make our way toward the back of the sanctuary. Everyone has circled up for the closing hymn. My dog and I take a place at the end of the line, the circle here petering out into a ragged spiral. I hold a stranger's hand with my right hand, Abbe with the other. Madrona is folded up in my purse. I look around the church to see—lined up along the walls, under the windows—a hundred familiar faces gazing into the center, their voices giving blessing to all that is animal, the animal blessing us in reply. I hoist a panting Abbe onto my hip, and we sway in perfect time to a song I have no idea how to sing.

Nominated by Bruce Beasley, Andrea H. Budy, The Sun

WHITE EGRETS

by DEREK WALCOTT

from EPIPHANY

I

Plod of a hoof in blood-crusted earth.
Clatter of a rivulet over bleached stones.
Black bulls trampling the shade of cork trees,
wind in the high wheat whispering like surf
in Sicily or the opening pages of Cervantes.
Two storks on the bell tower in Alcalá.
The boring suffering of love that tires.
Though you change names and countries, Espagña, Italia,
smell your hands, they reek of imagined crimes.
The cypresses suffer in silence, but the oaks, sometimes,
rustle their foliate lyres.

II

A train crosses the scorched plain in one sentence.
In the cork groves shadows rhyme with their sources.
No name except Andalusia would make sense
from the train window of horses and galloping horses.
Echoes and arches of Spain, the word *campagna*
you smuggled from Italy and its fields of sunflowers;
is there a tilde here for Anna or Anya?
Irises stipple the hot square in passing showers,
shadows pause in the sun's capework, ornate balconies rust,
the sunlight of olive oil slowly spreads in saucers
and loaves that are hard to break have a sacred crust.

Esperanza, cherished Esperanza!
Your lashes like black moths, like twigs your frail wrists,
your small, cynical mouth with its turned-down answer,
when it laughs, it is like a soft stanza
in a ballad by Lorca, your teeth are white stones
in a riverbed, I hear the snorting stallions
of Cordoba in heat, I hear my bones'
castanet, and a rattle of heels like machine guns.

III

Suppose I lived in this town, there would be a fountain,
the tower with two storks, I called them cranes,
and black-haired beauties passing; then again,
I wouldn't be living in a posh hotel. All of Spain's
heart is in this square, its side streets shot
and halved by the August sun. The bullring would be
closed until Sundays, heat
would scorch the park benches, and there would be a lot
of pigeons hopping on the cobbles with their pink feet.
I would sit there alone, an old poet
with white thoughts, and you, my *puta*, would be dead
and only half your name would be remembered
because by then you would have lost power
over my sleep, until all that remains
is the fountain's jet. Storks on the bell tower, or cranes.

IV

For the crackle and hiss of the word 'August,'
like a low bonfire on a beach, for the wriggling
of white masts in the marina on a Wednesday
after work, I would come back and forget the niggling
complaints of what the island lacks, how it is without
the certainties of cities, for a fisherman walking back
to this village with his jigging rod and a good catch
that blazes like rainbows when he shows it to you,
for the ember that goes out suddenly like a match
when the day and all that it brought is finished,
for the lights on the piers and for the first star

for whom my love of the island has never diminished
but will burn steadily when I am gone, wherever you are,
and for the lion's silhouette of Pigeon Island,
and your cat that presumes the posture of
a sphinx and for the long, empty sand
of your absence, for the word 'August,' like a moaning dove.

V

The chessmen are as quiet on their chessboard
as those life-sized terra-cotta warriors whose vows
to their emperor with bridle, shield and sword,
sworn by a chorus that has lost its voice,
echo in that astonishing excavation.
Each soldier was a vow, each gave his word
to die for his emperor, his cause, his nation,
but still to stand still, breathlessly erect
as his own effigy that silence will select
and station like a chessman on a board.
If vows were visible we would see ours,
the way these changeless chessmen stand in the light
vowing eternal fealty to a cause
whose queen you are, vigilant through the night,
and suffering silently from love's deep curse,
that not all the clamour of battle can set right,
only the chessmen's silence, while trees toss
on the lawn outside with the music that is Time's
and vows that die and harden in their loss,
while a sable blackbird twitters in the limes.

VI

This was my early war, the bellowing quarrels,
at the pitch of noon, of men moving cargoes
while gulls screeched their monotonous vowels
in complex curses without coming to blows;
muscular men swirling codfish barrels
and heaving rice bags, who had stunted nicknames,
who could, one-handed, hoist phenomenal rolls
of wire, hoist flapping galvanise with both arms

52

to pitch it into the hold while hooks and winches
swung nearby. At lunch they ate in the shade
of mountainous freight bound with knots and cinches,
ignoring the gulls with their boulders of bread.
Then one would be terribly injured, one lose a leg
to rum and diabetes. You would watch him shrink
into his nickname, not too proud to beg,
who would roar like a lorry revving in the prime of his drink.

VII

When light fell on the bushes around Soufrière,
it was orderly, it named what it fell on—
hog plum and zaboca, dasheen, tannia and melon,
and between the hills, the orange and vermilion
immortelles that marked the cocoa's boundaries.
We stopped there, driving in prolonged stupor
at perfection framing itself, like the light
that named the town walls of the Marque, the shore
of the nibbling Adriatic, that made me elate
as a windblown chicken hawk, or an eagle's emblem
over Aquila, or where a hidden, guttural brook
recited 'Piton Flore, Piton Flore,' cedar, cypress and elm
speak the one language, the wind, from a common book,
open at summer. I stopped and listened to them.

VIII

We were by the pool of a friend's house in St. Croix
and Joseph and I were talking; he stopped the talk,
on this visit I had hoped that he would enjoy,
to point out, with a gasp, not still or stalking
but fixed in the great fruit tree, a sight that shook him
'like something out of Bosch,' he said. The huge bird was
suddenly there, perhaps the same one that took him,
a sepulchral egret or heron; the unutterable word was
always with us, like Eumaeus, a third companion,
and what got him, who loved snow, what brought it on
was that the bird was such a deathly white.
Now when at noon or evening on the lawn

the egrets soar together in noiseless flight
or tack, like a regatta, the sea-green grass,
they are seraphic souls, as Joseph was.

IX

I hadn't seen them for half of the Christmas week,
the egrets, and no one told me why they had gone,
but they are back with the rain now, orange beak,
pink shanks and stabbing head, back on the lawn
where they used to be in the clear, limitless rain
of the Santa Cruz valley, which, when it falls, falls
steadily against the cedars till it mists the plain.
The egrets are the colour of waterfalls,
and of clouds. Some friends, the few I have left,
are dying, but the egrets stalk through the rain
as if nothing mortal can affect them, or they lift
like abrupt angels, sail, then settle again.
Sometimes the hills themselves disappear
like friends, slowly, but I am happier
that they can come back, like memory, like prayer.

X

All day I wish I was at Case-en-Bas,
passing incongruous cactus which grows in the north
in the chasm-deep ruts of the dry season
with the thunderous white horses that dissolve in froth,
and the bush that mimics them with white cotton
to the strengthening smell of kale from the bright
Atlantic, as the road-ruts level and you come upon
a view that dissolves into pure description,
a bay whose arc hints of the infinite
and Africa. The trade wind tirelessly frets
the water, combers are long and the swells heave
with weed that smells, a smell nearly rotten
but tolerable soon. Light hurls its nets
over the whitecaps and seagulls grieve
over some common but irreplaceable loss
while a high, disdainful frigate bird, a *ciseau*,
slides in the clouds then is lost with the forgotten

caravels, privateers and other frigates,
with the changing sails of the sky and a sea so
deep it has lost its memory of our hates.

XI

My climate now is the marsh, the leaden
silver water that secretes in reeds
or moves with a monody that happily might deaden
endeavour and envy and the waste of noble deeds
for reputation's sake, my frenzy is stasis,
like a shallop with a staved-in hull.
I fly like the slate heron to desolate places,
to the ribbed wreck that moss makes beautiful,
where the egret spreads its wings lest it should totter
on the aimed prow where crabs scrape for a perch,
all that vigour finished with which I sought a
richer life to this halfhearted search.
I am thinking of a specific site
that is Hunter's Cove, away from the road
and traffic, of a marsh in marsh-light
with charging dusk and the boom of a toad
in the reeds at the firefly-flecked night
and a heaven improbably swayed in mirroring water.

XII

The nausea of horror continued as he read
and wrote and read and wrote in the iron-railed
Spanish hotel with wrought-iron pergolas
in its inside courtyard, at how often he had failed
with women, in a bullfighting town, Merida,
its ruined amphitheatre ringed with silent olés
for the flourish of his thoughts, for the self-murder
of his pitiable jealousy. Time might deliver
him of his torment, Time that had gnawed at the stone and
eaten its heart. You, my dearest friend, Reader,
its river running through reeds and lights on the river
by the warp of a willow coiled like an ampersand.

Nominated by Epiphany

RETREAT

fiction by WELLS TOWER

from MCSWEENEY'S

I HAD NOT SPOKEN to my brother Matthew in thirteen months when he telephoned me last autumn.

"Hey there, buddy. Ask you a question. What's your thinking on mountains?"

"I have no objection to them," I told him.

"Good, good," he said. "Did you hear I bought one? I'm on top of it right now."

"Which one? Is it Popocatepetl?"

"Hey, go piss up a rope." The mountain didn't have a name, as far as he knew. He said it was in the north of Maine, which is where he'd been living since July. Wind was blowing into the phone.

"You didn't move again."

"Oh, yes I did," said Matthew. You could hear he was talking through a grin. "I'm gone, little man. Must have been certifiable to stay in Myrtle Beach so long."

Maine sounded nice, I told him. Could he see the ocean from where he was?

"Hell no, I'm not on the *coast*," he roared. "I'm through with coasts. Didn't move twelve hundred miles just to come up here and bark my shins on a bunch of Winnebago people in lobster bibs."

Then his tone softened and he told me that the winter was coming, and that he'd like to see my face before the snows sealed him off from the world.

I said I probably couldn't spare the time, and Matthew began to emit an oral brochure of the property's virtues, its bubbling brooks, forests, and glassy ponds, and the "bold, above-canopy views" from his cabin on the summit, which he described to the last nailhead and bead of caulk. "And I got a guy out here with me who's your type of man. My buddy Bob, my neighbor. I've got him working on the crib. Outstanding guy. Mathematical opposite of those douchebags down in Myrtle. You guys could talk some good shit together. Let me put him on."

I tried to protest, but Matthew had taken his ear from the phone. The sound of a banging hammer rose in the receiver. Then the banging stopped, and a thin, chalky voice came on the line. "Yup, Bob Brown here. Who'm I talking to?"

"This is Alan—"

"Not Alan Dupree?"

"No. I'm Matthew's brother. I'm Alan Lattimore."

"Well, I can believe that over Alan Dupree. Good to know you."

The hammering started up again, and Matthew came back on the line.

"That's the wild man for you," Matthew said with a kind of chuckling pride. "Just him and me—pretty much a two-dude nation is what we've got out here. You'd go bananas for it. When can we put you on a plane?"

It was hard not to share Matthew's pleasure at his departure from Myrtle Beach. The world he'd inhabited there was every bit as worth fleeing as a Vietnamese punji trap—a shadowless realm of salt-scalded putting greens, of russet real-estate queens with sprawling cleavages pebbled up like brainfruit hide, of real-estate men with white-fleeced calves, soft bellies, and hard, lightless eyes, men who called you "buddy-to" as they talked up the investment value of condominiums already tilting into the Atlantic.

I would have applauded Matthew more heartily for abandoning his life down there had he not already insisted, over the years, that I applaud him for dropping out of law school at Emory, for quitting a brokerage in Memphis, for pulling out of a venture-capital firm he'd launched in Fort Lauderdale, for divorcing his first wife (a quiet, freckled woman I'd like very much) on the grounds, as he put it to me, that she was "hard of hearing and her pussy stank," and for engaging himself to Kimberly Oosten, Esq., the daughter of an Oldsmobile dealer in Myrtle Beach.

You could trace Matthew's rotations to his early days at school. He'd been an awkward boy, eager to be liked, with eyes as large and guileless as a mule's. He spent his school years chasing acceptance to one social set or another—gerbil enthusiasts, comic-book collectors, the junior birders, the golf club, the hot-rod men, et cetera, without much success. He had a way of coming off as both fawning and belligerent. He was routinely ridiculed and occasionally beaten up by the boys whose friendship he most ardently pursued. His discarded careers notwithstanding, Matthew, at age forty, had accumulated a good amount of money, and I imagine could have bought himself permanent membership in whatever society he liked. But it seemed to me that years ago, this had stopped being the point. Somehow, he'd gotten to a place where he wasn't happy if he didn't pause every four or five years and abort the life he'd had before. After a few years of living comfortably in a place, he would grow restless and hostile, as though he suspected he was being deliberately swindled out of the better life owed to him someplace else.

I live in Arcata, California, where I earn a slim livelihood as a music therapist, an occupation of so little consequence in my brother's eyes that he can never seem to remember exactly what it is that I do for a living. Though I did not have spare time or money to squander on a trip to Maine, as Matthew's pitch wore on I found it heartening that he had once again called me, the sole emissary from his past, to preside over his latest metamorphosis, and in the end I booked a ticket.

I left the first Thursday in November, along a cheap and brutal route. I flew out of Arcata midday to the San Francisco airport, where I spent four listless hours in the company of a man with a wristwatch the size of a plaster ceiling medallion. He tugged ceaselessly at the thighs of his trousers, currying the spare fabric into a blousy pavilion at his crotch. "Edward is really riding roughshod when it comes to our intentionality" is a sentence I heard him utter in two different conversations on his cellular phone. I caught the overnight flight from San Francisco to Boston, hunkered in the lee of an enormous woman whose bodily upholstery entirely swallowed our mutual armrest. I had no place to rest my head. She saw me eyeing the cushioned cavern formed by her shoulder and wattle, and she said, "Go on, stick it right in there." I did so. The woman gave off a clean, comforting aroma of the sea, and I slept very well.

From Boston, I caught a dawn flight to Bangor. In Bangor, I was ushered onto a tiny six-seater that sat on the tarmac for two hours while a mechanic who did not look fifteen peered learnedly at the wing. At last, the engines cranked, and the plane lifted in quavering flight for northern Aroostook County.

Unimaginable vastnesses of spruce and pine forests passed beneath the plane, unbroken by town or village. We landed at an airport that was little more than a gravel landing strip with a Quonset hut off to one side. A solid chill was on the air. The four people I'd flown in with grabbed their luggage from where an attendant had strewn it on the blue gravel, and jogged for the parking lot. The small plane absorbed a fresh load of travelers and vanished over the spruce spires on shuddering wings.

I walked to the shoulder of the country boulevard that ran past the airfield and waited for my brother. Ten minutes went by, then fifteen, then twenty. As the time passed, I was gored repeatedly by a species of terrible, cold-weather mosquito I had never come across before. In the time it took to beat one of their number to death, a half dozen more would perch on my arm, their engorged, translucent bellies glowing like pomegranate seeds in the cool white sun.

I'd been smacking mosquitoes for three-quarters of an hour when a red Nissan pickup truck with darkly tinted windowglass rounded the curve. It pulled to a stop in the far lane, the calved asphalt on the shoulder crunching under its tires. Matthew stepped out and crossed the road. His appearance startled me. In the year since I had last seen him, he had put on a lot of spare flesh—a set of jowls that seemed to start at his temple and a belly that could have held late-term twins. His extra weight, and the milky pallor of it, conveyed an impression of regal corpsehood, like the sculpture on the lid of an emperor's sarcophagus. I felt a mild rush of worry.

"You're late," said Matthew.

"I've been standing here for forty-five minutes."

He snorted, as though forty-five were an insufficient number of minutes for me to have been kept waiting.

"We showed up here two hours ago. Now the whole day's shot to shit."

"Look, Matthew—"

He broke in.

"My point, Alan, is that I don't just sit around out here with my hand up my ass. I had plenty on my plate today, but instead we had to come in to town and wait around, and now Bob's drunk and I'm half in the bag, and now we won't get anything done at all."

"That's good," I said. "Because I asked them specifically to hold the plane just to piss you off. I'm glad it all worked out."

"You could have called me with the status, is what I'm saying." He took his cell phone from his pocket. "Telephone, you know? They're great. You use them to tell things to people who aren't where you're at."

I wanted very much to smash my brother's nose. I picked up my bag instead. "Screw it, you asshole," I said. "I'll leave. I'll take the next plane out."

I'd walked three steps when Matthew grabbed me by the back of the neck and spun me around. His anger had evaporated, and he was giggling at me now. Nothing delights my brother like the sight of me in a rage. He kissed my eye with a rasping pressure of stubbled lip. "Who's an angry little man?" he cooed at me. "Who's an angry little man with fire in his belly?"

"I am, and you're a big fat cock," I said. "I didn't ride a plane all night to take this crap from you."

"He's all upset," said Matthew. "He's a frustrated little man."

He grabbed my duffel from me and, still laughing, marched toward the idling truck.

Through the pickup's open door, I saw the form of a man in the passenger's seat. He was slight and so deeply tanned that he was hard to make out in the dim interior.

"Alan, Bob—Bob, Alan, my baby brother," he said, though I stand six foot three, beneath a head of thinning hair, with violet half-moons of adult fatigue under my eyes.

Bob nodded once. "Good to know you, baby brother," he said. His voice creaked like an over-rosined bow. "And as the French have it, *bienvenue.*"

"Bob's a very slick ticket," said Matthew, tossing my bag into the bed with a thud. "He's a man of the world."

"Slick as a brick, and a genius in the bargain," said Bob. "I'm often told I should be president."

Matthew levered the driver's chair forward so that I could crawl into the cab's tiny rear compartment. Three large-bore rifles lay across the gun rack: the old Weatherby .300 magnum Matthew had claimed without asking from our father's estate, a sleek, black fiberglass rifle with a Nikon sight, and a cheap-looking 30.06. I had to crane my neck forward to keep my hair from touching the oiled barrels. The truck rolled onto the road.

Bob leaned around the seat to talk to me. He was older, in his sixties, I supposed. His rucked brown cheeks were roughened with whiskers the color of old ivory, and sparse white curls poked out from under his baseball cap. "I *should* be president," Bob continued. "Don't you think? Tell me, baby brother, would you or would you not give this face your vote?" He showed me a set of teeth that looked artificially improved.

"I'd have to know where you stand on the issues," I said.

Matthew cut me a look in the rearview mirror. "I'd appreciate it if you wouldn't get him started, really."

"Alan has every right to be apprised as to where I stand," said Bob. He tapped a philosophical finger against his pursed lips and pretended to ponder his platform. After a moment, he said, "Well, here's something: I believe that anybody who wants to ought to be able to drink a cocktail with the commander-in-chief and ask the man what's what. Once a week, we hold a lottery and an ordinary citizen gets to sit down for drinks with the president. The citizen brings the booze. The constitution doesn't provide for people going around getting soused on the taxpayers' dime."

"Fair enough."

"Number two: Every municipality in the United States has a cookout the last Sunday of the month. The grills are set up on the public square. You bring the fixings, the government brings the charcoal. Why not? It's good for the community."

"Sounds sensible," I said.

"And I'm proud of number three. The federal government imposes a single sensible standard for menus in Chinese restaurants. It's my position that if you walk into the goddamned Noodle Express in Toledo, Ohio and order a number forty-two, you know that's going to be the Kung Pao Chicken, rain or shine. Any chef who won't play ball gets a kick in the rump."

"It sounds like a hell of a country," I said.

"You're damn right it does," Bob said, his voice rising. "And I've got a cabinet all picked out. You know that girl from the tire commercials? Well—"

"I'm sorry, I'm sorry," said Matthew. "But is there any way you could please shut up with this? I apologize, Bob, but how many times have I heard this bit? Just change up the fucking jukebox, please."

Bob gazed back at Matthew in wordless malice. I gathered that in the three weeks since he'd called me, the "two-man nation" he and Bob had started building here was already showing signs of ugly schism.

Matthew steered the truck through a rural abridgement of a town—a filling station, a red gambrel-roofed barn with a faltering

61

neon sign identifying it as a pizza restaurant, and a grocery store with newspaper coupon circulars taped to the window glass. At last, Matthew spoke, trying to dispel the sour silence that had congealed in the cab.

"Hey, Alan, you didn't say anything about my new truck."

I told him I liked it.

"Just bought it. Best vehicle I've ever owned. V-6. Sport package. Got a carriage-welded, class-four trailer hitch. I'd say you're looking at a three-ton towing capacity. Maybe three and a half."

"You're really not going back to Myrtle Beach?" I asked.

"Why would I? Stick a fork in me, as far as that town's concerned. I dissolved the partnership. Hugh Auchincloss—"

"The notorious Mister Auchincloss," said Bob wearily. Matthew narrowed his eyes at him, as though he was going to say something, but didn't.

"Yes, Hugh Auchincloss, the conniver. Because of him, I took a hard fucking on this EIFS deal."

"On what deal?" I said.

"EIFS," said Matthew. "Exterior Insulation Finish System. Non-breathable synthetic cladding. Fake stucco, is what it is, and the deal is, it fosters mold." Matthew held forth at cruel length on the perils of EIFS and moisture intrusion and the tort liabilities involved in selling condominiums that were rotten with noxious spores. Hugh Auchincloss had evidently overseen the sale and construction of five infected buildings. He had homeowners coming at him, claiming respiratory ailments, and a couple talking about brain damage to their infant kids. The courts had handed down no penalties yet, but Matthew was sure there wouldn't be much left of him when the attorneys' knives stopped flashing.

"And Kimberly, the engagement?"

"Who, Kim Jong II?" he said in a low growl. "She's done. Dead to me."

"Why?"

"She's a gold-plated bitch is why, with an ass like a beanbag."

"You left her?"

"Something like that."

In my opinion, this was not sad news. I'd met Kimberly once, over dinner at a high-class restaurant a year ago in January. I remember that she said that she wished Matthew "would quit being such a Jew" when he declined to order a $90 bottle of champagne. Then she told us about her brother, a Marine pulling his third tour in Iraq. She said she endorsed his idea for bringing the insurgency under control, which, if I was hearing her right, involved providing drinking water only to those districts that could behave themselves, and permitting the rest of the country to parch to death or die of dysentery. Kimberly was a churchgoer, and I asked her how the water tactic would square with "Thou Shalt Not Kill." She told me that "Thou Shalt Not Kill" was from the Old Testament, so it didn't really count.

"I'm sorry," I said. "I really saw that one working out."

Matthew took a tube of sunflower seeds from the ashtray and shook a long gray dose into his mouth. Then he spit the chewed hulls into a paper cup he kept in a holder on the dash.

"To be honest with you," he said after a time, "I just don't see the rationale for anyone purchasing a vehicle that doesn't come with a carriage-welded, class-four trailer hitch."

Bob lit a cigarette and rolled the window down. I heard the sharp lisp of beer cans being opened. Bob handed one to Matthew and one to me. Then he turned around in his seat and asked me, "Baby brother, would you like to see a magic trick?"

"Sure," I said.

He picked up an orange from the floor of the truck and held it out to me.

"Feast your eyes on it, touch it. Get the image firmly in your mind. Got it?"

It was a navel orange, flattened slightly on one side.

"Now watch closely," he said, and threw the orange out the window of the truck. "Presto," he said.

"You just tossed my fucking orange, Bob," said Matthew. "I was looking forward to eating that."

"And so you can," said Bob. "Whenever you want it, it'll be waiting for you right back there."

Matthew steered the truck through a narrowing vasculature of country roads that wound into high-altitude boondocks, past trailer homes and cedar-shake cottages with reliquaries of derelict appliances and discarded automotive organs in their yards. He turned at last down a rilled trail of blond gravel. High weeds grew on the spine between the tire tracks and brushed the truck's exhaust system with a sound of light sleet.

Bob watched the forest going by. "Once we get Alan's gear stowed, we should head to the lake and get some shots in."

"Not me," said Matthew. "We already shitcanned four days this week, and nothing. I've got a house to finish up. You want to go out, go."

"You know," said Bob, "if you weren't such a know-it-all son of a bitch, you might pay some heed to the fact that it's pretty much last-chance-thirty out here as far as getting something in the freezer this year. I don't think we've got seven good days left in the season. I like to eat meat in the wintertime. Stovewood is hard on my teeth."

Matthew shrugged, but Bob had warmed to his topic, and poured forth a suite of recollections of the bitter winters he'd endured out here and the miseries of waiting for the thaw without a freezer brimming with game. Ten miles of dirt track lay between Bob's house and the blacktop road. From Matthew's cabin, it was closer to eleven, and twenty more into town. When the snow was up to the eaves of your house, you couldn't ride into town for groceries any time you felt like it. It was all right by Bob if Matthew wanted to spend his winter making the frozen trek for supermarket pork chops that tasted like silly putty while Bob fattened up on homemade venison sausage and kidney pies.

"You've lived out here awhile?" I asked Bob before the two men's bickering could start up again.

"I spent my childhood running these woods," he said. "My family owned all of this."

"When was that?"

"Well, until your father half persuaded it away from me."

"You want it back? Make me an offer," Matthew said. "I'll let you have it cheap."

Matthew braked the truck at Bob's house, a khaki modular home at a fork in the track. Bob made no move to get out. "Go on," said Matthew. "Don't let us keep you from making your big kill."

Bob squinted at the sky, which was opaque and the color of spackle. "Rain coming."

"Come on now, Bob, don't let a little moisture hold you back," said Matthew.

Bob did not get out. Matthew winked at me in the rearview. "Bob can't actually shoot, is the problem. His eyes are bad. He couldn't shoot his way out from under a wet napkin."

"I'm going to have them tuned up soon," said Bob. "As soon I get used to the idea of somebody chopping up my eyeballs I'll have them good as new."

"Are you staying or going?"

64

"What's for dinner at your place?"

"You know what: beef stroganoff."

"Hm. Stroge again. I'd hate to miss that. We'll hunt tomorrow. Drive on, sir."

The truck bumped along the path and up Matthew's "mountain," which turned out to be a low-lying hill not much loftier than a medium-volume landfill. Matthew's cabin stood in a granite clearing at the summit. Beyond it, sunlight flamed the dark surface of a pond. The cabin, to my surprise, was a modest, handsome structure built of newly peeled logs and roof shingles the color of fresh pine needles. One curious thing was that the gable ends and eaves were trimmed out with a fussy surfeit of gingerbread curlicues, ornate scrollworks, and filigreed bargeboard, giving the place the look of a tissue-paper snowflake.

"This is amazing," I said. "You built this, Matthew?"

"It was mostly Bob," Matthew said, as though it were an accusation. "Bob called the shots."

"It's a hell of a good-looking place."

Bob's features lifted in an elfin smile. "The secret ingredient is wood," he said.

Matthew led me up the front stairs, along a gangplank nailed over the bare joists of the porch. In contrast to the cabin's outward fripperies, its interior was close to raw. The floors were bare, dusty plywood and half the walls were unfinished, just pink insulation trapped behind cloudy plastic sheeting.

"Just to spite me, Bob won't hang sheetrock," said Matthew. "All day long, I'm in here, mudding joints, and he's out there with his jigsaw turning my house into a giant doily. I get after him about it, but he threatens to quit and not come back."

Matthew let out a mirthless chuckle, and with the instep of his boot he herded a pile of sawdust against the wall. "It's pathetic, isn't it? I don't guess this is where you saw me winding up."

"I'm being honest, man," I said. "I think you've got a great spot. Once you get the finishing touches on it, you'll have a little palace out here."

His vast head tilted in a leery attitude, as though he couldn't be sure I wasn't making fun of him, so I went on. "I'd kill for something like this," I said. "Look at me. I live in a studio apartment above a candle shop."

Matthew's wariness relaxed into a kind of smirking disgust. "You're still renting?"

"Yes."

"Jesus Christ. You're how old, thirty-seven?"

"I turned thirty-eight in August."

"You got a girlfriend?"

"No."

"No shit? Still nobody since what'shername? Nothing on the side?"

"No."

Matthew raised his eyebrows, gazed at the floor, loosed a long sigh. "Well, fuck," he said. "I guess things could be worse."

I spent the afternoon with Bob, finishing up the porch, while Matthew worked indoors, where he kept up a steady racket, dropping tools and swearing importantly. The boards Matthew had bought for his porch were so drastically buckled that to make them lie straight you had to strain against them until you were purple in the face. While I was grunting over a plank that was warped to a grin, Bob raised his hammer and said, heraldically, "I proclaim this to be the sorriest excuse for a piece of one-by-six decking ever touched by human hands, and I proclaim Matthew Lattimore the cheapest, laziest son of a bitch to ever tread the grand soil of Maine."

I laughed, and then I brought up something that had been on my mind. "Hey, Bob, what'd Matthew pay you for this place, if you don't mind the question."

"I do not. He paid me one hundred and eighty-nine thousand dollars in green cash."

"Ah," I said.

"How's that?"

"Nothing," I said. "I'm not surprised. You can always trust my brother to leave you holding the brown end of the stick."

"Oh, I've got no complaints," Bob said, and then drove another nail home. "The land's close to worthless, as a matter of fact. The county put its pecker to largeholders like myself. They require fifty-acre plots to build out here. You can't subdivide it. Can't develop it, can't anything with it, and it's already been timbered to hell. I got a fair price. In exchange, I've got retirement, sir! I've got new teeth in my head and a satellite dish. No, if Matthew hadn't come along when he did, I'd be at the bottom of the proverbial well of shit."

Matthew stepped onto the porch with a flask in his hand.

"So, Alan," Bob said. "You're from California. What part did you say?"

I told him that it was the northern part.

"Ah, the north! Now that's real fine. What do you do up there? I suppose you run around with men."

"I do what?"

"That you're a homosexual, sir—a queer, a punk, one of the modern Greeks."

I wasn't sure how to take this. I assured him I was not.

He nodded, and slapped another board into place. He took a nail from a pouch on his belt and sunk it in a single pistonlike stroke. "Oh no? I used to be one myself, or half of one, at least. In my twenties, I lived with my ex-wife in Annapolis, Maryland. We had a good friend in the naval academy, a corporal with a head of blond hair and a prick like a service baton. We used to take him home and wrestle him, if the mood struck us of a Saturday night."

Matthew leaned against the doorjamb and drank deeply from the flask. "He's not joking, by the way," said Matthew. "He really used to do that sort of thing."

"Oh, I did, by God, I did," said Bob. "Yes, I have fucked and sucked all across this noble land, from the burning Mojave sands to the clement shores of Lake Champlain. I took a turn with all who would have me—man, woman, and child; bird, leaf, and beast."

"God have mercy," said Matthew.

I was enjoying Bob, so I urged him on. "And what now, Bob? Have you a steady mate out here?"

He set the hammer down. "I do not, Alan. I don't have the need for one. That's why I returned to my ancestral land like a doomed old salmon-fish. I've learned in my old years that I don't really care for people. I don't like *Homo sapiens*, and I don't like to have coitus with them. Church is for noodleheads, but I'll agree with the Holy Rollers that intercourse is deplorable—somebody climbing all over you, trying to get themselves a gumdrop. Repulsive. The last time someone tricked me into it, I was angry for a week. No, sir, I'm off it for good. Of course, unless Matthew makes me a tempting offer some chill midwinter night."

"Oh, would you please shut up," Matthew said. His cheeks stood out in little quaking hillocks. For an instant I thought he would break into tears. "Oh god, my life is on fire."

We had our dinner on the porch, where a soft, warm wind was blowing in. We ate beef stroganoff that Matthew made from a kit, and drank cold gin from coffee cups because Bob felt that eating "stroge" without gin to go with it was like a kiss without a squeeze.

"Alan," Matthew said.

"Yes," I said. "What is it?"

"That money, your money from Gram Gram. Have you got it still, or did you blow it already?"

I told him that I hadn't done a thing with it at all. It was sitting in the bank.

This news invigorated him. "What is it, twenty thousand or so?"

"Yes." It was closer to forty, but I saw no need to mention that.

"Outstanding, because there's something I've been meaning to bring to your attention."

"What sort of something?"

A slow wind rattled the leaves still clinging to their limbs. On the crest of the hill, a flock of bats tumbled in the day's last light.

"This is the thing," he said. "Now listen to me. How many guys like us, like me, do you think there are out there? Ballpark figure."

"What does 'like us' mean?"

"I'm talking about jackasses who marriage isn't working out for them, they've got jobs that make them want to put a bullet in their face. Guys out in wherever, Charlotte or Brookline or Chattanooga, sitting there watching their lawns get tall. Just broke-down, broke-dick dudes with nothing to look forward to. How many guys like that you think there are?"

"It'd be tough to put a number on it, Matthew."

"Bet you there's twenty million of them, maybe more. What do these guys want? Bunch of half-dead Dagwoods. They don't want much. What they want is to do like me, come out somewhere like this, get away from all the bullshit, is all they're after."

He went on to spin a vision in which this very mountain would be gridded into a hatchwork of tiny lots, and on each lot would stand a tiny cabin, and in each cabin a lonely man would live. He was going to start a website, place ads in the back pages of men's magazines. As early as next spring, these desolated men would flock here by the hundreds to dwell in convalescent solitude, with Matthew as their uncrowned king. It would be a free and joyous land, a place where the thrill of living, unknown since childhood, would be restored to one and all. He would set up a shooting range and snowmobile trails. He might even open a mountaintop saloon where he'd show movies in the summer, and where touring bands would play.

"I'm serious," he said. "It's happening. I've already got some people on the line. I ran it past Ray Broughton, and he was wild about it. Broughton, and Tim Hayes, and Ed Little. All of them are crazy about it. They're all in for fifty."

"Fifty what?" I said.

He gave me a look. "They already sent the checks. But my point is I could let you in, even just with that twenty. If you could kick that twenty in, I'd set you up with an even share."

"I can't do it."

"Sure you can. You're not losing any money here, Alan. I'll cover it myself."

"Look, Matthew. I don't have investments, don't have a 401(k). If my practice tanks, that twenty thousand is the only thing between me and food stamps."

Matthew held up his hand, his fingers splayed and rigid. "Would you shut up a second and let me talk? Thank you. The thing you're not understanding here, Alan, is that I *make* money. I take land, and a little bit of money, and then I turn it into lots of money. That's what I do, and I am very, very good at what I do. I am not going to lose your money, Alan. What I am probably going to do is make you very rich. Now, if it wasn't for that fucking monkey Auchincloss, I wouldn't be coming to you like this, but here we are. All I'm asking is to basically just *hold* your twenty grand for a couple of months, and in return you'll be in on something that could literally change your life."

"I can't do it," I said.

He took a breath, his nostrils flaring. "Well, goddamit, Alan, what can you do? Could you go ten? Ten for a full share? Could you put in ten?"

"I'm sorry—"

"Five? Three? Two thousand? How about eight hundred, or two hundred? Would two hundred work for you, or would that break the bank?"

"Two hundred would be fine," I told him. "Put me down for that."

"Let's don't borrow trouble," said Bob. "No point in fighting over something that could never happen in a million years."

"Oh, it'll happen," said Matthew. "And I'd appreciate it if you kept out of something you don't know anything about."

"First off, there's a fifty-acre—"

Matthew swatted the idea out of the air. "Irrelevant. You file a variance, is all you do. Pay a few bucks, go to a hearing. You're done. The county's starved for development. Tax base is on the respirator. It'd sail through like corn through a goose. I'm quoting the guy at the county on that."

Bob mulled over this. "It still wouldn't work."

"Don't get down on it, Bob," said Matthew. "There'd be something in it for you, too. Who do you think would build the cabins? You'd have more money than you'd know what to do with."

Bob shook his head. "It still wouldn't work," he said.

"You've got no expertise here, Bob," Matthew said. "It's *already* working. The wheels are rolling. The ball is in play."

Bob was quiet for a moment.

"Well, for one thing," he said, "I think you'd be looking at a serious fire hazard, having all those people up here."

Matthew coughed in scorn. "What, lightning? Chimney fires? Bullshit."

"Yep, there's that," said Bob. "But what I've got in mind, if you tried to bring a couple hundred swinging dicks in here, I think what I'd probably have to do is go around with a gas can and light everybody's house on fire."

"Don't be an idiot," Matthew said.

The sound of Bob's laughing echoed in his coffee mug. "You don't know anything about me, Matthew. You don't know what I'd do."

"Here's what *I'd* do," said Matthew. "I'd crack your head open, and then I'd have you put in jail and by the time you get out you'll be wearing diapers, if that sounds like your idea of a good plan."

Bob drained his gin. Then he licked his plate a couple of times, set it down, and fixed Matthew with a smile. "Do you know who J. T. Dunlap is?"

"The guy at the service station? The guy with the bubble in his eye?"

Bob's perfect smile didn't fade. "That's right. Go ask J. T. Dunlap what went on between his brother and Bob Brown. He'll tell you some things you ought to know before you go around making threats."

For all the joy that Matthew finds in provoking other people, he has never been a violent man. My brother is comfortable only in contests he is sure to win, and the chaos of physical violence muddies his calculi of acceptable risk. In his school years, I had seen Matthew run from boys whose throats he could have danced on rather than take his chances in a fight.

Matthew chewed his bottom lip and stared at Bob with cautious, hooded eyes. Then he stood up and hurled his plate against the side of the cabin. It bloomed into smithereens just below the porch light. He stood there long enough to watch a pale clod of creamed noodles fall wetly to the floor. Then he walked inside, slamming the door hard enough to make the gutters chime.

Bob clicked his tongue and said it was time to turn her in. He stood and held his hand out to me. I took it with some reluctance. "So we'll see you dark and early, then," said Bob. "And if Mister Grouchy Bear isn't in a mood to hunt, then you and me will just have to go ourselves. *Bonsoir.*" Bob straightened his cap and winked at me and strolled into the night.

Matthew's only furniture was the sheetless mattress he was sprawled on in the center of the living-room floor. He did not stir when I came in. I folded myself into the warm embayment formed of my brother's knees and outflung arms and fell into a sturdy sleep.

The door creaked open before dawn. "Out of the fartsack, gentlemen," said Bob, clapping his hands. "Come on, get to it, boys."

Bob tramped to the stove. He lit a lantern and boiled water for coffee. I rose and dressed. The air in the cabin was dense with cold.

Matthew hadn't moved. I rocked his shoulder with my foot.

"Leave me alone," said Matthew.

"All righty," Bob said brightly. "The big man's sleeping in. Alan?"

I nudged him again. Matthew sighed a quick, harsh sigh and got up with a crashing of bedclothes and thudding of knees and feet. He pulled on a camouflage bib, a parka, and an elaborate hunter's vest, busy with zippered compartments, ruffled across the breast with cartridge loops. Matthew retrieved the guns from the pickup and carried them to Bob's old white Ford, which sat in the driveway, an aluminum skiff on the trailer it was towing. We climbed in and rode off down the hill. I sat wedged between Bob and my brother. Matthew rested his head against the dew-streaked window, drowsing, or pretending to. Bob was ebullient. Last night's hostilities seemed to have passed from his mind. He prattled at a manic clip on topics ranging from rumors of prehistoric, sixty-foot sharks living along the Mariana Trench to the claim of a Hare Krishna he had met that poor black Americans were white slave owners in their prior lives.

We rode for half an hour on a two-lane state highway, and then Bob turned the Ford down a narrow road, where the leprous trunks of silver birch flared in the headlights. The road carried us to the shore of a lake. Bob nimbly backed the trailer to the water's edge and winched the boat down a mossy slip into the water. Bob and I carried the gear into the boat. Matthew took a seat near the bow with the guns across his lap, facing east, where the sky was rusting up with the approaching dawn.

Bob pulled the cord on the motor, and the skiff skimmed out of the cove. We headed north, hugging the shore, past worlds of marsh grass, and humped expanses of pink granite that looked like corned beef hash. After a twenty-minute ride, Bob stopped the boat at a stretch of muddy beach where he said he'd had some luck before. We pulled the skiff ashore, and Matthew and I followed Bob into the tree line.

Bob browsed the woods on quiet, nimble feet, stopping now and again to check for sign. At the edge of a grassy clearing, Bob waved us over to have a look at a pine sapling whose limbs had been stripped by a rutting buck. He knelt, and scooped a handful of deer shits into his palm. He raised his hand to his face with such savor and relish that for a moment I thought that he was going to tip the turds into his mouth. "That's fresh all right," he said, and cast them away. "I think we'll make some money here."

We sat in ambush back in the trees, in view of the wrecked sapling, and waited. A loon moaned on the lake. Crows bitched and cackled overhead. Before the dawn had fully broken, a fine, cold rain started sifting down. We drew our collars in. The rainwater slid from our chins down the front of our shirts. Nothing moved in the clearing. After two hours, a sparrow walked out of a bush and then walked back in again.

Far be it from me to guess at what goes on in my brother's rash head, but it seemed to me that the black and hollow silence enclosing him that morning was something new for him. In Matthew's idle moments, I could usually see on his face the turnings of distant gears—negotiations being schemed over, old lovers being recalled, iced tumblers of strong alcohol being thirstily imagined. I had never seen his face this way before, slack and unblinking, a vacant, lunar emblem of irreparable regret.

"Doing okay?" I asked him.

"Yeah, of course," he said in a listless monotone. "No sweat."

It took Bob until ten o'clock to decide that nothing was happening for us there. We trudged back to the skiff, and Bob drove us to the far end of the lake, where he knew about a big deer stand which would at least get our asses off of the wet ground. Instead, we killed another couple of hours huddled together up there in the stand, spying down on some empty woods while the sky kept leaking on us. I didn't talk and neither did Matthew. At one point Bob said, "This is why they call it hunting," and an hour or so later he said it again.

Around noon, Bob broke out the lunch he'd brought along, which was bologna sandwiches with cold wads of margarine lumped under the soggy bread. Out of swooning hunger and politeness, I ate my sandwich. Matthew took one bite of his and pitched it off the stand. Bob saw him do it but didn't say anything.

We got back in the boat and thrummed out over the lake, which was stuccoed just faintly with light rain. We skimmed across the broads to a wide delta where a river paid out into a marshy plain, a spot where Bob claimed to have killed a buck four or six or eight years ago. The bank sloped up to a little rocky promontory. We hiked up there and got down behind some big white pines. We hadn't been there long when Matthew sat up, rapt. "There we go," he said.

On the far side of the delta, a large bull moose had stepped from the tree line and was drinking in the shallows, maybe three hundred yards away, an impossible distance. "Jesus, shit," Bob said in a whisper, and then he made an urgent motion for one of us to slip back down the bank and get the moose into clear range. But Matthew seemed not to hear. He got on his feet, raised his rifle, took a breath, and fired. The moose's forelegs crumpled beneath it, and an instant later I saw the animal's head jerk as the sound of the shot reached him. The moose tried to struggle upright but fell again. The effect was of a very old person trying to pitch a heavy tent. It tried to stand, and fell, and tried, and fell, and then gave up its strivings.

Matthew rubbed his eye with the heel of his hand. He gave us a quizzical look, as though he half suspected that the whole thing was a trick that Bob and I had somehow rigged up. It surprised me that he didn't promptly launch into the gloating fanfare and brash self-tribute that generally attend the tiniest of his successes. "Trippy," was all he said as he gazed toward his kill.

"One shot—are you shitting me?" said Bob. "That's the god-damnedest piece of marksmanship I've ever seen."

We made our way down to the carcass. The moose had collapsed in a foot of icy river water and had to be dragged onto firm ground before it could be dressed. What a specimen it was, shaggy brown velvet go-ing on forever, twelve hundred pounds at least, Bob guessed. Matthew and I waded out to where the creature lay. We passed a rope under his chest. We looped the other end around a tree on the bank, using it as a makeshift pulley, and then tied the rope to the stern of the skiff. Bob gunned the outboard, and Matthew and I stood calf-deep in the shallows heaving on the line. By the time we'd gotten the moose to shore, our palms were puckered and torn raw, and our boots were full of water.

Matthew took Bob's hunting knife and bled the moose from the throat, and then made a slit from the bottom of the rib cage to the jaw, revealing the gullet and a pale, corrugated column of windpipe. The scent was powerful. It brought to mind the dark, briny smell that seemed always to hang around my mother when I was a child. Gorge rose faintly in my throat.

Matthew's face was intent, nearly mournful, as he worked, and he didn't say a word. Gingerly, he opened the moose's belly, careful not to puncture the intestines or the stomach. With Bob's help, he care-fully dragged out the organs, and Bob set aside the liver, the kidneys, and the pancreas. The hide proved devilishly hard to remove. To get it loose, Bob and I had to brace against the creature's spine and pull with all our might while Matthew sawed at the connective tissues. Then Matthew sawed the hams and shoulders free. We had to lift the legs like pallbearers to get them to the boat. Blood ran from the meat and down my shirt with horrible warmth.

When we had the moose loaded in the boat, the hull rode low in the water. So the bow wouldn't swamp on the ride back to the truck, Matthew, the most substantial ballast of the three of us, sat in the stern and ran the kicker. Clearing the shallows, he opened up the throttle, and we sped off with a big white whale's fluke of churned water arcing out behind us. The wind blew his clotted hair from his forehead. The old unarmored smile I knew from Matthew's early childhood brightened his face. His lips parted in the familiar com-pact bow. He raised his eyebrows and wagged his tongue at me in pleasure. There is no point in my trying to describe the love I can still feel for my brother when he looks at me this way, when he is briefly free from worries over money, or his own significance, or how much liquor is left in the bottle in the freezer. Ours is not the kind of brotherhood I would wish on other men, but we are blessed with a single, simple gift. Though sometimes I think I know less about

Matthew than I do about a stranger passing on the street, when I am with him in his rare moments of happiness, I can feel his pleasure, his sense of fulfillment, as though I were in his very heart. The killing had restored him, however briefly, to the dream of how he'd imagined life would be for him here. As the skiff glided over the dimming lake, I could feel how satisfying the gridded rubber handle of the Evinrude must have felt humming in his hand, and the air rushing through his whiskered cheeks, drying the moose's fluids and the brine of his own exertions. I could sense the joy of his achievement in having felled the animal, all the more pure because he had not made much of it, and his pride in knowing that its flesh would nourish two men until the spring.

With the truck loaded, and the skiff rinsed clean, we rode back to Matthew's hill. It was past dinnertime when we reached the cabin. Our stomachs yowled. Matthew asked if Bob and I wouldn't mind trimming and wrapping up his share of the meat while he put some steaks on the grill. Bob said sure, but that before he did any more work he was going to need to sit in a dry chair for a little while and drink two beers. While Bob was doing that, Matthew waded into the bed of the Ford, which was heaped nearly flush with the maroon dismantlings. With the knife in his hand, he browsed the mass. Then he bent over, sawed at the carcass for a while, and then held up a tapered log of flesh that looked like a peeled boa constrictor. "Tenderloin. You ever seen anything so pretty, Alan? If you had a thousand dollars, you couldn't buy yourself one of these, not fresh anyway."

He carried the loin to the porch and lit the grill. With a sheet of plywood and a pair of sawhorses, Bob and I rigged up a butcher station on the driveway in the headlights of Bob's truck.

I'd had enough of work by then. A swooning fatigue was settling on me. Not long into the job, I was not sure I'd feel it if I ran the knife into my hand. Bob, too, was unsteady on his feet. When he blinked, his eyes stayed closed a while. We had been at it for a time, when I began to take conscious notice of the dark aroma that had been gathering by degrees in the air around us, a sour diarrheal scent. The awful thought struck me that the old man, in his exhaustion, had let his bowels give way. I said nothing. A while later, Bob wrinkled his nose and looked at me. "Are you farting over there?" he said.

I told him no.

"What *is* that? My God, it smells like someone cracked open a sewer." He sniffed at his sleeve, then at his knife, then at the block of meat in front of him. "*Hruk*," he said, recoiling. "Oh, good Christ— it's off."

He went around to the truck bed and stood on the tailgate, taking up pieces at random and putting them to his face. "Son of a bitch. It's contaminated. It's something deep in the meat."

I sniffed my fingers, and caught a whiff of grave breath, the unmistakable stink of decay.

Out on the porch, Matthew had a radio turned up loud, and had set out a bottle of wine to breathe. On the patio table, three filets the size of wall clocks rested on paper plates, already pink and sodden. Matthew was ladling out servings of yellow rice when we walked up.

"Not possible," he said calmly, after Bob broke the news. "We broke it down perfectly. I'm sure of it. Nothing spilled at all. You saw."

"It was sick," said Bob. "That thing was dying on its feet when you brought it down."

"Oh, bull-*shit*. You figured that out, how?"

"Contaminated, I promise you," said Bob. "I should have known it when the skin hung on there like it did. He was bloating up with something, just barely holding on. The second he died, and turned that infection loose, it just started going wild."

Matthew rubbed his thumb across the slab of meat he'd intended for himself, and licked at the juice. "Tastes okay to me," he said. With a brusque swipe of his knife, he cut off a dripping pink ingot. He speared it with his fork and touched it to his tongue. "Totally fine. A little gamy, maybe, but they don't call it game for no reason. What?"

He licked it once more and then he squinted at the meat, the way a jeweler might look at a gem he could not quite identify.

"Poison," said Bob.

"No big thing, we go back out tomorrow," I said. "You'll get another one, no sweat."

But Matthew was not listening. He cocked his head and held it still, as though the sound of something in the woods beyond the cabin had suddenly caught his ear. Then he turned back to the table and slipped the fork into his mouth.

Nominated by McSweeney's

METHODICAL

by BOB HICOK

from GREEN MOUNTAINS REVIEW

A famous serial killer poured acid into the holes
he'd drilled in the heads of stunned men,
creating zombies to play with, which is serial killer
genius. I'm not sure who did this, I think Dahmer
but I don't care to do serial killer research,
the sawing and biting, the bodies under porches
tire in gruesome repetitiveness: even the bestial
becomes bland. But think about this: there's getting
the drill from the work bench or buying
the drill, there's choosing the size of the bit,
one-eighth or three-sixteenths,
there's putting the bit in the chuck
and tightening it with the key, there's plugging
it in, there's an extension cord possibly and possibly
lighting has to be taken into account. And this:
there's the moment when the bit rests against
a skull, a human skull, inside of which
dreaming resides, and the wiring which means beauty,
thirst. How does the next step happen, is the message
sent to the muscles of the finger, contract?
And think of this: there's the idea and the pencil
for the sketch, there's the blue print and the factory,
there's the shell and the guidance system, there's the sky
and the plane, possibly clouds and possibly clouds
above the clouds, there's the command and the yes

77

to the command. And this: there's the moment
when the bomb has nothing against anyone, when it's not
sound or blaze, and someone is walking home from work,
along a road she's trusted her whole life,
and the end of things begins but she doesn't know
a famous serial killer is above her, that death
will arrive from miles away, pushing a scream
ahead of it, the tear in the air healing almost as soon
as it happens, the pilots horizon bound,
wearing suits designed to keep them from being crushed
by the pressure of what they do.

Nominated by Dick Allen, Fred Leebron, Edward Falco,
Linda Gregerson, Green Mountains Review

NORTH OF ORDINARY

fiction by JOHN ROLFE GARDINER

from THE AMERICAN SCHOLAR

$\mathbf{W}$HEN PETER ASKED, "Do you mind?" Heather only looked down at the empty seat beside her. The men and women of the Freedom College debate team with their faculty adviser, Mr. Abel-Smith, and a dozen supporting students were scattering themselves through the chartered bus in the apparently random way required of young people who do not hold hands or tempt each other with tricks of dress or bare skin (Romans 12:1, 6:13; Ecclesiastes 3:1). Each stricture or directive at their small, new college in the Virginia Piedmont was traced to scripture.

Peter tossed his head, and continued down the aisle.

"Oh, sit," Heather said.

He turned back to join her. A virtuous gesture, he thought, though a little risky, befriending this provocative young soul who hadn't many friends. He only meant to chat with the woman who'd been so candid describing her high school career to his roommate, Jason. There were complaints that the tight-fitting clothes she wrapped on her appealing figure were unfair to the men on campus struggling to remain pure till marriage. To Peter she was a puzzle of talent and irritability. He knew she had little patience for the college's custom of mutual correction.

It was already dark, and the chartered bus with plentiful extra seats and soft, sound-absorbing upholstery offered a sense of privacy that made Peter more comfortable in her company for the hundred-plus miles up the Shenandoah Valley. There were students who would correct him for sitting next to this gifted debater, the one Ja-

79

son had taken to calling "Ahab's wife," his barely disguised way of calling her a Jezebel. She was only a sophomore, too new for campus-wide notoriety.

Peter had overheard a girl talking about the way Heather altered her outfits, gathering her blouses at the waist for extra shaping. He gave her a pass on the clothes but was curious about her purpose here where students were being trained with a Christian imperative for careers in government and media. When she came she must have known that all faculty signed a pledge to teach every subject as an extension of the Testaments, Old and New. She must have signed the statement of faith required of all students, one that said Satan was here in the flesh on campus and walking among them.

That afternoon Heather had helped the debate team to victory, defending the proposition "Arctic Penguin, Proof of Intelligent Design." In a break with custom, the topic was announced only when the teams took the podium. Heather volunteered and without preparation destroyed her opponent's evolutionist argument by giving a train of statistical impossibilities and presuming his familiarity with Beysian probability theory. The whispered encouragement of the opponent's cocksure teammates gave way to groaning as their sure thing turned to doubt on his tongue. Later, when she was required to take the opposite position, she prevailed again. Afterward, Mr. Abel-Smith said they could all learn something from Heather—the way she carried the opposition's metaphors to absurd limits while mining her own conceits with caveats against similar attack.

"The valley's beautiful along here," Peter said. "Too bad we can't see it."

They were passing the turkey farms of Harrisonburg, but it was beginning to rain. Sliding rivulets of water on their window were the only visible scenery. She said he'd have to do better than that, if he actually wanted to talk. As a senior, Peter was a little insulted. Other women at the college had told him they liked the way he'd changed over several years from a lean and taciturn Christian soldier into a fleshier, more likable New Testament sort of guy, and this new idea of himself had loosened his tongue. He had to be careful. Jason had corrected him more than once for his erratic approach to the other sex, losing his sense of proportion in the excitement of a moment when a lighthearted jest could be taken for hitting on a fellow student.

80

The blast of an air horn beside the bus startled them. Their driver cursed, changed lanes, and accelerated.

"They're good," Peter said, "the bus drivers."

"Really?"

"It's the trucks' day," he explained. His father was an information officer for the state police, so he knew what he was talking about. On a short-staffed Sunday night like this one, their cruisers disappeared from Interstate 81, leaving the Virginia stretch of the highway to the mercy of the tractor-trailers. Their long, drafting caravans were like trains that refused to uncouple, hogging the passing lane, uphill and down. Their speed, which could pass 90, was governed only by the boost or drag of gravity.

"God's speed? Godspeed to them?"

Her subversive cynicism was another trait that ought to be corrected (Galatians 6:1–2). But not by him. Not if there was a chance to draw her out, to get to the bottom of her testy dissatisfaction, or maybe to coax another confession of the way she used to behave in high school.

Mentor, or just perversely curious, he hadn't time to ask a first question before they were thrown forward against the seat in front of them. A second force pressed him against her, and for a while they were moving north, sideways. Light flashed through the windows left and right, strobing over mouths tight-lipped and then suddenly agape. The rotation continued, and Heather was pushed against him. When the bus came to rest at last, it was still foursquare on its tires but facing south in the breakdown lane, a line of trucks blowing by on their right, unaware of the feat that had taken place in front of them.

A shaken Mr. Abel-Smith offered a piety for their deliverance, and within a half-hour they were moving north again, with Peter and Heather rearranged in their seats. Thrown against her in the long skid, he was making amends, establishing with his eyes a modest do-not-cross zone between them. Thinking Heather might have softened in their sudden fortune of mutual salvation, he suggested an exchange of spiritual histories.

She said, no, she'd rather not.

He persisted. In his case, he said, it was not so much a conversion as a confirmation of things that were already testifying silently in the world around him. "You know, 'only more sure of all I thought was true.' Like that."

If his eyes had not been closed in a moment of inner peace, he'd have seen her pushing a forefinger down her throat, suggesting a productive gagging before she sank deeper into her seat, and said, "Hello?"

Faddish sarcasm, too, deserved correction. Why couldn't they all just speak the truth in love as the college asked of them? This was referenced in the student manual: Matthew 18:15–17. Instead she began to question his worldview. "Why do you think they chose that topic for debate? They thought they'd make us look like a bunch of cloacas, that's why."

Did he really think she *believed* what she'd first argued that afternoon? Did he think laying an egg and balancing it between webbed feet and a warm underbelly to keep it off the Arctic ice till it hatched could be proof of a thoughtful designer? And, by the way, did he think, as one of their professors taught, that more developed animals ran faster to escape the Flood and thus reached higher ground and a more exalted place in the fossil record before they were caught and layered over.

Better, he thought, she should keep her voice down. A girl had moved into a seat across the aisle one row behind them with an ear wired to one of the little music compacts. In a community alert to error, he knew this could be a cover for eavesdropping. But Heather wouldn't stop.

"What's your major?"

"Government." He was writing his senior thesis on mistaken assumptions about the separation of powers.

"Really? Have they taught you yet where the idea comes from?"

"Deuteronomy 17" he said, "14 through 20."

"Do you even know what that says?"

Peter reached for the *vade mecum* King James in his cargo pocket, turned on the light over their seat, and began paging forward.

"Don't bother." She closed the little Bible on his moving finger and offered her own translation of the passage. "It says when you get to your promised land, choose a king. Not a stranger but one of your own tribe. And not someone who'll take all the horses and wives and gold for himself. When the king's on his throne, he'll write down the statutes and read them every day. And stick to them."

"And?"

"And? And isn't it a light-year stretch from there to a prescription for the three branches of government? Like looking at a few stars incredibly far apart and tying them together as Orion's belt. Convenient if they actually lined up with each other. Leave it to our chancellor to connect the dots."

"Against Doubt, Vigilance," the college motto, was all that came to Peter's rescue. Like others, he was troubled by the doctrinal war spreading over the campus. Two of the most respected professors had published an essay in the college's periodical, *Faith Today*, asserting that most of the truth and knowledge on which civilization rests was the gift of irreligious men. General revelation they called it. Their contracts were not being renewed for the next academic year. Other professors were leaving in protest, and a number of students too.

"Why are you here?" he asked.

She explained how her parents' congregation in Presque Isle had raised tuition for one of their young people to go to Freedom. For her, it was this or stay home in that bleak corner of the country. She could have taken courses at the local campus of the University of Maine, where the motto was "North of Ordinary." Being the brightest thing their little church had to offer, she had come by default, she said, leaving behind the sons and daughters of potato farmers so that she could join the scrubbed-up faithful like Peter from all over the country.

"The brightest and most in need of . . . correction?"

"People have been talking about me?"

At that moment, with half the trip still ahead of them, Heather seemed to shed her debater's armor and become a wistful seeker, the woman Peter had hoped to befriend and debrief on the homeward journey. Her head was bent forward, offering a silhouette in contemplation. She was already violating the no man's land he'd arranged for them. With a forefinger at her temple, she twisted a dark curl as she began to describe a boy from the potato fields of Aroostook County, the one who had almost derailed her college plan.

She turned in the seat to face him and, as she spoke, reached over now and then to touch his shoulder, giving tactile sincerity to a developing confession. There was nothing very impressive about her, she said, except that she had gigabytes of extra memory, hardly taxed by her education so far. She was challenging Freedom to overwrite her hard drive with their chapter and verse.

A few miles later her dangling foot brushing against his calf was given a mechanical innocence by the occasional extra vibration of the bus. She said that the people she met in the village coffee shop (where else could they gather off-campus without some sort of apology?) didn't ask why she'd come to Freedom from a high school in northern Maine. No, they wanted to know why the campus was so eerily barren.

It was true. You could drive the bypass highway next to the college several times a day and not see anyone. Not even someone walking between the several brick buildings. Not a puddle, not a tree, not a soul on the leveled and reseeded plane. Not just intimacy discouraged, or hidden, but anything that might excite a corrective glance kept safely out of sight. Besides, the majority, the ones who weren't taking their secret lives off campus, were in their rooms, deep in study.

Yes, she said, it was surprising how much time and intellectual energy was spent parsing inherited truth, while ignoring the manifest evidence in the world around them.

"Do you talk this way to everyone?" he wanted to know.

She hooked a finger over his belt and gave a little tug, as if to ask for a measure of understanding. Peter thought of changing seats, but there was a story going forward. The Aroostook farm boy's name was Franklin. She'd known him as a childhood playmate; she was the one who went for help when he cut his forehead on a barn nail. She moved a finger carefully across Peter's eyebrow, showing exactly where the accident had left a scar and how close the child had come to losing his eye.

The farm boy, she said, had grown into a big, friendly man-child, a tease-absorbing pal to all, with deep, dark eyes that you might mistake for the tools of a penetrating intelligence if you hadn't been sitting in the same classroom and seen him blinking in the panic of an academic challenge. She was justifying her advances to the hapless schoolmate with the excuse that he actually understood more than he could ever explain.

Franklin looked like a great big country-music star, she said. Huge hands, all calloused. Tall and narrow waisted, with lots of hair for a country boy. He hadn't a clue about how to respond to her. Much too cautious to touch her. Embarrassed by his clumsiness, he'd have to be invited. Even so, there was some competition for his attention. Most all the girls liked him for refusing to be drawn into the intrigues of the class bully.

Heather must have known how condescending all of this sounded and how little her apologies could do to excuse the way she'd pushed the helpless Franklin into intimacy. She admitted it seemed banal to her now, not just that she had shed her superiority for him along with her clothes, but how predictably unsatisfactory the episode had been. How unpleasant in fact. And how tedious all the apologies when she tried to convince him of her remorse. Franklin and his family were members of the same congregation that sent her here. She'd pleaded with him not to confess the seduction to his parents and, for God's sake, not to their pastor.

So, she said, they'd had her family's Jeep while her mother and father were away for the weekend, visiting in Greenville. She'd taken him to their property on Echo Lake for the submarine races. And once there it was as if he was actually watching for periscopes, staring straight ahead at the water, which offered not a ripple. She was forced to make a game of it—dare, double dare. I'll remove this, you remove that. He wouldn't start; she had to. And not with a barrette or a shoelace. Blouse first thing, then her jeans. Franklin was paralyzed until she began to whimper and reprove. How could he leave her at such a disadvantage?

"In a Jeep?"

"You know, in his lap."

Peter didn't know, but he noticed the girl behind them, across the aisle, had removed her earpiece. She was moving to a seat farther back. The rain stopped as the bus reached Winchester and turned east toward their Piedmont campus, and he began to correct himself for letting her go on, for a curiosity that sullied him by proxy. There was no excuse for the way he pried further when she was so clearly finished with her story. By then she was maybe oblivious of his company, busy with herself, cleaning her nails, one by one, scraping under each with a nail of the opposite hand.

Something she'd said begged an explanation, but would anyone else believe he was only probing for the moral of her story when he asked: "What do you suppose made it unpleasant?"

She snapped up from her grooming and stared at him. She was looking out the window when she finally answered.

"For God's sake! He was clumsy! It was painful!"

She kept her back turned, gazing through the window at the rain-freshened night. Finished with him, she was turning her scorn to the abuse of the landscape, the backlit windows of a thousand houses, "a measles of development" on the fields surrounding Freedom. "Is this Christian habitation? Is this Christian stewardship of the land?"

When the bus reached the college, there was a little crowd waiting for them on the sidewalk. Dr. Edwards, the chancellor, was there and Mr. Rhoden, vice president for student life. Word of the near tragedy had arrived ahead of them. The students had come out of their dorms in pajamas and sweaters. A few held up signs of congratulation. Stepping off the bus, aroused against conscience by all the casual touching, Peter reached for something to surprise her. A joke, that's what he intended, something to reverse their positions, turn their conversation upside down, and make her laugh.

"So you want to hook up later?" he asked.

Whether she only smirked or actually chuckled at the thought, he couldn't tell.

Jason wanted to hear all about it. "You sat next to her on the way home? Off the map, isn't she?"

"Not that far."

Peter's Monday classes oppressed him. He listened to Dr. Koh, the departing political science professor, defend his distinction between general and special revelation. It was a logical man's duty to find truth on or off the Christian reservation, he said. A woman left the classroom close to tears. Did others wish to leave? Two more walked out. "Good," the professor said, "I'll assume the rest of you agree with me."

Later in the day Peter's scripture section met for discussion in the village coffee shop. He was embarrassed by their reading aloud, their confident parsing, their testimonials reaching and overreaching, their affirmations imposed on all the tables in the room. His silence was remarked on by the other students and corrected by one, who suggested his reticence was tantamount to disagreement with their consensus that "through a glass darkly" was more suggestive of refraction than opacity, that they were not meant to feel blinded but able to see truth long before Judgment Day through a transposition of the light allowed them.

He could imagine Heather's scathing review of their sophistry and even saw himself cheering her on. He was nursing yesterday's adventure—pleasure and bruises. He wanted to see her again, to find a way through her armor, down to the honest if mistaken core that drove her candid tongue, to be her full confessor, to share the weight of her past, even if it stained him. Today his sense of worth seemed tied to her, resting on her approval, her friendship, her admiration of his intellect as a peer. He thought of asking his parents' permission to court Heather.

He was called to the Administration Building by a student messenger in the middle of his afternoon government lecture. Mr. Rhoden was waiting with Peter's dossier open on his desk. Surprised by the half-dozen pages in his file, he saw his photo clipped to the top sheet, a thinner self, three years and at least a thousand caramel lattes ago. His old grin was almost as wide as his jaw; a Windsor knot dwarfed his Adam's apple, sport jacket square at the shoulders, hair slicked down; a believer reporting for duty. But ready today, if pushed, to defend to the college Heather's gift of wide knowledge, even if it had to be classified as general revelation. He didn't intend to lie for her; neither would he impeach her.

"You know what this is about?"

"The woman from Maine?"

"You don't know her name?"

"Heather." He tried to explain his confused admiration. Not in trouble was she? He had nothing to say against her.

Rhoden gathered up Peter's file, as if giving it another chance, but his eyebrows did a doubtful dance, and one by one the pages fell again. "All about me?"

"You have a history of this sort of thing. If you want to stay, you'll have to apologize. Not just to Heather. To the whole college. Your parents will have to be told."

Peter went first thing to Heather's dormitory. Would the girl by the house phone please call her down to the lobby? He waited a half-hour. Women passing on their way to the student lounge would not look him in the eye. Eventually, one told him he ought to leave. Heather was paged again. Maybe he should come back another time. No, he'd wait. Another reluctant intermediary went upstairs to try. Heather, she said, would not come down. She was afraid to be seen in conversation with him.

Doors along the first-floor hall opened in curiosity and closed in embarrassment. If he sat on the visitors' sofa, it might look like he was waiting for one of these women to join him for academic discussion. There was no use pretending that. His pout of injured rectitude was being taken for the expression of a penitent. He supposed his nervous innocence, if read by a lie detector, would send the recording pen into guilty oscillation. Still reluctant to leave, he begged a wary freshman to deliver a note. "What did you tell the dean?"

This time the response came quickly, printed in block capitals, as if it would be dangerous to allow him a sample of her handwriting: "THE DEAN CALLED ME IN. HE SAID I SHOULD WATCH OUT, AND YOU HAVE A HABIT OF THIS."

Peter phoned home to head off the dean's call, but it was too late. No, he told his parents, he hadn't harassed the woman. " 'Hooking up' doesn't have to mean that. It was a joke. She knew it was a joke."

His father wasn't easily put off. "You meant actually hooking up, but it was a joke? Or did you mean why don't we talk later, and it was innocent and didn't have to be a joke?"

"You're confusing me," Peter said. "They won't even tell me who reported this stuff."

In the week that followed, he had only occasional glimpses of Heather in the cafeteria. With a remade reputation as a victim, she was gathering new friends, who positioned themselves on either side and across from her at the table, protecting her while she sat vulnerable in a public space; their baleful glances warned Peter to keep his distance. He'd been removed from the debate team and barred from extracurricular activity while the case against him was prepared for the student judiciary.

Peter didn't care what Rhoden thought. Rhoden was an ass. Whatever was in Peter's files, no accusers had identified themselves, and there could be no action against him based on hearsay. If Heather had allowed this storm to gather, he doubted she would ever testify against him. He'd been told she was all innocence in front of the dean. She'd said she'd thought Peter must be joking. Peter could take comfort in the fact that she would not testify against himself, but he wanted more than that. He was still angling for her kind regard. He asked another girl on the debate team to question Heather, to see how things stood now that a week had passed, and to bring him a report. Which was strangely unfriendly: "The eunuch's lost his voice and sends a carrier pigeon?"

With more time to reflect, his parents took Peter's side, counterattacking with a letter to the dean, citing slander—"he has a history of this sort of thing"—passed from Rhoden to Heather and circulated among the students, defaming their son among his peers. Besides, they argued, the original report of harassment hadn't come from the girl herself but had been made by a third party and passed to a fourth, then a fifth before it reached the dean. Peter had a copy of the letter with his father's comments for him in the margins:

> No wonder they can't get accreditation.
> Why don't you come home?
> Tuition refund?

There was only a semester left before his graduation, and Peter was holding out for his government degree. With the legal leverage identified by his father, he supposed he could force the college to let him walk with his class. In the meantime they couldn't make him apologize. While the chancellor and his professors argued over the moral authority of St. Augustine, Peter shared the details of his predicament with Jason, who could do no more than point to St. Matthew's forecast of rain that would fall on the just and the unjust.

On his way to dinner one evening Peter found a note hanging from the slot in his mailbox: Waiting for you at Rock Faith in the Rapture Room. Call yourself The Tongue.

Signed, Candy Cane.

He folded and tore, folded and tore, until his fingers lacked the strength to go on, and tossed the dirty confetti to the ground.

He knew when to enter the cafeteria, the quarter hour after six, when Heather would already be seated in the farthest corner of the room at a table informally reserved for Eden's Fruit, the college maskers and their techies. This group, too, had been attracted to Heather, maybe hoping their sympathy would lure the talented girl into the drama club in time for the spring Passion. A step up for her, Peter thought—from Jezebel to Magdalene—if that's what they had in mind. She seemed to be doing most of the talking, provoking laughter, making theirs the loudest corner of the room, taking scant notice of his lonely meal.

He usually finished studying around midnight and unwound on a solitary walk around the perimeter of the campus. It was a rectangular stroll bounded by the bypass highways, two country roads, and a Christmas tree farm, which in the brief history of the college had already become mythic cover for broken rules and promises, reputed trysting ground of a famous romance between two high-ranked stu-

dents—an Executive Office intern and a Justice Department parale-
gal. They are now married, presumed penitent for the unsanctioned
courtship, and moving up in Christian-influenced governance.

Peter, who passed beside the artificial forest almost every night,
understood the exaggerated reputation of the place, even if he once
heard light laughter and moaning from several rows deep in the
spruce. He carried a small flashlight in his pocket but was reluctant
to use it, despite his college-entrance oath to shine a light wherever
Satan might be found in the flesh in his college.

The end of his walk took him back across the center of the campus
past the two women's dormitories and under Heather's room, where
he was now in the habit of looking up for the silent news from a win-
dow. Open or closed? Heather's air fresh tonight or conditioned?
Lights on, off? Was she awake behind the curtains, tucked away in
bed?

Peter's final semester dragged on, with Heather always a step out
of reach or turning away before he could beg a word with her. She
did appear in the spring Passion, not as Magdalene as he'd imagined
her, but cross-dressed as Thomas, darkened with charcoal, and made
up to have the doubting apostle appear more sinister than Judas. He
watched her, too, behind the college podium in another debate, her
eyes dancing past her opponent, capturing the hall, while first she an-
nihilated an odious phantom called the unitary power of the execu-
tive as a creation of megalomaniacs mad with Potomac Fever, and
then resurrected it as the implied intention of three founding fa-
thers, with several references to the Federalist Papers.

In the week before graduation, Jason went home to Maryland to
study. Peter, with no one in the room to correct him, used his free-
dom aggressively. On the way back from his midnight walk, he called
up to the open, fully lit window:

"Heather!"

She appeared in a loose shift, hugging herself. But seeing him be-
low, she threw her arms theatrically wide, draped a half-covered bo-
som over the sill, and called down: "Is it Peace, Peter?"

Confused, he had no answer.

She laughed, closed the sash, and pulled her shade. Her lights
went off, and so did others, until the whole dormitory loomed dark
and accusing over him.

"Is it peace?" He'd heard this before but couldn't place it.

Back in his room, he opened his concordance and found the words in II Kings with an answer: "What peace, so long as the whoredoms of thy mother Jezebel and her witchcrafts are so many?" And further on, almost the same question was asked by Jezebel herself, before she was thrown from her window and eaten by dogs.

He couldn't sleep on that. Nor had mutilation destroyed the invitation in his mailbox. Without Jason over his shoulder, he was free to roam the ether and risk his hard drive to the nasty kind of attack that could linger in its memory, even if he was lured only once to the wrong place.

Peter easily reached the Rock Faith site where he knew other Freedom students had found the solace of righteous company. He could argue that it was his duty to expose whoever would defile that refuge. Clicking on the Rapture Room, he was further reassured by a screen promising privacy in a 'personal corner,' where they offered him a last chance to turn back. Cancel or Continue. He made his choice and watched the forefinger of his right hand type the name she'd given herself and then, more slowly, the name she'd given him.

His father had been right; the college had abused him. He could say he only persevered against their damning accusation to earn his degree, so that his years there should not have been completely wasted by an overzealous dean or a rash ultimatum of his own. By comparison with the last month, his whole career at Freedom seemed of little significance. Nothing of moment, as long as Heather, whom he admired beyond reason and in defiance of his alleged faith, refused him the courtesy of a simple conversation, her confession of *his* innocence, even a sign of regret.

His signal must have alerted the receiving computer. His respondent was awake and typing:

"I thought you'd forgotten me. Are you ready to play?"

"No."

"You're no fun."

"Who are you?"

"Do you know what Professor Koh calls government majors? He calls them the chancellor's eunuchs. What are you wearing?"

"Who are you?" he asked again.

"As if you didn't know. Wait a minute. There, that's better. I was too hot."

"It's the middle of the night. I must have woken you."

"So imagine me now."

"I won't imagine anything."

"No, I don't suppose you will. Why did you wake me up?"

"I want to talk about Jezebel. I never called anyone that."

"Look, do you want to be stupid all your life? Don't you see what's happening here? The best people are leaving. Anyone with intellect is made to check logic at the door."

"What if I print this and take it to the dean?"

"The correspondence of Candy Cane and The Tongue? I don't think so."

Heather was gathering more attention as a martyr to Peter's effrontery. In the last week of the term he was called to answer the testimony of two more unnamed women who accused him of stalking the sophomore from Maine, harassing her at night from the sidewalk under her window. Near the top of her class, she'd never lost a debate. To her following of sympathizers, she had come to Freedom for protection from a predatory world, from a high school where she'd been date raped by a big tricky farm boy named Franklin, and was looking now for sanctuary in a community of truthfulness and humility.

The graduation tent beside the highway looked like the pointed drum of shiny plastic you'd see over a modern minicircus. Underneath, Peter was walking with his class. He wondered if the scroll they'd present him would be blank. Even with the diploma in hand he was wary, searching it for the tricky placement of a Latin negative, *non est*, or something like that.

The night after graduation he stayed on in his dorm to confront Heather one more time, even if just in the ether. Not to renounce duplicity so much as to marvel at the Trojan horse on which she'd jumped the college gate, the ease with which she grazed among the faithful. She gave no quarter, but congratulated him as one of the chancellor's freshly papered eunuchs before the Rapture Room went dark.

Nominated by The American Scholar

AMERICAN INCOME

by AFAA MICHAEL WEAVER

from POETRY

The survey says all groups can make more money
if they lose weight except black men . . . men of other colors
and women of all colors have more gold, but black men
are the summary of weight, a lead thick thing on the scales,
meters spinning until they ring off the end of the numbering
of accumulation, how things grow heavy, fish on the
ends of lines that become whales, then prehistoric sea life
beyond all memories, the billion days of human hands
working, doing all the labor one can imagine, hands
now the population of cactus leaves on a papyrus moon
waiting for the fire, the notes from all their singing gone
up into the salt breath of tears of children that dry, rise
up to be the crystalline canopy of promises, the infinite
gone fishing days with the apologies for not being able to love
anymore, gone down inside earth somewhere where
women make no demands, have fewer dreams of forever,
these feet that marched and ran and got cut off, these hearts
torn out of chests by nameless thieves, this thrashing
until the chaff is gone out and black men know the gold
of being the dead center of things, where pain is the gateway
to Jerusalems, Bodhi trees, places for meditation and howling,
keeping the weeping heads of gods in their eyes.

Nominated by Pamela Stewart

BENDITHION[1]

by HARRISON SOLOW

from AGNI

VULCANS HAVE AN INNER EYELID.

In one of the episodes of *Star Trek*, Mr. Spock is invaded by a fatal parasite on a remote planet. Exposure to high-intensity light appears to be the only cure—a treatment that would blind humans. Because of Vulcan physiology, however, a hidden ocular membrane descends to shut out intrusive rays, and Spock emerges intact, undamaged by his contact with an alien world.

It turns out that *y Cymry*[2] have an inner eyelid as well. More like an obfuscatory veil than a solid barricade, it allows the Welsh to see out, but effectively shades the inner self from the eyes of the inquisitive, casting all that is behind it in shadow. It is a dusky looking-glass, presented innocently enough to the stranger, deceptively luminous and reflective, its transparency clearly controlled by time and measured, in nanobytes, by trust.

Take the matter of the sandwiches.

Some time ago, I was writing an article on our postmaster Timothy who also happens to be a world class tenor,[3] and whose longstanding habit was and is still to have sandwiches sent in (a rather grand term for one of the postmen walking down the road two hundred yards and picking up a paper bag) from The Sosban Fach.[4]

---

[1] Bendithion means "blessings" in Welsh, though without a particularly religious connotation. It is the title of my forthcoming epistolary novel.
[2] Y Cymry is pronounced "uh Cumree" and means "the Welsh people."
[3] Implausible but true. Long story.
[4] Fach is pronounced vahch with the "ch" as in the Hebrew "challah" or the Scottish "loch."

"Sosban," as most people call it, is a tiny restaurant in our village, staffed by a bevy of ladies (in aprons patterned with teapots) with exceptional *Cymreictod*[5] and an uncanny radar for the "news" so cherished by our postmaster. Every morning someone from the post office phones in an order according to the number of people on duty that day, and at about 11:20, someone, usually Alun, picks it up.

In trying to inject a little human interest into this article, and to round out the very limited information I had theretofore been given, I sat down with these formidable ladies late one afternoon, in the post-lunch lull, with a cup of tea, to elicit what I mistakenly assumed to be some innocuous information on our mutual friend.[6]

It doesn't take much to get a story out of a Welshwoman. Or man either. The oral tradition is strong. So, I prepared comfortably (and somewhat smugly, I see now) for the cornucopia of tales my simple query, "Can you tell me a little about Timothy?" would undoubtedly engender.

"Lovely voice, hasn't he?" is the first comment—soon to become a refrain.

"Yes," say I, "Extraordinary. But what would you say, apart from his voice, are his main characteristics? I'd like to know more about his personality—how you see him."

"Oh, he's lovely, really, isn't he?" is the next response—met by a general chatter of agreement and vigorous nods.

"Like, how?" I ask.

"Very good to his mother, he was," one of them says, sagely.

As a number of vicious criminals have been documented to be good to their mothers, this doesn't seem to be anything significantly illuminating to put into an article, but the little silence that follows this in deference to his recent loss makes me hesitate. In their silence, my own silence rises to enclose me, my connection to Timothy reforms and I once again feel his grief.

My heart beats more slowly. More heavily. More insistently. More collectively. I feel myself losing identity. One or two of the women stare at me as if to absorb—or as if to detach—me from the group. I

[5] Welshness (pronounced "come—rike-toid." Sort of.)
[6] I use the phrase "mutual friend" with some reservation, since there are minute and invisible gradations of friendship and none of them have anything to do with the sort of tribal connection that the people in my village have with/to each other. My connections are more diverse, isolated. I am not part of that matrix. My connection to Timothy is explained elsewhere.

am not sure which. No one yet knows my identification with Timothy. I decide to keep neutral. I shake myself free.

"Yes, I'm sure he was," I say briskly, as if that knowledge and that loss weren't beating in my veins, "But I'm trying to describe him *in himself* so to speak—do you know what he feels strongly about—either positively or negatively?"

"Oh we haven't got anything negative to say about him," says one. They all shake their heads firmly.

"No—no—I don't mean that. I mean does he have strong feelings or opinions for or against anything that you know about?"

"He likes glass. He has a lovely glass collection. Pink. Have you seen it?"

"No, but that isn't quite what I meant." Still, I make a clear tidy note on my pad: collects *pink glass*? "You see, that's the sort of thing I can ask him about, actually, but thank you for telling me," I try to clarify, though I am beginning to see that they all know exactly what I mean. "I need your impression of him—any stories you can tell about him that would show what kind of a man he is."

"Cranberry," a voice at the corner of the table sings out. It sounds like "Crrrrrahnbuddy"—a musical, multi-textured sound that seems to consist of many more syllables than it actually has. I stop for a moment—take pleasure in this small Welsh song and then say:

"Cranberry what?"

"Glass," she says, again with multiple resonance. "Cranberry glass. He collects it."

"Look . . ."

"He was on *Sunday Request* yesterday," Bronwen interrupts. "I put down my brush straightaway and sat right down there in the kitchen and listened. Gives you a lump in the throat, doesn't he?"

Having had to stay inside for a whole day while my swollen eyes returned to normal on more than one occasion after listening to Timothy sing, my "yes, he does" seems inadequate, but I know if I recount my own experiences, then the conversation will dive into waters I would prefer to stay out of at the moment, so I just add, "I want to know what he is like as a person—not just a singer. Does he have any passions or causes, or personality traits that you would think of in describing him?"

Silence greets that little question. I think it must be the word "passions" and I instantly regret my vocabulary.

96

They all look into their teacups.

"Well," comes a voice from the middle of the group. "We don't know him very well."

This is a bit much for a Californian who is used to five-minute friendships. Ten-minute commitments.

"Come on! You've all known him for decades—you talk to him almost every day! You know his family, friends, the organizations he belongs to—his church, the town—his interests. I'm not going to say anything bad about him. I just want to know what he is like—quiet, funny, energetic, political . . . that sort of thing."

They raise their heads. In six pairs of eyes, that inner eyelid has descended. Almost translucent, but filtering out any real visual communication, a cloudy opacity has replaced the usually warm, communicative, merry eyes of my companions. Oddly, they all seem to have turned into one collective person.

"He's not quiet," someone says timidly. I am not sure who.

"But not a loud man," someone else replies. Again, though I am right there in front of them, I can't quite distinguish individuals from the group. It is uncanny.

"No, no," they all agree. "Not loud. He's lovely, really. Lovely voice." This produces a chatter of agreement and a launch into a discussion about who likes what song best and why.

"You know the one I like," Rhiannon says, briefly emerging from the crowd. "The one about Ceredigion Bay" ("Hen Fae Ceredigion"). She starts to sing it. One or two of the others join in. The rest close their eyes and hum along. I have to admit, they *can* sing, and I am lulled into this atmosphere of cohesive, peaceful harmony for a moment or two before trying to resurrect my sinking interview.

"Okay," I say. "You all know me. I've been coming here for almost three years. We've spent more time together than I have with some of my actual friends back home. Look at me. Look at my face. Do you see anything in it that says I want to portray Timothy in a bad light? Do I look like I am here to harm this man? I love this guy. I'd marry him tomorrow if I could. Today. Here. Right now."

There is a little squeal and a flurry of shifting attention.

"Could we be bridesmaids?" Marlene pipes up.

They are all instantly diverted and suddenly the mood changes. This is no longer "an interview." It's fun. It's "the girls." It's a hen party.

"What should we wear?"

"I want to make the cake."

"Oh I love a good wedding cake. I made my Betty's cake, you know."

"No!"

"I did. I went to Price's, got those little stands . . ."

"Oh wouldn't she make a lovely bride then for her postmaster?"

"Lovely couple," someone says.

"But who would we get to *sing* at the wedding?"

They all collapse in laughter.

"I'm not kidding," I say. "It's not a joke. He's a rare person."

"Oh we know," says Gwawr. "I'd marry him just for the voice."

"You're a pretty rare person, yourself," Bronwen says. "Thank God. We wouldn't want a lot of you loose, would we?"

A shout of laughter follows this, over the detailed recipe that someone is giving someone else for wedding cake. I catch "two dozen egg whites and one yolk"—think to myself, "that can't be right"—and then:

"I'd marry him for the glass," Marlene puts in.

"Well you can't have him," I say, crossly. "He's mine. Besides, you're the bridesmaids. Look," I entreat them, "Let's get back on track. We all love him. And we want everyone else to love him too when they read about him. So—can I get some opinions from you— his friends, neighbors, acquaintances, fellow villagers, about what he is really like? That's all. Nothing bad. I wouldn't do that. You can read what I write about you before I send it to the magazine if you like."

"Oh we know, *bach*,"[7] the most motherly of the group reassures me. "You wouldn't do anything like that. But we really don't know anything that you could write about. Nothing interesting. You'll be sure to mention the Sosban, though, won't you? How much he likes our sandwiches?"

"Well, I'm not writing an ad for the restaurant, but okay—I'll mention the name if I ever find anything to write about."

In the absence of any other information, at least I'll have to have some words to fill up the space. That gives me an idea. Perhaps I can ease into a more informative conversation another way.

[7] Pronounced like the surname of Johann Sebastian. It literally means "little" but is colloquially an endearment—"little dear," "little darling," etc.

"You do have great sandwiches," I say truthfully, but a little too brightly. "I like the Coronation Chicken. What's Timothy's favorite?"

They look at each other, then at me, and it is clear that the hen party is over. In unnerving unison, the inner eyelids descend once again.

"Oh, I don't think we could say, bach," Gwawr says. "It wouldn't be right."

"*What?*" I feel like Alice in Wonderland—confronting six waning Cheshire Cats.

"We really can't say," Blodwyn echoes.

I don't think I have heard right. I think of the intimate details I have heard from relative strangers in America—not to mention the talk show mentality and the general prolific "sharing" that seems to be culturally requisite these days in so many societies. There's no point in going there, so I just make mild protest.

"But why not? People order things in restaurants in public all the time—out loud. Everyone can hear what they order."

"*He* doesn't," they say. "It's on the phone, see?"

"It wouldn't be right," someone repeats.

Now it is my turn to be silent. I truly cannot think of anything to say in the face of this otherworldly delicacy. This time warp into ancient tribal reticence. This great collective cloud of irrelevant privacy.

"It's only a sandwich," I end up protesting feebly, but I know I have lost. "How can it hurt anyone to know what kind of a sandwich a guy likes?"

I wish they would talk to me about this man's beauty—his incandescent voice, his whirling white glowing personhood—the feel of his presence in the town—the something inside him that they know I see—that I know they see and that has drawn us together in mutual appreciation at this very table. It is of course, that exact something that makes them unwilling to talk about him—even so simple a thing as his sandwich. I need to write about this—this what? Modesty? Clannishness? Protectiveness? Mistrust? Cultural reluctance? But I can't. Not yet. They won't tell me anything. They won't even confirm what I already know.

"Well, but we don't know—do we?" says Gwawr, breaking my silence and vigorously nodding at the others. "There's an order put in, see, for all of them. We don't know *which* sandwich he would eat."

That remark seems to meet with great approval around the table—its cleverness and spontaneous parry are admired, as indicated by the appreciative glances in Gwawr's direction and a peek at me to see if I am swallowing that one. I'm not.

"Okay, ladies. I'm finished here. I know that you know and you don't want to tell me and that's okay. No problem. I'll just ask him myself."

This admission of defeat is greeted with generous, supreme relief, another round of tea, and the lifting of the veil, so to speak. The unclouded eyes reappear, conversation perks up, we exchange news and gossip on every subject except Timothy, and we have an excellent visit.

When I see Timothy next, I ask him, not that I'm interested, what his favorite sandwich is. His eyes start to cloud over until he remembers he knows me better now, and suddenly, they clear up. I watch this transformation and reversal, fascinated. And very pleased. But apparently he doesn't know me quite well enough at that point.

"Well," he says, slowly, "I don't like cheese."

~

No one ever asked why I couldn't marry him, by the way. But there is a reason: Timothy already belongs to me, to my race of opacity and denial, to my heritage of heads in the sand, to my bloodline of hope and first stars in the night sky. He is my kinsman, my comrade, my brother, my friend. Marriage would be a lesser bond between us. We are the shielded, the tender, the trusting, the blank-faced children in rooms of adult construction, easily bruised, easily frightened, easily led by pipers onto imperfect paths—Hansels, Gretels, Pinocchios, babes. This is our tribe.

We do not burst into the world unafraid, unreluctant, resilient, cheerful, impervious, as some do. We come unwilling into the light. We look back. And unless we are transformed by fortune or misfortune, or stay close to our origins, we wither in the noonday suns of the worlds outside or go mad. Our skins are too thin. We cannot take much light. And so we shield our eyes.

It is true that my Timothy, born and bred in Wales, and I, from a separate realm altogether, cannot claim common kingdom. But in the order of taxonomy, our species is the same. What he shares with his compatriots is residence behind the smokescreen. What he shares

100

with me is why. For unlike those lovely ladies of Sosban Fach, it is not that we wish not to be seen. It is that we wish not to see.

We were all born with those eyelids. I lost mine long ago in a land of midnight sun, transformed by necessity and the acid tongues of the English. Timothy, still living in the house where he was born, kept his intact. He still uses them when needed. Thank God, no longer with me.

~

This is the trouble with writing from the outside: meeting the shells of others with the shell of oneself. The truth is, I don't care about the information I seek at all. It is meaningless. Sandwiches, birthdates, glass, other people's opinions about someone I know as intimately as a pregnancy, as privately as a birth. Stories, tales, incidents, facts.

I know next to nothing about Timothy. But I have never believed that knowing about anyone was of any value. He knows next to nothing about me. And what he does know is misleading. Facts mean nothing. They knew that, the ladies of Sosban. They all know it. I asked for facts. They gave me facts. Not the ones I asked for, but facts all the same. They are all interchangeable, these little blocks of information. One person likes chicken. One dislikes cheese. "Facts, facts, facts, Mr. Gradgrind." What do they mean?

There is a world of difference, or rather a difference of worlds, between what is outside and what is behind these eyelids we were given to use or to lose as our separate lives unfold. One is the world of *knowing about*. The other is a world of *knowing*. This is the difference between Wales and everywhere else I have been. This is why I am here.

~

What all this means, then, is that I ended up with an article of almost no *factual* information. And yet, it contains more *actual* information than any other article I have written. This is it:

Princeps Cantorum

My first interview with Timothy Evans consisted of his telling me absolutely nothing for as long as possible while looking at me nonstop with bright, round, heartbreaking eyes over a mug of milky coffee. He answered no question with any relevant information, asked nothing of me, even when invited in desperation to do so to give us *something* to talk about, and never took his eyes from my face, while seeming not to look at me at all.

I started with a list of forty questions. After one look at his face at the fourth question, I slipped it into my briefcase and just sat and stared back. A few minutes later, largely to deflect the attention of other diners, I tried spontaneous questions, directly related to the amorphous comments I had received from him thus far, and somehow that didn't work either.

I'm not sure how he did it, even to this day, three years and a lifetime later when we have become so intrinsic to each other, except to say that generations of Welshmen beat in his blood and if you know what that means you know he could have done nothing else. Not then, anyway. I see now, of course, that that little I-Thou session set a precedent for the future. We still don't talk much. But we share a lot of silence together.

My name is Harrison Solow. I come from Los Angeles and I've never seen, met, known, or heard anyone in the world like Timothy Evans. And unless you live here, in this remote and somewhat implausible Welsh village where Timothy and I live, then neither have you.

Timothy is our postmaster. He sells stamps, issues various baffling permits, collects payments for bizarre things like television licenses and road tax and other nanny-like little punishments which the British government delights in inflicting upon its citizens. (By the way, *never* mistake "Welsh" for "English." It's far worse than mistaking a Canadian for an American, and in my opinion—having lived for some years in Canada—with good cause.) Timothy makes tea for his employees in the back room every morning, wears what appears to be the same sweater every day, and goes home to an empty house every night.

He goes home, as well, to acres of soft emerald fields full of the Shetland ponies, Torwen sheep, and Bantam hens that he breeds and cares for single-handedly every morning, some noons (during lambing), and every night of his spectacularly mysterious life.

He also has a voice that comes pretty close to what "Let there be Light" would have sounded like had it burst forth from the lungs of an anthropomorphic god in the act of creation. And pretty close to Light itself.

Let me say at the outset that this is not an objective account. I am absolutely committed to celebrating this man's voice. It is flawless, haunting, and irrefutably magical. You won't be the same after you've heard it. No one else is. And you will have probably wept through every unblemished note. Everyone else does. Of course, right now, "everyone" doesn't constitute a lot of people. This voice is one of the best (and deliberately) kept secrets in the world, as is so much about Wales. But that's about to change. I'm about to do a little "let there be light" in America, myself.

Wales, it is true, is known for its musical contribution to the world—Tom Jones, Bryn Terfel, Charlotte Church, the famed Welsh men's choirs, and to be accurate, almost every Welsh man, woman, and child you will ever meet inside Wales or out. They seem to be genetically programmed with music. But this—this is a voice beyond music. This is incandescence.

And lest one think that this is just the hyperbole of an isolated crank, esoteric music-buff or besotted fan, let me hasten to offer prolific, dispassionate, expert, and critical proof:

There is an astonishing tradition in this land of "mists and mellow fruitfulness" called the Eisteddfod. Pronounced "eye-steth-vod," it hails from 1176 when the great bards of Wales would gather in the halls of their kings to praise the virtue and valor of these leaders in poetry and song—and it is still in full flower today.

Of course, there are other things to praise these days, and the Eisteddfod system (local, regional, national) is now a much broader arts competition, open to all Welsh speakers, but the tradition is the same: literary and musical excellence. Excellence, by the way, means "Excellence." The standards are extremely high. Judges are severe and winners usually go on to make their mark in the world.

Poets, writers, and musicians are crowned after an exacting elimination process, and as they take their place on the Eisteddfod chair, they are honoured by a host of children who dance before them in praise. The first time I saw this, I was struck as silent as Timothy in his first interview.

I worry about Wales, actually. It is such a small country, so overshadowed by the England that has historically sought to absorb, assimilate, disempower, and eradicate it as a separate culture; so invaded by the rising influx of non-speakers of its language, dismissive of its heritage; and so eroded by bland blanket EU policies that take into account nothing that is unique or culturally significant about its mighty Celtic identity. But when I saw the Eisteddfod, I stopped worrying. "A country that cherishes its language this much—a country that sends its children to dance in homage to a writer and to sing to the land—to recite love poetry to their grandmothers and to cry over lost miners—all in an astonishing flowering of talent—will survive," I wrote to a friend. "My heart is at rest after seeing these children. They all have Timothy's face."

This is not simply sentiment. The dedication, the discipline, the talent, and the sincerity of these performers are all astounding. But what is more astounding, what is, in fact, strangely powerful is what they sing and write *about*: their mothers, their fathers, their families, their land, their history, their princes and bards—their farms and rivers, birds, air, and butterflies—their God, their homes, their children, their language, and their wild, rolling seas. And the most powerful thing of all is that these subjects of which they sing are all the same entity. None is separate from the other. I don't know how I know this but I do.

This is Wales in secret flower. Very secret. There is no video you can buy to relive these shining performances. There's nothing much on the website that gives anyone a real understanding of the magnitude of this event. It lives in the silence and memory of its people who return from their brief glory to take up their lives again in the farms, schools, businesses, industries (and post offices) they came from. It's a Welsh thing. Daily life is just more important.

There are of course consequences of extraordinary performance. People win real honors: writing is published, musical careers are launched. But by and large, it is an ephemeral cultural celebration. For the people, by the people, and of the people of Wales.

Then there is the International Eisteddfod, which is quite a different thing: open to all countries and all languages, it gives rise to some of the best international performers in the world.

Luciano Pavarotti competed in and won the International Eisteddfod in Wales one golden year of his life. So did Timothy Evans, which, by the way, is not his only resemblance to the Master with whom he is perpetually and favorably paralleled. Of course, Timothy has won every award for which he has ever competed. His house glitters with silver cups and prizes, including the most prestigious and coveted one: *Princeps Cantorum*. Colloquially translated as

"The Best Singer" or "*The* Eisteddfod Voice," this means not that he earned first place for a tenor in a competition with other tenors in his minute country, nor that he won first place in a competition among the tenors of the world. No.

Princeps Cantorum (literally "First Cantor" or "Foremost Poet") is the honor that goes to the single best voice—out of every soprano, tenor, bass, baritone (and all other variations) from every one of the forty-seven competing countries of the world. The fairest of them all. Timothy stopped competing after that.

Unlike me, Eisteddfod judges are dispassionate, exacting, experienced musicians without a shred of empathy for anything but perfection. They found it in Timothy Evans. All I have is the desire to do something about it. Unlike Timothy Evans.

Naturally, Timothy has been besieged over the years by offers to manage, train, market, and sell him to the world outside Wales. Unnaturally, he has refused every offer. If there was one question in my first interview with Timothy that I hammered to death, it was, in response to these refusals, "why?" And if there was one question I didn't even think to ask in our last interview, it was "why?" After living here for three years, I know why. And it is as unfathomable a question for me now as it was for him then. Still, I should at least record what he said:

He said, "Because I like it here."

That was the Chauncey Gardener answer (in toto) that he stuck with for about eight months. When he felt he knew me a bit better I got the second (Alice in Wonderland) half:

"Because if I went somewhere else and did other things, I would end up not being me, wouldn't I?"

I have to say that Welsh answers like these, which are really not answers at all, are one of the reasons I make my home here. Answers like questions, silence that speaks, empty houses that are simultaneously full, and an entire country that is hidden from view even while you inhabit it are the stuff of dreams for a writer.

I confess that I threw in that "empty house" deliberately. For, Timothy has never married. He lived, from birth, with the woman who bore him: his mother, his friend, his lifelong companion, until he lost her not long ago. And so, that house is truly empty for him. It has an echo now, not unlike the resonance in his voice that preceded his grief. There is, in Welsh, the untranslatable word *hiraeth* (hear-eye-th). It is not emptiness, exactly. It is not quite longing. Nor does it exist outside a Welsh heart. It is more like the heart that surrounds longing—that organic hungering vessel without which emptiness would not exist. I wanted that word "empty" to say something. I wanted to indicate by merest of allusions where this voice comes from. It has always come from hunger. It has always come from emptiness. It has always come from hiraeth.

What I mean by this is that there has always been a singular purity in his voice, an enigmatic otherworldliness, the consequence of a great deal of time spent in an unfilled space, alone. Timothy's world is essentially a world of one.

For me, however, when Timothy is home, the house is full. When he is in the village, the village is full. When he sings, the world is full—of beauty and of something else that has no name. He has a quality of extension that admittedly takes some receptivity to feel, but once felt, is never forgotten. And he doesn't even have to *be* there to do it.

Not long ago I sent a CD of Timothy's songs to a colleague, an entertainment manager in Las Vegas. Her job is to say no to ninety-nine percent of the professionally prepared bios, promos, packages, reels, DVDs, and CDs that cascade over her desk daily. Only because we are friends did she patiently (and I am sure skeptically) agree to listen to Timothy's lone CD (*sans* bio/photo/video/hype), one of his six locally produced recordings with a selection of twelve mostly obscure (to Americans) songs sung entirely in Welsh. What happened when she did so astonished her, puzzled Timothy for the thirty seconds he put his mind to it, and didn't surprise me at all. She cried, of course. But that's not all.

When she closed the door to her office one winter afternoon and put on the CD, somehow, at about the sixth song, this sophisticated, critical entertainment professional found herself reaching out to the CD player with her hand as if to find him, touch him—to make some connection with something that has no name. She rested her hand on the CD player in a kind of self-comfort until the last sweet notes faded away.

She said afterwards that when she realized what she had done, she felt a little lame. Shaken. Odd. She called him "gorgeous and rare." She said there was something in his voice that she had never heard before. She said she wants him but doesn't know what to do with him. (I know what she means.) Then, like the rabid researcher she is, she immediately sought out and listened to six CDs of world-famous tenors—some of whom she has booked for full-blast Las Vegas concerts—just to make sure—just to compare her reaction to them with her reaction to Timothy Evans.

There was no comparison. For as successful, popular, famous, and supremely talented as these tenors were, she found that, in her words, she "understood them."

"I know where they are coming from, who they are singing to. They're singing to me. But I don't understand Timothy. Who is he? And who is he singing to?"

The answer I gave her, without consulting Timothy, who would have said what he always says (nothing), was this: He is singing to that empty house and to those emerald fields that surround it. He is singing to himself and to the country that no outsider sees. He is, above all, singing to Wales itself.

The very reason for his magnetic effect on people is that he is *not* offering an I-Thou personal relationship to his listeners—he is offering transport to another world. He is the key to a secret garden, a rabbit hole, a yellow brick road, a starship, the door in the wardrobe, the back of the North Wind. An audible alchemist. A Gabriel at the gates. He isn't singing to you or to me. He's singing *for* us—on behalf of us, because we can't sing ourselves into a wonderland on our own.

The fact is, Timothy isn't even there when he sings. He told me once, in a whisper, that he sometimes "goes away" when he is singing. "Sometimes," he said, "It frightens me a little."

~

This is our postmaster. In a village of twelve hundred people. Selling stamps.

I can't stand it.

And so, I went to Timothy last month and asked him if, despite his having turned down everyone in the music industry who had contacted him in the last two decades, he would let me bring him to America to sing (in English) if I could find a suitable venue. He said yes. Just that. One word. "Yes." A few minutes later he produced his only caveat. "If you'll bring me back."

Nobody understands why after all this time he has changed his mind. Of course, no one really knew what was in his mind to begin with. Least of all me. But it has something to do with his empty house, something to do with me, and something to do with the revolution of the spheres, for lack of a better phrase. It's just time. He knows it. That's Timothy.

He seems unperturbed about this *volte face*. He knows he can sing anything that a lyrical tenor can sing. Anything. Anywhere. Anytime. For anyone. From opera to Christmas carols, from "Love Changes Everything" ("Serch Sy'n Newid Popeth") to the love theme from *Titanic* to ancient, contemporary, arcane, and traditional Welsh songs. He already has. He has that supreme confidence of the pure of heart, the sublimely talented, and the very young. Whereas, in fact, he is nearer forty than thirty, stout and fair, with a touching, untouchable dignity and lungs like a lion.

I should have said earlier that he was trained in his youth, or rather in his earlier youth, by Gerald Davis, the principal tenor of Covent Garden. Although it probably wouldn't have mattered if he wasn't. This voice was born, not manufactured.

Our entire village, by the way, acts as a collective and very protective chicken with one amazing chick. Timothy is known to and beloved by a vast, complex network of neighbors and relatives who consider him their personal property—so much so that when I first asked to interview people about Timothy, they all agreed, all kept their promise, all were warm and friendly, and all said nothing worth recording about him. No actual information passed their lips.

Timothy has hundreds of cousins, thousands of admirers, and one perfect best friend, Alun, who works with him side by side, day by day in the post office. Alun (pronounced Ah-lin) is another treasure in our village. If I weren't writing about the voice of an angel, so to speak, I would most certainly write about the heart of one—and it would be Alun's. He is also the only person out of all the people I interviewed who would actually tell me anything about Timothy. He said one thing, and that was that Timothy was "the kindest person in the world," which says as much about him as it does about Timothy. But it illustrates something about what people think is important here. Trust, privacy, cohesiveness, friendship, solidarity, kindness, family, work, moderation, repetition, economy of expression certainly—and, of course, daily life.

I suppose now is the time to explain what's in it for me.

Basically, nothing. I'm here writing a book about Wales and lecturing in the University in our town. It's just that Timothy is my childhood sweetheart. And you do things for the inhabitants of your childhood that you just don't do for anyone else. It was Timothy of course who came up with this wacky label, in his quiet, uncanny way:

"I think we are childhood sweethearts," he announced one day over tea, apropos of absolutely nothing. He looked at me thoughtfully for a moment, smiled with exceptional sweetness, went back to his tea and said no more. I was instantly riveted of course. Diverted. Enchanted. Prepared, as writers are wont to be, to discuss this fascinating concept, this emotional connectional time-warp in all its delicate intricacy. But you can't have a conversation with Timothy when he is finished talking. Or listening. So that was about it. Anyway, I knew what he meant.

Ours is one of those decorous, old-fashioned, inexplicable relationships that develop at times between kindred spirits and have nothing to do with sex, something to do with romance, and everything to do with love. We know each other too well from a past we never shared to be called merely "friends," and we are too chivalrously attached to one another to be anything else. Almost all women will know what I'm talking about and I won't speculate about the perception of men.

And it doesn't matter that we were born on two separate continents in two different decades and met only three ancient years ago. It's not our fault. So "childhood sweethearts" it is. But even if we were merely on nodding terms, even if I did not like him at all, I'd still do my best to see this voice launched into the wider world. It would be criminal not to.

Not unexpectedly, Timothy maddeningly has no website, no email address, no promotional package, no music manager, no publicist, no lawyer, no long-term contracts—almost everything is done by word of mouth on an individual basis as is often the (barely believable but nevertheless true) custom here. He just has me. But he'll go where he is meant to go, because things happen that way in this land of King Arthur, Merlin, and magic. And so we will come to America.

I don't know how he will fare, this Pan, this man-child, this Adam before the apple, this Innocent Abroad. We'll have to make sure that he doesn't "end up not being him," although I think he's pretty safe. It's not that he hasn't been on tour before. He has sung the length and breadth of Wales in halls that resound not only with his voice but also with the response of his audience, awash in tears. His concert diary is as full as he wants it to be. And he still turns down most requests.

He has also sung in other countries on several tours—to sell-out crowds—but always to Welsh-speaking venues, for Welsh expatriates. Each time he has stayed in his hotel room until curtain time, sung stunningly on stage, and gone back to his (empty) room. Each time he has opened a door to a land of enchantment for others. This time, I want him to open it for himself.

Nominated by Agni

LOVE IN THE ORANGERY

by AIMEE NEZHUKUMATATHIL

from THIRD COAST

When you see a seventy-pound octopus squeeze
through a hole the size of a half-dollar coin, you

    finally understand that everything you learn about
    the sea will only make people you love say *You lie.*

There are land truths that scare me: a purple orchid
that only blooms underground. A German poet

    buried in the heart of an oak tree. The lighthouse man
    who used to walk around the streets at night

with a lighted candle stuck into his skull. But winters
in Florida—all the street corners have sad fruit

    tucked into the curb, fallen from orangery truckers
    who take corners too fast. The air is sick with citrus

and yet you love the small spots of orange in walls
of leafy green as we drive. Your love is a concrete canoe

    that floats in the lake like a lead balloon, improbable
    as a steel wool cloud, a metal feather. This is the truth:

I once believed nothing on earth could make me say magic.
You believe in the orange blossom tucked behind my ear.

Nominated by Beth Ann Fennelly, Third Coast

ACROSS THE UNIVERSE

fiction by ANDREW MCCUAIG

from BOULEVARD

BEFORE I WAS EVEN TEN YEARS OLD, I was considered a prodigy at the piano. I never considered myself one, but my teacher, tiny Mrs. Chin, seemed to, and because she treated me the way she did, my parents grew to think I was talented in some mysterious, magical way, since neither of them were musical at all. Today if you sat me down and asked me to sightread something I'd be hard-pressed, but at the age of nine music was my second language. Sometimes even my first.

Mrs. Chin only had about ten students at any given time, and I suppose I was her best, though she had many who were older, six or seven years older, who were obviously playing more difficult music. But at every year-end recital she placed me last, after the big kids, and it never seemed to surprise or bother anyone. Every month there were little "workshops" on Saturday morning where all her students would gather in her basement and play for each other on one of her two grand pianos. Parents weren't invited. She'd give us a lesson on Liszt or Mozart, then play us some music on her black record player, pointing out interesting things with a tilt of her head, her finger raised. Then we'd each play the piece we'd memorized for that month and finish off with some juice and cookies. In June, the points we had earned throughout the year were tallied and I would win a rather cheap trophy, about six inches high, with a composer on top and my name engraved below with the year. The third year this happened—the bust was of Bach, I remember, big hair and all—one of the other parents, Renee Jacobs' mom I think it was, approached me and shook my hand, then made a snide remark to my father about my being a "charity case," or maybe it was "a sweepstakes winner"—something like that. My dad smiled awkwardly and looked at his feet, said something like, "I guess so." He was a Professor of Religion at Kalamazoo College and hated confrontation. If my mother had heard the remark it would have turned ugly.

My mother once called Mrs. Chin in the middle of dinner to shout at her to mind her own business or she wouldn't get ours. In the fall I played soccer and in the spring I played tennis. One day during a lesson Mrs. Chin told me that if I wanted to be a success at the piano I needed to cut out these other things; that they were for children. I had a future as a great artist, but if I didn't commit myself at a young age it would never happen. For me, playing the piano was something I liked to do, something I did well, but it was just one of many things. In most ways I was an average little boy. I shrugged and went on playing, but when I casually told my parents at dinner what Mrs. Chin had said, my mother threw down her napkin and, while my dad said, "Laura, Laura, wait until you calm down," she called up my teacher and let her have it. I was quiet and embarrassed, but also exhilarated. My sister Darlene, who was sixteen, was beaming—*here* was something to tell her friends. Before my mother slammed down the phone she told Mrs. Chin her services wouldn't be needed anymore.

I missed two weeks of lessons, during which I played every afternoon anyway because I needed to get the pieces right for myself. One afternoon, at the end of this stretch, I felt my mother standing beside me and I looked up. I wanted to ask her how long she had been standing there. For a while we just looked at each other. When she spoke it was almost a whisper.

"You play very nicely. Sometimes I don't even notice."

I put my hands on my lap and waited for her to leave.

She went into the kitchen and called Mrs. Chin. I listened with my fingers on the keys. My mother spoke in a quiet humble voice and did most of the listening.

When I let myself into Mrs. Chin's house the following Tuesday—it was always Tuesday, for eleven years, always Tuesday at four o'-clock; I'd let myself in the back door, walk through her kitchen and down the linoleum basement stairs—she was waiting in her chair beside the first grand piano. She was smiling warmly. She motioned to the piano and told me to play whatever I had been working on. I remember I played a Haydn sonata, a difficult piece with a final scherzo that was especially tricky but fun. I played the whole thing pretty well and when I was done she was laughing and wiping her eyes, telling me welcome back, welcome back. I was nine.

I enjoyed the piano, especially Mrs. Chin's two twin black grands, and I could make the keys do what I wanted. I could pick out a melody the way I suppose some kids can throw a curve ball or wrist a puck shoulder high past a goalie. There was an ease to my playing that I've encountered very rarely in my life. Athletes talk about being in the *zone*. I once played a pickup game of basketball in my twenties where everything I threw up went in. I suppose I had entered a kind of fluky zone that day, but it was much more legitimate when I was a boy sitting at the piano.

Once, Mrs. Chin got out some very advanced Mendelssohn and asked me to give it a whirl—just for fun, she said. It was five o'clock—our lesson was basically over—but I guess she was curious. I checked the key and tempo—key of D, two sharps; Moderato, *walking pace*, something I could do. The piece began with a long run in the right hand before the left-hand chords came in, plinking like the chords of a harp, just a touch of pedal to let them resonate. Then the left hand started in with runs of its own while the right did its own thing. As I leaned forward doing these things, I felt myself enter the zone. From time to time Mrs. Chin would say, "Careful now, not too fast," but her shaking fingers waiting to turn the pages for me made me want to go faster. I finished with a flourish, an uncalled for *fortissimo*, pumping the pedal slightly to make the keys ring.

That was pretty fun, I thought.

She looked at me curiously for a while, then told me that that's the piece I was going to play at the Western Michigan Bach Sonata Competition. I stared back at her, then shrugged and said Okay. Then I thought of something else: "But it's not Bach," I said. I thought it was a good point, but she laughed and hugged my shoulders and said it didn't matter, that students could play anything, it was just the name.

In the fall of 1980, the dark days closing in, I started visiting my mother in bed. She had been sick for six months with an unknown disease that kept her weak and bed-ridden. In retrospect, she probably had Chronic Fatigue Syndrome, but we didn't have that vocabulary then. We all thought she was going to die, but no one ever talked about it. In the afternoons, right after school, she'd invite me into her bed to hold me, and she'd tell me stories and have me imagine things. I knew she was going to die but I didn't know when—that very day, or a month from now, no one knew—and so I held onto those moments fiercely and never wanted to leave. I was ten.

It was Thanksgiving morning when it started. My dad had re-learned cooking since my mother took sick in April and he was down-stairs cooking the dinner, determined to make Thanksgiving *normal*. My sister Darlene was seventeen and never home. I don't remember one conversation about anything with her during this time. My dad, even with his religious background, never discussed my mom's illness directly. All we talked about was what I must do, or more accurately, what I *couldn't* do: Don't climb the stairs that way, your mother's asleep. Don't clank the dishes like that, you'll wake up your mother. Don't practice right now—don't you know your mother's resting?

I know now that he was suffering and that he dealt with what was going on in his own way, but he was no comfort to me then. I believe he was more open with his students about what he was going through than with his own children. In his classroom, where the audience and subject were supplied for him, he must have lectured about God and God's will, or if there was any such thing as God's will. What Luther would say on the subject, or Matthew, or St. Paul, his favorite, and what gave him his Ph.D. I realize this all now, but at the time I thought he was a stone.

With the smell of turkey and squash filling the house, I wandered upstairs in the late morning. My parents' bedroom door was open but the room was dark. It smelled of hand lotion and sickness. I stood in the doorway and looked in. My mother was lying on her side, fac-ing the door with her eyes closed. I thought she was asleep, but after a while she opened her eyes and asked me to come lie down with her.

I lay down on the covers and she caressed my hair. "My big boy," she said. "You're getting so big. Is Daddy doing okay with dinner?"

"I guess so."

"Have you been helping him?"

"A little." Though I hadn't helped at all—he had never asked. He was preoccupied with doing everything and had barely spoken to me, aside from telling me not to play the piano. I had watched some TV—the Detroit Thanksgiving Day Parade, and an animated story of how Squanto had taught the first Pilgrims to put a fish in the ground with each seed of corn. I had wandered into the backyard and found myself plucking the last dozen leaves off our Japanese maple. Then I had come upstairs.

"Are you going to eat dinner with us?" I wanted to know.

"Yes. Daddy will carry me down. I'll put something on and he'll carry me down."

"Why don't you go to the hospital and get better?" I said. She was still stroking my hair—we were both facing the doorway and I could feel her warmth through the covers and through my clothes. Her hand stroking my hair made me close my eyes.

"They don't know what's wrong with me," she said. "They can't do anything for me there, and I'd rather be home."

I wanted to ask her if she was going to die, but that wasn't allowed. You could think something all you wanted to in those days, but you couldn't say it. You had to let it gnaw at you until you were broken and bloody inside. That was being strong and big; that was being good, and I wanted to be good.

"Why don't you come in here and cozy up with me," she said then. "Take off your pants. They might be dirty."

I was ten. I was too old to be going to bed with my mother, and yet not old enough for it to be sexual. It wasn't sexual at all—yet it was, of course. It was intimate—maybe that's the best word. We shared the same space, the same warmth. She asked me to turn so my back was to her, and then she snuggled up to me so that I felt her breasts and stomach against my back and her hand on my hip. She was burning up. "Isn't this nice?" she said.

"Yes."

"Let's pretend we're in a tent and it's winter out and we're lost," she whispered. "We're out on the frozen tundra and if we don't cuddle together for warmth we'll both die." She lifted the covers over our heads. "Can you imagine it?"

I didn't speak. It was winter in Michigan. The sun never seemed to show its face, and it was a cold dark night by dinnertime. We were used to this and didn't complain; this was Michigan and we were tough. So it wasn't difficult for me to imagine that we were huddling for warmth, huddling together for our lives. There were times I absolutely believed these things to be true.

We may have fallen asleep. After a while she asked me how my Mendelssohn was coming along. The competition was December 20th, the second darkest day of the year—about three weeks away. I said okay, but the truth is that I didn't get to practice enough because I

116

wasn't supposed to wake her up. I didn't tell her this, but she must have guessed. "Play it for me now," she said.

"Now?" I didn't want to leave her.

"On my leg."

So I turned around and played the whole concerto—all three movements—on her thigh with both my hands. She laughed now and then; she said it tickled. I laughed myself when it was over.

"I think you only missed a couple notes," she said, and we smiled at each other in the near-dark.

"You come do that every day and I'm sure you'll be a big hit," she added.

After a while I said, "You won't be able to come, will you?"

"No, I'm afraid not. But we'll see. Maybe." And she kissed me.

My father appeared in the doorway. His face was dark and obscure and behind him a dim light shone. "What's going on in here?" he said.

"We're just cuddling," my mother said casually. "He was playing his concerto for me." We both giggled a little.

He must have been confused—we were not a touching family, much less a cuddling one—but said nothing for a long time. He stood scratching his head in the doorway, slender and bearded and about six-four. I haven't come within three inches of his height. Now, as an old man, he's shrunk some, but he's still taller than me.

Finally he spoke. "Richard, why don't you get dressed and go downstairs and practice for real now, on the piano, now that your mother's awake?" He pointed the way out the door, waiting for me. "Then we can eat."

He watched me put my pants on and pull up the zipper.

Darlene drove our dad's old Pacer to the high school and would have driven me, too, if I had wanted it. But I preferred to walk. I preferred, in fact, to walk alone. My school was about six blocks away and if I opened the door and some neighbor kids were walking by I'd wait for them to pass before going outside. I sang softly to myself as I walked, my feet keeping the tempo. My hands in my pockets would finger the keys, work out difficult passages over and over. I would challenge myself to get it right; tell myself I couldn't take another step until I got it right. I remember being late quite a bit.

And I remember the slush and the ice and the dreariness. The one busy street I had to cross was cracked and crumbling, with last summer's weeds dead and brittle but still there. There was gravel and gum and wet paper trash and dog waste at my feet, but there was also the thin branches of winter trees tangled like pick-up sticks against the sky. When the snow fell I tried only to look up, to see the flakes flutter toward me like stars hurtling through space. I'd pick out individual flakes in the distance and will them into my mouth.

Sometimes I'd make up new songs. A melody would come to me, and I knew just where the notes were. With my hands in my pockets, I'd picture the keyboard and the keys I had to touch. These tunes would come to me abruptly, kick around in my head for days, and then suddenly disappear to be replaced by another.

In the afternoons, after school, I would let myself into our quiet house and walk straight upstairs. She was usually asleep, but didn't mind me waking her. "Hello, Richard," she'd say. And she'd unfurl her blanket like a giant wing.

We'd lie together, me always on the outside, facing the door, my mother holding me from behind. Sometimes we'd sleep. It was warm and peaceful. At some point she always asked me to play for her, and we'd both move so I could play on her leg, or sometimes on her back. She always found this funny. Some days she'd ask me to sing along with the playing. One day I remember playing something new, one of the songs that had been kicking around in my head.

"Can you sing it to me without playing?" she wondered.

"I'll try," I said—but I couldn't: the melody wouldn't come if the hands were still. I played it again with my fingers across her back—it was a slow, comforting ballad in G major, my favorite key. When I was done she said how beautiful it was. She hugged me and called me her little composer.

"Did you write that for one of your girlfriends?" she wondered.

"No," I said.

"Don't composers write songs for people? You mean to say that beautiful tune is for no one at all?" She was teasing me.

"It's for you," I said.

"That's nice," she whispered. "Play it for me again." And I did.

I seemed to know instinctively not to tell anyone about our afternoons. By the time Darlene and my dad came home just before dinner, I was in front of the TV watching "Gilligan's Island" or "Lost in Space," doing my math homework and snacking on pretzels.

One morning, my mother asked me into her bed before school. My sister and father were downstairs. I told her I had to go to the bathroom first, and by the time I walked back to her room (I thought of it as *her* room) my father was standing in the doorway talking to her. When he saw me coming he turned and wondered what I was doing. "I was just going to say goodbye to Mom," I told him, but he shut the door and said no, I wasn't: "Mother's tired, and you're running late again. Now run along. Let's move it."

"See you after school, Richard," she called from behind the closed door.

"Let's get a move on," my father said, shooing me away. "Get your coat on."

On December 8th, my clock-radio alarm clicked on to tell me that John Lennon was dead. The words came to me in the dark before I was fully awake, and I remember jolting up and spinning around in my bed to listen. When the facts sunk in, I remember burying my head in my hands in my cold room. I didn't even know I cared.

At the breakfast table, Darlene and my dad already knew. They were listening to the radio as my dad got breakfast ready. Darlene stared off. She had bought his latest album, "Double Fantasy," just a few weeks before. My dad kept shaking his head, but when the radio played "Strawberry Fields Forever" he lost it a little and had to leave the room. When he came back he was all business.

At school, our principal Mr. Naylor came on the speaker after the first bell and made an announcement. He said that by now everybody had probably heard the news: John Lennon had been shot outside his apartment in New York City late last night. He was rushed to the hospital but didn't make it. He was forty years old. Mr. Naylor said that most of us kids might not know exactly who John Lennon was, but that all of our parents and all the teachers in the school had grown up listening to him and that he meant a lot to many people. He said that everybody had their own favorite Beatles song but that he would like to play his, "All You Need is Love." As the song played, our teacher, Mrs. Hilgers, hid her face behind her hands. Even some of the kids were crying.

After school, I walked down Mrs. Chin's basement stairs and took my seat at the piano. She looked at me for a minute, then asked if I was okay. I said I was. The concerto, she reminded me, was less than two weeks away, and she wanted to hear the whole thing. I had had the piece memorized for a while now, and I started in on the first movement, absently, not fully concentrating. The keyboard seemed new to me, since I hardly played on one anymore. For at least a week I had been playing only on my mom's leg and in my own pockets: practicing yes, but only on the walk to school, in the small dark holes of my coat pockets. Now the keyboard seemed stretched out in front of me, too large, hard and shiny.

Mrs. Chin gave me instructions as I played, now and then raising her voice, almost shouting instructions, drawing me back to my task. This was something new; she usually let me go, but now she was a high-strung coach laying down the law. Midway through the second stanza I sort of froze. I don't quite know what happened. I was playing as if on auto-pilot, then all of a sudden I didn't know what note came next. There was this awful pause, the last note—a high D—ringing in the air. I hit it twice more, trying to jar my memory. It was something I had never before experienced; then the notes came and my fingers did their work.

When I was done, Mrs. Chin chastised me. Her Chinese accent, usually hidden or subdued, came out of nowhere as her voice rose. Either I was going to play the piece the best it could possibly be played or I wasn't going to play it at all! Don't think I was going to this competition automatically. I owed it to Mendelssohn, and to myself, to play my best. Anything less was unacceptable. But, she said after a long pause, if I *did* play my best, great things would come to me. It would be a day we would never forget.

"That's all for today," she informed me. Stunned and embarrassed, I put on my coat, gathered up my backpack, and slunked up the stairs.

"You come to play next week or we're not doing this," she told me.

The next week I nailed the whole damn thing, like an Olympic gymnast, not one flaw—I did it for Felix and his sad brilliant sister Fanny, and for my parents and for Mrs. Chin, and for the Gipper and the rest of the team, and maybe even for Darlene and pitiful Mrs. Hilgers—but that night, as Darlene washed the dinner dishes, I sat down in front of the piano, not knowing what was about to happen. I turned back the keyboard lid, stared at the keys, and started to play a very slow version of "Across the Universe." I wasn't sure I knew it all, but the notes came and the words came too, and I was singing and playing in B-flat of all things. By the second verse, my sister had turned off the water to listen, and my dad was standing in the doorway to the living room. When I was done, he looked at me strangely. "That was beautiful," he said. "Wh-where did you learn that?"

"I just picked it out," I said.

He nodded, and I realized that he was afraid of me.

The morning of the competition, my dad told me he'd try to get there, but he had to teach a class at the same time and didn't think he could get out of it. Why did they have such an important event, he wondered, in the middle of the afternoon on a weekday? Before she left for school, Darlene gave me an envelope and told me to look at it later. I opened the envelope on my way to school. It was a little good luck card, homemade. I hardly even knew her handwriting. It said good luck, and then, "You keep me sane during these crazy times. Love, Darlene." I didn't even know she noticed me. I shoved the card in my back pocket, where I sat on it all day, even at the piano in Hearns Auditorium six hours later.

Mrs. Chin was waiting in the school parking lot after lunch, as planned. She seemed nervous, her hands tapping on the steering wheel, her eyes flitting around. I buttoned the top button of my white shirt and fished in my backpack for the clip-on tie I was told to wear. We drove to campus, not too far, to Hearns Auditorium, where just two hundred yards away my father was teaching a seminar.

We were directed to a large check-in room where stuffy-looking adults with nametags took our coats and signed us in. We were told to enter the auditorium quietly, and only between performances. Contest participants should sit near the back and leave inconspicuously as their time approached. I was told to leave right after a boy named Paul Montrose played Schubert's Quartet in B Minor, a piece I recognized from one of my Saturday workshops. I was to go out the main entrance and circle around, following the signs back stage. There I would find some water, bathrooms and, for those "on-deck," a quiet room to gather my thoughts. At the very end of these instructions, the woman smiled abruptly and wished me good luck.

The auditorium was very still, even though half the seats were occupied by children. A boy about my age was standing beside his piano, taking an awkward bow. He was wearing a tuxedo, and quite suddenly I was scared about the whole thing. It didn't seem fun. No one was smiling, though the most beautiful music was being played. I was quite certain, watching the next girl, that we all played better in our socks, the smells of dinner enveloping us, our sisters doing their homework on the couch. The girl on stage was about twelve; she wore a white frilly dress, stockings and black shoes. Her hair was done up in ribbons. She was playing a Bach sonata competently, though without much feeling, but then somewhere in the third movement she stumbled. She repeated herself, then stumbled again; then the reality of her situation—that several hundred people were watching her—made her suddenly contort her face and turn to her teacher. She spread her hands open but received no help. She repeated the previous phrase for the fifth or sixth time, then stood up and walked off stage. As she reached the edge of the curtain we all heard her break into tears.

There was a murmur, then a mumbling, then a late but respectful smattering of applause. I clapped seven times myself, and looked over at Mrs. Chin, her hands in her lap. Her face was firm and hard and she was shaking her head almost imperceptibly. It seemed more a shake of disgust than pity.

We listened through ten more performances, over an hour. Some kids were confident and played wonderfully, making the instrument ring and sing, while others were stiff and nervous as hell, and their performances were filled with errors. At least two kids left the stage in tears, and it occurred to me that this was some kind of torture for them; that we were being forced on stage to satisfy some need or emptiness in the lives of our parents, or in my case, my teacher.

Paul Montrose was a seventeen year-old with wild hair and long tails on his tux who reminded me of Van Cliburn. He took a low bow before sitting down—something none of the smaller kids did. He played with a flourish, lifting his hands high over the keys, but his fingerings lacked subtlety: he was playing like a football player. Mrs. Chin leaned over and told me I better make my way back stage. She reminded me of the *rallantando* of the third movement, to play my *pianissimos* the way they were written, and to pause between movements. She said she was proud of me and that I'd do fine. Then she squeezed my arm and told me to get going.

The next thing I remember I was being told to come along, that I was up. I was directed on-stage, where I stood dumbly beside the piano looking out on the crowd. I was aware of my ridiculous tie and my sister's note in my back pocket. I felt very small and young. But when I sat down all that disappeared. I took my time adjusting the seat and finding my place. The keyboard was shiny from sweaty fingers, and when I placed my fingers on the keys their blurry mirror image reached out to me.

Everything faded away but the music, but I don't think it was because I had entered the *zone*, or that I was in some way gifted; I believe I simply did not care enough to be worried. I wasn't nervous because I suddenly didn't care whether I won or not, or what people thought of me. For a time I felt a connection to the composer—noble, too-good-for-this-world Felix at thirty-seven, heartsick from his sister's death, on the verge of death himself. All time and place seemed to drift away and I was simply bringing those old notes, his handwritten vision to life. I closed my eyes and leaned into that vision; I could almost feel him with me, and we were alone. But then at the *rallantando* of the third movement something unforeseen happened. I consciously slowed my chords as Mrs. Chin had reminded me to do; slowed them way down, an overly dramatic *molto rallantando*, and just at the very slowest point, just before the right hand takes up the new melody and brings it back to tempo, I hovered. And in the emptiness of that lull my mother's song filled it—the song I had played for her in our tent and had kept playing over these last few weeks. I don't know where it came from—all I can say is that Mendelssohn was there and then he wasn't and my mother's song filled the gap and it all seemed to flow and fit. My right hand rose the octaves plucking out three-note major chords, then turned into a slow contrapunctual melody that I had played so many times in my coat pockets on the way to school, and had sung for my mother as I played on her thigh and that I still, even today, think of as a beautiful and mysterious melody, a tune of sadness and comfort and longing and loss, of our sad cold house and the bleak sky and the branches of our little maple scratching at the air. For maybe three minutes I played this melody, until it too moved into a *rallantando* and ended somberly with a strange two-handed chord that was not quite major or minor. At that point the Mendelssohn was lost. I felt a momentary regret, not for myself or Mrs. Chin, but for Mendelssohn himself—but it couldn't be helped. When the last notes spread throughout the auditorium and died out on the dust I lifted my hands and stood up.

Confused faces stared at me. Someone clapped, then another, and soon I was being given a short ovation. I saw the judges consulting with each other; one of them shook his head and made a face. I stood long enough to pick out Mrs. Chin about ten rows back (she had moved closer to see me). Her mouth was open slightly and her hands were folded together loosely at her chest as if in prayer.

We didn't stay for the awards ceremony. The sky, when we left the auditorium, was the color and texture of wet cement. Though not much past three, it was almost dusk. Streetlights were on, and students trudged head down through the slush to their overheated dorm rooms.

Mrs. Chin hadn't said a word to me. She drove slowly, and I fully expected her to just take me home and drop me off. But then she said, "How about we get a bite to eat. Do you like Wendy's?"

"Sure," I said. I held a certificate in my mittened hand, a manilla paper rectangle stating my participation in the 13th Annual Western Michigan Bach Sonata Competition. My name was written in rather sloppy calligraphy in the very center, and at the bottom, on two lines, was the date, December 20, 1980, and someone's illegible signature.

"You can take your tie off if you like, Richard," Mrs. Chin said. "You look very uncomfortable." She smiled at me.

"Okay," I said. I unhooked it and loosened my top button. Then I rehooked the silly thing onto the vent in front of me. Mrs. Chin laughed.

It wasn't until we were sitting together at Wendy's that she addressed what had happened. "I'm trying very hard to understand you," she said.

I sipped my Frosty and fingered some fries, not knowing what to say. Mrs. Chin wasn't eating, and her face seemed too close to mine across the small table. I knew I had to say something but I didn't have the words.

"What happened up there?" she asked me directly. "Did you just—forget?"

"No," I said, shaking my head—but then I was lost again. My mother's melody seemed to come naturally out of the *rallantando*, as if Mendelssohn himself had written it. But how could I explain that?

She waited, trying to maintain her smile but mostly looking confused. "Then what happened, Richard? What happened up there?"

I couldn't answer, except to say, "I don't know. I'm sorry."

She nodded, leaned back, then leaned toward me again. "Was that your own song?"

"Yes."

"Was it—? Did you compose that right then, on the spot?" She seemed almost frightened. When I said no, that it came to me about a month ago, she nodded. She asked me if I had known, ahead of time, that I was going to play that; had I known beforehand that I

124

would *abandon* (as she put it) the Mendelssohn we had worked so hard on?

"No," I answered simply—and it was the truth. "I'm sorry," I repeated.

"Well, so am I," she said.

We sat in silence for many minutes. Finally, she asked, "How are things at home? Is everything all right?"

"Yes," I said, and she nodded.

"I'm sorry your mom and dad couldn't make it."

I shrugged and sipped my Frosty. Outside it looked like midnight, our reflections clear and colorful in the glass.

"Well, you have absolutely nothing to be ashamed of," she said, standing up. She looked at me as if she had granted me something and I should be grateful. But I was just confused: I wasn't the least bit ashamed, just sorry I had let her down.

My mother didn't die. Not that winter, not that spring—not until I was twenty-eight and living in California with my family, my wife Jessica and our boy Franklin. We moved back to Michigan during her illness—lung cancer, though she never smoked. We rented a house in Kalamazoo and helped my dad take care of her. When the end was near we all knew it and said our goodbyes. She had a living will and hospice care, and died in her bed, the same bed I had shared with her for about four months when I was ten.

On a windy day in April, 1981, I realized my mother was not going to die and that maybe she was not even sick. There was still no diagnosis, but now it didn't seem to matter. She was getting stronger every day; she made it downstairs to dinner more regularly, though she never cooked and had trouble walking upstairs after the meal. I climbed the stairs that windy day and kicked off my muddy shoes inside her door. I remember they smeared the baseboard. I put my backpack down heavily, waking her. I watched her stir, and said, "When are you going to get better?"

She lay on her back, her eyes closed, and I asked her again, louder this time. She opened her eyes to look at me.

"You're not even sick, are you?" I said.

She threw back the covers and swung her legs over the side of the bed. She sat there, rubbing her face, ignoring me.

"*Are* you?" I shouted. Still she rubbed her eyes, and I kicked her on the shin with my bare foot, hurting my foot more than her. She dropped her hands and stared at me then, bleary-eyed, dazed, maybe even a little bored.

"I hate you," I said.

She studied me a long time, and then she said: "I don't hate you, Richard. But I don't want to cuddle with you today, or ever again. You're getting too big, and it's not right." Then she stood up, stretched, and I watched her walk out of the room and down the hall. I picked up my shoes and backpack and walked downstairs. It was over.

In June, just as school ended, she regained her strength, and by the end of summer it was as if nothing had ever happened. Our mother was back, but it was more than that: She had never been gone.

When I was a teenager we fought terribly, sometimes screaming venomous words at each other, even throwing things. I spent most of my time at my girlfriend's house. My father worried about us, but could do nothing. "You two have your own strange relationship," he told me once. Throughout it all, I played, but as I mastered more and more difficult pieces it seemed more like a chore than a pleasure. And so I quit, without fanfare, a month after graduation.

I moved out as quickly as possible. I went to Northwestern and met my wife and later moved out to California. I didn't make peace with my mother until the very end. I stood by her bed three days before she died, and told her I loved her. I kneeled and played my song for her on her pale, limp arm. She smiled through the drugs and we kissed. I caressed her hair and she closed her eyes.

Today I don't play at all, except during the week before Christmas, when I pick out Christmas carols without music. The tunes all come back to me, but sometimes I have to fudge the words, which can be funny. Franklin sits on my lap and sings along in his three-year-old yodel. Sometimes he leans forward and pounds his fists on the keys. I smile and let him.

Nominated by Wally Lamb, Richard Burgin, Boulevard

OLIVE TREES

by LOUISE GLÜCK

from THE THREEPENNY REVIEW

The building's brick, so the walls get warm in summer.
When the summer goes, they're still warm,
especially on the south side—you feel the sun there, in the brick,
as though it meant to leave its stamp on the wall, not just sail over it
on its way to the hills. I take my breaks here, leaning against the
    wall,
smoking cigarettes.

The bosses don't mind—they joke that if the business fails,
they'll just rent wall space. Big joke—everyone laughs very loud.
But you can't eat—they don't want rats here, looking for scraps.

Some of the others don't care about being warm, feeling the sun on
    their backs
from the warm brick. They want to know where the views are.
To me, it isn't important what I see. I grew up in those hills;
I'll be buried there. In between, I don't need to keep sneaking
    looks.

My wife says when I say things like this my mouth goes bitter.
She loves the village—every day she misses her mother.
She misses her youth—how we met there and fell in love.
How our children were born there. She knows she'll never go back
but she keeps hoping—

At night in bed, her eyes film over. She talks about the olive trees,
the long silver leaves shimmering in the sunlight.
And the bark, the trees themselves, so supple, pale gray like the
rocks behind them.

She remembers picking the olives, who made the best brine.
I remember her hands then, smelling of vinegar.
And the bitter taste of the olives, before you knew not to eat them
fresh off the tree.

And I remind her how useless they were without people to cure
them.
Brine them, set them out in the sun—
And I tell her all nature is like that to me, useless and bitter.
It's like a trap—and you fall into it because of the olive leaves,
because they're beautiful.

You grow up looking at the hills, how the sun sets behind them.
And the olive trees, waving and shimmering. And you realize that if
you don't get out fast
you'll die, as though this beauty were gagging you so you couldn't
breathe—

And I tell her I know we're trapped here. But better to be trapped
by decent men, who even re-do the lunchroom,
than by the sun and the hills. When I complain here,
my voice is heard—somebody's voice is heard. There's dispute,
there's anger.
But human beings are talking to each other, the way my wife and I
talk.
Talking even when they don't agree, when one of them is only
pretending.

In the other life, your despair just turns into silence.
The sun disappears behind the western hills—
when it comes back, there's no reference at all to your suffering.
So your voice dies away. You stop trying, not just with the sun,
but with human beings. And the small things that made you happy
can't get through to you anymore.

128

I know things are hard here. And the owners—I know they lie
    sometimes.
But there are truths that ruin a life; the same way, some lies
are generous, warm and cozy like the sun on the brick wall.

So when you think of the wall, you don't think *prison.*
More the opposite—you think of everything you escaped, being
    here.

And then my wife gives up for the night, she turns her back.
Some nights she cries a little.
Her only weapon was the truth—it is true, the hills are beautiful.
And the olive trees really are like silver.

But a person who accepts a lie, who accepts support from it,
because it's warm, it's pleasant for a little while—
that person she'll never understand, no matter how much she loves
    him.

Nominated by Katrina Roberts, Jessica Roeder,
Philip White, Philip Levine, Threepenny Review

THE HEIR

fiction by JACK LIVINGS

from A PUBLIC SPACE

THERE ONCE HAD BEEN A TIME Omar looked forward to fighting the Chinese the way he looked forward to a good meal or sex. But lately he'd been letting his men take care of the dirty work. He could no longer bear the awful smell of the Chinese, their coarse gestures and smacking lips. To make matters worse, everyone was plotting against him—his own people were working with the Chinese to engineer his downfall, he was sure of it. Even Bola, the Mongolian henchman so stupid he hardly knew his own name, had made a play for the old gangster's throne. Not to expect treachery from his men would have been to display a gross misunderstanding of human nature, and Omar wasn't anyone's fool. But he had begun to question his ability to defend himself from their plots. Some of his men would cut their own mothers' throats.

Omar ran the west end of the Ganjiakou market, which was known as Uyghurville. There the crowded market stopped abruptly at an invisible line on the road. Chinese there, Uyghurs here. From the Chinese side, it was possible to look into Uyghurville and see a few shirtless men tending pit ovens outside the mutton and noodle restaurants, old people moving slowly and without intent down the pockmarked road, expats looking to score hash. Bicycle tires and old shoes lay strewn across the roofs of the low buildings. Curtains of acrid steam poured from the paper plant at the neighborhood's edge. Farther west the poorest of the poor had slung tarps at the feet of massive hills of garbage. Uyghurville was unquestionably the worst place in the world, and it remained perched on the edge of oblivion by a mix of swindle and violent refusal to submit to the Chinese city surrounding it.

For years residents of Beijing would not go there for fear of being robbed or killed. There had been uprisings and bombings. The Public Security Bureau, a paramilitary force known for its enterprising use of torture as a public relations tool, regularly conducted sweeping acts of brutality in Uyghurville. Old men disappeared only to reappear months later with weeping stumps for legs. Women were destroyed with lead pipes. In some circles there was discussion of who had struck first, but no one involved in the fight cared one way or another.

The violence advanced and receded like floodwaters.

Then Omar struck a deal with the PSB officer in charge of minority control: in exchange for monthly "advisory fees," the PSB would publicly declare the neighborhood rehabilitated and safe for commerce. Uyghurville hosted a ceremony with ethnic dancing and speeches touting a new era of progress. Chinese cadres, like lions at the kill, hunched over meals of spicy lamb. Later, Uyghur girls were brought in. Though the cadres' eyes lit up at the sight of that primitive flesh, only a few partook, and the rest thought them perverse for doing so.

For a while everything ran smoothly. PSB officers walked the beat and the neighborhood attracted the faddish attentions of Chinese bohemians, the children of high-ranking officials, the first wave of Chinese entrepreneurs. Expats hung around the noodle and mutton places smoking with the kitchen boys. The restaurants kept up their monthly payments and almost overnight the atmosphere of menace began to lift. But it wasn't long before the deal started to unravel. The cadres were swept up in a corruption scandal and replaced with a new band of bureaucrats who as their first order of business doubled the protection fees, reasoning that since they had been clever enough to survive the scandal, they were worth twice as much as the morons who'd been kicked out of office. This sort of Chinese logic made Omar want to shoot himself in the head.

On this point alone Omar and his grandson saw eye to eye. The Chinese were pigs. No amount of money could make up for the defilement they heaped on the Uyghurs. At one point, the government had welded the neighborhood's manhole covers in place and diverted the sewers when the PSB discovered that gangsters were using the tunnels as escape routes. Consequently, shit ran in the streets and

131

Uyghur children died from diseases. Only Omar and a few others had proper homes. The Chinese robbed everyone blind, and no one could save enough to improve his lot. They lived like animals, sleeping in their noodle shops, atop laminate tables. At night, the floors belonged to the rats.

He ordered the restaurants to stop making payments. The Chinese were already bleeding them dry. Soon the PSB patrols thinned and the neighborhood began to slip back into the sea. There were rumors the Chinese had marked Omar for death. People joked that it was better not to stand too close to Omar in case an inept Chinese sniper had been assigned to the case. With him out of the picture, the Chinese could bulldoze the neighborhood and put up skyscrapers. There was no question about that: the land was worth something, even if the people weren't.

It was with dark pleasure that Uyghurville's residents repeated the gossip about Omar. He wielded absolute power over the neighborhood, and for that they blessed him, feared him, and wished him dead all in the same breath. He was famously vengeful and he had a long memory. Once, a Kazakh had brushed against Omar's wife in the market. The man apologized profusely, prostrating himself, delivering gifts in the following days. It's nothing, Omar had said. He waited ten years to pour hot lead down the Kazakh's throat. In the meantime, he did business with the man, ate at the same table, shared the pipe. The Kazakh had come to feel that he could depend on Omar. This was how Omar operated. He took the long view.

By summertime, the rumors that had simmered for months were being served up as fact: Omar was as good as dead. He didn't pay it any mind. There was always something in the air.

Every night Omar took a walk, as much to assure the neighborhood that he was very much alive as to survey his domain. He wore large square sunglasses, a blindingly white skullcap, patent leather shoes. On this particular night, he was engulfed by a double breasted suit that hung on him like a hospital gown. A small velvet bag filled with his enemies' gold teeth chattered in his pocket. His capos trailed behind him, and behind them, a few little boys, like gulls in the wake of a garbage scow, worrying the men for betel nuts.

The sun had dropped between the paper plant's stacks, tinting the sky the color of a bloody wound. A hot wind pressing down from above flooded the street with steam.

Despite the PSB pullout, the restaurants were packed on this hot summer night, the streets swarming with Chinese, Uyghurs, expats, shady looking in-betweens. "See," Omar thought, "it's worked out fine." When he passed by, the wranglers who pulled in customers kept up their patter—"Come! Come!"—but maintained a respectful distance. Foreigners and Chinese stared openly at this slice of local flavor, the crowd parting to allow him passage.

Near a pile of trash at the edge of the neighborhood Omar passed by some off-duty PSB. They were young and stiff, swallowed by their green woolen uniforms, and absolutely terrified of this place, which lay between their station and the dormitory where they lived. Only through great restraint did they manage to keep from holding hands, as some officers would have done. Two had reached a compromise and walked with their arms locked at the elbows. It was obvious they were only kids, but Omar never let them out of his sight. Children always ran the revolutions, and in the old days these animals would have worked him over with their clubs. He knew they had a nose for his blood. Sure enough, as they passed by, one jumpy recruit thumped his stick against his woolen leg.

Omar was sick of it. He'd been dreaming of open skies and the steppes. The intimacy of emptiness. Endless rivers and the shallow arc of the horizon. It had been thirty years since he'd breathed air so clear a man could detect the hint of a cooking fire an entire valley away. He blamed these fantasies on his grandson, who had been threatening to go home to Ürümqi. The young man was spineless but hot-blooded, and these days they avoided each other except to argue.

After strolling the neighborhood for a while, Omar settled into a table at his usual haunt, where a bad thing happened. A kitchen boy who had no friends among the other boys, seized by a lunatic scheme to prove himself worthy of their respect, stuck his penis into a steaming bowl of noodles meant for Omar. The other boys made such a ruckus that Omar's guards stormed the kitchen. They hoisted the boy onto a table and pinned him there. Instantly the restaurant was empty as a windswept plain.

Slowly, perhaps with a hint of weariness, Omar rose from his chair. Standing over the boy, he opened a delicate knife shaped like a crescent moon and sliced open the boy's pants. He carved the air above the rubbery nub of flesh and stroked the boy's hairless abdomen with his hard fingers, but he felt he was doing it for the benefit of his men, who seemed pleased to have interrupted such an obvious act of disrespect.

"This sort of thing never used to happen," Omar said.

"Please, uncle," squealed the boy.

Omar was distracted. He needed to eat. "What's to be gained by cutting you up?"

The boy whimpered for mercy.

"Everyone thinks I've gone soft in the head. This is bad for you, understand? It means that I might have to make an example of you."

"Uncle, please."

Omar looked around at his men, their faces those of expectant children. "Have you seen that new movie?" Omar said. "The one about those Yakuza? To punish disloyalty they split it from stem to stern."

Urine spurted from the boy and darkened the table.

Omar was seized by a sudden and deep sadness, and he turned away in shame. His men made a huge fuss about the piss. This is only a boy, he thought. A boy.

"Change this one's diaper and send him back to the kitchen," Omar said. Then, to the boy, he said, "Keep that thing in your pants or you'll lose it." He stroked his cheek with the back of his hand. "Bring me another bowl," he said.

As a younger man he would sooner have castrated the boy than spat on the floor. Maybe he was getting soft in his old age. But what was the point of thinking about it?

The boy, trembling, one hand clutching the waist of his pants, returned with a fresh bowl of noodles. Omar pressed a twenty-Yuan note into his palm. He looked carefully at the boy's anguished face, into the black waters the boy didn't even know existed within him, and as if a tumbler had fallen in a lock, with a crisp, unbroken motion Omar cracked him on the side of his head with the knife's ash handle. The boy's lips parted, he wobbled, then dropped to the floor. The other kitchen boys pried the money from his fist and dragged him away, his pants around his ankles, his eyelashes fluttering. It was done and Omar would not think of it again.

After Omar returned home from dinner, he had one of his men fetch his grandson, who was sitting on a crate outside a restaurant down the street, watching the world go by. Anwher was twenty-five, uncomfortable in his own skin. His sharp cheekbones launched straight out from his deep eye sockets like a pair of cliffs, and, like most young men, he spent the bulk of his time cultivating an air of internal discord, which made him look superficially haunted.

134

"Boss wants you," Omar's minion said.

"He can wait," said Anwher.

The thick-necked goon stayed where he was, silently exuding thuggish authority.

"Fine," Anwher said. Without a word, they started back toward the house. Anwher studied the man's gait with an almost scientific attention to the roll of his massive shoulders. No one stood in their way, and before long they were at Omar's house.

The man stopped at the door and stepped to the side. Anwher went in and sat on the floor by a low table.

Omar sat drinking his tea for a while, sizing up the boy.

"So?" Omar said.

"So what?" Anwher said.

"Busy out there tonight."

Anwher nodded and took a cup of tea.

Omar sighed. He considered himself an able communicator, but the boy was impossible to talk to. He was lazy as a rug and responded neither to reason nor violence. What once had been a gap between them had become a canyon.

"It's hopping," Anwher offered. "A human farm. Eat, shit, screw. All day, all night."

"Perhaps if you did something besides sit on your ass all day, you'd have a different take on things," Omar said.

Anwher set down his cup and made moves to leave, but Omar held up his hand.

"You have a point," Omar said. "But you might show a little respect for your home."

"Ürümqi is my home."

"This again," Omar said.

"Always. Don't act surprised," Anwher said. "I'll go like a ghost in the night."

"You should write that down," Omar said. "Hand me the smoke." He slowly brought an unlit pipe to his lips and blew through it, moving with the measured patience of a man who routinely found himself talking to people too stupid to come around to his point of view. Anwher dropped a leather pouch into his grandfather's palm.

"And what will happen to the business when you go?" Omar asked.

"Maybe this stomach ulcer will clear up, is what will happen. I can't believe I've lasted this long. If I had any sense I would have bugged out years ago."

Anwher looked out the top of his head when he said this, gauging his grandfather's reaction as best he could without making eye contact. He was ready to run, but Omar said nothing. Then the old man motioned for a knife.

Anwher pulled one from his pocket, snapped it open, and with a flourish presented the handle.

"Where's yours?" Anwher asked.

"Left it at a restaurant," Omar said. He gouged at the pipe with Anwher's knife, the blade rasping against the bowl. "This pipe is a piece of junk."

"It's fine."

"Really? Look at this. It's clogged solid. What am I supposed to do with this?" Omar paused to stab at it some more. "What to do? Cleaning it properly will destroy it. You see what I'm saying?"

"Yeah, I see."

"Ürümqi's not the way you remember it," Omar said.

"It's not the way you remember it, either."

"No Uyghurs left there, you know," Omar said. "It's slope city now. They turned all the Uyghurs into Chinese. You have to cut them open to see the difference."

"You don't say."

Omar stopped working on the pipe and looked at his grandson. "The Chinese have black blood. That's the truth."

"Sure," Anwher said.

"Go to Kashgar if you want to be a man. Go someplace you can behave like a noble human being."

"We'll see. I'm overflowing with noble ideas."

"You're overflowing with something."

"You wouldn't joke if you knew how serious I am about this."

"Really?" Omar grinned. "You're serious? Should I call you a cab?"

"Don't tempt me."

"Boy, I give up. You have my blessing," Omar said, chuckling and rolling his eyes. He knew the boy would never go through with it, and that was fine because he wanted him nearby where he could keep an eye on him. He was a caged bird and he'd get eaten alive in Ürümqi.

Omar turned his attention back to the barrel of the pipe. The blade hitched against a lump of carbon fused to the shank. Eventually he gave up on the pipe and located a container of snuff. He scooped one long pinkie nail through the powder.

"Don't think I won't do it," Anwher said.

"What's that?" Omar said, grinning.

"Leave," Anwher shouted. "I'll do it."

"I'm sure you will," Omar said. He wrinkled his nose and brought another scoop of snuff to his nostril, inhaled, and waited for the blur to settle into his brain. With his free hand he felt around behind him for a pillow. "Off to see your boyfriends tonight?"

Anwher stood up, shaking his head and smiling crookedly, amazed as ever at the old man's capacity for provocation. "You truly know how to injure a man," he said. "Good night, Grandfather. Blessings upon you."

"Get a haircut," Omar called after him. "You look like a girl." The boy had always been a torment. He took a beating without a word, afterwards never showing any sign of anger. Shot in the head, he'd rise up to commend his assassin. It had occurred to Omar that this trait was the mark of the divine—who else but a truly spiritual man could be so guileless?—but it was dangerous to be known as a forgiving man. Forgiveness had no place in this world. He wasn't going to be around forever. What would the boy do then?

Omar rummaged around for another pipe and smoked some hash. Before long he was asleep, his hands tucked into his jacket in case a hungry rat picked up the smell of food on his fingers.

• • •

The restaurant across the street kept a little monkey. Most of the time it lazed on the warm brick by the pit oven eating Kishu oranges, occasionally rousing itself to harass a customer. It would steal parcels and toss them onto the hot coals where the nan baked.

When Anwher emerged from his grandfather's quarters, he saw the monkey preening the fur on its peach-size face, and he looked around for some trash to fling at it. The hunk of tire he found flew over the monkey's head and thudded against the restaurant's tin roof. The owner came out with fists raised, ready for anything.

"Why? Why?" said the poor man, mortally wounded for the thousandth time.

Anwher shrugged and started up the street.

"Worthless," the restaurant owner shouted. "You're a piece of shit!" As always, Anwher pretended not to hear and disappeared into the crowd.

He wandered deep into the Chinese market, his hands stuffed in his pockets so no one could accuse him of anything, and he tried to walk proudly, meeting the eyes of any Chinese who looked him in the face. The market smelled of garlic and rotten cabbage and was lit by strands of light bulbs drooping over the street. He caught sight of his barber working behind a cart stacked with chicken cages, and he abruptly turned on his heel and cut through the crowd.

The broad-faced Chinese man was moving gracefully around his customer, a mound of flesh who had established himself, like the cap of a mushroom, on a low wooden stool. From time to time the customer gave his newspaper a shake to clear the hair clippings. Otherwise he was still as a mountain. The barber combed and trimmed in silence, his hands gliding about the man's enormous head. Anwher waited quietly, in a strange communion with the barber, those conjurer's hands, the unmoving customer, until an old auntie pushed him out of the way.

"You're spooking the chickens. Go wait over there," she said to Anwher, pointing at a stool with a folded bib atop it. "I'll get to you in a minute."

He ignored her.

"You deaf?" the auntie said. She held her left hand, palsied and shaking violently, to her ear. Then she recognized Anwher and said, "For a little extra, I'll cut with the right." She laughed like she was choking on a bone.

He knew this woman. Like all Chinese, she was working an angle.

"There's only one thing you get paid extra for," Anwher said, "and you're so old I'd probably fall in."

The woman squinted slightly. "Get out of here. We don't serve your kind."

"Sure you don't."

"A haircut's not what you need. Maybe a hatchet between the eyes," she said evenly. Anwher lifted an eyebrow and tried to stay cool. The barber and his patron both looked up slowly, as if they'd been disturbed from the mutual appreciation of a huge, tranquil painting.

"Everything okay, Ma?" the barber said.

"This Uyghur," she said.

The barber limped over, his comb and scissors by his side. He hadn't received enough iron as a child and his legs were crooked. "It's no problem. I know this gentleman." He craned his neck to see the sides of Anwher's head. "Little shaggy on the sides."

138

"Yeah," said Anwher.

The barber assessed him. "Don't tell me you've started picking fights with old ladies?"

Anwher coiled slightly. "How was I supposed to know she was your mother? Now I know."

"Hey, don't take it so seriously. I'm just messing with you. We're okay, right?"

"It's fine," Anwher answered.

"That's the spirit," the barber said. Then he held up his comb and scissors and said, "We aim to please."

"I don't go looking for fights," Anwher said.

"Of course not. Have a seat over there and I'll be with you in a minute," the barber said. He made a playful jab at Anwher's shoulder, and the young man juked like a prize fighter. The barber smiled and held out his hand for a shake. Anwher rolled his shoulders and tugged on his lapels. Among the Chinese he had no friends, but in this predictable monthly transaction there was a sort of comfort, one that relied on the rules of commerce to insure that the razor the Chinese man put to his throat would never draw blood. There was, Anwher reasoned, no point in this Chinese doing him any harm. He tipped well and treated the barber like a valued servant. But the old woman had thrown the balance, and Anwher hated her for it.

"Come on," the barber said. He limped over to a stool and snapped out the bib, shaking it playfully for the young bull. Anwher sidled over and the barber tied the bib around his neck. He went back to his other customer.

"It's the heat," the barber said softly. "I saw two old ladies beating each other with their canes yesterday." The fat man chuckled, his paper rattling as he heaved.

"I don't notice it," Anwher said, but as soon as he'd spoken he wished he hadn't. He'd meant to sound gruff but it had come out sounding childish, impatient.

"Lucky man," said the barber. "Always better to close one's eyes than curse the darkness."

The barber's mother had been studying Anwher all this time. "I never forget a face," she said, shaking a stubby finger at him.

"Take it easy, Ma," the barber said around the comb clamped between his teeth.

Clearly the old woman was deranged, but Anwher couldn't catch the barber's eye to confirm it. The barber cut merrily along while his customer read the paper. The chickens scratched in their cages.

• • •

The old woman had spent a fair amount of time in Uyghurville. Those people didn't frighten her. And she knew exactly who this was in front of her. She had given herself to his grandfather in return for a lamb for her son's wedding. The other Chinese girls acted superior to the Uyghurs and complained about every little thing, but not her. She did what was asked, and she got repeat business.

That had been years ago. Sometimes she saw the old gangster in the street. She didn't step aside. A rich Uyghur was still worth less than a Chinese whore.

The boy's grandfather had been rough with her, but she hadn't complained. Afterwards they had lain in his murky room, a place composed entirely of desperate corners light could not find, angled shadows where anguish had taken up residence. It made her skin crawl: everywhere the spirit of the dead wife.

After a while, the old man had called out and the boy silently appeared at their feet. He had a shadow of hair on his upper lip. She pulled the sheet over her breasts.

"Take a go at this?" the old man said.

The boy shook his head.

"Come on, I'll show you how. You put your little worm in the slit." He tore away the sheet and grabbed her between the legs.

The boy shook his head, his eyes down.

"Faggot," Omar said.

She set her jaw in case he decided to strike her. People were like that.

Instead he made a sudden lunge at the boy, but Anwher dashed out of the room before Omar's feet touched the floor.

The gangster shook his head. "This is the sort of crime that has been visited on me every day of my life. I should get it over with and buy him a man," Omar said. He went on and on, talking, talking about the boy, the dead wife, business trouble.

As his semen dried to a crust on her thigh, it pulled tightly at the delicate hairs there. He had gone at her with all the hatred he could muster. She hadn't complained.

From the other room came the sounds of the boy crying, and the

140

old man had stopped talking. He sat up and told her to get dressed.

With only a blanket wrapped around his waist he'd led her outside. At the restaurant across the street, the lamb carcass had been skinned, gutted, and strung up by its hind legs from the eave. The monkey was making a show of poking at the milky eyeballs, then leaping back to cower behind its owner's legs. In the heat the carcass had begun to sweat and a small crowd gathered as she'd struggled to get the slick body from the rusty hook and into the wooden cart. Without anyone's help she managed to wrestle the viscous thing down. Her clothes clung to her body like a caul. After she'd loaded up and gotten a little ways down the street, the gangster stepped through the crowd and called her name. "Tight Chinese hole," he shouted after her, his fingers forming an O. The crowd laughed. She'd gripped the wooden cart handles and leaned towards the Chinese end of the market.

She knew all about this Uyghur in front of her.

· · ·

From his stool Anwher catalogued the tools at her disposal. She had scissors. A razor lay on a corroded tray nearby. Rope lay coiled at the foot of the chicken cages, which were stacked in a bank high enough to conceal him from the crowd. Even if he cried out, no one would hear him over the noise. This was his usual means of entertainment. He imagined his own horrific death and cultivated baroque fantasies involving a funeral march through the market. Everyone would be sorry, especially his grandfather, whose heart would break when he gazed upon the beautiful corpse.

After a while, the dim light and heat overpowered him and he dozed off and dreamed about a huge pillowed room filled with bodies twisting like lizards around each other. There were no faces and he lay with women and men alike and never needed to stop.

When he awoke, the barber was close to him, studying his face. Anwher smelled garlic on the man's breath. He glanced down to make sure his erection wasn't showing.

"You have a noble nose," the barber said softly.

Anwher wiped his face with his hands. The barber stepped back and began to move his arm. The razor slapping against the strop sounded desperately final.

"Tilt," the barber said, applying two fingers to Anwher's chin. A

141

metal pot was steaming over a fire, and the barber plucked out a hot towel. He laid it over Anwher's mouth and went back to sharpening the blade.

"This makes some people nervous," the barber said.

"Not me," Anwher said into the towel.

The barber got down to business and neither one said a word until he was done.

Actually, it was the old woman who spoke first. "How fetching," she said. "The boys at the Secret Garden will love it." The barber's scissors snapped around Anwher's head, touching up the tight crop.

"She's bad for business," Anwher said.

"Hm," said the barber.

"All right, that's fine," Anwher said. The barber pressed a small plastic mirror into his hand. He inspected the cut, then rose from the stool and worked at the bib's knot. He fumbled with it long enough to become aware that everyone was looking at him. "Allow me," the barber said. It was off instantly.

Anwher held out a twenty, a generous sum. He wasn't sure why he'd offered more than usual. The barber bowed.

"If the old woman hadn't shot off her mouth it would have been forty," Anwher said.

She looked up from her bowl of noodles. "Hey, young man, no hard feelings. It's on the house."

"Very funny, Ma," said the barber, flashing the banknote at her. For a moment something other than composed serenity flashed across his face. Then it was gone, replaced by the set line of his mouth.

"What? Speak up," shouted his mother. "We're not so bad off we need dirty money."

The barber winced. Grasping Anwher's hands in his own, he said, "Good night. Be well. See you soon."

"Listen to me," his mother said. "We don't need money from that piece of filth. Give it back. Don't make me embarrass you in front of these people."

The barber tried to laugh, but it was a weak, nervous effort and hardly any sound came out at all. Gingerly he ventured a hand forth to pat Anwher on the shoulder, then thought better of it. "She's not well," he whispered.

"No shit. Who is she to be talking about filth?" Anwher said.

"Accept my apologies. She's like a naughty child. It happens. It's the heat. The heat does terrible things to an old mind."

"They say the murder rate goes up when it's hot," Anwher said in a tone meant to be menacing. As usual, it hadn't come out right.

"That's true. It's a fact," said the barber. When Anwher didn't respond, the barber added, "It makes us all do things we don't mean."

For reasons Anwher couldn't quite comprehend, the barber's obsequious behavior angered him. He was like a fat bottle fly buzzing over a plate of food, its mere presence ruining the entire meal. "She's no different in the dead of winter," Anwher said. "I can tell these things about people. Bitter old bitch."

The barber stared back at him.

"Look here," Anwher said, crowding the barber, "I don't go looking for fights."

"No one's looking for a fight."

"You should keep her on a leash," Anwher said.

"Beg your pardon," the barber said, backing away. "Beg your pardon."

"That's all you have to say about it? You're a shitty son," Anwher said. "Worthless." Anwher couldn't abide weakness. "Your mother is a whore," he said.

The barber nodded.

"She's a whore," Anwher said.

The barber said nothing.

"You're not telling him anything he doesn't know, boy," the old woman said.

"Shut up," Anwher said. Looking back at the barber, he said, "How much? It's by the hour or what? Doesn't matter. I'll just take my whore right here. That okay with you?"

The barber remained bent at the waist. It was a while before he spoke, and when he did, he addressed himself to the hard earth. "Discuss business matters with her."

"Unbelievable," Anwher said. "Can you believe this?" Anwher looked around for an answer, but the fat man appeared to be engrossed in his newspaper, and the old woman had a crazy grin on her face, so he looked back at the son.

Eventually the barber said, "I know. It's hard to believe."

"You need to have your head checked," Anwher said.

"Haircut's on the house," the barber said. He forfeited the bill without looking up. "Please go."

After spitting twice on the ground at the barber's feet, Anwher left. The barber's mother, still grinning ever so slightly, turned to the fat man, that seemingly permanent fixture atop his stool. "That was quite a performance, hm? Did you see that? He walked off without paying. Those people would rob their own kin."

"Ma," the barber said. "Don't."

The fat man shook his head and hauled himself off the stool.

"Ma," the barber said.

"I could give you more than a haircut on the house, you know," she said to the fat man.

He made a show of shuddering.

"You're not much to look at yourself," she shot back.

"I have my charms," he said.

"So does a rattlesnake," she said.

"Aw, you don't mean that," the fat man said. "Come file a report in the morning. We'll take care of the rest."

• • •

They came for Anwher while he slept and dragged him from his low bed by a rope twisted around his neck. When they started to beat him the garrote slipped a bit, and in this way he avoided asphyxiation.

They threw him in the back seat of a Volkswagen sedan, a standard unmarked PSB vehicle. Two men sat on either side of him, their large thighs pinioning him. He tried to screw open his swelling eyes, but couldn't see a thing. His ears rung and his face throbbed in time with his heartbeat. They were rolling now, the compartment filling with cigarette smoke that stung the raw tissues of his esophagus. Something cold and hard was in his mouth. One of the men began to punch him in the head.

He awoke in a cell, which in the darkness he first mistook for his room at home. The confusion didn't last long. The scrape of metal buckets on concrete echoed through the cellblock as prisoners passed around the pot to relieve themselves. His body was numb until he moved against the concrete floor and the net of agony tangled around him tightened. He remembered where he was. Slowly, he drew into a ball and wept.

• • •

Omar had stood in the doorway and watched them take his grandson. He could have screamed and waved his arms like a woman, but what

144

good would that have done? Gotten him a broken jaw, probably. He knew how this worked and he kept his distance. Just to be sure, the Chinese had stationed one of their thugs by him, and weapons were made obvious, but he wouldn't have moved even if he'd had an army behind him. It was everyone's fate to be dragged off by the Chinese. Omar, of course, viewed fate as little more than a starting point at which one began his negotiation with the universe. Everyone but Anwher, it seemed, knew how this worked. He'd struggled and made it worse for himself.

Omar went to the slot in the floor and counted out a decent payoff. They'd be sure to liberate him of anything valuable he carried in, so he removed his watch and gold chains and dropped them in the hole.

Then, outside to have a smoke and wait for daylight. He blew out his nostrils and packed the pipe. The monkey across the street was curled on a blanket beneath a window. Omar squatted down and watched the sleeping animal's dim form.

• • •

Alone in the cell, Anwher had backed his spine tight against the concrete seam of a corner. His face had become a mask of dried blood and sweat. The unrelenting ammoniac stench of public toilets was thick on the air. Guards' voices echoed through the corridor. When the prisoners moved, they moved in silence while the guards stamped beside them, shouting, "March, convicts!" Anwher envisioned his own grotesque death, but stripped of the chorus of sympathy usually humming in the background. *Allah, mercy, I beg you.* Despite the heat, he was freezing, so cold that he felt his hands might snap off like twigs. He knew he was waiting to be retrieved, and that alone kept him awake, his eyes sweeping the dim cell for movement. Finally, the door opened and two guards dragged him to the wash room where they told him to strip, which he did, as they dumped bucket after bucket of stinging water over his head. He dressed with the agonizing deliberation of an eighty year old, and they dragged him off to another part of the prison. The barber and his mother were there.

When he came into view, the old woman did a little dance. "That's the one," she said. "Hey there, Uyghur. How's life?"

"Cut it out," a guard said. "That's inappropriate."

Another guard shook Anwher by the arm. "You stole from these people?" Anwher tried to catch the barber's eye, but the man was looking everywhere else. He'd made his decision. Anwher let out a low moan.

"Oh, that's definitely the one," the old woman said. "Coward."

The barber lifted his head to say something, but she cut him off. "You had your chance," she said.

The guard directed himself at Anwher. "You've stolen from a Chinese citizen," he said, "and have damaged the reputation of your minority group."

The old woman laughed.

From behind them a voice boomed, "Behave, all of you." A round man filled the doorway and moved slowly into the room. His face was slick with sweat and the top of his coat was unbuttoned to reveal a roll of flesh at the base of his neck. At first the face was only vaguely familiar to Anwher. This was the commanding officer, that much was clear, and when Anwher placed him he shrunk back against the guard, who pushed him away. It was the fat man with the newspaper. "This is a crime against the People's Republic," the fat man said, "and it will be dealt with according to proper procedure."

"They said it was on the house," Anwher whispered.

"On the house?" the fat man said to the barber. "Is that right? For the record, did you say that?"

"You were sitting right there," said his mother.

"We need to establish the facts."

"Do we look like we're running a charity?" she said, then paused to consider the rules of the game. She had to be sure no traps were being laid for her before proceeding. "Did you hear me say it was on the house?" she asked the fat man.

"I don't recall," he said, his face impassive. It was enough to satisfy the woman that she wasn't going to land in a cell herself. "You understand this kid is connected?" the fat man said.

"Like I care. He walked a tab. And he insulted me."

"Besmirched your good name, did he?"

"You were there," she said. "You heard what he said."

"For the record," he said.

"A whore. He said I was a whore."

"Imagine."

She crossed her arms and gave the fat man the evil eye.

This went on for a while, the fat man extracting his pound of flesh, Anwher attempting invisibility, the old woman needling them both.

The barber watched dumbly from the side. Eventually the fat man got bored.

"I'm sure he'll gladly pay a fine plus what he owes you," he said to the barber's mother. "Justice done?"

"He steals from me. He threatens me. He calls me a whore in the open market and you let him go free?"

"I'm sure you've been called worse," the fat man said. "Don't push your luck." He waved at the door. "Take him back to his cell and get this citizen her money."

• • •

The fat man had been promoted hastily in the wake of the corruption sweep. His ascension to the rank of commanding officer was the result of good timing and the luck enjoyed by those who kept their mouths shut and carried out orders. But his men made farting noises when he walked by, and some still called him Fatty Bo to his face. This bothered him.

He had his orders from the new regime and had been waiting for an excuse to move against the old gangster. One could never be too careful. Things had to look right. He'd told the old woman what to do: make your claim, file a report, allow the process to take hold.

Of course, these civilians don't take orders. She'd crashed into the station like it was 1967, invoking Maoist slogans and a bunch of stuff she'd heard on the radio. "Seek truth from facts," she kept yelling. Before he knew it, the entire station was peering around doors and over the tops of their reports to see what was going to happen next. His men didn't bother to hide their snickering faces. "They're taking over," she screamed. "Threatening old women!"

He bellowed at the corporal to escort the old woman to the prisoner. The man took his time leading her away, and Fatty Bo had to yell at him again. The corporal's hangdog face hardly registered the abuse, which the other men found hilarious. And the son—there he was, trying to put enough distance between himself and his own mother to signal that their simultaneous arrival had been a coincidence. Fatty Bo motioned him over.

"She's really got a wire up her ass," Fatty Bo said.

"It's the heat," replied the barber. Fatty Bo waited, but that was all the son had to say on the matter. Why she wanted the Uyghur strung up was a mystery, but it sure wasn't because the Uyghur had called her a whore. She wanted this kid out the back door in a body bag. So be it. Embarrassing, yes, to be subject to a crazy old woman's whims, but good luck all the same. Fatty Bo was self-sufficient enough to summon some intellectual appreciation for the situation. It was a blessing, is what it was. Bastards wouldn't call him Fatty Bo after he burned Uyghurville to the ground.

• • •

Omar went to the PSB station alone, having left the payoff with one of his toughs stationed down the street.

Every cop in the place jammed into booking to eyeball him. It took two hours to fill out the forms because his Chinese was far from perfect and one of the cops dumped tea on the papers just as he was finishing. This was part of the process and Omar dutifully requested new forms, for which he was charged a Yuan and a half. Hunched over like a schoolboy he began again, pausing occasionally to brush their cigarette ash from the backs of his hands. After the forms, they made him strip and open his orifices in front of everyone before handcuffing him to a radiator in a stifling reeducation classroom. None of this was new to him.

After an hour in that swampy air, his skin had the consistency of boiled chicken and his tongue was so swollen he had to hang his mouth open like an imbecile. A young officer came to fetch him. "Here now, Uncle, take my arm," the officer said gently, "and we'll go see the prisoner." He led Omar through a series of iron doors, until finally, through a forest of bars, Omar spotted Anwher slumped against the wall, lifeless as a coat left on the ground overnight.

Fatty Bo appeared and offered Omar a thermos of water, which the old man guzzled. Anwher watched the men from his corner of the cell. "This can't be pleasant for you to see," Fatty Bo said.

"It's a shame," Omar said. He had developed a nonchalance when dealing with the authorities that was by this time as automatic as breathing. A man had to wait out the Chinese, figure out their game. Only after carefully considering the options would Omar step forward to engage them.

"Prisoner, hup to," shouted Fatty Bo. He took the younger officer's baton and dragged it across the bars. "Up! Up! You have a visitor."

"Go in and get him," Fatty Bo said to the younger officer. A few bold prisoners strained to see from their cells, but the majority hung

148

back, out of sight of the officers. A sidelong glance from a PSB and you'd be carrying rocks for a month.

The young officer nudged Anwher with the baton and said, "Come on now. Don't try Fatty Bo's patience."

"Use the proper form of address in front of the prisoner," Fatty Bo shouted.

The young officer shrugged. "Come on now," he said. "Quit playing." When Anwher refused to budge, the officer, embarrassed to find his kindness rejected, jammed the baton into the prisoner's ribs. "Up," he demanded. Still, the prisoner refused.

Fatty Bo's nostrils flared at this display of ineptitude. Bands stood out in his neck. "Get out," he said, shouldering the young officer aside.

"Boy, don't be an idiot," Omar said under his breath. There was nothing he could do. Fatty Bo pinched Anwher's ears with his thick fingers and wrenched him into a standing position.

"He's got spirit," Fatty Bo said, as if holding up a prize piglet.

"He's an idiot," Omar said.

"If you say so. We should discuss his case." Fatty Bo unsnapped the leather holster on his hip and patted his pistol.

"What's that all about?" Omar said.

"Just watch yourself, okay?"

"Let's discuss the boy's case," Omar said. A gun wasn't necessary for these negotiations and it surprised him that the officer had put it into play. But the Chinese were good at psychology. They had hundreds of clever tricks to knock their detainees off balance.

"His file was called up for a minor charge," said Fatty Bo, "but some research turned up unpaid license fees." He graced the younger guard with a wry smile. "What is he? A raisin salesman?"

"A furniture importer," Omar said. "We can take care of this quickly."

"I haven't even told you how much he owes. How much do you think he owes?"

"In range of three thousand," Omar said quickly. He didn't care what the officer was claiming the boy had done. The officer would have the money and Omar wasn't going to stand in his way.

Fatty Bo chewed on it for a moment. "Damn close. It's good that you're on top of his business."

"Four," Omar said.

"Look, it's a symbolic act. A measure of good faith." Fatty Bo focused intently on Omar, his eyes narrowing.

"I wouldn't call it symbolic," Omar said.

"Can I tell you something about myself?" Fatty Bo said. "I'm an unlikely success, you know? The odds were staggering. I was very sick as a child. As scrawny as him." He tipped his chin at Anwher. "Unable to defend myself. Can you believe it, looking at me now? Things change."

"Things change," Omar said.

"And listen to this: my father was taken by the Red Guard, strapped to a log, and pushed over a waterfall," Fatty Bo said. "My mother and I lived like a couple of rats in a hole. If someone had told me I'd be here today . . ."

"You'd never have believed it," Omar said.

"Yes! Exactly." Fatty Bo looked at Omar appreciatively. "You haven't had an easy life, either, but look at you—you've done well for yourself. That's why I feel I can talk to you. So what's money between two men like us? My men tell me you didn't even raise your voice to them. You spoke without speaking, right? It impressed them, I'll tell you that much. When was the last time you woke up bloody in a jail cell? Not in my lifetime, am I right? That's a mistake you only make once. But this poor boy. This generation worries me. They're soft. None of this 'eat bitter' bullshit for them. He'll never be able to hold your empire together by himself, that's what you're thinking. Not that there haven't been dangerous homosexuals—remember Queen Li? That guy and his fucking wooden knives!"

Omar kept his eyes level and his hands by his sides.

"You're worried," Fatty Bo said. "Let me put your mind at rest." But that was all he said. He expelled a weary sigh.

"He's been saying he wants to move back to Ürümqi," Omar ventured.

"Is that a fact?" Fatty Bo said.

"It is. He's had it almost as bad as you and I, so it's understandable."

"I very seriously doubt that."

"When he was a child in Ürümqi. Both of his parents. My daughter—" Omar brought his finger across his neck.

"No," Fatty Bo said.

"Yes. Truly. Killed in the street."

"By Chinese?"

"Yes," Omar said.

"That's no surprise. They used to send the top notch psychos out there. All this bad blood is their fault. Everyone got off to a terrible start."

"And still, the boy wants to go home."

"If only things could have been different early on," Fatty Bo said.

"I've told him to stay here, but he's a grown man. He can do what he wants."

"It's too late to change the course of history. Isn't that what they say?"

"He's a grown man, but I'm responsible for him." Omar brought his hands up, as if to apologize for this indissoluble family bond. "I can have the money here very quickly," he said.

"That's a good idea. You should pay the fine and I'll let the boy go." Fatty Bo leaned toward Omar and put his mouth close to his ear. "You understand I'll have to interrogate him. To appease the men. They're animals. No ability to recognize the nuances of the situation. Our history creates expectations."

Only the four of them—Omar, Fatty Bo, the younger officer, and Anwher—were there in the corridor.

"You'll do what's expected," Omar said.

Fatty Bo sighed and held his gun out to the younger officer. "Give me your stick. And don't let this old man get the drop on you. He's got a trick or two up his sleeve." The younger officer nodded gravely.

Standing over Anwher, Fatty Bo slapped the baton into his meaty hand. "Now, young man. Whenever you're ready to apologize for your crime, let me know." Anwher scrambled into a corner, but Fatty Bo was all over him. With a great sweeping arc he raised the stick above his head, then brought it smashing down on Anwher's back. "This is unnecessary," Fatty Bo said to no one in particular. Beatings no longer interested him the way they once had. But a man did his duty.

He hit Anwher until the Uyghur stopped struggling, and by that time his own back was starting to seize up. It took all of his concentration to ignore the pain. He tried to swing from the hips to minimize the cramps.

He directed some shots to Anwher's head, the baton reverberating sharply in his hand. Then he stopped and looked at Omar. Omar met his gaze but said nothing.

Anwher was making noises. It could have been an apology, but

Fatty Bo's back was killing him, the muscles yanking like someone snapping out a wet cloth, and he couldn't think about anything but the cramps. He tore open his jacket to reveal a sweat-stained T-shirt underneath and attacked with a dull furor, the blows momentous, every one a raging earthquake. Anwher's hands crept over the floor, as if he were trying to drag his ravaged body out of the cell, out of the station, away from Beijing entirely. In his homeland, a man could walk in a deep valley for days without encountering another soul.

"Why?" Anwher cried, his voice suddenly clear.

Fatty Bo stopped long enough for Omar to respond to his grandson. When the old man said nothing, Fatty Bo looked up. "This can go on indefinitely," he said.

Omar knew it could.

"So be it," Omar said. "Show us what you're made of."

Nominated by A Public Space

FATHERS

by JOSEPH MILLAR

from FORTUNE (Eastern Washington University Press)

All year they've given things away:
lipsticks, stockings, movie tickets,
wiper blades and cigarette money.
At dawn they stand over our sleeping bodies
gazing into our faces, into the future.
Then they stay outdoors after dinner
smoking, watching the road turn dark
and they don't want to come back inside.

Ten thousand of them have rested later
under a gray coat still wet with rain
in their belt buckles and reading glasses,
their hatbands and tobacco smells.
When they fall asleep
night collects in their palms,
miles of track turn bright with dew
and a net of stars rises
over the river. They hear a voice
asking for order, asking for quiet
while the world tilts away from the sun
and the shadows grow long at the end of fall
over the wisps and stubble,
over the dust and chaff.

Nominated by Rick Bass, Jack Driscoll, Christopher Howell, Dorianne Laux

NORTH OF

fiction by MARIE BERTINO

from MISSISSIPPI REVIEW

THERE ARE AMERICAN FLAGS on school windows, on cars, on porch swings; it is the year I bring Bob Dylan home for Thanksgiving.

We park in front of my mom's house, my mom who has been waiting for us at the door, probably since dawn. Her hello carries over the lawn. Bob Dylan opens the car door, stretches one leg and then the other. He wears a black leather coat and has spent the entire ride from New York trying to remember the name of a guitarist he played with in Memphis. I pull our bags from the trunk.

"You always pack too much," I say.

He shrugs. His arms are small in his coat. His legs are small in his jeans.

"Hello hello," my mother says as we amble toward her.

"This is Bob," I say.

My mother was married with a small son in the Sixties and wouldn't recognize the songwriter of our time if he came to her house for Thanksgiving dinner. She has been cooking all morning and all she wants to know is whether somewhere in his overstuffed Samsonite my friend Bob has packed an appetite.

He has. "We're starving," I say.

The vestibule is charged with the cold we have brought in. She puts her finger to her lips and points to the dark family room. I can make out a flannel lump on the couch. "Your brother is sleeping. We'll go into the kitchen."

The kitchen is bright with food: cheeses, meats, heads of cauliflower, casserole dishes. My mother wipes her hands on an apron she's had for years. "I wanted him to have his favorite foods before he leaves. For Iraq." She pronounces it like it's something you can do. I run, I walk, Iraq. "Bob," she says, "do you know how to behead a string bean?"

She arranges Bob Dylan at the counter with a knife and a cutting board. I excuse myself.

The downstairs bathroom is lit by a candle. Over the toilet seat, an American flag.

When I return, there is a new voice in the kitchen. I am in time to hear my mother say, "He came with your sister," referring to Bob, who has amassed a sorry pile of gnarled beans.

"Jeeeeesus." My brother recognizes him immediately. "It's nice to meet you." They shake hands. "Wow, man, wow."

My brother's face is blurred with nap, but in his eyes grows an ambitious light. It is a spark that could vanish as quickly as it came or succeed in splitting his face open into reckless laughter. I know it can go either way.

I make my voice soft. "Hi there."

"Hey." My brother turns, lifts his nose and sniffs. His smile recedes. "Still smoking?"

I nod. I say, hopefully, "You met Bob."

He nods.

"Can you beat that?" I say.

"I didn't know it was a contest." His smile is gone.

My mother leans over Bob, to re-explain how much of the string bean is "end."

"I thought you would like to meet him," I say.

He shrugs. "I thought it would just be family."

I can tell when Bob Dylan needs a cigarette. We excuse ourselves before dinner to the backyard, where everything is dead. In the corner near the fence is a pile of lawn ornaments my mom will put up in the spring. She's had everything for years. The newest thing is the dining room table, a mahogany affair, and even that is allowed in the house only two days a year: Thanksgiving and Christmas.

Bob Dylan never has his own cigarettes. I thought this was charming at first.

"We're going to get you a pack today, buddy." I hit mine against the inside of my wrist and unwind the plastic. I brought Bob here to

155

remind my brother how he used to be, before American flags and Iraq. I thought at least it would give us something to talk about. I give myself the length of a cigarette to admit it: my plan is not going to work.

Bob and I smoke on the edge of the yard. There are no lights on at the Monahan's house, our neighbors. They normally go to a cousin's in New Jersey for Thanksgiving.

The grass is frozen. Every so often I stamp on it to hear the crunching sound. Then, without speaking, Bob Dylan and I have a contest. He expels a line of smoke clear to the middle of the yard. "Damn," I say, when mine dies not three feet in front of me. He exhales again, this time surpassing mine by yards. "Damn," I say. He is good at this, but he has years on me.

We go back in.

"Isn't it wonderful?" my mother says. "The whole family around the table."

My brother is wearing new clothes. I am spooning mashed potatoes onto my plate when I ask, "When do you leave?"

"Two weeks."

"Isn't it wonderful?" my mother says again. "They let him have a good Thanksgiving dinner before he goes."

The presence of Bob Dylan seems to make my brother anxious. Our dinner conversation is punctuated by his glares toward Bob, as if I have brought him here as another fuck-you: look at the friends I have made in New York City. Thankfully Bob is oblivious, admiring each string bean on all sides before plunging it into his mouth.

Later, there is an argument. There is something my brother wants me to admit and I won't. Bob Dylan ends up with a busted lip.

My mother wants us to sit back down and eat the turkey. She is trying to hold a bowl of corn and pull me back into my chair.

I say, "Bob, let's get out of here."

It is cold, but there is sun. Bob Dylan and I drive through dead trees and I point out personal landmarks that make this Not Just Any Neighborhood. This is where I got my first kiss; this is where I worked that summer; this is where I went to school.

There's the hospital where I was born. Small and curled like a comma, smears of mustard-colored hair, there's the hospital where I was born. My brother was at home on the stoop, passing out candy cigarettes to the other six-year-olds.

My car rattles on an overpass. Below Bob Dylan and me sweep the arms of the turnpike. Over our left shoulders, north of the city, nothing.

"You used to be able to see the Vet from here," I say, as if I'm narrating. "Great times had at the Vet. Years ago on Opening Day, a big fight broke out on the 700 level. *The Daily News* got a picture of my brother."

A curious train runs next to my car. It ducks me, reveals to me its silver flanks through the trees, and ducks me again. It plunges farther into the crunch as I turn off. The sky is blue.

I stop at a red light on the Boulevard. A man on the median is breathing into his cupped hands. He is selling roses.

Someone in the car in front of me calls to him. It is my brother, ten years ago.

He is fighting with my mom, and I am in the backseat, caught up in being eleven, ignored and ignoring. My mom's cheeks are wet.

He asks how much the red ones are.

"On second thought, it doesn't matter," he interrupts himself, and buys twelve. They are wrapped in plastic and smell like exhaust, but it ends the fight.

This happened years ago. He is a good son. My brother is a good son.

The light changes to green. I make the turn.

On one of the lawns facing the Little League field, an older couple is hauling leaves to the curb in a quilt that is too nice to be used in this way. Their progress is slow, but they couldn't have asked for a better day. It is cold, but there is sun lighting up my windshield, warming me at red lights. The sky is blue. The turkey is steaming on its plate.

Do they hope to clear the lawn of every leaf before the kids arrive? This is one of those unrealistic expectations parents have. That their children will be smarter than they are, or will like each other, that no Thanksgiving dinner will ever be interrupted by the hard sound of someone upending a chair.

There are too many leaves. Bob Dylan and I both know: they will never get all of them cleared in time.

There are American flags on buses, on coats, on bandannas tied around the necks of golden retrievers. Hanging from every tree, reflected in every window.

Bob Dylan is upbeat. His lip has stopped bleeding and he wants to know, Do I consider myself to be an American Daughter?

I have been vaulted from the Thanksgiving table. What's more American than that? How many people have left their steaming homes to drive around and think about old things? I pass car after car.

Outside the Slaughtershouse Bar, the pay phone hangs from its cord. There I am six years ago, an unimpressive fifteen. No breasts, arms and legs beyond my control, making a phone call to my brother in the middle of the night.

"Stay right there," he says. "Don't do anything stupid."

I walk in place to stay warm. Every so often a car drives by and hurls its lights at me. Ten minutes later he pulls up, brakes sharply.

"I ran away and I'm never going back." I am crying.

He waits for me to fix the long strap over my shoulder before he pulls away.

I look at him, then at the road, then at him.

"Are you going to yell at me?"

"Do you know what tape this is?" he says.

I listen. There is music playing.

"No."

"It's *The Freewheelin' Bob Dylan*."

"Oh," I say. "What's that?"

"Bob Dylan."

"Right."

We watch the road in silence.

"Are you going to take me home?"

"More people should listen to Bob Dylan," he says.

He drives to the Red Lion diner. We sit in the big plastic seats and give the waitress our order. He buys me a bowl of French onion soup.

"I'll take you home tomorrow," he says. "You can stay at my place tonight."

Suddenly, it is a new, dangerous night, one that will not end with me at my mother's house. I give him a sloppy, generous smile. He glares at me.

A man at the counter says to the waitress, "I hear they're talking about exploding it and putting up two new stadiums."

The waitress seems impressed. "Yeah?"

"No," the man says. "Not exploding. What is it when it goes in-stead of out?" He makes a motion with his hands, lacing his fingers into one another over and over.

My brother smiles at me. "Imploding," he says.

"That's it." The man swivels to look at us. "Imploding. They're gonna sell tickets. Get a load of that."

My brother takes a large bite of his cheeseburger. He puts a finger up, to signal to the man, the waitress, and me to wait. "They'll never fucking do that," he says, when he has the meat in his mouth under control.

The man isn't convinced, hacks into his hand. "That'll be a Philadelphia event. All of us tailgating to watch a stadium implode."

My brother is certain. "No fucking way they'll do that. This city is nothing without the Vet."

The man shrugs. "They've already done it. They signed contracts and everything."

"Who are you, the mayor?"

They both laugh. My brother's teeth are stained with meat.

The door slams and rattles the ketchup bottles. A tall girl stands in the doorway of the diner unwinding a scarf. Then, she seems to make her way toward our table.

My brother scrambles to make room for her in the booth. "I'm glad you came," he says.

"No problem." She sits down and is face-to-face with me. I don't know where to look.

He gestures as if I am a mess on the floor. "My sister."

"Nice to meet you. I'm Genevieve." She pulls her scarf from her neck, and I am able to see how red her hair is. It is the closest I have ever been to someone who looks like they could be famous.

"Genevieve and I work together." My brother is having a hard time swallowing. "I have to take a leak," he says.

When he is gone, she looks at me, and I look at my soup. Her per-fume smells like *Vanity Fair* magazine.

"I heard you ran away," she says.

I nod.

She drags one of my brother's french fries through a hill of ketchup. "I ran away once. I got all the way downtown. I got scared and called my mom."

"Really?"

"I called her from Wanamaker's."

159

"Was she mad?"

"Oh boy. She was so mad, she sent my dad to come get me. He bought me a slice of pizza."

She has impressive eyebrows. What could I say that would mean anything to her? I decide on an idea I had been toying with since the ride over, the beginning of a line of thinking.

"You were freewheeling." I am careful to laugh after I say it like I don't mean it, in case she rolls her eyes.

"That's right," she laughs. "Like Bob Dylan."

"Oh. Do you like him?" I say it like, Nothing much to me either way, toots.

"Are you kidding?" she says. "He's my favorite."

"He's mine, too," I say. I am not lying.

"You should talk to your brother." She tilts her pretty eyebrows toward the men's room. "As of last week, he had barely even heard of Bob Dylan."

I chew a piece of cheese, and she arranges a stack of creamers. "Are you my brother's girlfriend?"

When she opens her mouth I can see all of her teeth. "You'd have to ask him," she says.

My brother returns from the bathroom, wiping his hands on his jeans. His hair is wet.

"Let's go," he says. "*Saturday Night Live* is on."

He lives in a crumble of an apartment next to the diner. Trucks turn into the parking lot and light up his front room, waking up whichever one of his friends is sleeping there.

We sit in his basement, and he howls through the entire show. I look back at him, and he wipes tears from his eyes. After it is over, he throws a pillow at me. He and Genevieve go upstairs.

"Night, Squirt."

I sleep on the couch in his front room. The headlights from the trucks scan me in my sleep.

The next day, he drops me off at our mother's house.

"Kiddo," he calls me back to the car.

"What?"

"Don't ever fucking do that again."

His face is twisted. I assume with worry.

"Don't worry about me," I say. "You don't have to protect me. I can take care of myself."

He spits. "Come here," he says. I lean into the car, and he lays his hand on my arm, no trace of expression around his eyes or mouth.

"I mean," he says, "don't ever fucking do that to Mom again."

I go inside. My mother pulls at her hair and weeps in a slow collapse against the wall of the kitchen.

This is my high school. This is my first play. Here are the good grades, the medals, and the prom. This is the scholarship to the private college and here is the field where, in my cap and gown, I hugged my teachers good-bye. There were no friends. "So long," I say. "I'm going to New York City."

This is the gas station where my brother worked until he and the owner had a "difference of opinion." This is the hardware store where my brother worked until he told the manager to fuck himself. This is the auto parts store that gave him a job because he and the owner went to the same high school. Philadelphia is a network of my brother's buddies. He doesn't stay unemployed for long.

The first year I live in New York, I find a job I still have. He calls every so often to ask if I have seen any celebrities.

If the people at the convenience store on Bloomingdale Road are surprised to see the bloated Voice of a Generation using the candy display to scratch the low part of his back, they keep it to themselves. Bob Dylan has been looking for Tootsie Rolls for ten minutes. He's wild over them, but they appear to be out.

I leave him to it. I am happy to be with the people on Thanksgiving, albeit the ones who do not think ahead. There is something reassuring about being among strangers on a national holiday. In the cereal aisle, the mood is decidedly last-minute.

"Can you use Corn Flakes instead of bread crumbs?" a man in slippers asks his bored-looking teenager. "I feel like you can, but I don't want Mommy yelling at us when we get home. Go ask the cashier." The son shuffles off.

Bob is grouchy and empty-handed when he returns to me.

Seeing him, the man with the canister of Corn Flakes asks himself a question I cannot hear.

Then he says to Bob, "Oh, jeez. Aren't you Vincent Price?"

This has been a problem before. I pray Bob hasn't heard, but the man says it again, louder, as if remembering Vincent Price is deaf. He taps Bob's shoulder a couple times and calls for his son. "Get a load of Vincent Price!" he says.

This is all Bob needs. First his lip is busted, then no Tootsie Rolls, now this. He screws his hand into a punch and lurches toward the man who, almost as an afterthought, performs a delicate side step. Bob's momentum hits the candy display, and he falters, swiping at the ground with his feet, trout-sized chocolate bars slithering down his faded coat.

The teenage boy is back. "What happened, Dad?"

The man is dumbstruck, joyous. "Vincent Price just tried to punch me, and he missed!"

Someone got us while we were sleeping, so this Thanksgiving is the year of the American flag. There are American flags on overpasses, tricycles. There are American flags printed on condoms at the counter of this convenience store; *America will screw you hard*.

Bob Dylan mopes in the car. I feel saddled with him now. He was supposed to create some sort of lather, and he barely summoned enough energy to behead a pile of string beans. I buy him a magazine, a Liberty Bell key chain, Band-Aids shaped like pieces of bacon, and a pack of Camel reds. They are parting gifts. In line, I try to catch his eye through the window, but he is sulking and won't look up. Bob Dylan can be a real baby.

My brother's car is gone when I pull into my mother's driveway.

There is a picture in her garage: a stop-motion account. In the first panel the Vet is whole, intact. In the second panel there is smoke around the eastern wall: a stadium with a headache. In the third panel it is half obscured by the smoke, and so on.

My mother is at the table drinking. She has poured one for me before I come in, stamping off mud and leaves.

"Where's your friend?" she says.

"Dropped him off at the train."

She nods, and senses my apology before I have time to form one. "I don't want to hear it," she says. "You should try to get along with your brother."

On her collar, a pin as small as a thumbprint, the shape of a flag.

"I'm sorry," I say, and then I can't stop saying it.

We tailgated all day but it wasn't until the second inning that he told me about Genevieve leaving for school in Vermont.

"Said I was narrow-minded because I never went to college," he said. "Said the experience would have done me good. What fucking experience? What kind of experience is in Vermont?"

His fingers strummed his knees. By then he had cultivated hard knots of muscles up and down his arms and legs, making him look in motion even when he was sitting.

"Maybe she won't like it," I said.

"Maybe fuck her."

He was dating girls from the neighborhood and had gotten one of them pregnant. He told me like it was something he had forgotten at my house. It was one of the only times I had seen him in years, and I felt him slipping through me even as he sat next to me. I held onto his arm. "You could have something real and true."

"It's the size of a pea," he said, like a punch line.

When the fight below us broke out, I grabbed his arm. "Don't go down there," I said. "Please," I said. "Please."

He shook me easily. "Get off me, punk."

His friends pushed him into the aisle and down the steps. People were already on the field swinging at each other. I kept an eye on his blue hat until he came to the lip where the bleachers met the field and he had to jump. I caught glimpses of blue here and there until the press of bodies moved him too far away, and he became indistinguishable. There were fields of him. Fields and fields.

I found him outside the stadium. Flanked by his friends, he held up Chris Monahan's T-shirt to a gash in his head. When he caught sight of me he smiled right through all the blood, proud of himself. His face lit up so pretty and so fast that it made me light-headed. I swayed.

He needed it, so I gave him the money. After that, he made himself into a secret, answered his phone rarely and then not at all.

Finally, my mother's voice through the phone in my New York kitchen. "Your brother has enlisted. Your brother is going to war. Your brother is in the Army, and they are sending him to war. Come home for Thanksgiving. We are going to have Thanksgiving. Before he leaves, we will have one last . . . we are going to have Thanksgiving."

"No, Mom, you're wrong. No one is going to war," I say. "No one is going to war." I keep saying it after she hangs up.

There is an aunt who escaped to California, but she exists mostly in postcards, so it's four of us for Thanksgiving dinner. My mother,

Bob Dylan, my brother and I sit around our nuclear table, making bland, unseasoned comments and doling out corn and mashed potatoes.

Then my brother says, "When's the last time you visited?" He is not looking at me as he rolls the sleeves of his flannel shirt, but I know it's me he's talking to.

I pretend to think about it. "Good question. I don't know."

"Five years, you think?" He passes the string beans to Bob Dylan, who takes a liberal spoonful.

"Maybe." I shrug.

"Maybe," my brother says. "Mom, don't you think it's been five years?"

"Don't know," she says. "Glad she's here, now, though. Let's pray before we forget. Bob, would you like to lead us in—"

"Bob's a Jew," I say.

Bob laughs, I laugh. After thinking about it, my mom laughs.

My brother stabs at a pile of dark meat, securing three pieces onto his fork. My last remark bothered him. Not because it might have offended Bob, but because I am trying to be funny. I am his sister, and I know this.

He makes his voice sound light, as if suggesting a swim. "Oh, do Jews not pray?"

I say, "Do Army people pray?"

My mother folds her hands. "I'll pray," she says. "Dear God, we are all of us going strong. Keep my baby safe in I-raq and keep my other baby safe in New York and thank you for sending us a helpful dinner guest on such an important night for our family." She winks at Bob who, to my confusion, blushes, and I wonder: is my mother hitting on Bob Dylan?

A quick amen and it is over. We eat what we have deposited onto our plates. Ours is an eat-it or wear-it family, so I check to make sure Bob Dylan has not taken too much.

My brother sees this and rolls his eyes. "Thought you'd come back for Chris's funeral," he says.

I say, "I sent a card."

"Oh, a card. Well, then."

My mother layers finger-sized pieces of white meat onto Bob Dylan's plate. She says, "I don't know if you do this in New York, Bob, but in this family we have a tradition: after dinner we compete to

164

break the wishbone. The person who ends up with the biggest piece has a year of good luck. What do you think about that?" She wants Bob Dylan to be interested; she wants him, or anyone, to wrestle with her over a dry, cracked wishbone, to fight over a year of good luck, to take it outside if necessary, she wants to lose both of her terry cloth slippers in the struggle, she wants us all to share a big laugh over it. My mother is not afraid to make desire plain on her face, a trait shared by neither of her children. It makes her seem vulnerable to attack, and I can't look straight at her while she waits for the words of Bob Dylan.

I am proud of Bob. He begins to eat the turkey noisily, signaling to her with a thumbs-up, another kind of answer.

"Did they write back?" my brother says.

"Did who write back?" I say.

"The Monahans. Did they write back to your card?"

"They may have. I didn't really keep track." This is a lie. I checked my mailbox twice a day.

"I wonder why they didn't write back. Their only son killed in Iraq, and you send a card."

My mother says, "Okay, everyone."

"Were you too busy hanging out with Bob Dylan in New York?"

"I have a job," I say.

"And I am the loser with no job," he says, as if we are introducing ourselves to guests. "I guess that is some kind of New York etiquette, Mom, and we just don't get it. Neighbor dies, send a card. Big dinner, bring a stranger. Why don't you just admit it: you don't like it here."

A shiver of my mother's hand holding the gravy boat produces a small jangle on its plate. She places her left hand on her right to say to it, Be calm. I realize I am signing up for a life of disappointment if I ever think my brother will appreciate a gift I give him. The desire to please him wobbles, an amorphous yet contained thing, easily trashed, like the cranberry sauce no one eats. It is a boozy feeling, making me capable of inducing great hurt.

"Don't worry," I say. "If you get killed in Iraq, I'll come home for the funeral."

I am standing, then he is standing, his napkin clinging to the waistband of his jeans.

My mother is suddenly fluttering with activity. "I have an idea," she says, almost screaming. "Let's do the wishbone now." She throws her napkin on her chair and darts into the kitchen, where we hear a clattering of utensils. Then she emerges, a small, gray V in her hand. "Who wants to?" She looks at me, her eyes pleading. "Let's you and me do it."

I say, "Are you serious?"

"We're doing this now?" My brother grins.

"Yes, now," she says, her face wild. "Now."

My brother and I share a look.

"This is crazy," I say. "In the middle of dinner?"

"Now." She turns to Bob. "What do you say, Bob? You and me!"

Bob Dylan has no designs on the wishbone. He shakes his head.

"Well, I'm not doing it either," I say.

My brother wipes his mouth with his napkin. "Jesus Christ, I'll do it. Me and you, Mom."

My mother cheers. "Let me warn you," she says. "I've been practicing."

"I'll keep that in mind," he says, grabbing one end of the wishbone.

"Are we going to do this right here?" I say, but they have already started, my mother and brother on either side of the table, pulling.

Bob and I remain seated. He reaches over me for the gravy.

After a moment, my brother says, "This is taking forever, Mom."

"Maybe it's not completely dry." My mother leans forward over the table, her American flag necklace idling over the cranberry sauce. "Give up?" she says.

"Never. Battle to the finish."

It goes on, neither side showing any progress.

My mother says, "This is a good one!"

Then, my brother pulls his arm away from my mother in a sharp motion, forcing her farther over the table, and the V between them cracks. She is thrown backward with the release. Her limbs go into a frantic star position, and she brings her elbow solidly into the mouth of Bob Dylan. The force of it upends the front two legs of his chair, Bob Dylan teeters, and it seems he will topple over. But, I am on my feet, and I catch him.

"Oh shit," I say. "You're bleeding, Bob."

My mom disappears into the kitchen. I hear the faucet go on, and a clattering of silverware.

My brother laughs, and I turn on him. "You did that on purpose."

He throws his hands up. "How would I know that would happen?"

166

"You knew Mom would do that!"

He waves me off. "Shut up, punk."

Bob Dylan paws at his busted lip, touching it with his callused fingers, then showing himself the blood. My mother comes out with a wet cloth and kneels next to him. There is no more hope anywhere on her face. Someone is bleeding at her Thanksgiving table. "I am so sorry," she says. "I am so sorry."

I say, "It wasn't your fault, Mom. Just a small gash. No harm done." I am lying. It is a small gash, but I know Bob Dylan will be relentless about it, looking at it from all angles in every car window and mirror we pass for the next five days.

"Now you can say you gave Bob Dylan a fat lip," says my brother.

"You hit Bob Dylan," I say. "You did."

"Are you on another planet, punk? Mom hit Bob Dylan."

"Stoppit," she says, quietly, still kneeling. "It was my fault."

"Are you happy?" I say. "What a jerk."

"Everyone just sit down and eat, please."

My brother obeys. He replaces the napkin on his lap, primly spears a string bean and places it in his mouth.

"At least," he says, "I'm not a fucking phony."

I look to my mom for some clue she knows I am being maligned, but she is staring out the window to a ratty tree that has gotten rid of every leaf except one. Her hands are still folded, but she has freed her index fingers. She stares past us to the point on the lawn where winter is advancing on her family so fast that she has time to do nothing except tap her index fingers with the nonchalance of someone deciding whether to add eggs to a grocery list.

Bob Dylan holds the washcloth to his lip with one hand and with the other pats down his denim shirt where he will, I am certain, not find cigarettes.

"Bob," I say. "Let's get out of here."

The day after Thanksgiving, my brother and I move the table into the garage. We maneuver it around the corners of our house without speaking. It is thick between my hands and I worry I will drop it. When we finally put it down, there is a moment when it is the only thing between us.

He says, "Mom needs to clean this garage," the same time I say, "Don't do anything stupid over there." I don't know if he hears me.

We rub our chapped hands.

I say, "I brought Bob Dylan here for you. To make you happy."

His eyes move over the tools hanging from nails on the wall. The hammers, the wrenches, the screwdrivers.

"So what," he says. "You want a fucking medal?"

Nominated by Ron Tanner, Mississippi Review

WHAT THEY'RE DOING

by DAN ALBERGOTTI

from THE CINCINNATI REVIEW

They're bulldozing the cheap apartments
where the young Chinese couple were slaughtered
on Veterans Day. They're hauling away broken,
blood-stained bricks. They're making business decisions.
They're making children who will piss in the river
and ride their new bicycles down the center of the street
on Christmas Day, grinning, baring sharp little teeth.
They're taking children to church and singing hymns.
They're becoming Christian soldiers, marching as to war.
They're carrying a cross before them like a scythe.
They're entering holy cities in armored personnel carriers.
They're accomplishing missions, declaring victory,
saying *amen, amen*, meaning *so be it, so be it*. And so it is.

Nominated by Natasha Trethewey, Stuart Dischell, Colette Inez

SHADOW BOXING

by JEREMY COLLINS

from THE GEORGIA REVIEW

Study people's success stories hard. Study their failures even harder.
—Sylvester Stallone, *Sly Moves: My Proven Program to Lose Weight,*
Build Strength, Gain Will Power, and Live Your Dream

The original *Rocky* was released in 1976; I was born the same year. In a weirdly literal sense, we've grown up together. We recently turned thirty, and neither of our prospects look good. *Rocky* has to contend with the films Stallone has made since; I have bad knees, student loans, and credit card debt. What keeps me up nights, though, is that I've yet to publish the book I've been writing for ten years. I'm not sure how healthy it is to inventory one's life next to that of a movie or a celebrity, but I can't tell my story without telling Stallone's. I know how strange (or, in the words of *Rocky III*, "mentally irregular") that sounds, but I have Stallone to blame. He introduced me to the world of stories—and, later, when I was nineteen years old, *Rocky* taught me something about grieving. I'm too old to be looking to Stallone or *Rocky* for inspiration and guidance, but I do. I'm hard-wired. I've heard or seen *Rocky* thousands of times; I can't prove this, but it's true.

I.

In 1982 the Academy Award-winning *Rocky* was the CBS movie of the week. I was six years old and enraptured in front of the television when my parents told me it was time for bed. Kicking and crying, I refused my mother's appeals that I listen to a story from the pile of books by my bed. As a child, I was an insomniac with an imagination. I saw snakes in sock piles, legions of monsters poised under my bed,

170

bats inside my closet. To get me to sleep, my parents had to do some hefty reading. On that night, though, I didn't want a child's story. I wanted to know what happened to the man in the baggy gray sweat suit. I'm not sure what it says about Stallone's film that it captured the imagination of a six-year-old, but as my parents tucked me in, my father promised to tape the rest.

We didn't own a VCR and wouldn't until 1988. My father taped the balance of *Rocky* (even editing out the commercials) by resting a tape recorder next to our imitation oak television. The next night and countless nights that followed, I fell asleep to—and in—the world of Rocky Balboa: the sounds of Rocky wishing his pet turtles (Cuff and Link) good night, pounding his fists against raw meat, and jogging down the streets of Philadelphia.

The tone and shape of Stallone's voice became part of my inner world—*What about my prime, Mick? At least you had a prime! I didn't have no prime. I didn't have nothin'!*—and by the time I was nine years old, I'd memorized the last hour or more of *Rocky*. My recall was robotic. I'd perform scenes for third-grade classmates, complete with Stallone's slurred speech and the facial features I had to imagine. The story cast a spell over my young life. *Rocky* was like an imaginary friend, a portable book on tape playing inside my head.

There are probably several things wrong with a savant-like child quoting *Rocky*. Looking back, I know my biggest problem was that I thought Rocky won the fight at the movie's climax. If you close your eyes to the movie's final ten minutes and just listen, it's hard to tell who wins. During those nights, I was usually fast asleep even before the opening bell of the fight in which Apollo Creed would be declared the winner.

The audiotape of *Rocky* faded with my early teenage-hood, my idea of Rocky replaced by our VCR and the bloated spectacles of *Rocky II*, *Rocky III*, and *Rocky IV*. I watched these over and over after school until my parents got home from work. In each sequel, when the final bell rings Rocky is unbroken, smiling, blowing kisses. My classmates and friends also watched these sleek major motion picture sequels. We purchased the soundtracks at record stores and watched the gory fight scenes in slow motion. The voices of the original *Rocky* began to disappear.

When I was thirteen, the original *Rocky* came on television again. For the first time, I *saw* the movie. The experience was strange. Everything seemed dark and grungy. I felt as though I were watching some forgotten dream of my own or an old home movie. I mouthed the lines before they were spoken, and I watched each character closely. Rocky didn't resemble the bodybuilder Stallone of the sequels. He looked like a club fighter with a slight gut. I should've been prepared when Rocky lost, but I wasn't.

Growing up in the suburbs in the 1980s meant growing up a winner. Ronald Reagan had declared the Vietnam syndrome over. Bruce Springsteen's "Born in the U.S.A." wasn't a defiant song of protest, but a patriotic, kick-ass rock anthem. The Huxtables on *The Cosby Show* suggested mothers and fathers could be successful lawyers and doctors and yet always at home. Donald Trump was on his first wife and first millions. Greed was good. Image was everything. Homelessness, hunger, and AIDS were rumors to those of us wandering the neighborhoods and shopping malls of metropolitan Atlanta. Watching the original *Rocky* end in defeat reeked of some other era, some other country, and some other people who were unsure of themselves. The Rocky I knew was a winner, just as I knew I was a winner. I didn't want this new knowledge. I wasn't ready for it. It was like discovering that Santa Claus isn't real, that the Virgin Birth and the Resurrection are metaphors, and that all of our heroes are ultimately human.

II.

Rocky VI, officially titled *Rocky Balboa*, has been lauded for its humanity. A December 2006 issue of *Newsweek* called it "a provocative exploration of heroism and aging . . . a poignant exit." In the movie, Rocky's wife and number one fan, Adrian, has died (from, Rocky tells us, "woman cancer"), and Rocky has to deal with "the beast inside of me." To "purge" his grief, Rocky fights an exhibition bout against a champion thirty years his junior. (Watching the film, I tried to imagine what percentage of sixty-year-old widowers would handle the loss of their wives by taking their shirts off and punching other men in the face.)

The film explores grief about as deeply as does *Bambi*, and perhaps not as well, but Stallone has taken the reviews in stride. He's appeared at *Rocky VI* openings worldwide, complete with a Botox smile and his fists up, as a spokesman urging aging baby boomers to still "follow their dreams." The tag line on the DVD version says, "Never give up. And never stop believing." The movie's message seems to be, "It's never too late to be naive."

When I walked into the theater last December, I knew better than to expect *Rocky VI* to explore grief. But I wanted it to, because grieving has been on my mind for the past ten years. I've been trying to write a book about it. Ten years ago my best friend and college roommate, Jason Kenney, was killed in a single-car drunken driving accident. He was the driver and I was his passenger.

Both of us were believers. Rocky believers. As boys we held boxing matches in Jason's basement, taking turns being Rocky. To get pumped before basketball games in junior high, we'd watch *Rocky IV* over and over, and during timeouts of close games, Jason would quote lines from the movie to break the tension. Years later, our answering machine in college played the opening bars from "Eye of the Tiger," the theme song from *Rocky III*; at Young Harris College, our small two-year school tucked away in the Appalachian Mountains of northeast Georgia, we ran each morning on a narrow mountain road, thinking ourselves not unlike Apollo Creed and Rocky on the beach in that movie. Our shared affection for Rocky was based more on nostalgia for the cartoonish, oversized Rocky of the sequels than for the Rocky of the original film. But we loved thinking of ourselves as underdogs who only needed to dig a little deeper to overcome any obstacle.

The accident left me with a broken nose, a crushed right shoulder, and a shattered left foot. I was covered in road rash—bruises, cuts, scrapes. But my injuries seemed embarrassingly minor. Jason's death was immediate. A few weeks later I returned to Young Harris. I requested a single room and found that at night, after I ran out of Percocet, I couldn't sleep.

I'm not sure how many times I watched *Rocky* in that tiny room. I don't know how many times I saw Rocky wake up at four in the morning to the insipid talk on his radio alarm clock, stumble out of bed, drink raw eggs, stretch, and then hit the ground running. I don't know how many times I watched him run past the statue of George Washington and then up the stairs of the Philadelphia Museum of Art and raise his arms in the air. I'm not sure how often I saw Rocky get the holy hell beaten out of him by Apollo Creed. But I watched the movie over and over because I was afraid that if I didn't I'd act on my other fantasies and throw in the towel.

I find it hard to call any moment in front of a television screen "spiritual," but watching *Rocky* kept me afloat through those nights.

Rocky's refusal to submit to disaster helped me to invite pain, to see what it could teach. For a year after Jason's death, I didn't laugh or cry. The people I loved the most couldn't touch me. The promises and assurances of the church seemed suddenly out of Disney. But *Rocky* gave me an escape and a dogged hope that I could move into tomorrow.

In time, I started looking for a way to mourn Jason and give grief a shape. I shot baskets each night in the run-down gym where we'd played one-on-one. When the pins were taken out of my left foot and my rehab was done, I ran in the mornings up and down the same mountain road the two of us had run. I also discovered the kindness of an English professor who gave me books to read. I read and ran and played basketball for Jason. I made mourning my mission.

Grieving was often simply a matter of endurance, of putting one foot in front of the other, but in time I found my horizons expanding. I'd discovered something through reading. In books I found a kind of temporary immortality where characters and scenes seemed more real than reality. In books like *The Great Gatsby* and *A Separate Peace* I found echoes of Jason. I didn't want him to disappear. I decided I would become a writer. The week after I graduated from Young Harris I drove to the Kenney's house in Atlanta and promised Mr. Kenney that I would write a book about his son.

III.

That summer, while wandering a used bookstore in the Atlanta suburb of Decatur, I stumbled onto Stallone's *Rocky: The Movie Scrapbook*, published the year after *Rocky* was released. I was set to enroll at the University of Georgia as an English major—to make good on my promise—when I found Stallone's strange book, which outlined the story of his creation of *Rocky*. I sat down in the aisle and read the entire thing. It wasn't hard to read the short book (with photos) in a single sitting; it was hard not to be inspired.

Stallone recounts his twenty-ninth birthday party as the turning point in his creative life. He was broke and unemployed. His wife was broke and pregnant. They lived in a garage in Los Angeles, and Stallone was trying to make it as an actor and writer. In L.A. he'd landed a few television commercials as well as a part in *The Party at Kitty and Stud's*, a soft-core porn film later released as *Italian Stallion*. The work didn't pay better than had his jobs in New York (lion cage cleaner, fish-head cutter, bouncer for an apartment slumlord). His biggest scores were minor roles in *The Lords of Flatbush* and Woody Allen's *Bananas*. The phone wasn't exactly ringing off the hook. In fact, it had been disconnected.

As Stallone blew out the candles on his twenty-ninth year, he promised himself that he'd make a deeper commitment to his writing. The next day he bought spray paint and blacked out the windows to his garage home. He got rid of his television and "entered the subterranean world of writers." With a nineteen-cent Bic and a forty-nine-cent yellow legal pad, Stallone got to work. He didn't panic. He didn't go to film school. He didn't enroll in a creative writing program and take out a student loan. Instead, he wrote and kept on writing.

Stallone's writing was, in his words, "pretty juvenile stuff." He wrote short stories. He wrote television sitcoms. He wrote screenplays. He wrote pages and pages that led nowhere.

Stallone needed a spark, needed a subject, and both arrived one day when a friend gave him a ticket to watch a closed-circuit broadcast of a boxing match at the Wiltern Theater in L.A.

The year was 1975, and the fight featured Muhammad Ali against Chuck Wepner, whose career record was an unremarkable 31-17-2. Wepner had two nicknames. He was from Bayonne, New Jersey, and was called "the Bayonne Bleeder." He was also known in boxing parlance as a "tomato can"—which, no matter how you hold it, is never very threatening.

The boxing world wasn't exactly holding its breath for the matchup between a champion known as "The Greatest" and a challenger considered a "tomato can." Las Vegas oddsmakers were less likely to take bets on who'd win the fight than on whether Wepner could survive three rounds. The odds said no.

Wepner was battered and bloodied throughout the fight, but he kept coming out of his corner for more. In the ninth round, Wepner landed a shot to Ali's ribs and, for the first time ever as heavyweight champion of the world, Ali went down. Wepner went to his corner and said, "Hey, I knocked him down," to which his trainer reportedly said, "Yeah, but now he looks really pissed off." Ali got up and won on a TKO in the final round's last seconds. Wepner had gone the distance with Muhammad Ali in a display of sheer will.

Watching the fight back in L.A. was that struggling writer, and B actor, who was about to sell his dog. He went home, picked up his yellow legal pad, and on a diet of coffee and NoDoz stayed up for eighty-six hours writing. Stallone took his ninety-page script to Irwin Winkler and Robert Chartoff, producers at United Artists; he knew them from his many failed casting calls. According to legend, both producers were impressed and offered Stallone $25,000 for the rights to the script. Stallone agreed, as long as he could act in the lead role. They refused, and so did he.

Allegedly the bidding soared to $100,000, to $250,000, to $360,000. United Artists' studio chiefs were certain they could land Al Pacino, James Caan, or Burt Reynolds for the role of Rocky, so they were willing to substantially increase Stallone's checking account balance, which at that point was $106, for the rights to a script they thought would be a hit. But Stallone held his ground. If he couldn't be Rocky, there'd be no deal. Stallone's perseverance paid off. Chartoff and Winkler went to bat for Stallone and convinced United Artists to let him star in the lead role. The movie was given a budget of $1 million, the union minimum.

Rocky was filmed in twenty-eight days. Most of the scenes are first takes. Some of the best dialogue, especially between Rocky and Mickey, is ad-libbed. But these rough edges give the film its charm and suggest something closer to a play than to a major motion picture. Of Stallone's claim to have written the screenplay in three and a half days, Pauline Kael wrote in the *New Yorker*, "Some professional screenwriters, seeing what a rag-tag script it is, may think that they could have done it in two and a half. But they wouldn't have been able to believe in what they did, and it wouldn't have gotten the audience cheering like *Rocky* did."

I felt like cheering in that used bookstore as I read Stallone's story. I wanted to cheer for Stallone and myself. I'd found a blueprint, a plan to follow by the letter. Here was how I'd write a book about Jason. What I didn't see was the most important lesson of the creation of *Rocky*: some things, perhaps the best things, cannot be taught.

IV.

Writing takes time, and good writing is earned a word at a time. That lesson isn't profound, but it can take a lifetime to learn. When I headed to the University of Georgia, I plotted a writing course like Stallone's. I rented a studio apartment in a run-down part of Athens' west side. The place had one window—two feet by two feet (with

176

bars)—directly overlooking the scrap yard behind a glass shop. I slept on a bare mattress on the floor. No television. No Internet. I cleared my desk and set out to write a book about Jason's short and troubled life, and my experience of mourning in the mountains. I knew Stallone had written *Rocky* in eighty-six hours. I was willing to give myself a little more time, but not much.

I wrote and wrote and had no idea what I was doing. I wrote five or six hours at a time: descriptions, sketches, explanations of emotions. On the wall beside my writing desk, I kept three pictures. One was of William Faulkner as a young man in New Orleans in snappy tweed, holding a pipe. He is smiling, ever so slightly. The second picture was of a young Hemingway fishing a stream in Upper Michigan around 1913. The current is running against him—pooling at the backs of his knees. His mouth is slightly open in an expression of concentration and care. Next to Faulkner and Hemingway, I tacked a photo of Rocky Balboa on the stairs at the Philadelphia Museum of Art, his hands in the air, exalting.

After a year of working, I wasn't satisfied. My writing was confused. Unruly. I figured I wasn't working correctly. I decided to improve my writing habits by reading everything Hemingway and Faulkner wrote. Pyramids of books took over my room. I also decided what I needed was to make a commitment more truly like Stallone's. I needed to surrender totally. I wanted to make my life about willpower. I decided to be alone. I broke up with my girlfriend. I stopped calling friends back. I didn't make social plans because I had *other* plans. I wanted to prove I had the will to write a book.

I set two goals. I decided I'd write three pages a day for one hundred days, and I signed up to run the Philadelphia Marathon, which ended at the steps of the museum. I wanted my training to be strenuous. I figured here was a natural goal for a writer—running a marathon—and that somewhere in the silence and solitude of the road, words would fill my consciousness. The right words. Poetic words. Lean, sharp, lovely words.

I spent weeks running and writing. Sometimes I ran for miles on small country highways past fields and farms as the sun rose. Sometimes I woke and wrote for blocks of eight hours. I wrote pages without paragraph breaks and ran so far I stopped counting miles. When I wasn't running or writing, I read biographies of Hemingway and Faulkner. I slogged through *The Sound and the Fury* and *Islands in the Stream*. I read and reread Stallone's story about the creation of

Rocky. I stared at the pictures on my wall. I wrote plans for writing. Outlines. Charts. I made lists of titles for my book. Occasionally, I'd have to take a break from reading about writing and crank out my three pages. I'd hold the pages up to the light, call them good. I posed in the mirror and practiced the expression I wanted on the back of my book.

I devoured everything I could about Hemingway and Faulkner. Interviews, biographies, critical essays. I figured I'd wasted time by not knowing the essentials, the secrets. Hemingway and Faulkner knew the secrets. I was going to discover them too.

Here's what I found.

Hemingway: Write it first in pencil, then again with a typewriter. It's better to type standing up. It's nice and pleasant to work in clean cafes. Good to keep a horse chestnut in one pocket. A rabbit foot in the other. Harder to write in the summer. Too hot. Easier in the fall and best in the mornings. Stop when it's going well so you'll know what happens next. When you're done, take a walk. Read a book. Make love with the woman you love. Watch people do things they enjoy and understand. But when you're done, don't talk about your writing. Don't listen to others talk about your writing. Don't think about your writing.

Faulkner: Write when the feeling is hot, the material alive, while you are demon-driven (you must be demon-driven), and make sure you read, read, read—read everything! Think of yourself always as an amateur: don't think of writing in terms of duty or profit, but as a game of tennis, as fun. Realize that the longer sentence can be a metaphysical exercise in expressing our desire to outrun life's brevity, and that reality will always fail to be commensurate with this desire—as it will with so many other desires of the human heart. Don't be a "writer" but always be writing. Summer is a good time to write because the blood boils in the veins. Whether you are in the saddle of a horse or leaning on a fence, always carry a pencil and paper because you never know when inspiration might strike. But don't spend too much time thinking about writing; otherwise, you'll never get started.

I wrote these maxims down and spent a lot of time—too much time—thinking about writing. But I still wrote my three pages a day. I took a notebook everywhere. I wrote in the mornings and the evenings. I wrote between classes and during classes. I scribbled notes on scrap pieces of paper while working at a local bookstore. I stayed up late and woke up early, in the shadow of the glass shop, writing.

I'd have trouble calling those pages a continuous narrative. The writing was scattered, unfocused. I couldn't decide how to tell Jason's story. I didn't trust my own voice, so I wrote it as a novel and then as a screenplay. I wrote short stories from a third-person point of view, referring to my character as "the young man" and Jason as "the friend." I wrote our story as a cycle of poems. Some of them kind of rhymed.

> I loved my friend,
> but wait,
> stop.
> No more.
> Jason was not a metaphor.

I took writing classes and was too thickheaded to listen to the sound criticism from my professors. Instead, I listened to my peers' encouraging feedback ("Great! I really like the dialogue on page 7!"). But, after a while, it was hard to feel encouraged. When I got honest, the sheer amount of really bad writing I'd done seemed an overwhelming testament to how shitty a writer I was. I'd finished a first draft (titled "Mountains Like Waves") and was tempted to burn it. When I looked at a book like *The Sun Also Rises* or *As I Lay Dying* and then at "Mountains Like Waves," the gap seemed insurmountable. But I kept writing.

I kept writing because I liked the clean feeling at the end of a day's work. I kept writing because occasionally I'd write a sentence or even a paragraph that surprised me. I kept writing because I had a promise to keep. And if I felt spent and wasn't sure what to write next, I'd copy pages and pages of Hemingway and Faulkner. Over time, I copied all of *The Sun Also Rises* into my computer. But when the hundredth day arrived and I packed for my Philadelphia pilgrimage, I'd written three hundred pages. Of something.

V.

When Rocky hits the pavement running at that ungodly morning hour in Philadelphia, he's alone. When I hit the Philadelphia streets early on a November morning, I was surrounded by people. Waves

179

and waves of people. Strangers. I'd spent the last six months in solitude—reading alone, writing alone, and running alone; being surrounded by thousands of other marathoners made me seasick.

After a few miles—past old churches, past Chinatown, past Independence Hall and the Liberty Bell—I found my legs. The morning was bright and cold, and I was startled to be in a city that dripped history on every block. I ran those first half-dozen miles in a touristy reverie, until two older women ahead of me in matching pink Nike jogging suits began talking.

By their accents I could tell they were indigenous to the South. While growing up I'd seen their types in the Atlanta malls: goose-stepping housewives power walking past food courts and department stores. Their conversation hooked me. I could've moved to the sidewalk or to the other side of the road, but I didn't. I'd forgotten what it was like to listen to voices other than ones on a page.

In the South, many of our conversations move horizontally: Who is getting married to whom? Who got into what school? Who didn't? Who is getting a divorce? And who isn't? I took a strange pleasure from listening, and in spite of my reticence I almost introduced myself. Then they began talking about art. The subject was Russian literature. The subject was Oprah's Book Club.

The Golden Girl with the purple fanny pack and white headband did most of the talking. She mused about Anna Karenina's suicide and Tolstoy's peasant life in Russia. I wanted to gag. What did they know about sacrifices for Literature? They discussed Oprah's charity work and her long-distance running. I wanted to gag again. What did Oprah know about running? We ran along the Schuylkill River, and they gushed about Oprah's performance in the Chicago Marathon—four hours and twenty-nine minutes. "Now, that's just *so* amazing," the woman with the purple fanny pack said. Four hours. Twenty-nine minutes. The time seared itself into my head. I checked my Ironman watch and did some frenzied math. By mile twelve, I was slightly ahead of Oprah's pace. Barely. I looked again at my watch, took a breath, and sprinted past the Golden Girls.

I ran fast. I ran far. I ran as if my identity as a man depended on it.

No one ever warns you about bleeding nipples. When you sign up for a marathon, no one pulls you aside and discreetly warns you to cover your nipples with Band-Aids. The cold and constant friction between the fabric of my shirt and my nipples rubbed them raw. The pain wasn't terrible, but at mile eighteen the pain was a new one in a growing list—shinsplints, dehydration, sore knees, cramp in left foot. *My nipples are bleeding*, I kept thinking as I ran. It was absurd enough to make me want to quit. I thought of explaining to friends and family why I'd traveled so far only to stop, but *My nipples were bleeding* didn't quite contain the gravity I needed. I kept running and tried to imagine Rocky saying, "Yo, Mick. Bad news. Can't go anymore. It's my nipples. Gotta throw in the towel."

At mile nineteen, I had to piss. Bad. So bad it burned. But when I stopped inside a Port-A-Potty, I couldn't go. Nothing. At mile twenty, I was run-walking. My legs locked up. They felt like pieces of wet firewood. I told myself to snap out of it. I told myself to run. I'd played basketball my whole life. I'd survived football two-a-days. I was an athlete, damn it. But soon I found myself stopped, out of gas, at the foot of a big hill. *No mas.*

From the bottom of the hill, I could see the chubby runners in front of me making their way to the top, where volunteers manned a water and Gatorade station. Marathon volunteers might be the friendliest people in the world—to call them eternal optimists would be to greatly understate their enthusiasm for your running. I heard the cheers for the runners ahead of me:

"Way to go! . . . Only a few miles . . . Looking strong!"

I'm not sure how I looked as I dragged myself to the top of the hill, but I remember the voices.

"Are you OK? Do you want us to call an ambulance?"

I grabbed the hem of my shorts and leaned over. Before I could tell them, *Yes, yes, please call an ambulance, preferably one with a bed*, I felt a hand on my shoulder.

"Here, man. Eat this."

I looked up and saw a Good Samaritan in a Columbia fleece pullover. He wore a well-trimmed beard and a look of concern. He opened his hand and revealed what looked to be a small packet of toothpaste.

I stared at his offering.

"Take it."

I reached for the packet and held the cold plastic container in my hands.

"Eat," he said.

I studied the small plastic tube.

"What is it?"

"Electrolyte gel," he said. "Banana flavored."

I tore the plastic open with my teeth and squeezed the goo into my mouth. Banana flavored electrolyte gel tastes like what you might imagine. Pasty. Astronaut food. I smacked my gums. He handed me a paper cup of water and then another. I looked at the people on the shadow-covered sidewalk. I thought about curling up next to them in the fetal position.

"OK?" the man asked.

Before I could tell him "Not OK," the Golden Girls came swishing by, smiling and waving.

"I have to go on," I said.

Something like applause came from the volunteers as I began to jog.

I caught up with the Golden Girls and ran alongside the woman with the purple fanny pack. "Well, hey!" she said.

"Howdy."

She reached into her pack and held out a piece of gum.

"Dentyne?" she asked.

"Thank you."

We talked and chewed Dentyne for six miles—jogging at a steady pace—discussing books and movies and their homes in Tennessee and mine in Georgia. We talked about the South and Atlanta and how much it has changed in good ways, but how sprawl and traffic are taking over. We talked about their children, who were my age and attending college in North Carolina. We talked about Philadelphia. "You know," the woman with the purple fanny pack said, "I don't care what they say. These people here are awfully friendly." We rated the hoagie shops in South Philly as if we were experts. We named our favorite Founding Fathers.

Before I knew it, we crossed the finish line. We didn't hold hands, but we did gather for a photo beside the statue of George Washington in front of the museum.

Alone, I virtually crept up the famous stairs, my knees creaking with each step. As I plodded upward, my hands against my nipples. I tried to imagine what Stallone had felt when he reached this spot in 1975. He'd come so far from the boy who was teased because of his slurred speech (caused by a forceps blunder at birth) to the Writer Who Refused to Sell Out or Give Up. I tried to think of my book draft at home. I'd done it. Three hundred pages. But what had I done? I'd created a hodgepodge of Hemingway and Faulkner, mimicking their moves but never catching their music. I tried to bask in the glory of finishing the marathon. I looked out on the Philadelphia skyline and took a deep breath. The only thought I could muster was that Oprah had beaten me by twenty-one minutes.

When I got home I took down the picture of Rocky. Later I took down Hemingway and Faulkner, too. I've tried to keep a lowercase *e* for the epiphany I had that day in Philadelphia while inching my way back down those stairs. I gained an awareness I suspect Stallone resists: no matter how much your abs resemble a six-pack, no matter how far you can run or how strong or great you feel, physical fitness can't take the place of art. Or, as Hemingway once wrote, "Do not mistake motion for action."

VI.

I'm not sure why I take Stallone's perpetual sophomore slump personally. His is a minor nobility compared to that of other megastars from the 1980s. He hasn't joined a cult (Tom Cruise) or married an actress from the WB network (Tom Cruise) or jumped up and down on Oprah's sofa (Tom Cruise). He's never owned a pet monkey (Michael Jackson) nor made a movie with an orangutan (Clint Eastwood). He has yet to blame the Jews for any world war (Mel Gibson), and his father isn't alleged to have ties with Nazi Germany (Arnold Schwarzenegger). Maybe, in considering the autumn of Stallone's career, I should remember Nietzsche's warning not to confuse an artist's work with his life. But where else can one look when there's no more art?

Remembering the artistic achievement of Sylvester Stallone isn't easy. There's so much to forget—*Judge Dredd, The Specialist, Demolition Man, Cliffhanger, Stop! Or My Mom Will Shoot, Tango & Cash, Lock Up, Over the Top, Cobra, Rhinestone* (with Dolly Parton), all three Rambo movies, and Stallone's directorial effort, *Staying Alive* with John Travolta. But at this point in his life, he has almost unlimited resources and time. He could start a film company à la Clint Eastwood and Sean Penn. He has options. Or to think of it another way: Stallone once wrote for eighty-six consecutive hours and produced an Academy Award-winning film. Why couldn't he then write consistently, even if slowly, for thirty years and produce a few more good ones?

Maybe it has something to do with the sunshine, palm trees, and Beverly Hills. About his time in Hollywood as a writer, Faulkner said,

"Existence evaporates, slips from your grasp in all this sunlight. Experiences become fashions and styles, everything is a pattern for some facetious evasion . . . nothing ever happens and then one morning you wake up and find out that you are sixty-five."

Stallone's own evasions of writing are numerous. Toward the end of his 2005 self-help/fitness book *Sly Moves*, Stallone lets us in for a closer look at three days in his life. The view isn't exactly pretty, but it's revealing. He spends most of his time at Gunnar Peterson's private gym, noticing, "It's a beautiful place to work out and a lot of celebrities go there, as well as some 'normal' people." I'm not sure who these "normal" people are, but look, there's Jennifer Lopez! "She's very serious about fitness." And Kim Basinger! "My wife thinks she's the most beautiful woman in the world, and part of her secret is that she's committed to working out on a very regular basis." There are all sorts of beautiful people and all sorts of adventures in name-dropping. "Once, Jennifer and I were at the gym with Jamie Lee Curtis, Angelina Jolie, Jennifer Connelly, and Christina Applegate . . ."

What's most depressing about this "book" is that people are sized up with a fascist zeal for health. Stallone makes the classical Greek blooper of mistaking beauty for truth. His own obsession with appearances makes us wonder, to say the least, about the levels of Stallone's self-consciousness. While reading *Sly Moves* I was reminded of something a friend told me years ago upon seeing Stallone (unlit cigar in mouth) walking through a Las Vegas casino.

"He wears elevated shoes, Jeremy. Elevated shoes."

I refused to believe then that Stallone would wear designer shoes to compensate for his height (five feet eight inches) just as I've refused to believe that Stallone wouldn't take writing seriously. Now the situation seems clear: Stallone is too worried about the impression he's making ever to tell another honest story. In the book he writes that every day "I am reminded how much bad food is out there. Everyday is like walking through a minefield. You need to be careful with bagels. Cream cheese will hurt you."

Our failures often give way to strange neuroses. Perhaps working out and being fit is Stallone's penance for wasting his time and talent. Hemingway, late in his life, wrote in a letter to a friend, "The time to work is shorter all the time, and if you waste it you feel you have committed a sin for which there is no forgiveness." Maybe forgiveness is what Stallone seeks.

We seek forgiveness when we've failed a better version of ourselves, and Stallone is better than his Fitness High Priest persona. In a 1998 interview with Susan Faludi for her book *Stiffed*, Stallone commented on his willingness to put on weight for the movie *Copland*:

> I don't want to put down working out, it's good, but you become incredibly self-conscious. You are always aware of yourself . . . everything is display. You take a serious gym rat, a man who lives in a gym, it's like, what do you do with it? You've got it, but it comes out in this vanity thing. You qualify for nothing—like the Chippendale dancers. It's like the orchid; it's so gorgeous but it's a parasite. It lives off of everything but what it is.

Deep down, underneath Stallone's chiseled features, tanning cream, and Botox, there exists a heretic of his own faith. When *Copland* flatlined and Stallone was shunned by Hollywood producers, he told Faludi, "I see everyone else working and I'm not doing dick. I'm in total limbo. I'm a man without a country. It's a scary thing to have all these accolades and then to have nothing." In a sense, we're back at the beginning—*What about* my *prime, Mick?*—and our ears perk up. We're back in the presence of conflict. Stallone is no longer a man with answers. He's someone with pain and experience. Someone who might have a story to tell.

That was almost a decade ago. Nine years is a long time—plenty of time to start a magazine, star in a reality television show, write a fitness book, and make *Rocky VI*. Why has Stallone allowed himself to become so distracted? I've called Stallone's agency several times in an attempt to speak with him; I'm still waiting to hear back. Stallone seemed willing to talk with Susan Faludi years ago, so I e-mailed her agent to see if Faludi could shed some light on Stallone's inactivity. My e-mail request earned a brief reply to the effect that Faludi was too busy to assist me. This polite rejection didn't exactly discourage me. I was glad someone was getting some work done.

Nine years might be a long time, but ten years is longer. I've had a decade (some 88,000 hours) to finish my book. After graduating from Georgia, I stayed in Athens for a few years, working odd jobs and taking some courses in religious studies at the university. I worked on my book about Jason, but with diminishing returns. Frustrated, I headed west and enrolled in a creative writing program. I graduated in the spring of 2007, but without my book finished, my diploma feels about as significant as the paper it's printed on. I did, however, finish a new draft. It's the fourth with a beginning, middle, and end. It's flawed, but it has a voice. A voice I can recognize as my own.

I've given up the frantic writing sessions, the all-nighters. I don't do marathons anymore—either at my desk or on the road. I've gradually come to see that writing is as much about imagination, spontaneity, and being vulnerable as it is about will. I haven't finished my own book yet, but I don't type out other people's books anymore.

When my writing is going well its pace resembles that of the Golden Girls. The speed is steady, the steps are the same. Wake up. Write for two or three or sometimes four hours, then go about my day. I teach writing courses at a local university and community college. If I have to prep for classes in the mornings, I fit the writing in at night. I often take Sundays off, especially during the NFL season. I tell myself this staying steady is healthier. I hold to the advice of Flannery O'Connor: "I try to write a little bit each day." But there are times when this doesn't feel like enough.

Each year, Mr. Kenney and I get together for lunch, often in Atlanta. Each year he asks—politely—how the book is going. He doesn't prod. He doesn't pry. He doesn't ask for a word count. Each year I tell him, "Steady, steady."

During our last lunch, he nodded when I gave my annual answer. He then told me that he'd read recently that Louis L'Amour wrote more than sixty books in his life. That was at least a book a year, Mr. Kenney said, encouraging me to read L'Amour and take a look at his life. I almost said that what L'Amour wrote wasn't real literature, but I stopped. Anyone who's spent time thinking about the inner life of Sylvester Stallone has no business critiquing others' sentimental loves. I simply nodded, and Mr. Kenney encouraged me to keep after the writing—then picked up the check.

There was no venom in Mr. Kenney's comment about L'Amour, but there was a bite. His words left a mark that I carried into my viewing of *Rocky VI*. For weeks afterward, I found myself thinking about my latest draft of the book, Stallone, work habits, and integrity. Now, instead of working on the next draft, here I am writing about Sylvester Stallone. But I've also kept writing about Jason, and I like to think that last year Mr. Kenney was also telling me, "Get it out. Be done."

So I work on—letting Stallone, Faulkner, and Hemingway ride off with L'Amour into the sunset—trusting the steady slowness of my muses, the Golden Girls in pink Nike jogging suits, to light the way home.

VII.

Walking out of *Rocky VI*, I forgave Stallone. It wasn't hard. I've been forgiving him for a while. I'm still just a Rocky fan, though I can't say I "enjoyed" the movie. Out of some dogged loyalty I needed to see it—and a week later I needed to flush it by putting the original *Rocky* in the DVD player on my computer and hitting PLAY.

I still love the original *Rocky* for what it doesn't do. *Rocky* refuses to be a sports movie. Unlike the leads in *Knute Rockne: All American*, *The Natural*, *The Karate Kid*, *Hoosiers*, *Rudy*, *Cinderella Man*, and *Seabiscuit*, Rocky doesn't suddenly receive inspiration and discover the faith needed to win. He's a realist. He knows what's coming, and he gets his face caved in.

Defeat and loss are our most honest teachers. Stallone once knew this, or at least his film did. *Rocky* begins with a black screen, a trumpet call, and then bold white letters announcing R-O-C-K-Y as we hear the dim beat of voices, the low rustle of a crowd. Are we in a revival tent? A subway station? Then a mural on the wall comes into focus as a Byzantine image of Christ holding the host and the cup. We wonder if we're in a church or cathedral until we see fight fans, cigarettes hanging from their mouths, hurling obscenities at two half-naked men locked in a violent dance. Rocky is battling Spider Rico in a club fight.

The brief juxtaposition is clear—this is my body, this is my blood— and our beginning points to the end. This won't be a story of victory, but of the redemption that's found in defeat.

When Christ makes his debut as a literary character—in the Gospel of Mark, circa AD 70—the production is all wrong. The oldest Greek manuscripts read as if written by a sixth grader on speed. The original ending, however, is almost perfect. When the women arrive at the tomb with spices, they don't find a risen Lord. They find a young man dressed in white who says Jesus isn't there. Unlike in the other gospel sequels or the gory action blockbuster *Revelation*, we don't find a ghostly Jesus wandering through doors, showing off his scars, or riding the white horse of Apocalypse. Instead, we're left to imagine all sorts of things as the women rush away from the tomb, terrified, amazed.

At the end of *Rocky*, Rocky doesn't stand over the broken monsters Clubber Lang (*Rocky III*) or Ivan Drago (*Rocky IV*). He doesn't jump into the air when the bell rings. He doesn't give a post-fight speech to the Kremlin on the dangers of nuclear proliferation. He barely knows where he is. His trainer, Mike, helps him take off his gloves. His right eye is destroyed. The left eye doesn't look much better. Reporters bark out questions, but Rocky only responds, "Adrian! Adrian!"

The shot cuts to Adrian, who's yelling for Rocky as she pushes through the crowd.

"Rocky? Rocky!"

"Adrian?!"

"Rocky?!"

"Adrian?!"

"Rocky?!"

As Adrian rushes toward him, her red beret gets knocked off, but she keeps running until she makes her way into the ring.

"Adrian."

"Rocky."

"Where's your hat?"

"I love you."

"I love *you*."

She falls into his sweaty, meaty embrace. We realize, at this moment, *this* is the moment toward which the entire movie has been building. Adrian and Rocky sway in an embrace as the ring announcer delivers the news: Apollo Creed is our winner. Rocky doesn't seem to hear as he rests his heavy hand against the back of Adrian's head and inhales. Pulling her closer, he shuts his eyes and breathes out. Freeze the shot. Fade to black. Cue the music. Roll the credits.

Before I try to canonize *Rocky* or Sylvester Stallone, I should stop. I've probably already said too much. But I owe Stallone a thank you. I'd like to buy him a beer. Or maybe a post-workout-recovery fruit smoothie with glucosamine and protein powder. *Rocky* helped me through the night when I was a child and carried me through those other days and longer nights. And for a moment in his life, Sylvester Stallone was more than equal to the demands of the task, equal to the art.

Nominated by Pamela Stewart, The Georgia Review

AIRPORT ECONOMY INN

by TOM SLEIGH

from THE VIRGINIA QUARTERLY REVIEW

No one speaking, nothing moving

except for the way the snow keeps falling,
its falling a kind of talking in the dark
while all across the valley we keep on sleeping

in the separate conditions of our dreaming.

His face all overgrown with concern

the newsman's mouth says whatever it's saying,
explosions going off, sound turned down, wind
ripping at some twanging strip of metal.

My friend's voice keeps murmuring in my head,

murmuring she's stressed by going out

with two men at once, worrying they'll cross
and she'll lose them both, she's starting
to drink and smoke too much, love's

making her a liar, a chimney head, an alky.

No one speaking, nothing moving but snow

falling, falling, burying this motel
with its take-out menu, *New Standard Bible*,
checkout time 11 A.M.,

smiley face envelope to leave the maid a tip:

out in the hall someone's pounding

on the ice machine, one hand beating rhythm to
fuck it fuck it fuck it fuck it . . .
Reveries of living here year after year,

scalloped walls, cottage cheese ceiling,

plaster hands praying on the checkout counter,

complimentary doughnuts hoarded in the ice bucket
DO NOT DISTURB credit card imprint
Room 401's one of our regulars

. . . food, god, death, money, a TV clicker

to push the world back and bring it closer,

fantasies of lust so ridiculous and charmed
you need two king beds and a mirrored ceiling.
No one speaking, nothing moving

but for the screen lighting up with bombs falling
through shifting fortunes of the soldier

on a stretcher, body gone limp,
lost in glare spilling off a Humvee's side
that keeps hearselike pace with the stretcher moving

above the stretcher's shadow.

No one speaking, nothing moving,

my eyes close, I drift and doze,
dissolving to jags, chunks, splinters,
flake piling on flake erasing diamond-cut angles

of every crystal swirling through streetlight

before fading back into parking-lot gloom as these lines stretch out

and return to the margin
as if nothing can stop this pattern
from repeating, words

telling it in irregular shifts of rhythm

while the crawl keeps crawling at the bottom of the screen.

Nominated by David Wojahn, Lloyd Schwartz, Grace Schulman,
The Virginia Quarterly Review

TABRIZ

fiction by ELIZABETH TALLENT

from THE THREEPENNY REVIEW

DAVID PAWSON, heartsore in the way of old activists, a stooped, unkempt forty-eight, leafs through his so-called love life for precedent and finds none. (Waiting in a parked car induces introspection.) The other guys in EPIC share the leanness of long outrage, frequent marathons, and enduring luck with women, but obsession has not been good to David's relationships, his days spent tracking the toxins that bleed through watersheds, questioning children in hospital gowns printed with teddy bears, inking cancer clusters onto topo maps, bringing his peculiar skillset to bear, his milky mildness, what his second ex calls his anti-charisma, the hangdog air of bewilderment that makes even dying children strive to enlighten him, the harmlessness that glints through his wire-rimmed specs when he shakes hands with some CEO or other, except that mostly they know better, now, than to let a bigwig sit down with David. Don't even wave when you pass him in the courthouse hall, they're told. Despite his scruffiness—one judge told him to get a haircut—he is sleek in pursuit, righteous, relentless, a scorner of compromise, a true believer.

Whose own luck with women was flawed, which was why God invented joint custody. David loves his two sons with the appalled passion of a dad whose work acquaints him with small coffins. From his right hand to the hollow of a kid's well-worn glove runs a taut thread of inevitability, the ball held aloft and swivelled—*Dad, look!* In the making of a boy psyche this is the key phrase. It's David's job to arrange plenty of occasions for its happy utterance: *Dad, look!* His rendition of *Goodnight, Moon* is famous for the oinks, whistles, and cheek-pops enhancing the line *Goodnight noises everywhere*. He's fed trembling white mice Coca-Cola from an eyedropper for the sake of fourth-grade science, though his coworkers' connections in the Animal Liberation Front would rip his heart out and nail it to the front door—*Environmental Protection Information Center*—if they knew.

His abuse of white mice—with their tiny old-lady hands! their suffering docility!—is a rare departure from the party line. Though they have long since abandoned ecotage, the five members of EPIC hold fast to their ancient intimacy, to their affinity-group habit of staying up until two or three, baring their souls, though they do so now under the harassing buzz of office fluorescence, tipped back in ergonomic chairs, feet up on desks variously dishevelled or anal (David's: anal), when in the old days it was T-shirts printed with raised fists, Levi's out at the knees, scuffed boots, a high-desert campfire sucked toward the moon, shooting sparks. Ice may be melting out from under polar bears, breast milk brims with mutagens, but change hasn't touched EPIC, not deeply, not at the level where they are bonded. At David's wedding last Saturday, they slouched in attitudes of conscientious celebration. They kissed the bride, they sang David's praises and then told her when she was done with this loser to give them a call, they stuck orchids behind their ears, but at the deepest level there was a shimmer of apprehension. They'll never sling an arm around his shoulder with a brother's manic affection or confess their own romantic fuckups, not if David's with Jade. Between brothers, there has to be parity in terms of fucking up, or another dynamic sets in, ordinary rivalrous maleness with its assessing squint, and the phenomenon of Jade, the fearful symmetry of teeth and cheekbones, plus the fact that she's on the other side, the sexiness of her being, basically, the enemy, can neither be assimilated nor forgiven.

The wedding's meticulously repressed question: What does she see in him? In his rented tux, David had shrugged, reading minds he'd been reading half his life. They could have a little more faith, though. For a profoundly good man to find love shouldn't strain credulity. David caught himself thinking *profoundly good* and palmed his thinning fair hair in a manner Jade recognized as embarrassed or sad. She'd lifted her brows: *What's wrong?* He'd slung her over his arm, leaned in as if kissing were drinking, held her practically horizontal until people said *Aww*.

But it was a moment's uncensored private felicity to have meant it: *profoundly good.*

He's earned it.

What he regrets now is not that thought but the ruefulness of his gesture, palming his hair—the mild, contrite, revisionist embarrassment, so that she'd had to lift her brows, to wonder what was wrong when nothing was.

In the arroyo a couple of wrecked trucks sail past a rusted washing machine, a tilted, doorless refrigerator, tires of various sizes and degrees of rottenness, a cathedral window's worth of shattered glass and the jutting wing of a small plane. The boys love coming here, because nowhere else are they permitted such an array of dangers— prickly pear, stained underpants, rusty nails, rattlers. Actually, the altitude's too high for rattlers, but the boys reject this fact. Before he lets them out of the car, David lectures. Careful, careful, careful, the poisoned echo of little white coffins. Down in the arroyo, out of his sight, they look after each other, a good thing for them to learn. They are stepmothered now, in fairy-tale jeopardy, though in taking them on Jade has shown an easy, can-do confidence. She read up on stepparenting, and it turns out that beauty figures even here, in the reconfigured family calculus, the boys defenseless as their father. David would have explained himself as, romantically, a hanger-back with a slow heartbeat, somebody who feared to tread. In work he was fanatical, devoted, but as a husband he was often described as *just not there*, and he had accepted as deserved the amicable breakups of marriages one and two. Then came Jade: they had gazed, eaten, drunk, fucked, the usual plot, but then fucking took over and they fucked their way deep into a tranced adoration, discovering there this secret status in being the two of them, this insolent sexual satisfaction coexisting with the improvisational restlessness of genius, this safety, this bliss exempt from inhibition and nagging history, neither one bothering, neither needing to explain their *hasty* marriage, because it was natural to want to seal such transcendent fucking with that cultural kiss of approval, dubious though you were, otherwise, about that culture.

Crossing to the arroyo's edge, he can make out the boys' voices, and guesses they're intent on intergalactic slaughter. Lasers, viruses, dirty bombs—their games incorporate everything there is to fear. This is good for them, David believes.

Hey, Shane.

Edmund.

He calls the ill-assorted names—ranchhand, dandy—chosen by two of the three women he's loved, and, from the hush that follows, figures he's been heard. A scrap blows by, and David stomps. This is the usual lawlessness, the regular Joe's cost-effective contempt for the environment. People find this shattered-glass wasteland irresistible: free dumping! Showing a perverse initiative, somebody has carted an oil drum out to the tip of this stony spur where the road dead-ends. The innocent human love of shortcuts accounts for a lot of devastation, David thinks. The ADD species, distracted from the story unfolding down at the level of chromosomes or up in the ozone. He himself is persistently, doggedly, *profoundly* good, thus exhausted, more and more tired of the long odds, the moated, slit-windowed, lawyered-up enemy: how long before they wear him out? He releases his scrap to the wind, which gives it a good shake before whisking it away. As if a signal has been given, more bits and pieces tear loose from the mess and veer past like animated confetti, the dervish blowing by, revealing that an object he had mistaken for a jutting plank or beam is in fact a furled rug. It seems undamaged, and as David puts an arm around it and levers it out, a kamikaze egg carton rears up and crunches into his shoulder. He has to squint, studying the oil drum's seethe: tin cans, a partially melted telephone, a doll's head trailing singed acrylic hair, a coil of filthy rope, a shirt stippled with blood, a clock, rain-fattened paperbacks, eggshells, ashes, a melee of electrical wire, a high-heeled shoe. As he works it loose, the rug dislodges a cascade of junk that tumbles along the ground, light bits scattering, heavier things rolling this way and that. Something, an envelope, wings past, nicking the corner of his eyebrow. *Ow.*

"—wouldn't *be* anybody." Panting. "Left to. Operate. Lasers."

"Wrong! Somebody lived! 'Cause they hid in—" They come clambering up the slope.

"—caves—"

"—that, like, connect, a whole underground—"

"—*city*—"

Reaching the arroyo's rim, the half brothers come to a halt and stare.

Squatting, David peels back a corner of the rug. With only a few square inches revealed, the pattern seems familiar, your hometown light-grid glimpsed through the window of a tilting plane.

195

"Hey, guys," he says. "Look what I found."

For a breezy minute they ponder the scene, litter skittering and dodging past. The moon catches their eye-whites. Two hours' reckless play brings out the brother in them.

"So?"

One brother's cool slides its knife-blade through the bonds of pairdom.

"Show some fucking interest in what Dad found whycantcha."

Ordinarily, and despite the unfairness of enforcing rules in this male wilderness, David would have to deal with *fucking*. He does a quick check. Edmund does not appear hurt, only newly severed from his older brother. His eye-whites glitter. Not with boredom, either. Freshly relieved of intimacy, both boys are radiant. David gives the rug a good yank, and it thumpingly unrolls.

"Wow."

"Wow."

David sits back on his heels, trying and failing to understand, to account for this departure from ordinary life, the rug's fanatically executed geometry interrupted just at the point of frigidity by winding, organic movement, delicate leaves, impish involutions, this diversion, this near escape from paralysis part of its tale, its secret proffered with the bristling incomprehensible beauty of bees dancing within a hive or a thicket of sinuous branches, vision inspired by the challenge but the mind's movements tentative, repeatedly stubbed out, this agitating impenetrable beauty the work of how many nights and days, its blood reds and ominous crimsons contending with, outnumbered by, a choir of blues, azure, jay feather, turquoise, baby blanket, forget-me-not, but to number them like that, to try to say what they're like, that's merely a poor, doomed attempt to domesticate them. They are gorgeous blues, and they assail peace of mind. In the center there is an oval where nothing happens, visually, and this is the grainy indeterminate fawn of animal camouflage, of a doe fading into underbrush, and what appears to be peaceful is really another wild evasion.

Edmund, at nine still sometimes playing the baby, hangs an arm around his neck. "You pulled that out of the garbage, Dad?"

"It shouldn't have been in there."

Shane leans into David from the other side. "Why was it, then?"

"I have no idea." Because it can't be explained. No taint of yeast or compost, no halitosis of slowly souring milk carton, no oil-drum dankness mars the rug's dry, antique compound of *grass, twine, stone floor*.

Edmund says, "I want to look in the can."

"Honey, there's nothing else in there, and we've talked about syringes and dangerous sharp things and how the guys handling garbage wear gloves."

"You didn't have gloves."

He tries a technicality and some italics, an old parenting tactic. "I wasn't reaching *down* into the garbage, the rug was right on *top* and I carefully carefully *carefully* pulled it out."

"Dad, I really really need to see."

Father and son go over and peer down into the oil drum: garbage. "Okay?" David says.

Behind them Shane wings stones at the drum until David says, "Cut it out *now*." Shane pitches a last defiant stone and the drum gives off the resonant *gong* of a bull's-eye. Edmund runs back to try to match this feat, and David decides to let them have at it, because what can they hurt? He rolls the rug up tight and improvises a kind of fireman's carry. The metal whines when the stones whang against it. The brothers have refined their aim, and as David labors under the weight of the rug he takes immense pleasure in his boys' prowess. Hunters. He's the father of a pair of slender, moonlit, stone-throwing boys: there may be no deeper pleasure on earth. He pauses to admire them. They sense this. It throws their aim off. They want to be fatherless, motherless, outcast, a cunning tribe of two, their terrible prey—black, squat, stinking like a bear—moaning when it's dinged. Before they can leave this place, the spirit of the bear that the oil drum mysteriously incarnates must be stoned back to the underworld. If there were no boys throwing stones, that spirit would never have emerged from the underworld in the first place, but put a stone in a boy's fist and the old world breathes out reeky ghosts. The Pleistocene lives on in the heads of boys. In fact, three-fifths of EPIC believes that we're headed back that way: when weather chaos descends big-time and the center cannot hold, humans will regroup as hunter-gatherers. That's the optimistic view. What the other fraction of EPIC believes can't be voiced, since (David is one) they are fathers, and certain thoughts are forbidden to fathers. *Extinction. Annihilation.* Nestled, still tightly rolled, in the rear of the station wagon, the rug's strangeness is muted: it could be rightfully his, bought and paid for. David calls for the boys to *get into the car* but fi-

197

nally has to start the engine—David's own dad's long-ago threat—before the boys climb in. They're overextended, he figures, long past the time when they should have been freed of the intensity of their love for each other by the bleating electronic triviality of Gameboy.

"It's skanking up our car," Edmund complains, and Shane chimes in, "It smells all old."

"Hey, does everything have to be new? Plastic? Old's not such a bad smell, is it?"

Pleading is always a wrong move.

"It's not ours." Edmund, doing a good imitation of Jade. She's new enough that they shouldn't be able to mimic her this well, and the boys' deft appropriation of Jade's voice and style when they want to drive home a point slightly worries David, and feels unfair, as if he's being ganged up on.

"It's ours now, sweetie."

Sweetie is fatal, registered in jolting silence. Jolting because the next thirty miles are so bad, the road seeming as lost as a road can get, running aimlessly along and then madly swerving, barely managing to avoid outcrops of rock or steep drop-offs.

"You mean you can just take anything out of the garbage, whoever left it there, and if they want it back you can say no, it's yours?" Shane, bent, at eleven, on discovering the moral workings of the world.

A hard curve, and as he slows the car, David tries his mostly successful good-father voice. "Look, I don't want you going through *any* garbage *ever*. You never find anything good."

"*You* did."

"*You* did."

Jade says, "It must be worth a fortune. Twenty or thirty thousand dollars, even, depending on how old it is. Somebody's going to want it back. Because how could it have been left in a garbage can? The whole thing sounds fishy. I've never seen anything like this except in a museum. And why didn't I know that you go for these drives? Was this a thing you did before?" Before her. "Were you just having a really bad day? Is something going on?" *Do we have secrets now?* "The rug is a problem, David. There's been some kind of mistake, because this isn't the sort of thing that gets thrown away, not ever. You took it? What made you think you could just walk off with it?"

"What question do you want me to answer? It clearly *had* been

198

thrown away. At the end of a dirt road in the middle of nowhere. Nobody was coming back for it. It was getting dark."

"I just think you were a little hasty," she says, "impetuous," and he shouldn't be flattered, but he is. "Draw me a map of how you get there?"

Her love of proof, documents, evidence, is very like his, and on the back of an envelope he sketches a map, the journey's last leg a squiggle meant to indicate arduousness, an x for the oil drum.

"This is where you go? There's nothing there."

He's surprised to be off the hook about the rug, and relieved. "That's what's good about it."

"Did you think about us?"

"A little."

"You figured us out."

"Absolutely."

"How do you know nobody was coming back for it? Maybe they're there now, looking, and it's gone."

Cross-legged on their bed, husband and wife consider the rug unfurled across the tiles of their bedroom floor, and he watches, under the lowered lids of her downward gaze, the REM-like movements of her eyes as she reads, or tries to, the rug's branching and turning and dead-ending intricacy, its profusion of leaves and petals or the geometric figures that might be leaves and petals, which the gaze barely discerns before relinquishing them back into abstraction. Jade, leaning forward, her elbows on her knees, frowning, her right breast indented by her right arm, her shadow thrown across him because her reading light's on, her backlit profile showing the radiant lint of her upper lip, the contour of her jaw, the length of her throat, the cunning hollow at its base with her pulse, barely visible, thrumming across it, and below that the contour of the heavy breast, the nipple's surprising drab brown color, the unaroused, modest softness of its stem, its wreath of kinked hairs. Best of all, in love, in what he's experienced of love, are those moments when you can watch the other's self-forgetful delight.

She says, "I have to tell you something."

In his work, he's a good listener. More than that, he solicits the truth, asks the unasked, waits out the heartsick or intimidated silences every significant environmental lawsuit must transcend. Someone has to ask what has gone wrong, and if the thing that's gone wrong has destroyed the marrow of a five-year-old's bones, someone has to *need* that truth or it will never emerge from the haze of obfuscation. But this isn't work. This is Jade.

"I'm a little afraid," she says. "I know that's not like me. Scared."

"Of me? I love you."

"I'm a Republican."

Simply, instantly, he believes it. He's been blind to the syllogism chalked on the board: Caius is a corporate lawyer. All corporate lawyers are Republicans. Caius is a Republican. Someone had partially erased it, one or two swipes with the side of a hand, but it had been there all along, visible through the cloud of denial. The dismay he wants to keep to himself is instantly transmitted to her.

"I knew you couldn't handle it. I knew it would be this *thing*."

"So you waited until we were married?"

"Until I thought you could deal."

"I can't *deal* with dishonesty."

"Then try seeing the honesty in coming out to you. I knew it was a risk." She sucks on a lock of black hair, then yanks it from her mouth, disgusted with her needy, uncharacteristic confusion.

"I knew I was in for it."

"I'm in the wrong? That was fast."

"Righteous indignation. Your default position." She takes hold of his wrist, and when he winces, lets go. "David. Say the rug was in the office of some Los Alamos scientist, and one day somebody ran a Geiger counter over it, a random check, a sweep, 'cause they're human, accidents happen, and despite the most meticulous precautions—"

"They're not meticulous enough," he says, and he knows.

"—traces of uranium stick to the soles of somebody's shoes and get tracked across the rug, and out of fear for their jobs they decide to dispose of the rug quietly, in this furtive undocumented way, the sort of thing you're always telling me about. You, the expert on how these things get into the air and the water and into people's houses, you bring it home with you, with no explanation for the sheer unlikeliness of something this beautiful being left in a trash can. You must see what I'm saying. The rug could hurt us."

"You're what's hurt us. Your dishonesty."

"My taking a little time to tell you a difficult thing. A private thing. Because my beliefs are my own, and I could've gone on keeping them to myself. But you and I tell each other everything."

"Obviously not."

"We do," she says. "We can."

"There's nothing wrong with this rug," he says. "You're being paranoid."

"You want to call an intuition paranoid, *you*? And my concerns? You want to blow them off?"

"Yeah," he says, and from pure meanness, blows across his palm and waggles his fingers.

He's let down when, without another word, Jade turns out the light. If they were both wolves they'd be lying just like this, their eyes slitted, their fur on end. How about a little red-in-tooth-and-claw sex? He wants her. But who is she? She may intend to amend the Constitution to rule out gay marriage, or drill for oil in the Arctic Wildlife Refuge. How can he fuck someone who wants to drill for oil in the Arctic Wildlife Refuge? All the same, he's hard. Arctic Wildlife Refuge or not, he's got an erection. Post-coitally, he can convince her that caribou have rights to their ancient migratory routes. He's not sure where she is in her progress toward sleep, and when he leans over her, the intense repose of her body on the bed tells him she's wide awake. This treachery—another in her string of deceptions—exhausts him, and he gives up. He's asleep.

Before dawn he's startled by her cry. He can't make sense of her naked, placatory stance in front of his computer, or his own accusation: "What did you do?" His voice is harsh, his body recollecting their fight before his brain does.

"I walked across your rug and must've picked up some static electricity, because when I touched the computer, I got a shock, and—"

Naked, he scrambles from the bed, the rug's nap pricking the soles of his feet.

"—it crashed. It made this little match-strike sound, and the screen went black. David. I wasn't going to look."

Well, then, what was she doing there? He never tells her anything about his work. He's tediously ethical that way. She may end up representing a corporation he's going after.

"I wasn't going to look."

The repetition really scares him.

Her fingertips patter across the keyboard: nothing. Frustration tenses her freckled shoulders as she leans over his computer, and her hair sticks up in tufts, dirty with yesterday's gel. There's even a tiny tear in her panties. Nobody would hire her to represent a major corporation if they saw her from behind like this. His chest hurts. Not this morning—not some heart thing. No, it's okay, his heart. It's just that his chest has constricted with frustration and another emotion, darker, more energetic, beating away. Wham wham wham. Violence is awake, that instant neurochemical transport to the Pleistocene. Fury.

"This weird thing happened."

Sunday afternoons the boys and their belongings trek back to Susannah's, according to an agreement hashed out with Nina, Edmund's mother, an academic on a year's sabbatical in Paris. David sits with Susannah on the back steps, the boys dodging through the neglected garden whose sunflowers are ten feet high, yellow petals tattered and their brown, saucer-sized centers under attack by sparrows.

"—never make it out alive unless—"

"—we find a way to neutralize—"

Jade walks across the rug, acquiring a crackling charge of electrons, and these leap from her fingertips to his keyboard, cases compromised, the irreplaceable interviews, the meticulous documentation, zapped, and yeah, he has some of it on disks, but not all, a rare failure of meticulousness.

"No way I'm gonna resurrect this thing," said the consultant, after twittering away at the dead keyboard with the skewed persistence of a dog using its hind paw to get at the itch behind an ear.

"The guy I've always relied on, he couldn't fix it," David says. "What freaks me out is, she never goes near my computer. She has no business touching it."

"Maybe she was looking for incriminating email. That's the usual reason for fooling around with the other person's computer."

"It's not like that."

"It's always like that. She could be looking for email from a previous relationship. Like with me. She could want to know what things were like between us."

"I don't think so. She hasn't wanted the lowdown. She sees me and her more as a clean-slate kind of thing." Or a lightning strike. An angel's wing passing over their upturned faces.

From the shoes ranged on the wooden step—shoes with neon glyphs, striped shoes, shoes with soles thick as antelope hooves, shoes bristling with spikes—Susannah chooses one whose laces are a gray snarl maddening to contemplate, and begins, with her dirty nails, to pick the knot. She says, "You don't know her very well."

202

Angry at her superbly divorced reasonableness, the very quality he loved a moment ago, he says, "The rug is evil."

"Oh, David. Things aren't evil. People are. And not that many of them, though I can see why your line of work makes you think otherwise."

Evil: he had continued pecking at the keyboard as if lucky ineptitude could conjure, from the dark portal, the blip of returning consciousness. Jade—exasperated by his manic persistence, in which she rightly detected an element of anger directed at her—left for work. In the fugue state of technological thwartedness, he heard the *scream*, shock blazing down every dad-nerve, and danced backward to see out the French doors: Edmund hanging from a branch of the apricot tree, screaming at his own daring. With this innocent howl in his ears, David lost his footing, and in a slow-motion trance of remorse went over backwards. Falling, he seemed to view himself from above, and if he was helpless, his arms flung out and his mouth gaping, the back of his head about to connect with the floor, he was also suspended in a peaceable realm that had detached itself from terror. There was time to marvel at this double consciousness before the floor slammed it out of his skull.

"My God," Susannah says. "You could have been really hurt"—and her palm on his nape radiates solicitude, but this kind of comforting costs her nothing, really: she can do it in her sleep. With the broad Norwegian planes of her wide-open face she's so different from Jade, so *accessible*. "But you're okay," she says confidently. She turns his wrist to read his watch, and the kitchen telephone rings. The screen door bangs behind her long, freckled legs.

"Hi.

"You can't?

"You can't?

"I know but why does that have to—

"I know it is but why—

"I know.

"I know.

"I said I *do* know.

"Yes.

"I will.

"I won't.

"Me too.

"Me too. Bye."

She's high enough from this clichéd, abortive exchange to sit down beside David and confess, "I think I'm in love. After all this time. I mean, you've been through two wives since me. My turn, I guess." The smile she gives him is expectant, but he's having trouble reconciling the two realities, the reality before she vanished into her kitchen and this new version, because weren't they still, until this confession, still, really, in spite of everything, *married*? She has eluded him, slipped away taking her critical possessive practical generous irreplaceable and beautifully *accessible* love with her, and David says miserably, "Oh."

"*Oh?* After I listen to the wonders of your lovelife for *six* years? *Oh?* That's not trying, David. That's not even—nice. *Oh?* That's cold."

"I need to ask you about something."

Such a transparent grab at her vanished attention: she grimaces, exaggerating the expression but truly pissed off. "Were you even listening?"

"You're in love. And it's, from your side of the conversation, kind of complicated."

"When isn't it complicated."

He *uh-huhs* prevaricatingly.

She says, "Right. Marrying somebody you don't know. That's nice and simple."

"I'm in trouble, Suse."

"You know, you are utterly, confoundingly selfish." But she's curious. "What kind of trouble?"

"This is a what-if. What if someone you were in love with turned out to be a Republican? How bad would that be? Would it be something you'd leave them over?"

"That couldn't happen."

"Sure it could."

"Nope. Because when you're talking to a Republican, you can't talk long before you hear something, some opinion, that makes your blood run cold. Like what Emily Dickinson said about poetry? It's poetry because it makes you feel like the top of your head's come off? That's how you know it's a Republican." As she's been talking, she's been processing. "*Jade's* a Republican. David? She would be! But you're an activist, you can't possibly—whoa. Whoa! This *changes* things."

"Of course it changes things." But he's confused. "What things?"

"How does she discipline, David? Are there bedtime prayers? I can't believing how trusting I've been, how naive. Intimidated! I was intimidated by her. I never really believed she liked the boys. She was probably pretending to be into them out of some kind of phony family-values baloney. Or to get you."

"Hey, you've seen her with the boys, you know she's—" Well, wasn't Jade a little cold, really? Confident, but maybe a little off-hand? It had seemed a consequence of her heavy workload, merely. "Suse, Suse, please. Come to the house. Because I don't know whether I'm crazy to think the rug might be—" He can't say *evil* twice in one conversation.

"It makes no sense to blame the *rug*. Blame Jade. That's what you're trying to avoid with this obsession. You're resisting taking a good look at a relationship that was flawed from its very—"

"If you look at it and say, *there's nothing wrong with this rug*, that's all I need."

"Um, is that how obsessions work, really?" She snaps her fingers. " 'Snap out of it, guy'? That works?"

In her twice-weekly trips to his house to retrieve or deliver the boys, she has waited, eyes averted, outside the front door, and now, entering this bedroom, his and Jade's, Susannah is struck by emotions David should have foreseen: jealousy, confusion, vengefulness. She gives the rug a perfunctory once-over, but the unmade bed gets her complete, anguished attention, and then, oh shit, an actual, daunting bra of Jade's, silky cups upturned, and Susannah sits down on the rug and begins to cry. David rubs at the ill-shaven patch on his chin, weathering the storm, riding it out on his end of the rug. At last her crying peters out in breath-catches and hoarse cries. He tears a tissue from a box on the nightstand and offers it.

"Thanks." She blows her nose and shudders.

"Want to tell me what's going on here?"

"It wouldn't help."

"Want to try?"

"You *tricked me*. You went ahead and made this other life, and you're hopeful. I was used to you being more or less despairing."

He doesn't want to sit down beside her. On his feet he has a little distance from the rug's malign influence, which she's succumbed to. At the same time, it's a little sexy, standing over Susannah like this, her head at crotch level. He quashes the thought.

"I could make some prediction, if I were mean-spirited. She's got to be against the Endangered Species Act, right? For opening wilderness to logging—how will you stomach that? I could predict that nothing will ever be the same between you, that you'll never really trust her again. But I don't know her—that's obvious. I may not know you, either, is the strange part. See, I always thought that in life there was one person you got to know everything about. You get your one person, and it doesn't really matter whether you end up living with them or not, because the way you know that person, nothing can undo or diminish it. It's not a consolation, exactly. No more than gravity's a consolation. It's just a fact, that there's one single person out of everyone on earth who is your own private safe person, who you can talk to in your head and know what they'll say. After we broke up, you were still my one safe person. You know? But if *you* can turn out to have a Republican wife and attribute a run of bad luck to an evil rug, I guess I don't know anything about anyone, not really. I'm in love and now you've made it so I have to distrust him. Will you tell me something, David? Tell me. Did I *know* you? Was I your person?"

Because if he answered her honestly the answer would be *no*, because he can't bear to hurt her, from pure reckless solicitude he rubs a palm down his fly. "Suse. Do you want to do something?"

"I want to do something," she says, standing. "I want"—and, optimistically unzipping, he's staggered by her swift backhanded blow, by the moan of protest that is neither his nor hers, causing them to turn, the ex-husband and wife, to find their child standing in the doorway in his pajama bottoms. "Honey," David says, "Shane," but after a long and disbelieving gaze that pivots from mother to father and father to mother, Shane bolts. David caresses his jaw and says softly, "Wow."

"David. Let me take him home. I need to talk to him. Let me have this."

He lets her have this. Edmund, discovered in the boys' room, turns piously cooperative, as if to preserve what's left of his family's sanity. Jackets are tugged on, backpacks snatched up, as if the house is on fire, Susannah and the boys fumbling their way out the front door when they encounter Jade. The women's voices spar in a little ecstasy of mutual dislike. David stands there, apprehensively feeling his jaw, holding his own, if barely, against an onslaught of guilt. Before it can drag him under, he sits down. Here is the rug. He straightens glasses knocked cockeyed by Susannah's blow and runs a hand along its nap. Real. Real enough. Threads ran one way, a warp, and another, a woof. Jade slams the front door. "What's going on?" she calls. "What happened?" He closes his eyes to postpone her interrogation, meanwhile attending to the ringing in his ears.

"Shit!"

She does the instinctive hopping step that keeps one foot from touching the rug, and at first he thinks she has converted hostility into a droll, rigid dance like a sandhill crane's.

"What happened?"

"I stepped on something. Was there glass in this rug? Oh, why didn't we vacuum?"

The trash can: the poisonous seethe of its debris. David is half sick with guilt, driving her to the emergency room, because some shard from that roiling cauldron has driven itself into her darling foot, because he brought the foul thing home in order to impress her, to prove he is not merely a tired foot-soldier slogging through muddy depositions but a hero capable of wresting beauty from chaos. She has suffered for his vanity. The doctor is a sleekly handsome Indian with a tranquilizing lilt but Jade won't melt, and when the doctor leaves the cubicle and David explains in a low voice that the rug is behind everything that has happened she shivers and commands, "Shut up." The handsome doctor enters then, bestowing on David a discreet frown of sympathy, an acknowledgment that Jade is not the only person suffering in this harshly illumined but far from sound-proof cell. To explain that he's fine, David touches his swollen jaw with two fingers, *this?*, and shrugs, *this is nothing*, and this time when the doctor frowns, there is no sympathy in it: submit to spousal abuse if you will. A blush creeps up Jade's throat and tints her ears, her shame exacerbated by the doctor's indifference, for he, assuming she is a highly troubled individual, ably ignores her, bending to his task. Extracted from her heel, brandished under the hooded medical lamp, is a sliver of rusted metal. She can't remember when she had her last tetanus shot. Hatred figures in the look she gives David as the needle goes in.

"We need to talk."

"I can't. Work."

"Do you feel like things are falling apart. *Flying* apart?"

Her left foot in a steep high heel, the injured right mummified in stretchy bandages and jammed into a scuffed moccasin, she faces him asymmetrically. "Do you know why they do this? Make the bandages this sick *beige*? It's the shade of cadaverous Caucasian flesh. It's an intimation of mortality. It's so you wrap your rotting foot in your own future dead skin." In frustration, she kicks off the high heel and tries a flat. "I did hear what you said, and yes we'll talk, but I'm twenty minutes late, and I've got the Kelsis thing."

"Kelsis?" he calls. "Kelsis?"

"The thing," she calls over her shoulder. "The thing I told you about."

The thing she didn't tell him about.

He needs to collect his wits, to shave delicately around the swollen hinge of his jaw, to negotiate rush-hour traffic with Zen serenity, to sit down at his desk and plot the decline of the black-footed ferret. He needs the escapism inherent in any ordinarily bad day. After lunch, he opens a fat packet that informs him he's been hit with a SLAPP suit. Nobody else in EPIC is named in the suit, but he is married to a lawyer, and would solicit her ultra-competent advice except that, this morning, she said something about Kelsis, a little mining operation near the Arizona border whose radioactive runoff has been turning up in wells in the next county. Even worse, his records for the Kelsis suit, like all the files on his computer, have vanished. He goes through his desk drawers hoping to find penciled notes or a backup disk holding some pertinent trace, but no, there's nothing, and in trying to reconstruct the basic outlines of the case, he naturally loses track of time, and it is well after midnight when David turns the key in his front door. As was his habit on certain dire nights in his other two marriages, he eats a bowl of children's cereal over the kitchen sink, and when he glances into their room, Jade is sitting up in bed, a legal pad against her knees, spectacles on her nose, and though she knows he's there, she doesn't stop writing. This means either that she's hot after an idea or that last night's grievance—the belief that he caused the needle to pierce her foot—has festered during ten professionally hostile hours at Pox, Welt, Scorch & Fray. The rug has disappeared from the floor, he notes. The door to the boys' room is ajar, their nightlight on, Shane's bed dishevelled, because Shane is a poor sleeper, rousing and turning at the slightest of sounds—the back of his mother's hand connecting with his father's jaw, say. Neither boy is there, of course. There's no telling when Susannah will entrust them to this household again. The nightlight is a nautilus shell shielding a tiny bulb, and by its glow, David sits in the corner, wishing he could get the boys back. If he only had his boys here, asleep in their beds, he would know how to begin to set the rest of his world right. He would start with the beautiful sleep of his children and work outward.

When she hears him come in, Jade continues to study her legal pad with an undeviating frown, and figuring that he has little to lose, he lets his anger show. "What did you do with it."

She takes off her glasses, folds them, sets them on the nightstand. He might be some witness she's treating to this stilted performance whose essence is her offended disbelief. "You use that tone of voice?" When he doesn't answer she says, "You wanted it gone. You told Susannah it was evil."

"You talked to Susannah?"

"I called her to ask what was wrong when they were leaving last night."

"What did she say?"

He's invested this question with a little too much anxiety, and she frowns. "She said to tell you Nina called. From Paris. She's flying home and she wants to take Edmund back with her for the rest of the year. Evidently I'm not to be trusted with either child."

"But the guys have never been apart."

"It looks like they will be, now. Because I'll make them say bedtime prayers for the health of George Bush. I'll knit them little American flag sweaters, and mock Darwin." She sucks on a lock of black hair, catches herself, spits it out. "When you didn't come home, and you didn't call, and your cell went right to voicemail, I couldn't just sit here stewing, could I? I followed your map. It was a long drive, it took me an hour each way, but I thought things would calm down if you knew the rug had gone back where it came from. Please, David, try for some perspective. It's an inanimate object. It can't hurt us. Only we can hurt us."

"We *are* hurt, because, Jade, politics—they're not in some little box with the lid shut tight. They're beliefs. They figure in what we do all day long. At least in what I do. I live my politics. And how do you think we're doing, Jade? As far as honesty goes. On a scale of one to ten, with ten being the most transparent mutual trust, and one being despicable, self-serving deception."

"You want transparency? Because I look at you, David—how enraged you are—and I think maybe, maybe in keeping my beliefs to myself I was preserving a necessary degree of mystery. Don't you think an interrogating, pulverizing righteousness like yours could doom a marriage? It's wilderness we measure the oppressiveness of civilization by, isn't that the EPIC line? So isn't a marriage measured by its secrets? You were used to such com*pliance*, with Susannah. After her, Nina, Shmina, who from everything you say and despite her supposed feminist credentials was basically this *mouse*. Now there's me, and, right, you and I don't know everything about each other, and we never will, and we're not meant to. You're leaving? David?"

The road unwinds before him in moonlight, rough as ever, only half familiar, and he takes its curves too fast, absorbing the adrenaline hit whenever a clump of cholla looms in the headlights, or a redoubt of sandstone. Once a coyote ghosts across the road, and the station wagon fishtails to a halt, swallowed in its own dust. The wipers squeal, clearing the haze, dirty rivulets rippling horizontally as David picks up speed, the desert laid out for him in luminous swipes, loss a particular taste in his mouth, a rank, rising bitterness he can't swallow away, his heartbeat manic, though it had been calm while he stood listening to Jade. There are no boys in the car to heed the warning but David lectures. Careful, careful. You'll get there. You'll find it. It was there once, it will be there again. Have a little faith, he lectures.

But the oil drum perched on the spur of rock is empty, turned over on its side, rocking when he nudges it with a toe, its trash blown over the rim, he supposes, scattered across the floor of the arroyo, rags fluttering from prickly pear, shards variously glinting, like the lights cupped in travelling waves. She left the rug here, she said. That must have been about dark. It's unlikely that anyone has driven the road since then. The wind has been hard at work, lashing and moaning: could the rug have been lifted and sailed over the rim? Here is the trail, wide enough to suit deer or two small boys, a little tricky for a grown man, stones kicked loose by his missteps, preceding him in clattering showers, his descent entirely audible, if there was anyone to hear. The interior of that tilted refrigerator is pierced by spokes of moonlight: bulletholes. Paperbacks cartwheel past, shedding pages. When he picks his way among the wreckage, he meets another moon, hanging in the unsmashed headlight of a wrecked truck, the starry refraction of a light coming from some earthly source. David makes for that glow, sheltered under the tilted wing of an airplane. The pain in his back is worse, but apart from that, he feels good, looser, a little winded but freer, defiant, trying to recall the last time he pursued something, some aim or intention, under the night sky. *Twenty years ago*. With the other four, his brothers, prowling a mesa in the dark, tossing survey stakes over the rim after pouring sugar in a backhoe's gas tank. Nothing he does now can compare with the satisfaction of that sabotage, with its clean, unequivocal high. He's grown old, tame as office air, carrying the dead carcass of skepticism on his shoulders. Jade had revived him, for a time. *Ow*. When a chip of stone grazes his chest, its sting—and the primal weirdness of being struck by a flying object in the dark—brings David entirely awake, but when he squints around, there's only the gusting sand, cholla rearing up spookily to his left, his shadow dipping and lengthening as he hikes toward the glow—a campfire, maybe. Something pelts his chest again, then his arm, and before he can shield his eyes he's hit by a whirlwind of grit and twigs. Bewildered, he walks right into it, grazed, poked, showered with debris, leaves, twigs, and scouring sand. If she were with him, Jade would hide her face against his chest, and he'd shelter her as best he could, her ferocious lawyer-hair lashing his face, and even with the wind whipping and scouring they could achieve a kind of safety. David reels along blindly, and from the way his lungs strain he understands he must be crying out, though he can't hear anything over the wind. This is what he has seen happen to small bald-headed children: death blows you away while you struggle, the truth, the outrage, dying in your throat. Flinging a last handful of grit, the blast relents. David has passed among the cholla unscathed, and here is the shelter under the airplane's wing, from which a lantern is suspended, shining down on a boy and a girl, entwined on his rug, its arabesques dimmed, its choir of blues bleached to lunar grays and faint violet. The boy is fast asleep, but the girl is awake. She tightens her arms around her boyfriend, and lifts her chin defiantly. She's got the inky hair favored by punked-out runaways, a fright wig trailing sharp fangs over her forehead, the pinched-together brows and eyeholes whose expression can't be deciphered. When he takes another step toward his rug, she flashes a palm. Stop. He takes another step, and gets both palms. She wants nothing more than to stop him, and he stops. It all stops, moon, love, breath, heartbeat. David sprawls there, feeling the hardness of the ground, the nerve-revival of panic, the terror that she won't know what to do, that she's stoned and can't help. The wind dies down and the moonlight blinks and he doesn't know what comes next on earth. No one knows. But there are footsteps coming toward him, if there is any chance of saving a life through the sheer force of one's love for it, he is already saved.

Nominated Atsuro Riley, The Threepenny Review

POSTHUMOUS MAN

by DAVID BAKER

from THE SOUTHERN REVIEW

I hate the world.
I have come to the edge.

Our neighbor's white
bean field in a snow fog.

Three weeks of it
shedding in the warmth

like smoke from fire
lines set against the trees

or the season's
cold boredom with itself.

Mud in the white
field. A hump of gray snow.

Nothing is there.
I hold the dog tight

on his leash. Gray
snow: gray coat, rising now

—scuffed like a bad

rug, scruff-eared—so we watch

nothing rise in
the white bean field and shake

off a night's sleep
and sniff, sniff, peer over

at us. Winter
wrens in a fluff. Rustle

of bramble. He
trots off at precisely

one hundred and
eighty degrees from where

we emerged from
the woods, into the woods . . .

The long-married abide in privacy
longer and longer. That's one irony.
After hearing the coyote crying
a week, ten days, maybe more, late at night
through the glassy air, crying like a bird
his song among the billion stars, we saw him
sunning asleep in the neighbor's old field.

And he woke. And saw us. And, unafraid,
loped off. We rise each morning alone from
the shape of our bodies in flannel sheets,
burrow beside burrow, where we dream of
running, bleeding, food, feral sex, each
to his or her own outlandish nightlife.
We walk in the world, we sip our coffee

at a clean glass table, we love our child.
Then come to an edge, where the world

meets the soul, and the soul knows once more
what it holds, such capacity
to inflict harm or injury, easy
as a snowfall and fog's long rise back.
It does, or does not, again and again.

I hate the world:
It batters too much the

wings of my self-
will. He's writing to Fanny

a few weeks cold
after the nightingale.

He hears it sing
in lone, full-throated ease.

And knows himself
grown spectre-thin. Even

in sweet incense,
full summer, his sadness is

a bell's birdcall
tolling him *back from thee*

to my sole self!
He'll sail himself, next year—

a man post-
poetry and posthumous,

too numb to feel
the sun over Naples,

to heal his
scavenger lungs. His hands are

white cold. His nails
are ridged, like a field.

He writes, to Brown,
were I in health it would

make me ill. And
means, of course, his heart's lack

—white trees, white waves—.
It is death, without her.

I hear behind me winter wind. It whips
the sycamores, whose leaves are large as sheaves
of paper, brittle-brown or blowing down.
It whips and shakes the blanched-bone trunks of beech.
Despite the cold it's humid, a warm
exhaust of fog and breathing of the mud.
Back down the path I cut all summer, down

the ridge and up the drumlin rise beside
our creek, you're reading. Or you're watching out
the windows where I've vanished with the dog.
I've learned when I should leave. There's privacy
you crave, as I do. The irony thereof.
It is my source of fear. The sheltie wants,
growling at his leash, loose. I won't let him—

the coyote would kill him simply.
So we watch. Long snout. Bone-slender, his high
rear hips. He's a reel of fog unspooling
toward the far, half-shadowed rim of trees.
Uptick of grackles, more wrens—. He's loping.
Now he's running through the field toward the woods.
By the time he is halfway, he is gone.

Nominated Michael Waters, Jane Hirshfield, Susan Hahn,
Khaled Mattawa, Linda Gregerson

RICKSHAW RUNNER

fiction by NAOMI J. WILLIAMS

from THE SOUTHERN REVIEW

WHEN I BRING THE CAR AROUND for Mr. Chaplin he is not at all ready to go but still dressed as Tramp and talking with people on set. He sees me and shouts, Kono, I need a driver in this scene, come quick. But I stay in the car and shake my head no. I'm in dead earnest, he says. After foolishness last night, I wonder how he still is so demanding. But ever since he starts making this movie, *The Kid*, he loses all his sense. I keep shaking my head no, and he says, Be a good chap, Kono, just drive past the camera. I tell him it is too dark anyway for more shooting, and this makes him angry. Now you tell me how to make pictures, is that it? he says. But cameraman laughs and says Kono's right, Charlie, too dark now, go on home.

In dressing room I help Mr. Chaplin out of costume. I am sorry, I say. He hands me Tramp wig and says, I ask too much, Kono. This is true, but I tell him, For me I would not mind. And he says, I know, I know, the formidable Mrs. Kono forbids it. I put wig in box and cane on peg and wonder about this word, "formidable." I do not know meaning, but it sounds like my wife. Three years before I have small part as driver in Mr. Chaplin's movie *The Adventurer*, and I like it very much, especially making thirty dollars for two days' work—usually one whole week I work as chauffeur to make this money. But my wife finds out, and she says to me, Toraichi, you don't bring shame on family like this! Acting not respectable work, Mr. Chaplin may be very rich but he comes from nothing.—So my acting career is very short.

When Mr. Chaplin is dressed, I drive him from studio. On our way

217

out I see light on in kitchen of big studio house where I live with my wife and baby boy, and I wonder if they have dinner yet. I go south on La Brea, and when I turn left onto Wilshire I say to Mr. Chaplin, I think she will not be there tonight. But he does not answer. I look back and he has on hard thinking face, like when he is having new idea for scene or new picture, and then he does not hear anything what I say. But when we come close to Oxford Street, he suddenly curls up on backseat of car and asks in small voice, Is she there, Kono? Is she there? It is pitiful for grown man to hide from his own wife like this. Every time he does this I want to hit him on his head. But I tell him again, No worry, she will not be there, and when I see corner I say, See, no one there.

Actually there *is* someone, but just Japanese gardener gathering rake and shovel in front of house. The gardener looks up at the car, and first I think he is admiring it. It is big 12-cylinder Locomobile, very impressive. But then he looks down street and back, and I think maybe he knows. Gardeners know many things what goes on around neighborhood. But this man does not know what happened last night. I can tell gardener man just like I tell Mr. Chaplin, She will not be here. Tonight she still is laughing about last night, how much trouble she cause me and Mr. Chaplin. Tomorrow night maybe she will feel sad again, have her driver bring her to corner of Oxford and Wilshire to see Mr. Chaplin go by. But tonight, no. The gardener turns back, and I see it is me he is looking at, not the car and not Mr. Chaplin. He seems familiar and it is not good kind of familiar. Then Mr. Chaplin says, Get us out of here, Kono, drive like hell—what he always says—and I do.

I take Mr. Chaplin to Los Angeles Athletic Club on 7th Street. This is where he sleeps instead of home with Miss Mildred. Then I drive home and I pass Oxford Street again, but this time no one is there at all, not Miss Mildred in her car and not gardener with his look that I don't like.

When I get home my wife does not say welcome home like in Japan when the husband returns, but Oh good, it is just you. I say, Who else you expect? And she says, You know what I mean. She sets pot on stove to reheat dinner, and I sit at kitchen table. I already tell you it will not happen again, I say to her, and she breathes out through her nose to show me she is not believing. When Mr. Chaplin first give to us the big house on studio lot, my wife and I sometimes eat meal in front of giant fireplace in living room. But then Mr.

218

Chaplin start visiting with girlfriends, different one every time, and he wants us to serve dinner then leave while he has romance by fire. I finally tell him, Mr. Chaplin, this is insult to my wife. He frowns and says, Oh Kono, what a prig you are. But he stops visiting. We never use living room since; we go in there only to dust furniture, we never sit on sofa.

My wife hands me doorknob. Upstairs bathroom, she says. Our studio house looks very nice, like mansion of rich person. But carpenters who build it used to building sets what look good in movies, not to last long time. So everything is always breaking: doorknob falling off and window slamming down and roof leaking. I fix it tonight, I tell her. The stair railing is loose, too, she says. I will look later, I tell her. And she says, No, Toraichi, you cannot fix, you talk to carpenter. I say nothing. She knows I hate to talk to set carpenters.

She brings me rice and miso soup and fish, then sits down across from me. So what happen last night? she asks. I wish to change subjects, so I say, Do we know Japanese gardener who works on corner of Wilshire and Oxford? My wife thinks a minute and says, No, there was problem with Japanese gardener last night? I say, No, no, not at all. You come home after midnight, she says. You sit here at table and drink. I know, this morning I wash glass.

I don't say: I spend last night with Mr. Chaplin snooping divorce reason for him. What kind of man spies on wife, hoping he find she is with another man? Last night we sneak to his house and he stands on my back to look through window and watch Miss Mildred drinking tea with young man, but no kissing or even holding hands. This is big disappointment for Mr. Chaplin. Then this large man drags us out of bushes; he points gun at me and asks what the hell we are doing and calls Mr. Chaplin you little runt. We run back to the car and Mr. Chaplin tells me, Go back and offer big man fifty dollars to spy for us. I say, Are you crazy? But Mr. Chaplin insists, and I go back and gun points at me again. Mr. Chaplin always says Miss Mildred is stupid, but I disagree. Big man turns out to be private dick who Miss Mildred hires to spy on Mr. Chaplin spying on her, and young man in house is just brother of friend she invites to make Mr. Chaplin jealous. I go back to car and tell Mr. Chaplin he hires me to be driver, not spy. I say, My ancestors are samurai, this work too low for me. And he says, You come from samurai, Kono? Well, I'll be goddamned. I can see he likes this idea of samurai chauffeur.

I cannot tell my wife any of this. Man should never say something to

219

wife without he knows what she is going to say back. Maybe my wife will be serious and say, Toraichi, time to quit job with Mr. Chaplin. Or maybe she will feel angry and say, Why you not ask him for more money, you big fool? Or maybe she will be scared if I am shot, maybe she starts to cry.—No, that will not happen. That is American woman way. More probable my wife laughs and says, Just like Mr. Chaplin's picture! Or laugh harder and say, What good joke! You tell Mr. Chaplin you are *samurai*? I don't want to hear any of these, so I say nothing.

After I finish dinner, I take doorknob and go upstairs, and my wife washes up very noisy, how she does when she is angry. At end of hall I look in bedroom of my son. He is asleep in crib with his mouth little bit open and all his blankets off. I spread out yellow blanket that is gift of Miss Edna Purviance, who is star of so many Mr. Chaplin's movies. She likes my son. Every day she asks, How is my little friend Spencer? and sometimes stops by house to see him. Mr. Chaplin likes children, too, but it is hard for him to see my son. When he is born I ask Mr. Chaplin, It is OK we call him Spencer? Because Spencer is middle name of Mr. Chaplin. And his eyes fill with tears, only second time I see Mr. Chaplin cry, and he says, Of course, Kono, I'm honored, and he gives me one hundred dollars but never comes to see the baby.

Before I leave Spencer I push on model airplane I make to hang over his crib. Maybe Spencer will become pilot when he grows up. One time in the past I want to be pilot. When I first come to southern California, I study at aviation school in Venice. But then I bring wife over from Japan. I know this woman always, our families engage us when we are children. But she surprises me very often after we marry—not nice and quiet like at home, but speaking her mind on many things. She says, Toraichi, you don't make me widow with flying business. You get a real job, like other Japanese here. And that is how I end up with Mr. Chaplin.

Next morning when I leave house I see neighbor with ladder and hammer and something rolled up on front lawn. I hope they will not hang big sign to embarrass Mr. Chaplin. These neighbors are not happy about studio right next door and never friendly to me or my wife. I think to tell Mr. Chaplin, but when I get to the club he comes out with big grin and talks about splendid breakfast he ate and what glorious day to be alive, and I forget about neighbor. Because this kind of happy Mr. Chaplin always means trouble for me.

On way back to studio we pass house on Wilshire and Oxford and I see gardener again. This time he is digging large hole in front yard, like to plant bushes. He has white cloth tied around his head with knot in front. His clothing are Western but headband Japanese, and now I am sure I know this man, but I am glad he does not notice me. Maybe this man sail on *Empress of China* with me second time I come to America. My first trip I had nice cabin, but second time I foolishly lose money in Yokohama and have to take steerage. How can I know they don't provide blanket for steerage? A miserable trip. My shipmates all Japanese peasants, very poor, hoping to be farmers in America. This gardener, maybe he was one of them. Maybe I stole blanket from him. Then Mr. Chaplin says, Kono, have you heard a goddamn thing I've said?

Now I listen and Mr. Chaplin is telling me he wants to move new actress into Miss Purviance's dressing room. *What* new actress? I ask. And Mr. Chaplin says, A charming young girl I need for new scene in *The Kid*. Miss Purviance will not like, I tell him, and he says, She'll be fine, Edna's a champ, and I say again, Miss Purviance will not like. And now we are near studio, but I am so worried about Mr. Chaplin's plan I forget to check what next door neighbors are up to.

Miss Purviance does *not* like. She stomps around while workmen move her things, and then she sits in chair and refuses to talk and is mean to new girl. New girl turns out to be only twelve. Her name is Lillita MacMurray, and I remember now she comes with mother to see Mr. Chaplin for part in his picture. Now Mr. Chaplin gives her dressing room and makes new scene just for her. The scene is Tramp's dream with everyone dressed up as angels and flying around studio on wire. Lillita is angel, too, but I don't know if she is good angel or bad angel. She seems to be tempting Tramp and Tramp enjoys very much. I see face of Mrs. MacMurray. Now she is maybe not so happy about daughter working with Mr. Chaplin.

It is strange, strange scene, but Mr. Chaplin does not hire me for opinions, and anyway I am busy. There are guests of Mr. Chaplin on set I need to take care of. Also Jackie Coogan, who is the Kid, gets splinter, and this boy who plays big fight scene for Mr. Chaplin with no crying screams and screams while I take out tiny splinter. Then Miss Purviance disappears and I must find her before she comes back drunk. I also try to find set carpenter, but they all are too busy for me. Then Miss Mildred calls twice, and I am so ashamed to talk to her, but here is where poor English and mysterious Oriental attitude become very useful. She says, Kono, you *do* give my messages to Mr. Chaplin, don't you? And I say, Mr. Chaplin very great man, very busy man.

I go home for lunch, and there Miss Purviance is with Spencer on her lap. Oh, Kono, she says, don't look grumpy, I'm having fun. My wife hands me letter that arrives from Japan. I read over my lunch and Miss Purviance says, What's wrong, Kono—bad news? And I say, No, because letter is from my mother and full of good news: maple trees so pretty this fall and my brother working hard, nice harvest from bamboo grove and my school friends all with good success. But there is underneath meaning: You belong here, not in strange land with no weather. And why you let younger brother take your place in family business? All your old friends do better than you.—Bamboo is only small part of family business, but my mother always mentions to remind me when I was teenager and stole bamboo to pay for good time, drink with geisha in town, and make my father to send me to America. I wonder again about gardener on Wilshire and Oxford. Maybe he is former worker from bamboo grove. Maybe he help me take bamboo and sell. Maybe he lose job then come to America. I don't know. I don't remember where I see that man's face before.

My mother has very good writing, lines all straight up and down, no sloppy characters, the date in Japanese style—Taisho 9, ninth year of Emperor Taisho reign. She wants I not forget how to be Japanese, but I no longer count years by emperor reign. I hear this emperor is insane anyway. To me it is 1920. Or maybe Chaplin 4, for how many years I work for Mr. Chaplin. Chaplin 4. Why not? He is crazy also.

That afternoon when I drive Mr. Chaplin from studio lot, my wife waves to me from front porch. I slow the car and she calls in quiet voice, Hello, Mr. Chaplin, and he nods and takes off his hat for her. Then she tells me in Japanese, Don't forget tonight we go to Little Tokyo festival. She looks like she will say something more, but she does not. I nod and say, Yes, festival—to show I remember. But my wife knows I have forgotten. I often forget things I don't want to do.

I turn left out of lot and slam my foot on the brake. Mr. Chaplin almost falls off seat and shouts, Confound you, Kono, what on earth? I point up to giant banner on next door house.

JAPS KEEP MOVING!
THIS IS A WHITE MAN'S NEIGHBORHOOD.
Member, Hollywood Protective Association

Here is what my wife wants to tell me, I think. Mr. Chaplin says, Kono, they're idiots, pay them no mind. I tell him, Easy for you to say—I am only glad my son is too young to read. But it is mistake to mention about Spencer. Mr. Chaplin stays silent for moment, then he says, Kono, I'm late.

It is cloudy, and I am happy if it will rain and this ruins festival. I am thinking about rain when we pass house with Japanese gardener. I slow down to look for him, feel half disappointment, half relief that he is not there. But then Mr. Chaplin says, What the hell, Kono, get us out of here, and I look up and see the car of Miss Mildred parked on Oxford with stony face driver in front and Miss Mildred in back. She is so pretty with brown hair waving around her face and big eyes little too close together and so sad. I have not really looked at her since funeral last summer for her baby boy. He was born in July, just four months before Spencer, and Mr. Chaplin says, Won't it be nice, Kono, our children running around studio together? But Mr. Chaplin's boy has stomach problem and dies after only three days. After funeral Mr. Chaplin lies down on backseat of the car and cries like little boy while I drive for long, long time. People say sad times bring people close together, but this is not true for Mr. Chaplin and Miss Mildred. Mr. Chaplin, he puts all his sad feelings in *The Kid*. I don't know what Miss Mildred is doing.

Unfortunately, there is no rain and I take my family to festival. It is festival of local association of Japanese from Hiroshima. My wife thinks it is so important Spencer will know Japanese culture and meet other people from Hiroshima. But it is not real Japanese culture, these festivals. Today is not even real Japanese holiday. And Little Tokyo is not Hiroshima. Anyway, why I want to talk to Hiroshima people? If I want that, maybe I stay in Hiroshima.

We go to the stall selling *okonomiyaki*, and we see people we know. All the women are maids in Hollywood or Beverly Hills, and their husbands are gardeners or cooks. One man with very red face who smells of *saké* says, What are you here for, Kono? I thought you become big movie star—and everyone laughs. I say to him, Is it true L.A. cops follow your red face to find Japanese speakeasies? Everyone laughs again, but then they start to ask, Does Charlie need Japanese actor? or How about free tickets for Charlie's next picture, Kono? These people all laborers back in Japan, I would not be friendly with them there. They are people my family might hire. I say excuse me and turn to leave, only to find that gardener from Wilshire and Oxford in my way. He looks at me with sideways smile, then lets me pass by. And he says in loud Japanese, Ah, that one is too grand for us. Now not just his face but his voice familiar, too.

I ask my wife, Who is that man? She says, I find out for you, and disappears with Spencer into crowd before I can say no. I walk through street past many stalls of Japanese food, but I am not hungry. Then small parade starts with young women doing traditional dance, and I think of Miss Mildred, who is same age as these girls but already married and lose not only child but love of husband, too. After dancers comes noisy group of men in festival coats and carrying heavy *mikoshi*, festival shrine. They pass me and I see gardener man, his tan face strains under weight of *mikoshi*, and I suddenly remember this same face straining under different weight. I turn around to leave, but it is too crowded. My movement only gets attention of gardener. Driver man, he calls out panting. Maybe *this* town needs buses, too? How about it, driver man? He laughs as parade moves on. I fight through crowd and find my wife, who reports the man is called Sato, and in Hiroshima he—. I know, I say, he was rickshaw runner. Oh, she says, you already know. Why do you ask me if you know?

On the way home Spencer falls asleep on lap of my wife. When we pass next-door neighbor's house we say nothing. But I know she is thinking about big sign, and I know she knows I am thinking same thing. That kind of silence very loud sometimes. At home our telephone rings like maybe it is ringing long time. Only person who calls at night is Mr. Chaplin, and it is always emergency. I answer while my wife carries Spencer upstairs to bed. Where have you been? Mr. Chaplin shouts into phone, and before I explain he says, Mildred's sued for divorce. This is what he hopes for so much all these months, but now he sounds not so happy. Do you hear me, Kono? he shouts. She'll ruin me, she'll take *The Kid*, I have to get out of California— tonight. Tonight? I say, and he says, Yes, goddamnit, tonight. When I hang up I go upstairs and tell my wife I have to leave, am not sure when I will come home. She says, If that man tells you to jump off bridge, you will do it. And she closes the door without good night.

I leave to get Mr. Chaplin from the club. Clouds have cleared up

224

and it is pretty night with almost full moon. I pass house on Wilshire, and there is now new palm tree, good size, in front yard. This gardener Sato, who was rickshaw runner in Japan, is strong man. Rickshaw runners, they have hard job to run all day long pulling people behind them. They either be very strong or die early. This man Sato is strong type. I know, because one time I see him push the motor bus into ditch.

When I was seventeen, after bamboo fiasco and my first time in America, I go back to Japan and try to stay in good graces of my father. He help me and my friend start bicycle shop in Hiroshima and we do it for one year, make pretty good money. But I want to fly and bicycles not so interesting to me even though I know about Wright brothers, how they start with bicycle shop, too. My friend and I, we use profit from bicycle business to buy sixteen-passenger motor bus. Motor buses have engine and take passengers, so I figure I am one step closer to airplane. We decide to start bus service from Hiroshima to Kobe. It is optimistic time for me. My father starts to talk to me again at dinner, and my mother not always sighing when she sees me. The English I learn in America I start to forget.

In those days there are not very many cars in Japan, so the motor bus is exciting thing to see. We arrange for grand opening of bus line and many people come, all our friends and family and also townspeople. But we have no experience, we don't understand we make enemy of rickshaw runners. Big gang of runners come from Hiroshima and Kobe and all towns in between. We recognize them right away— they wear half-length kimono, brown or gray or blue, over dark leggings and straw sandals, and *hachimaki* headbands across forehead. They surround the bus and nobody stops them. Maybe at first people think they are part of entertainment of the day. Maybe I think so, too.

But then this Sato points to me and my friend, and shouts to crowd, These rich schoolboys have such fancy ideas, ehh? And everyone except friends and family start to laugh, because common people, they always ready to clap hands when good people succeed, but even more ready to clap when they fail. Then Sato points to the bus and shouts, Think this foreign devil wagon can beat us? And nine or maybe ten runners with Sato start to push against the bus until it is rocking back and forth. They push and push and push together until the bus tips over and there is huge dust cloud. When it is clear we see the bus is off road and down in the ditch. The crowd shouts and claps because show is even better than they expect. If it is not my bus I will also be impressed, maybe also clap and shout. But I only think that later. At the time I am angry, and I yell and yell while Sato and his men run away. They are good runners, of course, and we do not chase after them.

My father arranges for workmen to drag the bus out and sell to someone else. Then he says, Toraichi, you join family business, but I say, No, father, I go back to America, and he nods and holds out his hand and I see he has already money for my passage. That is last time I take money from him, and I spend on drink and good food in Yokohama. Maybe I think, If I have no money for ship, I will not have to leave. But then I wake up the morning *Empress of China* is due to leave and I have nowhere to go, so I end up down in steerage. And I never return again to Japan. Only thing I do what I am supposed to do is marry my wife. But she is raised to be rich merchant's wife, not wife of chauffeur. She never expects to be waitress in her own home. She does not expect to live in house where rich man comes to entertain girlfriends. She never thinks to work for man of so low birth. I do not know how to fix for her.

All I can think is how I would enjoy striking Sato in his face. Why he is here? Does he follow me to Los Angeles to insult me more? No, this cannot be. I think rickshaw runners win that day in Hiroshima, but now they are losing. More and more cars in Japan, more railways and streetcars, less and less rickshaws. So he ends up here, too. But there are no rickshaw runners for rich people in Los Angeles. Here rich people have chauffeurs.

When I collect Mr. Chaplin, he is very nervous, never stops talking, sometimes laughs and sometimes groans, and always telling me drive faster. I give him brandy what I keep in the car, and then he calms down little bit. Studio house is very dark as we drive onto lot, and I think of my wife probably not asleep in bed upstairs. I park outside production building, then we quickly load many thousand feet of film into big suitcases, not real leather. They are very heavy to move. *The Kid* is longest movie Mr. Chaplin makes so far, and I think maybe it is longest movie anyone ever makes. When we go to the car I find on driver seat a package wrapped in Japanese cloth; inside is rice ball for me and sandwich for Mr. Chaplin. Ah, Kono, Mr. Chaplin says, your wife, what a gem. He takes long drink from flask and says, To successful marriage. I ask, Where to, Mr. Chaplin? And he says Utah, my friend, Utah. The upstanding Mormons will protect me from my divorce. Then he gives big laugh.

We pull out onto La Brea, and I don't want to see that big sign next door, but I cannot help to look. Beautiful night to run away, Mr. Chaplin says, and his cheerfulness makes me angry. I stop the car and turn around, point back to studio house. Your house is very pretty on outside, Mr. Chaplin, but we can live at another place, I tell him. He says, Good God, Kono, not threatening to quit again? I say nothing. What is it—you want more money? he asks, and I think no, that is not what I need. I need for doorknob to stay on and neighbors not to hate us and boss not to make me spy on people and for rickshaw runners to stay in Japan. But I still say nothing. And he says, Consider it done—God knows you deserve it after tonight. He takes another bite of sandwich and says, Do tell Mrs. Kono thank you for me. Then he finishes his drink from flask and says, Now drive like hell, Kono, get us out of here. So I turn on the car again and drive toward desert.

Nominated by Nancy Richard

CHANCES ARE,
LAFAYETTE, INDIANA

by SARAH GREEN

from THE GETTYSBURG REVIEW

You may have visited this strip club
advertised by one high heel, a line
of automatic cursive on the back page
of the college news. I can't remember

if the dancer's stockings show their seams.
We don't see beyond her ankle in the square
white box. What she is and isn't wearing,
how long she can stand, balancing

there. Maybe she's busy filling in the rest
of that sentence: *Chances are, you won't go home
with me. Chances are, I'll get into business school.*
And what business would she start? Don't

say *risky.* You know she's smart, bored, trying
to quit smoking. It isn't sad if we imagine
that she's young—as young as chance,
and as distractable. Chance is an amateur.

Chance hangs out on the back roads.
I had my chance, people say, like they've lost
an umbrella. Chance was just here, but we
keep getting caught in the rain. Chances are

won by some guy in your old neighborhood
at a Dominican store with a Red Sox photo,
a flag in the same frame. Chance is opening
a restaurant near you.

Nominated by Marianne Boruch

LOVE BADE ME WELCOME

by CHRISTIAN WIMAN

from THE AMERICAN SCHOLAR

THOUGH I WAS RAISED in a very religious household, until about a year ago I hadn't been to church in any serious way in more than 20 years. It would be inaccurate to say that I have been indifferent to God in all that time. If I look back on the things I have written in the past two decades, it's clear to me not only how thoroughly the forms and language of Christianity have shaped my imagination, but also how deep and persistent my existential anxiety has been. I don't know whether this is all attributable to the century into which I was born, some genetic glitch, or a late reverberation of the Fall of Man. What I do know is that I have not been at ease in this world.

Poetry, for me, has always been bound up with this unease, fueled by contingency toward forms that will transcend it, as involved with silence as it is with sound. I don't have much sympathy for the Arnoldian notion of poetry replacing religion. It seems not simply quaint but dangerous to make that assumption, even implicitly, perhaps *especially* implicitly. I do think, though, that poetry is how religious feeling has survived in me. Partly this is because I have at times experienced in the writing of a poem some access to a power that feels greater than I am, and it seems reductive, even somehow a deep betrayal, to attribute that power merely to the unconscious or to the dynamism of language itself. But also, if I look back on the poems I've written in the past two decades, it almost seems as if the one constant is God. Or, rather, His absence.

There is a passage in the writings of Simone Weil that has long been important to me. In the passage, Weil describes two prisoners who are in solitary confinement next to each other. Between them is a stone wall. Over a period of time—and I think we have to imagine it as a very long time—they find a way to communicate using taps and scratches. The wall is what separates them, but it is also the only means they have of communicating. "It is the same with us and God," she says. "Every separation is a link."

It's probably obvious why this metaphor would appeal to me. If you never quite feel at home in your life, if being conscious means primarily being conscious of your own separation from the world and from divinity (and perhaps any sentient person after modernism *has* to feel these things) then any idea or image that can translate that depletion into energy, those absences into presences, is going to be powerful. And then there are those taps and scratches: what are they but language, and if language is the way we communicate with the divine, well, what kind of language is more refined and transcendent than poetry? You could almost embrace this vision of life—if, that is, there were any actual life to embrace: Weil's image for the human condition is a person in solitary confinement. There is real hope in the image, but still, in human terms, it is a bare and lonely hope.

It has taken three events, each shattering in its way, for me to recognize both the full beauty, and the final insufficiency, of Weil's image. The events are radically different, but so closely linked in time, and so inextricable from one another in their consequences, that there is an uncanny feeling of unity to them. There is definitely some wisdom in learning to see our moments of necessity and glory and tragedy not as disparate experiences but as facets of the single experience that is a life. The pity, at least for some of us, is that we cannot truly have this knowledge of life, can only feel it as some sort of abstract "wisdom," until we come very close to death.

First, necessity: four years ago, after making poetry the central purpose of my life for almost two decades, I stopped writing. Partly this was a conscious decision. I told myself that I had exhausted one way of writing, and I do think there was truth in that. The deeper truth, though, is that I myself was exhausted. To believe that being conscious means primarily being conscious of loss, to find life authentic only in the apprehension of death, is to pitch your tent at the edge of an abyss, "and when you gaze long into the abyss," Nietzsche says, "the abyss also gazes into you." I blinked.

On another level, though, the decision to stop writing wasn't mine. Whatever connection I had long experienced between word and world, whatever charge in the former I had relied on to let me feel the latter, went dead. Did I give up poetry, or was it taken from me? I'm not sure, and in any event the effect was the same: I stumbled through the months, even thrived in some ways. Indeed—and there is something almost diabolical about this common phenomenon—it sometimes seemed like my career in poetry began to flourish just as poetry died in me. I finally found a reliable publisher for my work (the work I'd written earlier, I mean), moved into a good teaching job, and then quickly left that for the editorship of *Poetry*. But there wasn't a scrap of excitement in any of this for me. It felt like I was watching a movie of my life rather than living it, an old silent movie, no color, no sound, no one in the audience but me.

Then I fell in love. I say it suddenly, and there was certainly an element of radical intrusion and transformation to it, but the sense I have is of color slowly aching into things, the world coming brilliantly, abradingly alive. I remember tiny Albert's Café on Elm Street in Chicago where we first met, a pastry case like a Pollock in the corner of my eye, sunlight suddenly more itself on an empty plate, a piece of silver. I think of walking together along Lake Michigan a couple of months later talking about a particular poem of Dickinson's ("A loss of something ever felt I"), clouds finding and failing to keep one form after another, the lake booming its blue into everything; of lying in bed in my highrise apartment downtown watching the little blazes in the distance that were the planes at Midway, so numerous and endless that all those safe departures and homecomings seemed a kind of secular miracle. We usually think of falling in love as being possessed by another person, and like anyone else I was completely consumed and did some daffy things. But it also felt, for the first time in my life, like I was being fully possessed by being itself. "Joy is the overflowing consciousness of reality," Weil writes, and that's what I had, a joy that was at once so overflowing that it enlarged existence, and yet so rooted in actual things that, again for the first time, that's what I began to feel: rootedness.

I don't mean to suggest that all my old anxieties were gone. There were still no poems, and this ate at me constantly. There was still no God, and the closer I came to reality, the more I longed for divinity—or, more accurately perhaps, the more divinity seemed so obviously a *part* of reality. I wasn't alone in this: we began to say a kind of prayer before our evening meals—jokingly at first, awkwardly, but then with intensifying seriousness and deliberation, trying to name each thing that we were thankful for, and in so doing, praise the thing we could not name. On most Sundays we would even briefly entertain—again, half-jokingly—the idea of going to church. The very morning after we got engaged, in fact, we paused for a long time outside a church on Michigan Avenue. The service was just about to start, organ music pouring out of the wide open doors into the late May sun, and we stood there holding each other and debating whether or not to walk inside. In the end it was I who resisted.

I wish I could slow things down at this point, could linger a bit in those months after our marriage. I wish I could feel again that blissful sense of immediacy and expansiveness at once, when every moment implied another, and the future suddenly seemed to offer some counterbalance to the solitary fever I had lived in for so long. I think most writers live at some strange adjacency to experience, that they feel life most intensely in their re-creation of it. For once, for me, this wasn't the case. I could not possibly have been paying closer attention to those days. Which is why I was caught so off-guard.

I got the news that I was sick on the afternoon of my 39th birthday. It took a bit of time, travel, and a series of wretched tests to get the specific diagnosis, but by then the main blow had been delivered, and that main blow is what matters. I have an incurable cancer in my blood. The disease is as rare as it is mysterious, killing some people quickly and sparing others for decades, afflicting some with all manner of miseries and disabilities and leaving others relatively healthy until the end. Of all the doctors I have seen, not one has been willing to venture even a vague prognosis.

Conventional wisdom says that tragedy will cause either extreme closeness or estrangement in a couple. We'd been married less than a year when we got the news of the cancer. It stands to reason we should have been especially vulnerable to such a blow, and in some ways love did make things much worse. If I had gotten the diagnosis some years earlier—and it seems weirdly providential that I didn't, since I had symptoms and went to several doctors about them—I'm not sure I would have reacted very strongly. It would have seemed a fatalistic confirmation of everything I had always thought about existence, and my response, I think, would have been equally fatalistic. It would have been the bearable oblivion of despair, not the unbearable, and therefore galvanizing, pain of particular grief. In those early days after the diagnosis, when we mostly just sat on the couch and cried, I alone was dying, but we were mourning very much together. And what we were mourning was not my death, exactly, but the death of the life we had imagined with each other.

Then one morning we found ourselves going to church. *Found ourselves.* That's exactly what it felt like, in both senses of the phrase, as if some impulse in each of us had finally been catalyzed into action, so that we were casting aside the Sunday paper and moving toward the door with barely a word between us; and as if, once inside the church, we were discovering exactly where and who we were meant to be. That first service was excruciating, in that it seemed to tear all wounds wide open, and it was profoundly comforting, in that it seemed to offer the only possible balm. What I remember of that Sunday, though, and of the Sundays that immediately followed, is less the services themselves than the walks we took afterwards, and less the specifics of the conversations we had about God, always about God, than the moments of silent, and what felt like sacred, attentiveness those conversations led to: an iron sky and the lake so calm it seemed thickened; the El blasting past with its rain of sparks and brief, lost faces; the broad leaves and white blooms of a catalpa on our street, Grace Street, and under the tree a seethe of something that was just barely still a bird, quick with life beyond its own.

I was brought up with the poisonous notion that you had to renounce love of the earth in order to receive the love of God. My experience has been just the opposite: a love of the earth and existence so overflowing that it implied, or included, or even absolutely demanded, God. Love did not deliver me from the earth, but into it. And by some miracle I do not find that this experience is crushed or even lessened by the knowledge that, in all likelihood, I will be leaving the earth sooner than I had thought. Quite the contrary, I find life thriving in me, and not in an aestheticizing Death-is-the-mother-of-beauty sort of way either, for what extreme grief has given me is the very thing it seemed at first to obliterate: a sense of life beyond the moment, a sense of hope. This is not simply hope for my own life, though I do have that. It is not a hope for heaven or any sort of explainable afterlife, unless by those things one means simply the ghost of wholeness that our inborn sense of brokenness creates and sustains, some ultimate love that our truest temporal ones goad us toward. This I do believe in, and by this I live, in what the apostle Paul called "hope toward God."

"It is necessary to have had a revelation of reality through joy," Weil writes, "in order to find reality through suffering." This is certainly true to my own experience. I was not wrong all those years to believe that suffering is at the very center of our existence, and that there can be no untranquilized life that does not fully confront this fact. The mistake lay in thinking grief the means of confrontation, rather than love. To come to this realization is not to be suddenly "at ease in the world." I don't really think it's possible for humans to be at the same time conscious and comfortable. Though we may be moved by nature to thoughts of grace, though art can tease our minds toward eternity and love's abundance make us dream a love that does not end, these intuitions come only through the earth, and the earth we know only in passing, and only by passing. I would qualify Weil's statement somewhat, then, by saying that reality, be it of this world or another, is not something one finds and then retains for good. It must be newly discovered daily, and newly lost.

So now I bow my head and try to pray in the mornings, not because I don't doubt the reality of what I have experienced, but because I do, and with an intensity that, because to once feel the presence of God is to feel His absence all the more acutely, is actually more anguishing and difficult than any "existential anxiety" I have ever known. I go to church on Sundays, not to dispel this doubt but to expend its energy, because faith is not a state of mind but an action in the world, a movement *toward* the world. How charged this one hour of the week is for me, and how I cherish it, though not one whit more than the hours I have with my wife, with friends, or in solitude, trying to learn how to inhabit time so completely that there might be no distinction between life and belief, attention and devotion. And out of all these efforts at faith and love, out of my own inevitable failures at both, I have begun to write poems again. But the language I have now to call on God is not only language, and the wall on which I make my taps and scratches is no longer a cell but this whole prodigal and all too perishable world in which I find myself, very much alive, and not at all alone. As I approach the first anniversary of my diagnosis, as I approach whatever pain is ahead of me, I am trying to get as close to this wall as possible. And I am listening with all I am.

Nominated by Mark Irwin, Katrina Roberts, Diann Blakely, The American Scholar

SATURDAY NIGHT

by ELEANOR WILNER

from POETRY NORTHWEST

Moonlit rocks, sand, and a web of shadows
    thrown over the world from the cottonwoods,
        the manzanita, the ocotillo; it is
the hour of the tarantula, a rising
    as predictable as tide, irritable as
        moon drag. And if this were
an SF film, the spider would be
    huge as a watertank, it would loom
        red-eyed and horrible, its mandibles
wet with drool or blood, and screams
    would be heard as it stumbled
        through the cactus and the brush,
trees upended, small bodies
    crunching in its path; in the distance,
        police cars, lights flashing, sirens blaring,
would be tearing down the highways,
    dust rising in their wake, and cars
        would begin streaming from distant
cities, the terror growing with each
    report of it—the creature, like a figure
        from the bad conscience of the race,
hungry, hairy, would be coming
    for every blonde, she, hiding in a million
        bedrooms, breasts heaving under
filmy white lace . . . but now as the film

runs down, in a rush of stale air
     the hydraulic spider deflates, the saline
leaks from the implants of the bed-
    room blonde, the moon's projection
       clicks off, and the night is as it was,
       a place where fear takes its many
       forms, and the warships gather in
       a distant gulf, where a small man
       with more arms than a hindu god,
       has set a desert alight, and grief blooms;
while here, the theaters are full
    of horror on the screen, and you can hear—
     over the sinister canned music,
the chain-saws, and the screams—the sound
    of Coke sucked up through straws,
      your own jaws moving as you chew.

Nominated by Debra Spark, Marianne Boruch, Poetry Northwest

PROGRESSIVE DINNER

fiction by JOHN BARTH

from NEW LETTERS

1. HORS D'OEUVRES & APPETIZERS

"**H**EY, ROB! Hey, Shirley! Come on in, guys!"

"And the Beckers are right behind us. *Mwah*, Debbie! *Mwah*, Peter!"

"Come in, come in: Name tags on the table there, everybody. Drinks in the kitchen, goodies in the dining room and out on the deck. Yo there, Jeff and Marsha!"

"You made your taco dip, Sandy! Hooray! And Shirley brought those jalapeño thingies that Pete can't keep hands off of. Come on in, Tom and Patsy!"

TIME: *The late afternoon/early evening of a blossom-rich late-May North Temperate Zone Saturday, half a dozen springtimes into the new millennium. Warm enough for open doors and windows and for use of decks and patios, but not yet sultry enough to require air conditioning, and still too early for serious mosquitoes.*

"So: Did you folks see the SOLD sign on the Feltons' place?"

"No! Since when?"

"Since this morning, Tom Hardison tells us. We'll ask Jeff Pitt when he and Marsha get here; he'll know what's what."

"The poor Feltons! We still can't get over it!"

"Lots of questions still unanswered there, for sure. Where d'you want this smoked bluefish spread, Deb?"

"In my mouth, just as soon as possible! Here, I'll take it; you guys go get yourself a drink. Hey there, Ashtons!"

PLACE: *908 Cattail Court, Rockfish Reach, Heron Bay Estates, Stratford, Avon County, Upper Eastern Shore of Maryland, 21600: an ample and solidly constructed two-story hip-roofed dormer-windowed Dutch Colonial style dwelling of white brick with black shutters and doors, slate roof, flagstone front walk and porch and patio, on Rockfish Cove, off Heron Creek, off the Mattahannock River, off Chesapeake Bay, off the North Atlantic Ocean, etc.*

"So, Doctor Pete: What's your take on the latest bad news from Baghdad?"

"You know what I think, Tom. What all of us ivory-tower-liberal academics think: that we had no business grabbing that tar-baby in the first place, but our President lied us into there and now we're stuck with it. Here's to you, friend."

"Yeah, well: Cheers? Hey, Peg: We all love our great new mail-boxes! You guys did a terrific job!"

"Didn't they, though? Those old wooden ones were just rotting away."

"And these new cast-metal jobs are even handsomer than the ones in Spartina Pointe. Good work, guys."

"You're quite welcome. Thanks for this, Deb and Pete and everybody. *Mmm!*"

"So where're the Pitts, I wonder?"

"Speak of the Devil! Hi there, Marsha; hi ho, Jeff! And you-all are . . . ?"

OCCASION: *The now-traditional "season"-opening Progressive Dinner in Heron Bay's Rockfish Reach subdivision, a pleasantly laid out and landscaped two-decade-old neighborhood of some four dozen houses in various architectural styles, typically 3-bedroom, 2 1/2-bath affairs with attached two-car garage, screened or open porches, decks and/or patios, perhaps a basement, perhaps even a boat dock, all on low-lying, marsh-fringed acre-and-a-half lots. Of the nearly fifty families who call the place Home, most are empty- or all-but-empty-nesters, their children grown and flown. About half are more or less retired, although some still work out of home offices. Perhaps a third have second homes elsewhere, either in the Baltimore/Washing-*

ton or Wilmington/Philadelphia areas where they once worked, or in the Florida coastal developments whereto they migrate with other East Coast "snowbirds" for the winter. Half a dozen of the most community-spirited from the Reach's Shoreside Drive and its adjacent Cattail and Loblolly Courts function as an informal neighborhood association, planning such community events and improvements as those above-mentioned new dark green cast-metal mailboxes (paid for by a special assessment), the midsummer Rockfish Reach BYOB sunset cruise down the Mattahannock from the Heron Bay Marina, and the fall picnic (in one of HBE's two pavilioned waterside parks) that unofficially closes the "season" unofficially opened by the Progressive Dinner here in early progress.

As usual, invitation notices were distributed to all four dozen households a month before the occasion, rubber-banded to the decorative knobs atop those new mailboxes. Also as usual, between fifteen and twenty couples signed on and paid the $40-per-person fee, the others being either bespoken already for the scheduled evening or simply disinclined to this sort of thing. Of the participating households (all of whom have been asked to provide, in addition to their fee, either an hors d'oeuvre/appetizer or a dessert, please indicate which), six or seven will have volunteered to be hosts as well: one for the buffet-and-bar opening course presently being enjoyed by all hands, perhaps four for the sit-down entrée (supplied by a Stratford caterer; check your name-tag to see which entrée house you've been assigned to), and one for the all-together-again dessert buffet that winds up the festive occasion. The jollity of which, this spring, has been somewhat beclouded—as was that of last December's Rockfish Reach "Winter Holiday" party—by the apparent double suicide, still unexplained, of Richard and Susan Felton (themselves once active participants in these neighborhood events) by automobile exhaust-fume inhalation in their closed garage at 1020 Shoreside Drive, just after Tom and Patsy Hardison's elaborate Toga Party last September to inaugurate their new house on Loblolly Court. Recommended dress for the Progressive Dinner is "Country Club Casual": slacks and sport shirts for the gentlemen (jackets optional); pants or skirts and simple blouses for the ladies.

"Hi there. Jeff insists that we leave it to him to do the honors."

"*And* to apologize for this late addition to the guest list, and to cover the two extra plate charges, and to fill in the name tags—all

240

courtesy of Avon Realty, guys, where we agents do our best to earn our commissions. *May I have your attention, everybody?* This handsome young stud and his blushing bride are your new about-to-be neighbors Joe and Judy Barnes, formerly and still temporarily from over in Egret's Crest, but soon to move into Number Ten Twenty Shoreside Drive! Joe and Judy, this is Dean Peter Simpson, from the College, and his soulmate Deborah, also from the College."

"Welcome to Rockfish Reach, Joe and Judy. What a pleasant surprise!"

"Happy to be here. . . Dean and Mrs. Simpson."

"Please, guys: We're Debbie and Pete."

"*Lovely* house, Debbie! And do forgive us for showing up empty-handed. Everything happened so *fast!*. . ."

"No problem, no problem. If I know Marsha Pitt, she's probably brought an hors d'oeuvre *and* a dessert."

"Guilty as charged, Your Honor. Cheesecake's in the cooler out in our car for later at the Greens'; I'll put these doodads out with the rest of the finger-food."

"And *your* new house is a lovely one too, Judy and Joe. Pete and I have always admired that place."

"Thanks for saying so. Of course our daughters are convinced it'll be haunted! One of them's up at the College, by the way, and her kid sister will be joining her there next year, but they'll still be coming home most weekends and such."

"We hope!"

"Oh my, how *wonderful* . . . Excuse me. . . ."

"So! Go on in, people: Jeff and Marsha will introduce you around, and we'll follow shortly."

"Aye aye, Cap'n. The Barneses will be doing their entrée with us, by the way. We've got plenty of extra seating, and they've promised not to say that our house is the Pitts'."

"*Eew,* sweetheart: *You* promised not to resurrect that tired old joke! Come on, Joe and Judy; let's get some wine."

("You okay, hon?"

"I'll make it. But that Daughters thing really hit home."

"Yup. Here's a Kleenex. On with the party?")

HOSTS: *The "Associates": Deborah Clive Simpson, 57, Associate Librarian at Stratford College's Dexter Library, and Peter Alan Simpson, also 57, longtime Professor of Humanities and presently*

*Associate Dean at that same quite good small institution, traditionally
a liberal arts college but currently expanding its programs in the sci-
ences, thanks to a munificent bequest from a late alumnus who made
a fortune in the pharmaceuticals business. The Simpsons are child-
less, their only offspring, a much-prized daughter, having been killed
two years ago in a multi-car crash on the Baltimore Beltway during
an ice storm in the winter of her sophomore year as a pre-medical
student at the Johns Hopkins University. Her loss remains a trauma
from which her parents do not expect ever to "recover"; the very term
closure, so fashionable nowadays, sets their teeth on edge, and the co-
inciding of Julie's death and Peter's well-earned promotion to Associ-
ate Dean has leached much pleasure from the latter. Nevertheless,
in an effort to "get on with their lives," the Simpsons last year
exchanged their very modest house in Stratford—so rich in now-
painful memories of child-rearing and of the couple's advancement
up the academic ladder from relative penury to financial comfort—
for their present Rockfish Reach address, and they're doing their best
to be active members of both their collegiate and their residential
communities as well as generous supporters of such worthy organiza-
tions as Doctors Without Borders (Médecins Sans Frontières), to
which it had been Julie's ambition to devote herself once she attained
her M.D.*

"So we bet those new folks—what's their name?"

"Barnes. Joe and Judy. He's with Lucas and Jones in Stratford, and
she teaches at the Fenton School. They seem nice."

"We bet they got themselves a bargain on the Feltons' place."

"More power to 'em, *I* say: All's fair in love, war, and real estate."

"Don't miss Peggy Ashton's tuna spread, Rob; I'm going for an-
other white wine spritzer."

"Make that two, okay? But no spritz in mine, please. So, Lisa:
What were you starting to say about the name tags?"

"Oh, just that looking around at tonight's name tags reminded me
that friends of ours over in Oyster Cove told us once that nine out of
ten husbands in Heron Bay Estates are called by one-syllable first
names and their wives by two-syllable ones: You Rob-and-Shirley, we
Dave-and-Lisa, et cetera."

"Hey, that's right; I hadn't noticed!"

"And what exactly does one make of that sociocultural infobit, *s'il
vous plait*?"

"I'll let you know, Pete-and-Debbie, soon's I figure it out. Meanwhile . . ."

"What I notice, guys—every time I'm in the supermarket or Wal-Mart?—is that more and more older and overweight Americans—"

"Like us?"

"Like some of us, anyhow—go prowling down the aisles bent forward like *this*, with arms and upper body resting on their shopping cart as if it were some kind of a walker. . . ."

"And their fat butts waggling, often in pink warm-up pants. . . ."

"Now is that nice to say?"

"It's what Pete calls the American Consumer Crouch. *I* say 'Whatever floats your boat. . . .'"

"*And* keeps the economy perking along. Am I right, Joe Barnes?"

"Right you are, Jeff."

"So, Deb: *You* were saying something earlier about a long letter that Pete got out of the blue from some girl in Uganda?"

"Oh, right, wow: *that*. . . ."

"Uganda?"

"I should let Pete tell you about it. Where are you and Paul doing your entrée?"

"Practically next door. At the Beckers'?"

"Us, too. So he'll explain it there. Very touching—but who knows whether it's for real or a scam? Oh, hey, Pat: Have you and Tom met the Barneses? Joe and Judy Barnes, Tom and Patsy Hardison, from Loblolly Court."

"Jeff Pitt introduced us already, Deb. Hello again, Barneses."

"Hi there. We've been hearing great things about your Toga Party last fall! Sounds cool!"

"All but the ending, huh? We can't *imagine* what happened with Dick and Susan Felton that night. . . ."

"Has to've been some kind of freak accident; let's don't spoil this party with that one. Welcome to Rockfish Reach!"

"Joe and I love it already. And your place on Loblolly Court is just incredible!"

"Jeff pointed it out to us when we first toured the neighborhood. Really magnificent!"

"Thanks for saying so. An eyesore, some folks think, but it's what we wanted, so we built it. You're the new boss at Lucas and Jones, in town?"

"I am—and *my* boss, over in Baltimore, is the guy who stepped on lots of folks' toes with that tear-down over in Spartina Pointe. Maybe you know him: Mark Matthews?"

"Oh, we know Mark, all right: a man after my own heart."

"Mine, too, Tom: Decide what you want, go for it, and let the chips fall where they may."

"Well, now, people: Excuse me for butting in, but to us lonely left-wing-Democrat dentist types, that sounds a lot like our current president and his gang."

"Whoa-ho, Doctor David! Let's not go there, okay? This is Lisa Bergman's husband, Dave, guys: He pulls teeth for a living."

"And steps on toes for fun. Pleased to meet you, folks."

"Entrée time in twenty minutes, everybody! Grab yourselves another sip and nibble, check your tags for your sit-down dinner address, and we'll all reconvene for dessert with the Greens at nine!"

"So, that Barnes couple: Are they golfers, d'you know?"

2. ENTRÉE

The assembled now disperse from the Simpsons' to shift their automobiles or stroll on foot to their various main-course addresses, their four host couples having left a bit earlier to confirm that all is ready and to be in place to greet their guests. Of these latter, four will dine with George and Christie Walsh on Shoreside Drive; six (including the newcomer Barneses) with Jeff and Marsha Pitt, also on Shoreside; eight (the Ashtons, Bergmans, Greens, and Simpsons) with Pete and Debbie's Cattail Court near-neighbors Charles and Sandy Becker; and ten with Tom and Patsy Hardison over on Loblolly Court. Stratford Catering's entrée menu for the evening is simple but well prepared: a caesar salad with optional anchovies, followed by Maryland crab cakes with garlic mashed potatoes and a steamed broccoli/zucchini mix, the vegetables cooked in advance and reheated, the crab cakes prepared in advance but griddled on-site, three minutes on each side, and the whole accompanied by mineral water and one's choice of pinot grigio or iced tea.

The Becker group all go on foot, chatting together as they pass under the streetlights in the mild evening air, their destination being just two houses down from the Simpsons' on the opposite side of the cul-de-sac "court." To no one in particular, Shirley Green remarks, "Somebody was wondering earlier whether the Barneses got a bargain price on the Feltons' house? None of our business, but *I* can't help wondering whether the Beckers' house number affects *their* property value. . . ."

"Aiyi," Peggy Ashton exclaims in mock dismay: "*Nine-Eleven* Cattail Court! I hadn't thought of that!"

If *he* were Chuck Becker, Rob Green declares to the group, he'd use that unfortunate coincidence to appeal their property-tax assessment. "I mean, hell, Dick and Susan Felton were just two people, rest their souls. Whereas, what was it, three *thousand* and some died on Nine Eleven? That ought to count for something. . . ."

His wife punches his shoulder. "Rob, I *swear!*"

Walking backward to face the group, he turns up his palms: "Can't help it, folks: We accountants try to take everything into account."

Hisses and groans. Peter Simpson takes his wife's hand as they approach their destination. He's relieved that the Barneses, although certainly pleasant-seeming people, won't be at table with them for the sit-down dinner to distress Debbie further with innocent talk of their college-age daughters.

The Beckers' house, while no *palazzo* like the Hardisons', is an imposing two-story white brick Colonial, its columned central portico flanked by a guest wing on one side and a garage wing on the other with two large doors for cars and a smaller one for golf cart and bicycles. The eight guests make their way up the softly lighted entrance drive to the brightly lit main entry to be greeted by ruddy-hefty, bald-pated, silver-fringed Charles Becker, a politically conservative septuagenarian with the self-assured forcefulness of the CEO he once was, and his no-longer-sandyhaired Sandy, less vigorous of aspect after last year's successful surgery for a "growth" on her left lung, but still active in the neighborhood association, her Episcopal church in Stratford, and the Heron Bay Club. Once all have been welcomed and seated in the Beckers' high-ceilinged dining room, the drinks poured, and the salad served, their host taps his water-glass with a table-knife for attention and says, "Let's take hands and bow our heads for the blessing, please."

The Simpsons, seated side by side at his right hand, glance at each other uncomfortably, they being non-believers, and at the Bergmans, looking equally discomfited across the table from them. More for their sake than for her own, Debbie asks, as if teasingly, "Whatever happened to the separation of Church and Dinner Party?" To which Charles Becker replies smoothly, "In a Christian household, do as the Christians do," and takes her left hand in his right and Lisa

Bergman's right in his left. David shrugs his eyebrows at Pete and goes along with it, joining hands with his wife on one side and with Shirley Green on the other. Peter follows suit, taking Debbie's right hand in his left and Peggy Ashton's left in his right; but the foursome neither close eyes nor lower heads with the others while their host intones, *"Be present at our table, Lord / Be here and everywhere adored. / These mercies bless, and grant that we / May feast in Paradise with Thee. Amen."*

"And," Paul Ashton adds at once to lighten the little tension at the table, "grant us stomach-room enough for this entrée after all those appetizers!"

"Amen and *bon appetit*," proposes Sandy Becker, raising her wineglass. "Everybody dig in, and then I'll do the crab cakes while Chuck serves up the veggies."

"Such appetizers they were!" Lisa Bergman marvels, and then asks Paul whether he happens, like her, to be a Gemini. He is, in fact, he replies: "Got a birthday coming up next week. Why?"

"Because," Lisa declares, "it's a well-known fact that we Geminis prefer hors d'oeuvres to entrées. No offense intended, Sandy and Chuck!"

Her husband winks broadly. "It's true even in bed, so I've heard— no offense intended, Paul and Lisa. . . ."

Sipping their drinks and exchanging further such teases and pleasantries, all hands duly address the caesar salad, the passed-around optional anchovy fillets, and the pre-sliced baguettes. Although tempted to pursue what she regards as a presumption on their host's part that everyone in their community is a practicing Christian, or that because the majority happen to be, any others should join in uncomplainingly, Debbie Simpson holds her tongue—as she did not when, for example, the neighborhood association proposed Christmas lights last winter on the entrance signs to Rockfish Reach (she won that one, readily granting the right of all residents to decorate their houses, but not community property, with whatever religious symbols they cared to display), and when the Heron Bay Association put up its large Christmas tree at the development's main gatehouse (that one she lost, and, at Pete's request, didn't pursue it, they being new residents whom he would prefer not be branded as troublemakers). She gives his left hand a squeeze by way of assuring him that she's letting the table-grace issue drop.

"So tell us about that strange letter you got, Pete," Peggy Ashton

246

proposes. "From Uganda, was it? That Deb mentioned during Appetizers?"

"Uganda?" the hostess marvels, or anyhow asks.

"*Very* strange," Peter obligingly tells the table. "I suppose we've all gotten crank letters now and then—get-rich scams in Liberia and like that?—but this one was really different." To begin with, he explains, it wasn't a photocopied typescript like the usual mass-mailed scam letter, but a neatly handwritten appeal on two sides of a legal-size ruled sheet, with occasional cross-outs and misspellings. Polite, articulate, and addressed to "Dear Friend," it was or purported to be from a seventeen-year-old Ugandan girl, the eldest of five children whose mother had died in childbirth and whose father had succumbed to AIDS. Since their parents' death, the siblings have been lodged with an uncle, also suffering from AIDS and with five children of his own. Those he dresses properly and sends to school, the letter-writer declares, but she and her four brothers and sisters are treated harshly by him and his wife, who "don't recognize [them] as human beings." Dismissed from school for lack of fee money and provided with "only two clothes each" to wear and little or nothing to eat, they are made to graze the family's goats, feed the pigs, and do all the hard and dirty housework from morning till night. In a few months, when she turns eighteen, she'll be obliged to become one of some man's several wives, a fate she fears both because of the AIDS epidemic and because it will leave her siblings unprotected. Having (unlike them) completed her secondary education prior to her father's death, she appeals to her "dear Friend" to help her raise 1,500 Euros to "join university for a degree in education" and 1,200 Euros for her siblings to finish high school. Attached to the letter was a printed deposit slip from Barclay's Bank of Uganda, complete with the letter-writer's name and account number followed by the stipulation "F/O CHILDREN."

"How she got *my* name and address, I can't imagine," Pete concludes to the hushed and attentive table. "If it was in some big general directory or academic Who's Who, how'd she get hold of it, and how many hundreds of these things did she write out by hand and mail?"

"And where'd she get paper and envelopes and deposit slips and postage stamps," Lisa Bergman wonders, "if they're so dirt poor?"

"And the time to scribble scribble," Paul Ashton adds, "while they're managing the goats and pigs and doing all the scut-work."

Opines Rob the Accountant, "It doesn't add up."

"It does seem questionable," Sandy Becker agrees.

"But if you could see the letter!" Debbie protests: "So earnest and articulate, but so un-slick! Lines like *We do not hope that our uncle will recover*. And *I can't leave my siblings alone: We remained five and we should stick five*."

Taking her hand in his again and using his free hand to make finger-quotes, Pete adds, "And, quote, *Life unbearable, we only pray hard to kind people to help us go back to school, because the most learnt here is more chance of getting good job*, end of quote."

"It's heartbreaking," Shirley Green acknowledges. "No wonder you-all have so much of it memorized!"

"But the bottom line," Chuck Becker declares, "is Did you fall for it? Because believe me, it's a goddamn scam."

"You really think so?" Dave Bergman asks.

"Of course it is! Some sharpster with seven wives and Internet access for tracking down addresses sets his harem to scribbling out ten copies per wife per day, carefully misspelling a few words and scratching out a few more, just to see who'll take the bait. Probably some mid-level manager at Barclay's with a PC in his office and a fake account in one of his twelve daughters' names."

"How can you be so *sure*?" Lisa Bergman wants to know.

With the air of one accustomed to having his word taken, "Take my word for it, sweetie," their host replies. Downtable to his wife then, "Better get the crab cakes started, Sandy?" And to the Simpsons, "Please tell me you didn't send 'em a nickel."

"We didn't," Debbie assures him. "Not yet, anyhow. Because of course we're leery of the whole thing too. But just suppose, Chuck and everybody—just *suppose* it happens to be authentic? Imagine the courage and resourcefulness of a seventeen-year-old girl in that wretched situation, with all that traumatic stuff behind her and more of it waiting down the road, but she manages somehow to get hold of a bunch of American addresses and a pen and paper and stamps and deposit slips, and she scratches out this last-chance plea for a *life* . . . Suppose it's for real?"

"And we-all sit here in our gated community," Lisa Bergman joins in, "with our Lexuses and golf carts and our parties and progressive dinners, and we turn up our noses and say, 'It's a scam; don't be suckered.' "

"So what *should* we do?" Paul Ashton mildly challenges her: "Bet a hundred bucks apiece on the *very* long shot that it's not a shyster?"

"I'm almost willing to," Shirley Green admits. Her husband shakes his head No.

"What we *ought* to do, of course," Dave Bergman declares, "is go to some trouble to find out whether the thing's for real. A *lot* of trouble, if necessary. Like write back to her, telling her we'd like to help but we need more bona fides. Find out how she got Pete's name and address. Ask the American consulate in Kampala or wherever to check her story out. Is that in Uganda?"

"You mean," his wife wonders or suggests, "make a community project out of it?"

Asks Debbie, "Why not?"

"Because," Rob Green replies, "I, for one, don't have time for it. Got a full plate already." He checks his watch. "Or soon will have, won't we, Shirl?"

"Same here," Dave Bergman acknowledges. "I know I ought to *make* time for things like this, but I also know I won't. It's like demonstrating against the war in Iraq, the way so many of us did against the war in Vietnam? Or even like working to get out the vote on election day. My hat's off to people who act that strongly on their convictions, and I used to be one of them, but I've come to accept that I'm just *not* any more. Morally lazy these days, I guess, but at least honest about it."

"And in this case," Chuck Becker says with ruddy-faced finality, "you're saving yourself a lot of wasted effort. Probably in those other cases too, but never mind that."

"Oh my goodness," his wife exclaims. "Look what time it is! I'll do the crab cakes, Chuck'll get the veggies, and Paul, would you mind refreshing everybody's drinks? Or we'll never get done before it's time to move on to Rob and Shirley's!"

3. Dessert

The Greens' place on Shoreside Drive, toward which all three dozen Progressive Diners now make their well-fed way from the several entrée houses to reassemble for the dessert course, is no more than a few blocks distant from the Becker and Simpson residences on Cattail Court—although the attractively winding streets of Heron Bay Estates aren't really measurable in "blocks." Chuck and Sandy Becker, who had earlier walked from their house to Pete and Debbie

Simpson's (virtually next door) for the appetizer course, and then back to their own place to host the entrée, decide now to drive to the final course of the evening in their Cadillac Escalade. The Greens themselves, having left the Beckers' a quarter-hour earlier to make ready, drove also, retrieving their Honda van from where they'd parked it in front of the Simpsons'. The Ashtons, Paul and Peggy, walk only far enough to collect their Lexus from the Simpsons' drive-way and then motor on. Of the five couples who did their entrée at 911 Cattail Court, only the Simpsons themselves and the Bergmans decide that the night air is too inviting not to stroll through it to Rob and Shirley's; they decline the proffered lifts in favor of savoring the mild westerly breeze, settling their crab cakes and vegetables a bit before tackling the dessert smorgasbord, and chatting among them-selves en route.

"That Chuck, I swear," Lisa Bergman says as the Beckers' luxury SUV rolls by: "So *sure* he's right about everything! And Sandy just goes along with it."

"Maybe she agrees with him?" Peter suggests. "Anyhow, they're good neighbors, even if Chuck can be borderline insufferable now and then."

"I'll second that," Dave Bergman grants. Not to walk four abreast down a nighttime street with no sidewalks, the two men then drop back a bit to carry on their conversation while their wives, a few feet ahead, speak of other things. Charles Becker, David goes on, likes to describe himself as a self-made man, and in considerable measure he is: From humble beginnings as a small-town carpenter's son—

"Sounds sort of familiar," Peter can't help commenting, "except our Chuck's not about to let himself get crucified."

"Anyhow, served in the Navy during World War II; came home and went to college on the G.I. Bill to study engineering; worked a few years for a suburban D.C. contractor in the postwar housing boom; then started his own business and did very well indeed, as he does not tire of letting his dentist and others know. No hand-scrawled Send Me Money letters for *him*. 'God helps those who help themselves,' et cetera."

"Right: the way he helped himself to free college tuition and other benefits not readily available to your average Ugandan orphan girl. Hey, look: Sure enough, there's Jeff Pitt's latest score. . . ."

Peter means the SOLD sticker on the FOR SALE sign (with *The Jeff Pitt Team* lettered under it) in front of 1020 Shoreside Drive, the former residence of Richard and Susan Felton. The women, too, pause before it—their conversation having moved from the Beckers to the Bergmans' Philadelphia daughter's latest project for her parents: to establish a Jewish community organization in Stratford, in alliance with the College's modest Hillel club for its handful of Jewish students. Lisa is interested; David isn't quite convinced that the old town is ready yet for that sort of thing.

"The Feltons," he says now, shaking his head. "I guess we'll never understand."

"What do you mean?" Debbie challenges him. "I think *I* understand it perfectly well."

"What do *you* mean?" David cordially challenges back. "They were both in good health, comfortably retired, no family problems that anybody knows of, well liked in the neighborhood—and *wham*, they come home from the Hardisons' toga party and off themselves!"

"And," Peter adds, "their son and daughter not only get the news secondhand, with no advance warning and no note of explanation or apology, but then have to put their own lives on hold and fly in from wherever to dispose of their parents' bodies and house and belongings."

"What a thing to lay on your kids!" Lisa agrees. The four resume walking the short remaining distance to the Greens'. "And you think that's just fine, Deb?"

"Not 'just fine,'" Debbie counters: "*understandable*. I agree that their kids deserved some explanation, if maybe not advance notice, since then they'd've done all they could to prevent its happening." What she means, she explains, is simply that she quite understands how a couple at the Felton's age and stage—entering their seventies after a prevailingly happy, successful, and catastrophe-free life together, their children and grandkids grown and scattered, the family's relations reportedly affectionate but not especially close, the parents' careers behind them along with four decades of good marriage, nothing better to look forward to than the infirmities, losses, and burdensome caretaking of old age, and no religious prohibitions against self-termination—how such a couple might just decide Hey, it's been a good life; we've been lucky to have had it and each other all these years; let's end it peacefully and painlessly before things go downhill, which is really the only way they can go from here.

"And let our friends and neighbors and children clean up the mess?" David presses her. "Would you and Pete do that to us?"

251

"Count *me* out," Peter declares. "For another couple decades anyhow, unless the world goes to hell even faster than it's going now."

"In our case," his wife reminds the Bergmans, "it's friends, neighbors, and *colleagues*. Don't think we haven't talked about it more than once since Julie's death. I've even checked it out on the Web, for when the time comes."

"On the *Web*?" Lisa takes her friend's arm.

Surprised, concerned, and a little embarrassed, "The things you learn about your mate at a Progressive Dinner!" Peter marvels to David, who then jokingly complains that he hasn't learned a single interesting thing so far about *his* mate.

"Don't give up on me," his wife recommends: "The party's not over."

"Right you are," Debbie agrees, "literally and figuratively. And here we are, and I'll try to shut up."

The Greens' house, brightly lit, with a dozen or more cars now parked before it, is a boxy two-story beige vinyl clapboard-sided affair, unostentatious but commodious and well-maintained, with fake-shuttered windows all around, and on its creek side a large screened porch, open patio, pool, and small-boat dock. Shirley Green being active in the Heron Bay Estates Garden Club, the property is handsomely landscaped: The abundant rhododendrons, azaleas, and flowering trees have already finished blossoming for the season, but begonias, geraniums, daylilies, and roses abound along the front walk and driveway, around the foundation, and in numerous planters. As the foursome approach, the Bergmans tactfully walk a few paces ahead. Peter takes his wife's arm to comfort her.

"Sorry sorry sorry," she apologizes again. "You know I wouldn't be thinking these things if we hadn't lost Julie." Her voice thickens. "She'd be fresh out of college now and headed for med school!" She can say no more.

"I know, I know." As indeed Peter does, having been painfully reminded of that circumstance as he helped preside over Stratford's recent commencement exercises instead of attending their daughter's at Johns Hopkins. Off to medical school she'd be preparing herself now to go, for arduous but happy years of general training, then specialization, internship, and residency; no doubt she'd meet and bond with some fellow physician-in-training along the way, and he and Debbie would help plan the wedding with her and their prospective

252

son-in-law and look forward to grandchildren down the line to brighten their elder years, instead of Googling *suicide* on the Web. . . .

Briefly but appreciatively she presses her forehead against his shoulder. Preceded by the Bergmans and followed now by other dessert-course arrivers, they make their way front-doorward to be greeted by eternally boyish Rob and ever-effervescent Shirley Green.

"Sweets are out on the porch, guys; wine and decaf in the kitchen. Beautiful evening, isn't it?"

"Better enjoy it while we can, I guess, before the hurricanes come."

"Yo there, Barneses! What do you think of your new neighborhood so far?"

"Totally awesome! Nothing like this over in Egret's Crest."

"We can't wait to move in, ghosts or no ghosts. Our daughter Tiffany's off to France for six weeks, but it's the rest of the family's summer project."

"So enjoy every minute of it. Shall we check out the goodies, Deb?"

"Calories, here we come! Excuse us, people."

But over chocolate cheesecake and decaffeinated coffee on the torchlit patio, Judy Barnes reapproaches Debbie to report that Marsha Pitt, their entrée hostess, told them the terrible news of the Simpsons' daughter's accident. "Joe and I are *so* sorry for you and Peter! We can't *imagine*. . . ."

All appetite gone, "Neither can we," Debbie assures her. "We've quit trying to."

And just a few minutes later, as the Simpsons are conferring on how soon they can leave without seeming rude, Paul and Peggy Ashton come over, each with a glass of pale sherry in one hand and a chocolate fudge brownie in the other, to announce their solution to that Ugandan Orphan Girl business.

"Can't wait to hear it," Peter says dryly. "Will Chuck Becker approve?"

"Chuck schmuck," says Paul, who has picked up a few Yiddishisms from the Bergmans. "The folks who brought you your dandy new mailboxes now propose a Rockfish Reach Ad Hoc Search and Rescue Committee. Tell 'em, Peg."

She does, emphasizing her points with a half-eaten brownie. The informal committee's initial members would be the three couples at dinner who seemed most sympathetic to Pete's story and to the possibility that the letter was authentic: themselves, the Bergmans, and of course the Simpsons. Peter would provide them with copies of the letter; Paul Ashton, whose legal expertise was at their service, would find out how they could go about verifying the thing's authenticity, as David Bergman had suggested at the Beckers'. If it turned out to be for real, they would then circulate an appeal through Rockfish Reach, maybe through all of Heron Bay Estates, to raise money toward the girl's rescue: not a blank check that her uncle and aunt might oblige her to cash for their benefit, but some sort of tuition fund that the committee could disburse or at least oversee and authorize payments from.

"Maybe even a scholarship at Stratford?" Paul Ashton suggests to Peter. "I know you have a few foreign students from time to time, but none from Equatorial Africa, I'll bet."

"Doesn't sound impossible, actually," Peter grants, warming to the idea while at the same time monitoring his wife's reaction. "*If* she's legit, and qualified. Our African-American student organization could take her in."

"And our Heron Bay Search and Rescue Squad could unofficially adopt her!" Lisa Bergman here joins in, whom the Ashtons have evidently briefed already on their proposal. "Having another teenager to keep out of trouble will make us all feel young again! Whatcha think, Deb?"

To give her time to consider, Peter reminds them that there remains the problem of the girl's younger siblings, whom she's resolved not to abandon: *We remained five and we should stick five*, et cetera. Whereas if she "went to university" in Kampala for at least the first couple of years, say, she could see the youngsters into high school and then maybe come to Stratford for her junior or senior year. . . .

"Listen to us!" he laughs. "And we don't even know yet whether the girl's for real!"

"But we can find out," David Bergman declares. "And if we can make it happen, or make something *like* it happen, it'll be a credit to Heron Bay Estates. Make us feel a little better about our golf and tennis and Progressive Dinners. Okay, so it's only one kid out of millions, but at least it's one: I say let's do it."

"And then Pete and I officially adopt her as our daughter," Debbie says at last, in a tone that her husband can't assess at all, "and we stop eating our hearts out about losing Julie, and everybody lives happily ever after."

"Deb?" Lisa puts an arm around her friend's shoulder.

"Alternatively," Debbie suggests to them then, "we could start a Dick and Susan Felton Let's Get It Over With Club, and borrow the Barneses' new garage for our first meeting. Meanwhile, let's enjoy the party, okay?" And she moves off toward where the Pitts, the Hardisons, and a few others are chatting beside the lighted pool. To their friends, Peter turns up his palms, as best one can with a cup of decaf in one hand and its saucer in the other, and follows after his wife, wondering and worrying what lies ahead for them—tonight, tomorrow, and in the days and years beyond. They have each other, their work, their colleagues and friends and neighbors, their not-all-that close extended family (parents dead, no siblings on Debbie's side, one seven-year-older sister of Peter's out in Texas, from whom he's been more or less distanced for decades), their various pastimes and pleasures, their still prevailingly good health—for who knows how much longer? And then. And then. While over in Uganda and Darfur, and down in Haiti, and in Guantánamo and Abu Ghraib and the world's multitudinous other hell holes. . . .

"They had *nothing* like this back in Egret's Crest, man!" he hears Joe Barnes happily exclaiming to the Greens. "Just a sort of block party once, and that was it."

"Feltons or no Feltons," Judy Barnes adds, "we've made the right move."

Nearby, florid Chuck Becker is actually thrusting a forefinger at David Bergman's chest: "We cut and run from I-raq now, there'll be hell to pay. Got to *stay the course.*"

"Like we did in 'Nam, right?" unintimidated Dave comes back at him. "And drill the living shit out of Alaska and the Gulf Coast, I guess you think, if that's what it takes to get the last few barrels of oil? Gimme a break, Chuck!"

"Take it from your friendly neighborhood realtor, folks," Jeff Pitt is declaring to the Ashtons: "Whatever you have against a second Bay bridge—say from South Baltimore straight over to Avon County?— it'll raise your property values a hundred percent in no time at all, the way the state's population is booming. We won't be able to build condos and housing developments fast enough to keep up!"

Peggy Ashton: "So there goes the neighborhood, right? And it's bye-bye Chesapeake Bay. . ."

Paul: "*And* bye-bye national forest lands and glaciers and polar ice caps. Get me outta here!"

Patsy Hardison, to Peter's own dear Deborah: "So, did you and Pete see that episode that Tom mentioned before, that he and all the TV critics thought was so great and I couldn't even watch? I suspect it's a Mars-versus-Venus thing."

"Sorry," his wife replies: "We must be the only family in Heron Bay Estates that doesn't get HBO." Her eyes meet his, neutrally.

Chuckling and lifting his coffee cup in salute as he joins the pair, "We don't even have *cable*," Peter confesses. "Just an old-style antenna up on the roof. Now is that academic snobbishness, or what?" He sets cup and saucer on a nearby table and puts an arm about his wife's waist, a gesture that she seems neither to welcome nor to resist. He has no idea where their lives are headed. Quite possibly, he supposes, she doesn't either.

Up near the house, an old-fashioned post-mounted schoolbell clangs: The Greens use it to summon grandkids and other family visitors in for meals. Rob Green, standing by it, calls out *"Attention, all hands!"* and when the conversation quiets, "Just want to remind you to put the Rockfish Reach Sunset Cruise on your calendars: Saturday July Fifteenth, Heron Bay Marina, seven to nine p.m.! We'll be sending out reminders as the time approaches, but *save the date*, okay?"

"Got it," Joe Barnes calls back from somewhere nearby: "July Fifteenth, seven p.m."

From the porch Chuck Becker adds loudly, "God bless us all! And God bless America!"

Several voices murmur "Amen." Looking up and away with a sigh of mild annoyance, Peter Simpson happens at just that moment to see a meteor streak left to right across the moonless, brightly constellated eastern sky.

So what? he asks himself.

So nothing.

Nominated by Kim Addonizio

LOVE, OR SOMETHING

by CHRIS FORHAN

from PLOUGHSHARES

The way, at last, a sloop goes sailorless and bobs at the dock,
    swathed in darkness,
the way waves swell and, swelling, slay themselves—
water, whatever you want, I want to want that.

A nickel's in the till, then it's not, it's in a pocket, forgotten,
and the pocket's in a laundry chute. A puddle's in the parking
    lot, drying
to a ring of rust, asphalt buckling from something under it.

Conspiracy of earth and air in me, slip me your secret,
    I won't fret,
you want me stoneground, I want to want that. I want
the fire to find me ready. Let it be not scorn or pluck

I summon as I'm swallowed—I'm sick of pluck. Let it be love,
or something like it, assuming love is to the purpose, assuming
I'm not being maudlin, merely human, to bring love up.

Nominated by Judith Kitchen, Mark Halliday

WINDOW OF POSSIBILITY

by ANTHONY DOERR

from ORION

W E LIVE ON EARTH. Earth is a clump of iron and magnesium and nickel, smeared with a thin layer of organic matter, and sleeved in vapor. It whirls along in a nearly circular orbit around a minor star we call the sun.

I know, the sun doesn't *seem* minor. The sun puts the energy in our salads, milkshakes, hamburgers, gas tanks, and oceans. It literally makes the world go round. And it's huge: The Earth is a chickpea and the sun is a beach ball. The sun comprises 99.9 percent of all the mass in the solar system. Which means Earth, Mars, Jupiter, Saturn, etc., all fit into that little 0.1 percent.

But, truly, our sun is exceedingly minor. Almost incomprehensibly minor.

We call our galaxy the Milky Way. There are at least 100 billion stars in it and our sun is one of those. A hundred billion is a big number, and humans are not evolved to appreciate numbers like that, but here's a try. If you had a bucket with a thousand marbles in it, you would need to procure 999,999 more of those buckets to get a billion marbles. Then you'd have to repeat the process a hundred times to get as many marbles as there are stars in our galaxy.

That's a lot of marbles.

So. The Earth is massive enough to hold all of our cities and oceans and creatures in the sway of its gravity. And the sun is massive enough to hold the Earth in the sway of its gravity. But the sun itself is merely a mote in the sway of the gravity of the Milky Way, at the center of which is a vast, concentrated bar of stars, around which the sun swings (carrying along Earth, Mars, Jupiter, Saturn, etc.) every 230 million years or so. Our sun isn't anywhere near the center, it's way out on one of the galaxy's minor arms. We live beyond the suburbs of the Milky Way. We live in Nowheresville.

But still, we are in the Milky Way. And that's a big deal, right? The Milky Way is at least a major *galaxy*, right?

Not really. Spiral-shaped, toothpick-shaped, sombrero-shaped—in the visible universe, at any given moment, there are hundreds of thousands of millions of galaxies. Maybe as many as 125 billion. There very well may be more galaxies in the universe than there are stars in the Milky Way.

So. Let's say there are 100 billion stars in our galaxy. And let's say there are 100 billion galaxies in our universe. At any given moment, then, assuming ultra-massive and dwarf galaxies average each other out, there might be 10,000,000,000,000,000,000,000 stars in the universe. That's 1.0×10^{22}. That's 10 sextillion.

Here's a way of looking at it: there are enough stars in the universe that if everybody on Earth were charged with naming his or her share, we'd each get to name a trillion and a half of them.

Even that number is still impossibly hard to comprehend—if you named a star every time your heart beat for your whole life, you'd have to live about 375 lifetimes to name your share.

Last year, a handful of astronomers met in London to vote on the top ten images taken by the Hubble Telescope in its sixteen years in operation. They chose some beauties: the Cat's Eye Nebula, the Sombrero Galaxy, the Hourglass Nebula. But conspicuously missing from their list was the Hubble Ultra Deep Field image. It is, I believe, the most incredible photograph ever taken.

In 2003, Hubble astronomers chose a random wedge of sky just below the constellation Orion and, during four hundred orbits of the Earth, over the course of several months, took a photograph with a million-second-long exposure. It was something like peering through an eight-foot soda straw with one big, super-human eye at the same wedge of space for eleven straight nights.

What they found there was breathtaking: a shard of the early universe that contains a bewildering array of galaxies and pregalactic lumps. Scrolling through it is eerily similar to peering at a drop of pond water through a microscope: one expects the galaxies to start squirming like paramecia. It bewilders and disorients; the dark patches swarm with questions. If you peered into just one of its black corners, took an Ultra Deep Field of the Ultra Deep Field, would you see as much all over again?

What the Ultra Deep Field image ultimately offers is a singular glimpse at ourselves. Like Copernicus's *On the Revolutions of the Celestial Spheres*, it resets our understanding of who and what we are.

As of early April 2007, astronomers had found 204 planets outside our solar system. They seem to be everywhere we look. Chances are, many, many stars have planets or systems of planets swinging around them. What if *most* suns have solar systems? If our sun is one in 10 sextillion, could our Earth be one in 10 sextillion as well? Or the Earth might be one—just *one*, the only one, *the* one. Either way, the circumstances are mind-boggling.

The Hubble Ultra Deep Field is an infinitesimally slender core-sample drilled out of the universe. And yet inside it is enough vastness to do violence to a person's common sense. How can the window of possibility be so unfathomably large?

Take yourself out to a field some evening after everyone else is asleep. Listen to the migrant birds whisking past in the dark; listen to the creaking and settling of the world. Think about the teeming, microscopic worlds beneath your shoes—the continents of soil, the galaxies of bacteria. Then lift your face up.

The night sky is the coolest Advent calendar imaginable: it is composed of an infinite number of doors. Open one and find ten thousand galaxies hiding behind it, streaming away at hundreds of miles per second. Open another, and another. You gaze up into history; you stare into the limits of your own understanding. The past flies toward you at the speed of light. Why are you here? Why are the stars there? Is it even remotely possible that our one, tiny, eggshell world is the only one encrusted with life?

The Hubble Ultra Deep Field image should be in every classroom in the world. It should be on the president's desk. It should probably be in every church, too.

"To sense that behind anything that can be experienced," Einstein once said, "there is a something that our mind cannot grasp and whose beauty and sublimity reaches us only indirectly and as a feeble reflection, this is religiousness."

Whatever we believe in—God, children, nationhood—nothing can be more important than to take a moment every now and then and accept the invitation of the sky: to leave the confines of ourselves and fly off into the hugeness of the universe, to disappear into the inexplicable, the implacable, the reflection of that something our minds cannot grasp.

Nominated by Dan Chaon, Orion

BLINDNESS

by CIARAN BERRY

from NOTRE DAME REVIEW

Whether arrived at in the womb or through old age,
　　or because hatred in a hoop skirt and whalebone corset
　　　　has been welcomed as honored guest into your home,

the result, it seemed, was much the same: a darkness
　　emphatic as when the clock's short arm breaks back
　　　　an hour to let the shadows loose over the lawn, to make

welcome the fall's first frost. In double science after lunch,
　　one boy argued it would happen if you touched yourself
　　　　too much or spent too long before the goggle box—

revenge of the body on itself by way of an unraveling
　　within the tissues, humors, rods and cones, so that
　　　　the soul's supposed door could no longer open to usher

in the objects of desire, to carry word and image upside
　　down into the flesh. Those fledgling years the sightless
　　　　were a nation unto themselves, their flag crow-black,

their head-of-state the shopkeeper, whose eyes were like
　　two hardboiled eggs without the shells stirring below
　　　　the jars of clove rock and jawbreakers arranged in rows

across the shelves; whose identical twin was taciturn,
    pure strange, forever, it appeared, *staring* into space.
        They knew far more, I guessed, than we could know

about the grave, about the afterlife, and how the world
    could be so cruel, why in the third act, the seventh scene,
        of the play we were reading that year in school,

the King's daughter must conspire with her husband the Duke,
    who will use just his fingernails to gouge out the Earl's eyes,
        leaving behind these two bloody sockets a loyal servant

will dress, as best they can, with "flax and whites of eggs."
    Our teacher, whose vision was perfect, swore the walk
        to Dover's chalk cliffs, its "crows and choughs," was
            metaphor

for something or other of how the future would describe
    its arc, whispering softly into our ears, then leading us away.
        Later, he told us of the cloistered monk who kept a poker

in the fire until it glowed a bright orange and he applied it
    gently to both eyes, so that the dark he craved would be
        seamless, so that he could not lose his way to what he saw.

Nominated by Eamon Grennan

UNCLE

fiction by SUZANNE RIVECCA

from NEW ENGLAND REVIEW

SHE TOLD THREE MEN. The first stopped sleeping with her right away. Not because she was tainted or anything, he explained. It just put images in his head that were counterproductive to sustaining an erection. He felt terrible.

The second man asked a lot of questions. She didn't want to tell him—this was on the heels of the first man's reaction—but he treated her like the burial site of an ancient civilization; he dug for clues with a sweaty-palmed reverence and did not stop until he held it triumphantly aloft, that sordid tidbit like a saber tooth. He was interested in breeding. He didn't want to marry into a flawed tribe; and for months she wished herself dead and him weeping at her bedside.

The third man was different. He said it wasn't her fault. He said it had happened to him, too, although in less severe form: a random crotch-grab in a public restroom, the culprit a classic drooler in a trenchcoat with one rheumy eye. He had been fourteen and he punched the man in the face, fled the room, hid and cried and told no one. He was, he said, ashamed. He should have run to the nearest authority and turned the drooler in. The unchecked drooler could be fondling innocents at this very moment. He was so vehement on this point that she saw his terrible question coming at her like the fin of a shark, and she shrank inside but there was no escape. "Did you ever tell the police?" he asked, and when she said no, he scolded her for being a passive accomplice to countless evil acts. "You know his name," he said. "You know his address. It's unconscionable!" He continued to ask, "Did you call the police yet?" until she refused to see him.

They were kind men. They deplored sexual deviance. The third one once said to her, "You know what I think of rape scenes in movies? It's like someone put a big, beautiful birthday cake right in front of me and took a shit on it. It's like someone shitting on my birthday cake," and she scoffed at him for trivializing the issue, but at the same time felt oddly defended and grateful.

They were all kind. But she decided never to tell another one.

It did not define her; the men never understood this. She did things. It was not the sum of her because she made herself do things, stitched a personality together out of extracurriculars and carefully chosen proclivities. She hated Christmas and proclaimed her aversion loudly. She ran in the ravine. She was a person who ran all the time and had complicated shin issues. She made a lot of tea and learned the names, origins, and fermentation processes of each varietal. She did crosswords in ink and finished nearly all of them. She read. She loved novels in which people were genteel in their desperation and drank a lot of tea and spoke with dispirited eloquence.

Even with all of these diversions, she often thought about what the third man had said. She couldn't help thinking of it, because he kept calling to reiterate it.

"Just tell me his name," he said over the phone. "Just a first name is all I need. I'll do the rest."

"The rest?" she said. She was stirring sauce on the stove.

"The rest," he said.

She switched off the heat and visualized the third man's lips close to the receiver and moving emphatically, like a cinematic tight shot of a villain demanding ransom. "If you're thinking of the police," she said, "it's pointless. We're talking about twenty years ago. I was in grade school. There's a statue of limitations."

"Statute," the third man said. "But it doesn't matter. Whether he's actually *arrested* or not doesn't matter. The thing is to let him know it's not okay. To let him know he's being watched. It's a deterrent."

She remembered how the third man had once turned to her while she was reading and said in a voice flat with impersonal awe, "Your face is beautiful." He said it as if her beauty was the beauty of a dead thing, a butterfly framed and dried; it could do neither of them any good.

She said, "He isn't even around any little girls anyway." She kept stirring because she didn't know what else to do. "I was the only niece. He has no daughter, no granddaughter. He's not like your guy. He's not a roving weirdo running all over town." Her voice roughened.

They argued some more and she hung up, then poured her sauce over cooled pasta and vegetables and sat down to eat. She wondered why she was able to eat after this conversation, and if it meant something was wrong with her. Coiling the noodles around her fork was absorbing. She became lost in the round green integrity of a single pea, cupping her attention around it like hands, and when she disengaged herself she realized her dinner was cold and the dining room window was dark.

She put her fork down and sat back. The people across the courtyard were celebrating a birthday. Their lives seemed constructed of smartly colored geometric shapes. Through a bright square of window she saw a woman walking like a bride while carrying a blazing wheel of cake. The man she was walking toward was grinning, receptive, saving up breath for his big part, and when she placed the frosted circle in front of him he reared his head back, dragonlike, and extinguished all its light.

✻

A month later, her lease ended and she did not renew it. She moved to a new apartment in a half-gentrified part of town that smelled of hops and oatmeal from the nearby breweries and Pillsbury plant. There were train tracks everywhere. Children dangled off corroded jungle-gyms. The neighborhood had the carved-out, makeshift feel of a hobo camp and she found it surprisingly soothing, the shambling lullaby of the trains at night, their *click click click* hypnotically monotonous as a skipping record, the starchy soup of fog in the morning. She biked to work every day past an abandoned casket factory, rows of moldy Victorians, morning glories entangled in fences and opening their blowfish mouths in the light.

She told herself she had moved to escape the attentions of the third man. She enjoyed imagining him learning about her relocation secondhand and marveling at the ingenuity and resourcefulness it took to orchestrate an entire move without telling a soul or asking for help.

For a while she felt safe. But her new place—a big shotgun flat in a converted rooming house, with spiky stucco walls and bad wiring—

266

was uneasily silent. No matter how often she made tea and how invitingly she decorated her bed, she was plagued by waves of heartsick edginess, like a passenger who'd waited hours for a train only to realize that she'd been in the wrong depot all along: a sickly, hollow dawning. She ran more than ever. In her dreams she kept missing crucial appointments by a slim margin of time, and woke each day with a sore jaw from grinding her teeth. She waited for the third man to find her, or at least send an emissary. But no one called.

When the phone finally rang, it was her mother.

"Do you still want those dishes?" her mother said.

She began to cry. As always during displays of emotion, a specter hovered in the cool lobby of her brain, waiting for the signal to step in and put a stop to it.

"Oh, honey," her mother said. "What can I do? Don't you like your new apartment? You were so excited about it."

She swallowed air and said, "It's dirty. It's so dirty here, I've cleaned and cleaned and I'm not the one who made it this way, you know I'm not a slovenly person, I don't live in squalor—"

"I know that, honey," her mother said. "You're a very clean person. Remember how you used to vacuum the whole house when you came home from school, before I got home from work? I remember how nice it was to come home to a freshly vacuumed house. Remember how mad you'd get when Dad would step all over the carpet with his shoes on and ruin your beautiful vacuuming job? You did such a good job."

She laughed weakly. "I was a weirdo," she said.

"No," her mother said adamantly. "You were a good person and a helpful person."

"I cared so much about the vacuum," she said, and began to cry anew. The image of herself in the house where she grew up, making back-and-forth furrows like a plow horse, felt horribly vulnerable. She knew she was being self-indulgent, but she didn't want the ghostly bouncer to step in yet.

"Why don't I come over?" her mother said. "I'm going to stop by and we'll clean the place together. You just need some help, honey. You just need help."

"I do," she said. "I do."

The mother waited until after a great deal of cleaning had been done—the blinds taken off the windows and soaked in the bathtub, the baseboards scrubbed, the ceiling fans dusted—before telling her about the uncle.

"What I was told," she said, wiping her forehead carefully, "is that he got religion."

The daughter looked out the living room window, toward the casket factory and the Grain Belt brewery. The air smelled of refrigerator and leavening. "What sort of religion?" she said.

The mother looked down at the gleaming baseboards. "I don't know, that doesn't ever mean a particular creed, does it? 'Got religion'? It's sort of like a generic born-again thing I guess. Not some theology you actually study." She picked up a dirty sponge and tossed it aside. "All I know is, he's going to these churchy meetings and he's taking it very seriously. That's what Amelia says."

The stucco wall looked like white meringue stiffly whipped into peaks. She sometimes felt the urge to put her tongue to it.

"I'm telling you this," her mother said, "because he may be coming here. He may seek you out."

The daughter laughed. "Seek me out?"

Her mother laughed too, flailing one wrist in a minimizing gesture, loose with uncoordinated relief and anxiety. "I don't know. There's some emphasis on making amends. They talk in these strange pilgrimage terms. So Amelia says."

They sat in silence for a while. Her mother kept glancing sideways at her with anticlimactic intakes of breath, as if about to speak. Then she blurted out, "Grandma said once. 'If I were you I'd keep her far away from him. I just don't have a good feeling.' Or something like that. But you always wanted to be with him!" Her eyes stretched wide. "I thought she was just thinking the worst, you know how she is. She's always having a bad feeling about something and she's never right. I thought, 'the kid *wants* to be around him, what could he possibly be *doing* to her that's so bad?' She's the one who always said, 'Two signs a man will make a good husband: if he's good to his mother and kind to animals.' And he was both. My sister wouldn't have married him otherwise. He was both."

The daughter had once called her mother a bad mother and made her cry. She didn't want to do it again.

She said, "How does he even know where I live?"

Her mother flicked a foot up and down and did not answer right away. Then she said, "Amelia asked for your new address. I didn't really think twice; what was I supposed to say? She sends birthday cards every year, you know that."

In the silence the ceiling fan rollicked round and round, its unsteady revolutions oddly comic. It seemed to be winding up for a dramatic liftoff and the daughter almost laughed. Then a thin peevish misery, runny as yolk, spread over her. It was all very banal. The sun was boring, bland with midday virtue; there were ants on the floor and the clicking of the trains was depressingly productive and brisk. She had a sense that this encounter was not what it should be. Things should feel sharper in general right now, and less like cardboard. Life should seem much less ridiculous, more urgent than it did when her mother finally looked her in the face, not reaching out but backing away now, each breath between words a frantic hand-flap, a shooting away: "I always wanted to know, honey, what *was* it? What could it have been? When you kept being around him. When you just kept coming back!"

The daughter wanted to say, "I didn't."

But she had. She had gone back again and again: to pretend to understand his stories and laugh at what was supposed to be funny and to be lifted like a sack, with an affectionate casualness that proved her lightness, her doll-like simplicity, the reassuring physicality of someone else's entitlement to her. She had never since been borne into the air with so little ceremony.

What she said was, "Shut up." She imagined her own eyes pale and lizardlike, looking at the mother. "Will you shut the fuck up?" she said, her voice louder this time. The mother looked out the window and didn't say anything.

Over the next few weeks she thought a lot about handicrafts. At work she was competent, researching government grants with the whimsical earnestness of the postgraduate. Her co-workers were progressive women in their mid-thirties and avuncular, aging gay men; they all liked her and indulged the precocious sass that emerged after her trial period of anxious sweetness ended. Gainful employment was still a dress-up game, one she was good at. Lately, though, she found herself looking forward to returning home as soon as possible in order to devote her full attention to thinking about handicrafts until she cried.

She couldn't understand the sudden poignancy of the subject. But it was something she needed, in the artless prodding way of a food craving: to be filled with a grief whose origins were both dubious and concrete, to absorb the sad wobbly essence of these unloved objects until she spilled over with it.

So each evening, as dusk curtained the house and the phone did not ring and the boxcars trundled off to Santa Cruz and Burlington and Alberta, she sat on the floor against the couch and inhaled the sawdusty yeast smell and thought of body parts made of clay, baked in kilns, and ineptly glazed. An impression of her seven-year-old palm overlaid with a sheen of sickly lavender finish. They punched a hole so it could be hung at holidays, a disembodied emblem of the universal sign for *stop*. There was also a plaster cast of her right foot, painted streaky blue with acrylics. And the clay bowl she'd grandly visualized as so beautiful had emerged lumpish, thumbprints baked into its clumsy sides. Her silkscreens always turned out backward, as did her woodblock prints. She could not cross-stitch. Was so inept at making a friendship headband out of yarn that the Girl Scout leader, a horsy blond matron who volunteered her time out of an honest faith in the character-building properties of female bonding of the rustic and homespun variety, gave up and made one *for* her because everyone had to have one for the Friendship Ceremony and the situation was clearly hopeless.

She held each failed object, sharp with the crystalline sterility of an art-class slide, in her mind's eye and squeezed, extracting its emotional pulp: the ache of having tried too hard, aimed too high, wrapped up loose ends in a slapdash of despair. Thinking of the crafts all together in a gallery of shame made her weep as she had never wept before: loudly, with copious amounts of mucus she did not bother to wipe off. Nor did she hide her head in her arms, just walked around the house like that, doing menial tasks and cooking dinner and brushing her teeth, all the while thinking of malformed crafts and bawling.

If she stopped for a second, she was unsure what to do next. Usually the only thing that made sense was to go to her bed and make herself come over and over, not languorously, not ardently, but like a rat pressing a lever. Once in a while she felt a tiny stun gun of clarity right after she came. In these moments the stopper of her numb chemical bath jostled loose, and she would regard her hands with a sober appreciation for their perfection and dexterity. The sensitivity of their little hairs. Their cunning joints. Then she would remember the clay hand and start sobbing again.

She bounced back and forth between craft-weeping and masturbation, clubbing herself dumb with the crudest of sensations, until one day she couldn't. One day the crafts didn't make her weep anymore and her groin was too tender to touch.

It was a Saturday morning. She sat back against the headboard and assessed her surroundings with the grim, bloodshot closure of a drunk coming out of a bender. The body's capacity for dissolution had been exhausted. Her options fanned out, cryptic as tea leaves. She called the third man.

"What the hell?" he said. "Your phone's been off the hook for weeks."

"It's not off the hook; it's disconnected. I moved."

He asked where and she described the trains and the factories and the bread smell. She made him laugh once or twice. Then there was silence and he said, voice dipping in a nakedly aggrieved way that made her feel scarily womanly and responsible, "Well, why are you calling me now? Since you didn't even bother to mention you were moving."

She stood up, put a hand between her legs, and was bemused by the leaping, responsive pulse of herself: some gamely wagging trouper under the rubbed-raw skin. Her body was a perplexed animal, ever ready to serve. It forgave everyone everything.

She said to the third man, "I have something you want."

"What?" he said, wary; she was never one to be coy about sexual matters.

She said, "A name. And an address."

✳

His face had lost its customary zealotry. Stripped of it he seemed washed-out and sheepish: the mild-mannered alter ego of his former self. He wore a puffy coat she did not recognize.

"Is it really that cold out?" she said, gesturing toward the coat. He caught the screen door with his elbow and shuffled into the kitchen.

"I rode my bike," he said. "The wind." She stuck a teabag in a cup of boiled water and told him to sit down in the living room; he did, sticking his hands between his thighs to warm them: an uncharacteristic and studied gesture.

He took the cup she offered and said, "How's the job?"

She said, "I'm doing a grant to stop world hunger."

271

"Has it stopped yet?" He sipped.

"No. It will." She had the sensation that someone who knew her well, a sister if she had one or a close high school friend, was watching this exchange from above and snorting in disgust at both of them.

The third man eased himself off the couch and sat crosslegged on a floor pillow. "This apartment's weird. Your other place was nicer."

"This is cheaper."

"It really does smell like beer outside."

"Yeah, well, it could smell like something worse."

The third man pressed his lips together and separated them with a popping sound. "So," he said, eyeing the cracked plaster of the living room wall, "you have a name for me?"

"Guess what it is." She deliberately flattened her voice so it wouldn't sound like some flirtatiously sassy challenge.

He shrugged. "I don't know. Larry?"

She shook her head.

"Bert?"

"No one is actually named that."

"Yes, they are," he said. "I've known people named Bert."

She looked at him and had the urge to go running, right then, in the ravine, past the rained-on mattresses and trembling footbridge, the graffitied rocks and the flashers, bouncing complicit glances off the other runners as her rib cage lifted and lowered, her heart giddy and always the awareness of her own breath as a precious and fallible commodity.

She said, "I don't think I'm going to tell you."

She expected a scene, but he shrugged. "Well," he said, "can't say I'm surprised."

She snorted. "What, you just thought I wanted an excuse to lure you over here?" She thought, *what an inane encounter*, over and over.

He stood up and dusted off his pants for no reason. "I don't know. It didn't really matter. I've been worried. I just wanted to see if you were doing okay, I guess."

She stared at him. She had the sensation she was shrinking. "Okay?" she said.

He nodded.

"You're not a vigilante anymore?"

He shrugged again. "I still think he should go to jail. But I'm done with the whole thing about me being involved in putting him there. I think I was kind of infantilizing you. You know? It's up to you to come to terms with this thing how you see fit, is what I mean." He spoke without looking at her, and fidgeted with the zipper of his jacket.

She had never hated him before; she did now. She hated him and wanted to see his old rage so badly, his inner light lurid as swamp gas, the fathomless oil slicks of his dilated pupils. She saw now that his eyes were a temperate shade of blue she recognized as a popular hue for the shutters of tract homes on her childhood cul-de-sac. She scrutinized him for a trace of the taut, hunted shiftiness men's faces assume when they are driven to be with her and don't know why. It was never sweet. They were never besotted, just stiffly, sullenly advancing as though shoved toward her from behind. Sometimes they looked at her like an animal eyeing an untrustworthy trainer; other times in a gauging, measuring way, like she was an obstruction they needed to lift and move to get what they wanted.

And although there was nothing of this in the third man's face, although he just stood there in her living room looking gamely uncomfortable, she came forward and pressed her palm against his crotch. She looked down at it. And when he put his hands on her shoulders and said, "What are you doing?" she fumbled with her belt buckle, heard its gratifyingly heavy clink, began to unzip.

Her breathing was perfectly even, as though she had been granted a surgeon's access to her own insides, lifting and lowering her ribcage tenderly with both hands and guiding banners of breath in and out of her throat like a fire-eater. For a few seconds she knew the shamanesque power of them all: the man in the bathroom, the flashers in the ravine, the uncle with his wormy silk-sweater smell and his aura of raspy restless movement like a cricket's legs scraping, the ease with which he reached into himself and split the seam demarcating what he did from what he was. Then got up the next day and ate cereal. Petted dogs. Engaged in the poignantly vain grooming rituals of a middle-aged man: the inspection of gums, the sculpting of sideburns.

The third man peeled her hand off and said, "I'm not doing this with you." He sounded resigned yet rehearsed, as though he'd glumly anticipated having to say this.

She stepped back. "Then why the fuck did you come over here?"

The third man picked up his backpack and looped it over one shoulder, his shutter-colored eyes flat, his voice tight. "I told you. To see if you were all right."

273

"I'm better than you are," she said. "You're fixated. You belong on *Oprah*."

He was walking toward the door now. When he reached the big double oven he backed against it and looked down at her and said, "What happened to me wasn't much."

"Can't quantify it," she singsonged, wagging a finger.

He just kept talking. "What happened to you was bad, though. I used to think you should go get vengeance. Not just for yourself. For everybody. But I can't make you into this poster child. It needs to be under your own jurisdiction. Or it won't count."

"You're like a shitty fortune cookie."

He shrugged. She didn't remember him being such an inveterate shrugger. He had always been too incapable of concession to shrug even in casual conversation.

"I'm sorry," he said. Then he opened the door. She stood on the back porch and watched him cross the parking lot, his back sloped like a mountain climber's, a carriage both braced and slouchy. He swung one leg over his bike. She thought of his meditative, bittersweet ride home to his normal-smelling neighborhood, a sage's flinty smugness in his eyes, the wind in his righteous hair. She thought of several things she could yell after him. But all that came out was something she hadn't known was on the tip of her tongue: the uncle's name and address, over and over. Not yelled but simply thought, and long after he rode away.

*

There were three men and that was all. The third was the last one told.

Eventually she saw other men, and kept her mouth shut through Oscar-winning movies in which innocents were diddled; through endless televised parades of Very Special Victims; through the initial ten seconds of sex that were always fraught with panic, her heart whinnying, pawing, walleyed. She gentled it down and kept moving. She did things, tending her body with the disinterested briskness of a nurse. To friends, she alluded comically to a three-week stint in which she cried nonstop about handicrafts. She omitted the compulsive masturbation and came off as endearingly vulnerable and daffy, even as her inner abacus clicked coldly with each deposit and return, each ally enlisted.

She recognized that she was a person of limited means.

About six months after the third man's visit, she was running in the ravine when a man stumbled out of the underbrush with his pants around his ankles. She stopped and looked at him. Birds chirped. The air around her seemed to soften, deliquesce with sweet rot. A mother duck and three ducklings glided through the Mississippi. The man had freckled thighs and was knock-kneed. His eyes, deep-set and brown as the river, met hers, and he flushed, looked back and forth and suddenly covered himself—not shamefully, but with a whiplash grab of self-preserving instinct. Then he turned about-face and blundered back through the brush, clutching at the waistband of his khakis.

He seemed less of an exhibitionist than an apparition, some feral creature separated from his tribe. She pictured more of them back there, hunkering fearfully and waiting for her footsteps to fade. She imagined what otherworldly powers they superstitiously ascribed to her by firelight, how they warned their young and disbanded camp at the scent of her. The next day she said to a co-worker, "Some naked guy popped in front of me in the ravine, but as soon as he saw me he looked all horrified and ran away. I didn't know flashers were so discriminating." The co-worker, one of the funny gay men with whom she pored over celebrity gossip magazines in the lunchroom, said the flasher likely wasn't a flasher at all and that the ravine was notorious for illicit gay-sex trysts; didn't she know that? She shrugged. She was inexplicably disappointed.

The next day the uncle came.

Somewhere in her brain, she had mislaid his significance. His face, bobbing up the back porch stairs, was blandly ubiquitous as a television personality's. But then he said her name.

Conventional wisdom claimed smell as the beeline to memory, but for her it was the sound of her own name on someone's tongue: a calling card coded with sensory nuance, redolent of the nature of their claim on her and their preferred method of collection. He rapped on the screen door. It never occurred to her not to let him in.

The uncle made a fussy show of scraping his shoes on the doormat and clapping his hands against his lapels. He looked the same. She hadn't seen him in five years, having evaded family reunions and holiday galas since the age of eighteen.

"May I come in?" he said, although he was already in.

"Yeah," she said. She flapped an arm toward the dining table. She didn't know what to say next, so she said, "Want some water?"

"No, no, no; no trouble on my account, please." There was a charged subtext to this, employed like a flexed muscle.

She leaned against the sink, arms crossed. He stood by the refrigerator with his hands at his sides. "My mother said you might come," she said.

"Yes," he said. He kept looking at her searchingly. He wore a good-quality coat with a hood. It was beige and belted tightly. His hair was slightly grayer and his eyes were still round and harmless-looking, with jaunty little eyebrows like a dog's vestigial markings. He didn't smell the same though. There had been an acidic sharpness. It was gone.

The uncle cleared his throat. "I've been trying to start a clean slate with my life," he said. "Your mom may have mentioned it." He waited for affirmation. She said nothing. He went on, "It's a time of transformation, and part of that is trying to make things right with those I've wronged. And I know it must be upsetting for you to see me. And I wrestled with this, you have no idea; I asked myself is it selfish to go to her, to dredge this up? Do I have any right? And maybe I don't. Maybe I don't. But this is not about reducing karmic debt; please understand that. This is not something to cross off a to-do list. This," he said, inhaling as if about to plunge underwater, "is the central black hole of my life."

She sneezed violently. "Excuse me."

"Bless you," he blurted. He seemed grateful for the opportunity to bestow this benediction.

"Look," she said, tucking her hair behind her ears, "this really isn't necessary."

He looked down. "Would you like me to leave?"

"I don't care," she said. "If this is a big thing for you, say what you need to say. Go for it."

"I appreciate it," he said. His constant head-bobbing and knee-jerk deference made her feel like a guru in a kung-fu movie, attended by a bowing, scraping apprentice. She smiled coldly. She articulated the action to herself as she performed it: *I am smiling coldly.*

"I don't want to just make a speech at you," the uncle said. "I was hoping we could have kind of a give and take." His voice tilted up. She recognized it, that cocksure wheedling.

"I don't think so," she said. The crispness of her own voice made her stand up straighter.

The uncle's round eyes began to fill up, taking on the hazy mirage-like illusion of movement that preceded full-fledged weeping. Then he blinked the water away. "All right," he said. He looked down at his galoshes. She remembered how his vacated shoes and his socked feet used to give off an earthy, pungent odor, not unpleasant, the expansive warm smell of something tightly contained and suddenly freed.

"I just want to say one thing," he said. His round eyes were stricken. He extended an arm as though tempted to grab her for emphasis, but quickly withdrew it. "What I did to you," he said, "was not your fault. I know . . . I've read the literature. I know a lot of people grow up thinking there's something wrong with them. That they're to blame. And they are *not*. It was me, it was all . . . my sickness. It could have been anyone. You were there, and you were—accessible. That was it. That was *it*." He made a slicing gesture, then winced at his own immoderation.

She pictured him reading the literature. She had read it, too. Then she said, "I'd feel better if it did have something to do with me. Is that sick?" The uncle took a breath to speak and stopped short. He was at a loss.

He opened and closed his mouth. He took a step forward and back again.

Then he did a strange thing: he bowed his head and covered his eyes with his hand.

She leaned against the stove and watched him for a while, earnestly but without investment, the way children watch parades and inaugurations and tedious civic rituals in general. The uncle's fingers dug hard into his temple.

The niece thought of self-defense. She wondered if this was a dangerous situation; technically, there was a lawbreaker and a deviant in her home. But she could see that something in him had shut against her. And not only against her but against a lot of things, and she was just one of them, an emblem he distorted at will, a monster disarmed. He had to turn her into this. And for a moment she felt that he had succeeded: her hands were folded in front of her, her chin pointed down, and she thought she must resemble an old daguerreotype she saw long ago in a textbook, a pioneer woman on a prairie: salt of the earth and grimly unsexed, frozen in the eternal posture of one who bears up, bears up, bears up, then dies.

The uncle was now sitting on a wooden chair as though a giant hand had dropped him there by the scruff of the neck. He rubbed his forehead with thumb and fingers. His flesh pleated and reddened. He was right there in front of her. She thought of him having sex with his wife. She stared at his hands. They were small hands, chapped and pinkish with spatulate fingers and broad nails, and the first time they touched her—the back of the neck, brushing—she had not been afraid.

She had never been afraid of him. What she felt now, what she had always felt, was collusion: uneasy, dead-eyed, and leaden. It began in the back of the throat and slowly sifted downward, dragging heaviness to her base like a punching bag with a weighted bottom, rooting her to the ground with the knowledge that she belonged in this kitchen with this man, that she was born here and would die here and that there was no other scenario in which she would ever be so wholly herself.

She coughed and the uncle looked up. He looked at the corner of the wall where two cupboards met.

"Well, I don't know," he said finally. "I don't know what you want to hear from me. I don't know if I'm just making this worse than it needs to be." He wasn't pleading now. He was just looking at her sanely and tiredly. He was trying to reason with a tiresome woman. She realized that he was wondering what he ever saw in her.

The niece started rubbing her own chest: not sensually, but like she was applying an unpleasant-smelling but curative poultice. The uncle's face sharpened in genuine surprise. As she rubbed she said, "Do you remember that white cat that used to roam around Grandma and Grandpa's neighborhood, the albino one? And you told me about the ghost tigers and I didn't believe you. I thought you were making them up for the longest time. But then, and this was my first year at college, I saw some at the Toronto zoo. They were very ghostlike. It was like seeing a herd of unicorns. It was quite a shock."

The uncle opened his mouth and closed it. Her hands moved down to her groin and she rubbed that too and felt a small cheap hit of comfort. She concentrated on this.

She suddenly couldn't stop talking.

"Do you think about it?" she said to the uncle, flatly and nasally. "How many times in a week do you think about it?"

"I don't—I mean, I think about what I did to you often—think about the *damage* of it, the—" The uncle lobbed the words, trying to stand his ground, squinting at her now as if he could force her back into focus, his focus, the one he'd donned that morning with his galoshes and muffler and pleasant cologne.

The walls of the kitchen seemed to narrow around them and she moved closer, feeling taller and wider, her shadow throwing darkness over him like a tarp.

"What are you doing?" the uncle said. She stepped forward, not rubbing anymore. She could think of nothing else to say so she just stared at the uncle's face, and after a few moments she found it, the look she'd searched for in the third man: the taking-over and the leaving behind. The bullish emptiness of the eyes. It was there. Then it wasn't; his face seemed to skip a frame and he was turning around, the uncle, he was clutching at his collar with one hand, he was moving toward the door.

"I'm sorry," he said, not looking at her. "I'm sorry."

He did not sound sorry. He threw the words like baking soda on a grease fire.

He was another chastened, decent man who closed the door without slamming it and walked through the rain to his sad car. It was so stupid it was criminal. The car revved up and crunched over gravel.

The kitchen grew chilly. As darkness set in she wrapped her arms around her torso. She continued to stand there like that, because it was cold. Because she could hear the train's *skip, skip* like a bad heartbeat, and she knew the morning glories were closing their throats for the night, and because it was hard, in that clenched fist of twilight, to imagine doing anything else.

Nominated by New England Review

DREAM

by PAUL HOSTOVSKY

from BLUELINE

You're alive and riding your bicycle
to school and I am worried about you
riding your bicycle all the way to school
so I get in my car and drive like a maniac
through the dream over curbs and lawns
sideswiping statuary and birdbaths along
the way frantically seeking you everywhere
the rear wheel of your bicycle disappearing
around the next corner and the next and then
I am riding a bicycle too and sounding
the alarm which sounds like a bicycle bell
so no one believes it's an alarm and I pedal
faster and faster my knees bumping up against
the handlebars which by now have sprouted
ribbons with pompoms and a basket attached
with your lunch inside and I'm pedaling to save
my life and your life and finally when I find you
in the dream you aren't dead yet you're alive
and a little angry and embarrassed to see me
all out of breath on a girl's bicycle holding
your lunch out in my hand trembling with joy

Nominated by Blueline

ELEVEN WAYS TO CONSIDER AIR

by BRANDON R. SCHRAND

from ECOTONE: REIMAGINING PLACE

I.

OF ALL THE ELEMENTS in the American West romanticized in the nineteenth century, air is perhaps the most curious. Gold, copper, silver, and water certainly top the list in many ways and rightfully so. The notion of water in the arid West, for instance, lived long (indeed too long) in the Victorian imagination before it was recognized, finally, by some, as a resource with a rarity on par with some hard-rock minerals.

One of the greatest stories about illusory water beyond the one hundredth meridian concerns the Buena Ventura River that supposedly coursed across the alkali desert of western Utah before eventually crashing into the Pacific. Cartographers plotted the river carefully, Mormons told tales of its azure waters, and settlers wandered the desert in vain seeking the faintest sign of its meandering breadth. Trouble is, no such river ever existed despite the stories, despite the maps. It was a myth.

Air, though, was the most egalitarian of elements, and it was purer in the West, people thought, than anywhere else. And it was for the taking. One did not need a sluice box, smelter, or pickax to extract it from the sky. One need not go mad in the desert with a bogus map looking for it. All one needed was a set of lungs to process its infinity.

Seldom did a nineteenth-century travel writer pass through the West without gushing about the pure mountain air. Consider Horace Greeley, who had this to say in his 1860 account, *An Overland Journey*. "Brooks of the purest water murmur and sing in every ravine;

springs abound; the air is singularly pure and bracing." Likewise, in *Mountaineering in the Sierra Nevada*, published twelve years later, the swaggering adventure-crat, Clarence King, waxed this way: "After such fatiguing exercises the mind has an almost abnormal clearness: whether this is wholly from within, or due to the intensely vitalizing mountain air, I am not sure." My favorite, albeit lesser known period author, Captain John Codman, traveled west in 1873 and took up lodging in my hometown of Soda Springs, Idaho, a settlement tucked in a sagebrush valley in the southeastern corner of the state. In *The Mormon Country*, published a year later, Codman wrote that in Soda Springs he had "nature in her wild majesty, [and] an elastic, stimulating air."

The mountain air in the West was not there merely to enjoy for its "bracing" freshness; it was literally prescribed for one's health, as if it could be bottled and sold. Silas Weir Mitchell, a physician of prominence toward the end of the nineteenth century, was well known for his "rest cure" (treating women for their so-called "hysteria") and most notably here, for his "fresh air therapy." If a man felt glum, soft, or, god forbid, effete, Mitchell sent him packing for the West where a stark encounter with rugged landscape and exposure to the wild air would restore his machismo faster than he could say "Buena Ventura." Mitchell's most well-known client was none other than Teddy Roosevelt.[1]

It is not known whether John Codman consulted Dr. Mitchell before boarding his Pullman Palace Car to the land of enchanted air, but it is clear that the idea of fresh-air-as-medicine was a priority for the fifty-nine year old blue-blood. His close friend and former Mormon prophet Heber J. Grant once remarked that Codman "suffered from asthma, and he discovered he was better at Soda Springs, Idaho, than at any other place" in the world. The message seemed clear: Go West, old man. Get some air.

II.

During the early summer weeks of 1950, the Monsanto Chemical Company broke ground at the very northern edge of Soda Springs.

---

[1]If Mitchell were alive today, he might be pleased to know that canned oxygen is now sold over-the-counter and is gaining wide popularity in chic venues known as oxygen bars. Recently, the convenience store Seven-Eleven Japan stocked its shelves with canned oxygen and is now awaiting profits from those seeking a hit of vigor.

There, at the northern city limit in a brushy stretch of grazing land amid knuckles and ridges of basalt, the company erected a phosphorus furnace plant above the subterranean layers of ore they planned to reach, exhume, and process. Since that summer, Monsanto has dominated the landscape, economy, and cultural fabric of the southeastern Idaho town. Monsanto *made* the town, people say.

And should anyone forget the company's imprint on Soda Springs, custom-made trucks carry cauldrons each filled with six hundred cubic feet of molten, radioactive byproduct, or slag, and slop the refuse down a tailings slope into a waste lagoon.[2] This quasi-lava flow occurs five times an hour, around the clock, day after day, year after year. As a boy growing up there, I used to think it was spectacular, a man-made volcano in my back yard. Actually, the slag's peak temperature is about equal to a volcanic lava flow, topping off at 2,552 degrees Fahrenheit.[3] The slag pours and pours. And the air and the junipers and the silvery sagebrush and the streams and the yawning fields of winter wheat turn wild shades of orange. The townspeople pace the streets and sidewalks daily hunkering under that glow-dome, that pulsing spell of false luminosity. Night becomes day. The daylight is widened. And the air is not elastic or stimulating. It is acrid.

III.

When I was seven, I stopped breathing and was rushed to the emergency room where I was revived on a cold table. I was not in Soda Springs, Idaho, at the time, but in Richland, Washington. We had moved to that desert town two years earlier when my stepdad got a job at the Hanford Nuclear Reactor Project as an electrician. I re-

[2]Rock that contains trace elements of elemental phosphorus is processed in the electrical arc-furnaces as a means to extract the phosphorus, while silica and carbon are added to the mix to jettison any impurities. The by-product of this process is a gray, rocky, vitrified slag material that contains uranium and radium. For years, the city of Soda Springs eagerly used the slag as roadfill, foundation mix for schools and houses, sidewalks and bridges. In 1990, the EPA warned residents of Soda Springs that they were at a greater risk of cancer due to the low but ubiquitous levels of radiation around town.

[3]Only once has a man tipped his truck over into the magmatic sludge. I was in high school at the time and remember the day the story spread through town. The unimaginable had happened. That night I drove out to Monsanto and stood in its radiated glow, watching. I was haunted and unendingly fascinated. I imagined how his flesh must have poured from his bones, how the bones became smoke, how the smoke rose in a solitary plume and thinned on an ordinary wind. The slag had erased him. Only the carcass of his truck was recovered. The tragedy did not, however, interrupt the five-count rhythm of the day.

member the respirators he brought home and how they made him look terrifying, like an insect.

I had cousins who lived in Richland and it was at their house during a sleepover that my respiratory system shut down in the middle of the night. I shot up in bed, straight as a broomstick, and tried to draw a breath, but to no avail. I tried to scream for help but no sound escaped. So I did the next best thing: I pounded on the headboard and walls. I beat my fists into the mattress. In seconds, my aunt Marcia rushed in, while my uncle Jack a police officer, called the ambulance. After that I remember only fragments: the crowded ambulance, its strange half-light, my aunt's gown, hushes, and a hand to my forehead. I wore an oxygen mask the color of seawater. This time I looked like the insect and it was no less terrifying.

In the hospital, I could breathe again. I sat on the cold empty table, feet dangling over the edge, shirtless, my small chest heaving. A doctor orbited the table with a clipboard and stethoscope and asked a battery of questions, most of which my aunt could not answer. My parents, she had said, were on their way. That was the first time I had ever heard the words *asthma attack. Severe.*

Shortly after the attack, Mom scheduled a doctor's appointment where she faced her own barrage of questioning: "Do you or your husband smoke cigarettes?"

"Yes."

"Both of you or just one of you?"

"Both of us."

"Do you smoke in the home or outside?"

"At home. In the home."

Mom, I could tell, was uncomfortable.

"And the car? Do you smoke in the car?"

"Yes."

The doctor scribbled in his notepad, thumb-clicked his pen, pocketed it, and told me that I could put my shirt back on. "Mrs. Schrand, considering Brandon's history of allergies and his asthma, I strongly recommend you and your husband change your smoking habits at once. He has difficulty breathing under the best conditions. Having to breathe in the constant presence of smoke is like, well, it's like breathing with a piano on your chest." I stared at my plaid pants and my Big Bird sneakers and imagined what it might be like to have a piano sitting on me.

Mom usually cracked the window when she smoked in the car, but that day, on the way home from the doctor's office, she rolled the window all the way down. After that, she stopped smoking in my bedroom too.

IV.

Seneca, the ancient tragedian, orator, and writer, also suffered from asthma. He noted that of all illnesses that had visited him, asthma was the most menacing. "One could hardly, after all, expect anyone to keep on drawing his last breath for long, could one?. . . This is why doctors have nicknamed it 'rehearsing death,' since sooner or later the breath does just what it has been trying to do all those times." But he did not acquiesce to the haunting "squall" of asthma. Instead, he defied it, dared it to take him while he was sleeping: "I shall not be afraid when the last hour comes." Unlike Seneca, I feared the last hour, entertained nightmares about the last hour, recurring ones that replayed the scene at my aunt Marcia's house.

V.

Air, it seems, is not easily won in my family. We lived in Richland, Washington, for only three years before Dad was laid off from Hanford, forcing us to vacate our white, two-bedroom clapboard rental and move back to Soda Springs. There, my grandparents owned an historic three-story brick hotel, café, and bar right downtown and had enlisted my parents to help run the place. It was a family business in the strictest sense, and we all lived there, squared away in apartments on the ground floor. Because my grandparents' apartment was larger, though, I lived with them.

A few years before my asthma attack, my grandfather was diagnosed with emphysema, and although he quit smoking his Winstons, he refused to go on oxygen. His doctor urged him, emphatically, to use it, supplementally, at least at night. It would help, he said. Afraid of becoming dependent upon a tank, afraid of that kind of entrapment, my grandfather dug in and tried to fight the disease. Inevitably, though, he lost ground as everyone knew he would. Drawing a full breath became more and more labored. By the time we moved back to Soda Springs, a cold green steel cylindrical tank filled with pure oxygen stood at the head of his bed. As a child, I was vaguely frightened of this armless gargoyle that towered in my grandparents' room. It looked like a beheaded soldier, a robot, or a bomb that could explode at any second.[4]

Only those patients who have advanced emphysema need supplemental oxygen, but all sufferers will need it eventually. The disease is particularly troubling because the lungs lose their elasticity. Those afflicted with emphysema are encumbered with the haunting reality that it is not just a progressively arduous task to draw a full breath, but it is inordinately difficult to exhale the breath once they have taken it.

My grandparents tried everything to outpace his degenerative respiratory condition. They tried steroids, exercise, inhalers, herbal remedies, prayer, anger, denial. At one point they drove to Mexico to look for large and inexpensive quantities of cortisone, a drug, they were told, offered relief for various victims. While some days were better than others, we all knew that eventually my grandfather's fears would come true: he would rely on an oxygen tank for the rest of his life, And that this disease would kill him.

If my grandpa smoked before he volunteered to fight in World War II, he smoked twice as much by the end of the war. There is little doubt that smoking led to and caused his disease. But for years after the war, his lungs saw no reprieve. He harvested grain on combines without cab enclosures, mowing through thunderheads of splintery chaff and grain dust. And when he wasn't attending to the ranch, he worked at Monsanto where columns of smoke filled the sky and thickened the air.

---

[4]An aside: When I was in elementary school, I formed a club based on Bertrand R. Brinley's children's books, *The Mad Scientists' Club*. The books centered on a smart but goofy cast of characters who hatched hair-brained ideas with intent to help their nostalgically named town of Mammoth Falls. Their plans and schemes always backfired, of course, but these "failures" did not deter them from trying other experiments. Fully taken by these stories, I started to hatch some schemes of my own. One involved building a rocket out of my grandpa's oxygen tank. I cobbled together a launchpad out of two pallets, four cinder blocks, and scrap lumber. On notebook paper, I sketched a number of designs and schematics. Each one, however, hinged on the same ignition theorem the rocket would launch if I knocked the valve off the tank with a twenty-pound sledgehammer. It would have to be a clean strike. One hit. The fear of a spark and a certain explosion, however, distressed me greatly and caused many sleepless nights. The launch was canceled indefinitely. I don't think it ever occurred to me, though, that it would have been my grandfather's air I was shooting into the horizon, his part-time life support system that would have surely exploded in our driveway.

Like Mom, who had stopped smoking in my bedroom when I was diagnosed with asthma, Grandma also quit smoking her Bel-Air Menthols in their bedroom when Grandpa was hit with emphysema. I will not soon forget the artwork that adorned her cigarette packages. A crisp blue windblown sky feathered with a light, airy wisp of a cloud. The very package was the image of the freshest air imaginable.

Best of all, the packages came with coupons that could be redeemed for merchandise from the company's glossy-slick catalog. Grandma collected the coupons and one summer, gave me two shoe boxes filled with rubber-banded bundles that I mailed off to the Raleigh Bel-Air company in exchange for a red Tasco telescope with a black tripod and a yellow-and-blue two-person inflatable rubber raft complete with oars and air pump.[5] Combined, the two items required over two thousand cigarette coupons. I was ecstatic. I raced my bike over the sidewalks to the post office daily to see if any large boxes awaited me. Day after day, I returned home winded and disappointed.

The day my raft and telescope arrived, however, marked the day I redoubled my efforts to collect more coupons. At night I lay in my bed beneath a large skylight and flipped through the merchandise catalog, my wish book. And five times an hour the skylight would glow orange, coloring, if only faintly, the glossy catalog pages I thumbed through and marked with a ballpoint pen. I circled the full-color pictures of binoculars, compasses, bicycles, watches, radios, a color TV Math problems—columns of addition and subtraction—riddled the margins. So many coupons for the compass left only so many for the FM radio Possibilities abounded. The cardboard carton that held my new batch of coupons was pathetically empty, however, so I pestered Grandma making certain that every coupon was accounted for. "How many packs did you smoke today, Grandma?" I would ask, beaming. It was our running joke. "I can only smoke so many a day, you know!" She would say, and laugh.

---

[5]It is probably safe to say that few people today pay much attention to the common air-pump, but there was a time when its early incarnations generated a great deal of scientific discussion. The Honourable Robert Boyle, for instance, who is largely credited as the progenitor of modern chemists, was fascinated with the air pump. In 1657, he happened across an early model of the air pump—created by Otto Von Geuriecke, a German physicist who experimented with, among other things, vacuums and generators—and worked for two years on improving the contraption. And by 1659, Boyle had completed the new and improved "machina Boyleana," which led to a number of significant experiments on the properties of air. The common air pump was integral to those experiments.

VII

On bright afternoons, I visited with Grandpa in his bedroom. He had an adjustable bed that, when elevated, made it easier for him to draw and release his breath. Their bedroom had a large window and the two of us would sit on the edge of his bed, share a bowl of cherries, spit the stones into the waste basket, and talk on all matters of the world—whether or not ESP was real, would California sink in the big quake, would Russia launch a missile at the US, and would Soda Springs be a target? All the while his oxygen hissed in the background. Sometimes I set up my telescope in his room so I could look through his window. Once, while I dragged the lens across the horizon, my eye intent on anything and nothing (usually a stand of cottonwoods or a skein of geese over distant brushy hills), and while my fingers dialed the fine-focus knob, Grandpa popped me on the head playfully. I looked at him, blinking. I was standing on his oxygen hose. "Oh, sorry," I said. "I didn't know."

Asthma does not affect the tissues in the lungs like emphysema. Asthmatics struggle to breathe because the bronchi in their lungs narrow and restrict airflow. Many people who suffer from asthma rely on aerosol inhalers when they feel particularly short of breath, like I did when I wrestled in junior high school.[6] I remember the gymnasium where we practiced and how the air was heavy and humid and odorous, and how it hung like weather. Thin, smallish, and light on my feet, I could sprint as fast as anyone on the team, at least for the first half-dozen wall touches. Then the ceiling lights blurred yellow while my chest burned and I would invariably fall behind the rest of the team, gradually at first (I can still hear my coach, a balding man built like a meat locker: *Come on, Schrand! Pick it up!*), and finishing last, sucking the sour air. My lungs felt raw and shredded. I would stumble to the court's edge and snatch up my inhaler and blast its foul gas into my throat. I hated that inhaler, though, because it was viewed by my coach and teammates as a weakness, an excuse, some-

---

[6]During the composition of this essay, I came down with bronchitis, and was prescribed an inhaler in addition to the usual regimen of antibiotics. "Because of your history with asthma," the doctor said, regarding the inhaler. I checked the active ingredients for oxygen, but found none. Instead, I learned that the L-shaped canister contained a "microcrystalline suspension of albuterol in propellants [trichloromonofluoromethane and dichlorodifluoromethane] with oleic acid." Whatever *that* is, you won't find it among Seven-Eleven Japan's chic assortment of canned oxygen.

how emasculating. As the corridors in my lungs closed in on themselves, I understood what it must be like to have someone stand on my oxygen hose.

VIII.

Seneca did not have an inhaler. Nor did asthmatics in the nineteenth century; rather, they had the West. They had places like Soda Springs, Idaho. My grandfather had Soda Springs, too, but one day decided that the air was better elsewhere than it was in his hometown. And just like that, without ceremony or explanation, he and my grandma packed their red Volkswagen Rabbit and drove into the desert southwest, and settled for the winter in Bullhead, Arizona. They moved not for the weather, but for the air—his fresh-air cure. "He just knew he could breathe better there," Grandma often says. "And what the hell? It was worth a shot."

My grandfather stopped breathing and died in a fluorescent-lit hospital room on the night of January 4, 1986. I was fourteen and remember clearly the moment he flatlined and how Mom ran out of the room, sobbing. I also remember not knowing how to react, so I didn't. I just remember the sound and Mom bolting, her face in her hands. And how the oxygen kept hissing long after he was gone.

It is summer. Almost twenty years have passed since my grandfather died. I sit in my grandmother's house and talk loudly because she is losing her hearing. My two children are not with me, so she smokes in the living room. When my wife and I visit and the kids are with us, Grandma retreats to her bedroom, shuts her door, and smokes quietly there, hidden away. Other times she will slip out the back door. When we stay over we pitch a tent in the backyard in the cool open air. My grandma doesn't mind. It relieves her some because she is hyper-conscious of her smoking. Four years ago she spent over one hundred dollars on an air purifier. The next year she bought another at nearly four hundred dollars. She cleans the filter obsessively while we are there. She asks us time and again, "Can you tell a difference? Does it seem better in here?" And time and again we nod eagerly and say *Oh, yes. My! A big difference!* In reality, though, we cannot detect a change at all. I still find it difficult to breathe in her house and everything smells like smoke. The furniture, walls, carpet, everything. I used to joke that even the tap water smelled like cigarette smoke. I often wonder if her air purifying contraption is as bunk as the Buena Ventura, if it might be this century's mythic "fresh air cure."

This time back though the mood is slightly strained. Her breathing, I've noticed, is labored and heavy, her coughing fits, violent. And although I notice for the first time that an inhaler sits on the kitchen counter near her glass ashtray, I say nothing. I ignore it because she does not want to talk about it. Earlier in the morning she had gone to the doctor and was told that she may very well have emphysema, but he wasn't certain.[7] To be certain, he sent her home with a monitor that would track the flow of oxygen in her bloodstream. She is supposed to use it at night. "They want to see if I need oxygen. What a bunch of crap." She is obstinate. "At my age? What the hell is the point?"

IX.

The mythology of the American West, which is an extension of the larger American mythology that begat it, goes like this: the land and the air and the watersheds and the species and everything down to a singular broom of spindly bog sedge, are ours. It has all been willed to us by some greater power, and it is all there for our taking. Manifest Destiny told us that the American West was the Garden of Eden all over again, a notion nineteenth-century travel writers like Horace Greeley, John Codman, and Clarence King promoted variously. To suggest that we have abandoned the garden mythology for a land-wise, water-wise, air-wise ideology is foolhardy. Manifest Destiny still runs in our blood, and is the blank check that funds strip-mining, feedlots, and agrigiants. And mitigative measures such as reclamation do little to offset the consequences of our dominant mythologies. After all, reclamation presupposes that whatever is being reclaimed was ours to claim in the first place. We believe this mythology so entirely that we have created a federal agency—the Bureau of Reclamation—in its honor.

Evidence that threatens to unravel our garden mythology—that suggests that the pristine is polluted, that the virgin is penetrated, or

---

[7] For reasons that aren't exactly clear, emphysema is more common in men than it is in women, a fact that offered some hope for my grandma's health.

that the Buena Ventura was imaginative—is very often met with denial, derision, or dismissiveness. Consider, for instance, a recent AP article about the air quality in Soda Springs: "People living in the area of Soda Springs . . . have a health risk score that is nearly 109 times higher than the national average for other neighborhood tracts included in the 2000 census. The Soda Springs census tract ranks 283rd out of the nation's 65,443 census tracts for the highest risk of industrial air pollution in the country."

The article cites the air in my hometown as the thirteenth most polluted in the nation. It also says that federal regulators point to two culprits behind this diseased air: Monsanto and Agrium, a local corporation that produces industrial amounts of fertilizer.

Three days after this article surfaced, I scanned this headline in the *Caribou County Sun*, my hometown's newspaper: "Monsanto Circulates Fact Sheet to Correct Health Risk Story." The "fact sheet" was released hours after the AP article appeared, and no one in Soda Springs questioned, at least publicly, the veracity of the document. Monsanto's message was clear and unwavering: *The AP article was absurd. It was flat wrong. Their data modeling methodology was botched; nothing could be further from the truth.*

I was troubled for any number of reasons. The intriguing way the paper framed the debate: the "fact sheet" correcting the "story." Monsanto's lightning-fast reaction. The sweeping assurances, the brio in their insistence. The fox insuring us the henhouse is ship-shape, that Eden is still Eden, and that all is well.[8] But I was most troubled by what was not said, by the holes in the logic. The AP story, as they termed it, may very well have been flawed. The data could have been skewed. But this is hardly a yes-the-air-is-polluted, no-it's-not dilemma as Monsanto's fact sheet would have us believe. I am not a scientist, but I can say with some certainty that data sets—especially those dealing in parts per million—rarely work in absolutes, but rather gradations. Maybe the air in Soda Springs is not the thirteenth most industrially polluted in the nation, but could it be the sixteenth or seventeenth, or fifth for that matter? It is difficult to know. What is not difficult to know, however, is that the air in Soda

---

[8]Monsanto is not beyond reproach in the arena of environmental matters. For over four decades they knowingly saturated the small town of Anniston, Alabama, with PCBs (carcinogenic industrial coolants) by unloading "millions of pounds" of the waste into landfills and streams. They were sued and fined seven hundred million dollars in human and ecological damages. Anniston is now virtually uninhabitable as a result of the contamination.

Springs today is not the same elastic air John Codman once sought to relieve his asthma.

X.

It is commonly known that coal miners used to truck caged canaries into the mines as instruments that warned of imminent danger. The canaries' hypersensitive respiratory systems could detect a sudden shift in the air quality, and should the shaft fill with carbon monoxide, the canaries would tip over, giving the miners their short, albeit only, chance to evacuate.

On an already-hot morning in August of 1996, Scott Dominguez, an old high school friend of mine, did not have such a chance to evacuate. He had gone to work that morning, like he did every morning, at Evergreen Resources, Inc., a Soda Springs company that converted mining by-product trucked in from Kerr-McGee (another local operation) into fertilizer. That morning, Scott's boss, Allen Elias—an industrial tycoon infamous for violating multiple environmental safeguards—ordered Scott to clean the sludge out of the bottom of a twenty-five thousand gallon tank. Elias sent Scott into the tank without protective clothing, and when Scott asked for a respirator, his boss seethed: "There's nothing in that tank but mud and water. It's as safe as ordinary shampoo."

Fearful of losing his job, Scott descended into the darkness of the tank. Armed with nothing but a fire hose and broom, Scott went to work. But it wasn't long before he knew something was wrong. By the time two of his co-workers started yelling down into the tank, Scott had already pitched face-first into the gray sludge. An ordinary canary would have been dead once it was lowered into the tank because it was filled with hydrogen cyanide gas. Scott suffered irreparable brain and physical damage. The EPA launched an investigation into Evergreen Resources, and the case climbed to the US Supreme Court. Now Elias sits in a Texas prison and Scott struggles day to day with speech and motor skills.

I cannot pass over the haunting irony of Evergreen as the name of a company that converted waste into fertilizer and nearly killed its employees in the process. If there were ever an ideological disconnect between our mythology and the results of that mythology, Evergreen

292

Resources might typify it. Doesn't the name "Evergreen" connote notions of perpetuity and fecundity? Couldn't the company also be called The Perpetual Garden? Maybe so. Another example of this disconnect is shown in a recent Kerr-McGee television commercial. It shows a mountain desert brushed with fields of snow. A Bel-Air blue sky. Wild horses thunder across the open space and then slow, stop, and nudge what is presumably a natural gas plant. The assuring voice-over—set against some faintly patriotic background music— talks of fuel exploration (mining) and wild nature (streams, meadows, air) existing as one, not as strange bedfellows but as lovers. The machine courting the garden.

XI.

We need the miner's canary as metaphor. We need it for the short term. The warning. The alarm system telling us that the air is no longer air, that night has become day, and that the Great Buena Ventura runs not through Utah's west desert, but through Eden, and that its headwaters are found in our imaginative dreams. What is most important though is that we find a canary for the long term, one whose respiratory system is hypersensitive to changes that can and will occur hundreds of years from now. We need a metaphor that will free us from our indenture to mythology. But as long as we can walk to our faucets and expect water, and as long as we can trust cigarette packages and fact sheets, Monsanto, Hanford, and Evergreen, and as long as we can step outside and expect the air to be there, pure and bracing, the mythology will march on with real consequences hanging in the balance.

Nominated by Robert Wrigley, Jeff P. Jones, Daniel Orozco, Ecotone

YOU HAVE FLOWN TO THE DANGEROUS COUNTRY

by ELIZABETH SPIRES

from THE NEW CRITERION

You have flown to the dangerous country,
how easily you have left this life behind,
this street, this quiet city street,
where letters arrive each day dependably,
where trees make a canopy in summer,
and winter, it is winter now, possesses a cold clarity.

But in the place where you are there is heat,
there is hunger, and the trees have been cut down,
and dogs, there must be dogs, slink out of the night's
blackness, teeth bared, and the sound of drumming penetrates
your sleep even when there are no drums. And slowly,
you begin to forget the words we are used to saying here,
they speak another language there, a language that has no place
for words like *snow* and *safety*, a language I will never know
because I have never been to the dangerous country,
                                    and I do not think I will go.

I think of a tear in a curtain, a jagged man-high tear,
that you step through easily, without a glance backward,
because you are drawn to the dangerous country,

to the need and the want and the hunger,
and to something more that I cannot name.
I feel such a distance, such an unreality,
when I think of you in the dangerous country,
with the heat and the dust and the dogs,
the drums and the knives, the nightmares and the screams.

But I tell myself there must be birds and flowers,
rare flame-colored exotica surrounding tiny pastel houses
that a child might draw, there must be children flying kites,
running along a curving shore where watercolor waves
wash up in shades of ultramarine, there must be
painters painting paintings of it all, and laughter
and singing, because people laugh and sing everywhere,
                                    O tell me that they sing.

Do the people there, do they ever ask you
what it is you mean by *winter* and by *snow*,
by *safety* and by *silence*? Do you try to explain?
And then I begin to wonder what it is to be safe,
do I feel safe here, and is there safety anywhere,
as I move through the rooms of this house, drawing the curtains,
the street so quiet now, and twilight coming on.

Nominated by Michael Collier.

ELDER JINKS

fiction by EDITH PEARLMAN

from THE ANTIOCH REVIEW

GRACE AND GUSTAVE were married in August, in Gustave's home—a squat, brown-shingled house whose deep front porch darkened the downstairs rooms. The house lot had ample space for a side garden. But there were only rhododendrons and azaleas, hugging the building, and a single apple tree stranded in the middle of the lawn. Every May Gustave dragged lawn chairs from the garage to the apple tree and placed them side by side by side. When Grace first saw this array, in July, she was reminded of a nursing home, though she wouldn't say anything so hurtful to Gustave—a man easily bruised; you could tell that from the way he flushed when he took a wrong turn, say, or forgot a proper name. So she simply crossed the grass and moved one of the chaises so that it angled against another, and then adjusted the angle. "They're snuggling now." The third chair she overturned. Gustave later righted it.

They had met in June in front of a pair of foxes who made their own reluctant home at Bosky's Wild Animal Farm on Cape Cod. Gustave was visiting his sister in her rented cottage. Grace had driven in from western Massachusetts with her pal Henrietta. The two women were camping in the State Park.

"You're living in a tent?" inquired Gustave on that fateful afternoon. "You look as fresh as a flower."

"Which flower?" Grace was a passionate amateur gardener as well as a passionate amateur actress and cook and hostess. Had she ever practiced a profession? Yes, long ago; she'd been a second-grade teacher until her own children came along to claim her attention.

"Which flower? A hydrangea," answered Gustave, surprised at his own exhilaration. "Your eyes," he explained, further surprised, this time at his rising desire.

Her tilted eyes were indeed a violet-blue. Her skin was only slightly lined. Her gray hair was clasped by a hinged comb that didn't completely contain its abundance. Her figure was not firm, but what could you expect.

"I'm Grace," she said.

"I'm Gustave," he said. He took an impulsive breath. "I'd like to get to know you."

She smiled. "And I you."

Grace was employing a rhetorical locution popular in her Northampton crowd—eclipsis: the omission of words easily supplied. Gustave, after a pause, silently supplied them. Then he bowed. (His late mother was Paris-born; he honored her Gallic manners even though—except for five years teaching in a Rouen lycée—he had lived his entire life in the wedge of Boston called Godolphin.)

Grace hoped that this small man bending like a headwaiter would now brush her fingers with his mustache—but no. Instead he informed her that he was a professor. His subject was the history of science. Her eyes widened—a practiced maneuver, though also sincere. Back in Northampton her friends, there were scores of them, included weavers, therapists, advocates of holistic medicine, singers. And of course professors. But the history of science, the fact that science even had a history—somehow it had escaped her notice. Copernicus? Oh, Newton, and Einstein, yes, and Watson-and-What's-his-name. "Crick," she triumphantly produced, cocking her head in the flirtatious way. . .

"Is your neck bothering you?"

. . . that Hal Karsh had hinted was no longer becoming. She straightened her head and shook hands like a lady.

Gustave had written a biography of Michael Faraday, a famous scientist in the nineteenth century, though unknown to Grace. When he talked about this uneducated bookbinder, inspired by his own intuition, Gustave's slight pomposity melted into affection. When he mentioned his dead wife he displayed a thinner affection, but he had apparently been a widower a long time.

In Northampton Grace volunteered at a shelter, tending children who only irregularly went to school. "Neglected kids, all-but-abandoned by their mothers, mothers themselves abandoned by the kids' fathers," she said. Gustave winced. When she went on to describe the necessity of getting onto the floor with these youngsters, instructor and pupils both cross-legged on scabby linoleum, Gustave watched her playfulness deepen into sympathy. She'd constructed an indoor windowbox high up in the makeshift basement schoolroom; she taught the life cycle of the daffodil, "its biography, so to speak," including some falsities that Gustave gently pointed out. Grace nodded in gratitude. "I never actually studied botany in my university," she confessed. The University of Wichita, she specified; later she would mention the University of Wyoming; but perhaps he had misheard one or the other—he'd always been vague about the West.

A lawyer friend of Gustave's performed the wedding ceremony in the dark living room. Afterwards Grace sipped champagne under the apple tree with Gustave's sister. "Oh Grace, how peaceable you look. You'll glide above his little tantrums."

"What?" said Grace, trying to turn toward her new sister-in-law but unable to move her head on her shoulders. A Godolphin hairdresser had advised the severe French twist that pulled cruelly at her nape; Henrietta had urged the white tulle sombrero; Grace herself had selected the dress, hydrangea blue and only one size too small. Her grandchildren, who with their parents had taken the red-eye from San Francisco, marveled at the transformation of their tatterdemalion Gammy—but where had her hair gone to? "What?" said the stiffened Grace again; but Gustave's sister forbore to elaborate, just as she had failed to mention that Gustave's first wife, who had died last January in Rouen, had divorced him decades ago, influenced by a French pharmacist she'd fallen in love with.

Gustave and Grace honeymooned in Paris, indulging themselves mightily—a hotel with a courtyard, starred restaurants, a day in Givergny, another in Versailles. They even attended a lecture on the new uses of benzene—Gustave interested in the subject; Grace, with little French and less science, interested in the sombre crowd assembled at the Pasteur Institute. They both loved the new Promenade and the new Musée, and they sat in Saint Chapelle for two hours listening to a concert performed on old instruments—two recorders and a lute and a viola-da-gamba. That was the most blissful afternoon. Gustave put the disarray of their hotel room out of his mind,

298

and also the sometimes fatiguing jubilation with which Grace greeted each new venture. Grace dismissed her own irritation at Gustave's habit of worrying about every dish on the menu—did it matter how much cream, how much butter, we all had to die of something. Light streamed through the radiant window, turning into gold his trim mustache, her untidy chignon.

And now it was September, and classes had begun. Gustave taught Physics for Poets Mondays, Wednesdays and Fridays at nine, The Uses of Chemistry those same days at ten. He taught a graduate seminar in the Philosophy of Science on Thursday evenings. The first two weeks the seminar met in the usual drafty classroom. But then Grace suggested . . . Gustave demurred . . . she persisted . . . he surrendered. And so on the third week the seminar met in the brown-shingled house. Grace baked two apple tarts and served them with warm currant jelly. The students relived last Saturday's football game. Gustave—who, like Grace, professed a hatred of football—quietly allowed the conversation to continue until everyone had finished the treat, then turned the talk to Archimedes. Grace sat in a corner of the living room, knitting.

The next day marked their first separation since the wedding. Gustave had a conference in Chicago. He'd take a cab to the airport right after the Uses of Chemistry. Early that morning he'd packed necessary clothing in one half of his briefcase. While he was reading the newspaper she slipped in a wedge of apple tart, wrapped in tinfoil. After they kissed at the doorway his eye wandered to the corner she had occupied on the previous evening. The chair was still strewn with knitting books and balls of yarn and the garment she was working on, no doubt a sweater for him. She'd already made him a gray one. This wool was rose. His gaze returned to his smiling wife. "See you on Sunday," he said.

"Oh, I'll miss you."

She did miss him, immediately. She would have continued to miss him if she had not been invaded, half an hour later, by two old Northampton friends bearing Hal Karsh. Hal was visiting from his current perch in Barcelona. He would return to Spain on Sunday. Hal—master of the broken villanelle, inventor of the thirteen-line sonnet; and oh, that poetic hair brushing his eyebrows, hair still mostly brown though he was only eight years younger than Grace. Those long fingers, adept at pen and piano but not at keyboard—the word processor was death to composition, he'd tell you, and tell you why, too, at length, anywhere, even in bed.

Gustave's upright piano could have used a tuning. Grace had meant to call someone, but she had been too busy putting in chrysanthemums and ordering bulbs and trying to revive her high-school French. The foursome made music anyway. Lee and Lee, the couple who brought Hal, had brought their fiddles too. Grace rummaged in a box of stuff not yet unpacked and found her recorder. Later she brewed chili. They raided Gustave's *cave*. They finally fell into bed— Lee and Lee in the spare room, Hal on the floor in Gustave's study, Grace, still dressed, on the marital bed. Then on Saturday they drove to Walden Pond, and to the North Shore; and on Saturday night Cambridge friends came across the river. This time Grace made minestrone, in a different pan—the crock encrusted with chili still rested on the counter.

Hal wondered what Grace was doing in a gloomy house in a town that allowed no overnight parking. Such a regulation indicated a punitive atmosphere. And this husband so abruptly acquired—who was he, anyway? "She picked him up in a zoo, in front of a lynx," Lee and Lee told him. He hoped they were exercising their artistic habit of distortion. Hal loved Grace, with the love of an indulged younger brother, or a ragtag colleague—years ago he and she had taught at the same experimental grade school, the one that demanded dedication from its faculty but didn't care about degrees. (Hal did have a master's, but Grace had neglected to go to college.) Hal thought Grace was looking beautiful but unsettled. Did her new spouse share her taste for illicit substances, did he know of her occasional need to decamp without warning? She always came back. . . . When Hal had mentioned that the Cambridge folks would bring grass, Grace's eyes danced. Well, nowadays it was less easy to get here. In Barcelona you could pick it up at your tobacconist, though sometimes the stuff was filthy. . . .

This batch was fine. They all talked as they smoked; and recited poetry; and after a while played Charades. It was like the old times, he thought. He wished Henrietta had come along, too. "I have no use for that fussbudget she married," Henrietta had snapped. But the fussbudget was in Chicago.

It was like the old times, Grace, too, was thinking. And how clever they all were at the game; how particularly clever in this round, Lee and Lee standing naked back to back while she, fully clothed, tra-

300

versed the living room floor on her belly. Odd that no one had yet guessed "New Deal." Odd too that no one was talking, though a few moments earlier there had been such merry laughter; and Hal, that man of parts, had put two of his fingers into his mouth and whistled. At Lee? Or at Lee? In silence Grace slithered toward the hall, and saw, at eye level, a pair of polished shoes. Pressed trousers rose above the shoes. She raised her head, as an eel never could—perhaps she now resembled a worm, ruining the tableau. The belt around the trousers was Gustave's—yes, she had given it to him; it had a copper buckle resembling a sunburst within which bulged an oval turquoise. When it was hanging from his belt rack among lengths of black and brown leather with discreet matching buckles, the thing looked like a deity, Lord of the closet; now, above dark pants, below striped shirt, it looked like a sartorial error, a *mésalliance*. . . .

Scrambling to her feet she found herself staring at Gustave's shirt. Where was his jacket? Oh, the night was warm, he must have taken it off before silently entering the house fifteen hours before he was expected. Her gaze slid sideways. Yes, he had placed—not thrown—his jacket on the hall chair; he had placed—not dropped—his briefcase next to that chair. She looked again at her husband. His exposed shirt bore a large stain in a rough triangular shape—the shape, she divined, of a wedge of tart. She touched it with a trembling forefinger.

"That tender little gift of yours—it leaked," he said.

He surveyed his living room. That naked couple had attended his wedding, had drunk his champagne. A pair of know-it-alls. Their names rhymed. The other creatures he had never seen before. A skinny fellow with graying bangs advanced toward him.

"Gustave, I want you to meet—" Grace began.

"Ask these people to leave," he said in a growl she had never before heard.

They seeped away like spilled pudding . . . Lee and Lee, first, dressed in each other's clothing, clutching their overnight cases and instruments, kissing Hal on their rush toward their car and its overnight parking tickets. They didn't kiss Grace. The Cambridge crowd didn't kiss anybody. But Hal—he stood his ground. He was a head taller than Gustave. He extended a hand. "I'm—"

"Good-bye."

"Listen here—"

"Get out!"

He got out, with his satchel in his left hand and, in the curve of his right arm, Grace. At the last minute she turned as if to look at Gustave, to plead with him, maybe—but it was only to snatch up her pocketbook from the hall table. Next to the pocketbook she saw a cone of flowers. Sweet peas, baby's breath, a single gerbera. An unimaginative bouquet; he must have picked it up ready-made at the airport stall.

Gustave climbed the stairs. The guests had apparently cavorted mostly on the first floor; except for the two unmade beds in the spare room, the only sign of their occupation were towels like puddles on the bathroom tiles. He went into his study and his eye flew to the bookcase where, in manuscript between thick bindings, stood his biography of Faraday, still in search of a publisher. No one had stolen it. On the carpet lay a book—open, face down. He leaned over and identified it as a Spanish grammar. He kicked it.

Downstairs again, he heated some minestrone—he had not eaten anything since his abrupt decision to abandon that boring conference and come home early. The soup was tasty. He looked for a joint— how sweet the house still smelled—but the crowd had apparently sucked their whole stash. He did find, in one corner, a recorder, but he couldn't smoke that. He put all the plates and glasses into the dishwasher. He tried to scrub the remains of chili from a pot, then left it to soak. He vacuumed. Then he went upstairs again, and undressed; and, leaving his clothes on the floor—these gypsy ways were catching—slipped into Grace's side of the bed. With a sigh he recognized as an old man's, he flopped onto his back. His thoughts—which were uncharitable—did not keep him from falling asleep.

But a few hours later he found himself awake. He got up and went through the house again. He threw the Spanish grammar into the trash bag he had stuffed earlier and lugged the thing out to the garage, knowing that anyone who saw him in his striped pajamas under the flood light at three o'clock in the morning would take him for a madman. So what. Their neighbors considered them a cute couple; he had overheard that demeaning epithet at the fish market. He'd rather be crazy than cute. He relocked the garage and returned to the house. And surely he had been deranged to marry a woman because of her alluring eyes. He'd mistaken a frolicsome manner for lasting charm. She was merely frivolous; and the minute she was left unsupervised. . . . He stomped into the living room. That rose-colored garment-in-progress now shared its chair with a wine bottle, good vineyard, good year . . . empty. He'd like to rip the knitting out.

The yarn would remain whorled; he'd wind it loosely into a one big whorl. When she came back she'd find a replica of Faraday's induction coil, pink. Come back? She could come back to collect her clothing and her paella pan and the bulbs she kept meaning to plant. He picked up the sweater. It would fit a ten-year-old. Insulting color, insulting size . . . he went back to bed, and lay there.

Grace, too, was awake. The hotel room was dark and malodorous. Hal slept at her side without stirring, without snoring. He had always been a devoted sleeper. He was devoted to whatever brought him pleasure. Under no circumstances would she accompany him to Barcelona, as he had idly suggested last night. (He had also suggested that she buy the drinks at the hotel bar downstairs; she supposed she'd have to pay for the room, too.) Anyway, she had left her passport next to Gustave's in his top drawer. She hoped he'd send it back to her in Northampton—she had not yet sold her house there, thank goodness, thank providence, thank Whoever was in charge. She hoped he'd send all her things, without obsessive comment. She wanted no more of him. She wanted no more of Hal, either: it was enough that she had shared his toothbrush last night, and then his bed, and was now sleeping—well, failing to sleep—in one of his unlaundered shirts.

How hideous to have only yesterday's lingerie. Unshaved underarms were one thing: grotty underpants quite another. What time did stores open on Sundays? She'd slip out and shop, get a new sweater, maybe—that would pick up her spirits. She remembered the half-finished vest for her granddaughter she'd left on the chair; she hoped Gustave would send that back, too. . . .

"Amelie. . . ." muttered Hal.

"Grace," she corrected.

If only she were back in Northampton already, where everyone was needy and she was needed. She wished she had never visited that Wild Animal Farm at the Cape, had never paused to look at those foxes. She wished she had not married a man because he was learned and polite, especially since he had turned out to be pedantic and sanctimonious.

From time to time that Sunday Gustave thought of calling the lawyer who'd married them—she happened to specialize in divorce. Instead he read the papers; and watched the football game. What a sport:

303

force directed by intelligence. He prepared for tomorrow's class, the one in which he and the students would reproduce one of Faraday's earliest experiments in electrification. They'd all come carrying foil-wrapped water-filled film canisters with a protruding nail. These were primitive Leyden jars in which to store electricity. The electricity would be produced by a Styrofoam dinner plate nested in an aluminum pie pan—the kids would bring these friction-makers too. He went to bed early. He could see a low autumnal moon above the mansard across the street—well, only the upper half of the sphere was visible, but he could supply the rest.

Grace bought, among other things, a yellow sweater. She took her time getting back to the hotel. She found Hal showered and smiling. During a long walk by the river she listened to his opinions on magic realism and antomasia—she'd forgotten what that was, she admitted. "The use of an epithet instead of a proper name," Hal said. " 'The Fussbudget,' say. . . ." He told her of the Spanish medieval farsa, which was related to farce. And just when she thought her aching head would explode it was time to put him into a cab to the airport. He seemed to have enough cash for the taxi. He thrust his head out of the open window as the vehicle left the curb. "My apartment is near Las Ramblas, best location in Barcelona," he called. She waved. The cab disappeared, and her headache with it.

She went back to their room, now hers, and read the papers, and enjoyed a solitary supper in front of the TV, watching a replay of that afternoon's football game. Nice intercept! Such brave boys, there on the screen. But Gustave had been brave too, hadn't he, scorning *savoir faire* as he cleansed his house of unwelcome revelers. How red his face had become when Hal theatrically held out his hand . . . he'd felt wronged, hadn't he, or perhaps *in* the wrong; maybe he thought she'd summoned her friends, maybe he thought he'd failed her. If she ever saw him again she'd tell him about Hal's lonely rootlessness. She'd tell him about poor Lee and Lee's barn of unsaleable paintings, if she ever saw him again. . . . She put on her new nightgown and went to bed. She could see a curve of the dome of the Massachusetts State House, just enough to suggest the whole.

The lecture room was shaped like a triangle. The platform holding lectern and lab bench was at the apex, the lowest part of the room; concentric rows of slightly curved tables radiated upwards toward the back. Three students sat at each table. The professor stood at the lectern when he talked, moved to his lab bench for demonstrating. He and the students employed their identical home-made equipment. As he talked and demonstrated—creating the electric charge, storing it—the students imitated. There was expectant laughter and an occasional excited remark and a general air of satisfaction. Only a few of these poets might change course and become physicists; but not one of them would hold science in contempt. "Faraday made this experiment with equally crude apparatus," he reminded them. "And with faith that it would work. Faith—so unfashionable now—was his mainstay."

The woman in the back row, alone at a table, without pie plate or film can, wished that she, too, had the implements, that she could obey the instructions of the measured, kindly voice; but mostly she marveled again at the story that voice was telling of the humble young Faraday setting himself upon his life's journey. "He considered that God's presence was revealed in nature's design," wound up the little man. He looked radiant.

When he at last noticed the figure in the yellow sweater, he was cast back to an afternoon in Paris when the same glowing color had been produced by sun refracted through stained glass; and the lips of his companion had parted as she listened to winds and strings send music aloft. She had thrilled; she had become elevated; she had generously carried him with her. . . .

The lecture concluded to applause; the teen-agers dispersed; the professor materialized in the chair next to the visitor's.

They looked at each other for a while.

"I'm Grace," she said at last.

"I'm Gustave," and how his heart leaped. "I'd like to . . . get to know you."

Another long pause while he belatedly considered the dangers in so ambitious an enterprise; for he, too, would have to be known, and his shabby secrets revealed, and his out-of-date convictions as well. They'd endure necessary disappointments, and they'd practice necessary forgiveness, careful to note which subjects left the other fraught. Grace's mind moved along the same lines. Each elected to take the risk. Gustave showed his willingness by touching the lovely face, Grace hers by disdaining eclipsis. "Me, too," was all she said.

Nominated by Antioch Review, Joyce Carol Oates, Rosellen Brown

DOOR PSALM

by HEIDI HART

from EDGE BY EDGE (Toadlily Press)

There are the doors
in and out of the world:
the white bed,
the prison gate,
the still pool, deeper than it looks,
the heart valve open or shut,
the mineshaft,
the stone rolled from the tomb.

There are the doors
of the body:
the mouth that accepts
the drink at last,
the womb that lets in
and lets out,
the eyelid that lifts
in recognition.

There are the doors
you see with an inner eye:
the moment you pull up
a flower and fear
the ground has opened for you;
the wind that enters your room
and asks you
to leave the life you know.

Nominated by Helen H. Houghton

MORMONS IN HEAT

fiction by DON WATERS

from THE KENYON REVIEW

He that knoweth not good from evil is blameless.
> —Alma 29:5, The Book of Mormon

SUNLIGHT FLASHES OFF CHROME FENDERS, hitting Eli's eyes, blinding him. Eight motorcycles enlarge in the rearview mirror. Hot this morning, and warming up.

"More highway company," Eli says to Sutton, or to the steering wheel—whichever. This latest cache of sightseeing brochures is simply hypnotizing his partner. Sutton holds one by the edges, handling it like a delicate specimen. Splashed across another glossy pamphlet are different types of cacti.

"Forget about those, Sutton. Pay attention," Eli says. "You might learn something."

As the bikes approach, down goes Eli's window. He wants to side-glance that fine Harley craftsmanship. He wants to inhale, for a moment, the freedom.

"Chicks on motorcycles," Eli says, clenching the steering wheel. He can almost smell the armpits.

Leading the charge is a woman wearing square gunner's goggles. Eli clocks her at fifty, maybe fifty-five years old. Her cheeks are as red as her flapping bandanna, cinched tightly around her skull, and she commands with her chin, which she holds high, with attitude. She veers into the oncoming lane, and Eli marvels at her glistening biceps.

"Elder Sutton," Eli says, "I am experiencing a vision."

Sutton doesn't say anything, not that the kid would. Eli sets his jaw. Why can't he appreciate this impromptu, middle-of-nowhere, wet T-shirt contest? The woman's custom-made, turquoise low-rider has high, wide handlebars, and along with a rib-tight T-shirt, she and her companions wear sleeveless leather vests with cartoonish beavers on the back. Over the beaver's crazed, bloodshot eyes and squared buckteeth is the group's name, stitched in white: The Beaver Rockets.

When the last rider thunders past, she opens her throttle and her muffler explodes. Eli's eardrums palpitate. The women soon disappear into the shimmering highway, and again the desert is quiet, cleansed.

"Now that's the work of God," Eli says.

A bead of sweat disappears into Sutton's thin, wordless lips. If the kid has anything to say about what went down the previous night, in Eureka, he's saving it for the Celestial Kingdom.

"She was eighteen," Eli says, stating his case. "So just stop with your dumb look." And there is, always, a look. Sutton has a sharp, lordly nose that goes up whenever he's disappointed.

Eli, recalling what happened, grows tense and aroused. Desert daughters love opening their legs. He's learned that. He was two nights in Eureka when he met Emily, Emily Something-or-Other. The girl was a threat to any man with functioning testes: strawberry-flavored, bee-stung lips and a stomach as firm as watermelon rind. Last night, he fast-talked the girl out of a pair of rose-print panties. Then, this morning, shocked to realize his bareback, condomless mistake, he unleashed an incoherent but firm speech, insisting that she ingest six blue, oval, morning-after pills. Quite lucky, he lied to the pretty young stranger, he just so happened to work in pharmaceuticals.

"Guilty as charged," Eli says. "She was my Achilles. I admit it. Can we drop it?"

The missionaries flew out of Eureka, coursing along the furnace of Pancake Range. After a wrong turn back on 375, so-called Extraterrestrial Highway, Eli flipped a U and decided on 95 instead. He's aiming for distance, after all. Highway 95 is as flat and coppery as a penny.

Near Goldfield Summit, Eli stops to refuel at a highway gas shack. Prolonged drives make his muscles feel itchy and needled. He scours the trunk for his racquetball, something to squeeze. With all these Books of Mormon they ferry around, there's hardly space for luggage. A canister of motor oil has leaked all over one box. And, thanks to Sutton, the trunk is also filthy with brochures. Hundreds of them! Sutton collects and actually reads the stupid things, front to back. Eli's come across one from every country, an advertisement for Virginia City's Suicide Table, maps of isolated ghost towns. They've never been to Pyramid Lake or the Area 51 Mountaintop Lookout, and, Eli decides, they never will.

"Seen my racquetball?" Eli says, tapping Sutton's window. He mimes like he's rolling down an imaginary window.

Sutton throws a cold glance at him before returning to his brochure.

"Jesus. Let's not rush to the podium," Eli says.

Just look at the kid. Buttoned-up in a starched white shirt and a navy blue blazer. Scarecrow thin, size twenty-eight waist, Sutton could pass for thirteen. And his military-style haircut and glassine features certainly don't add any years. Oh, Sutton is Salt Lake City's foot soldier, all right. On hundred-plus days, during long hauls, he dresses in the required uniform. Even his goddamn name badge is always pinned on, per Church regulations.

Whatever sadist at HQ paired him with Sutton should be fired. After spending an entire year alone, the Church finally delivered Eli a partner. His partner turned out to be a dud. Eli wondered if he could ship him back. He was told that the kid was "shy." But Sutton isn't "shy." He's pathologically withdrawn. Sutton has spoken only a few dozen paragraphs, at most, but the sentences in those paragraphs aren't strung together. Each remark arrives startlingly, unattached to further conversation, each awkward syllable as unlikely as a snowflake landing in Death Valley.

When Sutton isn't looking, Eli scoops up an armful of pamphlets. He deposits them in a nearby trash can.

Eli settles behind the wheel, next to his monkish partner. Eli once read a magazine article about a man with severe epilepsy. Surgeons had to remove half of the guy's brain. When the patient awoke, he learned that the empty side of his cranium was filled with Ping-Pong balls. Three strands of light blond hair are caked to Sutton's forehead. Eli starts the car, wondering what's in there.

Eli has maintained a steady level of paranoia throughout his tour, sure that the higher-ups are watching him, keeping tabs. Hardwired in his DNA is the fuck-up gene. He understands this. It's always been his way. Surveillance could have started the moment he slaughtered his compulsory vows. Odd the way his sponsor, guy by the name of Jeremiah, never took him seriously after that.

Eli thinks about it from time to time. Perhaps he was a little too eager to enlist in the Church of Jesus Christ of Latter-Day Saints. And maybe he was too pushy by insisting on a mission. After all, LDS didn't find him. He flipped open the Yellow Pages and he dialed them. It was either LDS or the Jehovahs, Eli didn't care, but a nearby LDS Ward called back first. After his endowment ceremony, Church officials must have been stumped. What to do with a thirty-year-old, jobless divorcé who's been living in his brother's basement? Save his soul, yes. But send him where?

Eli excels at putting distance between himself and his problems. Take what happened with Margo, his ex-wife, for example. One affair at his real estate office melted into the next. Margo found out and yeah yeah: divorce. That made *número dos*. Shit, he needed to get his act together. Not long after she walked out (actually, she made him leave), he began paying more attention to the Church's bland TV commercials. LDS appeared to be a wholesome enough choice.

And his decision worked—for a while. The Church kept him on track his first year out in the desert. Eli actually began believing in this stuff. The Books were all around him, so he began to read. Salvation through purity through family seemed OK by him. He was cruising through this missionary thing. He was giving away Books faster than headquarters could ship them FedEx.

Of course, there were a lot of smoky bars amid the brush weed. Also lots of press-on fingernails in those honky-tonks. After pounding pavement morning till night, there was little for Eli to do in those backward towns in the middle of Nevada. The red-haired, bowlegged woman worked for the Bureau of Land Management. Her job, she explained, was exterminating a particular species of invasive thistle. Not that it mattered. What mattered was the morning he awoke next to her, her salty toe lodged in his mouth.

His budding faith incrementally flaked away, bleached by the sun, stripped off by harsh desert wind. Nothing was left for Eli back in Texas, in Houston, his hometown. Rather than abandoning his mission, he stayed the course. He remained in the desert. Besides, everything was all-expenses-paid. Looked at properly, he was enjoying an extended, two-year vacation.

All he had to do was dispense the Books. The Church was always sending him more, and still more, goddamn Books. He scattered them in places named Jackpot, Battle Mountain, and Manhattan, Nevada.

Highway speed signs read seventy, so Eli goes eighty-five. He wants half the state between him and this morning. That feat in Eureka has that one-two-three strikes ring to it. He thinks the stunt is grounds for excommunication. Eli mashes his heel into the accelerator.

Mud lakes and sand flats skate past the windows. A sea of sagebrush blurs into silver-green fog. Sun fries Eli's knuckles. Augusts are miserably hot. Nevada is long, empty roads, etched ridgelines, so much open blue.

Plastic grocery bags trapped by sage introduce the town of Amargosa, a minor highway pit stop cuddled by low hills. Eli slows down when he realizes the town is crawling with bikers.

Eight lady joyriders on a lonely desert highway are a welcome sight. But sixty-plus middle-aged women dangling from ape-hanger handlebars, their modified Hogs parked along the town's half-mile drag, make for an unexpected, discombobulating weirdscape. Amargosa is firing on all cylinders. It's as though he and Sutton have penetrated some sort of menopausal biker pod. Drug-thin gals in tight-tight tees idle next to large-boned women squeezed into jeans. Frontward denim pouches hold beery guts. Some of the women look terrifying, notably the gray-haired lady wearing the "Priestess" T-shirt.

Eli pulls to the side of the road, stunned.

"We have to keep driving," Sutton says unexpectedly. The kid blinks like there's sand in his eyes.

"You work," Eli says. "Did I forget to wind you?"

Sutton reaches for the gearshift, but Eli slaps at his knuckles. "Jesus H," Eli says. So many women, he wants to say. He says instead, "You are the worst evangelical I've ever met." He points out the window. "These are potential converts."

A Hi-Top Motel sits across the street. Three big-breasted women are loitering on the upper balcony. They're huddled around a ripped-open twelve-pack of beer. One of them waves, and Sutton blinks spastically.

Each small, desert town is a slow-mo rerun of the previous dusty stop, full of tedious chitchat and hundreds of miles before interesting new faces. It isn't a hard decision to make.

"We're staying the night," Eli says. "Too many hours behind the wheel," he says. "Plus, my heels ache." He cracks his large toe.

ʊʊʊ

In the motel's air-conditioned office, Sutton plucks brochures from a plastic rack. Not surprisingly, he's holding up his nose. The kid scrutinizes one brochure with a frog across its cover. He swipes several others and slips them into his blazer.

Thanks to the flock of bikers, it's the Hi-Top's last room. Every Hi-Top has the same flavor: bolted down TVs and cheap sunset wallpaper. This particular room smells like a difficult case of athlete's foot. Eli thinks it would be nice, just once, to open the door onto an ocean view. Oh to be able to inhale eucalyptus.

Sutton sheds his blazer and retreats to the bathroom, taking his brochures with him. He slams the door.

Most baby-faced nineteen-year-olds are awarded the primo assignments, two years' traveling around Argentina, Switzerland, the tropics. Eli, on the other hand, knew he was eleven years past the expiration date. A different set of rules applied. On the day he was given his Divine Assignment, he was escorted into a back room of his local Ward. He was handed a worn map of Nevada, keys to a used Toyota, and a credit card good at any Hi-Top Motel in the southwestern United States. The Church, he was quietly informed, was a majority shareholder.

The small parking lot is overrun with custom-made motorcycles. Eli stands gaga at the window. His lips are brackish from the long, face-melting drive, and he feels dehydrated, which always gives him a buzz. Mufflers rumble distantly.

The Beaver Rockets. He's never heard of the motorcycle club, or whatever they are. He spots the woman from the highway, Ms. Biceps, Ms. Red Bandanna, holding court from the seat of her lowrider. Her bandanna has disappeared, revealing licorice-black hair fashioned into a mullet, business in the front and party in the back. Others listen as she puffs on a cigar. The next time she lifts the stogie to her lips, clutching it, Eli's knees weaken. His thoughts drift. He imagines a life similar to hers, a life beside hers, a life without rules—gnats in his eyes, unpaid bills, arrest warrants with his name on them.

Eli's only successful conversion happened his first week, a Western Hemisphere record. Only one other missionary ever saved another

312

soul within the first seven days. But that was in 1977, in Phuket, Thailand, a different landmass, with completely different standards. So as far as Eli is concerned, it doesn't count. He wins.

For his record breaker, he brought around a copper-mine foreman from Cactus Springs named Ted Ringle and his non-English-speaking wife, Tanja. Ted Ringle explained, with a wink, that his new bride was mail-ordered and arrived via Turkish freighter.

Anyway, Eli was out to cut his teeth. He had something to prove. Fresh off a divorce, anointed with a purpose, he was soldier-ready.

For a week he showed up at the Ringles' apartment with Mini-Mart donuts. After reading the usual, best-of, all-time-greatest LDS hits from the Book, Eli would bow his head and say, "Let's pray." Good-spirited Ted Ringle would nod while his Slavic wife smiled. Bless her heart: she understood nothing. And whenever Ted Ringle posed one of the Big, Unanswerable Questions, Eli would pinch his chin and say, "That is interesting. That is very interesting." Eli learned the importance of validating without answering.

The newlyweds for Eli were a coup. They were everything the Church wanted, a happy, healthy couple on the verge of procreation. But after his first converts, Eli's luck ran out.

So he fine-tuned his advance. He tailored his routines. Each mark required a fresh approach. Conversion was a delicate con. Assumed godliness, thankfully, commanded a modicum of respect. If he had God on his bench (or when others thought he might have God on his bench), they sometimes listened.

Where to find the people, the hearts and minds, the converts? He attended town hall meetings, county fairs, and small-time rodeos. It took patience to sniff out the most attentive audiences.

Lonely old farts were a great discovery. They couldn't hurry away. On Saturday evenings, state-run nursing homes rolled out the bingo and pinochle, and Eli would show up, his face red and raw from having just shaved, and he'd wander around, pretending to be a lost grandson.

Naturally, old folks enjoyed their tall tales, too. Eli began to loathe the countless variations on World War II, childhood in Kansas, how-things-were yarns. He was shown plenty of embroidery and too much needlepoint. Then he began noticing the vultures, vultures of all sizes, during his long treks around the state. Their talons were always curled around power lines, perched as though recharging. The ugly birds fed off the weak. They too took advantage of soon-to-be carcasses.

Eli cooled it on the geriatrics. He returned to rural ranches and neighborhood grids. Dressed as he was, in a navy blue spokesperson get-up, a square, white name badge over his heart, he was a spot-on giveaway. The sight of him inspired grimaces. Women were nicer than men, and mothers he could talk to. But whenever one of them balked, he'd let loose with the scare routine.

"War, Ma'am," he'd begin. "This is war. And you and your lovely daughter here are in a foxhole. A hot bullet rips through her eye. That creamy scarlet hole is a horror show. That's right. Her eye hangs down her face like some broken jack-in-the-box coil. Bombs are concussing. Your daughter is moaning. So do you take Him into your heart? *Do you then?* To save your daughter's eternal soul?"

Rumor has it there are special departments in Hell set aside for the Sons of Perdition. If only Eli believed in quote-unquote Hell, if he just believed in quote-unquote the Sons of Perdition, he might be frightened away from his boozy mistakes. He was counting on the Church to clear the brush from his yard. Hellfire scare tactics work on others. Why not him? He knows officials in SLC wouldn't be pleased with his antics. Hell, they'd probably throw a few aneurisms.

Eli shuffles across the grubby motel carpet. He taps the wood of the bathroom door with his uncut fingernails.

"We haven't even touched these new boxes," Eli yells through the door. "What do they expect us to do? Eat them?" He's referring to the latest shipment. "I'm going out. Want me to grab some local leaflets? The usual?"

He hears the sound of a toilet flush. As usual, Sutton doesn't respond. Eli presses his palm to the door. He doesn't like Sutton. He doesn't understand him. Still, he feels somewhat protective of the kid. It's the same disturbing feeling that overcomes him whenever his brother leaves Eli alone with his retarded, helmet-protected nephew.

In the bathroom of the local Bongo Burger, Eli squeezes out drops of lingering guilt piss, inhaling the medicinal stench off the urinal puck.

He sets a gold-embossed Book on the toilet's lid in the first stall. He puts another in the adjoining stall. He leans one more against the faucet. Customers will have to move them. People love free things, right? Lately, this has been Eli's general strategy. Who cares if some

314

anonymous face then pops a Book or two in the trash? Not his problem. He's got all these goddamn Books. HQ keeps sending him these fucking Books.

There's not a single cloud in the sky, and an eastern breeze drifts in, carrying traces of smoldering sage. Sweat that hasn't absorbed into Eli's sacred garments settles in a wet sack around his groin. He's in a constant fight against rashes. He calls the long, funny underwear, which wraps his torso and ends at his knees, his Brigham Sweatbox.

Eli finds two metal newspaper boxes on Amargosa's strip of boarded-up storefronts. The *Daily Wart* sits beside a national newspaper with week-old headlines. He shovels a few Books on top of the national paper and the spring-loaded door slams shut. Yet another lazy tactic—but whatever.

As he's propping the other box open, a motorcycle appears alongside the curb. Its rim is polished to a mirror finish. Ms. Former Red Bandanna, Ms. Cigar Toker, Ms. Woman of the Highway, holds a bottle of beer.

"Toss me a paper?" she says to Eli. Two lime-green eyes, hooded by wild, untended eyebrows, overwhelm him. He stares at her like he's stupid.

"A newspaper please," she says again. She points at the local, the *Daily Wart*.

He fumbles, handing one over. Up close, the woman's triceps are stunning. Deep ravines line the backs of her arms. Her crinkly neck is absurdly out of place with the rest of her, or vice versa.

"Tina Pennybocker," she says to Eli in a rasp. "Tina was born in Amargosa."

She folds back the paper, and he's shown a thumbnail photo of a brunette with spectacular bangs. The brunette's hair crests like a breaking wave. It's a face only a mother could love. Unfortunately for Tina Pennybocker, her photo lies in the center of the obituaries.

"Tina's family plot is down the road at the cemetery," the woman tells him. "A damn shame the nearest minister lives in Tonopah. He called Joanna. Said he can't make it. None of us have much to do in the way of what he's about."

She runs her thick fingers through her mullet and takes a swig of her beer. There's a sudden thirst in Eli's throat. His uvula aches. Dusty goggles hang around the woman's furrowed neck, nestled inside loose cleavage, a soft, flabby, freckled wonderland.

His shirttails aren't tucked. Mustard stains decorate his collar, and his dress shoes are laughably tattered. His LDS name badge is long gone too, misplaced somewhere at Massacre Lake during an all-night bonfire with three Paiutes. He looks anything but pious. Still, getting interested, he glances again at the woman's low-cut landscape.

He says, "Actually, you're in luck." He places a Book on her rhinestone-encrusted saddleback. "I might be able to help," he says. "Eli," he tells her.

The woman's smile shows off a brown front tooth, a shade darker where it meets her gums. Eli always likes people better when they're a little broken.

"Your name?" he asks, and he gently takes her beer bottle. Church doctrine dictates absolutely no alcohol.

"Jane," the woman says. Then she adds, as though it's her surname, "from Wyoming."

Church doctrine also states no fornication outside the sacred bonds of marriage.

"The Lord visits us in unexpected ways," Eli says to Jane-from-Wyoming. He swallows a mouthful of piss-warm beer. That mouthful tells Eli he'd very much like another, and soon.

Nights like this, shrouded by amber lamplight, the idea of a next day does not exist. Jane-from-Wyoming chisels him down to basics. With her, he is just muscle, nerve, and nuclei. All night, motorcycles roam the street, their exhaust notes like Gatling guns, upending Eli's whiskey-sugared dreams.

Their brief get-to-know-you joyride into the tan hills beyond Amargosa segued into shots, cigarettes, and nibbles off her briny Wyoming neckline. Jane-from-Wyoming smells of seaweed, and when he melts into her large, lumpy breasts, he imagines swimming in an oil slick. Plaquelike odor rises from her decaying tooth, and her expert tongue probes like a lizard's.

In the middle of the night, Eli jolts awake. He sits upright. His throbbing erection pushes against the heavy bedspread. He is insanely thirsty; did he eat a sand castle? The room looks wicked, strange, as though he's seeing it for the first time through smudged blue lenses. Odd, too, the last time his rectum throbbed a doctor was checking for a leaky appendix.

Sutton marches out of the bathroom in tighty-whiteys. He wears only one sock. A bright fluorescent bulb illuminates steam billowing from the kid's shoulders. Like always, he's been showering, his fa-

316

vorite pastime when Eli's busy. Sutton pulls a cover from the other bed and yanks it into the bathroom.

Eli pinches up the sheet and studies his bedmate's cream-cheese body. Varicose veins line her thighs. He might as well be looking at a map of the country's interstate highway system. He is horror-struck. He is so turned on.

A night with Jane-from-Wyoming isn't life changing, but he will have to reevaluate things. At one point, he was sort of tossed in the air and thrown against the headboard, which accounts for his aching jaw. It feels like it's been broken and reset. The floor, strewn with condoms, is a spring break shoreline. Jane-from-Wyoming snores like a trucker.

She rolls over, taking the rest of the sheets with her. Eli freezes. How to turn the troublesome thing off? He needs a switch. She rolls again, and her hand lands on his sternum. As if sensing its animal heat, her fingers wander downward. She steers him like he's a joystick, a game, an object. He is powerless under her weight.

❧❧❧

In the morning, Sutton struts out of the bathroom, showered, dressed, and toothpasty. The knot in his tie is a perfect Windsor. The sight of his partner's early morning efforts rouses Eli's nausea.

"We're leaving," Eli says to Sutton. Eli rolls out of bed and begins picking clothes off the floor. There's a window in the bathroom. It's small, but they'll fit through. For some reason, Sutton starts arranging brochures on the other bed, fanning them out, situating them . . . just so. The kid probably read each one—fascinating!

"Are you showing the place?" Eli asks, growing more irritated. He can't find his necklace, a gold crucifix, his grapapa's.

Jane-from-Wyoming, bless her, tumbled out of the room before dawn. And she never returned. Eli parts the drapes. Beaver Rockets are gathering in the parking lot. He quickly shuts them. Sutton hovers with that nose of his.

"I don't need your jury-foreman attitude," Eli says. "I'm in the middle of a crisis. My grandfather's necklace. It's gone."

"You told her you're giving the sermon," Sutton says.

Eli snorts. How many lies has he used, and with less muscular women? He throws open the end table, and inside is a new Bible. Those goddamn Gideons. Eli's smacked with admiration. They are on top of it.

"That's pent-up sperm talk," Eli says to Sutton. "I'm not giving any sermon. In fact, we're leaving. Right now."

"You said," Sutton says. "I heard you through the door."

"Hallelujah, you talk," Eli says. "A miracle."

This new pain feels like studded plates pressing into his temples. Not to mention, Eli's left incisor is chipped. A quart of Blue Label: just about the right amount for him to tell Jane-from-Wyoming he'd give a sermon. Eli detests public speaking. Anxiety logjams the sentences in his throat before they ever reach open air.

Chewing on the side of his thumb, Sutton paces a figure eight. His willowy shoulders slump forward, and he looks exactly like the teenager that he is. The Church dispatches its lambs when they're only nineteen, the crucial years, when a young man's hard-on is at its hormonal and optimal peak. But Eli doesn't think Sutton ever ties off his own rope. They've shared the same room every night for the past 150 nights, their pillows mere yards apart, and Eli's never seen movement, or heard rustling, underneath Sutton's sheets.

Eli realizes he's laced his shoes wrong. He skipped holes on both feet. Already it's a horrible start.

Sutton says, "We're going to that woman's funeral."

Another divorce, followed by this missionary charade, barrels of bad decisions, and now that Sutton is finally speaking, he's high-minded. The total prick.

"I like you better when you're broken," Eli says. "Please shut up."

A wolfish glint lights up the kid's eyes. His shoulders pull back and his spine straightens. He charges over. Eli raises his arms in self-defense. But rather than a fist, Sutton comes up with a pair of size sixteen panties. They're yellow. He squashes them into Eli's nose.

"I know," Eli says. He sits on the bed. "I know, I know. This is worse than the hooker in Mesquite, isn't it?"

❧❧❧

A large contingent of beaver insignias has colonized the Hi-Top's parking lot. Eli's stomach drops when he sees this. More arrived during the night. Sutton shoves Eli out the door, where Jane-from-Wyoming is waiting next to her turquoise bike. Frayed denim cutoffs accentuate her strong, cellulite-padded thighs.

"You clean up," she says. Jane-from-Wyoming looks rested, considering.

"Splashed water in my eyes," Eli says.

Jane-from-Wyoming pats her hump seat. "Minister."

Eli hates her. Eli adores her. He feels chapped bodywide.

"I said," she says. Her lip rises like a curtain, parading her ugly tooth.

As he straddles the seat, Sutton thrusts a Bible at him. It's from the end table, those overachieving Gideons.

The kid says to him, "Do good."

A meandering motorcade has formed on the street. They drive to the front, assuming the lead. The smell of burnt asphalt yields to whiffs of peppermint coming off Jane-from-Wyoming's shampooed mullet.

A beat-up hearse soon rolls into town. Fingers point down the road, directing it to the lead spot, where Eli's afforded a first-rate view, beyond tinted glass, of a plain brown coffin. He's unable to attach any feelings to the thing. To him it's just a large box, nothing more. But he is startled when the driver suddenly leaps out, both thumbs raised, smiling wildly. Short, Latino, the guy's dressed in orange sweats. His socked feet are shoved into a pair of checkered, slip-on Vans with demolished heels. He wears them more like flip-flops, scraping the pavement as he walks. Obviously, the guy is thrilled to be around so much fringed leather and feathered hairdos. Eli's relieved when he sees Sutton, behind the wheel of the Toyota, at the rear of the motorcade.

"I apologize for taking advantage," Jane-from-Wyoming says over her shoulder. She squeezes his knee. "You're a man of the cloth. I understand. But there are times a woman needs a mercy fuck. Tina was a dear friend."

Eli says, for lack of anything, "Glad I could help."

"The bite marks will disappear," Jane-from-Wyoming adds. Before he can respond, she stabs the air with her fist. Engines rev, the deep reverberations begin. Eli's brain rattles in his skull. His testicles vibrate on the seat. He imagines this is how war sounds, mechanized and unrelenting.

The deafening swarm follows the hearse a quarter mile and turns down a dirt road, ending at Amargosa's cemetery, nothing more than a powdery scrap of land dotted with scorched weeds. Dominating an acre's worth of headstones is a granite obelisk engraved with the dead woman's name: PENNYBOCKER. It overlooks a sad excuse for a river. Eroded banks hold gray pools of stagnant water. Etched thickly at the base of the monument is the father's generic name, Edward William. Eli does the math on him. Dead twelve years. Her mother, Helen Douglas, followed seven years later. Plenty of room for Tina's four easy letters.

Four women with arms as burly as Jane-from-Wyoming's wrestle the casket from the hearse. They throw it onto a hoist perched over a freshly dug grave. The driver claps, slipping out of his shoe.

Eli can't find Sutton anywhere in the crowd. As the women gather, angling for position, shoulder to shoulder, he wonders how many more predicaments, how many more can he stomach? Deliver a sermon? Eli doesn't even know how, or why, Tina Pennybocker of Amargosa died. He figures he'll just say, Bless this, Bless that, Too bad for Tina, rev the Toyota's four cylinders, and haul ass out of town—next stop Elko.

These expectant eyes might as well be dentist drills. His heart beats in his throat, nearly sealing it. And his stomach squirts up a teaspoon's worth of bile onto the back of his tongue. He is 100 percent hangover emotional. Noxious exhaust fumes from the bikes swirl, and the glare off some lady's tachometer makes his eyes water.

Eli struggles, and he says, "The sky is hustling with light."

Hustling with light?

He finds faith difficult, if not impossible. Sure, he'd like to believe. When he signed the forms, when he joined the Church, Eli thought it might get the ball rolling. But it didn't. It hasn't.

He peers out over the mob of women. Pale morning light reddens above the hills. It's a commanding land, that's certain. Heat and infinite, forever sky. The West does have the best views. Nothing is more sacred than the sun, he thinks, spotlight on us all.

"Let us look up," Eli says. And a few naïve women actually do. His throat catches when he says, "Up at the sky." A sun-glare tear drips down his cheek. Jane-from-Wyoming, misinterpreting, lays her hand between his shoulder blades.

"It's not easy," she says, "I know." Eli briefly recalls the sensation of cold keys whipping his bare ass.

There's a tug on Eli's shoulder, and Sutton steps forward, his sleeves rolled up, lips pursed, his nose raised high. The teenager clutches the brochure with the frog on the cover. He stands before the women assuredly, as if, Bible open, he's behind a pulpit.

"Kid," Eli says.

Sutton stares back at him coolly, and then calmly, reading from his trifold brochure, he begins.

"Amargosa is home to one of the rarest forms of life in the world. Here, along a twelve-mile stretch of river, off Highway 95, down the road from Bud's World-Famous Sausages on a Stick, lives the Amargosa toad." The kid pauses, scanning the vellum paper with his thumb. The sun turns his hair entirely white.

"Amargosa toads are chubby and covered with warts," he goes on. "They're often different colors, beige or olive green, and always have a trim stripe decorating the back. Distinct for webbed toes, for tinted humps, and for black spots on its belly, this ugly but humble creature is truly one of nature's more peculiar sights."

Eli's clenched teeth begin aching.

"I didn't know Tina Pennybocker," the kid says, folding the brochure. "I didn't know there was a Tina Pennybocker until recently. But when I look at you, her friends, the grieving, it's clear that Tina Pennybocker was like the Amargosa toad." One woman releases a high gasp. The kid quickly says, in conclusion, "She was rare. Tina was special."

This draws appreciative sighs. Eli spots the Toyota out of the corner of his eye. He maps out a tiptoe escape route. Nearby, a breeze spins up a dust devil. Space opens up behind him, and he takes a step backward.

Tina's casket is lowered into the grave via steel crank, dusted soon after by fistfuls of dirt. Teary women line up and take turns bidding farewell.

Eli shuffles, he bobs, he weaves. While hiding behind a broad-shouldered woman, a safe distance from all the sobbing, he watches Jane-from-Wyoming tug at her shirt and scratch her collarbone. Wrapped around her thick, dinosaur-sized neck is a gold necklace, a crucifix. His. Grapapa's.

Eli says, "Oh, sweet fucking Christ."

A woman turns and shushes him. There's a chrysanthemum tattooed inside the rim of her ear, the only flower at the service.

Eli snaps his fingers, trying to signal Sutton. Instead, Jane-from-Wyoming notices him hiding behind one of her friends. A look of confusion spreads across her face and then rearranges into benevolence. Jane-from-Wyoming half-smiles. That tooth, so imperfect, so him.

Nominated by Ben Fountain, The Kenyon Review

RITUAL

by SUSAN MITCHELL

from THE AMERICAN POETRY REVIEW

as one who casts the word *bread* upon the word *waters*, testing

as one who not believing something will rise up from
those waters, but not disbelieving either
casts out her voice

as one curious or hungry or filled with longing breaks
off just the crust of a word, throwing
the way she threw as a girl when everyone

told her that was not the way
to throw and expecting little or nothing
looks into the blackness but the waves

are not black they will be deep
scummed violet and bronze
like a memorial forgotten
                                    would it have made a difference
if she had cast the word *thread* upon those waters
unspooling what she spoke sewing

knots and tangles into waves and might
thread return to her as *dread* or even *dead*

as one who does not know what it is she wants
but wants her wanting sanctified
and anointed with myrrh and futility black

the waves are black and laced with white
shrouds which pass
                      into nothingness and the way
a snowflake vanishes
into the waves her voice cast out from her

she has wanted so long such a lifetime not
knowing what it is she wants

as one who has eaten joy for no good reason
with no idea where it came from
and wept in her sleep forgetting afterward who

embraced her but the next day feeling the loss
as one who casts word after word
into nothingness fillets ruins of foam cresting

so the word *lover* vanishes into water
and with it go *fervor* and *savior forever*
and *elixir*
             as one who keeps opening and closing
so the word *birth* is buried in *earth* so
the word *breath* is lost in *death*

as one who waits to see the eyes of water
roll back into depth, who waits
to see the depth rolled back and parted so she

can fly through and thinks she sees wings
and knows herself deluded
even though she sees
                as one who marked off
her wanting who staked its boundaries and let
nothing cross over to staunch or squander it

as one who says I want therefore I am

as one who saw the word *bread* float in the word *water*
before they both sank under
the weight of her wanting

as one who thought she saw something leap
but it may have been the word *motion* coming back
to her shadow for shadow

what is the hunger to know the other's
hunger built up like an altar

sacrifice she understood the blood
of her hunger wanting hunger for hunger, its
teeth in her flesh the word *flesh* the word *hunger*

as one who the more she looked saw less
what little there was she messed into more mess
there was no depiction in it

what would it take to register the quickness
the alacrity to blow out

the candle of the waves the word *candle*

the voice of the waves the word *voice*

the living face of the promise of the voice

Nominated by Reginald Shepherd, Joan Murray

ESSAY ON WHAT IS WANT

by JOHN D'AGATA

from CONJUNCTIONS

W HEN MY MOTHER AND I first moved to the city of Las Vegas, we lived for several weeks at the Budget Suites of America, a low-rise concrete pink motel with AIR COND and WEEKLY RATES and a Burger King next door.

We started to look for houses in developments called "Provence," "Tuscany," and "Bridgeport Landing," wandering through their model homes on plastic carpet runners.

In the master bedroom suites there were books displayed, their dust jackets removed, their spines always up, their titles too faint to clearly read at a glance. In the mudrooms there were chalkboards with the reminder *Buy milk!* Mason jars of pasta in the kitchens neatly spilled. Ceramic white bowls for family pets on the floor. Silk flowers in blue vases on the dining-room tables sparkling with little specks of round plastic morning dew.

There were terra-cotta tiles, screened-in lanais, entertainment centers in every living room.

The model called the "Amador" had columns beside its door. The "Palomar" had room for four cars in its garage. And "Versailles," gleaming white, came with an optional motorized gate.

In every house were cookies in stainless-steel ovens that were baking golden brown for families never there.

"All you have to do," said one hostess in one house, "is pick your model and your lot, and then leave the rest to us."

During one of those summer mornings when we first had moved to Las Vegas, my mother and I stood in the dirt of that city while listening to a broker around some wooden stakes and flags, some white-chalked land plots and orange-painted pipes, trying to see what the broker saw as he motioned with his hands, as he motioned with his wrists and wriggly fingers in full circles, motioning before his face, above his head, and to my mom, motioning toward the west, and then to me, and off the lot, then motioning past the stakes, the whipping flags, the lines in sand, beyond to where some pocks of little yucca plants were blooming, their tiny white flowers that never open all the way, their wobbly tall stalks of puffy million-seeded pods, their sword-long fronds that always indicate a desert, fanning out beyond the yellow of the lot in which we stood, fanning north above the shadow cast down by a mountain, fanning up and fanning over, fanning down and fanning out, then fanning off the private acreage that defines Summerlin, the walled and gated community my mother came to live in: orange houses, green parks, a white clock tower at its heart.

"You gotta imagine the land out here without all these weeds and stuff," the broker told my mom as he kicked a yucca plant. "You're on your back lawn, iced tea, easy tunes, maybe a little water feature bubbling in the distance."

We stood there on a $100,000 one-eighth-acre lot because Ethan, my mother's broker, had said that living in this community would be like living in New England, our home for the previous four generations.

"I like to tell people," Ethan told us, "that more trees line the sidewalks of Summerlin per capita than any other neighborhood here in Las Vegas," a fact he was particularly sure of, Ethan said, because the builder of Summerlin, a corporation called "Howard Hughes," had surveyed the number of trees in the neighborhoods of other builders, divided that by the number of residents in each, then ordered sixteen percent more trees than the highest of those estimates.

In the Spanish, we were told, *las vegas* means "the meadows," a lush haven that was named in 1829 for the "miles of shaded peace it offered early pioneers."

That first Spanish scout who wandered into Las Vegas said that it appeared "like a godsend" to him, "a great lie within the desert," "unbelievable," "unexpected," "truly the surest proof that this land is touched by God."

We walked through the sand, onto sidewalk again, up the two steps into Ethan's red Chevy S-10, then drove across the yellow lots of yucca-dotted desert, past gray concrete walls that were still being built, then finished concrete walls being painted closer in, beige concrete walls keeping yuccas off lawns, beige concrete walls lined with saplings, lamps, and shrubs, beige concrete walls with red swing-set tops behind them.

"This was all green at one point, as far as the eye can see. Meadows . . . meadows . . . green meadows," Ethan said. "That's what Summerlin's all about, bringing all that nature back."

Now, in Las Vegas, there is a Country Club at the Meadows, a Golden Meadows Nursing Home, Meadows Coffee, Meadows Jewelry, Meadows Mortgage, Meadows Glass, Meadows Hospital, Automotive, Alterations, and Pets. The Meadows Country Day School is a private k through six. Meadows' Women's Center is in Village Meadows Mall. Meadows Trailer Park has a waiting list for lots. The Meadows Vista Townhomes are apartments near the mall. And the Meadows Church of Light has a Christ on its marquee.

Barefoot, white-ankled, he's teaching in a meadow.

When Summerlin was started in 1988, its developer said that it wanted to create "the most successful master-planned community in the United States of America," and as we entered the town's center, called the "Town Center at Summerlin," Ethan explained that the goal of the builder had already been surpassed, even with only two-thirds of the development complete.

"Someone moves into a new Summerlin home every two hours and twenty-two minutes," he said.

We circled in the town center at Summerlin's parking lot, idled behind a Lexus, beside a fountain, under sun. Then Ethan led us deeper into the center of the town, past Jamba Juice and Quiznos and Starbucks storefronts, past the life-sized bronze statues of a shopping mom and son, and into a green expanse called "Willow Park at Summerlin," a three-acre fluffy stretch of shrubs and white flowers and a long mattress lawn toward which Ethan spread his arms.

"This is what living in Summerlin is all about, my friends."

Acrobats in sequined shorts flipped backward down the lawn. A mime followed behind a man who licked an ice cream cone. A stilt walker, burger stand, barber-shop quartet. Children chased each other with their faces brightly painted. Dogs chased the children with their eyes as they heeled. Above the park on two white poles two banners stretched and waved:

SUMMERLIN NUMBER ONE! and

GUINNESS BOOK OF RECORDS WORLD'S LARGEST GROUP HUG.

"OK," Ethan said, "I'll be honest, with ya, right? It won't be like this every day that you're living in Las Vegas. But I just wanted to show you how much spirit we all have. You can tell that everyone's really psyched to be living here, right?"

Of the 335,000 acres that constitute the Las Vegas valley in Nevada, only 49,000 remain undeveloped. According to the Nevada Development Authority's *Las Vegas Perspective of 2005*, 8,500 people move into the valley every single month. It is the fastest-growing metropolitan area in America. As a result, the valley's shortage of land has become so pronounced that a local paper reported in 1999 that one new acre of land is developed in Las Vegas every hour and fifteen minutes, on each of which are squeezed an average of eight three-bedroom homes.

Indeed, even as early as 1962, when the population of Las Vegas was one-thirtieth its current size, the natural springs that fed the city's growing population noticeably began to dry, and then eventually were depleted, and then sank forever after beyond the reach of Las Vegas.

The city built a pipeline through the desert, therefore, running fifty miles into the city from Lake Mead, the artificial lake that was formed by Hoover Dam, the largest artificial body of water in the world. Today, the pipeline carries ninety percent of all the water that Las Vegas uses, although the lake that it's been tapping for over sixty-five years is eighty feet below what it normally should be, thirty-five percent beneath its usual capacity, losing about a trillion gallons of water every year.

During the summer my mother and I first moved to Las Vegas, the lake's surface reached what was being called locally "a potentially low level," but which hydrologists elsewhere in the United States were calling "the worst southwestern drought conditions in one hundred years" and "the worst drought conditions in five hundred years" and "not technically a drought according to the data," as one geologist wrote in 2005, because "the level of precipitation that has made possible the unprecedented growth in that city" has been a "phenomenal fluke," has been "wholly unnatural," is "not what a desert would normally be like."

"Almost a century and a half ago," wrote the geologist,

> when Las Vegas was discovered, an extraordinary cycle of rainfall was just starting in the area. It eventually would

328

bring an increase in annual precipitation and would cause, among other things . . . the appearance of "meadows" in the Las Vegas valley. . . . But vegetation like that just isn't indigenous to a desert. What's indigenous to Las Vegas is sagebrush and creosote and maybe a couple yucca. . . . [But] Las Vegas residents don't want to acknowledge that they're living in the single driest place in America, and this is what has caused in part the problems the city faces.

In response to the warnings of a drought that summer, the general manager of the Las Vegas Water Authority said that "the notion that we have only a finite amount of water, and that when that water is gone we'll have to stop our city's growth, is a notion that belongs in the distant past."

And so, we settled in.

We moved my mother's cat, her books, her pinball machine, the three floors and five bedrooms of boxes from home. We planted a tomato in a large pot outside, bought green plastic chairs and a table for the deck, hung drapes to frame the view of the fairway in the back, the green promise we couldn't play on but paid extra to live beside, and took a trip to see the lake that had made that promise possible, the blue shock in yellow rock that attracts more campers and boaters and fishers and swimmers and skiers and hikers and divers and scouts than any other national recreation area—seven million annual visitors on average—an estimate that the National Park Service raised to eight million visitors by the end of that summer, an increase that one ranger tried to explain was not caused by more campers or boaters or fishers or swimmers or skiers or hikers or scouts, but by amateur archaeologists, owners of metal detectors, history buffs, photographers, and those who used to live there.

For what attracted the extra million visitors to Lake Mead that year was not the usual lure of the lake's artificial beauty, nor its recreational usefulness, nor even just the novelty that such a lake could exist, but rather the simple fact that the lake was slowly dying, that as the city quickly drained it, the lake's level lowered, and there slowly reemerged from its sinking blue surface the far distant past of the city of Las Vegas:

a chimney stack from a concrete plant, poking higher and higher above the water every day, a giant complex of mixing vats and grinders that was built in the thirties to help pour Hoover Dam, and then closed once the lake that the dam formed rose;

the B-29 bomber that crashed into Lake Mead, the gray one from the forties that was left there by the air force, fifty feet below at the time of the crash, now twenty feet below, its tail fin just ten;

the sundae shop, the baker's shop, the grocery store, the bank;

the wooden Mormon temple, the Gentry Mining Inn;

the 233 crosses and stones, the crypts and the clothing, the necklaces and rings and nail frames around bones: every deceased resident of St. Thomas, Nevada, exhumed and zip-locked and reburied upriver, six days before the lake would swallow the town whole.

Even a five thousand-year-old city reemerged, the ancient Indian settlement called "the Anasazi Lost City," a name it didn't receive because the city had been misplaced, but rather because the city—up until that dry summer—had remained one of the country's only pre-Columbian listings to be cataloged as "submerged" on the National Register of Historic Places.

"We may not have a history that's as rich as other cities," said a megaphoned voice in Summerlin that day, "and we may not be the biggest in America yet, but, ladies and gentlemen, do you know what we are?"

What? yelled the park.

"We are the city of big spirit!"

Some dogs barked, the park clapped, Ethan cheered, and then he *wooed*. It was noon and a stilt-walker's legs were on the ground, heat was sweating lines down the faces of some clowns, dogs were lapping ice cream off the bushes in the park, and the megaphoned voice said, "All right, now, let's go!"

He assembled us into groups around the edges of the park, made a countdown, a joke, then fired a starting gun.

This was a city, it was suggested that morning, that often came together in community spirit. Earlier, the city had come together to watch the old Dunes Hotel be imploded in a gray cloud of smoke in twelve seconds. It had come together before to watch the Sands, Hacienda, and Landmark be imploded. And it came together at 2:30 one recent Vegas morning, in an estimated crowd of twenty thousand people, in order to watch the old Aladdin Hotel be imploded, an event that attracted three TV news copters, two dozen articles in local newspapers, special rates for hotel rooms overlooking the implosion, a six-course Implosion Dinner for Two, and 19,462 more people than the 538 Summerlin neighbors who convened on a morning with sun in a park to prove that Las Vegas had community spirit, an effort that they made on behalf of the city, but without the news copters or dinners for two or the 363 extra group huggers that they needed to unseat the current record-holding huggers, the nine hundred employees of Goldman Sachs in New York.

"That's OK," yelled the voice. "That's all right, it's all right. We have a contingency plan here. Hold on, folks."

We milled.

It was noon still, or later.

Someone's cell phone started ringing.

Ethan took his shirt off and wrapped its sleeves around his head.

"I'll get you back to the hotel real soon," he said. "Promise."

I heard two strollers on the asphalt of a path emit two screams without a response.

I watched a teenage boy try to walk out of the park, but a clip-boarded woman at the edge sent him back.

"If I could get some assistance from the band," said the voice.

And then the band began to play "The Hokey Pokey Song."

We stood there, five hundred, for about the length of a verse.

"You put your right foot in," sang the megaphoned voice, "you put your right foot out, you put your right foot in, and you shake it all about."

A woman behind Ethan said, "What the fuck?" and walked away. A group of several children beside my mom collapsed to the grass. Other kids were crying, rubbing paint from their eyes.

"We're almost there!" yelled the voice. "You won't regret it! One more verse! The World's Largest Hokey Pokey right here in Las Vegas!"

Nominated by Robin Hemley, Mark Irwin

JUST NOW

by PETER CAMPION

from POETRY

a ladybug, its carapace blown open
so a translucent trace of orange gleams
from its body, has ascended link by link
the smudgy silver curve of my watch band.
It must have helicoptered past the sill
while I was slumped here squinting in the paper
at the ashen packaging another bombing's
made of a minivan. Made available
in the photo like the homeless in a poem.
The pain is far away. But then for moments
utterly clear: molten metal guttering
down from the Milky Way to fall on us.
And sometimes, God, it lands with all its will.
My spluttered prayer for it to hold its distance:
how ludicrous to blurt it from this comfort.
Still it impels itself from me. Please stay
away from me. Please stay away from this
insectile soul who only weeks ago
was wind and shit and jasmine leaves and rain.

Nominated by Rosanna Warren, David Wojahn, Michael Collier, Atsuro Riley

BANG, BANG, IN A BOY VOICE

by AKHIM YUSEFF CABEY

from THE SUN

I had a fear based on prior experiences of being maimed.

In 1984, the year vigilante Bernhard Goetz shot four black boys on a New York City subway car, I was nine, and I loved to ride the subway by myself. The dingy trains were spectacular space rockets to me. When I rode them, I wasn't just going to Queens to visit my grandmother; I was saving the galaxy.

At eight I had hounded my mother every chance I got to let me take the trains by myself. Though she threatened me with ass whippings if I continued trying her patience, I wouldn't back down. "I ain't no little kid no more," I'd say to her as we waited for the number 4 train to arrive at the elevated subway platform near our home in the Bronx. Knowing she would never smack me in public, I'd fire off the names of mothers who allowed their sons to journey the city alone.

"Do I *look* like everyone else's damn mother to you?" she'd snap back as the train rumbled into the station. Then she'd snatch me by the wrist and fling me into an open seat on the car. For the rest of the trip to Long Island City, Queens, where my grandmother lived, she kept a hand clamped around the back of my neck. It felt as if she would hold on to me forever.

On what I thought of as special occasions, my mother and I would

The inset quotations are taken from a statement Bernhard Goetz gave to police after turning himself in for the shooting of four teenagers on a New York City subway. One of the teenagers Goetz shot is a distant cousin of the author. The two cousins have never met. — Ed.

take the train to Clancy's Pub on 52nd Street in Manhattan. Once inside the bar, she'd slip into a booth and have dark drinks with unfamiliar, stringy-haired men, leaving me unattended on a bar stool. While my mother giggled and leaned into those men's bodies, I plotted ways to sneak out and ride all the way back to the Bronx, just to prove to her I was a big boy and could do it on my own. I never got far before she yelled for me to get my behind right back on that stool. I'd slink back and stuff myself with maraschino cherries and green olives to spite her with self-induced stomachaches on the ride home. She'd just shake her head and tell me that I got what I deserved.

Though my tactics failed and I endured beatings, I was determined to wear my mother down. One morning, while I was playing with action figures in my room, making punching and gunshot noises, she walked in, sat down on the bed, and told me to listen up. Pulling me against her, she told me about Etan Patz, a six-year-old boy who'd been abducted from the SoHo section of Manhattan on May 25, 1979. I couldn't see her face, but I heard her words echo in her chest as she told me how that boy had pleaded with his mother to let him walk alone to the school-bus stop, only two blocks away. "He told her he was a big boy," my mother said. At first Etan's mother had refused, but eventually she'd given in. She'd escorted him downstairs and watched him until he reached the corner. That was the last time she ever saw her son alive.

My mother finished the story and squeezed me harder. She knew how I craved her touch, and I believe she clung to me that day because she hoped it might destroy my fascination with riding the trains. And I was mesmerized, and frightened, by the story of how Etan had simply vanished. But the second she loosened her grip enough for me to breathe, I cried, "I ain't six! I'm *eight*!"

She was off the bed in a second, and we were adversaries again. "Boy, did you not hear anything I just told you?"

I'd heard everything she'd said, but there was no way I would give in. In my mind, Etan was one boy, and I was another.

My mother and I continued to battle. I resorted to begging, falling at her feet, locking my arms around her leg and refusing to let go, even when she dragged me up and down the hall. For a while it looked as though I'd be her prisoner forever. Then, on my ninth birthday, in June 1984, she came to me and said, "It's time for you to learn them trains."

334

I aimed at the center of the body of each four.

If not for the reruns of *Star Trek* that I watched on an old black-and-white television with a clothes hanger for an antenna, the trains would've been just noisy, cumbersome machines to me. Inspired by the TV show, I flattened the cardboard tubes from two toilet-paper rolls, laid one against the other, and used duct tape to mold them into the shape of a phaser—the futuristic weapon wielded by the show's heroes. I imagined traveling the universe in a magnificent spaceship, responding at warp speed to distress calls from friendly worlds under attack. When I arrived at the planet, I'd puff up my chest like Captain Kirk and give long monologues about the importance of peace and tolerance. Only after negotiations had failed and the alien enemy had refused to compromise would I let fly the wrath of galactic justice. In my living room, I'd punch and kick and duck and dive and roll, then come up zapping the chair, the lamp, the potted plant. The bad guy always fell, and I was always the hero.

My mother had no idea I carried my "phaser" with me on the train to visit my grandmother. Every Friday, just before I left, she'd grip my wrist and move in close to my face, so we were eye to eye. "Keep out of your head, you hear?" she'd say, jabbing me in the chest with her forefinger. "Pay attention to the people around you. And don't be *messing* with nobody on them trains."

Her tone was serious, even harsh at times, and what I mistook then for her mistrust of me I now know was the sometimes necessary sternness of parenting. Regardless, I never wanted to disobey or disappoint her, so I promised to do exactly as she told me. I would be the best starship captain in the Bronx and a more loyal son.

And I was, until I got to the end of the block and turned the corner onto Burnside Avenue, toward the elevated train station. Once I was out of my mother's sight, the sensation of the phaser tucked in the waistband of my jeans was enough to override any maternal fidelity I had left. By the time the number 4 pulled into the station like a mechanical stallion—screeching and shaking the platform at my feet—I had no mother.

To get to Queens, I'd transfer to the underground D train at 161st Street—Yankee Stadium. The D was my favorite train, because after it made its last local stop at 125th Street—Harlem, it streaked through the tunnel nonstop for sixty-six blocks. I'd press my forehead against the window and get lost in the speed of the express run, hyp-

335

notized by the tunnel wall flashing by. I'd transform the tiny, third-rail explosions into force shields deflecting torpedo fire from an enemy vessel hot on our trail. When, after five long minutes, the D fell out of warp at 59th Street—Columbus Circle, I had to resist the temptation to get off and cross over to the opposite platform and fly back through the galaxy to 125th once more.

At the 47th-50th Street—Rockefeller Center station I hopped on the Q, a dull, ordinary train that brought me uneventfully to 21st Street—Queensbridge, near where my grandmother lived. The best I could do at that point was pretend the escalator up to the street was transporting me to the surface of an alien planet. When my feet hit the pavement, I was once again just the son of a worried mother, a boring boy armed with a toy.

> I wanted to murder them, to hurt them, to make them suffer as much as possible.

I can reasonably guess what was on those four black boys' minds on December 22, 1984, when Bernhard Goetz boarded the downtown 2 at 14th Street and took a seat: *We can take this white motherfucker.* Two of the teenagers carried screwdrivers in their pockets, which they were planning to use to break into the coin boxes of video-game machines. Goetz carried a loaded .38 pistol in his waistband. I also think I know what was going through his head before he stepped onto that train: *Never again will I be taken.*

According to an opinion by Chief Judge Sol Wachtler of the New York State Court of Appeals, this is how it went down: One boy stood to Goetz's left, another to his right. A third hovered near the doors. The fourth boy hung back. The boy on Goetz's left said, "Give me five dollars." Goetz pretended not to hear, and the boy asked again. That's when Goetz stood, pulled out the pistol, and fired four shots. The first teenager was hit in the chest. The second was hit in the back as he tried to escape. The third boy took a bullet that passed through his arm to his left side. The fourth and final boy retreated down the aisle. Goetz shot and missed; the bullet ricocheted off the wall of the conductor's cabin.

Goetz surveyed the three he'd downed and then fired a second shot at the last boy, who in the meantime had sat down. The bullet entered his lower back and severed his spinal cord.

After someone pulled the emergency cord, Goetz went between two cars, jumped onto the tracks, and fled.

"See," my mother repeated in the days that followed, shaking her head as though she'd known the shooting was going to happen all along. "*This* is the shit I'm talking about."

My stepfather offered a different opinion: "White man been trying to kill us for four hundred years."

My nine-year-old mind was filled with questions. Why did white *men* want us dead, but not white women? And why us? What had we done to them? And why four hundred years? Had we been friends four hundred and *one* years ago? One Sunday night my stepfather and I were watching a Giants-Redskins game, and during a commercial I asked him how what one man had done was the fault of all white people. "As a whole, they can't be trusted," he told me. His tone was matter-of-fact, and his voice seemed to come from somewhere else. What I really wanted was for him to tell me why men shoot boys, and why boys rob men on trains, and what it is about skin color that makes people so angry.

The first time I saw Goetz on the news, after he'd turned himself in on December 31, 1984, I was baffled. By then he'd been dubbed the "subway vigilante" and was being championed because he'd taken the law into his own hands and fought back against his attackers. But more than anything else, I was confused because he looked nothing like the tan, square-jawed action heroes I'd seen on TV. He had a pointed chin and crooked nose. His receding hairline made his forehead look huge, and the lenses of his glasses were the size of playing cards. He looked more like Murdock, the nerdy, mentally unbalanced character on the television show *The A-Team*. "Subway vigilante"? I was furious: I didn't care that he was white, just that his goofy-looking ass had become the hero of *my* trains! I cared even less, or didn't know how to care, that the boys who'd been injured were black, and so was I. I only wanted the trains all to myself again.

The citywide furor that followed the shootings soon faded. The volatility was still lurking, but after a few weeks my mother let me travel the city alone again by train, and that's all that mattered.

I had lunch one afternoon in Greenwich Village with my uncle, and afterward we walked to the train station, where he waited with me until the Bronx-bound C train arrived. Before I boarded, he took me by the chin and turned my face to his. "Be careful," he said.

I'd heard that phrase so many times—from parents, relatives, and teachers—that it had lost all importance. The words made no more impression on me than "Boy, you better clean that plate" or "Wash behind your ears." Nothing could compete with how invincible I felt on the trains.

When I got on the C that day, I expected it to shoot through the tunnel uptown, just like the D did when I rode it downtown. I scrambled into a window seat so I could lose myself in the magic of the tunnel wall. Which aliens would need to be rescued today? Which would need to get their asses blasted? As the train slowly climbed to warp speed, all else vanished.

After half a minute, though, the C slowed and came to a stop at 14th Street, the same train stop I'd heard mentioned on the news and in adults' conversations only months before. I fully expected to see Bernhard Goetz stroll onto the car and take a seat next to me. I was grateful when only unfamiliar people boarded and sat scattered throughout the car.

At no point did the C hurtle anywhere; it crawled from 14th to 23rd to 34th, traveling in tiny, agonizing increments, scooping up more and more bodies at every stop. That's what they were to me from 42nd to 50th to 59th to 72nd: faceless bodies interrupting my voyage. Then we hit 81st Street, and I realized the train was standing-room-only, packed with what seemed like all the white people in the galaxy. The bodies now had faces, bright as bulbs. I couldn't distinguish which of those white faces belonged to a potential killer and which didn't. They weren't clearly marked as evil, like the faces of the bad guys in my fantasies. They were just as plain as Goetz's.

Stay out of your head.

I remember wanting my mother. I remember wishing I had the power to disappear through the wall of the train. I recall fragmented details: A red shoe wilth an ice-pick heel. High-water slacks revealing white socks. Crackling cellophane. A brown department-store bag nestled between a pair of bare pink knees. At one point, I found myself staring at a man across from me. He stared back, and this made me wonder: had he already made up his mind to hurt me, because he believed I'd already made up my mind to hurt him?

Pay attention to the people around you.

But I closed my eyes, because I was too damn scared to keep them open. In order not to make a sudden move that might confirm that I was who they expected me to be, I rooted my feet to the floor and shoved my hands into my pockets. That's when I felt it: The plastic slickness of duct tape. The phaser. My weapon against the Federation's enemies. My head throbbed with fear. I wanted to pull the phaser out and show everyone that it was just make-believe and that I was a regular boy, but there was no way to tell how they would react. Instead I sat still and kept a tight grip on the toy gun.

And don't be messing with nobody on them trains.

When I got off at Yankee Stadium, I found the nearest bench and sat down as the other passengers climbed the stairs. Once I could be sure I was alone on the platform, I took the phaser from my pocket and held it in my hand like a weapon one last time. It felt heavy. I moved my forefinger along the peeling-tape trigger and made a blast noise, but it had ceased to sound real to my ear. At the foot of the staircase, I dropped the thing into a trash bin before taking the stairs.

I was halfway up when a train hurtled into the station along the middle, express track. I went back down and watched. The sight of it was still magic, but I was now aware that it was my mind which had made it so.

And as the D blasted out of the station—its slithering, magnificent bulk shrinking into the distance—I knew these sullied silver bullets would never be the same for me again.

> If I was a little more under self-control, I would've put the barrel against his forehead and fired.

My mother could not know what future violence would come for her son, only that, sooner or later, it *would* come.

She could not know that in December 1986, Michael Griffith would be severely beaten by a mob of white teenagers in Howard Beach, Queens, then chased onto the Shore Parkway and killed by an oncoming car. She could not know that in November 1987, fifteen-year-old Tawana Brawley would allege that white police officers had raped her, written racial slurs on her body, and then smeared her with feces. Later, when it would be revealed that the girl had lied, my mother would know even less what to say about the brutality we suffer due to race. Nor would she be able to explain why a gang of black and Hispanic boys would confess to raping and nearly beating to death Trisha Meili, a white woman who was out jogging in Central Park on an April night in 1989.

And what explanation would she be able to offer in August of that same year, when sixteen-year-old Yusuf Hawkins was shot to death by a member of an angry mob who believed he was involved with a white girl in the predominantly Italian neighborhood of Bensonhurst, Brooklyn?

What could she say about a future she knew was coming, but did not know when, or how, or what it would mean for her son?

I was fourteen the summer Hawkins was killed and Reverend Al Sharpton led a march through the streets of Bensonhurst in protest. I remember on the news the blotchy red faces of neighborhood residents who chanted, "Useless, useless," (a play on "Yusuf") as the marchers made their way down the avenue. I considered my middle name, Yuseff, as well as the infatuation I had with Alyssa Milano, the Italian American actress who starred in the sitcom *Who's the Boss?* The similarities were too close. I developed a serious fear of Brooklyn, believing that if I ever went there, I'd surely get my black ass killed.

It was shortly after that, while I was staying with my grandmother for the summer, that I became part of a bicycle crew in Queens. We were like a troop of brothers. About nine of us would gather on the basketball court before noon, the August morning air still cool on our bare legs and arms. By one o'clock the heat would be torching us as we looted tennis balls from public courts or lifted packaged cakes off the back of unattended delivery trucks. Mainly we cruised Steinway Avenue, rolling by on our bikes like a hungry pride of young lions. When we decided the day should be an epic one, we'd cross the Queensboro Bridge into Manhattan and ride several blocks to Central Park. We kept a lookout for loose change or dollar bills, and when we came up with nothing, we would watch for a sweet-looking girl whose behind we could rhapsodize about for the rest of the evening.

The camaraderie we shared was seductive, and for the first time in my life I understood what it meant to love someone other than a relative or the silent, pretty girl at the back of the class. These were my first true niggas, and my relationship to them was the initial demarcation of my blackness. I would've killed anyone who tried to take it away.

One evening about ten of us were hanging out in the courtyard of my grandmother's building in the Queensbridge Housing Project. We had our bikes flipped over on their handle-bars and were fixing flats, oiling chains, and trading parts. I haggled over an inner tube with a quiet, well-built kid named Ray. Our bartering turned sour, and we graduated to ranking on each other's moms. I was only an average ranker, and when the crowd that had gathered began laughing harder at Ray's jokes than at mine, I grew hot with anger. Ray let off several quick "yo' mama" jokes, and all I could come back with was that I was smart and he was dumb, that I was brown-skinned and he was dark-skinned—powerful insults for any black person in the boroughs. Ray just threw his head back and laughed as if none of it fazed him. "But, nigga," he said, "you talk white." The crowd exploded, laughing so hard they looked as if they were dancing. I fumed. Even worse than being dumb and dark was sounding like a white person.

"So you want to fight?" I heard myself say.

"Come on, then," Ray replied, so fast it was too late to pretend I hadn't challenged him.

We drifted onto the basketball court, the crowd following behind us. I held my fists just above my waist, like a martial artist I'd seen on television. Ray held his near his chin, like a boxer. I swung more like I was handling an axe than punching someone. Ray dodged every karate chop I threw and snapped my head back with three quick jabs, the last of which pitched me on my ass. The crowd went, "Ohhh!" Girls giggled. I staggered to my feet only to be dropped again with a flurry of blows to the cheek and temple. The next time I got up and tried to go at Ray, an adult held me back, saying, "It's over, little man. Give it up." I was deranged with anger, not only because I'd gotten beaten up, but because by beating me, Ray had revealed just how far behind I was as a boy—and as a *black* boy. Because there was no way I was going to lay a single knuckle on Ray's face, I roared the filthiest things I could think of about his mother and shouted that I wanted to kill his entire family.

After that night, my days of riding with the bike crew were over. For the next week I didn't set foot outside my grandmother's apartment, and when I did, it was to flee back to my own neighborhood in the Bronx. On the train ride home I felt I knew how my former friends back in Queens saw me: as a weak little bitch who talked like the people who'd killed Yusuf Hawkins.

Ray was on my mind for a long time after that. I couldn't let it go. I spent hours in front of the mirror mimicking his punches and preparing to use my fists more effectively the next time a conflict came to blows. I was never going to lose another fight. Maybe I couldn't be black in Queens, but I could still be black in the Bronx.

341

It didn't matter where in the city I was, though. I was plagued by memories of the beating I'd taken. Near the end of the summer, I snapped. One day the mentally ill aunt of a neighbor showed up at our apartment, saying she was an old friend of my mother's. My mother wasn't home, and I knew nothing about the woman's illness, so I let her in. When she said my youngest sister was *her* daughter and that she'd come to reclaim her, I realized I'd made a terrible mistake. "Get the fuck out," I told the woman, trying to sound ferocious, though my voice shook. "Now!" I added more forcibly, shielding my sister behind my leg. The woman was out the door in an instant, and I stood there, livid and confused and aware that my hands were growing hot.

Not thinking—or perhaps thinking too much—I grabbed the keys, locked my crying sister inside the apartment, and took to the street. The woman had reached the end of the block and was just turning onto Burnside Avenue. I sprinted after her and around the corner, catching sight of her as she was passing a Vietnamese fruit stand. When I was close enough to touch her, I said, "Hey, bitch." She turned, and, holding my fists like a boxer, I unleashed on her face.

After that I got used to the muffled clapping noise hitting someone made, and the feeling of my knuckles against a person's jaw. Not tough enough to be a true thug, I picked fights with boys I knew I could beat. I hit one kid because he called me a "wack-ass quarterback" after he dropped a touchdown pass I'd thrown during a game of two-hand touch. I hit another kid in the gut because I saw him wearing a hat I believed belonged to my younger brother. And during a remedial trigonometry class at my high school one Saturday, I went after the math teacher—a fat, balding, bitter white man—because he told me to get the hell out of his class if I was going to run my mouth instead of work on the equation he'd scribbled on the board.

These incidents took place in front of people I knew, and I was grateful for the audience. Though I'm not proud of who I was during those fights, there was no way I could have withstood another loss. If I had allowed myself to get duped by some crazy woman, wouldn't that have made me even more of an outcast than her? If I had let some white person disrespect me in front of a group of my peers, wouldn't that have made me even more of an Oreo cookie—black on the outside, white on the inside—than they already believed I was? I wanted to work my way back into the hearts of my people. All so many of us want is to blend in effortlessly, to attain that raunchy, odorous, and sometimes fabulous love I'd had with my bike crew. I found myself ready to take a person's head off in order to honor the group's code: *Be like us, or else.* Had I the power to tear open time and space and let that bike crew from Queens see me battling with a crazy woman, a hat thief, and a math teacher, I would've cried, "See! See how black I am! Look at me! Love me again!"

Had I a gun, I would've smoked all my enemies' asses.

Subsection 1 of New York State's self-defense law 35.15 states that a person may use deadly physical force upon another person if he reasonably believes such force is necessary to defend himself. What this emphasis on "reasonable belief" boils down to is: Would you have acted the same way under the same circumstances? A jury of Goetz's peers knew precisely how they would've behaved if they'd been carrying a gun and four black teenage boys had demanded five dollars from them on a subway car. And in June of 1987, Bernhard Goetz was acquitted of attempted murder.

For all that has been said about black boys from the hood, and all that continues to be said, our culture refuses to speak passionately about what it means to be a white person cast out from the hearts of *his* people. Had Goetz been robbed on the train that day, his whole self might have collapsed, just as mine felt like it had in Queensbridge when the crowd had roared with laughter after Ray called me white and then put me on my ass. Perhaps those black boys who asked Goetz for money represented every white face in his life that had long ago maimed his heart. Maybe when he got up and started firing, he was getting even with everyone who'd called him a "faggot," a "geek," a "pussy"; with every girl who'd grimaced after she'd caught him staring at her breasts. Maybe being able to stand over those boys' bleeding bodies allowed Goetz to think, *At least I ain't black.* Maybe he even hoped it would make his people love him again.

To praise or condemn Goetz's actions on the train that December day is to ignore how violence far too easily becomes the only way the desperate and wounded know how to react. And what all this demonstrates is that bloodshed ruins black people and white people alike, and isn't that what makes us the same?

But at some point I got off that train.

Growing up where I did, I've often wondered why I never killed a person, or at least committed a violent crime. Maybe I was afraid of the reciprocal harm that could have been done to me, or that the damage I caused would have landed me in prison and not at my computer writing, or in the street playing football, or in bed making love to a woman. I never consciously chose not to be violent. Rather I developed a strategy of fighting when necessary, and with appropriate force, and never in the name of racial redemption, and being willing to accept the consequences of my actions if this strategy failed. Who knows? One more knuckle sandwich here or there, and I might have been carrying a pistol in the waist of my jeans the way I once had a phaser.

Sometimes I imagine I'm on the train with Goetz and those four boys—Troy, Barry, James, and Darrell—that December afternoon in 1984. In my fantasy, Goetz and I are one. We are Captain Kirk, and we have the weapon: the .38 is in our waistband, a phaser resting comfortably against the hip or deep in a coat pocket. The scent of the gun metal and the feel of the wooden handle are rapturous. I imagine Goetz on the car that afternoon (sometimes he is a boy, sometimes he is a man) running, diving, ducking for cover, then coming up with pistol drawn and shouting, *Bang, bang!* in a boy voice as he guns down dark bodies. And later in my fantasy, when he is definitely a man and those boys lie bleeding at his feet, he looks up and out the train window at the wall whipping past at dazzling speed. He presses his face against the glass and marvels at the third-rail explosions, just another one among us who has ignored his mother's warnings to stay out of his head, pay attention to the people around him, and don't be messing with nobody on them—

If I had more bullets I would have shot them again and again and again.

Nominated by The Sun

DEVOTION: REDSHIFT

by BRUCE SMITH

from TIN HOUSE

Occurs when the light from an object is shifted toward the red
end of the spectrum: an increase in wavelength, a decrease
in frequency. And I saw the white horse in the fields
of central New York become at sunset a fiery red, light
from an object shifted and its rider was given power to take peace
from the earth and to him was given the tools of shock and awe,
and the power to break the seals as light from the objects shifted,
and the oil wells burned on the day of shock and awe. Redshift.
Guernica, April 1937. Redshift: Hiroshima, 1945,
when I was born in a dilation of time as the wavelength lengthened
and the creature said, "Come and see." And I heard, redshift,
Lord Amherst say give the blankets with the smallpox to the
    Indians,
redshift, and let the corpses dead of the plague be flung over the
    wall
by a catapult, redshift, and the Assyrians corrupt the wells and
    'Hannibal
fill the water jars with vipers. Shock and awe. My life is chemical
time and the moon turns a blood red, light shifts, skin blisters,
time dilates, the liver swells with toxins, and the sky rolls up like a
    scroll,
redshift, in shock and awe and I write on my skin on the red end
of the spectrum as my nation flings the corpses over the wall
and endows the spores that turn the skin to coal. And the sun
turns black like a sackcloth made of goat hair as the oil wells burn.

In Unit 731 the Imperial Army makes racial bacteria as I catapult
over the walls and the vector of my life is a vesper mouse,
and the target is my skin. And in the fields of central New York
I saw a riderless horse, a fiery red one.

Nominated by Alan Michael Parker, Chard de Niord, Diann Blakely, Tin House

PROWLERS

fiction by JACK DRISCOLL

from THE GEORGIA REVIEW

T HERE'S A LADDER that leans against the back of the house, a sort of stairway to the roof where Marley-Anne and I sometimes sit after another donnybrook. You know the kind, that *whump* of words that leaves you dumbstruck and hurt and in the silent nightlong aftermath startled almost dead. Things that should never be spoken to a spouse you're crazy in love with—no matter what.

Yeah, that's us, Mr. and Mrs. Reilly Jack. It's not that the air is thin or pure up here, not in mid-August with all that heat locked in the shingles. It's just that we can't be inside after we've clarified in no un-certain terms the often fragile arrangement of our marriage. And right there's the irony, given that we fill up on each other morning, noon, and night—excepting during these glitches, of course, when we reassert our separateness, and all the more since we've started breaking into houses.

B&E artists, as Marley-Anne calls us, and that's fine with me, though never before in our history had we made off with somebody's horse. Tonight, though, a large mammal is grazing ten feet below us in our small, fenced-in backyard. This kind of incident quick-voids a lease, and we signed ours ten months ago with a sweet-deal option to buy. A simple three-bedroom starter ranch with a carport, situated on an irregular quarter acre where in the light of day we present our-selves as your ordinary small-town underachievers. And that pretty much identifies the demographic hereabouts: white, blue-collar, Pet Planet employed. I'd feed their C-grade canned to my rescue mutt any day of the week if I could only sweet-talk Marley-Anne into someday getting one.

I drive a forklift, which may or may not be a lifelong job but, if so, I'm fine with that future, my ambitions being somewhat less than insistent. Marley-Anne, on the other hand, is a woman of magnum potential, tall and funny and smart as the dickens, and I buy her things so as not to leave her wanting. Last week, a blue moonstone commemorating our ten-year anniversary, paid for up front in full by yours truly.

Anything her maverick heart desires, and I'll gladly work as much swing-shift or graveyard overtime as need be, though what excites Marley-Anne . . . well, let me put it this way: there's a river nearby and a bunch of fancy waterfront homes back in there, and those are the ones we stake out and prowl.

The first time was not by design. The declining late winter afternoon was almost gone, and Marley-Anne riding shotgun said, "Stop." She said, "Back up," and when I did she pointed at a Real Estate One sign advertising an open house, all angles and stone chimneys and windows that reflected the gray sky. "That's tomorrow," I said. "Sunday," and without another word she was outside, breaking trail up the unshoveled walkway, the snow lighter but still falling, and her ponytail swaying from side to side.

She's like that, impulsive and unpredictable, and I swear I looked away—a couple of seconds max—and next thing I know she's holding a key between her index finger and thumb, and waving for me to come on, hurry up, Reilly Jack. Hurry up, like she'd been authorized to provide me a private showing of this mansion listed at a million-two or -three—easy—and for sure not targeting the likes of us. I left the pickup running, heater on full blast, and when I reached Marley-Anne I said, "Where'd you find that?" Meaning the key, and she pointed to the fancy brass lock, and I said, "Whoever forgot it there is coming back. Count on it."

"We'll be long gone by then. A spot inspection and besides I have to pee," she said, her knees squeezed together. "You might as well come in out of the cold, don't you think?"

"Here's fine," I said. "This is as far as I go, Marley-Anne. No kidding, so how about you just pee and flush and let's get the fuck off Dream Street, okay?"

What's clear to me is that my mind's always at its worst in the waiting. Always, no matter what, and a full elapsing ten minutes is a long

348

while to imagine your wife alone in somebody else's domicile. I didn't knock or ring the doorbell. I stepped inside and walked through the maze of more empty living space than I had ever seen or imagined. Rooms entirely absent of furniture and mirrors, and the walls and ceilings so white I squinted, the edges of my vision blurring like I was searching for someone lost in a storm or squall.

"Marley-Anne," I said, her name echoing down hallways and up staircases and around the crazy asymmetries of custom-built corners jutting out everywhere like a labyrinth. Then more firmly asserted until I was shouting, hands cupped around my mouth, "Marley-Anne, Marley-Anne, answer me. Please. It's me, Reilly Jack."

I found her in the farthest far reaches of the second floor, staring out a window at the sweep of snow across the river. She was shivering, and I picked up her jacket and scarf off the floor. "What are you doing?" I asked, and all she said back was, "Wow. Is that something or what?" and I thought, Oh fuck. I thought, Here we go, sweet Jesus, wondering how long this time before she'd plummet again.

We're more careful now, and whenever we suit up it's all in black, though on nights like this with the sky so bright, we should always detour to the dump with a six-pack of cold ones and watch for the bears that never arrive. Maybe listen to Mickey Gilley or Johnny Cash and make out like when we first started dating back in high school, me a senior and Marley-Anne a junior, and each minute spent together defining everything I ever wanted in my life. Against the long-term odds we stuck. We're twenty-nine and twenty-eight, respectively, proving that young love isn't all about dick and daydreams and growing up unrenowned and lonesome. Just last month, in the adrenalin rush of being alone in some strangers' lavish master bedroom, we found ourselves going at it in full layout on their vibrating king-size. Satin sheets the color of new aluminum and a mirror on the ceiling, and I swear to God we left panting and breathless. You talk about making a score . . . that was it, our greatest sex ever. In and out like pros, and the empty bed still gyrating like a seizure.

Mostly we don't loot anything. We do it—ask Marley-Anne—for the sudden rush and flutter. Sure, the occasional bottle of sweet port to celebrate, and once—just the one time—I cribbed a padded-shoulder, double-breasted seersucker suit exactly my size. But I ended up wearing instead the deep shame of my action, so the second time we broke in there I hung the suit back up where I'd originally swiped it, like it was freshly back from the dry cleaners and hanging again in that huge walk-in closet. We're talking smack-dab on the same naked white plastic hanger.

Now and again Marley-Anne will cop a hardcover book if the title sounds intriguing. *The Lives of the Saints*, that's one that I remember held her full attention from beginning to end. Unlike me she's an avid reader; her degree of retention you would not believe. She literally burns through books, speed-reading sometimes two per night, so why *not* cut down on the cost? As she points out, these are filthy-rich people completely unaware of our immanence, and what's it to them anyway, these gobble-jobs with all their New World bucks?

I'd rather not, I sometimes tell her, that's all. It just feels wrong.

Then I throw in the towel because the bottom line is whatever makes her happy. But grand theft? Jesus H., that sure never crossed my mind, not once in all the break-ins. (I'd say twenty by now, in case anyone's counting.) I'm the lightweight half in the mix, more an accessory along for the ride, though of my own free will I grant you, and without heavy pressure anymore, and so no less guilty. No gloves, either, and if anyone has ever dusted for fingerprints they've no doubt found ours everywhere.

Foolhardy, I know, and in a show of hands at this late juncture I'd still vote for probing our imaginations in more conventional, stay-at-home married ways. Like curling up together on the couch for Tigers baseball or possibly resuming that conversation about someday having kids. She says two would be satisfactory. I'd say that'd be great. I'd be riding high on numbers like that. But all I have to do is observe how Marley-Anne licks the salt rim of a margarita glass, and I comprehend all over again her arrested maternal development and why I've continued against my better judgment to follow her anywhere, body and soul, pregnant or not.

That doesn't mean I don't get pissed, but I do so infrequently and always in proportion to the moment or event that just might get us nailed or possibly even gut-shot. And how could I ever—a husband whose idealized version of the perfect wife is the woman he married and adores—live with that? I figure a successful crime life is all about minimizing the risks so nobody puts a price on your head or even looks at you crosswise. That's it in simple English, though try explaining "simple" to a mind with transmitters and beta waves like Marley-Anne's.

Not that she planned on heisting someone's goddamn paint, because forward-thinking she'll never be, and accusations to that effect only serve to aggravate an already tenuous situation. All I'm saying is that a bridle was hanging on the paddock post, and next thing I knew she was cantering bareback out the fucking gate and down the driveway like Hiawatha minus the headband and beaded moccasins. Those are the facts. Clop-clop-clack on the blacktop, and in no way is the heightened romance inherent in that image lost on me.

But within seconds she was no more than a vague outline and then altogether out of sight, and me just standing there, shifting from foot to foot, and the constellations strangely spaced and tilted in the dark immensity of so much sky. Good Christ, I thought. Get back here, Marley-Anne, before you get all turned around, which maybe she already had. Or maybe she got thrown or had simply panicked and ditched the horse and stuck to our standing strategy to always rendezvous at the pickup if anything ever fouled.

But she wasn't at the truck when I got back to it. I slow-drove the roads and two-tracks between the fields where the arms of oil wells pumped and wheezed, and where I stopped and climbed into the truck bed and called and called out to her. Nothing. No sign of her at all, at least not until after I'd been home for almost two hours, half-crazed and within minutes of calling 911.

And suddenly there she was, her hair blue-black and shiny as a raven's under that evanescent early-morning halo of the street lamp as she rode up to 127 Athens, the gold-plated numerals canted vertically just right of the mail slot. Two hours I'd been waiting, dead nuts out of my gourd with worry. I mean I could hardly even breathe, and all she says is, "Whoa," and smiles over at me like, Hey, where's the Instamatic, Reilly Jack? The house was pitch dark behind me, but not the sky afloat with millions of shimmering stars. I could see the sweating brown and white rump of the pinto go flat slick as Marley-Anne slid straight off backward and then tied the reins to the porch railing as if it were a hitching post. The mount just stood there swishing its long noisy tail back and forth, its neck outstretched on its oversized head and its oval eyes staring at me full on. And that thick corkscrew tangle of white mane, as if it had been in braids, and nostrils flared big and pink like two identical side-by-side conch shells.

I'd downed a couple of beers and didn't get up from the swing when she came and straddled my lap. Facing me she smelled like welcome to Dodge City in time warp. Oats and hay and horse sweat, a real turnoff and, as usual, zero awareness of what she'd done. Nonetheless, I lifted Marley-Anne's loose hair off her face so I could kiss her cheek in the waning moonlight, that gesture first and fore-most to herald her safe arrival home no matter what else I was feel-ing, which was complex and considerable. Her black jeans on my thighs were not merely damp but soaking wet, and the slow burn I felt up and down my spinal cord was electric.

But that's a moot point if there's a horse matter to broker, and there was, of course: Marley-Anne's fantasy of actually keeping it. Don't ask me where, because that's not how she thinks—never in a real-world context, never ever in black and white. She's all neurons and impulse. Factor in our ritual fast-snap and zipper disrobing of each other during or shortly after a successful caper, and you begin to understand my quandary. She does not cope well with incongruity, most particularly when I'm holding her wrists like I do sometimes, forcing her to concentrate and listen to me up close face-to-face as I attempt to argue reason.

Which is why I'd retreated to the roof, and when she followed maybe a half hour later, a glass of lemonade in hand, I said, "Please, just listen, okay? Don't flip out, just concentrate on what I'm saying and talk to me for a minute." Then I paused and said, "I'm dead seri-ous, this is bad, Marley-Anne, you have no comprehension *how* bad but maybe it's solvable if we keep our heads." As in, Knock-knock, is anybody fucking home?

She'd heard it all before, a version at least, and fired back just above a whisper, "I can take care of myself, thank you very much."

"No," I said, "you can't, and that's the point. You don't get it. We're in big trouble this time. Serious deep shit and our only ticket out—are you even listening to me?—is to get this horse back to the fuck-ing Ponderosa, and you just might want to stop and think about that."

She said nothing, and the raised vein on my left temple started throbbing as Paint thudded his first engorged turd onto the lawn, which I'd only yesterday mowed and fertilized, and then on hands and knees had spread dark red lava stones under the azaleas and around the bougainvillea. All the while, Marley-Anne had stood hyp-notized at the kitchen window, re-constellating what she sometimes refers to as this down-in-the-heels place where the two of us exist to-gether on a next-to-nothing collateral line.

It's not the Pierce-Arrow of homes, I agree. Hollow-core doors and a bath and a half, but we're not yet even thirty, and for better or worse most days seem substantial enough and a vast improvement over my growing up in a six-kid household without our dad, who gambled and drank and abandoned us when I was five. I was the youngest, the son named after him, and trust me when I say that Marley-Anne's story—like mine—is pages and pages removed from a fully stocked in-home library and a polished black baby grand, and to tell it otherwise is pure unadulterated fiction. "Maybe in the next lifetime," I said once, and she reminded me how just two weeks prior we'd made love on top of a Steinway in a mansion off Riverview, murder on the knees and shoulder blades but the performance virtuoso. And Marley-Anne seventh-heaven euphoric in hyperflight back to where we'd hidden the pickup behind a dense red thicket of sumac.

Nothing in measured doses for Marley-Anne, whose penchant for drama is nearly cosmic. Because she's restless her mind goes zooming, then dead-ends double whammy with her job and the sameness of the days. Done in by week's end—that's why we do what we do, operating on the basis that there is no wresting from her the impulsive whirl of human desire and the possibility to dazzle time. Take that away, she's already in thermonuclear meltdown—and believe me, the aftereffects aren't pretty.

She works for Addiction Treatment Services as a nine-to-five receptionist filing forms and changing the stylus on the polygraph. Lazy-ass drunks and dopers, jerk-jobs, and diehard scammers—you know the kind—looking to lighten their sentences, and compared to them Marley-Anne in my book can do no wrong. Her code is to outlive the day terrors hellbent on killing her with boredom, and because I've so far come up with no other way to rescue her spirit I stand guard while she jimmies back doors and ground-level windows. Or sometimes I'll boost her barefoot from my shoulders onto a second-floor deck where the sliders are rarely locked. In a minute or two she comes downstairs and deactivates the state-of-the-art security system, inviting me in through the front door as though she lives there and residing in such splendor is her right God-given.

"Good evening," she'll say. "Welcome. What desserts do you suppose await us on this night, Reilly Jack?"—as if each unimagined delight has a cherry on top and is all ours for the eating. Then she'll motion me across the threshold and into the dark foyer where we'll stand locking elbows or holding hands like kids until our eyes adjust.

At first I felt grubby and little else, and that next hit was always the place where I didn't want to fall victim to her latest, greatest, heat-seeking version of our happiness. I didn't get it, and I told her so in mid-May after we'd tripped an alarm and the manicured estate grounds lit up like a ballpark or prison yard. I'd never taken flight through such lush bottomland underbrush before, crawling for long stretches, me breathing hard but Marley-Anne merely breath-*taken* by the kick of it all, and the two of us muddy and salty with perspiration there in the river mist. No fear or doubts or any remorse, no second thoughts on her part for what we'd gotten ourselves into. It's like we were out-waltzing Matilda on the riverbank, and screw you, there's this legal trespass law called riparian rights, and we're well within ours—the attitude that nothing can touch brazen enough, and without another word she was bolt upright and laughing in full retreat. And what I saw there in front of me in each graceful stride was the likelihood of our marriage coming apart right before my eyes.

"That's it," I said to her on the drive home. "No more. Getting fixed like this and unable to stop, we're no better than those addicts, no different at all, and I don't care if it *is* why Eve ate the goddamn apple, Marley-Anne"—an explanation she'd foisted on me one time, to which I'd simply replied, "Baloney to that. I don't care. We'll launch some bottle rockets out the rear window of the pickup if that's what it takes." I meant it, too, as if I could bring the Dead Sea of the sky alive with particles of fiery light that would also get us busted, but at worst on a charge of reckless endangerment, which in these parts we'd survive just fine and possibly be immortalized by in story at the local bars.

"We're going to end up twelve-stepping our way out of rehab," I said. "Plus fines and court costs. It's just a matter of time until somebody closes the distance." All she said back was, "Lowercase, Reilly Jack. Entirely lowercase."

She's tried everything over the years, from Valium to yoga, but gave up each thing for the relish of what it robbed from her. Not to her face, but in caps to my own way of thinking, I'd call our prowling CRAZY.

So far we'd been blessed with dumb luck the likes of which I wouldn't have believed and couldn't have imagined if I hadn't been kneeling next to Marley-Anne in the green aquatic light of a certain living room, our noses a literal inch away from a recessed wall tank of angelfish. Great big ones, or maybe it was just the way they were magnified, some of them yellow-striped around the gills, and the two of us mesmerized by the hum of the filter as if *we* were suspended underwater and none the wiser to the woman watching us—for how long I haven't the foggiest. But in my mind I sometimes hear that first note eerie and helium-high, though I could barely make out, beyond the banister, who was descending that curved staircase. Not until she'd come ghostlike all the way down and floated toward us, a pistol pointed into her mouth.

Jesus, I thought, shuddering, oh merciful Christ no, but when she squeezed the trigger and wheezed deeply it was only an inhaler, her other hand holding a bathrobe closed at the throat.

"Sylvia?" she said. "Is that you?" and Marley-Anne, without pause or panic, stood up slowly and assented to being whoever this white-haired woman wanted her to be. "Yes," she said. "Uh-huh, it's me," as if she'd just flown in from Bangor or Moscow or somewhere else so distant it might take a few days to get readjusted. "I didn't mean to wake you," Marley-Anne said, soft-sounding and genuinely apologetic. "I'm sorry." As cool and calm as cobalt while I'm squeezing handful by handful the humid air until my palms dripped rivulets onto the shiny, lacquered hardwood floor. The woman had to be ninety, no kidding, and had she wept in fear of us or even appeared startled I swear to God the lasting effects would have voided forever my enabling anymore the convolution of such madness.

"There's leftover eggplant parmesan in the fridge—you can heat that up," the woman said. "And beets. Oh, yes, there's beets there too," as if suddenly placing something that had gotten lost somewhere, not unlike Marley-Anne and me, whoever I was standing now beside her all part and parcel of the collective amnesia.

"And you are . . . who again?" the woman asked, and wheezed a second time, and when I shrugged as if I hadn't under these circumstances the slightest clue, she slowly nodded. "I understand," she said. "Really, I do," and she took another step closer and peered at me even harder, as if the proper angle of concentration might supply some vaguest recollection of this mute and disoriented young man attired in burglar black and suddenly present before her.

"Heaven-sent then?" she said, as if perhaps I was some angel, and then she pointed up at a skylight I hadn't noticed. No moon in sight, but the stars—I swear—aglitter like the flecks of mica I used to find and hold up to the sun when I was a kid, maybe six or seven. I remembered then how my mom sometimes cried my dad's name at night outside by the road for all her children's sakes, and for how certain people we love go missing, and how their eventual return is anything but certain. I remembered lying awake on the top bunk, waiting and waiting for that unmistakable sound of the spring hinge snapping and the screen door slapping shut. I never really knew whether to stay put or go to her. And I remembered this, too: how on the full moon, like clockwork, the midnight light through the window transformed that tiny bedroom into a diorama.

"Emphysema," the woman said. "And to think I never smoked. Not one day in my entire life."

"No, that's true," Marley-Anne said, "you never did. And look at you, all the more radiant because of it."

"But not getting any younger," the woman said, and wheezed again, her voice flutelike this time, her eyes suddenly adrift and staring at nothing. "And Lou, how can that be so soon? Gone ten years, isn't it ten years tomorrow? Oh, it seems like yesterday, just yesterday . . . ," but she couldn't quite recollect even that far, and Marley-Anne smiled and palm-cupped the woman's left elbow and escorted her back upstairs to bed. Recalling the run-down two-story of my boyhood, I noticed how not a single stair in this house moaned or creaked underfoot.

Standing all alone in the present tense with that school of blank-eyed fish staring out at me, I whispered, "Un-fucking-believable." That's all I could think. As absurd as it sounds, these were the interludes and images Marley-Anne coveted, and in the stolen beauty of certain moments I had to admit that I did, too.

That's what frightens me now more than anything, even more than somebody's giant, high-ticket pinto in our illegal possession. But first things first, and because Marley-Anne's one-quarter Cheyenne she's naturally gifted, or so she claimed when I asked her where she learned to bridle a horse and ride bareback like that. In profile silhouette, hugging her knees here next to me on the roof, she shows off the slight rise in her nose and those high-chiseled cheekbones. She's long-limbed and lean and goes one-fifteen fully clothed, and I've already calculated that the two of us together underweigh John Wayne, who somehow always managed to boot-find the stirrup and haul his wide, white, and baggy Hollywood cowboy ass into the saddle. Every single film I felt bad for the horse, the "He-yuh," and spurs to the ribs, and my intolerance was inflamed with each galloping frame.

Perhaps another quarter hour of silence has passed when Marley-Anne takes my hand. Already the faintest predawn trace of the darkness lifting leaves us no choice other than to mount up and vacate the premises before our neighbors the Bromwiches wake and catch us red-handed. They're friendly and easy enough to like but are also the type who'd sit heavy on the bell rope for something like this. I can almost make out the outline of their refurbished 1975 midnight blue Chevy Malibu parked in the driveway, a green glow-in-the-dark Saint Christopher poised on the dash and the whitewalls shining like haloes.

Not wanting to spew any epithet too terrible to retract, neither of us utters a word as we climb down in tandem, the horse whinnying for the very first time when my feet touch the ground. "Easy," I say, right out of some *High Noon*—type western. "Easy, Paint," but Marley-Anne's the one who nuzzles up and palm strokes its spotted throat and sweet-talks its nervousness away. I've ridden a merry-go-round, but that's about it, and I wouldn't mind a chrome pole or a pommel to hold on to. But Marley-Anne's in front on the reins, and with my arms snug around her waist I feel safe and strangely relaxed, Paint's back and flanks as soft as crushed velour. Except for our dangling legs and how high up we are, it's not unlike sitting on a love seat in some stranger's country estate. Marley-Anne heels us into a trot around the far side of the house and across the cracked concrete sidewalk slabs into the empty street. Paint's shod hooves don't spark, but they do reverberate even louder, the morning having cooled, and there's no traffic, this being Sunday and the whole town still asleep.

Marley-Anne's black jeans are not a fashion statement. They're slatted mid-thigh for ventilation, and I consider sliding my hands in there where her muscles are taut, and just the thought ignites my vapors on a grand scale, everything alive and buzzing—including the static crackle in the power lines we've just crossed under, and that must be Casey Banhammer's hound dream-jolted awake and suddenly howling at who knows what, maybe its own flea-bitten hind end, from two blocks over on Cathedral.

We're slow cantering in the opposite direction, toward the eastern horizon of those postcard-perfect houses and away from the land of the Pignatallis and Burchers and Bellavitas, whose double-wides we've never been inside without an invitation to stop by for a couple of Busch Lights and an evening of small talk and cards and pizza. Guys I work with, all plenty decent enough and not a whole lot of tiny print—meaning little or nothing to hide. Marley-Anne negotiates their backyards this way and that. A zigzag through the two or three feet of semidarkness ahead of us, and the perfect placement of

Paint's hoof-pounds thudding down. A weightless transport past gas grills and lawn furniture, and someone's tipped-over silver Schwinn hurtled with ease, the forward lift and thrust squeezing Marley-Anne and me even tighter together.

There are no sentry lights or fancy stone terraces or in-ground swimming pools, though the sheets on the Showalters' clothesline seem an iridescent white glow, and when Marley-Anne says, "Duck," I can feel the breezy cotton blow across my back, that sweet smell of starch and hollyhocks, the only flower my mom could ever grow. Shiny black and blue ones the color of Marley-Anne's windswept hair, and I can smell *it* too when I press my nose against the back of her head.

There's a common-ground lot, a small park with a diamond and back-stop, and we're cantering Pony Express across the outfield grass. The field has no bleachers, though sometimes when I walk here at night I imagine my dad sitting alone in the top row. I'm at the plate, a kid again, a late rally on and my head full of banter and cheers and the tight red seams of the baseball rotating slow-motion toward me, waist-high right into my wheelhouse. It could, it just might be, my life re-imagined with a single swing, the ball launched skyward, a streaking comet complete with a pure white rooster tail.

But if you've been deserted the way my dad deserted us, no such fantasies much matter after a while. And what could he say or brag about anyway? Truth told, I don't even remember his voice. It's my mom's crying I hear whenever I think of them together and apart. He might be dead for all I know, which isn't much except that he sure stayed gone both then and now. Marley-Anne and I have never mentioned separation or divorce, an outcome that would surely break me for good. And the notion of her up and leaving unannounced some night is simply way too much for someone of my constitution to even postulate.

We slow to something between a trot and a walk, and Paint isn't frothing or even breathing hard, his ears up and forward like he wants more, wants to go and go and go, and maybe leap some gorge or ravine or canyon or, like Pegasus, sprout wings and soar above this unremarkable northern town. On Cabot Street, under those huge-domed and barely visible sycamores, Marley-Anne has to rein him in, and now he's all chest and high-stepping like a circus horse, his nostrils flared for dragon fire. He's so gorgeous that for a fleeting second

I want someone to see us, a small audience we'd dazzle blind with an updated Wild Bill story for them to tell their kids.

We look left toward the Phillips 66 and right toward the all-night laundromat where nobody's about. We keep to those darker stretches between the streetlights and, where Cass intersects with Columbus, there's the Dairy Queen with its neon sign a blurred crimson. The coast is clear, and we stop in the empty parking lot as if it were a relay station on the old overland route to Sioux Falls or San Francisco.

"So far so good," I say, and when Marley-Anne tips her head back I kiss her wine-smooth lips until she moans.

"Hey," she says, her mouth held open as if a tiny bird might fly out. "Hey," like a throaty chorus in a song. When I smile at her she half smiles back as if to say, We're managing in our way just fine, aren't we, Reilly Jack? You and me, we're going to be okay, aren't we? Isn't that how it all plays out in this latest, unrevised chapter of our lives?

I nod in case this *is* her question, and Paint pirouettes a perfect one-eighty so he's facing out toward East Main. Already one walleyed headlight wavers in the huge double plate-glass window of the Dairy Queen as that first car of the morning passes unaware of us. Otherwise the street is deserted, the yellow blinker by the Holiday Inn not quite done repeating itself. Above, up on I-75, a north-south route to nowhere, is that intermittent whine and roar of transport trailers zipping past. But there's an underpass being constructed not far from here, no traffic on it at all, and beyond that the sandpit and some woods with a switchback two-track that will bring us out to County Road 667.

Saint Jerome's Cemetery is no more than another half-mile distant from there, and I can almost smell the wild honeysuckle by the caretaker's shack, its galvanized roof painted green, and a spigot and hose and pail to give the horse a drink. The deceased are enclosed by a black wrought-iron fence, and there's a gate where we'll hang the bridle and turn Paint loose to graze between the crosses and headstones, and perhaps some flower wreathes mounding a freshly covered grave. Another somebody dead out of turn, as my mom used to say, no matter their age or circumstance, whenever she read the obituaries. Out of turn, out of sorts, just out and out senseless the way this world imposes no limits on our ruin—she'd say that too. She'd say how it grieved her that nothing lasts. "Nothing, Reilly Jack, if you love it, will ever, ever last." Then she'd turn away from me and on her way out glance back to where I was sitting alone in the airless kitchen.

And what are the chances that I'd end up here instead of in another life sleeping off the aftereffects of a late Saturday night at the Iron Stallion, where all the usual suspects were present and accounted for, and the jukebox so stuffed full of quarters that its jaws were about to unhinge and reimburse every drunken, lonely last one of us still humming along. But *here*, at 5:45 AM eastern standard, I kiss Marley-Anne again and our hearts clench and flutter, Marley-Anne shivering and her eyes wide open to meet my gaze. Paint is chomping at the bit to go, and so Marley-Anne gives him his lead, his left front hoof on the sewer cover echoing down East Main like a bell.

Already somebody is peppering his scrambled eggs, somebody sipping her coffee, and what's left of this night is trailing away like a former life. The house we lived in is still there exactly the way we left it, the front door unlocked and the pickup's keys in the ignition. *That* life, before those cloud-swirl white splotches on a certain pinto's neck first quivered under Marley-Anne's touch.

Nominated by Stephen Corey, Claire Davis, David Jauss, The Georgia Review

LICHEN

by ROBERT WRIGLEY

from MERIDIAN

Not moss but slower, a kind of lumpenproletariat
fungus come in bunches no one keeps an eye on.
Grandmother ones, grandfathers, though where they're at
they're babies, half birthed among a thousand tiny generations.

And lacey they are, tightly massive as minimal forests,
but always more beautiful the closer you look.
And holding the dew in billions of pin-prick droplets,
they drink their fill and wait, the very name meaning to lick.

Nominated by Katrina Roberts, Christopher Buckley, Claire Davis,
Jeffrey Harrison, Bruce Beasley, Kay Ryan

REASONS FOR AND ADVANTAGES OF BREATHING

fiction by LYDIA PEELLE

from ONE STORY

Shell

I meet the herpetologist on the bus. Rush hour is in its deepest throes, a snow storm has clamped down on the city, and the bus is packed with people in bulky coats, impatient and aggressive at the end of the day. Trapped at the center of the crush, I am starting to doubt that I will be able to hold it together all the way to my stop. Then a surge from behind sends me sliding into the man in front of me, and the flaps of a cardboard box he is holding pop open. I find myself looking down at a turtle, its shell mapped with orange and yellow and green. *A turtle!* I say as he gently folds the flaps back down. Then, shocked to hear myself unlock a door to conversation, *Do you mind if I see it again?* He opens the box just enough for me to see inside. *Are you particularly interested in reptiles?* he says kindly. *Absolutely*, I say, though it isn't true. I just want to keep looking at the turtle, which has drawn its head inside its shell, so utterly still and complacent in the midst of the chaos of the bus. *It's rare to meet young people with an interest*, he says. *Oh yes*, I say quickly, thrilled to be considered young. Then I look up at his face and realize how old he must be himself—grey beard, eyes big and watery behind thick glasses. *I'm a professor*, he says, *at the university. I've written a book you might find interesting.* He pulls a card from his pocket and points to the address with a shaky finger. *Drop by any time.*

Classification

Most nights, I don't sleep. Instead I lie in bed and page through my list of dread and regret, starting with my childhood and ending with the polar ice caps. Everything in between I file into something like schoolroom cubbies, marked with labels like Disaster and Desire. When my husband left, he told me he hadn't been happy in years. *Happy?* I thought. *We're supposed to be happy?* I was under the impression that no one was truly happy, given the raw materials we have to work with in this life. Since he's been gone, I keep the lamp on all night. I'd rather lie awake in the light and keep an eye on his absence than reach out in the dark, thinking he's there. The fact that I may do this for the rest of my life is unclassifiable, too much to bear. When the list comes to this I get up and sit at the kitchen table and watch the snow, the snow which seems always to be falling.

Navigation

After looming for weeks, the day of my office Christmas party arrives. Every year it is the same. We all bring our husbands and wives to a third-rate steakhouse and get drunk and have a gift swap. The husbands and wives stand around making awkward small talk, and we all compliment one another on how nice we look out of our office clothes, drinking swiftly and heavily, sick to death of one another. At the center of all this sits an enormous, blood-rare roast. Last year my husband stole a bottle of vodka off the bar and we snuck out to the back alley, where we wrapped up in his coat and tried to name the constellations we could see between rooftops. The thing I was most grateful for: he could look at any situation, no matter how dire, and instantly know the best way to navigate through. If I was lucky, I'd be pulled along with him. At five o'clock someone comes by my cubicle and reminds me brightly, for the third time today, about the gift swap. I reach into my bag for an aspirin and find the herpetologist's card. *I just remembered*, I say to no one in particular. *I have plans this afternoon.* I pull on my coat and hat and go, stumbling through the exhaust-stained snow. The university looms on a distant hill. When I finally arrive, it seems deserted, nothing but an expanse of iced-over parking lots. It takes a while to find the building whose name is printed on the herpetologist's card, and just as I am about to give up I see it, a low industrial structure that sits on the edge of the campus like an afterthought. Inside, the halls are ill-lit and empty. I follow the signs to the herpetology department. Down one flight of stairs, then another, then another. With each flight I grow warmer, strip off a layer—coat, hat, sweater, scarf. By the time I have found the herpetologist's office, deep in the basement, I am breathless and damp with sweat.

Anticipation

When I knock, the herpetologist flings open his door and beams at me, ushering me in. The tiny room is tropically warm, one wall lined with aquariums that glow with ultraviolet light. *This is my office*, he says proudly, *and those are my anoles*. He is wearing battered khakis and sandals with socks, as if he has just come in from a jungle expedition. The anoles give the room a frantic energy. They puff and posture, do push-ups, circle one another warily. Their bodies are sharp and lizard-like, the dulled green and brown of sea glass, and fans of brightly colored skin hang from their chins: red, purple, blue. *Do you want to hold one?* the herpetologist asks excitedly. When I step closer, their faces seem wise and irascible, and as they swivel their eyes I get the sense that they are judging me. But the herpetologist has already pulled the mesh cover off one of the tanks and is watching me expectantly. I reach in and make a half-hearted show of trying to catch one, my hand sending streaks of panic through the tank. I look at him and shrug. *Like this*, he says, and I see his hand slip in like a stealthy animal. Suddenly, an anole is clasped in his fingers, its head between his thumb and forefinger, tongue flickering, as startling as a bright scarf conjured in a magic trick. I gasp and find I've been holding my breath. *You've got to anticipate*, he says, grinning.

Raft

I come home to a red light flashing in the dark of the living room, a message on the machine from my husband. I have to play it twice, his voice slurred and halting. This is how it has been for several months: when he gets drunk, he wants to work it out. I call him back and tell him to come over, willing to take him any way I can get him. He arrives already bristling with defenses, a cape of snow on his shoulders. As we stand there in the living room, hashing it all out, I try to keep it together by fixing my eyes on the snow, watching the flakes turn to drops of water and then disappear into the fabric of his coat. A brand new coat, I notice, and I am sideswiped by an image of his new apartment, where I've never been, all the furniture I know he has treated himself to—top of the line, paid on credit, same-day delivery, as if he

364

can buy his way back to a beginning. Exhausted, I collapse into him, and he pilots me towards the bed, but when we make love I feel as if I am struggling for a grip on a slippery raft, trying in vain to pull myself up. Afterwards, we are lying side by side, not touching, when he turns to me and flexes the mattress with his fingers. *I know why you can't sleep*, he says. *It's obvious. What you need are individually wrapped coils.* When he falls asleep I turn on the light and watch his eyes flutter in a dream. I imagine all his women, in there with him. I close my eyes and picture them, one by one, lingering on the torturous details: their optimism, their young skin, their white teeth flashing as they smile at him across his expensive new bed. But in between, I find I keep seeing the herpetologist's office. It calms me, familiar, like an ill-used back room of my mind: the glow of the lamps, the dust-cloaked bookshelves, the anoles, a many-colored bouquet.

Adaptation

On the coldest day of December, the heat goes out at work. I sit hunched at my desk, freezing, my hands pulled up into my sleeves. I think about the tropical warmth of the heat lamps in the herpetologist's office. I get up, switch off the computer, and go. Outside, a thick sleet is falling, turning the city the color of asphalt. The cold air slices through my clothes. When I arrive I try to think up a reason for why I've returned, but the herpetologist takes my coat without question and in fact seems overjoyed to see me. *Let me show you the lab*, he says, clasping my arm. *Is it as warm as your office?* I ask sheepishly. *Warmer!* he says. *Come on.* Our shoes squeak on the linoleum as we walk down the long hall. No one else seems to be around. He opens the door of the lab with a key on his crowded key ring, and I feel my lungs bloom with the heat. At first, the room seems full of empty aquariums. Then, slowly, as the herpetologist leads me from one to the next, the animals reveal themselves. There is a sidewinder and a hellbender. There is a chuckwaller from Texas which, when it sees us, rushes between two rocks in its habitat and puffs itself up until it is wedged tightly in. There is a nightmarish creature from Australia called a thorny devil, with spines that have spines. Its Latin name, typed on a card taped to its aquarium, is *Moloch horridus*. In the next cage, a giant Gila monster sleeps under a heat lamp, its sides pooled out around it, *POISONOUS!* written in red on its card. A brilliant green gecko uses its tongue to wipe its eyes. The herpetologist's face is shining. *All these diverse adaptations, with one common goal,* he says. *To live to see tomorrow.* He turns abruptly towards the back of the room, tripping over a cardboard box full of crickets. *Come here*, he says, motioning with excitement, and I go to him and watch a barking tree frog, an impossible, unnatural yellow, delicately eat a fly out of his hand.

Natural History

My husband and I sit side by side on the couch, in the light of one lamp. We say the same things we always do, slicing back through the scar tissue in one another's hearts. *I've always felt,* he says, *that you never had any hope for us.* I stare silently at the puddle of melted snow around his boots by the front door, no idea where to begin. My hopelessness extends over the whole human race. We've mortgaged our lives, ruined the planet, and, with modern technology, rendered ourselves nearly obsolete. What is there to hope for? Who is equipped to take on what's to come? I saw our love as a fallout shelter for the future, and thought he did too. But all along he'd been with other women, with whom, he told me, he could have fun. *Fun.* When we make love I stare up at the ceiling, already imagining him pulling his pants back on, sliding into those boots, sneaking out soundlessly in the morning while I squeeze my eyes shut, feigning sleep.

Night Vision

I come home the next evening to find a dark snake draped across the foot of the bed. Motionless, waiting for my next move. I freeze, thrilled to the sheer shock of it. My pulse rips with terror and delight. Fingers quivering, I switch on the lamp. But it is only my husband's limp black sock, left from the night before. Caught where it landed when we pulled off our clothes once words had failed us, as they always have.

Spadefoot Toad

Walking home from work, I go far out of my way to pass the university. I descend the steps to the herpetologist's office with as much sense of purpose as if I have been given my own key. He is at his desk when I arrive, and sits back in his chair and quite naturally begins to tell me about the spadefoot toad. *You're lucky to see one in the wild,* he says. *They burrow deep, deep in the ground. They've been found,*

366

unscathed, among the embers of brushfires. *And,* he says, dropping his voice, leaning in close, *They freeze solid in winter. Solid. Like an ice cube. You could actually pick one up and throw it against a wall, and it would shatter.* As he says this, he makes the motion one would make to dash a frog against a wall, as if sidearming a tennis ball. His glasses slip off with the effort, and he fumbles for them with both hands. The silence that follows is intimate and close. Startled by it, I search his face, wondering if he notices it too. His grey beard is etched in red, annals of his younger self. *I tried to kill myself once,* I say. *When I was young. I jumped off a bridge into a half-frozen river.* The herpetologist is quiet for so long that I wonder if I shouldn't have said it, then wish I could take it back. Finally he says, *And were you shivering, when they pulled you out?* Of course I was shivering, I say, confused. He nods. *Trust the body, not the mind,* he says, smiling. *The body loves itself.*

Habitat

On Christmas Eve, I end up at another party. Every instinct says not to go, but it's Christmas Eve, I keep telling myself, and there's a possibility my husband may be there. I manage to pull on a dress and a pair of panty hose and go. By the time I arrive, tight packs of people are already impenetrably formed around the room, plates expertly balanced, voices tinkling. I find a drink and arrange myself near the hors d'oeuvres, where I keep an eye on the door and stab my drink with its tiny straw. As time wears on, my panty hose sag around my thighs, hobbling me there. I watch the faces around the room, wondering how everyone can be having such a good time, given the devastating stories I'm sure that they too all saw on the six o'clock news. The only thing keeping me going is the Christmas tree, which smells like bracing outdoor work, well-being and fulfillment. The hostess comes over and offers me another drink. *The tree smells lovely,* I say, motioning to it there across the room. *Oh!* she says gaily. *It's a spray!* and sweeps off to find my drink. I carry myself like a broken glass to the dark of the corner, where at least I can yank up my sagging panty hose. Sliding behind the tree, I see the holes in the plastic trunk where the wire branches screw in. A new low, I think, to be failed by a tree. I grasp a bough between my thumb and forefinger for balance and find that I am nonetheless searching its needles for any sign of life, hoping for anything, the blink of an eye, a flash of a disappearing tail.

367

A Gift

On Christmas morning I step out onto the stoop and find the herpetologist's book, laid carefully on a patch of white ice. A bright green chameleon is staring up at me from the dust jacket, its eye following my every move. When I pick it up I open to a mimeographed list of errata pasted to the flyleaf. The copyright date is thirty years old. I turn to the back flap, hoping to see a photograph of the herpetologist as a young man, but there is only a list of his degrees and credentials. On the inside front cover, there is an inscription made out to me: *with warmest regards*. Only then do I wonder how he found my apartment. I stay home all day and read it cover to cover. I read that, at ten weeks, a human fetus is nearly identical to a salamander embryo—gills, webbed hands, tail bud. I read that snakes have two hundred pairs of ribs and tiny, vestigial leg bones. I read all about hibernation and estivation. In the section on evolution, the move from life underwater to life on land, I read a chapter titled *Reasons for and Advantages of Breathing*.

Perpetuation

A bullfrog in a corner aquarium has laid her eggs. They float in a raft of jelly on the surface of the water, knocking against the glass. The big green frog courses around, kicking her thick thighs, oblivious to them. *In the wild, she'd be long gone by now*, the herpetologist says. *Her existence is a perpetual struggle. She can't be burdened by babies. But still, she must replace herself.* I think of all of us, people toiling to leave something to the world only to end up slowly poisoning it in the process. *What's the point?* I don't realize I've said it aloud. *Who knows?* the herpetologist says. He taps the glass. *Ask her.* I turn towards him. *Did you ever have children?* He shakes his head and with a smile tells me he's always been married to his work. *We never did*, I say. *My husband wanted to. But I just couldn't bring a child into this world. I don't know. Do you think I should have?* He shakes his head. *Should have, should have*, he says. *Look at her.* He taps the glass again. *She knows no such word as* should. *She knows only* can *and* do. I look down at the eggs. There must be thousands of them, each with a dark spot at the center like the pupil of an eye, and I am suddenly dismayed by the thought of the mother kicking away from them without leaving so much as a promise. *How many will make it?* I ask. The herpetologist ticks off the hazards that would face the eggs in the wild: flood, drought, pollution, construction, snakes, fish, turtles, toads, raccoons, other frogs. *The tadpole stage is even chancier*, he says, *and you can just forget about it when you're a froglet.* Then he says, *But at least one.* One? I think, looking at the mass of eggs with a sinking sense of despair. Which one? The lucky one?

Locomotion

On a day with little else to justify my getting out of bed, the herpetologist gives me a turtle skeleton. *A turtle's backbone is fused to its carapace*, he chants, *an arching armature for its armor.* The neck and leg bones are impossibly frail, fine as pebbles. They seem far too delicate to support the heavy awning of the shell. *Yes*, the herpetologist says, seeing me looking, *poorly designed for locomotion on land. No lateral possibility, with those bones.* He takes the skeleton from me and shows me how a turtle moves: lifting two legs, deliberately throwing itself off balance until it falls forward. Lifting the other two legs and falling forward again. Falling, picking itself up, falling. *Like this, the turtle has lurched its way through two hundred million years. Through all kinds of weather.* This strikes me as the most remarkable thing I've heard in months. *Humbling*, I say. *Yes! But think of your own skeleton*, he tells me. *The bipedal frame is a triumph of design. Thirty-two articulated vertebrae, all in a line. And at the tip, the unparalleled mass of electricity that is your mind. And you didn't even have to ask for it.*

Range

As I walk through the frozen city, I do think of it, my skeleton hanging in perfect balance. The bones of my toes and feet, flexing inside my shoes. I trace them up my shinbones, the long bones of my thighs, up the ladder of my spine. All the way up to the thought that I could walk for miles, hundreds of miles if I so chose, clear out of the city to a warmer place.

Company

On New Year's Eve I go out for a walk, just to breathe the sharp night air. People scurry through the street two by two, heads bent against the cold, wearing their best clothes. The men nervously check their watches as if there is a train to catch, headed for a fabulous destination. A man and a woman are leaning close to a shop window, looking in at something, their voices filled with delight. It is my husband with

369

a much younger woman, both dressed for a party. When he looks up and sees me, a strangled noise escapes his throat. *I don't want to see you any more*, I say, because it's all I've got. *OK*, he says, *alright*, not even pretending to put up a fight. As they walk away and join the disappearing throng on the street, I get the sense that the train is departing imminently, with no chance that I will be on it. I look in the window at what they've been examining. It is a glittering diamond and emerald brooch, something I myself have admired in the past. But now it seems gaudy and crude, and I realize I was expecting something infinitely more beguiling to be crouched behind the glass. I hear a noise behind me and wheel around, thinking that maybe he's come back, but it is just a lone crow, picking delicately through an overturned trash can. It feels as if we're the last two creatures left in the abandoned city, just me and this crow. Grateful for the company, I raise my hand. *Oh, hello*, I say.

Las Vegas Leopard Frog

There is a grainy black and white photograph of a frog taped above the herpetologist's desk. It is an ordinary looking frog. Beneath the photo hangs a narrow page torn from a field guide. I read it so many times I am able to repeat it from memory, or almost. It reassembles itself in my mind as a sort of a poem:

> *Last seen in 1942, long before worry about endangered species*
> *Probably extinct*
> *As the city of Las Vegas grew*
> *groundwater pumped out, springs capped*
> *hope for* Rana fisheri *was filled in with cement*
>
> *Discovery of a remnant population*
> *would be a herpetological event*

Deficiency

The herpetologist needs my help. *I wouldn't ask*, he says on the phone, *except that no one else is here*. A snake has just been brought in to the lab, a confiscated reticulated python that someone has been keeping as a pet. When I arrive, the herpetologist is standing in front of its tank, dwarfed by it. *I'm afraid it must be destroyed*, he tells me sadly. *It has an irreversible and degenerative vitamin deficiency, resulting from an inadequate diet. Nothing can be done.* I watch it

370

slowly map the terrain of its tank, staggered with disbelief that some-
one would keep such a massive, commanding thing in the house and
not take pains to see that it had everything it needed. *Ready to shed,
too,* the herpetologist says, pointing to its milk-white eyes. *Dull all
over. Would be brilliant in a week or two. I've seen them tie them-
selves in knots in an effort to shed the old skin. What a shame,* I say,
as the loss suddenly multiplies —the snake, and the newness the
snake won't have the chance to inhabit. *People,* the herpetologist
sighs. I help him hold the snake as he makes the injection, and in my
hands I feel a change in the taut muscles, the exact moment that life
leaves them. We hold vigil over the enormous body. The herpetolo-
gist looks stricken, drawn and old. *I don't know,* he says over and
over. *I just don't know.* I shove my hands in my pockets, wishing I
could give him something. We stand there together for a long time,
bewildered as two night travelers with a map they can't make out in
the dark.

Bloom

All night, I lie awake in the light of the bedside lamp, studying my
hands. What was it, exactly, that I felt pass out of the snake? The one
thing I know for certain: I've witnessed a slight parting of the curtain
that hangs over the unknown. By morning I feel a bloom of gratitude
for this which I wear, a bright badge, pinned to my chest for days.

Heralds of Spring

I leave my apartment at five to help the herpetologist with his morn-
ing feedings. So this is what it feels like, I think, to be out at dawn,
meeting the world head on. Salt trucks are rumbling by, preparing
the icy streets for the coming day. The sky is a color I've never seen
before. It is as if a corner of the city's grey overcoat has blown back to
reveal an orange satin lining. We drink Postum out of Styrofoam
cups. He apologizes that there is no real coffee. I tell him I don't
drink it anymore, a last attempt to reclaim sleep. *Good girl,* he says,
good girl. He pulls a record off the bookshelf and puts it on the
turntable. Through the scratchiness I hear a high pitched, insistent
whistle, like crickets, only the notes are rounder, wetter, like water
dropping from a leaf into a pond. *The dawn song of the peeper,* he
says, *the herald of spring.* He beams. *I don't think spring is ever com-
ing,* I say. *Nonsense,* he says. *And in a week or so, the students will
come back. I must say, as much as I enjoy the quiet, it does get lonely*

around here when they're gone. The students! The fact of them has never occurred to me. Now I see their bright eager faces, I see them shaking snow off their boots as they file in, listening raptly to the herpetologist in a lecture room, notebooks open, carrying him away in a wave down the hall. The record switches to the call of a bullfrog, mournful. I have the sudden urge to reach behind me and lock the door.

Secret

I want you to see something, the herpetologist says. *A secret.* He leads me to a door at the back of the lab that I haven't noticed before. He selects a large key from his ring and unlocks it. We step into a tiny antechamber, and when he closes the door behind us, we stand together for a moment in the utter darkness. Then I hear the click of a key in another lock, and we step through to another room, even darker than the first. He switches on a dim red light. As my eyes adjust I see a chest-high tank of water in the center of the room. We step to its edge. In the red light I can just make out something swimming around in the water, tiny ghost creatures with red ruffs of gills. *The Georgia blind salamander,* he whispers. *It exists only in the deep wells and subterranean waters of one particular farm in southeast Georgia. You're maybe the tenth person in the world to see one alive.* The salamanders seem to give off a light of their own, dark eye buds showing through the clear skin of their faces, their red gills waving like feathers as they weave through the water. For a heartbeat I forget myself completely. Then I catch my breath and say, *they don't even know we're here.* The herpetologist moves closer. I slip my hand in his. *I think I love you,* I say. He shakes his head firmly, as if it's the wrong answer to a question. *No, you don't,* he says.

A Herpetological Event

I stay late at work, in no state to face my dark apartment, overcome by a new sort of loneliness, one that seems as if it will outlive me. By the time I get on the bus, late in the evening, it is hushed and mostly empty, and I collapse into a seat near the back. As we rattle down the street I close my eyes and think of the blind salamanders, down there in their well in Georgia, far from the city, far from me. When I open my eyes I have long since missed my stop. I sit up in a panic, recognizing nothing outside. But then, as the bus voyages through unfamiliar streets, the salamanders come back like a dream. The darkness

372

deep in the earth where they've been all along. Arcing, looping, somersaulting through the water, somehow finding one another in the dark. Without any thought, care, or need for me. And for an instant, just before the bus turns on its loop, I catch a glimpse of the infinite. There I am inside of it, for one suspended moment —tiny, inconsequential, and utterly free.

Dawn Song

Late in the night a storm settles in on the city, throwing snow heavily against the windows and rattling them in their frames. My husband calls to tell me his power has gone out, asks if he can come over. *Just this one night*, he says. *I don't have anywhere else to go* I sit at the kitchen table waiting for him, listening to the silence of the streets, the weather too bad for even the plows to be out. Things are so still that I am startled to look down and see the collar of my robe quivering steadily with my pulse. He comes in with a red wind-burned face and cold clinging to his clothes. We sit side by side at the table, no words left for one another. Soon my power goes out as well and there is nothing for us to do but get into bed and huddle beneath the blankets, press tight together to conserve warmth. We make love, a matter of survival, our bodies desperate to generate heat. My heart pounds against his chest with the insistence of self preservation, tenacious and bright, as if it has shed a dull skin. It is still beating hard, determined, by the time he has fallen asleep. I sit up and try to make out his sleeping face in the dark, left with the unshakeable feeling that there is a stranger in my bed. Sometime before dawn I get up into the cold room and look out the window. The snow is slackening, but down the block, all the street lights are still off. In the darkness, the shine of the deep white drifts is the only thing I can make out. It seems to conceal a great mystery, the snow. I stand there watching, struck by the possibility of what might be hidden beneath. I watch for as long as I can stand the cold, knowing that by morning the trucks will have come to clear it all away.

Nominated by Andrew Porter, H. E. Francis, One Story

NO OTHER PARADISE

by KURT BROWN

from WATER-STONE

Pale dawn   then banks of cloud   shot with light
highway salted to a dry crust   the sun a white flame
but no ice   the river a broad   rippling scintillance
the skyline's jagged profit chart   we wake to our own reality
purely imagined   the ghost-life of money   war
history's fractured narrative   we had a paradise
it was around here somewhere   near blighted derricks
tankers   bloated with oil   on the far bank
more of the same   and where bridges stride
listlessly   above the waste   raw sky empty of wings

    ✿

standing here   in this city   this gray sprawling
dismasted island   made of baby carriages
and sunken rails   stink of scorched rubber   howl
of metal   Lucite   mortar   polymer   glass
horizon of stainless steel   chromium nickel towers
so high   they lean *in*   grid on grid   finials and brick
cladding   the vanished hulls   asphalt slips
once porcupined with spars   and under pavements
scooped   blasted interior of spongiform rock
city of tin cans   conurbation of exposed beams
men with lunch boxes   dining nonchalantly in air
lives teetering on pylons   and the sea's indulgence

    ✿

slurry on the river   a liquid gel   and in the park
pigeons huddle by a wall   heads stuffed back
into shoulders   like rolled socks   wind
veers down alleys and mews   hurdles buildings
spills into the city's mold   then hardens into towers
catwalks   parapets   buffeting the few
who scrabble home   or off to work   is it that difficult
to get from one place to the next   tall gusts
bludgeoning cornices   cabs   the decrepit façade
of Deutsche Evangelisch Lutherische Est. 1859
meanwhile   Miss Donna   "Mystical Astrologist"
deprived of customers   falls asleep over her cards

     *

snow circles the pediments   handprint of a child
on Fourth Street   filled with rain   sign on a cellar door
jazz until down   but dig in one corner and turn up houses
old pastures   parading troops   riots   slums
no longer crowded   to know is to guess   age on age
everything streams past this palimpsest   this eviction
of ghosts   and by the frigid beltways   prow
nudges prow   avenues come apart   the past is spliced
onto the present   the future snaps like a cable
nidus of incalculable ambitions   necropolis of dreams
now sunlight breaks fully on these stone embrasures

     *

no silence   but steady tumult   night or day
skirl of iron   blast of brakes   wrecking ball
and dredger   *listen*   someone's key rattles in a box
we were born here   passing through flesh
to become flesh   in the white rush of acetylene
the boom of freight   arriving in a bright arpeggio
of taxis   departing in the echo of announcements
I didn't do anything   he says   *I was half asleep*
then a gust of air   before the train arrives
bristling sound along the tracks   like hundreds
of tiny wires   shaken together   a secret scuttering
the bastard slipped out on me   doors close   everywhere
and in the freezing air   all that was never said
glitters louder than jackhammers   probing the street

there's always someplace else to be but where we are
hurrying uptown   hurtling down   highways
stream like gunwales   leaving our old address
while buses   slick as carp   nose down avenues
helicopters hop from stalks of concrete   even the earth
trembles underfoot   shuddering with departure
sky-hung scaffolding sways   settles under booms
and steel nets   coming and going   there are clocks
everywhere   circling the day   whistles   bells
schedules   printed with the details of ephemera
a nickel glints on the sidewalk   pressed into stone

pipes froze   windows cracked   it was that cold
laundry hung like sheets of metal on the line
later   soot   rain   the bald sun-scorched arcades
blood stopped in the arteries   the intricate veins
of the face   squalls   blizzards   a hundred winters
buried in the mind   *this isn't a city   it's the world*
built up   and demolished   icicled and white
someone skis down blanketed ravines   the abandoned
offices   exposed manholes breathing steam
and later   gelid bodies   brittle as petrified wood
appear like pharos   under elegant pyramids
makeshift ziggurats   a mummified doorman stamps
his feet   and takes a long-drawn   glittering breath

praise the filth   the narrowing   sexual nights
history's pages   thumbed over and over in the street
young girls trudge past   gloved hands locked   laughter
spangling the air   then a child   dragging a sled
such storms rise out of the sea   to reclaim the town
dragging it under a powdery   white   iridescent foam
praise the cinder   the compact   scalloped slush
the incalculable waste   box   and melon rind
greasy axle and lug nut   the flyblown   busted armchair
in which no one sits but the bleak   fugitive sun
praise ashcan and coal chute   brackish gutter and cracked
pane   how the brand-new passes through the present
to the harrowing   unspeakable dump   *don't let go*

they giggle   turning the corner with linked arms
if you lose someone here   you may never see them again

   *

angle of earth   and our distance from the sun
all these lives pitched outward   man in a penthouse
woman in 14-c   *it was around here somewhere*
higher and higher   time leans *in*   brimming the dank
projects   the rich basilicas   someone's hat
blows off and rolls down the street   who isn't a city
a generation   who isn't a graveyard   the flaking
broken stones   MOSCOWITZ   O'MALLEY
POUDELLE   VAN DER SLUIJS   VOSZKA
CHORBAJIANI   SUDHOLM   NJOKU-OBI   ZENK
passing through flesh to become flesh   mothers
strolling under bare trees   fathers turning in the long fall

   *

one shop trembles like a wick   windows
spewing flame   houses in surrounding streets
shudder together like dry leaves
sirens and alarms   walls reflecting strobe light
smoke billows out and pours into the sky   smell
of the eternal   scrapbooks   photos   letters
files crammed with documents   words beginning
to erase themselves   the past   lifting up and thinning out
the future   vast and blue   swallowing it whole   then nothing
but the pungent odor of burnt wood   water   sealing us back in

   *

Miss Donna   wakes in snowlight   no one there
only her cat   chary and alert   as though something might
happen   some restless apparition   or voice   *listen*
across the water   cannons rumble   as a ship arrives
ensigns aloft   and near the slips   drunken song
anarchy of gulls   fish market   pig stall   the butcher's
litter   this island itself a ship   breasting time
she hears it in the silent rocking of the shop   and now
as the wind luffs   rattle of cartwheel   bottle chink
blade drawn slowly over stone   sound of a dog
from a different century   shadows of flakes   drifting
down the wall   the insubstantial dead   the multitude

   *

if it's all glass   why can't we see through it
river to river   its febrile life exposed   tier on tier
into endless air   and when we come down
a little drink steadies us   anchors us again to the ground
whenever one of my friends succeeds   he says
a little something in me dies   ghost-life of numbers
all that abstraction   trapped in concrete   all
that sweat   that heartbreak   just as the hairs on the head
are numbered   the breaths we take   *going up*
we say   to spend our day   suspended   between
heaven   and earth   how the invisible   the bodiless
can crush us   story by story   floor by floor

    ✿

four a.m.   the savage markets   aproned men
in boots   haul fresh meat   hooked aloft   packed
plucked bodies   skinned sinew and scraped bone
a carcass swings   hacked open   to a lattice of ribs
across town   catfish lie   composed in steel bins
near moist hake   plush with oil   and knots of octopus
glisten in aluminum tubs   nothing can appease
the city's appetites   its cold lockers swung wide
mounds of bread   like fresh graves   stacks of lettuce
squash   potatoes   leeks   trucks arriving with the first
antiseptic light   the hauler's hands   bloody
with their work   the very stones stained with it
until their hoses wash them clean   and the river
profaned with garbage   drags its filthy body towards the sea

    ✿

praise the sewers   the black   scabrous buildings
praise billboards   their ripped   illuminated smiles
light erupts   spills from the center like fire
a spectral phosphorescence   leaching the ravenous dark
windows appear   statues in the park grow pensive
trees nudge each other   the moon swings on its black cord
and on avenues   thick with lights   chic salons
ignite cheap   heraldic logos   the city flings its halo
into space   a bright   tentative exhalation above the roofs
the shivering   muffled night   scarred with stars

    ✿

a hesitation   a hush   the rush of traffic slows
Miss Donna lights a candle   and stares into her own palm
on the next block   St. Bosco's Elementary   spills
children into the street   their voices   punctuate the dusk
mothers stroll under bare trees   and fathers turn
as though they could hear something   a bell ringing
in the next century   the ghost-life of war   *if you lose*
someone now   you may never find them again
for a moment   walls tremble   leaning into each other
as what-has-been   leaches into what-will-come
and in a mailbox   somewhere   there's a letter
written with a firm hand   bearing news that will wreck a life
meanwhile   wrapped in blankets   a bum stops
at the corner   and squints at a billboard for Clancy's Whiskey
"a little taste of heaven"   to calculate the angle of earth
his exact distance from the sun   in the morning
he'll emerge from his ziggurat of boxes   bored stiff
and chastened   ready to assume the blessings of his new life

❀

o fish-flanked city   crux of origins   locus of souls
we wake to our own reality   *just now   and always again*
train wreck   widow's cry   the murderous indictment
banks of light-shot   ineffable turrets   rise   the tide whelms
and pivots   praise the hustle   the shuck and jive
praise the boulevard's riot of light   who knows his homeland
from these littered streets   *hold on to your wallet*
and don't look no one in the eye   now night lowers
its thickening grit   and incoming flights   beacon the sky
who can tell his life from this rabble of announcements
from Sin City   "Open for Lunch"   Kotz Bros. Welding
Raju & Sons 24-hour Tow   HairHealth Inc.   Nick's Locks
and Hindleman's Smoke Shop   from no other paradise   but here

Nominated by Andrea Hollander Budy, Water-Stone

ERRANDS IN THE FOREST

by WILLIAM DEBUYS

from ORION

THE FOREST did not keep the body of the dead mare long. After two weeks, close to Christmas, when I returned to the knoll where I shot her, the skeleton was already picked clean. I had not imagined the hunger of the forest to be so swift. Coyotes must have done most of the work, vultures having migrated south, or perhaps a bear gorged on the carcass before heading to winter sleep.

A week later, I noticed that the tips of the short ribs had been gnawed away, and rabbit tracks dimpled the glaze of snow beside them. I had never thought of cottontails as scavengers, but here was proof. It seemed that every creature participated in the slow reduction and disassembly of the old mare's parts.

We called her Geranium. She'd been my kids' horse for six or seven years, after a well-earned retirement from service as a cow-pony in the rugged New Mexico high country of the Pecos Wilderness. The woman who named her—she was two owners removed from me—said one morning she went out to buy a pot of geraniums to brighten her kitchen, but when she came home she brought with her not flowers, but a compact, even-tempered mare about fourteen hands high.

A working horse takes a lot of pounding in its forelegs. Too many sharp turns cutting cattle. Too many long days up and down mountain steeps, sometimes with a rider, sometimes with a pack. Geranium's knees began to give out a few years after we got her. A few years more and the arthritis pained her so much she could barely hobble around to graze. I consulted a vet as well as my retired sheepherder neighbor, a lifelong horseman. They agreed that it would be cruel to put her through another winter on our little mountain ranch.

The vet offered to provide me the barbiturates to put her down, but I declined. That would have involved a backhoe and a giant grave, lest the drugs poison the creatures that came to feed on her. Instead, I waited as long into December as I dared and then led her one morning to a pretty knoll in the forest where I put a soft cloth over her eyes and unholstered the pistol.

On a horse, if you draw imaginary lines from the root of each ear to the opposite eye, the lines cross in the center of the flat plane of the skull. That is where you shoot a horse to kill it. And that is where I shot Geranium, who buckled and dove into the ground even before the gunshot's roar reached its peak.

Killing her was a wrenching duty, made of large parts of obligation and regret, and for months afterward I kept going back to the knoll where I left her.

All this happened a decade ago, and, in fact, I still go back.

One day, in those first months, I visited the knoll, approaching through a thicket, not by the path I used when I took her there. The head and spine were now yards from where she'd fallen, and a gristled leg had been dragged into oak brush. The winter was dry, and no snow lay on the ground to record the tracks of visitors. I left by the usual path, which was an alley through the scrub of young pines that guarded the site. Where the scrub opened out, something lay in the trail. Something white like a bone. Some piece of Geranium, I thought. But no, it was the skull of a cow. There was no mistaking that it had been placed to lie at the entrance to Geranium's death site. The cow skull was a funerary marker, and it had not been there long.

Any creature bringing the skull would have crossed a patch of bare ground, devoid of duff, where the only tracks were those I had left on earlier visits and the lighter, less distinct prints of coyotes and my own dog. In my years of wandering this patch of forest, I had rarely encountered sign of another person this far back from both the river and the road, and never had I found such sign in winter. I was sure no person had brought the skull to the entrance of the knoll. But I believed I knew the skull's origin.

Some years earlier a cow had died—or a dead cow had been discarded—at the head of a gully beside a logging road a quarter mile away. The carcass appeared in summer, when food was abundant, and the forest community dawdled in consuming it. For months the gully reeked. In those days I rode the logging track frequently, and I would kick my horse and hold my breath as I passed by. Back then I also collected skulls, and I kept my eye on the cow's, but it vanished before it was clean enough to take home. Now, perhaps, this was that very skull, reappeared.

Tales that cast coyote as a trickster abound in native lore. No other creature seems so instinctively inclined to mischief. The fox may be sly, but he is not bold enough for joking. The wolf is bold, but not light-hearted. Bear is both bold and strong, but too hazy-witted to deal in irony or symbolism. Cougar and bobcat, like all felines, are too self-absorbed. Among our cast of forest characters only raven also possesses the requisite curiosity and knack for mockery, but raven, being a bird, is too small for muscular pranks.

The business of the cow skull, however, was more than mischief. It was a declaration. I have encountered only one other statement of similar heft and seriousness, and coyote unmistakably was its author. I stumbled upon this message years ago in deep forest at the foot of a mountain. Scrub oak blanketed the upper slopes and made the area rich in acorns. And thick with bears. Within the forest I followed a well-worn game trail. Where this trail met another, there lay a bear skull, upside down, exactly in the center of the crossing. No other bones were close by; the skull had been brought there and conspicuously placed. It was old and whitened, and the base of the cranium had been opened and the brains eaten or rotted out. But the cranium was not empty. Bears no doubt think often, if fuzzily, about coyotes, and coyotes surely reflect even more upon the bears whose territories they share. In this instance a coyote that held strong views about its neighbors had deftly filled the cranium of the defunct bear with a compact mound of turds. The message was hardly subtle. It might have been a general statement about all bears or a more specific declaration about this particular bear, but in either case the author's point of view was unmistakable.

The shat-in bear skull having enlarged my idea of what a coyote might do, it did not seem a stretch to believe that a coyote might place the skull of a cow to mark the death place of a horse. I believe that a coyote did this in the same way that I believe in small miracles and in the frequent intendedness of coincidence. Odd, dreamlike things happen in the forest that beggar belief, and we learn only of a few, while explaining fewer still. When D. H. Lawrence wanted to invoke the mystery of the soul, he summoned the image of the forest. The image works because the reverse is also true: to invoke the mystery of the forest, only something as grand and inexplicable as the soul will do. Here is what he said:

"This is what I believe: That I am I. That my soul is a dark forest. That my known self will never be more than a little clearing in the forest. That gods, strange gods, come forth from the forest into the clearing of my known self, and then go back. That I must have the courage to let them come and go."

Lawrence's image of the soul is like the forest I think I know. It is a place more often dark than light, where the half-light of dawn and dusk lasts longer than in other places. It is a place where creatures on strange errands trot through the gloom bearing odd burdens and odder messages that are rarely deciphered. It is a place where bones and other strange things vanish and later reappear only to vanish again. But in the forest, as in the soul, nothing is lost. Or so I believe.

So it must be with the skull of the cow, which disappeared from Geranium's knoll three weeks after it was placed there. I have searched for it repeatedly, but I have not seen it again. It simply vanished, and when I noticed it was gone, the tracks in the mud and crusty snow revealed no more or less than they had before.

Nominated by Orion

RETURNING HOME
IN THE MG
JUST BEFORE DAWN

by GERRY LAFEMINA

from CHATTAHOOCHEE REVIEW

The last rags of cloud have dispersed
displaying the harvest moon's mandala burnished,
but seeming as far away
                                as a saxophone

a friend retired four years ago,
the one she sometimes pulls from the closet—not to play,
but rather to hear the reedy echo of song
lodged in its long esophagus.

Imagine that song is a hymn.
Imagine it is sung by a famished cat on the front porch.

Imagine it's sung by vibrations of the last struck chord
on that stand-up piano shoved in grandmother's living room corner;

sung by the engine at 4000 RPM;
sung by the grackle right before dawn.

How soon I return to the rind of this world—
the misgivings of sparrows and neighbor kids who wake
with my arrival; the lawn laminated with dew;

my house barren, shut down like a stage
but for the porch light

which ignites the safety net of a spider web
stretched tightly between the skeletal limbs of white birch.

Nominated by Lee Upton, Mary Ann Samyn, Michael Waters, Chattahoochee Review

THE EPICUREAN

fiction by LOUIS B. JONES

from THE THREEPENNY REVIEW

Whenever Candace Roan called me during the day (I was a construction laborer in that year while I planned to go back to school; and I existed in a state of constant romantic expectation, waiting for the ringing of a phone inside a foreman's trailer out on a job site somewhere, and for the foreman to emerge holding the cordless phone saying *It's for you*, begrudgingly), we would meet in her condominium above Highway 101, to eat one of her artfully cooked dinners, as prelude, while the steady river of freeway traffic below provided a kind of moral white-noise curtain I associate with that decade, when all the world seemed newcomers to California, all our souls bathed in a million headlights' combined glamour. She always sent me home before I might possibly fall asleep in her bed—she had a long drive herself, back to the Sunnyvale house where she lived—but for a while we would lie together and talk and—on this particular occasion—eat pears and grapes from a bedside bowl. I was ten years younger than she was. She worked during the day as a lawyer at a multinational accounting firm, wearing suits that repelled touch, but inwardly she was nagged by a talent for pleasure, captivating to herself. That was how I constructed her in my own mind. The truth is, I never did understand her, and still don't today: what put that light in her eye; what motivated her to shop for the ingredients and the fresh flowers and drive all the way up from Sunnyvale alone, and light the candles; or what she saw in me at all. Now I'm past her age at that time, and at least I know enough to see now how mysterious it all was, our appearances for each other, or for ourselves, every so often in that condominium borrowed from her corporation, white-carpeted, with window shades of hanging vertical plastic slats, a dining room table of glass. Beginning at dusk above the rivers of rush hour, with the choice of wine or the revelation of sherbet, concluding with talk against the bedstead among shifting dunes of our embraces in repose, the whole evening would elapse in wonderments—for example, I had never eaten an artichoke—until the end when I lay in bed beside her listening to her stories of daily events around her office. I felt large and happy and useful, eating grapes. She used to say this debauchery (as she called it) was a temporary stage her pilgrim soul was going through while she was newly divorced and still young enough, and she used a theological adjective for it, "Kierkegaardian." I'd known her when she was Candy Pfleger in our youth in Illinois; our families were members of the same church; she sang in the choir while I was a Sunday-school student, far beneath her notice then; Candy Pfleger was just as far above my notice; she made almost no impression in my memory. Then her family moved away to Cedar Rapids, Iowa.

Now out here in California, reincarnated for a time in a version of an inconsequential paradise, the most fantastic scandal, to me, about Candace Roan was that she had studied seriously to be a nun. A real Dominican nun. She had actually been in a convent. One night while we took bites of fruit and sipped sweet dessert wine in a shared snifter, she told me a story of something that happened during the year when she was on the brink of taking her vows. I had been teasing her about what a wonderful cliché it was, that a nun should disguise a sexpot, who, as on a night of full moon, at last scaled the high wall and got out on the streets and never looked back, devoting herself to sin. It provoked this response: she drew a breath and held it, thinking about whether or not to speak, and then she told me that she had once done something . . . evil. That pause was there. Evil is a simplistic or melodramatic idea, probably seldom useful in application, and she arrived at the word with some self-amazement, and some confusion, reluctant to settle such a stole around her own shoulders, her at-that-moment naked shoulders.

It was during her time in a San Francisco convent. To narrate, she took back her leg and her arms and sat up against the bedstead, and bowed her head to focus on the past, holding in both hands our misty glass snifter of wine. I saw I wouldn't get another sip. She was taking possession of it as storyteller rather formally. She said, first of all, nuns are not necessarily innocent in any special sense of the word: a convent is just another human institution, and those high walls of dirty yellow brick (on Geary Boulevard, beyond the big red Gap Superstore) enclose a society like any other, just as liable to meanness or injustice, politics or subterfuge, wit or pleasure or irony. Indeed, some of those women are very sharp and couldn't possibly dedicate themselves to "innocence," in any simple understanding. Innocence—she tagged the tip of my nose with a green grape, making me blink—is *mysteriously* distributed, both low and high in Creation. She certainly didn't think of herself as naïve, when she first arrived at the Convent of the Blessed Virgin Mary—an Iowa girl in San Francisco, doing three years of service in the world before her novitiate. Twenty-two was an age she considered replete. She had lived a full, happy, hedonistic life as a modern girl on a modern college campus. In Cedar Rapids all the usual versions of sin can be found: smoking marijuana in a dorm room, envying her friends' beauty or money, letting herself be taken to burlesque clubs on the Coralville strip, drinking Singapore Slings and sniffing lines of cocaine in a condominium swimming pool complex with a lonely older man, a man too old for such folly, a man who feels he has nothing at stake in his life; and among her girlfriends the pleasures of the dark heart, like malicious gossip or frankly revealing clothes or, for a while, systematically hurting the feelings of a rich handsome selfish Chicago boy. Everything. The whole world is right there in Iowa, the same satisfactions of vanity. And of course, as everywhere, the several possible sexual contortions. She'd been, during a time of early discovery, the sensualist that commercial culture urges girls to be—or at least she'd tried her best to be—though she couldn't help feeling secretly that, honestly, for women sex wasn't the great mind-emptying solution it seemed to be for men. In taking the chastity vow, she'd felt the most difficult trial would be, not to deprive herself of pleasure, but to deprive herself of children. She had come from a good family. She had had a warm, confiding relationship with her father, cut off by his too-early death. Also, she loved men, men in general, she loved being around maleness, which a number of nuns did not: a surprising number of nuns had had terrible early experiences. Perhaps her own men tended to be outside the norm, a bit thoughtful or impractical, or sad, or sensitive, rather than the louder, simpler, more aggressive type of male norm, whose nature seems imbued with a mysterious essential wrath, and whom she found herself steering clear of. They were fine. They were for other women.

I loved this aspect of Candace Roan's present day epicureanism, that she'd been dedicated to austerity once. What I wanted to know was, why did she enter the convent in the first place? What was it about her personality? She thought maybe what was different about her (if anything was "different" about her!) was that she had an irrepressible tendency to consider the long-term consequences of deeds, the consequences of people's lives. Even in the midst of pleasure's physical drama—as a girl in a Coralville, Iowa, motel room, or in the backseat of her traveling textbook salesman's car—she would find herself watching from above, as an out-of-body experience, and she pitied the struggle itself. Even at the supreme sexual moment, that fish-out-of-water moment, she saw the clinging soul as pounded away into an abyss. It amounted to a betrayal, *her* betrayal, of that already unhappy man, the traveling college-textbook salesman with the Springsteen tickets and the cocaine, who by his joviality always kept her at a distance. Having once pictured the sex-act that way, she couldn't shake it, the picture of his spiritual death at her lips. The word "sin" is too clumsy; the reality it tries to capture is subtle and fluid. To use the word was to handle one of the mysterious old chalices. (She looked up from the half-full snifter directly into my eyes and she said, "You won't understand this; but even to practice law is a perfect, masterful kind of sin. I mean, strictly in pure New Testament terms. As a lawyer I'm," she lifted her elbows beslimed, "deep in terrible sin and iniquity in the world. Sin is just the most . . . fantastic thing!") Her family hadn't been Catholic. On all sides for generations they were liberal Congregationalists who had no metaphysical interests. This religion was to her such an old museum, enshrining so many barbaric dioramas, so many traditional errors and lurid lights—to navigate its dark corridors required, of a modern girl, an openness to unprejudiced thought, as well as a personal, private, interpretive creativity, plenty of constant self-interrogation. She believed at twenty-two, when she came to the San Francisco convent, that she would be able to reconcile, within herself, all the paradoxes and fond hypocrisies, such as, for example, the glowing arrogance that furnished the spine of "humility"; the crazy *vengefulness* in good works, visible in some of the nuns; the men's politics in the Vatican, even the whole religion's historical origin in a sensationalized

389

Galilean rumor as hysterical and dubious as Elvis sightings. She had always seen all those problems, with perfect clarity. They were a part of *the world*. That is, they would be a part of any possible world.

But preserving a kind of "innocence" was exactly a Sister's main job too, preserving a kind of original integrity. There really is such a thing as "sin" moving in the world, beginning only as a shadowy whorl in the heart, but these little whorls result in real actions and events, the great weather-systems of envy and gluttony and sexiness we live in the midst of, and feel so unhappy inside of. When she first arrived in San Francisco she often found herself driving past the great bath houses and pleasure clubs—one on Market Street in a building whose glass door had torn-off corners of old posters Scotch-taped to its surface (a detail that always struck her as emotionally moving); another on Folsom in an ornate brick warehouse with arches like an ancient stadium, looking prosperous and Byzantine even in these latter days of the great venereal plague—and she could imagine in general what took place inside. Men in a state of loneliness—in a state of spiritual solitude in the midst of the crowd—inhaled or swallowed enough chemicals to numb themselves against knowledge or remembrance, and then, by rubbing, erased the soul. The moment of erasure, itself, was ecstasy, the ultimate. All else—at their jobs, or in their schools, or at home—they experienced as boredom, boredom their wives, boredom their children, boredom the newborn day, boredom the starry sky, boredom.

And it wasn't only the fun-seekers. They were the mere victims. She could also drive past the palaces of the rich, on San Francisco's hills, where lived the people she worked for today, guarding their money at the office of Gartner Sachs Boldon. But when she was twenty-two, she had located sin outside her own soul. And then one night, as she put it, God frightened her. In her bed at the convent one midnight, she had a dream, in which she was personally present at the Crucifixion—she was there in Jerusalem in the crush of the crowd—it was a cloudy, sweaty day on a muddy hill, and she was aware of perspiration inside her dress—and immediately she could see, first-hand, what had always been obvious but was never discussed: that it was exciting. That she wanted this. Our Lord, pinned back, had thrown aside his head to bare his throat, and he lengthened his belly and pushed his hip forward beneath the ragged cloth and the leverage-motion of a man's hips was something one recognizes in an instant. It was always so obvious. It hung above every altar. It was pleasure, this pain, and she herself, in the crowd on that stormy hill where black clouds swelled in the sky, was so excited her throat closed on itself, in the wish for the legionnaire's spear to tap again at the breast and make the hips lift harder.

Well, this was disturbing. It wasn't a nightmare at all, it was a dream of temptation. When she awoke, it was still there. It wouldn't go away. She set forth to spend a day inside the convent dwelling on the possibility that she was unworthy of any vocation—moving through her prayers and offices and classes, trying to be invisible along the convent's walls. *Cleaning* was what they did a lot of at the San Francisco BVM, a Dominican sister-convent to the Dubuque convent, cleaning for its own sake, in fourteen bathrooms with thirty-three toilet bowls distributed among three buildings. The work did bring a satisfaction to the worker on her knees after, say, a theology class in which her own brilliancy was exalted even above the quaint doctrines of the Church Fathers. The polishing of an old white hexagonal-tile floor made, on earth, a luster for a background, the better for God to observe the see-through soul, the soul of one asking to serve, the soul of one asking for simplicity. The chapel she felt unworthy to enter now, with this dream. But there were regular prayers and offices and meditations during the day; they were all unavoidable; she went in with downcast eyes, so dishonest her faith had always been. On the crucifixes of the altars, out here always more Hispanically lurid than Iowa crucifixes, the abdominal muscles were defined like rope-braids and the nipples explicitly pointed. She was in a kind of hell, in Augustinian terms: her natural sin, vanity, fixed her real distance from God.

But as the day went on, Freud had already saved her soul. Her undergraduate major had been pre-law, a choice made in remembrance of her father, who had had a law practice in Cedar Rapids before he died. But even for a pre-law student, it's hard to get through a modern liberal education without some exposure to psychoanalytic theory. It's modern knowledge: every possible perversion swims and evolves in the dark undersea we all contain. She was being warned. She'd seen herself as a simple thing. In driving past the late-night clubs of San Francisco, she'd believed she was giving little thought to what went on among the lost souls. But clearly her subconscious mind had considered it, in artistic detail. "The abyss" is in the convent, too. It's everywhere. It's in her bed where she lies down. Obedience and poverty are easy; chastity is a vow most mysteriously

391

complicated. In the Dubuque BVM, everyone knew who the lesbians were, a discernible group, almost enviable, for their shared secret, and for some sophistication they affected to have, or really did have; yet Candace had thought herself—quite charitably!—*better* than some of her sisters. She had thought she knew better than they, from examination of her own soul, that lust was the sister of pride, the embrace of a mirror-image. Vanity was the effigy there worshipped. The most austere command at the summit of the Gospel was the prayer always to disregard oneself, and empty oneself, to keep winning back one's usefulness as a vessel. God must use this vessel as it is, as He created it. At last she was able to tell that other human being in the confession booth behind the wooden grate, tell him that she had recognized depravity in herself, and that she had dreamed of depravity in the Savior.

Her sin was treated (by sleepy old Father Bernard, his bucktoothed lisp, his excess saliva) with a bored insouciance that was absurdly out-of-proportion—miraculously out-of-proportion—to her sense of her own monstrosity. He assigned her only the most routine penances. So that during the rest of that day, she caught herself being visited again by miscellaneous gladness, a common bird that alights everywhere. She didn't have to be told by Father Bernard, she knew for herself, that this was the beginning of a new responsibility. Her weakness would be a gift: it would make her stronger in service in the world. She applied in the office for social work, and the next day was summoned to discuss an assignment. Her undergraduate background in law would make her especially suitable for the work Sister Thomas had found for her. The convent worked with county and state agencies in providing aid for the families of inmates in prisons.

So it happened that, in the world, she met the actual man who went along with the dream. Mike happened to come along at a time when he could be a specimen of earthly love for her, as if the phenomenal world presents itself as a readily evolving hallucination whose purpose is to edify us. Candace took a sip of her dessert wine and paused in her story: once that name Mike had been spoken, her story faltered and developed a different pace, so that I myself, lying in her bed, became jealous of that name, though of course I knew I was not entitled to jealousy, a latecomer to her passion, a mere effigy (she'd used that word) in her wine-dimmed eyes, safe here in the future.

His name was Mike O'Callan, and he was twenty-six—four years older than she—but to her, he would always seem younger somehow, maybe because of his wiriness and his energy-level. He and his girl-friend lived in Marin County in a bad neighborhood. People in San Francisco didn't think Marin County *had* bad neighborhoods. But there it was: a few blocks of apartment buildings of brown stucco, with lived-in-looking parking lots, where lived-in-looking cars put down roots, beyond a section of body-and-fender shops, stereo-installation places, storefront offices for wiring money to Mexico. Mike was older than Candace but blessedly immature, Irish of com-plexion, pale and freckled. She portrayed him as having a thatch of black hair, so black it was blue, and dark navy-blue irises and wet-looking black eyelashes, and a repressed grin of hope. He was not tall, actually a little bit shorter than Candace, but he radiated brav-ery. He had the springy, coiled energy of a rock-and-roll drummer. Because that's what he was. Before his prison term, he'd been a drummer for several different bands concurrently. On his release he intended to go straight back to music. He seemed shy but he wasn't; and sometimes his glance upon her lasted too long. His prison term was for manslaughter. When she first saw him, it was through the glass barrier at the Marin County Jail, while he stood listening, impa-tiently, to his parole officer before his release. Mike's girlfriend Rosarita, standing beside her in the waiting area, gasped softly against Candace's ear in rapture, "Muy guapo, no? Muy listo."

"Sí," said Candace, agreeing, but falling. Immediately she recog-nized the possibility of weakness, but she didn't censor it, she cher-ished it as a gift from God. Something exalted and detached in her highest soul—a faculty of infinite discrimination, almost spiritually gourmet—saw this boy's body as a test. The simple word of Rosarita's—*listo*—was obscene in Candace's ear. In Spanish it meant *ready* as a particular type of intrepid male handsomeness; and he was, definitely, all that. Yet there was suddenly, in Candace's mind, an unavoidable channel leading straight from his "readiness" to the idea of her own vulnerability.

But she was an adult, an adult of some spiritual attainments, or at least pretensions to spiritual attainment. And her bones were formed in Cedar Rapids, not this place of unwise decisions. Though she wore no habit, she knew that on this scene she faded to the background colors of the general bureaucracy. Her intention was to be useful. She picked up Blame (that was the unfortunate name of the seven-

393

year-old girl Mike and Rosarita had adopted as a foster-child), and she pointed through the bullet-proof glass barrier and said, "Look, Blame, there's your dad!"—shifting the unexpectedly heavy girl to her hip.

Blame, who had learned skepticism too early, complained, "I don't see any space rocks."

A gift of genuine moonrocks had been promised her. Mike had claimed that the penitentiary was a very interesting place full of illustrious people, and that one of his fellow inmates during his Vacaville transfer was a former NASA engineer who owned moonrocks. He'd bring Blame a genuine moonrock from jail.

Blame was the reason Candace was here at all. The father had been Mike's brother. So Mike was an uncle to her during a period when both of Blame's parents were irresponsible. In the venereal plague that had fallen on San Francisco, both of the parents had died—having first christened her with that unhappy syllable, chosen for its mellifluousness and without regard to its meaning—so Blame was an orphan. Mike was the only one in the world she had. And he had already come to be responsible for her during the period of her parents' doomed hilarity. They expired within weeks of each other, and she became an orphan while her Uncle Mike was in prison.

Mike and Rosarita tried legally to adopt her but were denied, because Mike's murder conviction worked against him. Then they tried applying to be her foster-parents, which involves an entirely different and more lenient bureaucracy, and even though they weren't married, this effort succeeded. Rosarita was the foster-parent of record, and Mike's felony was ruled irrelevant. Candace, therefore, had come into their complicated lives as a representative of Catholic Relief, the agency that worked with the government to visit Blame regularly in her new home. Her job was to prevent the girl from reverting to the status "ward of the state." She was supposed to provide guidance and support and, minimally, interview Blame's foster-parents once a month to fill out a routine form. But frequently during the last few months, she had chosen to exceed her duty by coming over to babysit Blame and free up Rosarita, a single mother during these last months of "Michael's" prison term. (Rosarita insisted on calling him Michael, though he was utterly a Mike, from his jet-black tousled short haircut down to his canvas basketball sneakers.)

On their babysitting outings, Candace took Blame to the public library and the Discovery Museum and the Exploratorium. The child would allow herself to be led listlessly to each exhibit and stand before it with stubbornly averted eyes. Then they would visit—the one thing Blame liked—Baskin-Robbins 31 Flavors ice cream parlor, where she ate fast and hard in silence. She was a very dim-eyed little girl, but she would be beautiful, with blonde hair and dark coffee-colored skin, and high cheekbones like a Cherokee. Unfortunately, Candace had begun to notice a pattern: when she came to pick up Blame, Rosarita would be ready to leave the apartment, all dressed up in a blue brassiere, a red leather jacket, and a skirt of some elasticized material whose side-slit, when stretched against her thigh, looked like a bite ripped out. Now that Mike was getting out of prison, trouble was obviously coming. In which Candace found she felt strangely *complicitous*. And she was aware of the deep psychological question, how intentional are our accidental complicities?

When the armored door's lock was buzzed, a disgusted-looking policeman held it open and Mike flew out to Rosarita and they began kissing each other in that munching manner people learn from watching movie actors. Little Blame, standing alone, hung her head. Candace pulled the girl over, against her own hip. Rosarita actually started lifting her knee around him. Candace, in the audience along with Blame, began to feel as annoyed by the performance as the little girl obviously was. But she was better able to hide her opinion, and managed to beam maternally upon the porn.

They stopped kissing and Rosarita said, "This is the lady from Catholic Relief," speaking with prim resentment. Mike wasn't paying attention. He got down on his knees to hug Blame. He said sing-songily, "*Hiya, Daddy, d'ja bring me anything from jail?*"

Blame went limper in his hug, averting her face.

Mike stood up and presented himself to Candace, saying, "You're the Sister." His eyes met hers with suspicion, and vulnerability—and an overly long personal interest—quickly severed. O'Callan. He probably would have run into *Irish* Catholicism; there was something of that prepared disappointment in his eyes; and Candace made a nice smile for him, through the lacy mist of that particular set of prejudices. Together within that Catholic mist, Mike and Candace were joined by an understanding actually prior to, and deeper than, his relationship with Rosarita.

"Pleased to meet you," he said, and he told his little family, "So let's get out of here." His mouth was small and tender and mobile.

Against observing him too closely, Candace hooded herself, as they filed toward the elevator, she last of all, their shepherdess.

It was like a freight elevator, old and scuffed, oversized, its walls burnished by violence. The four of them stood in there, all sharing Mike's new freedom. On his forearm he carried a paper bag containing whatever they release you with. "Let's get a martini," he said. "Oh, before I forget"—he stood on tiptoe to reach into his jeans pocket, and he pulled out a little vial—"here's your rocks from space." He handed it to Blame.

Blame looked at the thing as if it smelled bad. It was a glass vial with a metal cap. The cap had a tiny rubber diaphragm, of the kind you can poke a syringe through. Inside were two pebbles. A strip of paper had been taped on the side reading, in ball-point pen, *"Lunar Basalt, U.S. Space and Aeronautics."*

If they were fake—of course, they had to be fake!—they were an artful fake. Candace considered Mike O'Callan from a longer perspective. His crime had been killing an acquaintance at a party. The whole story was something Candace had pieced together from Rosarita's not-very-objective narrative. One summer night there was a party in an apartment building on Conn Street, across from the 7-Eleven where the *campesinos* loiter each morning hoping for work. The party was in a ground-floor apartment, and Mike O'Callan had first impressed Rosarita Gustan by his manner of entrance; he pulled his motorcycle directly up onto the rear patio outside the sliding glass doors, and dismounted there. Rosarita's boyfriend of the time was David James, whom Rosarita referred to as if he were famous. *Oh, he thinks he's very hot because he has hair like Rod Stewart and he owns a drapery cleaning business. You don't know Rod Stewart. Rod Stewart sings 'If you want my body, come on baby, let me know,' and his hair is like all fwissh. But David James is a big shit. I'm sorry, Sister, but he is. His hair is exactly like Rod Stewart, with the bleach-blond and the teasing and the ratting, with the comb and mousse. Exactly the same. Forgive my language, Sister, but he was a shit truly.* In her work with Catholic Relief, Candace had been coming to see that the commonest factor in these tragedies was this self-absorption which manifested itself in the world as stupidity. There was no other word for it, for all these bad decisions, this deafness to reason. All originating in self-absorption. That and, of course, drug-abuse. Those are the two offices by which Satan, so to speak, works in the world, and which the justice system is beset by, and baffled by: drugs and selfishness. At this party on Conn Street, both of those elements seem to have been present. In David James's case it was alcohol and cocaine together in combination. In Mike's case it was a powder, common in California at the time, with the silly name of angel dust. Angel dust was compounded of PCP, which was a horse tranquilizer. It mostly had the effect of making humans supernaturally excited. Fights developed. Both medications numbed combatants to pain, while also blessing them with transcendent radiant strength.

At the Conn Street party, David James had been insulting Rosarita, in some fashion which Rosarita was too pious to describe in the ear of a nun. The trouble came when Mike O'Callan defended Rosarita's honor. Within the two boys' shared numbness, an angelic brawl ensued. David James went through the sliding glass door onto the rear patio, and then went on fighting while he bled. That was the cause of his death, hemorrhaging.

A large man who had been sitting in the corner all night—a man Rosarita said she had mistrusted as too mature for this crowd, too tall and big-around and humorless, too middle-aged and sober—stood up and waded in to separate the fighters. This was a remarkable detail in Rosarita's story. The man had kept quiet all night. He'd contributed nothing to the general celebration, and didn't seem to know anybody. He hadn't once moved from his corner chair. At this point he got up, crossed the floor to step out on the patio, and ended the fight, with a simple gesture of parting curtains. Which Rosarita demonstrated. He stood there in a traffic-cop posture for a minute, then turned away and sat back down and picked up his drink again. David James lay himself gently down upon the leafy, low hedges bordering the patio. Mike hopped on his motorcycle and stepped down on the starter and sped away, after having first given a long look at David James lying there. David James wasn't going to get up. Then in the lull while people were waiting for the police to arrive—when most of the guests had gone out to stand out front on the sidewalk with their drinks, and those holding drugs had vanished into the night, and somebody had cut the stereo, and one girl sat quietly crying on the shag-carpeted stair—in that quiet space, the big peacemaker sitting in the corner said the only thing he said all night: "It's always either a woman or a hat."

That was how Rosarita told the story. What Candace imagined most personally was Mike's escape by motorcycle, alone in the long dark alley behind Conn Street. It would have been two or three in the morning. All the windows at the backsides of the apartment buildings would have been dark, and his single trembling headlamp would have whitened trashcans and garage doors in his immediate future. The walls of the alley would have reflected back the roar, so that Mike was traveling in a tunnel of noise, a tunnel of his own making. *Everywhere I'm not, it's peaceful and people are sleeping, far and wide over the land.* That's what she pictured him thinking as he thundered up the alley. *Only where I am, only where I pass, is this roar and turmoil, this unfolding tunnel.* He was too young to have entered that tunnel. The death was an accident. But Mike was smart. When the police did come for him, he cooperated. He knew that, in the long run, he would outlive this mistake and make something better of his life. He was very smart indeed. You could see it in his eyes, their shy flicker, their obstinacy. He was so vibrant and tender and somehow humorous, in his nifty jeans and sneakers and T-shirt, it made her stomach all watery.

At last Mike did present himself as a test of Candace's faith. There came a day when she had to go on a long car trip with him, to Santa Rosa, to take his little girl to the Department of Health and Human Services. The trip was necessary to qualify Blame for social security payments. Because her biological parents had died of their immune deficiencies, she had to undergo a medical exam to qualify for state assistance. Blame herself didn't have an immune deficiency, but a complete physical was a requirement of the Child Welfare Board. The only state facility for such an exam was a half-day's drive away in Santa Rosa; and she was required to stay overnight in the hospital for a blood metabolism test; Candace had to be present as a case officer; Rosarita, on account of a girlfriend's bridal shower, was unable to come.

So it was just Mike and Candace, with Blame; and after they'd arrived in Santa Rosa, Candace's nun-like Ford Fairlane (property of the convent) broke down. In the medical clinic's parking lot, it wouldn't start. A tow-truck mechanic told them it needed a part that wouldn't be available until the following day, so Mike and Candace would have to stay in a motel. If this was a test of her worthiness for a vocation, then pure prayer would be the only guide, to pondering what is imponderable. The motel was a Best Western called "The Easter Bunny's Hole." It was thematically united by the image, everywhere on placemats and menus and on the tall highway sign, of a rabbit with a golf club, a kilt, and a tàm o'shanter. It was built around a paved courtyard where cars could be parked, surrounding a small central garden. The garden wasn't really a "garden" but an oval of blinding-white ornamental gravel, where two empty benches faced each other and topiary shrubs, which were once supposed to be animals, stood in disintegration.

Mike and Candace got there on foot, from the garage the car was towed to. He carried her briefcase for her, and she walked with her arms folded over the front of her sweater. It was like being in high school. Even the sound of the big dangerous freeway beside them made them children again. They ate dinner at a chain restaurant with orange upholstery, and then, as night fell, she and Mike went back to the motel to reserve two rooms. He telephoned Blame, who was happy in the hospital with TV and ice cream. After that, with a whole evening to kill, they went next door to a bar, where one of the two necessary conditions for a stupid mistake could be procured: an intoxicating substance. She felt safe with Mike. Rather, he seemed afraid of *her*—afraid of her holiness or impatient with cloistered innocence, what's the difference?

Oh, but she was afraid of him. His sense of humor was the dangerous part, it was so insolent. On the long drive north he'd done a lot of clowning around, mostly in trying to cheer up the stony, unforgiving Blame. He asked if Candace was "a novitiate or a novice or something," gesturing toward the absent habit, her bright hair. Candace, who was doing the driving (through what she discovered to be rather amazingly pretty, Iowa-like land north of San Francisco), explained that the novitiate comes later, after formal vows. This period of working for Catholic Relief in San Francisco was supposed to be her time of postulancy. Mike gave a little groan of recognition, "You're a postulant." Then he grumbled to Blame, "I'm a postulant, don't touch me—oh yuck!—I'm covered with little postules." He elbowed the girl sitting between them (who was not amused but grew all the more hollow-eyed, as if she were being personally mocked, as part of a long ongoing campaign of humiliation), and he started lifting his arms stickily, speaking in an English accent. "Whoops, uh-oh, I think I'm postulating. Sorry. I may have postulated on your upholstery. Just a little bit. Not much. I'm a postulant, you know." Blame shrugged in a show of irritation. Efforts at comedy were making the girl weakly *angry*, which perhaps meant her defenses were softening. How sweet was her rock-and-roll foster-dad, how courageous and delicate both. Candace drove along at the wheel just like a wife. Later at the motel desk, when she and Mike were reserving their (separate) rooms, he said, "Don't worry, you're safe with me. I wouldn't touch a postulant with a ten-foot pole. Really. No offense. It's true. I'd be afraid to wake up tomorrow morning and find I was postulating." It made the front-desk girl in her Best Western smock, typing in the reservation form, pause suspiciously.

When they got to the bar next to the motel, he ordered a double martini dirty. "Which is like plenty of olive juice." His looking nineteen was irrelevant. It arrived, and he took a sip. And though he couldn't have suddenly been drunk, it licensed him to mischief and he leaned back saying, "But you don't really *believe* all that."

He was referring to her vocation as a nun. In the car driving up through Sonoma County, he'd begun his campaign by saying she could be just as good a servant of God without joining an order and buying into all the Christianity. "There's that good ol' rule about always telling the truth," he said, "because of the tangled web we weave when first we practice to deceive."

"Deceive?"

"Deceiving the little people. Letting them think there's a god who pays attention. Or deceiving yourself. Calling it faith." This was a kind of mask he liked to wear: the defiant, the miscreant. The Lucifer mask. It seemed a way of asking for help or at least for serious engagement. She thought about his remarks while she was driving, and said after watching the road for a while, "Christianity binds me to a mystery. One *recognizes* that much of it is arbitrary, or simply invented by humans, or absurd. Tertullian said he believed *because* it's absurd. But it's a discipline. We're all living within a mystery, Mike. Even if you're not religious. Don't you agree?"

What she said had made Mike's eyes glow in slits, which might have been mistrust, or might have been admiration. He'd had no reply and only watched the scenery of Sonoma County go past. But now behind his silver martini in the bar's dimness, he wanted her to know he'd been thinking about it. He went on, "You're too intelligent. You're too intelligent to believe a rotten corpse will suck itself back together and start flying around. Everybody's too intelligent to believe that. The priests are too intelligent. The theologians are too intelligent. The Pope, and even every little believer, *everybody* is too smart to believe that. Not in their heart of hearts."

Before her cylinder of iced orange juice on the table, she folded her hands. "Okay, let me see if I can answer you," she said. "The tradition is *historical*." By historical she meant contaminated-by-the-world, in a sense she couldn't explain in five minutes over a drink. "The Church *grew*, in the hands of historical human beings just as fallible as you and I. Nevertheless, it's not for me to sit here in judgment and sort out the 'true' from the 'false,' according to my little categories. The human being is, like"—she flexed her shoulders within a straitjacket—"the human being lives inside this very limited set of perceptions. It's limiting. But if I know I'm limited, I can understand some things and *relax* in that assumption. And also I can do worldly work *within* that assumption. What's really amazing about all the . . . bullshit" (she made a pause, to indicate it really was an inappropriate word but also that she took some pleasure in saying it and wasn't incapable of mischief, wasn't one of the nuns who'd been called to the convent only because the world was an empty place for her), "what's really interesting, Mike, is that some of the bullshit may be true! Even all the miracle nonsense! Maybe, just to just go along with *life*, you have to be a little bit of an idiot." She presented herself: idiot—smile, shoulders, lips, breasts—and then, amending herself, grabbed the chilly pole of orange juice in front of her and pushed herself back on her side of the booth. Whenever other people were taking liquor she always got sympathetically more informal.

Mike said, "Right. So you preserve the lie to keep the little people faithful." He hadn't been listening at all. "You and the Pope, you all take the responsibility of being the liars, so the common people will have something to believe in. Like me with Blame's 'Outer-Space Rocks.'"

"Well *that*. Come on, Mike, that's different." She had chastised him the week before, for picking up ordinary pebbles from the prison-yard and calling them extraterrestrial. "That truly is a lie. In the long run, that's a disservice to the child. But religious myths—religious myths are different."

"Ah! Oh! Now they're 'myths.' "

"Religious *stuff* is different from bare-faced lies. It's a *fact* that those pebbles are not from outer space."

"They're definitely from outer space." His gaze was a little prolonged. He had a disturbing way of holding his attention upon her, as if they were talking about not pebbles but the inevitability of sleeping together. Surely it was only habitual with him and he had no notion of its effects in the world.

She thrust both her wrists between her knees and clamped her shoulders high, looking off to one side. "Mike, they're not from outer space."

He dove under the table. From the dirty floor he pinched up a bit of nothingness between his thumb and forefinger. He then held it up to her examination: "Look! Dust from outer space!" His arms floated up, to stir the outer space they were suspended in, even on this planet. "We are *in* the Void."

It was sweet, his little joke, it helped her to remember, he was like a child, like a little brother to her, there was no danger of sex here, she might be the younger one, but she was infinitely older in terms of spiritual responsibility. He had a marriage-like relationship with Rosarita. A very challenging relationship! They were trying to be parents to this girl. Yet, as things stood now, Rosarita and Mike could hardly even be worthy friends to each other. Candace's job was to help them, two of her fellow-creatures in danger, and she had been provided with a few tools, being from Cedar Rapids and working within the Church.

She resolved that she would pray for guidance tonight in earnest, in the mildew-smelling motel room.

She inhaled the wintry air at the surface of her orange-juice glass, all a-click with ice cubes, Iowa-February air at the rim.

Then Mike read her mind: "It won't last with Rosarita, you know," he said. "She's—you might say she's one of God's children who has many turns to take on a dark road before she'll come to the light."

Candace wasn't sure she herself wasn't being ridiculed.

He went on, "She means well. But she's pretty materialistic. No, I take it back. She *doesn't* mean well. Rosarita is one person who could use a little religion. Me and her are not simpatico. You know why we're together? Really? 'Cause I'm the hero who slayed the evil boyfriend. So we had to get together. It was so romantic. It was inevitable. The only problem is, she likes to party. And I'm a musician. Which is bad for her, 'cause musicians don't bring home enough money for the kind of partying she likes. See, I want to ask you something." He pushed his martini aside. "I want to ask you to let me still be Blame's dad. Rosarita and I are going to separate. That's inevitable. I'm moving out. But I want custody of Blame. I'll get an income soon. And Blame shouldn't live with Rosarita. That's a bad situation. You have the power. I know you do." He nodded toward the seat beside her, where her briefcase lay, her real date tonight. "You can just *tell* the county I'll be a responsible dad."

He leaned back and, in a single draught, took the rest of his double martini. He was too young to be drinking like that. It was all a part of his being so *listo* and foolish. Candace was weak from looking at him—at his sapphire-blue eyes in this amber bar—so that she had to look away, to let her vision drink of the lonely spaces of the earth, the emptiness of the world, that people daily thrust themselves through, the jukebox halo, the corridor to the bathrooms, the empty band-stand, the unforgiving white light of a "PHONE" sign.

She'd been foolish. There were spaces on the government forms and she should have long ago reported how the State of California's monthly three hundred dollars was being spent. It was mostly spent on Rosarita's clothes and drugs, while Candace's own money bought school supplies and shoes for Blame. She should have said all that specifically in the monthly expenditures form. But it would have caused Blame to be removed from the home, and all the visits would be over. So she was already compromised. And had been for months. She had been foolish and irresponsible, and Mike knew exactly why: there was that look in his eye, of confidence and sure traction. He said, "Hey. Why don't you have a real drink. I'll have a drunken nun on my hands. You're far from the monastery. I'll get you drunk so you'll promise to—well, basically *lie* to Child Welfare for me."

She almost could have ordered a drink. But that was identifiably the advisement of the devil because she'd never liked alcohol. She disliked even the taste unless it was buried under sugar and fruit juice. Therefore, she might have ordered a drink only as an active choice to blind herself. In her endangerment, as a kind of self-protection, she insulted him: "Charm will always be your impediment in life, Mike." She was still looking away from the table.

The insult worked. He didn't answer, but looked surprised, and then tried to drink from a martini glass where there was nothing left. She hated that, his being afraid of her. He cleared his throat and said, "I may not be perfect." The implication was that perfection was what *she* generally consorted with, up in her "monastery" on Geary Street, as he'd referred to it.

He said, "I'm just trying to be practical: practical about what's going to happen to Blame. She's not that adoptable. Face it. She doesn't make herself too attractive. She doesn't go out of her way. And besides, people only want little babies. People don't want a grown kid. And there's HIV. Nobody adopts a child whose parents were HIV-positive. By law they'd have to be told."

She could see what was happening: poor Mike loved that un-promising child. In his innocence he was entering that worldly ambush, love, actual love, its betrayals and inconstancies—for in fact, that little Blame was not going to return any gift of love. Candace despised her own failure of mercy, but it was the realistic truth. And it was her job here to be realistic, not sentimental.

"Why don't you and Rosarita try to get to know each other?" she said, with the sweetly flowing voice of hypocrisy. She didn't *want* those two to get to know each other and learn to stay together. In Rosarita, Candace had seen a certain something reptilian in the mouth and lips, beneath her cosmetics and hairstyle, something maimed and greedy that no spiritual counsel would ever repair. She disliked Rosarita—her slashes of make-up, her tits-and-ass, her little five-foot-one body grabbable like a phone receiver—and she wanted Mike to get away from her.

Yet she carried on with her speech. "You know what the Church's position is, on relationships that aren't working? First of all, get married. That would be fundamental. There's no progress until you're married. There isn't even any authentic *conversation* until you're married. Until you're married, you're not even really talking, honestly.

"Then when you marry, in God's eyes, you'd both enter into a sacramental state where all this deception and self-deception would have to stop. You'd be living within a promise. You'd be living within a mystery. You'd have to start working with her, and she with you. And learning about yourselves. And you'd be asking the divine will to work through you both . . ." Candace was a flute through which these meaningless formulae were passing, which might have the incantatory effect of making her believe too, because they *were*, if remotely, the truth.

"Neither of you is spiritually ready for a relationship. Really, *none* of us is ready. We're all still learning. We all need God's help. You and Rosarita together would ask for God's help, and the *three* of you then would make spiritual progress. Right now, unmarried, you're going to be in a state of sin and can't ask for blessings. You're living in untruth. The sacrament would show your commitment in God's sight." Her lips were saying this, but her arms and body wanted to move to comfort him, while he visibly shrank harder before her, his eyes dull upon his empty glass.

Somehow he must have signaled the woman behind the bar, who

404

nurselike brought him another double martini, which he gathered into the armful of tabletop he was poring over.

Then, just at the moment Candace could feel her whole body wanting to hold him, and be held by him, he said angrily, "Why do *assholes* and fucking bitches have any say over my life?"

Her only prayer, her only desire, had been to serve. She walked with her briefcase across the parking lot to the motel, to her room to pray, leaving Mike alone at the table after his outburst. On her knees, at the bedspread of green corduroy, with the flow of old smooth pebbles over her wrist and through her fingers, she let her lips carve the same ancient scarabs as ever, *now and at the hour of our death*, and *trespass against us*, the English translation of the Vulgate's extinct language. The more you repress doubt, the more it goes away in the wilderness to gather strength and return as an army with power and glory. So she needed to hold her doubt always openly before her, as her form of prayer. The motel ceiling plaster was textured, impregnated with little snowdrift-sparkles, yellowed over the years. A philosopher they'd been studying in an anthology this month—maybe A. J. Ayer or Martin Marty, one of the liberals—said something memorable on the topic of the Ontological Proof: It doesn't matter whether God "exists," because by faith a believer—an ardent woman on her knees in a motel room holding a plastic rosary—can *imagine* a God sufficient to "organize the psyche." Organizing the psyche was supposed to be enough. But an organized psyche, she felt now, amounted to faithlessness and lostness. An organized psyche is isolation. An organized psyche is hell. It was the cause of all her lonely doom, that she had an organized psyche. She stood up. She thought she would read the Bible. In the bathroom before the mirror, she put on pajamas and washed her face, and so by scrubbing went back to girlhood, bringing back a dullness in the skin to let the soul shine. She got under the covers, to read by lamplight. Her back was against the wall that divided her room from Mike's. She couldn't hear him in there. He was still in the bar drinking. The Pauline letters seemed quibbling and political, Ecclesiastes fatuous and terribly innocent, complacent. The Book of Job offered the usual familiar lines. She closed her old, creased, no-longer-lustrous Revised Standard Version and lay it down, its page edges dyed peppermint-red. In the bedside drawer was the common ugly green Bible, "Placed by THE GIDEONS," which turned out to be a King James version. She found herself reading in the middle of Genesis and came across a terrible sentence she'd never noticed before. So deep is that page, it keeps sending up beams from darkness and sunken facets as the light outside shifts. Or, maybe she was only a worried superstitious woman looking for signs in texts. After Abraham was told by God to take his only son Isaac up on the mountain to kill him as a sacrifice, the old man rose early in the morning. He laid the wood for the burnt offering upon his son to carry; and he took in his hand the fire and the knife. So they went, both of them together. And Isaac said to his father Abraham, "My father!" And he said, "Here am I, my son!"

The boy then asked, "Behold, the fire and the wood; but where is the lamb for a burnt offering?" The boy was asking that question in all innocent belief and trust.

The father's maniacal answer to his son—that God will provide the lamb—must have been spoken in an abyss of sadness, continuous with the abyss of the night sky over Moriah. His was no organized psyche. *God will provide the lamb.* That abyss was religion. It was obedience. She didn't *want* an organized psyche. The "self" is all we have here on earth, but it's what we're asked to give up, amounting to the most joyful obligation. As she lay there, she heard noises from Mike's room next door. A woman's giggles. Then the slam of the door.

Then somebody went past her window, a silhouette, past the drawn drapes. It was a female. Candace turned off the bedside light, and she slipped out of bed to look through the parting of the drapes.

The woman crouched at the ice machine scooping the cold treasure into a wooden night-table drawer. It was the bartender, from across the parking lot, the maker of double martinis. How quickly Mike had attracted her. And how subtly! They must have made their bargain by the surest of glances. Bringing him a second double martini would have been part of that secret communication. It must be this way always, with Mike. Females scheme to put themselves in his path. And so a man like him finds it hard to grow spiritually, his mind too readily emptied by the grab for the obvious handle. The woman ran back to Mike's room, the door slammed, and the bedsprings next door clanged. The walls were so thin, now Candace would have to listen to the sounds of love, inches from her own bed. Her first thought—which was forgivable by the Lord, as all things are forgiven by the Lord—was that she could crouch upon the bed and listen at the wall, in the kneeling position she preferred, and let her practiced finger in its piano-lesson posture keep striking the same middle C she'd discovered long ago in her childhood, because this was a lost moment, in a lost place. But she didn't do that—for in truth, no moment or place is ever lost. Nothing is lost. No one is lost. She put on her trenchcoat, over her pajamas, and she went outside.

On her feet, she wore her old flats. California summer nights were cold, not hot like Iowa's. She could spend an hour out here if she liked, sitting on one of the benches in the sad topiary garden in the middle of the parking lot. There are times for simply being still and waiting. This was surely one of them. Life is long. And the capacity for contemplation is the peculiarly human attribute, "an activity of soul in accordance with virtue," as the *Summa* declares, at a simplistic but surprisingly inevitable mountaintop of Christian ethics. She sat on the bench. The stars were few. Somewhere out there on the street, a car stereo was playing menacing hip-hop music—it was coming closer—then the boom of its bass (while she sat very still) passed by, like the plague that passed over in Egypt. It must be deafening inside that Japanese pick-up truck; she got a glimpse of the scrawny white boy inside alone, within his storm of revengeful music. The world is deep.

Maybe this was the guidance that was coming to her in the world: she would no longer be tempted by Mike. Mike was manifestly weak. There were probably drugs in the room. At least alcohol.

Consequently—and this was painful—she would have to make sure Mike was denied custody of the little girl who, at that moment, was sleeping hard alone in a hospital bed. She filled her lungs with air, because it would strengthen and refresh her, to have made that decision, though it would be sad for all concerned. Particularly for Blame. The long corridors of the state welfare system would take all hope from Blame but perhaps give her faith. In those corridors, she would be disappointed in human nature. And she would be disappointed in herself. That was a cost. It was Mike's loss that seemed the most terrible. He was so bright. It was such a waste. He was throwing so much away, in throwing himself away. Herself, she wasn't worried about. She knew she would be fine. She had recovered her humility. Her serenity of spirit.

She tucked herself deeper into her trenchcoat against the night air. That air, too, was God. Every atom of herself was God. As a way of saying goodbye to the whole situation, she leaned over and picked up a chunk of the ornamental white gravel from the ground and spilled it around on her palm, tilting her hand around, rolling it on its

407

facets, thinking of maybe pocketing it as a souvenir, because now, thanks to Mike O'Callan, she could see it as a rock that actually does exist in outer space. As does everything. That was a gift. Nobody but Mike could have seen it that way. It's wasteful the way some people decide to level off and stop growing. He had had a unique sweet insight: that the commonest pebble underfoot is suspended in original outer space at all times, fresh right out of the Big Bang.

"What did happen to Blame?" I said. Candace's story seemed to be over because she sat against the bedstead without adding anything more, cradling that little philosophical remark of her friend Mike. That little joke seemed to be, for her, the high point of the story. However, Blame was still a loose end.

"Yes, I know" was her response, self-accusatory. She was looking into her empty snifter.

Then she went into explanations. "The rationale at the time would be: God has His own ways of bringing everybody closer to Him, closer to God. Blame too. Me too. And Mike and Rosarita. Everybody's struggle in life is their own process of coming closer. I guess if I imagine the worst for her, she would have gone into the foster-care system. A series of situations, then." She smiled into her snifter but blearily, seeing those situations. "Of course, in the end we all get *absolutely* close. Guess nobody escapes that. Some just start sooner."

"So. That was the night you lost your faith," I gloated, wanting to tickle her, to cheer her. Telling this story had made her too serious and thoughtful. The night wasn't exactly young anymore, and the sound of the freeway seemed to counsel an eagerness: there was still time for more love, and love is scarce. It's like an economic good, in that way: scarce.

She said, "No, you never lose 'faith,' exactly. It's something that stays with you and just gets complicated. But I did realize that night, what saved me was my particular gift: that I didn't care about passion and the whole thing. Some women do have that as a determinant, passion, which in their lives they have to deal with. Even way back in Cedar Rapids. When I was pretending to be promiscuous. *Not* having that, it's really a blessing."

About this particular blessing, she looked permanently sad.

"You?" I leered, clowning, always clowning; my finger crept on her ankle. "Don't like passion?" Just look around: the sheets were tossed all over, the dining room table was still uncleared, my own body lay alongside hers. My happiest usefulness in the world was in my readiness to expand and fill any void, a readiness on a job site or on graduate-school applications, pure expansion. She turned and looked at me and my little joke, with a softening: I was like a nice beach she could sail close to but would never set foot on. I wasn't sure I liked that rather simplified view of myself. I added, "Maybe that was then," while my fingers went on walking, making a miniature threat to stalk up her knee. Candace always was fond of my sense of humor and she tapped me on the nose once more with a green grape, making me blink again within the mask of innocence she liked to keep me in during our time together.

Nominated by The Threepenny Review

THE OWL

by SUSAN STEWART

from AMERICAN POETRY REVIEW

I thought somehow a piece of cloth was tossed
into the night, a piece of cloth that flew

up, then across, beyond the window.
A tablecloth or handkerchief, a knot

somehow unfolding, folded, pushing through
the thickness of the dark. I thought somehow

a piece of cloth was lost beyond the line—
released, although it seemed as if a knot

still hung, unfolding. Some human hand could not
have thrown that high, or lent such force to cloth,

and yet I knew no god would mind a square
of air so small. And still it moved and still

it swooped and disappeared beyond the pane.
The after-image went, a blot beyond

the icy glass. And, closer, there stood winter
grass so black it had no substance

until I looked again and saw it tipped
with brittle frost. An acre there (a common

place), a line of trees, a line of stars.

So look it up: you'll find that you could lose
your sense of depth,

a leaf, a sheaf
of paper, pillow

case, or heart-
shaped face,

a shrieking hiss,
like winds, like

death, all tangled
there in branches.

I called this poem "the owl,"
the name that, like a key, locked out the dark

and later let me close my book and sleep
a winter dream. And yet the truth remains

that I can't know just what I saw, and if
it comes each night, each dream, each star, or not

at all. It's not, it's never, evident
that waiting has no reason. The circuit of the world

belies the chaos of its forms—(the kind
of thing astronomers

look down to write
in books).

And still I thought a piece of cloth
had flown outside my window, or human hands

had freed a wing, or churning gods revealed
themselves, or, greater news, a northern owl,

a snowy owl descended.

Nominated by Mark Irwin, Lucia Perillo

ZANZIBAR

fiction by BEENA KAMLANI

from THE VIRGINIA QUARTERLY REVIEW

SHEELA PAREKH had learned three inviolable rules about married life from her mother: (1) you must tolerate your mother-in-law; (2) you must protect yourself from a man's desires; and (3) you must have a good cook. She considered herself moderately successful with the first two. But their cook had just written to say that his ailing parents needed him now in his village and he would not be returning to Bombay after all. And this was causing her a great deal of concern.

The monsoons had not helped. It had been pouring for three months. Relentless downpours with drops like stones. She watched from the windows of their sixth-floor flat with her husband, Arturo, as the shantytown across from their apartment building was washed away into the Arabian Sea. "Where will they go now?" she said to him.

"Here. This is where they will come. To our doorstep."

Later that day, when she answered the doorbell, she thought Arturo had been right. This was probably the first supplicant from the slum come to ask for food and money. She looked at the man warily. "I am a cook," he said directly, "and I need a job." His neatness impressed her, and his cockiness. Since their cook had left, Sheela had kept her ears open for someone who could turn out reasonable meals and take care of the dietary needs of their diverse household without constant grumbling. She watched him rustle through a plastic folder he removed from under his arm. "I have testimonials," he said, handing her some papers.

The letterheads were impressive enough: TAJ HERITAGE HOTEL,

413

"Wait here," she said. She closed the door in his face and went to her husband. "Look at this."

He glanced through the papers. "Hmm, very impressive. Probably fake. Still, there's no harm in talking to the man. See what he wants."

"Will you come?"

"These things are best done by women," he said.

His name was Vincent. "I have fed kings and paupers," he said, showing a shy smile for the first time. "And both have gone away happy."

She liked both his name and his sudden flamboyance. "You are a young man," she said. "How would you have met kings?"

He said he had traveled the world in the company of great chefs. "I learned many things in my travels."

She nodded encouragingly, so he went on. "In Russia, I learned to stuff chicken with butter and parsley, and in Germany, to make onions into a stew. In France they know how to use liver, and in Britain, kidneys. In Italy they use hunting dogs to find a kind of mushroom that costs more than gold, and in Spain I learned fifteen different ways to cook octopus. For five years I traveled through Europe with a band of chefs who needed a quick learner, a sous-chef who cut and cleaned up quietly and wanted to learn as much as he could. Then I came back to Goa, to visit my ailing mother. I got married, had a daughter, and left them behind to come here to earn money to support them."

Sheela heard him with growing astonishment. Why was this man at her door, seeking work? "You should go straight to the Taj hotel here in Apollo Bunder," she said. "We could not pay you properly and we have no need of an international chef." And to further dissuade him she added, "Also our kitchen is very small. Our previous cook used to sleep on the floor in there. We have no separate servants' quarters."

"I can sleep on the floor," he said. "As for hotels, I am tired of working for hotels. I want to be on my own and I want to cook for a family."

She opened the door wider now, and ushered him in. He had mystified her, and she was curious enough about his intentions to detain him a little longer. "Wait here," she said to him again, leaving him standing by the windows, which looked out onto a filthy gray Arabian Sea, its surface pockmarked by the pelting rain.

Arturo said, "This is a kitchen matter. I don't want to get involved."

Sheela went back to the entrance hall and saw Vincent standing there by the windows. One had been left slightly ajar and a thin ripple of water raced along the edge, trickled down onto the stone floor. He clicked the window shut, and as he did so, she knew, suddenly, that he belonged here, in her home.

"My husband says that he would like to sample your food before we hire you," she said.

"Yes, that is essential," he said. "You tell me when I can cook for you. I am ready any time you say."

"Tomorrow the flat will be practically empty. Only my daughter and I will be here. I can show you where everything is in the kitchen."

"I will come in the morning, at nine o'clock," he said.

She took out a small pouch attached to her petticoat. "How much will you need to buy the food?"

"I have to prove myself first," he said. "The money will come later."

She puzzled over his response. "We don't eat kidney and liver," she said. "Or feet of any kind. No tongue. No brains. And my mother-in-law will not allow beef or pork. My husband is allergic to fish and all seafood. My daughter will only eat jam sandwiches. Otherwise we can eat anything."

"What do you want me to make?"

"You are the chef," she said. "You choose."

At nine sharp the next morning, the doorbell rang. When Sheela let Vincent in, she noticed the bulging rattan baskets he was carrying. There was also a canvas bag, small and neat like a visiting doctor's bag. "You are planning a feast, it seems," she said. "We are simple eaters, and we don't eat very much."

He followed her to the kitchen. Sheela saw the tiny, grimy kitchen through the traveled eyes of the chef, following his gaze as it lighted upon every well-worn surface there. There was a gas cooker, three copper-bottomed pots that had blackened with use, a ladle and a stirring spoon. A flat grinding stone and pestle for masala pastes, a large round tin with small containers of spices on the inside, and two glass bottles—one containing used vegetable oil, the other water—were arranged by the stove. "The old cook was used to his village ways; he didn't need many utensils or pieces of equipment," she said. Next to the kitchen was an alcove, which contained a fridge and a large sink for washing dishes. There was an earthenware jug into which water dripped through a filter. "All the water is boiled after it is filtered," she said. He nodded with approval. "If the water isn't pure, the food doesn't taste good," he said.

She watched him unpack his baskets. Finger-thin eggplants and young baby okra, cauliflowers tight and unblemished, tomatoes lusciously red and ripe, guavas and figs, apricots and lotus buds all unwrapped carefully from their newspaper, followed finally by a chicken that, judging by the drops of blood that clung to its skin, had been plucked only minutes before. With the old cook, she had never bothered to step into the kitchen; all his food tasted the same—edible but lacking in flavor. Now Vincent opened up the canvas bag and removed from it a big wood-handled knife, a whisk, a large four-pronged fork, and a small wooden bowl with a wooden hammer-shaped stick. "I cannot work without these things," he said.

Sheela said, "You have everything you need?"

"Yes. I will start now."

She left him to it.

Throughout the day, she wondered at the noises and smells that drifted out of the kitchen. At one moment, she smelled stewing figs, at another cauliflower roasting in aniseed. A sharp smell of lemon rind, then delicate buttery saffron steeping in warmed milk, followed by the winey-sour smell of pomegranate seeds crackling in fragrant oil.

She sat on a sofa in the drawing room and tasted the flavors on her tongue as if for the first time. And simultaneously she contemplated her household, the effects such vibrant food would have on them. There was first of all, the matriarch, Arturo's mother, a Goan by birth, a Hindu by inclination, now in the temple with her eldest daughter-in-law, whose driver had come early in the morning to pick her up for a day of shopping and prayer. There was her husband, Arturo, an engineer in the railways, a gentle man who did not know how the world worked and was consequently left feeling betrayed by all who surrounded him, and there was her nine-year-old daughter, Nandita, who was pulling at her shirtsleeve and saying, "What are kidneys, amma?"

"Nothing you will ever have to eat," she replied, realizing that the child had overheard every word uttered between her and their cook-to-be the first time he had entered their home.

The child, satisfied, turned back to her book, and disappeared, as they all did in this household, into her own world.

Her mother-in-law would berate the food, because it was not what she was used to. "At my age, I cannot expect my stomach to handle new things," she would say. Her husband would smile indulgently and say, "But how are we going to eat like this every day? It must cost a fortune." And her daughter would reject everything, as always, because it wasn't what her storybook heroes, George and the Famous Five, ate. She wanted potted meat and cucumber sandwiches and ginger beer, none of which Sheela knew anything about. So whom, really, was Vincent going to please? Her, just her, with her dulled taste buds yearning to be teased.

In the bedroom, the cleaner had gone under the bed with her long broom, fished out dust and other odds and ends that get swept there by the sea breezes.

"Memsaab," she called.

Sheela turned to her. "Kya hai?" What is it?

The woman held out a used condom. "Yeh?"

"Yeh kya?" she said. What about it?

"Yeh kya karoon?" What shall I do with it?

"Phenko, aur kya?" Sheela said nonchalantly. Throw it, what else?

The woman stared at her as she swept it up into her pan, her expression curious, challenging. Sheela turned away. Condoms are only used by prostitutes, the woman's expression said.

My husband visits other women, Sheela wanted to tell her, and I am simply protecting myself. But the woman would not have understood and it was easier to pretend that she didn't know what the woman was asking her. Their entire relationship was based on questions not asked, on answers not given. But the woman's expression bothered her all day. Whenever Arturo asked her why she was being so careful, she said only that they could not afford another child. In her heart she knew it was because of the prostitutes in whose arms Arturo lay, while pretending to her he was examining rail lines in Surat or Baroda.

That evening her husband brought home a high-ranking colleague. "With all this wonderful food in the house, we must have guests, isn't it?" he said to Sheela, as he introduced the man, a Mr. Vijay Seth.

"Vijay is the big chief in the signals department," Arturo said. "He is the man responsible for the trains arriving and leaving on time. He knows where every train is at any given moment. Deccan Queen, sir?"

Vijay glanced at his watch. "Approaching Ratlam in four and half minutes."

"And the Frontier Mail?"

"Leaving Mathura in seventeen minutes, as we speak."

"You see?" Arturo turned to Sheela. "He knows exactly where all the trains are, minute by minute. And not only that. He knows exactly how many bogies have been attached to each train—which ones are passenger bogies, which ones freight."

"That's exaggerating it. I don't know everything. I am at the mercy of the signal staff and they are all good fellows, I must say. But I, personally, am their manager, not the signal manager." Sheela liked his humility, so rare in a government body like the Railways, where everyone wanted to be the big man in charge. After Arturo served them drinks—they had gimlets, she stuck to her Limca—"let me spike it, Sheela," Arturo said; "No," she said, "I'll have it straight"— she left them and went into the kitchen to see how Vincent was managing. He was spooning out chicken biryani onto a flat platter; even in the weak fluorescent light of the kitchen, the saffron-smothered grains of rice glistened invitingly, the pieces of chicken moist with browned onions.

As they prepared for bed later that night, Arturo said, "That cook is a genius. Those were not ordinary chickens, Sheela. Anyone could see that. He must have gone to the Parsi Dairy Farm to buy them. And that was not our everyday saffron, I can tell you. Spanish, without a doubt."

"He knows what he's doing."

"Vijay was most impressed. Did you see his face? Every dish fit for a king, and he was the ruling rajah this evening. When Vincent brought out the mousse in that tall crust shaped like a pineapple— how did he do that, all those pastry leaves on the side—I knew the man was flabbergasted. For a change, I was not the ordinary man they think me to be, someone who doesn't know about good living. Tonight's dinner will make him see me in a new light."

"And he is such a good man," Sheela said. "You know, for tea he gave Nan jam sandwiches. She was so happy, eating everything for a change. We don't have jam in the house—he must have bought some for her."

418

"I was talking about Vijay, Sheela."

"I was talking about Vincent. What he did for Nandita, did you even hear me?"

"I did. It was very generous of him—but how are we going to afford this man? The ingredients alone will beggar us, never mind his salary."

Sheela noticed a new confidence in him—he had been proud to show Vijay that his house could turn out the kind of astonishing meal they had had that evening. Perhaps that was all that was wrong with their marriage—he needed to feel important, and this new cook, in one day, had provided him with a reason for claiming proud ownership of his home once again.

That night, Nandita, hearing the creaking bed boards in her parents' room, came in and stood by their bedside. "What are you doing," she demanded, and their gentle rocking stopped. "You're making such a racket, I can't sleep."

Sheela stared at Nandita. "We couldn't sleep," Sheela said finally. "We were tossing and turning like you do when you have a toothache."

Nandita shook her head. "Can you be quiet, please?" she said to them in her school principal's voice before flouncing out of their room.

Arturo put his arm around Sheela, as they both burst into laughter. "Shh," he said. "Miss Jones will be here again, if we don't behave ourselves." Sheela wondered at the lightness in his voice. The hopefulness had returned; she looked at him and he seemed to her once again the keen and passionate young man she had fallen in love with a decade ago.

As he was adjusting his tie in the mirror the next morning, Sheela said, "What are we going to do about Vincent? I will have to say something to him."

"Sheela, we can't afford him, it's as simple as that. Tell him to give us a bill for last night's dinner—and withdraw money from our savings to pay him. It must have cost quite a lot."

"Art, listen to me. I have thought about this very carefully." She felt the diamonds warming in her hand, their brilliant light now searing and onerous. "Arturo, we can afford to keep Vincent. There is a way."

"What?" he asked, surprise in his voice.

"These." She unclenched her hand and held out a pair of diamond earrings. Arturo's mother had given them to her when Sheela married Arturo. "I don't need them. They are beautiful, but they are only stones, after all."

Arturo gave her an astonished look. "But my mother," he said. "Nanubhai's craftsmanship."

"I know. But what Vincent has given us already is worth so much more."

"You're asking me to pawn these?"

"No," she said. "Sell them outright. We'll put the money in our savings and withdraw from it every month to pay Vincent's salary."

"And when it runs out?"

"We'll see then."

"And my mother? What will we tell my mother, who likes to see you wear them every day?"

"Tell her the screws at the back needed replacing. I don't know, Arturo. She's your mother. You sort it out."

So Vincent became part of their home. Sheela asked him to vary the menu to display his experience with international cuisines. "You can show off to us, and Nandita will learn something about how other people in the world, besides her beloved Famous Five, eat. It will be good for us all to learn."

At the first meal he cooked for them all, Vincent served a warm chicken mould, decorated with carrot slices and tarragon leaves. Mrs. Parekh the elder said, "When my digestive system packs up, you can ask him to cook this for me." They chewed the mashed-up chicken in silence until Sheela said, "I love the herb sauce that goes with it." *Hmm*, Arturo nodded. "It's different," he said. "It takes some getting used to."

Vincent made it a few more times—and then they were asking for it again and again. One by one, he produced dishes that might have been puzzling at first, but then dazzled them all. Cannelloni. Paella. Empanada Gallega. Baked stuffed fish. Lobster Thermidor. Zweibelfleisch with caraway dumplings. Chicken à la Kiev. Mushroom soup, pungent and creamy and earthy. And the desserts: light-as-air English puddings, mousses and soufflés, fruit tarts and cakes, the flambés—every evening he served a sweet dish that made mother-in-law go all soft and sentimental. "This man," she exclaimed, holding on to Vincent's arm, "is a gem." While Arturo's eyes glazed over and he sighed with satisfaction after a meal, Sheela felt her senses grow sharper, as if life was flowing in her veins again.

Within a few months of Vincent's arrival, it seemed to her that their table was the most exciting in all of Bombay. She had begun watching him as he cooked sometimes, dribbling olive oil drop by drop into beaten egg yolks, till the concoction became full and fluffy and was used for chicken or egg sandwiches for Nan to take to school. The incredible effort he expended just to make them all happy amazed her. And even as he brought worldly panache to their little home, Vincent somehow managed to bring back some change from the money she gave him for shopping in the market.

Arturo came home in the early evenings now, in time to do some homework with Nandita. In the past, he would return only when the household slept, and Sheela would hear the old cook shuffle to the stove to warm his dinner. Now every meal had become an adventure and, like them all, Arturo wanted to be there as Vincent unwrapped his treasures at their table.

Nandita followed him like a puppy. When she had to choose between French and German at school, Vincent said, "French is better. Their food is more imaginative." His statement was the deciding factor. Geography quickly became her favorite subject. For her tenth birthday, Vincent's present was a map of the world, with pasted-in spices, herbs, flowers, and fruits for the countries he had visited and learned to cook in. They invented a game that involved rubbing one's fingers over a country and doing a lot of sniffing. "Cloves!" someone would shout. "No, cinnamon!" "No, juniper berries!" Vincent joined in, often pretending he couldn't identify the smell of something, when everyone knew he had done all the pasting-in himself. Arturo thought the game was silly, but he played it with them all anyway, always losing by a large margin.

Soon all Arturo's colleagues were clamoring for invitations. In the year he had been with them, Vincent's food had only got better. Every dinner party was a triumph. When the chief engineer of Western Railways hinted through his underlings that he, too, was keen to sample the food at the Parekhs, Arturo came back from work more excited than she had ever seen him. "Sheela, the chief engineer has asked to come to dinner here. How could I have been so remiss? But at the same time, you tell me how someone in a subordinate position like me could invite the chief engineer to dinner? It isn't done."

Sheela and he puzzled over what should be done about this new turn in events. As it was, the many parties they now had to give had taken their toll, and she had cut back on other things. The money from the diamonds had long gone. She hadn't had the heart to tell Arturo that they were now dipping into their emergency funds. Nan's uniforms, a new mattress for her mother-in-law's bed, her monthly visits to Olga the hairdresser and Madame Marcel's beauty salon, such things had drifted away as easily as dreams about holidays away from the city. She had learned how to manicure her own nails and sent Arturo's shirts to be darned to spare the expense of buying new ones. And she had taken other salable bits of jewelry to the pawn-shop herself, to the odious Mr. Patel, who took them but always exclaimed, "Such a tregeddy, from people like your good self." The parties went on, for they gave Arturo much pleasure, and Sheela loved his new sense of well-being with the world.

But now came the chief engineer's dinner. Sheela took Arturo's gold cuff links to Mr. Patel. "No good," the pawnbroker said. "Eighteen karat." They were Victorian, family heirlooms. "It's not the gold," she said. "They are antique."

"Antique shantique—whatever it may be, we don't know anything about that. The gold has no value." She reminded him about the great deal he'd got two weeks earlier when she'd brought him the solid sterling silver candlesticks. "I let you have them for peanuts—I needed the money," she said. As if shaking off a guilty feeling, he reached for his wallet, licking a thumb with which he peeled off five hundred-rupee notes from a wad. She took the money with a hanky and hurried out of his shop. It was the exact amount needed for the chief engineer's dinner.

"This chief engineer is a bully," she said to Vincent. "He terrorizes everyone who works for him—he knows that ultimately he decides who stays and who goes."

Vincent understood the importance of the dinner immediately. "Leave it to me," he said.

Vincent began preparing for the dinner a week in advance. Small glass jars of pastes and marinades lined the kitchen windowsills. Fruits steeped in fragrant liquids and herbs filled bottles containing vinegars and oils. On one side of the kitchen floor, ripening on a bed of hay, lay mangoes, green figs, and pomegranates, which he turned daily to distribute their increasing sugar equally. Against the constant noise of chopping, grinding, and beating, Sheela cleaned the silver, ironed napkins, and filled the vases with tuberoses, humming all the while.

The chief engineer brought his wife and two guests from the Middle East, bright-eyed sheikhs with turbans and djellabas, and slippers with pointy curled-up toes. They were brothers and owned a couple of shopping malls in Dubai. They had come to find cheap labor. "Our country needs Indians who are prepared to work hard," one of them said to Sheela. "We give them houses and food and good salaries. They send money back home. Everyone is happy, isn't it?"

As they sat down to dinner, Sheela wondered whether the Arabs could eat the food. The chief engineer said, "We have heard so much about your new cook. Everyone marvels at his meals."

"Yes, we are lucky to have him," Sheela said.

Vincent brought in his first creation: a thin layer of flaky pastry on which lay a bed of fragrant creamy mushrooms, still bubbling in their sauce. Fresh mushrooms from the cool moist forests in the Ghats—how had he got these, Sheela wondered. They all ate in silence, chewing the mushrooms as if they had never tasted mushrooms before. Sheela saw the chief engineer grin, then his wife's thin grimace widen to a beaming smile. She was the kind of woman who seemed to exist merely to affirm everything her husband said or did. "Wonderful," the woman murmured, parroting her husband's pleasure. The complete turnaround was breathtaking, and Sheela could manage only a superficial nod of acknowledgment.

Next came a baked whole fish. A spicy sauce oozed out as Vincent filleted it at the table. For Arturo there was chicken marinated with figs. Besides being beautifully flavored, everything was cooked to the perfect consistency and texture—crunchy or crisp or melt-in-your-mouth or soft and creamy. As the platter of rice with pomegranates and nuts and saffron went round the table, Sheela noticed one of the sheikhs close his eyes, as if he had suddenly glimpsed heaven.

The chief engineer said, "Mr. Parekh, I have decided that our dinner for the GM will be catered by your wonderful Mr. Vincent. You must tell him he will have plenty of help, but it is his hand we want guiding the final preparation of the food." Then he added as an afterthought, "And don't worry about the cost. After all, it is the General Manager, not some petty official."

The chief engineer was notorious for getting his subordinates to prepare, and bear the cost of, special dinners given by his division.

He somehow made it seem like a privilege, so that no one would protest. Sheela, who had heard tales of his proverbial miserliness, said, "Vincent only cooks for us, Chief Engineer, he is comfortable here. He won't cook in other people's homes."

"Fine, then we will have the dinner here," the chief engineer said. "No problem."

In the stunned silence that followed, Arturo said only, "It is an honor, sir." Sweat had gathered in little drops on his forehead.

Sheela stared at the rose-pink strawberry soufflé that Vincent carried in for dessert. While everyone else at the table sighed blissfully with every spoonful they raised to their lips, Sheela had to force each bite down. They had exactly five rupees left from the sale of Arturo's cuff links.

The chief engineer took out a pouch of tobacco from his jacket pocket and filled the bowl of his pipe. Sweet tobacco fumes surrounded their table. "I must say, this is the best meal I have ever had," he said. "Arturo, you are a man of the world. I have underestimated you." Sheela saw her husband's face light up as soon as the chief engineer addressed him by his first name, and knew that the evening had surpassed his wildest imaginings.

"We must congratulate this chef," one of the sheikh brothers said, rising and rushing to the kitchen. His brother followed behind. Sheela rose, feeling estranged from everything around her. She went to the kitchen, to tell Vincent that tea would not be necessary, and saw that the sheikhs had put a small red velvet pouch on the preparation table. "You can open your own restaurant in Dubai," one of the brothers said. "We will rival Caravelle's cuisine. You will better their Monsieur Roux." To Sheela's surprise, Vincent replied, "I will need some time to think about this."

"We are at the Taj hotel for another three days before we fly back to Dubai. Come and see us there," they told him.

Later, Sheela saw Vincent empty the velvet pouch in his hand. Gold guineas filled his palm, clattered down to the stone floor. She stood there, watching him pick them up one by one. He was shaking his head sadly, as if a decision had already been made.

When Vincent told them all he was going to Dubai, Nandita asked, "Why are you leaving us?" Vincent looked as if he was about to cry. He said, "It's because I want to come back." He left soon afterward, refusing his pay for the month, a man heavy with burdens and anxious now to make a name for himself in one of the few places in the world he'd never been.

In a matter of weeks after Vincent's departure, Arturo's mother announced that she was moving to her daughter's flat. "Anita says that once her baby arrives, she wants me there and Ashok is a very good son-in-law. He, too, is insisting."

They went through the obligatory protests but Sheela could barely hide her relief. Sheela said to Arturo, "You must tell your chief engineer immediately that Vincent has left, thanks to his guests at our dinner, and that you cannot host the GM's dinner after all."

Arturo nodded. "Yes, I will have to break the news to him. Let's give it a day or two."

As she shopped for vegetables at Crawford Market, Sheela saw among the crowd a face she thought she recognized. It was Mrs. Mendoza, the chief engineer's wife. Accompanied by her cook, she was making the rounds past the vegetable and fruit stands, stopping to examine an apple or an eggplant with a long look down her nose. When she saw Sheela, she came toward her and said, "Poor pickings today, aren't they?"

Sheela nodded, feeling a slight twinge of guilt. Once this woman was as nothing to her. Now she was grateful to be acknowledged.

"How is your wonderful cook?" Mrs. Mendoza asked.

"He is no longer with us," Sheela said. "He has gone to Dubai."

Mrs. Mendoza said, "What a pity!"

"Yes," Sheela said.

"Did he go with the sheikhs my husband brought to your party?" she asked.

"It was bound to happen at some point," Sheela said. "You can't stop a man who wants to make his fortunes elsewhere."

The chief engineer's wife narrowed her eyes and scrutinized Sheela. "That's quite true," she said. "We are ruled by our circumstances." Then, abruptly, she gave Sheela a parting nod, and swept past her as if the small window for social banter between them had now closed. Sheela saw the driver open the door for her, the cook get in at the front. They were going home, she felt sure.

There and then she decided that she would apologize to the woman, make a plea to her for her help. Without giving it much thought, Sheela stopped a cab and gave the driver the chief engi-

425

neer's address. Inside the cab, hemmed in by the surge of traffic surrounding them, she felt confused and uneasy at the thought of trying to engage the sympathies of a woman she had openly ignored at her dinner party. Vincent's savoir-faire had rubbed off on her, and she had taken it on like a mantle, used it to moderate her own attitudes to all around her. While Vincent had come off brilliantly that evening, she herself had not. She had compromised the first duty of a good hostess—to make everyone around her feel welcomed and at ease in her home. The thought of bowing before this woman rankled her, but she knew what she had to do.

A maid let her in through the door of the chief engineer's flat and gave her a glass of water to drink while she waited in the drawing room. Sheela suddenly felt unkempt, awkward. She was wearing an old pair of trousers and a chikan kurta, and her feet were clad in fraying leather chappals fit only for shopping in markets.

Mrs. Mendoza swept into the room in a blaze of gold. She had on a saffron yellow sari with brilliant white borders and her shiny black hair was swept back in a French twist. Small golden pearls gleamed at her earlobes. "Yes?" the woman asked. "What can I do for you?"

It was the way she said it, that long look down her nose, as if Sheela were an eggplant she didn't like the look of. Mrs. Mendoza was sleek and resplendent, fresh and crisp in her starched, crackling sari, every inch the chief engineer's wife. Sheela rose. "I'm sorry," she said. "I'm very sorry. I don't know why I came." She made her way to the front door, aware of her leather chappals flapping loudly against the marble floor. "I shouldn't have disturbed you," she said, backing out of the house.

That evening she told Arturo their financial situation was dire and that something would have to be done. "We need a transfer out of here. They must have so many postings in far-flung places—let's go and make a new life somewhere else, Art. Bombay is beggaring us."

He said, "How much money do we have?"

"Not much," she said, fearing the consequences of telling him the truth.

"How much, Sheela?"

"We are broke, Arturo," she said, suddenly bursting into tears. "There is nothing left to sell."

"I see," he said. Then he walked out of the house.

426

"It's twenty-four miles off the coast of Africa," Arturo said to Sheela. "It's a small island. Zanzibar, it's called—yes, Zanzibar." He had been to talk to the chief engineer. "The Tanzanians want to link the island to the mainland by rail. No harm in giving it a shot. Look at our toy trains on those narrow-gauge tracks going up the mountains, right?"

Arturo forced a smile.

"That's right, Art," Sheela said. "That's right."

"Good engineering can achieve miracles, I always say."

"That's right," Sheela repeated.

"But you—you can't cook to save your life."

"I've been picking up things, Art. I can manage."

That night Sheela consulted Vincent's map. There it was—she could see it clearly. Just as Arturo had described it: a tiny island nestled against the coast of Tanzania. One of the places she had tasted at her own table, but never been. She ran her fingers across its surface and when she held her fingers to her nose, she smelled cloves, chocolate, oranges, myrrh, and something else that puzzled and delighted her—some mystery that she held on to.

It stayed with her through the dismembering of their home. One by one their treasured possessions went to other, less loving hands. Mrs. Barucha complained about the Grundig radio—"So big, where will we put it?"—even as she directed her servant to carry it away. Arturo's cherished Rolleiflex with the light meter suffered the same fate. "Who uses such contraptions these days, saab?" Mr. Singh said, putting down a few rupees for it. "These days it's all instamatic. Instamatic, saab, you know—click and out comes your picture. These things are from another age, saab. No value." Soon there was nothing more to sell or give away.

The night before their departure, Sheela went into the kitchen to make scrambled eggs. As she spooned the eggs onto paper plates and placed some slices of bread on each plate, she caught sight of a familiar bag sticking out from under the kitchen table. She brought Arturo and Nandita their meals, then hurried back to the kitchen. As she pulled it out, she knew it immediately. Vincent's canvas bag. She opened it up and there were the implements—the same five things he had produced the day he entered their home: the wood-handled knife, the whisk, the fork, the wooden bowl with the hammer. She stared at the objects as if they were relics from some long-gone era.

427

He's forgotten them, was her first thought. Then she knew that a cook as careful as Vincent would not have forgotten these things behind. He'd left them behind because he was coming back, as he told Nandita. And perhaps also for her, Sheela, for their new home, in a place none of them knew. Wondering, she went to the suitcase marked "Household goods," unzipped it and slipped the canvas bag in, a good omen for an uncharted future.

They ate sitting on the wooden chests that would accompany them to their new home. Chests filled with things they would need there—carpets and lace curtains, blankets, sheets and pillows, books and objets d'art. Sheela looked around the emptied hall and tried to remember how only a few weeks earlier it had been a place of plenty, where people had come to be filled with the tantalizing flavors of the food and the warmth of their hospitality. How could something good like that have ruined them, she asked herself.

Later, seated next to Arturo on the plane, she observed his tense, worried face. His eyes were moist as he watched Bombay recede from view. Nandita was reading, curled against the crook of Sheela's arm, buried in a world of lighthouses and pebbly English beaches. But for Sheela, the low thrum of the plane's engines was musical and lovely. She held her finger to her nose and breathed in the smell that still lingered there—that same mysterious aroma. She inhaled deeply and appreciatively. In Zanzibar, she would find that scent for herself.

Nominated by Wally Lamb, The Virginia Quarterly Review

THE WATER-BROOKS

by MARY KINZIE

from THE PARIS REVIEW

Slag and synthesis and traveling fire

so many ways the groundwaves of distortion
                                        pulse
            through bedrock   traffic   and the carbon chain
to be partitioned by result

particulate pollution   fine soot   fine biosolid dust   fine spark
                        of transuranium

water   out of breath   weighed down with nitrogen   water
            borne and water
                    ruining toxins
                                tending to methane
                        and sulfuric   that eats the hulls off ships

gases from fuels that fume above the pavement   then in
            backburn from the rockets aimed into orbit
                    falling down as watery
                                        jet thrust   everlastingly
                    degrading in a spittle of alpha particles

                    breathed out as from a mouth half-open during sleep

                            through the fetid afternoon
                                of future time

                                        Not to mention what
            they're hiding underground
                              down the unrenewable
                  reamed veins of oil and ore
                                        having siphoned out
                        the water to leave new kinds of moisture
            bonded to killer molecules and the god-tick

                  of radioactivity

In time nothing will grow out here but spiny cardoon and yucca
                                                    always
                  already stunned into sterility

But the young
                    the young on the highways now feel free as the breeze
            some with the windows down   the rust
                    eating at the grille   the tailpipe lacy
            others with smoked windows and polysemous
                          flames along the hood   or hubcaps
                    with a sluggish glisten of foil paint
                          to look like heavy alloy
            still others in cool models   gifts of parents   safety-heavy
                              with large salaries beneath them

      all weave in long inevitable ribbons   the young
                  with the also rapid middle aged   and the elders
                        rabid with longing that is a kind of greed
            and the truckers of unstoppable mileages
                                    and tonnage

all all

twine and re-form like sand moved by a whip
in a desert where soil is just a memory and the ground
            deep-stained   as are the cells   as is the
                      air
                            choked with an overcrossing

              threadwork of impurity
        about the heart and lungs
                                    over the
                            aquifers whose downward plumes
            trickle toward each other

and the thirsty dangers spread

            free as the breeze

Meanwhile the atmosphere so light you would not think
so many tons of lethal mist   gas   airborne speck   and effluent
could sit there

            hooked upon the lightness that we breathe

Where still the Lockheed Martins
                        pictured on their website
            in the aching blue   silvery as needles
thread the sky with slubs
            of vaporous kerosene   *(not pictured*
                            yellow as farmyard fleece
        that wind up
                somewhere else but in the very
                    system with the trees and frogs
                        and greasy updraft from the local takeout
                    that is ours
                our system
                    closed with us within it
        the private garden walled
                against derangement
                    hortus conclusus
        where a carpet of primulas once led from the virgin's hem
                to the flank of the reclining unicorn
                above the brook   should they be thirsty

nowhere *now* to go

although

the pilots and the smelters and executive engineers
        ingenious destructive boyish and not scrupled
gasp with delight
        projected on the clouds they leave behind

These were the men who made the movies too and the movie
                                 queens
like the most famous childless icon   Isis of availability
whose nervously brief wit
             could not sustain her when they dressed her up
                in undressed attitudes
        and made her up with the lipstick that looked as if it smelled
           like the enameled thimbles of pomade from France
opening   as Luca Turin might write   on the yeasty
                         topnote of a fresh
              gaufrette
        over a harsh residual
            like piss on tar   cut through
                by overwhelming funeral lily
Norman Mailer found it fetching
        and the Kennedys   who licked it off like honey

not her words were sweet but her surfaces and
        diminished hormones and pro forma
          happy welcome until
        Arthur Miller got her up in black and wrote her into the
Nevada desert   goddess on a sand shell   her face
        frowning in soft focus
           beneath her inkstroked lids   blond as a thistle

drying up

and driven tumbling   under the pillsmooth moon

Dusk   a frame of deceptive gold around each freeway lamp
        unholy halo of fine-ground debris
            and sulfurous moisture
                        and the   heat
            of short-chain fatty acids from the animal farms
              of Chino
        suspended in the clammy chill of not
            entirely night

The closer you come to each light
        the dimmer
            it seems to become

and the worse everything smells

Close-to
        beneath the choking yellow damp
                the tough evergreen
            of the hedges
        goes shapelessly black as if these were the door lids
              down to caves

so different from Wordsworth's golden mist
              that after the roaring in the wind all night
              shone on the wet green and on the hares
                  running so fast the mist flowed after them
        where a slow man went
                  bent
                    barefoot through the marshpools
                    of the rural nineteenth century

he who was so   glad
                of everything
        despite the paltry harvest of fresh leeches
                  with their accurate anesthetic
            which could be sold to healers
                    for his livelihood

But here against the boiling sound of cars

near the airport off route 10

no one's on foot

                  as if it were a kind of shame
                          to go thus unprotected
nobody walks

footsteps at the motel clatter quickly
                  up the thin but weirdly heavy stairs
           made of dried curds of vomit and soft drink
                  cemented into slabs and edged with metal
                then hung on curling sleazy wrought iron rods

to halt is fearful

nobody stops to see the moon

nobody pleasantly ambles forth
                  into the inland empire   chest high   arms free
      to take this air of ash and cadmium and air force base perchlorate
                into the flesh

nobody notices the noise of waters   without half-hearing
                          in the canyons
          the unwettable ravel of delayed-burn chaparral
                begin its slide

Lyke as the hart desireth the water-brooks
          the psalmist wrote
                through the clear cadences of Miles Coverdale
So longeth my soul after thee

another partition placed upon
                  the natural world   that put its faith
      in longing   in an animal

the hart with branching horns   whose instinct draws
          him to the pure low brook
                    no caravan or market dung has muddied
nor crag upstream comes into nor bubbling
     mineral or gas   or swollen corpse or even transparent
horde of genetically changing mayflies
                              to lay their eggs upon the still unsullied
emptiness of the quick aerobic water

          O God invisible as air

          My tears have been my meat

                              sweet
          because no noxious thing runs with them   only
          fragrant naïveté of the reflective midday when
          bank herb and wood flower and water from the pool
               can best be gathered
                                        also the knowledge
          that these gifts are tenuous and that the mouth
               and the harp
                    might soon be strange to play

for this was the tongue of English images
          wet with northern rainfall   and devotion   inland ocean
          freshet   and frequent rainbow and cold spring and not
     a place made mineral by thirst and harsh tectonics and
          in one prophet's warning

                    torrential landforms

     resembling Israel or Crete or dangerous like most
          sweet-looking blue-rose sunsets at the sea's edge

                    (where   yes   *One deep calleth another*

          beneath Laguna and Long Beach

Nominated by The Paris Review

THE VOICE OF THE PAST

by FLOYD SKLOOT

from COLORADO REVIEW

> *The past is never dead. It's not even past.*
> —William Faulkner, *Requiem for a Nun*

FACT-CHECKERS at the *New York Times Magazine* couldn't confirm my mother's pivotal story. She'd been, she always said, radio's "Melody Girl of the Air" in the mid-1930s, star of her own show on WBNX in the Bronx. Twenty-something and bound for fame, she was scheduled opposite Rudy Vallee, played the piano and sang, admitted she was better than Ethel Merman or Billie Holiday, and was the darling of George Gershwin and Cole Porter.

Wrapped in plastic bags on the top shelf of our hall closet was a short stack of scratchy 78-rpm records. She said they contained a selection of her best performances, and even though their tremulous soprano sounded nothing like her familiar smoke-shot contralto, I grew up believing her.

But at ninety-three, deep in dementia, my mother was losing the last link with her autobiographical self—the ability to sing—and was way beyond a final reckoning with the "Melody Girl of the Air" story. After she failed to perform in a scheduled talent show at her nursing home, I'd written a brief tribute to her life of song, and now the magazine was seeking verification of every point in my thousand-word essay.

They called the head nurse at the memory impairment unit, confirming my mother's presence there and her history of singing at the nursing home. Yes, she'd loved to perform and would sing or scat rather than talk. Yes, though she'd rehearsed as usual, she declined to show up for her talent show performance, refusing to leave the familiar sanctity of the unit. And, yes, a male resident did sing "Red River Valley" as part of the program. The fact-checkers determined that there was a striptease number in the Rodgers and Hart musical *Pal Joey*, though they grudgingly had to take my word that my mother performed it in the basement of our Brooklyn synagogue in 1955. But the key fact, the one on which the whole tribute turned, was the existence of my mother's radio show, and the *New York Times Magazine* could find no evidence of it. WBNX no longer existed, though they were able to verify that it had. But schedules and details of the station's 1930s programming were unavailable.

I maintained that even if it was untrue, even if my mother had lied about this fundamental aspect of her history, it would only underscore the power of her star-struck dreams. In the end, the editors decided to publish my essay despite the potential for factual error regarding the "Melody Girl of the Air."

It appeared on a summer Sunday in 2004, and early that morning I received a call from Howard "Pee-Wee" Kahn. A stranger to me, he lived in Boca Raton, was ninety, had read the essay, and was now finished crying.

"I used to drive your mother to the radio station for her shows!"

For most people, the past drifts off into haze, fading as they move toward the future. It's supposed to do that. "We forget because we must / And not because we will," as Matthew Arnold says in "Absence." Our brains would quickly be overloaded if everything that happened to us, everything we thought and felt, everything we saw and heard, remained vividly present. Only certain memories are retained, often the worst or best of our experience, burnt into our brain cells, the intense moments we keep returning to. This filtered, condensed version of our lives, though it can't possibly contain all our experience, is our essential Book of Self, our story.

But for some people, the past vanishes in a flash, explodes, sundered by traumatic brain injury or illness. The Book of Self comes unbound, its pages scattered, shredded, or vaporized.

In December 1988, a viral attack damaged my brain. It took the next fifteen years for me to master walking without a cane, and I still can't maintain balance with my eyes closed, or with my head tilted back and arms spread like a man welcoming the sunlight. My wife, Beverly, and I have lived in our new Portland home more than seven months now, but I routinely lose my way back once I've left the neighborhood. I continue to confuse words, assuring my in-laws that I've brought a clasp of tea along on our late-summer trip to ping fruiteries, rather than bringing a flask of tea as we pick huckleberries. I tell my daughter that it's been wealthy rather than lovely to speak with her on the phone. Which I suppose it has, since I feel richer in love. In a bustling restaurant, I bite my tongue—and need four stitches to close the wound—trying to talk and eat at the same time. When the phone rings while I'm making lunch, I put the receiver down on the countertop as I talk into a paring knife.

But the worst, most disabling damage remains the failure of my memory systems, both long and short term. My most intimate story, my sense of who I was, had been shattered in the aftermath of that attack, the past left in fragments I couldn't make cohere, the present vanishing in its own wake. I felt severed from myself, abandoned in alien territory. Memory, that familiar voice of the past in my head, went silent after I got sick. No, not silent exactly, but its sound became whispery gibberish, a mixture of occasionally recognizable words or phrases scattered among the nonsense and static. For the last eighteen years, I've been learning to find and retain that voice.

Without the power of memory, reading more than a paragraph or writing more than a few phrases are major challenges. Nothing connects to anything else. As I slowly regained the ability to concentrate and hold thoughts in mind, as I developed techniques to work with a brain that no longer functioned reliably, writing became a way to help me grasp, examine, and arrange surviving bits of the past.

I started with words, images, lines, disconnected notes that I wrote on index cards and filed in various folders: *Brooklyn*, where I was born in 1947 and lived until the age of ten; *Long Beach*, the Long Island suburb where I lived until high school graduation; *Baseball*, a passion throughout my life; *Summer Camps*. I had folders for *Mother*; *Father*; my brother, *Philip*; my daughter, *Rebecca*. A folder for *Franklin and Marshall College*, where I'd been a student in the late 1960s.

To stimulate recall, I listened to music from various periods in my life, doo-wop and show tunes and Chopin, campfire songs and the British invasion, Buddy Holly, the Weavers. I read out-of-print novels I'd read before but could barely remember, rented old movies and compilations of television programs, followed the least flickering of recall. Certain that the 1964 movie *Youngblood Hawke* had been important to me as a teenager, but unable to remember why or to locate a video, I read the Herman Wouk novel on which it was based. Partway through, as the title character publishes his first novel, I was overwhelmed with the sense of my seventeen-year-old self crying in the movie theater and thinking that the writing life would be for me. Even if I didn't look like the actor James Franciscus.

At the time I was beginning to do this work, my mother was slipping into dementia, her already shaky grasp of the past and the truth growing even more erratic. My brother was dying of kidney failure, his own memories compromised by the side-effects of dialysis and renal toxicities. Visits to his California apartment would often include long periods of silence, then a word or phrase from one of us might spark a glimmer of memory.

"I remember we used to go out with Dad on Sunday mornings," I murmured, sitting on the floor beside his recliner as he rocked. "We'd stop at a diner."

Philip nodded, his blind eyes shut, and said, "Toomey's." Suddenly I could see the diner whole: red leather stools circled by rippled chrome and supported by silvery pedestals, juke boxes at every table, the sign proclaiming *Special Today* that had nothing else written on it, the diner's air thick with breath and smoke and grease and sweetness. I could hear my father and brother, elbows on the red Formica counter, planning our adventures at Coney Island or Prospect Park, could glimpse Toomey himself skewering a customer's bill and slamming his cash drawer shut.

As I grew more able to piece together the fragments and finish a piece of writing, occasionally a poem or essay I published would find readers who knew me, knew my family, and possessed bits of the story I was seeking to assemble. They tracked me down, and soon I began to hear the voice of the past as something different from what I'd thought it was: a chorus, with soloists stepping forward, my own ragged voice growing more audible as it found its way back.

In early 2000, out of cyberspace blue, I received e-mails from Toomey's daughters. "I think your poem is very evocative of the diner as it was," Pat Toomey Noonan wrote. "My father, John, who is the fellow who skewered your bill, died in 1981." I was astounded. Through all the chaos of brain damage, I had remembered that detail correctly, having found it when the mention of a diner sparked my brother's lost memories. "Your images are all true," Peg Toomey Fisk wrote, a few days after her sister. She kept repeating the word *true*, and every time she did I felt like weeping because it was a confirmation that I did still have accurate memories, and that I was developing a way to locate them again, even if I couldn't easily put them together. "What rings so true to me," she continued, "is the serenity of the place. It's true; it was bustling, noisy, and reeked of that wonder-spattering grease, but I always felt at home there."

The idea that other people could not only be part of, but could also contain my memories, hadn't struck me before. They had sentences, paragraphs, sometimes whole pages of my Book of Self. In a very real sense, this experience of memory loss lifted me out of myself and made me part of something larger. Not just the community of the sick, but the wider community of selves.

There were letters, one by one, from the family who had lived in the apartment below ours in Brooklyn fifty years ago. The son, a contemporary of my brother, wrote of remembering my mother "at the piano, foot on the pedal, both hands on the keys, rising from the stool for a high note." So I hadn't been exaggerating when I told Beverly about that! The daughter remembered my father as a civil defense warden, wearing a white helmet and herding neighbors into the basement during midnight drills. I relished these sudden irruptions, the feeling that my past was alive and trying to find me, talk to me. That I was finding myself, and my story was beginning to cohere. That I had not lost all my memories, only the connections, the fit.

I received e-mails from three of my brother's early girlfriends, patching together a forgotten picture of him as an unlikely, overweight, teenaged Lothario. A woman from the Bronx, who had met our family at a Catskills summer resort, remembered my brother as "feisty in person as well as body." She also recalled coming to our Brooklyn apartment in order to meet Philip again. "I think he and I would've been good adult friends." This sense of my brother's charm brought me a fresh perspective, something I might never have had without hearing these voices from the past.

An e-mail from Aaron "Red" Bogart, the owner of a New Hampshire summer camp I attended in 1956, told me that he'd worked briefly for my father in the chicken market. "He was a hard worker, loved by all the Mafia women who came in to buy from him, and trusted implicitly." There was no one else alive in my life who remembered my father from that time, except me, and my memories were those of a small child who remembered his father's bloody apron and the cries of terrified chickens as he approached their coops. Red had met my mother before her marriage, coming to visit her brother at the family's fur shop. He found my mother "flirtatious and, I guess, looking to get married." He also found her unstable, "one tough customer to deal with," and thought she'd been spoiled by her parents.

440

But he also praised my mother's sense of humor and found her "always ready for a good laugh." Now that was news to me, and sad, suggesting that the years after Red knew her—when she married my father and had her two children—had taken away her laughter.

A letter from my childhood friend, Billy Babiskin, whom I hadn't seen in forty years, was addressed in part to my wife and daughter, filling them in on what I was like as a kid. "He could run like the wind," Billy told them. "My dad said Floyd had a rocket up his *toches*." And he remembered me singing "Sonny Boy" in a fundraising duet with my mother at the synagogue. Not, fortunately, the same one where she performed her striptease.

Within the space of five years, I received letters from the entire group of six adolescent friends who'd lived in my Long Beach neighborhood and with whom I'd played daily for so many years. Scattered now, they were not in touch with one another but had each found me. Larry Salander remembered the night my father died, and a walk we took along the beach during the eye of a hurricane; Johnny Frank remembered our summer jobs together, cooking at a beachfront fast-food grill or selling snacks on the shore from boxes strapped to our backs; Lester Silverman remembered my brother driving us to Nathan's for hot dogs and custard cones; Jay Shaffer remembered our late-night raid over the walls of the Lido Hotel to locate foreign agents, and the entire lineup from our slow-pitch softball team, names that brought back faces and events. Fellow summer campers from my years in the Poconos remembered running races and softball games I thought perhaps I'd imagined, lying in bed as I began the slow process of recovering myself. My folders were filling with vital bits of information, essential links to the things I myself remembered.

By 2004, when Pee-Wee Kahn called to talk about my mother's radio show, I was more delighted than surprised to hear from him, though I had not known of his existence before. Because clearly, as William Faulkner said in his 1951 novel *Requiem for a Nun*, the past wasn't dead at all. In fact, the past was so alive that I'd begun expecting it to find me, to assert itself, as long as I continued making the effort to gather up the fragments. This phenomenon is hardly unique to me, of course; many of us have found our pasts looking for us: an e-mail from a high school classmate, a letter from a retired teacher, a late-night phone call from a former lover, a daughter's early drawing tucked inside the pages of an old chapbook of poems.

441

After Pee-Wee told me about taking my mother to WBNX for her radio shows, I could hardly wait to send an e-mail to the *New York Times Magazine* fact-checkers. But then, when I asked how he'd come to know my mother, Pee-Wee said that he was a friend of her brother, Barney. My mother's brother was named Al, not Barney. Maybe at ninety Pee-Wee had his facts confused, maybe it wasn't my mother he drove to the station.

"Barney?"

"That's what we called Al, because with those eyes he looked like Barney Google from the comics."

"How well did you know him?"

"We met at summer camp. I'm telling you, we were like brothers. I'd stay over at their apartment three times a week."

Soon, Pee-Wee was telling me all about the "Melody Girl of the Air." It was, he thought, a ten- or fifteen-minute show. Songs and a little sit-com skit. My mother and her brother would work on the script as Pee-Wee drove them from Manhattan to the Bronx. "She'd play a few chords and sing a song or two, do this little comedy bit with the producer as her partner, then sing another song, and good-bye." He chuckled, coughed to clear his gnarled, knobby voice. "Your mother kept trying to convince Barney to come on the air with her. Take part in a skit."

"Did he ever?"

"Are you kidding? We'd go have a cup of coffee and pick her up after. But she'd nag her parents to make Barney do it."

The show, Pee-Wee thought, ran for a few months. The producer, another friend whose name really was Barney, got fired, and my mother's career was over.

"What was she like when she was in her twenties?"

Pee-Wee took a long breath. "Delusions of grandeur," he said. Then, after clearing his throat, he added, "Uppity, you might say. Let's put it this way. No man was good enough for the Melody Girl." For a moment, I wondered if this was the talk of a rejected swain. He seemed wistful, hurt, as if he'd taken her attitude personally. Had my mother's highfalutin ways broken hearts other than her own?

When I think of the voice of the past, I think of Pee-Wee's thick bass, the way it sounded swamped by all the years that have gone by, the way it seemed to rise from somewhere down below me. I also think of the clear, mellow soprano of Alice Sachs, who returned to my life in 2004 after an absence of fifty-two years. Her familiar snowy voice seemed to drift down over me.

In early February, I received a letter from Alice, who had recently moved to the Portland area and seen an article in the newspaper about my work. "Many, many, MANY years ago in Brooklyn," she wrote, "I knew a Skloot family—Lillian, Harry, Floyd, and Philip and her brother Barney." In the early 1950s, Alice had been married to the obstetrician who delivered me. Her husband had been part of the summer camp group, along with his cousin Red Bogart, Pee-Wee Kahn, and my uncle. It seemed so unlikely and so generous that these elderly people—scattered in New Hampshire, Florida, Oregon—all knew one another, all knew me and my family, all had lost touch, but had each independently come upon my writing and bothered to track me down.

Alice remembered my family vividly. "We were not close," she wrote, "but I remember how they looked and I remember, clearly, the apartment they lived in." And, as I soon discovered, she also remembered my mother so well that she could do a harrowingly accurate impersonation. A former actress and musician, and a practicing psychologist, Alice captured the tilt of my mother's head, her pursed lips, and widened eyes as she spoke in her faux continental accent. She enacted the familiar scene in which my mother would seek to charm her guests with talk of the theater or music, then suddenly stop and turn her head to shriek at my father, *Harry, shut your mouth when I'm talking!* then turn back to resume her hostess voice as if no interruption had occurred.

"Some friendships have a short shelf-life," she wrote. After her divorce, she lost touch with her husband's friends and never saw my family again. But now here was the Skloot name. I was a part of her memory as she was a part of mine, and we'd found each other again, jabbering of the past on the phone and then during dinner visits. Alice attended a reading I gave at Portland State University, and I loved hearing her laugh when I read about my mother's performance of the striptease number from *Pal Joey*. She remembered the event, too. She had also been at my brother's Bar Mitzvah in 1952. I found a photograph of her in the album commemorating that event and showed it to her when she came to dinner.

Beverly and I are driving south on 1–5, listening to a compilation of unreleased Crosby, Stills, Nash, and Young music. There are studio out-takes and sketchy experiments, alternate versions of familiar hits, songs that were never released, gorgeous guitar riffs, chatter. We're

443

singing along, reminiscing about where we were when we last heard this number, laughing as we head toward home.

The CD arrived in the mail from one of the fifteen-year-old boys, now fifty-two, who had been in my bunk when I was a counselor at Camp Echo Lark during the summer of 1970. I'd published an essay in *Colorado Review* about that summer, the rediscovered sense of community I found among those boys and the music they brought into my life, though I couldn't recall who had been the bunk's disk jockey. Then I received an e-mail from him, followed by a package of CDs he'd mixed to bring back my memories.

When "Everybody's Talkin' " comes on, a song I didn't know the group had ever recorded, I'm flooded with associations. Their distinctive harmonies put me back in the summer mountain air of Pennsylvania, playing baseball on the hard-packed infield dirt, and the song itself brings to mind, of course, the 1969 movie *Midnight Cowboy*, for which Harry Nilsson had recorded it. And I remember a moment I hadn't thought about in four decades, shortly after graduation from college and before the start of grad school, when I traveled in Europe and tried to supplement my savings by singing "Everybody's Talkin' " on a Copenhagen street corner.

When we get home, I make notes about that summer trip, and then get an e-mail from someone who had acted in a college production of *Measure for Measure* with me and remembered my "irreverence" as Pompey the bawd. This triggers a memory of trying and failing to recall that character's long jailhouse speech as I walked in the dense woods surrounding the house where Beverly and I lived for fourteen years.

It feels as if the past is all around me, whether I remember it or not. This has become a deeply familiar sensation over the last decade. As the British biographer and memoirist Michael Holroyd has written, "We live in a forest of family trees, and the branches reach out in complicated paths over unexpectedly long distances." I am so deeply connected to so many people, my past alive in theirs, yet only now, as I've worked to restore the fragments of my damaged memory, have I become aware of the ongoing flow between and among us, like swirling wind through the oak, fir, and maple trees around our house I have left behind but still inhabit in dreams.

Nominated by Richard Burgin, The Colorado Review

A BERRYMAN CONCORDANCE AGAINST THIS SILENCE

by ELENA KARINA BYRNE

from BARROW STREET

endlessly us undo
I have said what I have to say

against your silence-triumph

of the vanished on their uncanny errands
and up-lit, turned

and took a deep breath
                          for you

whereby we ripen
                          to have it out
and pace on in peace
if that's what you call it, kind suffering
                          our last bride

to letters and margin-omissions, to the pen falling asleep
in the hand of a friend
                          behind: me, wag. Here:

445

a bowl full of snow carried inside the house; one hundred
and fifty-five thousand black umbrellas opened and no water;

the image of the dead on the fingernail

of the closed fist of the dead; my head full of silkworm cocoons
thrown against the wall,

a strangeness in the final note.

Nominated by Angie Estes, David St. John, Kathy Fagan, Stuart Dischell, Barrow Street

CULTIVATION

fiction by SHANNON CAIN

from TIN HOUSE

ONE EVENING, Maury calls. Those public service announcements, he tells Frances, the ones about casual drug consumption supporting terrorism? Apparently they're working. Now his customers insist *their* marijuana be grown domestically. He needs the entirety of her last two harvests, which Frances estimates at roughly twelve pounds, counting the supply that's now curing in mason jars in her basement. "These people buy organic produce, if you know what I mean," Maury says. "They read the *New York Times*."

He'll pay her a thousand dollars a pound, but he wants her to deliver it. Here's the trouble: Memphis is fifteen hundred miles from Phoenix, and her three kids are home from school for the summer.

At the dinner table Frances says, "How about a road trip?"

The boys throw their hands in the air, cheering her. Todd, the six-year-old, her sports freak, the kid whose Little League coach is already planning his career, wants to know if they can sleep in a tent. The middle one, Robbie, who is eight and plays chess and computer games, says he guesses Memphis is cool. Emily inches one shoulder toward her ear, a half shrug that is one of her few signals of approval. She is fourteen.

Frances doesn't grow pot because she's a desperate single mother, though she is. She grows it to pay off her half of the thousands upon thousands of dollars in credit card debt she and her ex racked up during their marriage. Recently her minimum payments have become unreasonable. On three separate credit cards the Amount Due hovers resolutely above the ten-thousand-dollar mark, unaffected by

447

the enormous sums she sends each month. At 19 percent interest, she figures, Todd will have graduated from college before she pays off the debt. She'll still be wringing payments from her meager take-home as a per diem nurse on the oncology ward, digging herself fruitlessly deeper into the hole. In the memo line of her checks she scrawls her account number followed by *you fuckers*, an act which offers diminishing satisfaction with each new month. Lately she's had to rotate payments; she pays one bill, neglects the next. A shift in tone has occurred in the personalized notes printed on her bills: they've devolved from the tactful supposition of Frances's forgetfulness to the sinister hint of third-party collections.

So there's the money. Yet, also: there's nothing else in her life that offers the same satisfaction as the squat plants, the cultivation of perfect, tight, and tender buds, the recognition that she's expert at something. She grows weed and she grows children, but the weed doesn't talk back. The children make noise and messes. The weed is reliable. She feeds, she prunes, she waters, and uncomplicated as the sunrise, it grows.

Some of it she smokes, but who needs that much pot? She reaps three ounces per square foot every sixteen weeks, a yield right up there with the big guys. In her basement the plants fill a walk-in closet that she's double-dead-bolted against Emily, a kid who emerged from Frances's womb demanding to know everything.

Frances uses the Screen of Green method, which requires careful attention to the training of each plant for maximum light on the buds, and involves a complicated system of chicken wire, drip irrigation, grow lights, airflow fans, irrigation tubes, water pumps, thermostats, and exhaust pipes. Industrial-grade soundboard and weather stripping ensure that all this activity goes undiscovered by Emily. If she suspects anything, she hasn't mentioned it.

The promise of a cross-country adventure has excited the boys, requiring of Frances some serious bedtime cajoling. When all three are finally asleep, she goes to the basement to smoke her excellent pot, empties the dehumidifier in her drying cabinet, then pads barefoot through her double-mortgaged ranch house, back upstairs to their bedsides. She stands over their sleeping bodies. She bends close to their faces to peer at them in the dark. The eyelashes! The lips! She wanders from bedroom to bedroom. Their faces are never, during the day, as still as this. Emily's scowl is absent; she looks like she did in kindergarten, before Frances married the boys' father. Emily would hate to know her mother stares at her like this, big teenage girl that she is; she'd accuse Frances of invading her privacy. Frances absorbs the impossible beauty of her children. She gets teary with the joy of their existence and the delirium of primo homegrown.

The day before their trip Frances purchases an aerodynamic cargo carrier and a padlock. Inside the garage, she straps it to the top of the minivan and packs it with cardboard boxes of clothes the boys have outgrown and toys they've ignored for months. Together with these items she places two small nylon duffel bags purchased on sale at Target, one decorated with retro daisies and the other with soccer balls. Each contains six vacuum-sealed packages that weigh one pound apiece. She stayed up most of the night before with her vacuum sealer—purchased last year via infomercial—sucking the air out of ziplock freezer bags and wrapping them in duct tape. She closes the carrier and walks around the car, sniffing.

The next morning she assembles her children in the driveway. On the front lawn the boys are engaged in a vigorous game of "Slug Bug." undaunted by an absence of Volkswagens on their street.

Emily points to the cargo carrier. "What's in there?"

"Empty!" Frances says. "In case we want to do some shopping. In Memphis."

"We have malls here, Mom," Emily says.

Frances lets her gaze fall to Emily's torso. "What is that you're wearing? Some sort of dress, or what?" Some mornings it appears to Frances as if Emily's breasts have become larger as she slept. "Never mind," Frances tells her. "Come on, boys, let's hit the road."

In the car there are significant stretches of quiet. There is so much to see through the windows. Emily and the boys have their heads down, occupied with books or GameBoys or DVDs. Frances is struck with melancholy that no one in the car is in diapers anymore.

"You're missing this country!" she says. "Look outside, kids!" They must be climbing in altitude, for the landscape has become a hybrid of prairie and desert, long grass dotted with cholla cacti. Winds that don't seem to know which direction they're headed whip the grasses flat in great wide swaths of motion, exposing white underbellies, then tossing them upright, green again. Given all the gusting energy outside, it strikes Frances as strange that the interior of the minivan is so utterly without breeze. How completely a person can be insulated. "Look, guys!" she says. "Look how the grass is like waves!" Three blond heads turn to the left. Six green eyes register a view that fails to hold their interest.

"That's real nice, Mom," Emily says. She's reading *Herland* by Charlotte Perkins Gilman.

"Yeah, Mom, real nice!" yells Todd.

Frances remains silent for ten or twelve miles, until Todd informs her it's time to stop for lunch and besides he needs to poop. This sets off a round of butt jokes. From the back of her throat Emily offers a loud sigh.

"They can't help it," Frances tells her.

"Twerps," Emily says. "Brain-damaged cockroaches."

"Later on you'll love them," Frances says.

"Extremely doubtful," says Robbie, who was named, regrettably, after his father. It was still in the first year of Frances's marriage to him, even as she suspected the guy was fucking Emily's soccer coach. The kid won't let Frances call him Bob, Robert, or even Bobby. Todd, on the other hand, was a save-the-marriage baby, a fact for which she is only now on the verge of forgiving herself, thanks to expensive semiweekly therapy.

At the Burger King in Gallup, Emily studies the carrier and says, "Why don't we put the suitcases in there? We'd have more room inside the van."

"Plenty of room all around, sweetie," Frances says. Todd is grabbing for Robbie's milk shake, which Robbie holds maddeningly out of short arms' range. Todd's face has that pre-eruption expression. It's evoked so often by Robbie that Frances suspects he's trying for a record: how many times in one day can he make his brother wail in frustration? "Whoa, little dude," Frances says, and steers him toward the minivan. "You don't want that anyhow. Cooties on the straw and such."

Todd wiggles in satisfaction. He'll take the comment as evidence she loves him more than she does his brother. Which of course isn't true. Before the boys were born she couldn't bear the thought of loving another child the way she did Emily. But there they were, and she does. She searches the rearview mirror to give Robbie a wink but he won't meet her eye.

Frances needs to make a decision about lying to Emily. The kid's inquisitive nature has been bolstered lately by a sharpening sense of logic—that's what Frances gets, she realizes ruefully, for sending

450

Emily and the boys to decent schools—and an increasingly distrustful outlook on the world in general. Either Frances has to get much craftier about her basement activity or she needs to give up the deception entirely and tell Emily everything.

But it's the job of a mother to reveal truths to her children in increments they can handle. Last year when some kid on the playground called Robbie a "math dweeb" and he came home wanting to know what that meant, Frances didn't tell him about pocket protectors and rejection by girls and how high school is hell for kids like him. She told him only enough so he understood that the kid who had called him that name was confused and jealous and sad. Emily, though, is getting to the age when subtleties are important. At some point soon Frances will need to explain to her that the stuff they're teaching her in school about drugs ignores important shades of gray. As it is, she's learning there's pretty much no difference between pot and crystal meth. Frances would like to tell the zealots who champion the D.A.R.E. curriculum—the cops and vice principals of the world—about the cancer patients on her ward. How grateful the family members are when she pulls them aside in the hallway and tells them she can get them top-grade marijuana to ease the unbearable, humiliating nausea and build the appetites of their loved ones. How, handing her a hundred bucks—a substantial discount—for a baggie containing twenty joints, they sometimes cry with relief and gratitude. They hug her, the big suffering hugs of people whose nightmares are unfolding before them, and they tell her she's an angel. That God should bless her.

Robbie, on the other hand, would take in stride the truth about her basement endeavors. For a few miles Frances engages in a fantasy in which she and her grown-up son work together in a mother-son business. She'd do the cultivating; Robbie, his gift for numbers honed by advanced-placement math and an MBA from Yale, would handle the management side.

She looks at him in the mirror on the back of her visor. He is quietly placing tiny wads of chewed-up paper in Todd's hair.

"Emily," Frances says.

Emily sighs and saves her page with her finger.

"The cargo carrier," Frances whispers. "It's not empty."

"I knew it." Emily smiles.

It's so easy, Frances thinks. Their trust is always there, right at the surface, waiting. "I'm giving a bunch of your brother's old things away." She looks behind her, unnecessarily. "You remember Maury, my friend from college? He lives in Memphis now and he has a son and I told him I'd bring them some toys and clothes. Don't tell Todd and Robbie."

"Just as long as you don't try to give away Todd's baseball stuff," Emily says, her voice low. She opens her book and smiles into it.

Frances's supply of cheap tricks cannot, apparently, be exhausted. There is no shortage of law enforcement patrolling the American interstate system. Emily has empowered herself with a range of front-seat responsibilities, one of which is monitoring Frances's speed. "It's a construction zone, Mom," she says. "Fifty-five."

Normally Frances would arch an eyebrow and remind her who the mother is here, but she figures for the sake of harmony she can swallow a little teenage interference. At home Emily digs through the recycling bin to make sure each of the yogurt containers bears a number two triangle symbol. When the electric bill arrives in a pink envelope, the sign that it's overdue, she pulls it from the stack of mail spilling out of the wicker basket on the countertop—the basket Emily organizes on a regular basis, throwing out junk and sorting bills by their due dates—and shakes it at Frances accusingly. "How can you *forget* to pay a bill, Mom? How is that *possible*?" Once, Frances came home from work early and found Emily at the kitchen counter, frowning over a stack of credit card statements. The genetic source of all this angst is a mystery: like Frances, Emily's father—whom Frances hasn't seen since she was nineteen and pregnant—wasn't especially concerned about fiscal responsibility. She never knew him well enough to understand whether Emily's neuroses could have come from his side of the family. It doesn't much matter, though: Frances long ago gave up the struggle to get Emily to relax and act like a kid.

Given the odds, given a fifteen-hundred-mile road trip with the distraction of the boys in the backseat, it is bound to happen, and it does, in the early afternoon of day two, just west of Amarillo. Emily sees the flashing lights first. "Mom! Oh my God, it's a police car *right* behind us. What were you doing, ninety? Mom, he's pulling you over. Pull over! I can't *believe* this."

"Emily, honey. It's just a cop," she says as she guides the van to the shoulder. She does wish, though, that they weren't in Texas.

"What about that ticket when I was in sixth grade? You got points on your driver's license, didn't you? How many will you have now? I swear to God, if you lose your license my life is ruined."

"Deep breaths, sweetheart. Not a big deal. Not the end of the universe." She looks in the rearview mirror. The cop hasn't yet emerged from his car.

"Mom's in trouble!" Robbie sings.

"Shut up, butthead," Emily says. She's already going after her fingernails.

Frances cranes her neck to check on Todd. His mouth is in a serious line, his little forehead furrowed. "It's okay, lovey," Frances says. "Mommy was just driving a little too fast. I guess."

The cop is friendly enough. Emily looks straight ahead and grips her armrests. Frances did not, it turns out, see a sign that required slowing down for a high-wind area. Not able to miss the action, Robbie cracks open the rear window.

The cop looks past Frances, into the backseat. "How's it going, boys?" he says.

They squeak out a couple of tiny *okays*. They're such little ones, Frances thinks.

He hands her the citation. "What're you carrying up top?" he says.

"Just luggage," she says. "Camping stuff." She puts her hand near her jaw to hide the throbbing of blood through her jugular vein, then realizes touching your face is nervous body language and places her hand casually, she hopes, on the steering wheel.

"Look out for these winds," he says. "Sometimes these carriers can throw off your balance. A gust hits the car sideways and the extra height makes things tricky." He gives the carrier a knock with his knuckles. "Especially in these minivans. Slow down, ma'am. Have a nice day, kids."

They find a campground east of Oklahoma City at a place called Lake Eufaula. The boys indulge in another series of irritating wordplay jokes. Frances finds a spot near the water's edge, uncomfortably far from the parking lot, up an embankment, but at least a distance away from a family of speedboaters and a group of spirited college-age students with a huge cooler. She decides not to worry about leaving the weed in the carrier overnight. The boys attempt to pitch the tent, then give up and spend two hours smearing themselves with mud from the bottom of the lake, washing it off, and smearing again. Frances and Emily figure out the tent stakes and poles and loops.

They all roast hot dogs and marshmallows and Frances wishes her father were alive to meet his fine grandsons. They could use a grandpa, to play chess with Robbie and catch with Todd. She resolves to learn how to fish, to take them to a pond someday, give them poles and worms. She waits until she's sure the kids are asleep—the boys go down fast and solid but Emily tosses for a while—before she lights a joint and melts into campfire and stars and the lap of lake water. Finally she climbs into the tent and lies in her sleeping bag, listening to her children breathe.

In the middle of the night she wakes up to Emily groping around in the dark. "Where's the flashlight?" Emily whispers. "I have to pee."

"Damn, honey. I left it in the car," Frances says. "My keys—"

"They're in your jeans pocket," Emily tells her. The moonlight makes the tent nylon glow greenish. Frances finds her jeans, crumpled in the corner of the tent, and hands the keys to Emily. "It's in the far back—"

"I know where it is," Emily says, and zips her way out the door.

"Can you see? Is it too dark?"

"I'm all *right*, Mom." Emily's tone is designed to inform Frances she doesn't know a damn thing about her daughter and never will.

The boys are asleep on their sides, mouths open, Robbie's eyeballs active under his lids. Frances thinks about Emily making her way through the dark campground, considers climbing out of her sleeping bag to go with her to the cinder block toilet structure. You never know when drunken college boys are lurking in the woods. She could pretend she has to go also. Her mattress is softening from air loss, but she's still comfortable and sleepy and doesn't particularly want to get up. In the distance she hears the chirp of the minivan's alarm disengaging. Two weeks ago, doing the laundry, Frances found a letter from Emily to her most recent best friend, Breanne. It described a moment after band practice with a boy named Miguel wherein Emily's breasts were touched. Only the top half, her perfectly tidy handwriting was careful to note: no nipple.

That hardly counts, Frances found herself thinking. When Frances was twelve, her sixteen-year-old cousin Henry grabbed her breasts at an Easter picnic, zeroing in and twisting, and in return Frances whacked him on the temple with the hard edge of a tennis racket, a move that got her in huge trouble, given that the injury over which she'd retaliated had left no evidence of equal harm.

454

Emily's letter indicated nothing about the incident with Miguel being nonconsensual, a fact about which Frances feels both relief and foreboding. Her therapist later informed her that fourteen-year-old girls do not leave notes to their friends in the pockets of their jeans unless they're trying to tell their mothers something. Frances has yet to find a therapist who doesn't irritate her by pointing out the obvious.

Wide-awake, Frances waits for her heart to return to her from the dark woods. Finally she hears footsteps returning. "Sweetie?" she whispers. "Is that you?" But Emily doesn't come back inside. Frances unzips her bag, gropes for her shoes, and leaves the tent. She finds Emily standing at the edge of the water.

"Hey, baby," Frances says. "Not tired?"

"I was going to sit here and read." She shrugs. "Only the flashlight just died."

"Rats," Frances says.

"Why did you lie to that cop?"

Frances sighs. She's still feeling the effects of her bedtime joint. "I couldn't exactly tell him the truth in front of the boys. Plus, cops are always suspicious. He'd only have kept us sitting there longer, asking questions."

"Yeah, all those questions are real inconvenient," she says.

"What's that supposed to mean?" Frances says.

"Nothing. Whatever."

"Honey, listen, I wanted to talk to you about something." From across the lake she hears a Jet Ski. Some people don't know when to end the party. "Your school counselor called last week."

Emily expels a puff of air through her nose.

"She told me you brought a condom to school," Frances says.

"It was a dare." Emily sticks her bare foot into the lake. "That's the truth."

"Are you sure, sweetie?" You need to open these doors slowly, Frances thinks. Rushing headlong into a conversation about a certain boy and where his hands have been is a recipe for shutdown.

"That counselor is a bitch, Mom. She's out to get me."

"I wasn't terribly impressed with her either. But watch your language."

"She lies. Plus, she thinks all girls are boy crazy."

"Because you can talk to me about sex anytime you need to."

"Okay, all right. Just, okay. Gross."

Frances gives Emily a one-armed hug around the shoulders. It feels good to have broached the subject. "Okay, then," she says. "What about school, otherwise?"

"It's fine," Emily says. She grabs her hair as if to form a ponytail. She's done this since she was a little girl, as a way of occupying her hands. She'll smooth it and form it, work out the bumps, then let it go and start again.

"Classes okay? Teachers?"

"Why are you interested all of a sudden?" Emily's fingers catch on pillow knots.

"Here," Frances says. "Let me give you a braid." She takes Emily's hair out of her hands and begins to work it into a French braid, as if they're getting ready for a recital or someone's wedding. They face the water, Frances standing behind Emily, whose hair smells of green-apple shampoo.

"Can't beat moonlight on a lake," Frances says.

"You aren't even using a comb," Emily says. "It's going to come out crappy."

"Somebody you're looking to impress, out here in the woods?"

"Why are you always making fun of me?" Emily starts to jerk her head away, but her hair is entwined in Frances's fingers. Reflexively, Frances tightens her grip.

"I'm just teasing, sweetheart," Frances says. "But you're right. I'll try to stop doing that if it hurts your feelings." How did this child turn out so touchy? Frances mentally catalogs her own relatives, searching for someone prickly. Someone from whom Emily might have inherited all this sensitivity.

"Why didn't you get an abortion?" Emily mumbles, softly.

"What? You mean when I was pregnant with you? Emily! Aren't we done with that question?" Frances stops braiding and tugs Emily's hair to the side so she can see her face.

"Ow," Emily says. "Jeez. Never mind."

"I wanted you, that's why," Frances says. There's no reason to tell Emily that she nearly went through with the abortion, but then canceled her appointment, thinking her boyfriend might stick around if there was a baby. No reason for Emily to know that her mother was as typical and unoriginal and youthfully deluded as any other pregnant teenager in the history of pregnant teenagers.

"How did you know you wanted me if you didn't even know who I was?"

456

This child knows a lie, Frances thinks, and sighs. "I just knew, Emily." She needs to rethink her parenting strategy. She needs to adapt.

On the road the next afternoon, after a late start following a morning spent lounging at the campground, Todd says, "I want to call Daddy."

Frances believes in not withholding their father from them, so she hands back her cell phone and tells him to go ahead and call. Also, she wants the guy to be reminded that his sons think about him almost constantly. And that Frances is the kind of mother who goes to the trouble of taking her children on family adventures.

She doesn't remember, until it's too late, that Robbie Sr. knows the significance of Memphis. All those alarmists screaming about marijuana and memory loss might actually be on to something.

"Mom," says Todd. "Daddy wants to talk to you."

"You've got to be kidding me, Fran," Robbie says.

She hears music in the background, and voices. "Where are you, in a bar?" she says into the phone. "At one o'clock in the afternoon?"

Emily unbuckles her seat belt and climbs back to sit with the boys.

"It's an office party," he says. "Someone's birthday. Why do you say things like that when the boys can hear you? Jesus Christ. Tell me you're not going to see Maury. You're not bringing the boys to Memphis to see Maury."

"Oh, we're great," she says brightly. "They're having a great time." Frances peeks at Emily and the boys in her visor mirror. She's trying to get them to play "I Spy." Lately Frances has noticed Emily's worry attaching itself to the boys, especially when Frances talks to their father within earshot.

"I swear to God, Fran." Phone reception notwithstanding, Robbie sounds just like his sexy, flaky self, the kind of guy a smarter woman would have taken to bed but refused to marry. For most of her twenties Frances was brainless when it came to men. After she and Robbie had been dating for a month or so, he brought her to a spot in the Chiricahua National Forest where he'd been cultivating a plot of marijuana plants. It took them two hours to hike in, stepping carefully to avoid leaving a path. They picnicked at the edge of his plot. Backlit by the low sun, the dense buds protruted from each stalk like multiple furry penises. He explained that they were surrounded by females: that in the world of cannabis, women are the only desirable sex; that the male is mostly leaves and doesn't grow those dense, resinous floral clusters. "A male," he said, "carries genes that influence the quality of his female offspring, but on his own he's worthless. You grow him only to evaluate his potency. If you can use him to pollinate yourself some kick-ass girl plants, you keep him around." He lit a joint. "Then you clone your best girls and away we go." They got carelessly high, lying on a cotton blanket in the shade of his bright green plants. "Yep," he said, after they'd had the kind of slow-motion sex made more intense by the hypersensitivity of their mucous membranes, "the value of the male is defined by the quality of his daughters."

Listening to that silken voice now on the cell phone, Frances reminds herself that in the end she hated him too much to fuck him no matter how high she was. It took her years to discover that his countercultural attitude was nothing more than a cover for a lifestyle supported by credit cards and a refusal to take anything seriously, including their family.

"Just don't do anything stupider than you've already done," Robbie says. "I hope your barracuda divorce lawyer knows a thing or two about criminal law, because if you get busted everything's going to hell."

She flips the phone closed. For a brief beat in the visor mirror she and Emily look into each other's eyes.

Whatever happened to the good old-fashioned truck stop diner? Frances wonders. She envisioned root beer floats, milk shakes in metal mixing cups, she and the boys and Emily sitting in a row on chrome bar stools. But after another long day in the van, for dinner they've ended up, at twilight, in a convenience store truck stop that houses a series of miniature fast-food franchises. Emily wants a fish sandwich, Robbie a hot dog. These places, Frances is sure, are purposefully designed to split up the American family and, as an added annoyance, to cause mothers the special kind of anxiety that results from their children scattering in a public place. She follows Todd to a self-serve Slurpee machine and lets him pull the handle, releasing the slush into an Arkansas Razorbacks plastic cup.

They reconvene in a booth constructed of bright orange laminate with sticky brown soda rings on the surface. Robbie chose the spot, making a beeline for a table as close as possible to two cops sucking on tubs of soda, hunched over large quantities of fast food. Great, Frances thinks: a new fascination with the police. She sips halfheartedly on a Diet Pepsi.

Emily holds out her hand for the car key. She needs her backpack to go to the bathroom.

"What for?" Robbie says loudly. "You need a tampon?"

"Shut up, butthead," Emily says. Her period started only six months ago, later than all of her friends. Shortly thereafter Robbie pulled a Kotex out of the box in the hall bathroom and ran around the front yard with the pad stuck to his forehead. Frances can't tell whether his age-inappropriate fascination with menstruation is based on scientific curiosity or purely on the joy of irritating his sister.

Frances and the boys have finished their refreshments by the time Emily emerges from the bathroom. She's walking slowly and has an oddly serious look on her face. Frances begins to scoot out of the booth, to see what's the matter, when Emily opens her backpack and pulls out something wrapped in duct tape. A ziplock bag. Emily stops five booths away, looking Frances in the eye. The cops are seated exactly between them. She's openly holding the package of weed, but has kept the backpack positioned to block it from their view.

"Robbie put ice on my hair!" Todd yells.

Frances meets Emily's gaze. She stands up.

"Mom!" Todd says. "Tell him to quit it!"

"Hush now," Frances says. The boys crane their necks to see what she's looking at.

Emily hasn't moved. "Emily?" Frances says. "Honey?"

One of cops raises his head.

"What, Mom?" Todd shouts. "What's wrong with Emily?"

Emily stuffs the package into her backpack. She continues to look directly at Frances, whose lectures on the importance of maintaining eye contact have apparently not gone unheeded. On the way to the car, Frances's knees threaten to buckle.

Emily herds the boys into the van, gets them settled into the farthest seat back, the spot Todd calls the *wayback*. They hook into headphones with a Jackie Chan movie.

In the passenger seat Emily cries, quietly, for at least twenty miles. For fifteen minutes Frances does not acknowledge the tears of her firstborn. She tries to think about something else, but her mind settles on reasons for crying: skinned knees, lost toys, mean girls, absent fathers. A mother's comfort withheld.

"How did you get to it?" Frances finally says. On the opposite side of the interstate, headlights approach, then race on. All those people inside all those cars, hurtling across the darkened landscape.

459

"Last night. At the campground," Emily tells her. "I wanted to make sure you weren't going to give away any of my stuff. I just was looking for my stuff, Mom."

"I told you, Emily, I wouldn't give away your things."

"Why should I believe you? You lie to me all the time."

"I do no such thing, Emily. And we're not doing this right now. The boys."

"The boys, right. The boys." But Emily looks back at them too. She can't help herself, Frances thinks. This is a kid who needs to be in charge.

"I'm warning you, Emily. I swear to God. You have no idea. You think you're such a grown-up. Such an adult. Such the responsible one. Let me tell you. Let me say this."

"Shush, Mom," Emily says.

"Do you know anything at all about credit cards?" Frances says. "Do you know about 19 percent interest? Do you know how much, in dollars and cents, it would cost a single mother of three to pay off twenty thousand dollars? Take a guess. How many pairs of new sneakers is that? How many pounds of hamburger?"

Emily's mouth opens unattractively. Her jaw is being pulled down, Frances thinks, by the deadweight of all that ignorant righteousness.

"Would you at least whisper?" Emily says.

"Take a guess! How about mortgages? What do you know about mortgages?" It's possible Frances is now yelling. "What do you know about personal bankruptcy? And while we're at it, how about divorce? What happens, exactly, when the custodial parent is deemed financially insolvent? Any answers yet, missy? Anything else you want to add? Anything you can do better than me here? Maybe you'd like to drive this car? Get us to Memphis?"

It occurs to Frances to check the rearview mirror. The boys have removed their headphones and are peering over the seat in front of them at their crying sister. Two wrinkled brows, two pairs of startled eyes, two furry heads edged in light from the cars on the road behind them.

"It's okay, boys," Emily says. "I'm okay."

"Nothing to see here," Frances says. "Enough gawking."

At ten o'clock Frances pulls over at a rest stop outside Little Rock. While Emily and the boys are in the bathrooms brushing their teeth she calls Maury.

"I can't meet you in friggin' Arkansas, Fran," he says. "Jason has one of his god-awful violin recitals first thing in the morning. If I miss another one Eileen is going to divorce me. You're only two hours away, give or take. Ring the bell when you get here, wake me up. We'll have beds ready for you and the kids. Tomorrow we'll grill some burgers, the kids will go for a swim. Hang tough."

Emily and the boys climb back into their seats and Frances forces the car eastward. Were there a bridge over the interstate right here, a convenient way to turn around, she might yield to the urge to head back home. Instead, she tells the boys to take out their pillows and lie down. They drape a blanket over the seats and make a fort, which means she can't look at them sleeping. She lets them curl up with seat belts buckled around their waists and tries not to think about the reasons this is unsafe. Emily reclines the passenger's seat and falls asleep as well, or pretends to. She's such a little girl. Such a small, fatherless thing.

By midnight pretty much the only vehicles on the road are tractor trailers. Frances drinks coffee and thinks about life as a long-haul driver, how uncomplicated it must be. How quiet.

She takes the first exit after the enormous bridge across the Mississippi into Memphis. Mud Island Park is deserted. She finds a spot under a burned-out streetlight at the far edge of the park. She wants to be close to the water, to watch the current under the bright moon and appreciate its vast wideness. Suddenly she's no longer in a hurry to get to Maury's house. She'll sleep for an hour or so in this quiet van with her tousled children, their mouths open, their bodies having begrudgingly adapted to these makeshift beds. The boys' fort has collapsed; Emily's pillow has fallen to the floor. She is dreaming. Todd stirs, and raises his head. "Are we there?" She shakes her head, puts her finger to her lips and he's asleep again, too tired for curiosity.

Frances slips from the car and walks down a short path to the edge of the water. The river is flat and slow and wide, entirely as she expected. A barge passes, its lights distant and comforting.

Emily has never been good with life's gray areas. She's a child: children feel most comforted in the presence of clarity about right and wrong. Had Frances's marriage worked out, it's possible that Robbie's easygoing nature might have had a positive effect on Emily. During the final years, Frances thought the two of them were even starting to develop a mild respect for one other. But Frances is not Robbie, and she's not about to try parenting her daughter the way Robbie

461

might have done. Tomorrow she will take a walk with Emily, maybe take her to lunch, leave the boys with Maury and Eileen. They'll talk. She'll clear everything up.

She smokes a whole joint. She needs to sleep soundly, to dull the effect of the coffee and the discomfort of the driver's seat and the heaviness in her gut. In the morning she'll feel fuzzy-headed and drained, but for now she needs the familiar numbness of her own finely cultivated weed. A little smoke helps her, it really does, to put things in perspective, to keep the despair manageable. She stands there for a long time, watching the stillness.

Emily opens her eyes and watches her mother at the river's edge. She does not need to see the joint to know what's going on. And when the idea to toss her mother's marijuana into the actual Mississippi River comes into Emily's head, there is no chasing it out. Nothing else can be done. She thinks and thinks and thinks about it, and finally she cannot imagine their future unfolding any other way. After a while her mother returns to the van and Emily keeps her eyes closed and waits for her to fall very soundly asleep. She waits a long time. For a girl her age, Emily has an unusual capacity for patience.

Lately, at home, when Emily wakes up in the night, she experiences a desire to go to her mother's bedroom and climb into bed with her, like she used to do before the boys were born. It's strange how strong the feeling is. The night before they left on this trip, Emily even got so far as her bedside. When her mother's asleep she looks older, and just as impatient as she does when she's awake. Emily didn't get into bed with her mother, and now she wishes she had. Her mother is at her most gentle lying down. Emily remembers that tenderness and suspects that getting older means she can't really have it anymore.

In the driver's seat her mother sleeps with her head thrown back, her stale marijuana breath filling the car, looking as though nothing could wake her up. Certainly the soft click of the keys slipping from the ignition doesn't disturb her. Emily is careful to turn off the dome light before she opens the door.

She moves quietly, looking where she steps to avoid snapping twigs or sending a loose rock skittering. She's a careful girl; she's always been careful, and not very well appreciated. Her mother admires qualities that are not in Emily's nature: boldness and action and risk. But caution is important too, and responsibility. Someday her mother will realize this.

462

For the hundredth time that day, she thinks about Miguel. It's nearly eleven o'clock back home; he'll be in his room, playing video games. When her mom was at the river's edge Emily swiped her cell phone from the glove box. When she's done with the duffel bags she'll call Miguel, who will tease her about sneaking off to call him. He says she needs to quit being so good. She should skip doing her homework once in a while, for example. Also she should let him do more than she currently allows. Let him put it in other places; let him do it in different ways. He's seventeen, he's reminded her. He needs to experiment. She's always thought her goodness is the thing about her that keeps him around—that he wouldn't find her so mysterious if she weren't so good—but maybe she's been wrong.

The lock on the cargo carrier opens easily. The two duffel bags are just where she found them last. They aren't really that heavy. She pulls them out and sets them in the dirt. As she's easing the lid shut, she looks in the van's window and there's Todd, awake. He opens his mouth to say something and she puts her finger to her lips. Obediently, he shuts up. She moves quickly to the passenger door and motions him forward, smiling at him, raising her eyebrows. He loves adventures. He's really not such a horrible kid when you get him alone.

She holds the duffel bags in one hand and Todd's elbow in the other, helping him quietly down the path, away from the van. At the water's edge she gives him the daisy duffel; he'll be reluctant to throw away anything with soccer balls on it. She tells him it's full of zucchini and carrots. He believes her; he still trusts people.

"But it's wasting vegetables!" he says, delighted. He tries to swing it, to get some momentum. "It's heavy," he says, his little-boy forehead wrinkled in seriousness.

"Do this," Emily tells him, and she swings the other duffel around in a full-armed circle, a comic display of softball-pitcher enthusiasm. Todd laughs aloud.

In her pocket, the phone rings. Emily slings the duffel bag over her shoulder and fishes the phone out. Miguel wouldn't call her mom's cell phone, would he?

"Frances?" says the voice. It's Robbie. She's supposed to think of him as her stepfather but really he's nothing more than her brothers' dad.

"No, she's asleep," Emily tells him. "It's late here, you know."

"Is it Daddy?" Todd says too loudly, forgetting they're on a secret mission. "Let me talk to him!" He drops the daisy duffel in the mud and reaches for Emily's arm, tugging at her shirt.

"Is that one of the boys?" Robbie asks. "What are they doing up? Where are you?"

Todd dances in circles around Emily, trotting like a pony. "Daddy! We're by the river!" he yells.

"We're fine," she tells him, and hands the phone to her brother. "Keep your voice down," she says, and for good measure knits her eyebrows in exaggerated seriousness.

Lately Emily has begun to understand the tricky nature of mistruth, of roundabout deception. In real life people don't lie to you straight up. Miguel doesn't lie to her, not exactly. It's up to her to discover things. She has a gift for recognizing a half-truth. Last Friday Emily was alone with him on the couch in her basement and he swore he didn't *mean* to put it all the way in, not without the condom she'd laid on the table—and when they happen, these halfway lies, when she confronts him, he smiles at her, confesses, and is chastened, genuinely. She holds the power then: she's the one who decides whether he's forgiven. But what if she got pregnant? Would she end up with more power, or less?

Todd paces ten steps upriver to investigate the trunk of a fallen tree, chattering into the phone: baseball, video games, yesterday's speeding ticket. The kid doesn't get enough time with his dad. Emily sits on a rock that faces the river and opens the duffel, hunching over the bag to shield it from Todd's view. She pulls out one of the bundles, smells it, turns it over in her hands. She thinks about the time and energy her mother put into creating this tidy parcel of drugs and examines the package, how neatly and carefully it's been assembled. She did a nice job, Emily thinks, and then wonders why this is surprising. She zips it back inside the bag.

"Here," her brother says, handing the phone to her. He canters back up the riverbank, breaks a twig off his fallen tree, and uses it to poke at a patch of mud illuminated by moonlight.

"Emily?" his father says. "What's going on there? Todd says your mom and Robbie are asleep in the van? And you guys are near a river somewhere?"

"The Mississippi," she tells him.

"Is everything all right?"

"Sure," she says. The bag of drugs on her lap weighs, she guesses, a little bit more than a sack of potatoes.

464

"Are you crying? Sweetie?"

Emily tries to calm her breath. "She's such a liar," she finally says. Juxtaposed against all those years of thinking of this guy as an interloper between her and her mother, and the despair, then resignation, she lived through after the arrival of first one baby and then a second, Emily's disloyalty is both liberating and horrible. She remembers a day at the mall when Robbie convinced her mother that Emily was old enough to have her ears pierced. While the girl at the Earring Hut prepared the piercing gun, he winked at Emily, evidently trying to establish some sort of conspiratorial rapport. But she rolled her eyes, refusing to give him the satisfaction even as she bounced on the chair in anticipation.

Robbie sounds now like he's holding his breath. "What do you mean?"

"You know what I mean. The pot is what."

"Oh, Emmy. Damn." She hears the impatience in his voice.

"How much is all of this worth?" she asks.

"Honey, this isn't appropriate. Why don't you wake up your mom? I'd like to talk to her."

"I'm sitting here with two duffel bags full of marijuana," Emily whispers. She glances upriver. Todd is still occupied with his mud project, having abandoned the daisy duffel on the ground between them. She opens the soccer-ball bag, turning away again from Todd. "This one," she says, "has six packages in it, and each package is about the size of a brick. Like the red bricks on our back patio, only not so heavy. Just tell me. How much?"

He coughs, clears his throat. "Emily, listen to me. Put your mom on the phone."

"I'm about to throw it all in the river," she says.

"About twenty thousand dollars," he says. "Maybe twenty-five."

Emily inhales, but quietly.

"Listen," Robbie tells her. "You know your mother. Sometimes her judgment . . . well. She loves you, you know that, right? But she doesn't think things through. She goes headlong, consequences be damned. Responsibility isn't her strength."

"Like it's yours," Emily says.

"Okay, now . . ."

She twists around to check on Todd, who is gripping the daisy duffel at arm's length, whipping it in a circle parallel to the ground, his little body the fulcrum of a centrifugal spin. He stops, staggers, gives her a dizzy grin. "Put that down," she tells him. "Don't touch it." He grimaces at her and returns to his mud and twig. You needed to watch Todd every second: he was the sort of reckless kid who'd dash past you and fling himself into the water.

The muddy river glows orange in the Memphis night. "You people think I don't know anything," she says into the phone. "Mom thinks I have no idea. I can read, you know. I understand things."

"Would you wake up your mother, Emily? Would you please just put her on the phone?"

"I know how to balance a checkbook, for example," she tells him. She also knows how much money he sends them and when it's not enough and when it's late and what happens when her mother can't make a deposit. She taught herself how to go online and examine the bank accounts and credit card statements. After school, before her mother gets home from work, Emily logs in using the password she created and watches in dismay, and sometimes panic, as interest compounds and checks bounce and the late fees pile up. Last month she sent MasterCard two hundred dollars from her own savings. She went to the post office and converted her baby-sitting cash into a money order. Her mother didn't even notice.

"I'm not all that awful, you know," he tells her.

"I didn't realize we were talking about you," Emily says.

Robbie sighs into the phone, an irritating burst of static. Emily wonders if he's a little bit high right now. Wouldn't a sober person realize it's the middle of the night in Memphis and wait until morning to call? "Are you all right?" he says. "Have you spoken to your mother about this?"

"We've been talking plenty." But last night at the lake in Oklahoma, when Emily tried to confess she's been having sex with Miguel, when she tried to bring up the subject, her mother purposefully misunderstood. She closes her eyes and rests her head on her knees. What's a kid supposed to think when she asks her mother, What would happen if I got an abortion? and the woman pretends she heard a whole other sentence? Is a kid supposed to believe the weed is to blame?

Behind her, up the path, Emily hears the car door slam shut. At the same instant there is a splash in the river. She opens her eyes and turns upshore to see Todd, only steps away—how did she lose track of him?—jumping gleefully on the bank.

"What a pitch!" he yells, and cups his hands over his mouth, exhaling noisily to create the sound of cheering crowds. "Ladies and gennelmen! The kid does it again!"

"Todd?" Emily's mother calls. "Emily? What was that?" She runs down the path toward the water. Robbie emerges from the van, barefoot, following gingerly behind her.

A pocket of air inflates the round end of the duffel Todd has just thrown; it looks like a pink-daisy lily pad bobbing downstream. *Nice toss*, Emily almost tells him. The current is pulling the bag downstream and toward the center of the river, closer to her and yet farther away.

Her mother rushes to the bank and stands helplessly beside Todd at the water's edge, her hands on the top of her head. "Oh no, no, no," she says. She crouches in the mud. The resignation on her face, Emily notices for the first time, is that of a person for whom despair is part of the everyday. "Shit," her mother whispers.

Todd claps his hands over his ears.

Emily drops the phone, kicks off her sandals, and steps firmly into the river, wet silt slimy between her toes, the cold a surprise. She flops into the water belly first, and in a dozen certain strokes downstream catches the bag in her fingertips just as it loses the last of its air and slips under the surface.

When Emily turns toward the shore, eyes bleary with the Mississippi, her mother's moonlit face holds a curious mixture of admiration and terror. Which seems just about right.

Nominated by Katherine Taylor, Tin House

RAIN

by KEITH ALTHAUS

from ORION

Rain is the great transporter,
even before it arrives
its perfume slipped under the door
like a letter, an invitation
to rise as earthbound
drops descend like weights
backstage, that raise the scenery
and lift us out of easy chairs
and easy lives, to where
it never rains, is always parched,
a room cut off and boarded up,
where a single drop
placed on those lips
could bring you back.

Nominated by Orion

AVE MARIA

fiction by MICAELA MORRISSETTE

from CONJUNCTIONS

She herself could once have imitated the notes of any bird.
—James Burnett, Lord Monboddo
Of the Origin and Progress of Language

IN SUMMER, IN THAT COUNTRYSIDE, there was no dawn, but a sudden sun, that lashed out over the ridge, broke itself upon the sharp peaks, and poured down like rain. The fields swam with wheat, and the wheat bristled and stabbed at the onslaught of the day. On the edge of the fields was a tree, and the sun boomeranged off the glossy leaves and went pinwheeling back to the atmosphere. In the tree was a bird, and the sun sank into its matted hair, and oozed on its scalp. The sun trickled into the bird's eyes, and the bird raised a scabrous claw to wipe it away.

The ridge to the east, then the field, moving westward, then the tree; beyond the tree, a village. The village had not waited for the sun. It had already begun to draw its water, rob its chickens, stir its coals. Its air was greasy with candle smoke and bacon fat.

In the tree, the bird plucked a caterpillar from a nearby branch. With a nail, it split the caterpillar lengthwise; with a gray tongue, it licked the soft open stomach. The bird tucked the body of the caterpillar between its back teeth and its cheek. A breeze blew the smoke from the village into the tree and the bird sampled the smell. Its eyes were hard and beady. It stared at the roofs of the cottages and hunched its shoulders. Its heart beat very fast.

The arrival of this bird had driven away the other birds. They spiraled around the treetop, screaming and hissing. The bird reached out its claws to them. *Tweet, tweet,* said the bird. *Toowit, toowit. Caw, caw.* A parent whose nestlings remained several branches

469

above the head of the bird screeched and veered in to attack. The bird in the tree flapped its wings wildly before its face, but did not ascend.

A boy led his goats along the edge of the field. Approaching the tree, he watched the birds buzzing angrily around the crown and thought of flies on a corpse.

The bells of the village church were swinging. *Bong, bong,* said the bird softly. *Din, dan, don.* The throat of the villagers were throbbing with singing. *Ave Maria,* croaked the bird, *amen.* The goats were ripping at the wheat in a frenzy, and the bird could smell the dust raised by the clogs of the boy as he pelted down the path back to the village. The bird swallowed thickly. The caterpillar had turned sticky and tough in the back of its mouth.

The sun rose in the sky and melted, drenching the field and tree and village. A steady procession swam through the syrupy sun to the tree. The rays slithered off the bird's mangy plumage and plopped in long sebaceous strings from its branch to the ground. Observing several villagers reaching out their hands and handkerchiefs to catch these driblets, the priest issued his reluctant pronouncement: the goatherd had in his exulting innocence erred; this was no angel. The bird shifted on its haunches and splattered droppings onto the ground. A sharp jerk and shuddering twist took place inside it, like a hand wringing a goose's long neck. It teetered dizzily on the branch, and squeezed its claws tighter into the bark. *Ave, ave,* whispered the bird. *Tsstsstssss.*

A gendarme strode majestically into the scene. The bird watched his row of glittering buttons; the gendarme himself was a dark velvety cloth against which the buttons were displayed. A box was placed at the foot of the tree, the gendarme mounted it, hoisted himself to the first limb, and, clinging cautiously to the trunk, batted with his stick at the leaves above his head. With "astonishing speed" and "superhuman agility," the bird let go its branch, plummeted down in a flurry of snapped twigs, powdery lichen, and dead bark, yanked off a button from the gendarme's coat, scratched the gendarme's face, pulled the hair from his head, and clambered back up the tree. Reeling, the gendarme lost his grip and fell to earth.

The bird scraped out the caterpillar where it clung like cotton to the cheek and gums, and tucked the button in its place. The hot metal hissed slightly as it met the flesh, and the bird was rewarded with a small spurt of saliva. The bird swallowed this in clucking gulps. "It's cooing!" cried a child below. *Coo*, whispered the bird. It tucked the hair of the gendarme up safe in its nest, at the Y of the trunk and the limb. There was also a hawk feather, a sheet from an illustrated paper, a dead moth, and bits of a withered funeral wreath, once executed cunningly in the shape of a cross.

Word was sent back to the village that the apparition in the tree was not an angel after all, but a freak escaped from the carnival. Half bird, half human, gender as yet indeterminable, screened modestly by foliage. But tantalizing glimpses had been caught of cruel black talons; hair covering the body, stiff and coarse as quills; teeth pointed and curved like a row of little snapping beaks. As the farmers left their fields and the shopkeepers shuttered their windows for the midday break, the crowd swelled. Some villagers made attempts at capture: a broom was employed, a scythe, several stones. A cat summoned to its duty fled spitting, with its eyes starting out of its head. Seed was scattered on the ground, and everyone moved back a few steps, and waited, but the bird only abandoned its nest and climbed higher in the tree. When the breeze stirred the leaves the bird could be glimpsed, its neck craning, its face turned up toward the sky. The bird observed the passage of the clouds, but saw no pictures there.

The head of the bird was roiling with lice and it sucked hopefully at the ends of its hairs. The edge of a leaf scratched back and forth against its ear. The bark pressed red and white patterns in bas-relief into the legs of the bird and the bird prodded them, watching them swell and flush and fade. The bird's palms were covered with thick calluses and seamed with deep cracks and the bird moved the palms back and forth against its cheeks to feel the scratching. After a time it fell asleep. Whether it dreamed or not proves nothing.

Around the dinner hour, the gendarme reappeared, escorting Mme. J. Many of the watchers had departed by then; mostly children were left. One had speared an apple on a long stick and was poking it among the branches to tempt the bird. The gendarme had a pail in his hand. Shaking her skirts and fanning her face, Mme. J. banished the children and commandeered the pail. She had a jutting shelf of bosom and a wide, gliding stride. Her voice was calm and even. "I'm sure it's the same one," she said. She placed the pail at the base of the tree. It was full of cool water, and inside it swam an eel, dark and sinuous as smoke. "If it's her," said Mme. J., "she'll still have the shift we put on her. Not that she likes to wear it, but she wouldn't know how to take it off. Oh yes," she said, in response to the gendarme's in-

471

quiry, "my husband was going to report it to the mayor in the morning. But we only had her the one night. She was killing the rabbits in their hutches, and we were ready for her, and caught her. We got her locked in the shed, and got some clothes on her, and gave her a chicken to mangle—she only wanted meat, and only raw. But the next morning she was gone. She broke the lock on the door and the whole frame was dented and scratched—chewed maybe, even." Mme. J. and the gendarme settled themselves in the bushes. "But as you know," she murmured, "we live seventeen miles away, and not a stream between here and there, not a puddle even. Poor thing."

In the pail at the foot of the tree, the serpent luxuriated, stretching, stroking its coils against themselves, rolling, and flicking its muddy belly skyward. The bird cocked its head and heard the water sigh as it caressed the eel. It tilted its head the other way, but the faint whistle of Mme. J.'s breath was all one sibilance with the slosh of the water soft against the side of the pail. The bird dropped to a lower limb. Its feet curled and uncurled. The bird hopped quickly. It fluttered to the ground. It huddled very still in the roots of the tree. Its face was in the bucket, and its hands. Its mouth met the mouth of the eel. The eel's tongue flickered. The bird bit down. The eel slithered easily through its gullet and curled itself in the bird's stomach. The bird's face was in the pail, its eyes were shiny and unblinking underwater, then the snick of the noose pulled tight around its feet, and the fluster of wings as the hood slipped over its head.

M'sieu le Docteur ran his fingers over the sharp shoulderblades that jutted from the back of the bird. Solemnly, he counted the vertebrae of the spine. The anklebones were pronounced, like vicious little spurs. He placed his wrist against the bird's wrist, and waited for its pulse to slow to his. He scratched lightly at the horny, twisted black nails that arched from the bird's enormous thumbs. The knees were buried beneath deep, scaly pads. The smell of the body was pungent but surprisingly sweet, like fruit that has fallen and begun to ferment. M'sieu le Docteur probed at the temples of the bird and felt the blood trembling inside its brain. The bird chewed nervously at its foot, but was otherwise docile. Age was difficult to determine; hair was present around the private parts and under the arms, but the entire torso was hirsute. M'sieu le Docteur tapped at the rib cage; the bones tinkled: a brittle, hollow, tinny sound. A flea emerged from the ear of the bird and raced down its chest and stomach, diving into its navel for cover. The bird cupped its hand protectively over it. The lungs were sound. Excretions were normal, considering the raw diet. Ocular and muscular reflexes were satisfactory.

M'sieu le Docteur settled himself at the small table provided for him and observed the bird. As it did nothing but huddle, squatting against the wall, its arms around its knees, its chin pressed into the hollow of its neck, he turned away his eyes, took up his pen, and wrote:

> Upon the apprehension of an apparent specimen of *homo ferus* on the outskirts of the village of S—, I was summoned to evaluate the medical condition of the creature, with a view both to its health and to determining the span of the years it had spent in the wild. With the exception of severe dehydration, the physical examination revealed no disease. Regarding reports made in the last three years of a bird/wolf/ape/devil-like manifestation sighted in the woods and at least twice in the village streets, the physical mutations—presumably adaptations to facilitate a life comprised almost entirely of running, climbing, and hunting—are sufficiently advanced to suggest that the sightings may indeed be assigned to the individual I examined. Whether a child now no more than ten, and at the origination of the sightings only seven years old, could have sustained its own life and defended itself from predators for such an extended period is a question not easily resolved. Yet it is difficult to imagine that this individual spent so much as seven years in civilization, as it has so far betrayed no knowledge of any social convention or means of human communication.
>
> *Human qualities:*
>
> The physical form of the creature is by and large human and female, though some of its parts are of exaggerated size (thumbs, feet, knees), and though it does not put all of its parts to their accustomed uses (scratches head with

feet; runs on tiptoe with fingertips stabbing the ground at each pace; approaches unfamiliar objects and spaces mouth first, biting the bed, chamber pot, and my hand gently but firmly, in a spirit of investigation rather than attack). If it is in fact not of an altogether new species, then its peculiarities may be plausibly attributed not only to its savage lifestyle, but potentially to a state of idiocy, arising from its isolation or perhaps the original cause of its abandonment.

While there is no evidence that the creature has ever experienced any meaningful interaction with a human being, neither does anything strongly negate that possibility. If it has no idea of human diet, hygiene, language, tools, or customs, still it does not shy away from people as an animal of a truly undomesticated species might do. I have been able to closely examine the insides of the ears, the bottoms of the feet, the spaces between the toes, the back of the mouth, the roots of the hair, without opposition. Indeed the creature is perhaps more cooperative than the average human patient of its age. Now that it has resigned itself to its captivity, its stillness when touched is absolute, extending perhaps even to the quieting of its heartbeat. It bears an unnerving resemblance to the quail about to be flushed, more silent than death, but ready at any moment to explode out of invisibility in a hysterical churning of feathers.

General bestial qualities:

The creature's strength and agility are so remarkable as to be perhaps entirely beyond human capabilities, whatever the demands of the human's environment may have been. A gendarme who made the original attempt to communicate with it found, to his disadvantage, that it could race up and down the trunk of the tree in which it was discovered with all the thoughtless ease of an ant scurrying up a wall. The creature was coaxed from the tree and apprehended, but broke away from its captors en route to the jail, racing blindly (hooded) down the street with such speed that several women reported that the wind raised in

474

its wake snatched the caps from their heads. When a mastiff was released to bring down the escapee, the creature bludgeoned the dog so violently with its fists that the animal fell helpless in the dirt, and spectators reported that the prisoner appeared to be attempting to tear open the dog's throat with its teeth, though the hood prevented it from doing so.

The creature has eaten a great quantity of raw meat, and was observed to be greedily sucking the blood from the neck of a rabbit it was given to kill. Offerings of raw root vegetables such as turnips and potatoes have been accepted in a desultory manner. It repudiates all cooked meat, cooked fruits and vegetables, and grains.

Although words were spoken to the creature in several languages, it made no response. Its hearing does not appear to be impaired, however, as the squawking of a chicken outside the window claimed its immediate attention. The creature was spoken to harshly, soothingly, commandingly, imploringly, and in accents of terror, but its expression, or lack of one, underwent no change.

Particular avian qualities:

Tucks head under arm in repose or perhaps fear.

Frenzied attacks against mirror.

Nesting: Interested citizens come to view the creature have brought a number of items for its edification and amusement. Some, such as candy, India rubber balls, and chalk, have been ignored, but others are forming a pile under the washstand, where the creature likes to spend the night. These include: a rag doll, a handkerchief, a rosary, a sack of marbles, a robin's egg, and a small brass bell.

When awake, in constant motion, hopping from bed to floor to corner to door to stool to corner to washstand to bed to floor to door.

Beats hands lightly and repeatedly on window glass.

M'sieu le Docteur sighed wearily. Dusk had fallen while he worked out his report, and he had had to light a candle. He laid down his pen and passed his finger back and forth through the flame. After a while, the bird came up and did the same. M'sieu le Docteur stroked the bird gently along the jawbone and behind the ear, and scratched between its eyebrows. The bird chattered its teeth and made a whistling sound in its nose. M'sieu le Docteur continued to pet the bird until he saw its eyelids closing, at which point with great reluctance he draped the hood over its head, and called for the guard to hold the hood until he had gone, lest the bird discover the means by which he opened the door to gain the night.

The carriage went hurtling down the long, smooth drive that led to the palace of the Duke, and inside it the bird hooted loudly and preened itself. It ducked its head to snap in its beak the end of the satin ribbon Mme. J. had tied around its neck. The curtains revealed in snatches the leaves on the trees glowing deep gold and brown like brass buttons. Their shining was like the ringing of bells, and the bird jerked against the silken cord that tethered its ankle to the ring set into the floor of the carriage. "Tsk, tsk," said Mme. J., and the bird said, *TtTt* and gently knocked its head against the carriage wall. "Now, now," said Mme. J., and the bird blinked at her rapidly.

The Duke himself, the women with their long smiles and translucent hands, all the scuttling little boys, and the strolling gentlemen flocked around the bird and adored it. Mme. J. and the carriage went rattling back along the drive, farther into the distance, until they were a small black dot disappearing into the orange forest that swelled and thrashed like the sun. The bird watched them shrink and vanish before it veered off the veranda and went swooping to the garden the Duke had created for it.

A giant gazebo was erected, arches woven of twisting twigs crossed at the top and anchored in a generous circle in the ground. These were painted with gold leaf, and a swing was hung inside for the pleasure of the bird. A ladder, too, dangled from the top, woven of thick skeins of silk, and tangled with fuchsia, monkeyflowers, hibiscus, and trumpet vines. Beside the ladder, secured firmly to the roof, was the small canvas tent where the bird roosted for the night. When the breeze picked up, the garden burned with the clashing rays of a hundred small round mirrors that were suspended from the ends of thin silver chains attached to the framework of the gazebo. The bird went mad at these moments, leaping with open mouth to bite at the daggers of light where they stabbed the air. There was a splashing fountain, stocked with green frogs that eventually bred and escaped and were soon to be found in every room of the palace, between bedclothes, under cushions, and on tables.

Now the bird began each morning with a cool draught of water in which grapes or figs had stood. It was bathed in milk infused with lavender, and its eyelids, nostrils, and lips were dabbed with Armagnac until its eyes were wide and bright. A bowl of hot blood was brought to it, in which, on Sundays, snails were placed. The bird's hair was brushed until it crackled and the strands rose up into the air and clung to the fingers of its attendants. The hair was plaited loosely, pinned at the back of the neck, and brought forward over the ridge of the skull, swooping down in a thick curl to tease the bird's forehead. The bird wore a brass bracelet on its leg, and peach-colored hose, and long tunics with sweeping, wide sleeves in shining colors. The bird was ruby breasted, green backed, golden throated, chestnut barred, and flame crested. The little boys made chains of coins and wrapped them around the arms of the bird. When it flapped its wings it rang like a morning chorus of a thousand songs rising out of the wheat.

In the afternoons the bird took lessons in dancing. It learned to spread its skirts and arch its back and hurl itself in a circle. It turned its throat to the sky and lifted its arms behind it. Its neck grew long and active, writhing under its head, and its fingers could spread in a circle until the outside of the thumb and pinky were nearly touching. It could hurtle forward in strenuous crouching bounds, so that its legs seemed to buckle sickeningly beneath it even as it was already ricocheting back into the air. At the end of a performance it could bow to the audience in midleap, its feet kicking out and its knees tucking into its chest. The bird could sink into the ground with the graceful startlement of a gasp. It could tear at its hair and throw back its shoulders until it was two or three times its natural size.

At dinners the bird perched on a tall stool behind the Duke's chair and was fed morsels by the Duke's own hand. When not being fed, it leaned forward to nibble at his ear or curl its toes comfortably against his back. When the musicians came into the hall at the conclusion of the meal, the bird stood on the stool and keened sharply. All the musicians agreed with the Duke that the sound was uncanny, and they always played in the pitch the bird's screaming suggested. As the programs wound on, the bird would quiet, squatting back down on the stool, clucking its tongue against the back of its mouth, and pressing its face into the Duke's hair.

The bird grew pale and weak not long after the sun went down, so once the meal and entertainment had concluded, the bird would climb onto the Duke's back, and the Duke would bear the bird out into the garden, where it would climb the silken ladder to its tent. The little boys would release the rope and the great canopy would fall and slither over the frame of the gazebo, blotting out the moonlight that might play upon the hundred mirrors. The bird nestled into itself; it twitched at the feeble disturbance of its breath struggling against its feathers, and listened to the slug of its heart striking out at the other smothering organs. Its feet were curled so the toe-nails scratched the arch. When the bird's eyes closed, it felt the brief sting of the rough inner lid scraping against the lens. It watched red throb and cool, tiny black insects skating across the color, until everything was mottled and dull like mud. Cracks traced idly over the mud, portions of it shifted as if something were tunneling beneath, or a foot were pressing from above. Dark blots came, like drops of rain; a green tinge suffused the whole. A smell of slime and plant life. A kind of tilting in the mud, as if the bird had shifted its perspective. A comfortable tilting, a more agreeable angle, the mud oozed over the eyes of the bird and pressed calmly on its brain. The bird suddenly felt slippage, a plummet, groped wildly for its wings. Then there in its lungs was the aftermath of a tremendous sigh, and the canopy came whisking away and the sun was sharp with the smell of Armagnac, and lavender, and frothy blood.

The bird had clung to the finger of the Duke with its teeth, with all the strength in its jaw, but now its mouth was empty and the present the Duke had left on the desk, a nest woven of gold wire and containing two warm goose eggs for sucking, had vanished beneath the hand of the Mother Superior. "You must learn to be good and obedient," said the Mother Superior, "and raw meat and shiny toys are just the things to make you agitated. Here we live simply. The habit you wear will be rough, to scratch the itches before they start, and the food will be smooth and soft, to calm your temper."

The bird did not eat the stews and porridges, the salted biscuits or the sharp red wine, and after a week they twisted it in blankets and fed it through a funnel. At first the bird screamed so that the attending sisters could not even hear the chapel bells tolling for prayers, and an exorcist was summoned. Then its throat grew so raw that the brittle shards of sound twisted and dug at its gullet, and the bird quieted. Thick slicks of blood formed inside it and lurched their way out, stumbling from the mouth of the bird in clumsy belches and then in thundering gallops. During these red effusions the bird made a sound as if it were trying to speak through a gag. It licked at the blood clotting on its cheeks and chin, but the taste was rotten. Once the Duke was in the room, making a loud noise, the nuns spiraling away from him like dry leaves caught in a wind. He had the bleeding haunch of a rabbit, which he held to the face of the bird. Everything within the bird leapt and shrank at once in a terrible convulsion. Something held the bird and shook it for several minutes. It felt itself go upside down, then inside out. Then the meat was taken away and the Duke put the tip of his finger in the bird's mouth and sat like that for a while before he crept away. Not long after, a man came to draw the majority of the blood from the bird's body, and this afforded some relief. The bile of the bird became watery and pale and the bird enjoyed a faintness like the sensation of flying. Then like the sensation of sinking. Its body was covered with bruises; peering down, it saw itself hidden in a rose bush. The bird was molting. The air of the room was crowded with strands of its hair; sometimes the breeze picked these up and carried them out into the sky. The teeth of the bird dropped gently from between its lips and rolled onto its neck like a pearly collar. The sisters collected the teeth and also the nails and kept them in a leather pouch.

A sister was always with the bird. Sister Marie-Therese watched in the early morning when the bird was gray. Behind its veil of shadows, she saw its features released, dissolving and shifting, sweetly and gently. Then the light would come in fragments through the tree outside, picking out the beak, which would grow in response, and the eyelids, which glowed red. The bird was naked and pale in the dawn, and came into existence with the advent of the light, the ruff of its neck golden, its arms green as the leaves through which the sun struggled to meet it. The bird woke when the bells tolled for matins, and Sister Marie-Therese would bend over to hide its plumage under the brown blanket.

Sister Marguerite-Marie was most often there in the formless, endless afternoons. She brought lumps of sugar for the bird, sliding them to the back of its mouth. The bird stayed very still, waiting, and felt the sugar rearrange itself, biting at first at the bird's tongue, then spreading, investigating the pockets of the jaw, and traveling in a long procession of granules deep and down. The bird could feel the sugar burning all the way to the pit in the middle of it. Sister Marguerite-Marie told a story about a girl from China who had a beautiful bird that she loved very much but that one day escaped from its cage. In great distress, the girl resolved to visit a wondrous enchantress and beseech her help finding the bird. On the way, she met various animals in distress. A cat was trapped on an island in the middle of a lake. A rain-dragon was lodged in the arid earth. She helped the animals, and they gratefully came with her to the palace of the enchantress. The enchantress herself was like a bird, a giant blue-black crow. Her palace was of blue and white porcelain, and every inch of it was painted with blue birds. But the girl saw her bird pictured on the wall as well, and she understood that the enchantress had trapped all the birds of the air, and frozen them in the walls of her palace. The enchantress was just reaching out her long claw to snare the girl when the cat leaped up and swallowed the enchantress whole. Then the dragon flew into the sky, and rained down water on the palace, and the birds awoke, and turned from blue and white into every imaginable and unimaginable color, and rioted in the air, and the palace crumbled, and the girl put her bird safely back in its cage and they traveled home.

Sister Marguerite-Marie told the bird a story about a great flood that covered the entire earth. One man built a boat to weather it, and brought a male and female of every animal that existed onto the boat. Giraffes and dogs and unicorns. But there was only one dove in the world, and it could not come alone, so it snuck into the boat under an elephant's ear and stowed away. When the captain discovered it, he was wroth, and threatened to feed the dove to the lions, but the dove begged to be spared. So the captain banished the dove from the ship and said it might only return if it came bearing evidence of land. The dove flew over the formless, endless sea, in which no fish swam, and on which no sun shone, so that it could not even watch its own reflection, and after a time it began to doubt its reason, and to suspect that there had never been a ship, a captain, or an elephant, and that it was and had always been the only living creature in the world. And the dove nearly dashed itself into the void of the waters. But at that moment a giant finger pointed out of the clouds in the form of a beam of light and it lit on a sandy beach on the far horizon, and the dove struggled on, and plucked a twig from a tree on the beach, and without pausing for rest or refreshment, veered back to the ship, over the exulting waves. And the ship landed there, and all the animals were saved, and in gratitude to the dove the captain opened his chest and fed his own heart to the bird. And so the captain lived immortal in the dove, which, being the only one of its kind, could never die, but which, having the captain within it, was no longer alone.

Sister Marguerite-Marie told the bird a story about a hungry jackdaw that, observing how well fed was a family of quail, rolled himself in the dust until he was brown and presented himself as a quail. The quail took him in, and fed him and cared for him, until one day the jackdaw was so happy and comfortable that he burst forth in his chattering song. Immediately the quail recognized that he was a jackdaw, and pecking at him mercilessly, they drove him away. Miserably, the bird crept back to join the other jackdaws, but as he was covered with dirt, they took him for a quail, and attacked him, and bit him until he was dead.

Sister Marguerite-Marie and the bird ate sugar together all through the afternoon, and sometimes she would bring leaves of mint or basil and they would eat those too. Sister Marguerite-Marie would chew her leaves, but, as the bird no longer had any teeth, Marguerite-Marie would roll the herbs between her fingers until the leaf broke and the juice sprang out. She would rub her wet fingers on the bird's lips and nose and behind its ears. The juice would burn like sugar, and the world would be wet and sharp and green.

Sister Marie-Immaculate watched over the bird in the night, telling her rosary. The bird's eyes were open and the dark pressed against them as Sister Marie-Immaculate recited the Apostles'

Creed. The bird shifted slightly in the bed and curled its toes around the blanket as Sister Marie-Immaculate recited Our Father. Sister Marie-Immaculate said a Hail Mary for faith, for hope, and for love, and the bird clicked its tongue with the fall of the beads. Sister Marie-Immaculate gave glory to the father, and the bird meditated on the Joyful Mysteries, the Sorrowful Mysteries, and the Glorious Mysteries. Sister Marie-Immaculate offered the Fatima Prayer, and the bird whispered, *Oh, my Jesus.* Sister Marie-Immaculate said, "Hail, Holy Queen, Mother of Mercy, our life, our sweetness, and our hope," and the bird whispered, *Salve Regina.* The bird could hear the hiss of the beads sliding on the string, the scratch of the thumb of Sister Marie-Immaculate rubbing the wood. In the hair of Sister Marie-Immaculate was the ghost of incense; it was not like wood smoke; it was not like the petals of flowers that have fallen. On the breath of Sister Marie-Immaculate was the rough smell of red wine; the cold salve of lard; the thick odor of beans, like a woman's sweat; the powder of the wafer, like ancient dust. Sister Marie-Immaculate could smell the wool of her own underclothes, damp from the steam of the kitchen; the slick of oil on her face had a palpable weight. She could just see, in the bed, the white of the bird's face, a shock against the night, and the black holes of its eyes. She could hear, in its stuttering breath, a wakefulness. She began again. By the time she came to the Agony in the Garden, she could tell from the whistle in its nose that the bird was asleep.

The Queen of Poland came to visit the bird, and they took communion together. The Queen was disappointed that the bird could not hunt with her, for she had heard that it was faster than a falcon, and that it had returned the Duke's prey to his hand; nonetheless, she caressed it extremely. The bird said, *Gracious lady*, and if the Queen could not at first make out the words, when they were repeated to her by the Mother Superior she was greatly pleased, and favored the bird with a handful of gold coins, which the bird offered to the collection plate, excepting one that it kept in its nest. A poet came to see the bird and recited the poem he had composed in its honor and the bird nodded its head.

Mme. H. was engaged in writing a life of the bird. The bird was able to narrow down its origins to Martinique or Canada. The description it gave of its migration over the dark, inchoate seas was not included in the published work. A man with chapped cheeks and flushed, delicate ears founded a new philosophy on the bird. His coat was resplendent with buttons, but he did not offer one to the bird, and it kept its hands close by its side.

A journalist visited twice, each time with a different companion, each selected with a view toward the appetites of the bird. The first companion was a child, with crepe-like skin webbed with blue veins. Even the journalist was tempted to take a bite. The child's eyes were trembling in their sockets with fear, but the bird patted the fragile skull and begged the child not to be afraid. *God has changed me very much*, said the bird, and when Sister Marie-Therese repeated the words intelligibly, the child crowed with delight and crowded onto the lap of the bird to tug curiously at the long, mournful beak. The second companion of the journalist was a soft, sugary woman whose flesh spilled from her like cream from a pitcher, bubbling out of her clothes, overflowing her chair, in a generous profusion of fat. This time the bird shook its arms about itself in agitation, and had to be removed by the sisters. Marie-Therese informed the journalist that the bird had been overcome not by hunger but by nausea, and that it no longer ate meat in any form, preferring seedcake and communion wafers to all other food. Nonetheless, in the journalist's paper there appeared a long article about the vampirism of the bird, with references to pale young novitiates, and the bird was forced to write a letter to the editor.

After the bird was able to understand years and that they were passing, the Mother Superior invited it to join the convent, but the bird with sorrow declined. It was understood to say: *The rosary is circular and its decades therefore infinite. Nonetheless, eternity is not long enough to expunge the sins I committed when I was in the garden, refusing to eat of the tree that would teach me good from evil.* The Mother Superior spoke more plainly, explaining to the bird that since the death of the Duke, the bird's income would not suffice to cover its board as a guest of the convent. The bird took a small flat in the 12me arrondissement of Paris and placed an advertisement inviting the curious to come and wonder at what the glory of God had wrought in a savage creature.

The bird arranged twenty chairs in its drawing room and invested in a wardrobe of black silks and velvets, profuse with ruffles, and with long draping sleeves. However, many of those old enough to remember the bird's apprehension in S—found the six flights of stairs too difficult to navigate. Children would sometimes arrive in a giggling band, dart forward to capture a black feather from the bonnet of the bird, and scamper away in hysteria, without leaving any coins. Marie-Immaculate, now Christine, who had left the convent, came on Sundays to take the bird to Mass, bringing baskets of biscuits and wine and pickled cornichons.

The bird often rearranged its nest, polishing its buttons and coins, and crumpling its papers tighter into little balls. It sat with its arms on the sill of the window and sang *Je Mets Ma Confiance* and *Frère Jacques*. It kept a canary named Pierrot.

The bird took long naps in the afternoons. It awoke in the slanted light to see the flocks of dust motes swooping and diving in the breeze. It could feel the warmth of the day wriggling against its skin, tucked beneath its feathers. Twisting its neck to look through the window, it could see saints in white robes and angels with interminable wings drifting and sighing against the sky like clouds. Pigeons burbled comfortably in the eaves and the low hoots of the bird as it yawned did not disturb them.

The bird raked away the covers with its toes and drew itself up on its knees. It would not get out of bed that day to pray. Its chin nestled into its breast and it opened and closed its eyes, watching the light tangle in its lashes. It started and hunched at the sounds of steps in the hall, and continued to watch the door long after they had passed, tucking its hands nervously under its arms.

There were fleas in the bed and the bird watched avidly as they flashed into existence on knee or toe or pillow, blinked out, then reappeared on knuckle or elbow or sheet. One had bitten the bird on the shoulder, and it gnawed with satisfaction at the little welt. On the sidewalk below, a cat was crying forlornly. *Miao*, said the bird.

In the air was the smell of smoke, beer, leather, wet cotton on the line, the stinging scent of the soap with which the girl across the alley was washing her hair. Darker, heavier smells: the overripe peaches in the bowl on the bird's kitchen table, the patch of yellow mildew sprinkled across the corner of the ceiling, the odor of the bird's own

484

skin, sweet sharpness stabbing through a musky closeness, like mud slathered on leaves of basil and mint. The bird's stomach growled. The nails of the rats scratched as they bustled around inside the wall. The bird pressed its very hot palms against its very cold face and felt the temperatures exchange. Its fingers were stiff and cold. Its head was alive with fire. The bells of the church rang with a sound like sun shining.

Nominated by Mark Irwin

I DIDN'T SLEEP

by MARVIN BELL

from THE AMERICAN POETRY REVIEW

I didn't sleep in the light. I couldn't sleep
in the dark. I didn't sleep at night. I was awake
all day. I didn't sleep in the leaves or between
the pages. I tried but couldn't sleep
with my eyes open. I couldn't sleep indoors
or out under the stars. I couldn't sleep where
there were flowers. Insects kept me up. Shadows
shook me out of my doziness. I was trying hard.
It was horrible. I knew why I couldn't sleep.
Knowing I couldn't sleep made it harder to try.
I thought maybe I could sleep after the war
or catch a nap after the next election. It was
a terrible time in America. Many of us found
ourselves unable to sleep. The war went on.
The silence at home was deafening. So I
tried to talk myself to sleep by memorizing
the past, which had been full of sleepiness.
It didn't work. All over the world people
were being put to sleep. In every time zone.
I am busy not sleeping, obsessively one might say.
I resolve to sleep again when I have the time.

Nominated by Richard Jackson, Dick Allen, Mark Irwin, David St. John

THE RUSSIAN

fiction by ETHAN COEN

from ZOETROPE: ALL-STORY

I WAS THINKING about the ass of a woman I'd seen a couple weeks earlier on 34th Street when Hirsch rang:

"Busy?"

"Sort of."

"Come see me, anyway."

In his office he said, "Guy came in. Claims his wife's changed."

"Changed what."

"Herself. Different now. Wants to know why."

"Changed wife: we do this?"

Hirsch shrugged. "He paid."

"Who interviewed him?"

"Burns."

"Burns can't handle it?"

"Guy gave him the creeps. OK, who's this an impression of:" he stared at a point in space. " 'Is *this* it? Is *this* it? Is *this* it?' "

I shrugged.

"Ray Charles with a Rubik's Cube."

"Uh-huh. Where's Burns?"

"You're a detective. Find him."

Burns was in his office.

"So this guy," I said.

"Yeah. Boris Kshishnev." He pushed a file across the desk. "Daffy. Says his wife's changed. Yeah, right. Probably won't go down on him. Or maybe it's now she will. Anyway, I told Hirsch it was stupid. Won't do it."

"How come you get to not do it, and I don't?"

487

Burns shrugged.

" 'Boris.' What does he do, opera singer? Spy?"

"Computer shit. Like everybody now."

"Not you."

"Uh-huh."

"Or me."

"No."

"Or Ken Cassidy." We still had Ken Cassidy then, coming in at night to clean. He had diabetes.

"Yeah. No, Heh-heh. Fuck you."

"I told the man. The man Burns."

"Yeah, but Mr. Burns can't handle the case. Too busy. It's been re-assigned. To me."

"Stupid. I must say twice?"

"It's how we work."

"Stupid. Maybe I chose wrong agency."

"Maybe."

He stared at me. "My wife is Evelyn. She used to be good. Happy. Do this, do that. Now she sits home and eats chocolates."

"It happens."

"Not her!"

"But it *has* happened. It happens. She's depressed."

"I see," he sneered. "You are doctor."

"Don't have to be," I shrugged. "Eating chocolates."

"Is not like you think."

"Yeah yeah. She fat?"

"No."

"So, could be worse. Ha ha! I'll be frank, Kshishnev." This was not easy to say. "I don't know what you expect us to do."

"Learn! Learn!"

"Learn what?"

"Source of sedness."

"You ask her what's up?"

"Yeah, sure!"

"And?"

"She say, 'Don't talk to me, you big fet fuck.' "

She'd had a point. From Kshishnev's being in computers I'd expected a small clever ratlike Russian like the guy now, Putin. Instead he was of the large bearish ilk that slumps at the kitchen table in

488

a sleeveless undershirt, shoulder straps overwhelmed by backhair.

"Well . . . we'll see," I said.

The woman Evelyn was attractive. I fucked her, to gain her confidence. In bed afterward I asked what was up.

"What do you mean what's up?"

"I don't know. You seem quiet."

"We have to talk, now?"

"I thought women liked talking." I shrugged, "You know, personality stuff. So it won't be just an empty experience."

She stared at me.

Later I got up and looked around. Didn't see any chocolates.

My write-up was short since I left out the sex part, not certain it was ethical. Hirsch read it and grunted.

I said, "What now?"

He shrugged. "Beats me."

"What do I do?"

"I don't know. Improvise." He seemed nettled. "Uncharted waters. Wing it. He's paying."

I went to the Harvest House—the lunch counter at the Woolworth's, 48th and Seventh. This was back when they still had the Harvey. Much more reasonable than The Fiddler, on 49th. I had ham and two eggs over with rye toast, which if you order any other kind with eggs you're an idiot, in my opinion. I put a piece of ham on a toast half and an egg on top of that. I drew the knife across to release the yolk—sauce of a kind. I ate the thing knife-and-fork. The toast bottom is crunchy even buttered, even if you fork-spin a piece on puddled yolk. And the rye seed gives the dish character. If you go wheat or white I don't know what you've got. Plate of shit, basically.

When I'd finished the open-faced ham and eggs, I peeled a mixed-berry jam and spread it on the remaining two toast halves. Figured I'd revisit Kshishnev. I sat there, munching.

I asked Kshishnev for the names of Evelyn's friends. He said Carol Ott was her best friend and he spelled it for me. I didn't need him to spell Ott. He asked if there was progress.

"No."

"Does she have private pain?"

"Excuse me?"

489

"Does she have private pain. From where comes the sedness."

I stifled a belch. "We haven't established that yet."

"When will you esteblish?"

"Look, Kshishnev, I'm a private detective not the bus. These things don't happen on a schedule."

"But you have professional guesstimate?" He said his t's funny, as if his tongue liked hanging out with his teeth.

"No. I don't have a goddamn guesstimate. I'll keep you posted."

"I married heppy person."

"Yeah, well."

Guy gave me the creeps.

"Hey, Evelyn."

"Oh. You."

"Don't get too excited."

"Yeah, right."

I found her at the bar where I'd first tailed her and picked her up. Daylight now, in there, drinking, alone. Have I described the woman? She was pretty but her skin had a layer of fat that gave her features a putty look, like she got up in the morning and slapped her nose and mouth on any which way.

I said, "When'm I gonna see you again?"

"I'm right here right now."

"There's seeing and there's seeing."

"Look: don't press it."

"I wanna press it. I wanna jiggle it. I wanna make it stand up and sing Rigoletto."

"Yeah yeah."

This went on some more, but nothing doing. I changed tack. "You married?"

"Who isn't."

"But it didn't take."

"What do you mean it didn't take."

"You don't love him."

"Yes I do. I loved him the minute I saw him."

"Why."

"Do I love him?"

"Yeah."

"What's it to you?"

"I'm a student of human nature."

"You're a student of female anatomy."

"That too."

She looked at me. "He's sad."

"Sad."

"Yeah. Unhappy."

"Unhappy. As in, sad."

"Mm-hm. Nobody's sad like the Russians. Before Boris I just hung out with regular guys. Sought solace in intercourse. You know what solace is you ignorant fuck?"

"I know what the word means."

"Because I've read and shit."

"No, *I* know what the word means."

"Well so do I. But it wasn't enough."

"What wasn't enough?"

"Have you been listening?"

"You sought solace in intercourse."

"Uh-huh."

"And you felt—do I have this right?—you felt an emptiness. So you figured, I know, I'll find a mopey-assed son of a bitch to pal around with."

"Fuck you."

"That'll put me right back on top. Who needs laughs, I'd rather bang Eeyore."

"You understand nothing."

"I understand that it makes no sense. Nobody understands shit that don't make sense. Hence the expression It makes no sense."

"Fuck you. I'm tired of you."

She was one sour broad. "You are one sour broad."

"Go fuck yourself on a pogo stick."

Carol Ott was hitting thirty, hard. When she answered the door of the house in Kew Gardens she had a kid hanging from her tit and, from the noise, at least two more upstairs. Children, not tits. She invited me in, polite but hasty, like she had to get back to turn off the stove and finish a phone call and unload the dishwasher and wipe some kid's ass and then slap a chess clock.

"What's the deal with your friend Evelyn?"

"Are you a friend of hers?" she said. She sat behind an oilcloth-covered kitchen table, her lap bearing the baby up. "She's never mentioned you."

"A new friend." I tried to ignore the softheaded thing latched to her breast. "I just met her at a bar and we connected. What a great person. I thought I should get to know her other friends." Carol Ott twisted the baby and his head lolled like a drunkard's. Milk-squirt arced from her cleared nipple, drummed forward across the oilcloth, and then retreated. As Carol Ott hefted for a new grip the baby's goggling head swung out toward me and then back, slamming her tit. His gaping mouth re-clamped the nipple.

"Cute kid."

"Isn't he? What do you mean what's up with Evelyn?"

"She seems sad."

"Uh-huh."

Some thuds overhead and a shriek. Carol Ott didn't react.

"What do you think Evelyn's problem is?"

"Well, you know. You can't barhop at thirty like you did at twenty."

"But she does. I met her at a bar."

"Yeah, but now it's desperate. We used to do it together. Party party party. Then I met Mark Ott and she met Boris. Twenty, OK. Thirty, you need a center."

"What center."

"A center. Like I have Mark and the kids."

"She has Kshishnev. Kshishnev's not a center?"

"Not the one she needs, I guess."

"Is that what I'm supposed to say? She's got the wrong center?"

"Say to who?"

"People who ask, 'Hey, what's up with Evelyn?' "

"Who asks?"

"I do. I just did."

"Who are you again?"

"I told you. Friend of Evelyn's."

She looked at me, eyes narrowed. "Is something wrong with Evelyn?"

"See. You just asked me."

"Who are you again?"

I took the train back to Midtown, watching the standees swaying like kelp in a tide pool. I thought about Carol Ott and her house infested with children. I thought about the human ear, and what collects in it. I thought about the time I'd gotten drunk up in Utica and staggered into an alley and lifted the galvanized lid off a garbage pail and vomited, and something moved inside.

Outside the subway, at the top of the stairs, a vendor shoved a paper in my face and I shoved it back. A block away a raspy voice said, "Got any change, buddy? I gotta get to Chambers Street."

"Why."

The man worked bloodshot eyes to focus on me. "What?"

"Why do you gotta get to Chambers Street. You'll still be a bum on Chambers Street."

"Fuck you. I hope you get ass cancer."

People.

The street was loud with horns, and heat waves rose stinking like selfish prayer. This was a stupid case. What even made it a case? Kshishnev saying so? With his English? Did he even know what a case was? Or a private eye? Or a mystery for that matter? Some Russian guy saying something's a mystery don't make it any mystery. I'm sorry. I know what a goddamn mystery is.

I ducked into the Harvey House for more eggs. Farm-fresh eggs, the menu said. The word farm was supposed to make you feel good. Maybe it does some people. My uncle Hal was a farmer in southern Illinois. My folks sent me there once when they thought I should have a "farm summer." I was ten. Mother still thought of Hal as her little brother and not as a deranged Vietnam vet with a chip on his shoulder the size of a Zenith television set. He'd sit at the breakfast table blowing across the rim of his coffee cup, empty eyes on me seated opposite chewing stale store-brand corn flakes. After breakfast he'd set me to mindless chores. Never heard him laugh but once. There was a pony on the farm; god, I thought it was the most beautiful thing. Big eyes, round belly. I crawled on my stomach under the fence to get to it. Uncle Hal was watching but didn't tell me the fence was electrified. Well, I raised my ass up crawling and got a jolt that slammed me into the dirt. Didn't know what'd hit me. Raised up again and got slammed again. Probably did it four or five times before I got the sense of it and wriggled out backward. Uncle Hal was laughing a hard barking laugh, the same probably as when he tortured VC. Asked me how it felt getting my ass dribbled by a stock fence. Said he didn't know I had a thing for farms. Called me a ground-humper. "Young GH," he said. "Romeo. RJ Wagner."

Farm? No thanks.

I would go tell Kshishnev there was no goddamn case. I didn't care if Hirsch gave me hell. I'm a private detective not a monkey clapping cymbals.

The office of the little company Kshishnev worked for was in one of the printing buildings on 23rd Street. Somebody at the desk said he was on lunch break and suggested I try Billy's. I went down to the street and east on 23rd and turned up Sixth and at 24th went inside. This was back when it was still there, Billy's Topless. You could pass a pleasant lunch hour. Gone now. All gone. What they've done to this city is a shame.

It was cool and dark. Men at the bar sat looking up at a waitress dancing on the bartop, heads a-weave like charmed snakes. Kshishnev was not among them. My eyes adjusted and I spotted him in a back booth drinking and I slipped in opposite. He looked at me, then back down at his drink. "Mmph," he said.

"Hidy, Kshishnev."

"You."

"Yes, me."

"Is my fault maybe."

"What is."

"Evelyn," He sighed. "You walk in nature. See beautiful strim. Mountain river. Water sparkles. You want to kip. Fill bucket, take beautiful water home. What you got now. Water. Not sparkle-water. Bucketwater." He went on about bucketwater for two more drinks. Then he told me about his childhood dog Novotny. They'd had to amputate Novotny's tail because he wouldn't stop chasing it, chewing on it. After the operation Novotny would look for his tail and howl. Seeing a garden hose sent him into a frenzy. Describing Novotny took three more drinks. Then he told me about a cat down the street. The neighborhood boys would roll pieces of Scotch tape and pick up the cat and put a roll on each paw. The set-down cat would walk in place, lifting and planting his feet "like man in deep-sea helmet." This was where he started to lose me.

When we left the bar Kshishnev was reeling. On the sidewalk he blinked against the light and turned to me and hove to, bobbing on waves of alcohol. He stared as if trying to place me and finally said, "You have a-chee-ved your brief?"

I sighed. "Kshishnev, I ain't achieved shit. I thought you'd worked this out, how your wife turned into bucketwater. Or Novotny or something. Look, I came here to level with you. We don't do this. For what you got they have marriage counselors, clergymen, shrinks. Scams, all of them, in my opinion, but it's a free country and even foreigners and suckers and someone like you who's both can get up in the morning and hire any damn charlatan he wants and there's nobody can say him nay."

He stared at me for a long moment. Then he swung. A ridiculous punch that his clenching hand grabbed from the air way behind him; and when I sidestepped, it twisted his body well round. I pushed his near shoulder and launched a fist into his belly. It sank in deep, flesh closing over it, and for a panicked moment I thought he might have the wherewithal to gutmuscle shut and trap my hand, making me his prisoner or perhaps twin so that the two of us would grow old together fathering separate families and pursuing separate distinguished careers but physically linked and dressing alike and posing for formal photoportraits and defecating into commodes set side-by-side.

Instead, my hand withdrew. As Kshishnev bent hands to knees and tried to suck air I smacked down with my other hand, knuckles raking his nose. It gouted scarlet. He half-fell half-sat leaning backward, wearing a puzzled expression, one hand behind propping. After a moment he swapped supporting hands and raised the free one to his nose. He touched the nose, looked at the hand. Blood on the fingers, little pebbles on the heel of the hand where it had borne his weight. He sat forward more squarely over his ass so that he could pick the pebbles from his hand flesh, nose still gushing.

I walked away.

"What'd you do that for? Where are you? Fiddler?"

"Harvey House."

"OK. You win. I'll reassign it."

"Reassign it?! The case is over. I just belted the client around."

"Don't worry, he's a nut. And he was drunk, he won't remember."

"Boy, you don't quit. Who would you put on it? Whitliff?"

"Yeah, have to. Ain't got but the three ops, Uh . . . uh . . ." Hirsch sounded funny.

"You OK?"

"Fine."

"Whitliff's an idiot."

"He doesn't assault the customers."

"Doesn't help 'em either. This case is my aunt's balls."

"Great. Then Whitliff can't fuck it up."

"You admit it's cockamamy?"

"Ain't it obvious."

"But I can't tell Kshishnev."

"You did tell him."

"When he's sober."

"No. Come on. Umf. . ."

"You OK?"

"I'm fine."

"Ah, fuck it. OK. I'll finish it off. I'll fix it—Jesus, Ed, Whitliff's an idiot."

"You're a champ."

"Chump more like it."

"No no, really. Buh."

"Are you OK?"

On the train to Brighton Beach I looked at the light-box ads for Dr. Jonathan Zizmor. Wart removal. Picture of him, white smock, white smile. Eyelids down-slanted, mouth showing the whole Flatbush Cemetery. Begging to be pasted one.

Evelyn opened the door. She frowned, seeing me. I tried to picture her in her nonfrowning period, back when she was mountain water. Couldn't. "Look," she was saying, "I'm not interested in sex at the moment."

"Tell me what's bothering you."

"You are."

"Tell me what else is bothering you and I'll stop bothering you. Listen lady, you're causing a lot of trouble. Your husband is hiring people to find out why you're sad. He wants you to be up, you want to be down, you're at cross-purposes. The two of you are constipated, if you don't mind my saying so. You're stuck. You've got to change."

She stared at me. After a moment she turned and walked away but left the door open. I took it as an invitation to follow.

She was seating herself in the living room, gazing into space. Her hands plopped into her lap and lay there like a suicide's effects. I stood like a dummy and after a minute I sat too. We listened to the traffic from Neptune Avenue. A siren. Another siren.

She spoke without looking at me: "Who are you?"

"Private detective."

"Boris hired a private detective to find out what's wrong with me?"

"Uh-huh."

She smiled to herself. "What a nut."

496

"If it isn't working, why not dump him. What is he, king of the Hottentots?"

"I can't dump him."

"Why not?"

"He'd be sad."

"He is sad. He wouldn't smile if Jesus Christ came back and declared International Blow Job Day."

"Fuck you."

"On a pogo stick?"

"No. Regular fuck you."

"Now you're just being contrary."

She sighed. More traffic. Somewhere on the far side of the Earth the Chinese were gibbering. After a while she opened her mouth and said, "You look at things, you know they have an inner gravity. You can look at a table. Something's in there."

"In there."

"An inner solid thing it has. That keeps it from—floating off."

"If you say so."

"If it didn't have the solid thing it wouldn't be what it is. It would be something that could change—like you think I ought to." She almost smiled. "He won't change. He has that."

"Kshishnev. Like a table."

"Table, chair. A sad thing. That keeps him solid. Keeps him what he is. At a certain point you realize that the sad stuff is what the world is made of. And you stop running away from it."

"You stay put, feeling sad."

"You don't feel sad, you're made of sad. Just like the table. You accept it. I was happy once, yeah, I guess I was happy. But happiness fizzes off. It goes away because it isn't real. The sad thing lasts. You look at it, you know it's real. And the more reality a thing has the more it pulls at you." Her jaw worked. "I can't leave him because all that weight won't let me go."

"He's solid. Like a planet, pulling. Newton, so forth."

"Uh-huh."

"Yeah. OK. Now I get it. Why don't you write a poem about it."

"What?" She finally looked at me, interested.

"Write a poem. Give it to Kshishnev. Then the two of you can discuss it. And then fuck or whatever. Problem solved."

"I can't write."

"Then skip that part."

———

I went to the office, bilious, listening as acids squeaked through turns in my gut. It was late, after hours, but I wanted to write my final report—a blistering indictment of Ed Hirsch. I was going to rip him for taking Kshishnev's money and mocking our charter. We are private investigators. We are not for rent to every depressive with a hairy back.

I got off the elevator and stooped to work my key in the floor bolt of the glass double doors. Bent there, I heard moaning. I flipped the bolt and entered and walked slowly past the reception desk. I couldn't tell from whence the moans. The odd light still on showed the leavings of the day abandoned to Ken Cassidy, who would come in about one. The moans continued. They shortened, hiccuping, into sobs, and then smoothed out again. They paused, as if to collect force, and then resumed.

I tracked them past my office, past the kitchen alcove where coffee sat cold and burnt in the pot, past Burns's office door open to show a Tensor lamp glaring down at an empty desktop, past Whitliff's cubicle. I went past the two closed doors—stick man, stick woman—and past the desks where the secretary and accountant sit. Beyond, Hirsch's door was half open. His lights were off but the noise came from in there.

"Ed?" I pushed the door fully open and Hirsch looked up from behind his desk. His shoulders heaved as he panted. His face crumpled like a football half-deflated but his eyes were wide and glinting wet. "Ed? What the hell?"

He sucked in mucous. He opened one desk drawer and ducked his head as he poked around in it moaning. He shut the drawer. He opened another and withdrew a small packet of Kleenex and pinched one out. He clamped his nose and blew, waggling thumb and index finger to cross-clear his nostrils. He said "Guh!" and his jaw hung slack as he stared at the blotter in front of him. He winced at nothing and looked up at me.

"You know that I am a Jew!" he wailed, and then breathed hard, insucks rattling across deep-strung snot.

"Yeah."

"And you, you are a Christian, of some sort?"

"Right."

"And yet we are friends, are we not? There is a connection? Something that ties us together, sharing, buh-huh, buh-huh, sharing feelings—"

I'd had enough of this nonsense. "What the hell is this about, Ed?"

"My god, how can *we* be connected and not me and my *wife*? She's a stranger! She's a—GLARRUP!" A flapping in his throat like a clutch engaging. A long outgoing sigh like the wind in high trees. Then his shoulders bounced and he went *hurfl hurfl hurfl*. He looked up at me, hurt, as if these noises were one more unfair thing. "Pamela's leaving me!" he whinnied. "She told me today she's 'moving on.' 'Moving on!' After fourteen years and two children!"

"Waitaminute. She's trying to dump the kids on *you*?"

"What? No no. She's taking the kids."

"OK."

"But for god's sake! *Why*?"

"Why what?"

"Why would she do it? A good marriage, a good life, all thrown in the goddamn trash compactor! Turned into a ton of baled *crap*!"

A good marriage. At the office Christmas party three years earlier Pamela Hirsch and I had had a few. We'd snuck into an empty office wearing our party hats and holding paper plates of Christmas cake frosted white and pink. I'd hoisted Pamela's shirt and smashed the cake against her tits and fucked her, my hat's chin-string chafing my jaw.

"Look. It's over, Ed. You don't dwell on the how come. You move on, like the broad says."

"I can't move on! I can't move on! I'm stuck to her! Stuck!"

Had the whole world gone crazy? That night I went to the bar I go to. I picked up a redhead. At my place we did nasty things till orgasm grabbed us and we yelled holy hell.

The next morning she was in her underwear at the bathroom mirror, putting on lipstick. Her ass hung out of her panties, as asses will. I slapped it. The slap surprised her and the ass wobbled, unclenched. She turned to me, laughing, teeth flashing like ice in a bucket. Man: that hair, those lips. I yanked her panties down and fucked her again.

Goddamn. When I went into the office that morning I felt like a million bucks.

Nominated by Zoetrope

POEM IN THE MANNER OF COLERIDGE

by MATTHEW ROHRER

from RISE UP (Wave Books)

Of that house—that was more like frigid rooms
in a dingy, linoleum-tiled hive
and was home to manic ex-cons
—let us not banish that feeling, there, that we were
a miniature Earth, beset on all sides
by waves of dangerous subatomic
particles of other people's unease.
All things pierced by neutrinos but intact,
and our planetary defense was sound.
Let us recall the corner bagel place
with pleasure as a spot to occupy
the infant & me when a nor'easter
drove us away from the splintery gym.
Let us drink to the collapse of real estate.

Nominated by Wave Books

SCARECROW

Fiction by BETSY BOYD

from SHENANDOAH

RANDALL SCHROEDER'S BEEN DEAD for one week when his mother calls to invite me for dessert and to look through his things and take something I like. Mama, driving me to their farm, holds her cigarette out the window. The night is cold enough to hurt your hands and teeth, and our heater doesn't work. Mama asks me again if I think Randall meant to shoot himself in the head, and I tell her again that I have no idea. I wasn't there.

Ever since Saturday, the day Randall died, I know it sounds dumb but I've been trying to act like Christ, to stop hating people and wanting to rule over them and show them what's what. Mostly, it's to see if I can act like Christ, which is a way of being better and showing them what's what—but a subtler way. I hated Randall when he was alive. He had bowlegs and a petulant look. He acted like a macho ass. But it worries me now to think how I reacted the night of the school dance, the night he kissed my lips.

My little brothers sit buckled in the back pretending to shoot each other with their fingers, the younger one, Henry, repeating, "You dead!" in the same tone a person might say, "Congratulations!"

Pressing her thumb into my thigh, Mama reminds me not to tell Daddy about the smoking then grabs hold of my hand like a best friend. Now and then, she acts like a best friend to me.

Mama's wearing a pale blue sweater, and she's done her hair in ringlets with a curling iron. She may be fat, but she looks so pretty tonight. I know it's all for Mrs. Schroeder.

Out in the country in East Texas where Randall's family grows trees to sell to Georgia-Pacific, people don't know their neighbors, spaced miles apart as they are. Each farm drive has its own name: "Schroeders' Cove," Randall's sign reads, even though there's no water close by. At night, the fields grow so dark the only guides you can make out are highway lines and silver mailboxes. It makes you imagine the houses have crawled underground with the rabbits. It makes you imagine the grownups are expecting something savage to strike but haven't told the kids.

Mama's anxious, crunching M&Ms from a jumbo bag, tapping another cigarette from her pack. She tells me again that it is inappropriate of the Schroeders to ask me over when I didn't know Randall very well, especially when Daddy already paid his condolences. They aren't even members of our church—Mrs. Schroeder just shows up to sing soprano solos in the choir because she likes to collect a tiny paycheck and get attention. Mrs. Schroeder used to be Mama's bosom friend way back, but Mama eventually wanted nothing to do with her. It's not clear why. One time Mama told Daddy she'd lost respect for Mrs. Schroeder because she'd taken up with Kit, who was much younger and "tried too hard when he wasn't trying too little." Another time she told Daddy Mrs. Schroeder wanted her to feel like a poor, fat minister's wife. That's why she'd brought us that high-tech new microwave Mama didn't know how to use to save her life. And those size-eighteen jeans from Dillard's that were too big on Mama, thank you, and even a Thanksgiving ham. Daddy said she was too sensitive.

Mama exhales out the side of her mouth, producing a straight line of smoke.

"You scared to go inside that house alone?" she asks me.

"Why, aren't you coming?"

Now my brothers are singing "B-I-N-G-O" in the backseat.

"B-I-N-G-O," over and over . . . .

"Stop, y'all," I holler. And they lower their volume some.

"I need to run to the grocery before they close and buy lunch meat and stuff."

"Now you're not coming in, even though you did your hair?"

"If you're ill at ease—"

She knows that'll shut me up.

My teachers write compliments on my reports cards raving over my curiosity—they say I have a facility with language but talk too much. I like to know everybody, at least a little bit. I like to try everything. I don't like to get bored. I solve puzzles faster than most. I want to solve murders. I want to be a reporter and a novelist. I want to set records in track and field and get famous, but I also want to cure diseases.

I don't have friends at school, in part because I like to compete to be the best and people get annoyed by my drive, in part because I wear beautiful thrift store clothes sometimes years out of style. Kids call me Goodwill, as if that's original. They jam death threats under my locker door. Sometimes folks call me the daughter of Satan when I walk past, which really makes no sense; I'm the daughter of a minister, for Christ's sake. They think it's sick I have one green eye and one blue. They laugh at my homemade haircuts. No one understands my unstoppable power of will, except me and the man I'll marry, whom I have yet to meet. I try to be my own friend like Mama suggests, but of course I want to get asked to slow dance and French kiss like other sixth-grade girls. I want love—to give and receive it.

"No, I'm not a bit scared," I tell her. And then I tell myself.

Mama eases her noisy station wagon out the Schroeders' drive as I scramble up Randall's porch. Before I have a chance to knock, Randall's mother answers the door in a pink jogging suit, diamond stud earrings and clean white socks, which just about break my heart; I don't know why. I tell her I'm Sarah Jane in case she's forgotten. She smiles without showing teeth. She says, "Come in." Her short blond hair, combed behind her ears, looks greasy, and she's not nearly as curvy as she was at the Christmas play. Makeup shines on her cheeks, and I can see the line where the beige foundation ends, leaving her neck white and vase-like. Her nose reminds me of a deer's, and of Randall's nose, small and sweet. Mrs. Schroeder shows me through the entryway to the living room, which is the size of our two-car garage, carpeted maroon, with curtains to match. A leather couch divides into segments like a tapeworm. Mama won't be back for half an hour, but I don't want to dwell on that.

"You've been on my mind, Sarah Jane," Mrs. Schroeder tells me. She sits beside me on the couch with her pink painted hands in her lap.

The quiet feels worrisome. I'd pictured a room full of video games and fancy electronics and me taking my pick, but there's not a darn toy in sight. The hands of the wall clock look like butter knives ticking time at half-speed. Mrs. Schroeder touches my braid to move it from my shoulder to my back, and I jump. Then she sets her face in her hands and waits as though she's considering sliding it off.

503

"Was he unhappy?" she asks, face hidden, her voice cracking high.

I need to go to the bathroom in a big embarrassing way. What does she want me to say? Here's Randall: Everybody avoided him. He was hateful. He was aggressive as hell. Unpredictable. Loud. He liked to take any risk. He held onto open car doors, skied the gravel and screamed like a bandit. He also bragged nonstop—Randall told me once his father was a singer in a real band with real records out of Nashville. His daddy never visited him in Texas, so who knows if that's accurate. I'll have to remember to ask Mama. He said his stepfather Kit would give him anything he asked for, including chewing tobacco (which Randall brought to school), because Kit got depressed and had to spend days in bed with the blinds closed, not saying a word. As a way of redeeming himself, and showing his love, he'd give presents when he felt better. He wanted Randall to like him and accept him as his daddy, though Randall vowed he never would. Never. Sometimes Randall was kind to me; sometimes he was aloof as an old possum.

"Kit, where you at, sweetie?" Mrs. Schroeder calls to her husband. "We've got a guest."

"Right down, babe!" Kit shouts from upstairs.

"Did Randall seem depressed to you?"

"Not depressed exactly, no, ma'am."

The night of the Halloween dance and carnival, I was sitting by the punch bowl in my self-designed scarecrow costume trying to say the alphabet backwards, when Randall showed up dressed like Freddy Krueger with a striped shirt and cardboard blades for fingers and started talking to me like he sometimes did, like we were misfit brethren, like we were a couple of ghosts nobody else in school could see.

"Scarecrow, right?" he asked as he poured himself a cup of punch.

"Scarecrow."

"You got to spend the night minding your own business if you're a scarecrow."

Randall sat in the folding chair beside me, chugged his punch and started whistling along with the song that was playing, "All My Exes Live in Texas."

"You look good," I told him finally, because he did. He'd gone to the trouble of putting modeling clay on his cheeks. His neon sneakers were wrong, but I let that go.

When the music changed to Norah Jones, Randall asked me if I wanted to dance. I was so stunned I couldn't think what to say. I felt my power of will diminished at this moment—I didn't feel clear-headed but weak. Dances are so stressful. Part of me wanted to dance with him—or anybody—but another part wanted to laugh in his face and shun him. Annette Hollister, the most popular girl in sixth grade, was dipping herself some punch at the same instant, which influenced my answer, to be perfectly honest. There she was in her tight leather pants and witch's hat, her carefully crimped straw-berry hair falling down her back, looking like somebody off the cover of a fashion magazine.

Just the graceful way she dipped punch made me want to kick her bony butt. Billy Davis, this cute kid with white-blond hair who moved here from California in September, sneaked up behind An-nette and winked at me to be quiet and not give him away. Randall shot him the middle finger, which was uncalled for. They'd nearly had a fistfight over a water-fountain disagreement during P.E. that week. When Billy moved Annette's hair aside and kissed her neck, she turned around and Frenched him without a blink of hesitation, with a cup of juice in her hand and everything. It was beautiful. Then again, here's me in my scarecrow costume, straw taped to my base-ball cap, the rudest boy in school hot on my trail, the handsomest boy kissing another girl.

"Well?" Randall asked. "You want to dance or what, Sarah Jane?"

"No, thanks," I told him.

"Why? Why not? I like your costume—it's kind of kinky."

I hear the stairs creak and Randall's handsome stepfather appears. He nods hey. Kit used to be a night manager at Sizzler, but I heard he got fired for failure to show up once or twice. He looks like a hero in a movie, a good many years younger than Mrs. Schroeder—I've heard my parents figure up the numbers—with double-long legs, a thick head of black hair, eyes the color of toffee and pointy cowboy boots. Kit sits across from Mrs. Schroeder and me, searching her like waiting for a cue.

"You look real pretty, Sarah Jane," Mrs. Schroeder says.

"Thank you," I say.

"Nice duds," Kit says, dragging fingers through his wet hair.

My dress is too big for me and bell-shaped, which gives it a regal look. I like the effect—I pretend to be a scorned queen when I wear it to school—but I feel garish now wearing such a costume to visit a dead boy's house.

"What kind of ice cream do you like?" Mrs. Schroeder asks.

"Any kind," I say, "except I don't like nuts and fruit chunks."

While Mrs. Schroeder shuffles to the kitchen to dish my ice cream. Kit tells me snow is expected. Whispering, he says I ought to focus on the positive aspects of Randall's existence—we all need to—and not the quote fucked-up parts.

"Okay," I say.

"You were his girlfriend," Kit says, winking at me.

"His what?"

"You must have seen the good in him."

On Halloween—I didn't mention this before—I felt quite pretty when the night began and Mama dropped me off. I felt hopeful. I'd designed the scarecrow outfit carefully, with tufts of straw fastened artistically over a pair of denim overalls. Mama let me wear her black dancer's leotard, which fit tight as skin and enhanced my breasts, underneath. Daddy wasn't sure I ought to wear it, but Mama made the case that it was okay. She let me wear chocolate brown eye shadow and drew dark stitch marks across my lips with eyeliner. I looked attractive, like myself but not, like a beautiful new part of myself standing in for my unpopular Sarah Jane self. Though I'd fantasized Billy might fall head over heels in love with me, Randall was the one who noticed.

Toward the end of the night, Randall and I made eye contact from opposite corners of the gym. We were dancing fast like robots to a song by Beck with a thumping drum beat. It tickled us that we'd acted robotic at the exact same instant. The gym was full of boys and girls from all three middle grades dancing their dances in groups, some confident and graceful, some sluggish and self-conscious, dragging feet back and forth across the floor. Others stood locked in couple love, their bodies creeping close together in spite of the fast beat. Only Randall and I danced solo.

As Randall walked toward me, he kept his body in stiff robot pose, arms bent, hands flat, and I started to giggle. Something in me wanted him to keep coming. I stopped dancing, crossed my arms and waited, yellow and purple strobes lighting up my smile.

After Randall kissed my lips, I took his shoulders and kissed him back with a loud smack. Heck, I thought we might kiss longer, deeper—I wasn't even concerned other kids were laughing at us. Somebody said, "Gross, look at Goodwill," but I rose above it.

Then Randall turned and ran laughing like he'd pulled a prank.

Something in me felt so stung that a boy would give me my first kiss and jog away that I started to cry. I stood in the middle of the dance floor and sobbed like a baby. I said, "You ass, Randall Schroeder!" Billy noticed—he'd seen the kiss and all of it—and he went after Randall, out the door to the basketball-court blacktop and tapped him on the shoulder. In a quick crazy moment, I saw him tackle Randall around the waist and push him down onto the asphalt face first.

Mrs. Schroeder returns with the ice cream and sets it on the glass coffee table with a clink—a heaping mound of chocolate with cookies arranged around the rim, but I don't even feel like tasting it. She sits beside Kit this time with a hand on his thigh. He bobs his other thigh fast in that nervous habit men who wear cowboy boots seem to share.

"I know he didn't have many friends. But he told his daddy long-distance you two were going together," Mrs. Schroeder says. "We were real happy to hear it."

"Yes," I say, "so were we, as a couple, Randall and I."

Maybe it's the Christ in me telling this tiny lie. . . . I don't want to be the girlfriend of a dead boy, but I can relax knowing that's why I'm here. I feel I ought to go with it.

The ice cream calls my name, and I spoon it up.

"Did he seem peaceful to you, at least, once in a while?" Mrs. Schroeder asks while my mouth is full.

I nod big, remembering how scary it was to see Randall and Billy tumble across the blacktop in a ball, pulling each other's hair like a couple of professional wrestlers. Randall started to pound Billy's face when he got the chance, after he'd managed to pull off his Freddy fingers. Billy cried like a toddler and begged him to stop, even though at least a hundred kids stood there either slack-jawed or full of terrible zeal.

After I worked my way through the crowd, I begged Randall to stop.

I didn't shout. I spoke softly. I said, "Randall, this is beneath you."

"He had a large spirit," I tell Mrs. Schroeder, remembering my father's words on Sunday. "He was active, always running and squealing, having a good time."

"That's wonderful," she says, her eyes ready to spill.

Kit gets up then, walks across the room and peeks out the maroon curtains, maybe to see if my mother has returned. Mrs. Schroeder and I look at each other like a couple of friendly dogs, wondering if they ought to sniff each other.

"Still no snow," he says.

"I'm sure Randall planned to ask you to the formal," Mrs. Schroeder says.

"Oh, yeah. I encouraged him to, but he didn't want my advice," Kit says.

"He didn't suffer," Mrs. Schroeder says.

"Karin—" Kit cuts her off.

"Yes, ma'am," I tell her.

"He went like turning out a light," she says, snapping her fingers.

I wonder how she thinks she can know that, but of course I don't say.

Kit doesn't want to take a seat. He cracks his knuckles, walks back to check the window. He's a jumpy guy, and that takes away from his cuteness.

"Mrs. Schroeder," I say, turning the conversation like a boat, "when are you coming back to church to sing?"

"I don't know," she says. "I may not be able to sing anymore for awhile."

"I'm sorry about that," I say. "You sing so well—so big."

"You sure do," Kit says. But not in a real way, more like he's not listening.

"I go out to the barn, and I practice in there—I can get pretty loud."

"You sing like an opera," I say.

"I was singing when Kit came to find me. He'd been in the kitchen making a drink when the . . . . We're not sure how Randall got the key to the gun cabinet, but he was so mischievous. Randall knew he wasn't allowed to go near those guns."

She starts to cry pretty hard.

"Yes, ma'am."

"You want to see photos of our camping trip?" Kit asks out of nowhere.

"Okay," I say.

"She doesn't want to see those old pictures," Mrs. Schroeder says, wiping her wet eyeliner with her pinky nail. "You want to see Randall's bedroom, that's what you want to see."

In Randall's little room, which is decorated in a dark blue nautical theme, several ceramic lamps cast a dim light on Randall's charcoal drawings tacked to the wall and a few album covers of a country band called "The Randall Parker Five." Maybe his father had been in a band good enough to leave some dusty records behind. Randall was excellent at drawing, it turns out. It makes me glad to see that he had such a wonderful power all his own, when kids at school, me included, considered him a hopeless punk. He had a talent he worked on every night—a world to walk inside. I look at detailed sketches of robots, dragons, racecars, horses, ships—everything popping off the page, like a professional artist drew it. There's a spot-on sketch of Randall, bowlegs and all, titled, "Self-Portrait." There's also a sketch of me with my hair in braids. Good likeness, too, large nose, one eye green, one blue—I'm wearing my purple dress and a jeweled crown. Around my portrait he's drawn an ornate frame that reads: "Not Goodwill, Sarah Jane." Mrs. Schroeder takes out the pins and hands it to me. The drawing is nice, but what I can't get over is the beauty of the ocean painted on Randall's bedside lampshade.

"He painted that lampshade himself with a little old kit," Mrs. Schroeder says.

The drawing slips from my fingers, and Kit says, "Oops-a-daisy."

I bend down to retrieve it and spot a cigarette butt beneath Randall's bed—Kit probably sneaked him cigarettes, too. Kit wraps an arm around Mrs. Schroeder's shoulder, and I want to ask him about the smokes, and I want to know if he ever let Randall fire his gun. . . .

"Lord, your mama's in the drive, Sarah Jane," Kit says, pointing out the window.

"Let me see if I can talk her into some ice cream," Mrs. Schroeder says.

The night of the dance, after I said, "Randall, it's beneath you," he stopped pounding on Billy. He stood up and limped toward the chain link fence like a little old monkey. Mr. Perez, our principal, had just got wind of the vicious fight, far too late in the ordeal, wouldn't you know? He scurried toward Billy lying there on the ground, blood bubbling from his nose, while Randall climbed the fence and dropped on the other side.

After Randall got suspended for two weeks, I stopped talking to him altogether. He said, "Hey," to me once during lunch, but I didn't feel like responding. He tried once more. One afternoon I watched Kit pick up Randall in his black Toyota truck with the sticker that says, "Support Our Troops." Randall asked if he could ride in the back, even though it's a long way home and you have to take the crazy interstate, and Kit said, "I don't see why not," like a real baboon. Like he needed all the stepfather points he could scrape together.

"Yes, you rock, Kit!" Randall said, throwing his books into the back and tumbling in after them.

"Don't tell your mama," Kit called, so Randall could hear. Randall waved at me real big from the truck bed. He hollered, "You want a ride, Sarah Jane?"

I rolled my eyes and wouldn't humor him with an answer. As they drove off, I remember Kit revved the engine and screeched the tires to draw attention to Randall, who looked about as happy as a pig in shit, if you'll pardon the expression. All the bored, worn out kids waiting for their rides watched Randall roll past, sticking out his tongue.

I can hear women's voices lilt then drop low like mating birds down in the driveway. My mother and Mrs. Schroeder are getting reacquainted, doing their best.

Sitting on the bed, Kit licks his index finger and polishes the pointy tip of his boot. I mean he does this for ages and ages. The gesture feels to me like the thing he's doing to avoid bobbing his knee or walking circles, but maybe I'm thinking too much.

"Randall told kids you let him play with your handgun," I say brightly to Kit, like making normal chitchat, giving him the chance to deny it. It's a lie, but I feel there's no way to stop my mouth saying it. "He said you showed him how to load it. I know he tended to exaggerate."

He won't say a word, hands flat on Randall's bedspread, eyes on the floor.

"Sorry, sir, I shouldn't have said. . . ."

"It just fired off," Kit says, snot twinkling in his nose.

I wait because he's still going to talk.

"It hadn't *been* loaded. But he'd loaded it. I taught him how—for his birthday 'cause he'd begged me—and he'd loaded it by himself to show me he could. . . ." From the doorway, I survey Kit's hunched form. I bet it feels to him like we're on a ship he'll never be able to hop off. I bet he thinks he can't get forgiven for this.

"Jesus Christ, I couldn't believe it was loaded. . . ."

He needs to say something more. He looks at me across the room. I try not to look away. I try to put on a strong serious face that says he can tell this stuff to a child.

"What happened," I whisper, not as a question but a sentence.

"A boy wants to know how to shoot, you know?"

I nod, keeping my face as blank and unsurprised-looking as I can.

"Day Randall turned eleven, I took him into the woods, showed him how to load a twenty-two, said, 'Here, you try it.' But he didn't get it right. Dropped the gun on his sneaker. I said, 'Randy, that's the easy part,' trying to be funny but it didn't go over. He started acting nasty, and I said we'd better get on home."

Kit swallows. His Adam's apple bobs to the top of his throat. I want to shift my weight to my opposite hip, but I'm afraid to move a muscle and interrupt.

"Randall sulked for weeks 'cause I'd curtailed our hunting expedition. So me and him cooked up a deal: Next time Karin heads to choir we'll mess around in the woods, kill us some frogs, knock down Coke cans, whatever."

I try not to breathe too deeply, but I can hear my air going in and out.

"Karin's out in the barn singing, getting ready to go to church. I get the gun from the cabinet, lock it, plant the key at the bottom of my sock drawer, which, duh, Randall already knew damn well that's where I kept it, I guess. . . . Get the bullets from my desk. I go find Randall and ask, 'Hey, you want to load this thing or what?' I say it real cheerful and supportive with a smile. I mean we're excited to go into the woods, right?"

As he talks faster, his Adam's apple darts like it's coming off a slingshot.

"I go to Randall, 'Let me give you a refresher course first off on how to load.' And Randall laughs to himself. He has such a mischievous look on that face of his, you know? Like I should smell something's up, but I fucking don't. . . ."

Kit looks to me for confirmation, and I realize my mouth's hanging open.

"Not just mischievous," Kit says, "but proud . . . and joyful. Makes me happy he's happy, too, and allowing me to see the happiness in him. I say, 'Randall Schroeder, you're under arrest here today, son,' and point the gun at his little round face."

Kit is crying now, his lips forming a pale pink heart when he lets the tears come. It makes his voice jump high on certain words.

"It wasn't loaded, no way in hell! How? I wanted him to laugh till he peed his pants. You're under arrest! I don't remember . . . when did I pull the trigger, clowning? I can't see that part. I just remember how happy Randy looked one second but scared the next. For a millisecond, he looked scared. . . ."

511

Kit holds his knees beneath his chin like a kid. He's trembling, teeth knocking as if he's cold. Now he's not crying, just staring down. I don't know what to do next.

"You want me to tell Mrs. Schroeder for you?"

They're my words, but they surprise me.

Kit searches the ceiling, which is cracked in one spot. I slip off my Sunday shoes and walk toward him and climb on the bed, not to comfort him, because I wouldn't quite know how. I stand on the bed and pull the tacks from Randall's self-portrait because that's the drawing I want most—it's the best.

As I roll the picture up, I tell Randall something without words. I wanted him to like me, however much torment it involved. And I wish I'd been sweeter, even when he wasn't. I suppose it's the same thing I told him with my eyes the night I wore the sexy dancer's leotard, and he heard me and came to me across the gym floor.

"You want me to tell her?" I say to Kit, after I hop down and buckle my shoes.

He unfolds his long legs.

"I've tried, darlin'. I got to try again after you go home."

Kit scrubs his boot, stops, and tries to laugh one small laugh the way people will when they receive a cut or a burn—as if to say, "Look at that!" I'm frightened, but not of Kit exactly. He doesn't mean me any harm. Mama's car is still running in the drive. She's telling Karin something that takes time. It's only now I think to lean in and give Kit a hug, maybe the kind that sort of hurts or maybe just a quick one like ladies do after church.

Nominated by Jeffrey Hammond

GHOSTS

fiction by CHARLES BAXTER

from PLOUGHSHARES

O<small>UT ON THE FRONT LAWN</small>, Melinda was weeding her father's garden with a birdlike metal claw when a car drifted up to the curb. A man with brown hair highlighted with blond streaks got out on the driver's side. He stood still for a moment, staring at the house as if he owned it and was mulling over possible improvements. In his left hand he held an apple with teeth marks in it, though the apple was still whole. Melinda had never set eyes on the guy before. Her father's house was located in an affordable but slightly rundown city neighborhood with its share of characters. They either gawked at you or wouldn't meet your gaze. Many of them were mutterers who deadwalked their way past other pedestrians in pursuit of their oddball destinations. She returned to her weeding.

"Hot day," the man said loudly, as if comments on the weather might interest her. Melinda glanced at him again. With a narrow Eric Claptonish face, and dressed in blue jeans and a plain white shirt, he was on his way to handsomeness without quite arriving there. The apple was probably an accessory for nerves, like a chewed pencil behind the ear.

The baby monitor on the ground beside her began to squawk.

"I have to go inside," Melinda said, half to herself. She dropped her metal claw, rubbed her hands to get some of the topsoil off, and hurried into the house, taking the steps two at a time. Upstairs, her nine-month-old son, Eric, lay fussing in his crib. With dirt still under her fingernails, she picked him up to kiss him and caught a whiff of wet diaper. At the changing table, she raised her son's legs with one hand and removed the diaper with the other while she observed the stranger advancing up the front walk toward the entryway. The doorbell rang, startling the baby and making his arms quiver. Melinda called over to her father, whose bedroom was across the hall, to alert him about the stranger. Her father didn't answer. Sleep often captured him these days and absented him for hours.

She pinned the clean diaper together, and with slow tenderness brought Eric to her shoulder. She smoothed his hair, the same shade of brown as her own, and at that moment the man who had been standing outside appeared in front of her in the bedroom doorway, smiling dreamily, still holding the bitten apple.

"I used to live here," the man said quietly, "when I was little. This was my room when I was small." After emphasizing the last word with a strange vehemence, he seemed to be surveying the walls and the ceilings and the floors and the windows until at last his gaze fell on Eric. The baby saw him and instead of screaming held out his arm.

"Jesus. Who are you?" Melinda said. "What the hell are you doing up here?"

"Yes, I'm sorry," the man said. "Old habits die hard." The baby was now tugging downward at Melinda's blouse buttons, one after the other, which he did whenever he was hungry. "I heard him crying," the man said. "I thought I might help. Is that your father?" He pointed toward the second bedroom, where Melinda's father dozed, his head slumped forward, a magazine in his lap.

"Yes, it is. *He* is," Melinda said. "Now please leave. I don't know you. You're a trespasser. You have serious boundary issues. You have no right to be here. Please get the fuck out. Now." The baby was staring at the man. "I've said 'please' twice, and I won't say it again."

"Quite correct," the man said, apparently thinking this over. "I really *don't* have any right to be here." He made a noise in his throat like a sheep-cough. He had the unbudging calm of a practiced intruder. "Truly I didn't mean to scare you. It's just that I used to live here. I used to *be* here." Holding the apple in his left hand, he held out his index finger to Eric, and the baby, distracted from the button project, grabbed it. The man loosened the baby's grip, turned around, and began to walk down the stairs. "If I told you everything about this house," he said as he was leaving, "and all the things in it, you wouldn't live here. I'm sorry if I frightened you."

She followed him. From the landing she watched him until he had crossed the threshold and was halfway back to his car. Then he stopped, turned around, and said in a loud voice, a half-shout, "Are you desperate? You look kind of desperate to me." He waited in the same stock-still posture she had seen on him earlier. He seemed to be in a state of absolute concentration on something that was not there. People were getting into this style nowadays; really, nothing could outdo the urban zombie affect. It was post-anxiety. It promised a kind of death you could live with. He was waiting eternally for her to answer and wouldn't move until she replied.

"Yes. No," she called through the screen door. "But that's no business of yours."

"My name's Augenblick," the man said, just before he got into his car. "Edward Augenblick. Everyone calls me 'Ted.' And I won't bother you again. I left a business card in the living room, though, if you're curious about this house." He turned one last time toward her front screen door, behind which she was now standing. "I'm not dangerous," he said, holding his apple. "And the other thing is, I *know* you."

The car started—it purred expensively, making a sound like a diesel sedan, but Melinda had never known one brand of car from another, they were all just assemblages of metal to her, and he, this semi-handsome person who said he was Edward Augenblick, whoever that was, and the car, the two of them, the human machine and the actual machine, proceeded down the block in a low chuckling putter, turned right, and disappeared.

Picking up the baby, she went out to gather up her trowel and the birdlike metallic weeder. She would leave the weeds where they were, for now. Doing another sort of chore might conceivably restore her calm.

After taking the tools back to the garage, she surveyed her father's things scattered on the garage's left-hand side, which now served mostly as a shed. You could get a car in there on the right-hand side if you were very careful. Castoff fishing poles, broken flashlights, back issues of *American Record Guide* and *Fanfare*, operas and chamber music on worn-out vinyl, and more lawn and garden implements that gave off a smell of soil and fertilizer—everything her father didn't have the heart to throw away had been dumped here into a memory pile in the space where the other car, her mother's, used to be. Melinda put her gardening implements on a tool shelf next to a can of motor oil for the lawn mower, and she bowed her head. When she did, the baby grabbed at her hair.

She wasn't desperate. The almost-handsome stranger had got that particular detail wrong. A man given to generalizations might launch into nonsense about desperation, seeing a single mom with a baby boy, the two of them living in her father's house, temporarily. Eric pulled hard at her bangs. She was trembling. Her hands shook. The visitation felt like . . . like what? Like a little big thing—a micro-rape.

She had grown up in this house; he hadn't. It was that simple.

As if taking an inventory to restore herself, she thought of the tasks she had to perform: her property taxes would come due very soon, and she would have to pay them on her own house across town, where she would be residing this very minute if her father weren't in recovery from his stroke. She imagined it: her arts-and-crafts home stood empty (of her and of Eric) on its beautiful wooded lot, with a decorative rose arbor in the backyard, climbing in spite of her, in her absence. She missed its orderly clean lines and its nursery and its mostly empty spaces and what it required of her.

"Desperate"—the nerve of the guy.

Over there, at her own house, she would not be susceptible to the visitations of strangers. Over there, she would be walking distance from a local college where she taught Spanish literature of the nineteenth century—her specialty being the novels of Pérez Galdós. Over there, she was on leave just now, during her father's convalescence, while she lived here, the house of her childhood.

Looking at her father's ragtag accumulations in the garage, she worried at a pile of books with her foot. The books leaned away from her, and the top three volumes (*Gatsby*, Edith Wharton, and Lloyd C. Douglas) fell over and scattered. The baby laughed.

These garage accumulations exemplified a characteristic weakness of the late middle-aged, the broken estate planning of all the doddering Lear-like fathers. Still holding Eric, she sorted the books and restacked them.

Melinda's ex-husband had been a great fan of *Gatsby*. He loved fakery. He had even owned a pair of spats and a top hat that he had purchased at an antique clothing store. He had been the catalyst for a brief trivial marriage Melinda had committed herself to during graduate school. A month or so ago at a party where, slightly drunk on the chardonnay—she shouldn't have been drinking, she knew, she was still nursing the baby—she was telling funny stories about herself, and for a few moments, she hadn't been able to remember her ex-husband's name. Anyway, he was just an ex-husband. Now that she had the baby, solitude and its difficulties no longer troubled her. Her child had put an end to selfish longings. And besides—she was gazing at her father's old *National Geographics*—she had the languages. She spoke four of them including Catalan, which no one over here in the States spoke, ever; most Americans didn't seem to have heard of it. And of course they didn't know where it was spoken. Or why.

Her languages were a charm against loneliness; they gave her a kind of imaginary community. The benevolent spirits came to her in dreams and spoke in Catalan.

During her junior year abroad she had lived in Madrid for a few months and then in Barcelona, where she had acquired a Catalan boyfriend who had taught her the language during the times when he prepared meals for her in his small apartment kitchen—standard fare, paella or fried sausage-and-onions, which in his absentminded ardor he often burned. He gave her little drills in syntax and the names of kitchen appliances. He took her around Barcelona and lectured her about its history, the Civil War, the causes for the bullet holes still visible in certain exterior walls.

He had told her that anyone could learn Spanish, but that she, a stupendously unique and beautiful American girl, must learn Catalan, so she did. What a charming liar he'd been.

Time passed, she returned to the States, got her degrees, and then eighteen months ago, when she had taken a college group to Barcelona for a week, she had met up again with him, this ex-lover, this Jordi, and they had gone out to a tapas bar where she had spoken Catalan (with her uncertain grammar, she sounded, Jordi said, like a pig farmer's wife). At least with her long legs, her sensitive face, and her Catalan, she wouldn't be taken for a typical American, recognizable for innocence and obesity. Then she and Jordi went back to his apartment, a different apartment by now, larger than the one they had spent time in as students, this one near the Gaudí cathedral. Jordi's wife was away on a business trip to Madrid. Melinda and Jordi made love in the living room so as not to defile his marriage bed. Out of the purity of their nostalgia, they came at the same time. He had used a condom, but something happened, and that had been the night when her son was conceived.

She had never told Jordi about her pregnancy. He possessed a certain hysterical formality and would have been scandalized. As the father, he would never permit a Scandia-American name like "Eric" to be affixed to his child. God, he would think, had intervened. Sperm penetrating the condom would be so much like the immaculate conception that Jordi, a Catholic, would have trouble explaining it away. And because he wept easily, he would have first wept and then talked, the talk accompanied by his endearing operatic gestures. The sanctity of life! The whatever of parenthood. He had a tendency to make pronouncements, like the Pope. Or was this Spanish in nature? A Catalan tendency? A male thing? Or just Jordi? Melinda sometimes got her stereotypes confused.

Anyway, her news about the baby would have in all likelihood destroyed his marriage, an arrangement that Melinda supposed was undoubtedly steady, in a relaxed Euro sort of way, despite Jordi's one-off infidelity that particular night, with her.

Maybe he was habitually unfaithful. What was a married man doing with a condom in the drawer of the bedside table? Hidden but in plain view? Did husbands use condoms when making love to their wives? It seemed defeatist.

It was what it was. Still, she had loved Jordi once. She would say to her Catalan friends, "Have you seen his eyes, and those eyelashes?"—the most beautiful brown eyes she had ever seen on a man. He had other qualities difficult to summarize. All the same, men, at least the ones she had known, including Jordi, were a long-term nuisance, a drain on human resources. Whenever intimacy threatened, they often seemed unexpectedly obtuse. If you were going to couple with straight men—and what choice did you have?—you often had to deal with their strange semicomic fogs afterwards. Jordi snored and after lovemaking clipped his toenails. To quote one of them, the bill always came.

Anyway, she was not desperate. Melinda roused herself from her reverie. Augenblick! The stranger had got that part wrong, about the desperation.

She went back upstairs. She put Eric into his crib. Standing there, the baby occupied himself by listening to a white-throated sparrow singing outside the window. Across the hall, her father sat staring at his dresser. It had been positioned beneath family pictures—Melinda, her brother, her mother, and her father—hung in a photo

518

cluster where he could see them as he made his heroic post-stroke efforts to dress and to greet the morning. Behind the pictures was the ancient wallpaper with green horizontal stripes. He turned toward her, and the right side of his face smiled at her.

"Do you hear it?" he asked.

She waited. Hear what? The sparrow? He wouldn't be asking about that. "No," she said; the room was quite silent. Lately her father had been suffering from music hallucinations, what he called *ear worms*, and she wasn't sure whether to grant him his hallucinations or not. Did the pink elephant problem grow larger whenever, being affable, you agreed that there was indeed a pink elephant right outside the door, or shambling about in the street? "What is it? What do you hear?"

"Somebody far away, practicing," he told her. "A violinist. She's doing trills and double-stops. She's practicing someone-or-other's concerto in D. You really don't hear it?" Her father had not been a professional musician, but he had always had perfect pitch. If he heard music in D major, then that was the key signature, hallucination or not.

In the silent room, Melinda gazed down at her father, at his thinning gray hair, the food stains scattered on his shirt, the sleepy, half-withdrawn look in his eyes, the magazine now on the floor, the untied shoelaces, the trouser zipper imperfectly closed, the mismatched socks, the shirt with the buttons in the wrong buttonholes, the pre-cancerous blotches on his face, the half-eaten muffin spread with margarine nearby on the side table, and she was so overcome with a lifelong affection for this calm decent man that she felt faint for a moment. Her soul left her body and then came back in an instant. "Oh, wait," she said suddenly. "Yup. I do hear it. It's very soft. From across the street. You know, it's who, that scary brilliant teenager, that Asian girl, what's her name, Maria Chang. And I know who wrote that music, too."

"You do?"

"Sure," Melinda said. "It's Glazunov. Alexander Glazunov. It's the Glazunov concerto for violin in D major." She was making it all up as she went along.

"Yes," her father said. "Glazunov. The teacher of Shostakovich. That must be right." He smiled again at her. "But that concerto is in A, baby doll." Turning his head to face her at a strange angle, he

519

asked, "Who was that person who j-j-j-j-just came to the door? Did he come upstairs? Did he watch me? Did he come for me? Was it death? I was half asleep."

"An intruder," she said. "Somebody who said his name was Augenblick."

"Well, that's almost like death. What'd he want?"

"He said he used to live here. As a baby or something."

"Impossible. I know who I bought this house from thirty-five years ago, and it wasn't anybody by that name. Besides, that's not his real name. It's German. It means . . ."

"Blink of an eye," Melinda said. "An instant."

"Right. But he's lying to you. I never heard of any German person named Augenblick. It's a fiction, that name. There's no such name in German. It's total bullshit." He waved his hand dismissively. Since his stroke, her father had started to employ gutterisms in his day-to-day speech. His new degraded vocabulary was disconcerting. His mind had suffered depreciation. She didn't like obscenity from him; it didn't match his character, or what remained of it.

Her father's potted plant in the corner needed watering—its leaves were shriveling. Lately she had become a caretaker: Eric, and her father, and the lawn and garden out in front, and her father's house, and the plants in it—and if she weren't careful, that caretaking condition might become permanent, she would move into permanent stewardship, they would be her accumulations, and they would pile up and surround her. The present would dry up and disappear, except for the baby, and there would be nothing else around her except the past.

Downstairs on a side table was a business card.

Edward Augenblick
Investment Counselor
"Fortune Favors the Few"
email: eyeblink@droopingleaf.com

Anger spat up from somewhere near her stomach. "Fortune favors the few"! Damn him. And this zealotry from an intruder. At once, the languages roused themselves, spewing out their local-color bile. First, the Catalan. *¡Malparit. Fot el camp de casa meva ara mateix!* And then the Spanish. *¡Me cago en tu madre, hijo de puta!* What a relief it was to have other languages available for your obscenities. They pitched in.

A day later, she and her friend Gabrielle were walking in Minnehaha Creek, their pants rolled up, shoes in hand, Eric baby-packed on Melinda. They were searching the creek for vegetative wonders as they bird-watched and conversed. Melinda liked Gabrielle's bad temper and had befriended her for it. They had bumped into each other in a bookstore a year ago, and Gabrielle had cursed her affably. Melinda was bowled over by her comic vehemence and asked her out for coffee, an invitation that Gabrielle accepted. Gabrielle, a stockbroker, was now back from a cruise. She had planned to meet men. There hadn't been any available ones, at least none, she said, you'd want to take home or to converse with. All the cruise-males were old or stupefied by alcohol or money. She had been criminally misinformed.

"There's a blue jay," Melinda said, pointing. She splashed her feet in the water, being careful not to slip on the rocks.

"Did I tell you how all the staff spoke with an accent? Did I mention that?" Gabrielle asked. " 'Ladies and gentle, let me know eef I can help you in any how.' Their accents were worse during the winetasting session. 'Yooou like theeese vine? Have a zip.' " She walked up to Eric and kissed him on the ear. The baby giggled. " 'Hold theeese vine to the liiiight to determinate the lascivity.' "

"You should be more tolerant of foreigners," Melinda murmured, turning to face her.

"Why should I? I'm not like you. I'm a provincial. I put salt in my coffee." She looked at her friend. "You take that beautiful baby of yours around on your back just to flaunt him in front of me."

"No, I don't. Your leg is cut," Melinda said, pointing. "Where'd you get that mess of scabs?"

"Roses. I was staring at the clematis vine. Its growth habits were unpleasing. I held the ideal in my head so firmly that I obliterated awareness of the rest of the garden, especially the very large, known-to-be-violent rosebush between the clematis and me. I must have lunged at the vine. The rosebush grabbed at my leg, which continued to move. Seconds later I realized that the whole front of my leg had been savagely torn."

"Savagely torn? That's awful."

" 'Laceration' is what the form said, when I finally got out of the ER. I looked the word up, from *lacerate, distress deeply, torn, mangled.* Then I had a drug reaction to the prophylactic antibiotic. It sent me back to the ER. I couldn't walk."

"What's that?" Melinda nodded toward something growing in the creek.

"Watercress?" Gabrielle said. Her black hair fell downward as she bent to see it, and for a moment Melinda thought of Persephone on her way back from the underworld. She had the wildly intelligent eyes of a genius. "No, it's just an unknown, anonymous weed. By the way, how close are we to the Mississippi? I have an appointment. Well, *I* think of it as an appointment. You might not."

Melinda stood up straight, feeling the baby's weight shift. He was making sucking sounds. "I had a visitor yesterday. Well, not a visitor. A man, an intruder. He looked like Eric Clapton. He walked right into the house. He said he used to live there. But he didn't. He couldn't have. His name was Augenblick."

"You call the cops?"

"No."

"I would have," Gabrielle told her. "I'd have the law scurrying right over, with the cuffs and the beaters out."

"He said Eric's nursery had once been his own room. He said he knew things about the house, bad things. He said, this stranger, that I was *desperate*. Can you imagine?"

"He got the wrong address," Gabrielle said. "He meant me."

"Damn him, anyway," said Melinda. She pointed to an opening of the creek where the Mississippi River was visible. "There it is. There's the river. We made it."

"Yeah." Gabrielle slapped at a mosquito on her forearm, leaving a little smear of blood just above her wristwatch. "Is this about your mother?" she asked. Her tone was studiously neutral. "This is about your mother, isn't it? Maybe this guy lived in the neighborhood when you were growing up. Maybe your mother was known to him."

Melinda stopped and looked at her friend. Seedpods from a cottonwood overhead drifted down onto her hair and into the water. "Oh, well," she said, as if something had been settled. Melinda's mother had been in and out of institutions. Melinda refused to come to terms with it, now or ever; a mad parent could not be rescued or reasoned with. Things were getting dark all of a sudden. "I'm, um, feeling a bit lightheaded." She felt her knees weakening, and she made her way to the side of the creek, where she sat down abruptly on the wet sands.

"You aren't going to faint on me, are you?" she heard Gabrielle say, in front, or behind of, a crow cawing. "I'd appreciate it if you didn't faint on me, with that baby strapped to your back, and my appointment coming up . . ." The force of her friend's irritation drifted into her consciousness, as did her voice, someone turning the volume knob back and forth, as she held her own nausea at bay, her head down between her knees. Creek water was suddenly splashed on her face, thrown by her friend, to rouse her.

At certain times, usually in the afternoons, her father would ride the buses, but Melinda had no idea where he went, and he himself could not always remember. He said that he visited the markets, but one time he came back and said that he had knocked at the Gates of Heaven. He would not elaborate. Where were these gates? He had forgotten. Perhaps downtown? Many people were going in, all at once. He felt he wasn't ready, and took the bus home.

This traveling around was a habit he had picked up from his wife, whose wandering had started right after the death of their first child, Melinda's older sister, Sarah, who had died of a blood infection at the age of two. Her mother gave birth to Melinda and then went into a very long, slow, discreetly genteel decline. One day, when Melinda was eleven, her mother, unable to keep up appearances anymore, drove away and disappeared altogether. She was spotted in Madison before she evaporated.

Back in her father's house, Melinda went straight from the phone to her computer. She typed in Augenblick's email address and then wrote a note.

> hi. i don't know who you are, but you're not who you say you are, and my father
> has never heard of you or your family. i shouldn't be writing to you and i
> wouldn't be except i didn't like it that you said you knew me. from where? we've never
> met. you don't know me. i hardly know myself. kidding. i mean, i've met you and i still
> haven't met you. you're a ghost, for all i know.

She deleted the last three sentences—too baroque—both for their meaning and her responsibility for writing them. The joking tone might be mistaken for friendliness. She ducked her head, hearing Eric staying quiet (she didn't want to breastfeed him again tonight, her nipples were sore—but it was odd, she also had suffered a sudden brokenhearted need for sex, for friendly nakedness), and then she continued writing.

> as far as i know, the previous owners of this house were named anderson. that's who
> my mom and dad bought it from. 'augenblick' isn't even a name. it's just a german noun.
> so, my question is: who are you? where are you from? what were you doing in my
> house?—melinda everson, ph.d.

She deleted the reference to the doctoral degree, then put it back, then deleted it again, then put it back in, before touching the SEND button.

Half an hour letter, a new letter appeared in the electronic inbox, from eyeblink@droopingleaf.com.

> **THINK OF ME AS THE RAGE OVER THE LOST PENNY. BUT LIKE I TOLD YOU IM ACTUALLY VERY HARMLESS. W/R/T YOUR QUESTIONS, I CAN DROP BY AGAIN. INFORMATION IS ALL I WANT TO GIVE YOU.** eye two **LIVED THERE. HA HA.—TED**

The school year would be starting soon, and she needed to prepare her classes. She needed to study Peréz Galdós's *Miau* again, for the umpteenth time, for its story of a man lost in a mazelike bureaucracy—her lecture notes were getting mazelike themselves, Kafkaesque. And worse: bland. She would get to that. But for now she was waiting. She knew without knowing how she knew that when Augenblick came back, he would show himself at night, when both her father and her son were asleep; that he would come at the end of a week of hot, dry late-summer weather orchestrated by crickets, that he would show up as a polite intruder again, halfway-handsome, early middle-aged semi-degraded-Clapton, well-dressed, like a piano tuner, and that he would say, as soon as he was out of the driver's-side door of his unidentifiable car, perhaps hand-made, and had advanced so that he stood there on the other side of the screen door, "You look very nice tonight. I got your letter. Thanks for inviting me over."

These events occurred because she was living in her father's house.

"And I got yours," she said, from behind the screen. The screen provided scanning lines; his face was high-definition. "You're the rage over the lost penny. But I didn't invite you over. You're *not* invited. It wasn't an invitation." She hesitated. "Shit. Well, come in, anyway."

This time, once inside, he approached her and shook her hand, and in removing his hand, rubbed hers, as if this were the custom somewhere upon greeting someone whom you didn't know but with whom you wanted a relationship. It was a failed tentative caress but so bizarre that she let it happen.

"My father is upstairs," she said. "And my son, too. Maybe you could explain who you are?"

"This is the living room," he told her, as if he hadn't heard her question, "and over there we once had a baby grand piano in that corner, by the stairs." He pointed. "A Mason and Hamlin. I was never any good at playing it, but my sister was. She's the real musician in the family."

"What does she play?" she asked, testing him. "What's her specialty?"

"Scriabin etudes," he said. "Chopin and Schumann, too, and Schubert, the B-minor."

"She didn't play the violin, did she?"

"No. The piano. She still does. She's a pediatric endocrinologist now. Doctors like music, you know. It's a professional thing." He waited. "Ours was the only piano on the block." He glanced toward the dining room. "In the dining room we used to have another chandelier, it was cut glass—"

"Mr. Augenblick, uh, maybe you could tell me why you're here? And why you're lying to me?" She scooped a bit of perspiration off her forehead and gazed into his game face. "Why all these stories about this locality? Scriabin, Schubert: every house has a story. The truth is, I'm not actually interested in who did what, where, here." She saw him glance down at her body, then at the baby toys scattered across the living room floor. Her breasts were swollen, and she had always been pretty. She was a bit disheveled now, though still a beauty. "I'm a mother. New life is going on here these days. My son is here, my father, too, upstairs, recuperating from a stroke. I don't have time for a personal history. For all I know, you're an intruder. A dangerous maniac."

"No," he said, "I've noticed that. No one has time for a history." Augenblick stood in the living room for a moment, apparently pondering what to say next. At last he looked up, as if struck by a sudden thought, and asked, "May I have a glass of iced tea?"

"No." She folded her arms. "If you were a guest, I would provide the iced tea. But, as I said, I didn't invite you here. I don't mean to be rude, but—"

"Actually," he said, "you *are* rude. You wrote back to me, and that was, well, an invitation. Wasn't it? At least that's how I took it, it's how any man would have taken it." He pasted onto his face a momentarily wounded look. "So all right. So there's to be no iced tea, no water, no hospitality of any kind. No stories, either, about the house. All right. You want to know why I'm here? You really want to know why I'm here? My life hasn't been going so well. I was doing a bit of that living-in-the-past thing. I was driving around, in this neighborhood, *my* former neighborhood, and I saw a really attractive woman working in her garden, weeding, and I thought: *Well, maybe she isn't married or attached, maybe I have a chance, maybe I can strike up a conversation with that woman working there in that garden.* I wasn't out on the prowl, exactly, but I *did* see you. And then I discovered that you had a baby. A beautiful boy. You know, I'm actually a nice guy, though you'd never know it. I'm a landscape architect. I have a college degree. All I wanted was to meet you."

"You said I was desperate. You said you knew me. That was unkind. No. It was wicked."

"You *are* desperate. I do know you. Desperation is knowable."

"That's a funny way of courting a woman, saying things like that."

"We have the same soul, you and I," he said. He said it awkwardly. Still, she was moved, beside or despite herself. The sovereign power of nonsensical compliments: a woman never had any defenses against them.

"I don't know," she said. "Come back in a few days and tell me about the house."

"It's just an ordinary house," he told her, glaring critically at its corners. "Anyway, you're right, I never lived here. I lived a few blocks away."

"So make it up," she said. "You were going to make it up, anyway. Do what you can with it. Impress me."

The next time Augenblick came by, he brought a bottle of wine, a kind of lubricant for his narrative, Melinda thought.

They drank half the bottle, and then he began with the medical details about the house and what had happened in its rooms. There had been a little girl with polio who lived in the house in the 1950's, encased in an iron lung, with the result that her parents had been the first on the block to buy a TV set, in those days a low-class forgetfulness machine. In those days only two stations broadcast programs, a few hours in the morning, then off-the-air during the afternoons until four p.m., when the *Howdy-Doody Show*, *Superman*, and *Beulah* came on.

He touched Melinda's hand. From somewhere he poured her another glass of wine, a glass that she had taken down from her kitchen shelf an hour or two ago, and she took it. He did an inventory of ghosts. Every house had them. He told her that the living room had once been an organizing center for Farmer-Labor party socials of the Scandinavian variety, and that they had planned their strikes there, including the truckers' strike in the 1930's.

"Any violence?" she asked, taking the wine for her second glass.

"None," he said. As a little boy, he said, he had heard that there had once been a murder in these environs, and maybe it had been in this house. He wasn't sure. The body of the murder victim, it was said, had been propped up on the freezer, sitting there, and the police had come in to investigate after the neighbors had called in with reports of screaming, and one of the cops looked directly at the body of the murdered woman, her hair down over her face, and he hadn't seen it, and the police had left.

"Who are you?" Melinda asked Augenblick after they had finished the wine and he had concluded his story. Now they sat on the back porch in discount-store foldout chairs, and through the screens they could see her father's garage with the car on one side and her father's discards, his memory pile, on the other. "Because, right here, there's quite a bit about you that's completely wrong. You tell me a story, the absolutely wrong story, about happiness and a murder, and you say you know me and you say I'm desperate, and I think you said that you and I have the same souls, and your card claimed that you were an investment counselor, and then you informed me that you were a

527

landscape architect." Melinda put her tongue inside her wineglass and licked at the dew of wine still affixed there. "None of it adds up. Because," she said, "what I think it is, what I think you are, sitting here beside me, is a devil." She waited. "Not one of the major ones, in fact really minor, but one all the same."

Through the air pocket of dead silence the crickets chirped. Augenblick did not immediately reply. "Um, okay," he said.

" 'Okay'?"

"Yeah, okay. I used to be an investment counselor until I went broke. I couldn't part with the business cards. So then I went into planting things, landscaping. Not much income, but some. The life I have is modest. I have a kind of ability to, you know, hit the wrong note. Somebody once told me I was a borderline personality but not a success at it. And sometimes I tell stories that aren't quite true. Untruths are what I learned how to do in high school and never quite shook off."

"You should work at it," she said.

"I should work at it," he repeated.

"Was there anything, anywhere, you said that was true?"

"Yes," he said. "My name's really Augenblick. You and I have the same souls. I believe that. I still sort of believe that you're desperate. I used to live in this neighborhood. You had a mother once. I remember her. And actually, from the first moment I saw you, weeding out there in the garden, I haven't been able to stop thinking about you."

She waited. "Could we go back to the topic sentence?"

He leaned sideways in her direction. She could smell the wine on his breath. "About devils, you mean?"

"Yeah, that part."

"There are no devils anymore," he said. "There are only people who are messed up and have to spread it around. And they're everywhere. See, what you have to do is, if you're going to get it, you have to imagine a devil who is also maybe a nice guy." And he leaned over further, so that he almost lost his balance in his chair, and he gave her a peck on each cheek, a devil's kiss.

Making love to him (which she would never, ever do) would be like taking a long journey to a foreign locale you didn't exactly want to visit, like Tangier, a place built on the slopes of a chalky limestone hill. The sun's intensity would be unpleasant, and the general poverty would get in the way of everything. He would make love like a man who didn't quite know what he was doing and who would press that ignorance, hard, on someone else, specifically on her, on her flesh. Still, he would be careful with her, as if he remembered that she was still nursing a child. In the middle of the bed, she would suddenly recall that when she had first seen him, she had thought that there was nothing to him, and she would wonder if there was still nothing to him now. Whether he was actually named Augenblick, despite his claims, whether he did anything actual for a living, whether he would ever hurt her, whether he really might be a devil, though devils didn't exist. Because if they did, times would change and the devils would take new forms. If the name of God is changing in our time, then so are the other names. Then she would come, rapidly, and would forgot her questions the way you forget dreams. But it would never happen, not that way.

"You made love to him?" Gabrielle was outraged. The cellphone itself seemed to be outraged with her anger; even the plastic seemed annoyed. Melinda had called her friend in the middle of the night to consult.

"No, I didn't," Melinda said. "No. No love. But I did fuck him. I was lonely. I wanted to get naked."

"How was it?"

"Okay."

"Well, as the great Albert Einstein once said, 'Don't do that again.' "

She wondered if he would disappear. Everything about him suggested a vanishing act. He would not invite her to his house, wherever that was, nor would he ever give her an address. Like everyone else, though, he did have a cellphone, and he gave her the number to that. One night when he told her (she was lying in her bed, and he was lying in his bed, across town, and the phone call had gone on for over an hour), "I lived in your soul before you owned it," she decided that he was one of those crazy people who gets by from day to day, but just barely—he was what he said he was, a failed borderline personality. She resolved to tell him that she would not see him anymore, under any circumstances, but then he invited her to dinner at a pricey downtown restaurant, so she located a babysitter both for the baby and for her father, and when Edward Augenblick arrived to pick her up, she felt ready for whatever was going to happen, accessorized for it, with a bracelet of beautiful tiny gold spikes.

But in the restaurant, he played the gentleman: he talked about landscape architecture, landscaping generally, so that the conversation took a lackadaisical turn toward the work of Frederick Law Olmsted, and she talked about her work and her scholarship, about Pérez Galdós, the polite chitchat of two people who possibly want to get to know each other, post-sex, and she wondered whether they would ever talk about anything that mattered to them, and whether all his talk about souls was just a bluff, a conversational shell game. She was about to ask him where he had grown up, where he had been educated, what his parents had been like, when he said, "Let's take a walk. Let's go down to the river." The bill for the dinner came, a considerable sum, and he paid in cash, drawing out a mass of twenty-dollar bills from his wallet, a monotonous and mountainous pile of twenties, all the cash looking like novelty items, and Melinda thought, *This man has no usable credit.*

Across the Mississippi River near St. Anthony Falls stands the Stone Arch Bridge, built of limestone in the nineteenth century for the railroad traffic of lumber and grain and coal in and out of Minneapolis. After the railroad traffic ceased, the bridge had been converted to a tourist pedestrian walkway, and he took her hand in his as they strolled over the Mississippi River, looking at the abandoned mills on either side, and the rapids and the locks directly below.

"They don't manufacture anything here anymore, you know," he said to her, close to a whisper.

"The buildings are still here."

"Yes," he said, "but they're ghosts. They're all ghosts. They're shells."

"But look at the lights," she said. "Lofts and condos."

"They don't make anything in there anymore," he said. "Except babies, sometimes, the thirty-somethings. Otherwise, it's all a museum. American cities are all becoming museums." He said this with a wild, incongruous cheer, as a devil would. "Okay," he said. "I'll tell you one true thing. Listen up."

"What's that?"

"When I was a little boy, I lived three or four blocks down from where you lived. I've told you this. You don't remember me. That's all. You don't remember. I remember you, but you don't remember me. No one ever remembers me. One night I was playing in the living room, with my toy armies, and your mother came to our door. I think she was drunk. But I didn't know that. She rang the bell and she entered our house. My parents were upstairs, or somewhere. Your mother came into the house and looked at me playing with my soldiers, and she looked and looked and looked. She smiled and nodded. And then she asked me if I would like to go away with her, that she had always wanted to take a boy like me with her on her travels."

"How did you know it was my mother?" Melinda asked, between shivers.

"I was eight years old. Maybe nine. Everyone knew about your mother. Everyone. I had been warned. You knew that. Everyone knew that. But she had a nice face."

"Where did she say she wanted to take you away to?"

"She had this look in her eyes, I still remember it," Augenblick said. "You have it, too. She wanted to disappear and to take someone along with her. That night, it was going to be me. Your mother was famous in this neighborhood. But everybody thought she was harmless."

"Well, she was a success," Melinda said, the shivers taking her over, so that she had to clutch onto a guardrail. "In disappearing." She leaned toward him and kissed him on the cheek, a show of bravery. "Death is such a cliché," she said. "She disappeared into a cliché."

"Is it?" He wasn't looking at her. "That's news to me. She grabbed me by the hand and she took me for a walk and then she tried to get me into the car, but I broke her hold on me and I ran back to my house."

"Yeah," she said, dreamily. "Death. It's so retro. It's for kids and old people. It's an adolescent thing. You can do better than dying. *You're tired. But everyone's tired. But no one is tired enough,*" she quoted from somewhere. "Anyway, she disappeared, and so what?" It occurred to her at that moment that Augenblick might have leapt off the bridge to his death but that he had, just then, changed his mind, because she had said that death was a cliché. That was it: he looked like a failed suicide. He was one of those.

"She gave me the scare of my life," he said. "Your harmless mother. She scared everybody until she was gone. Shall we go back now?" he asked. "Should we go somewhere?"

"No," she said. "Not again. Not this time." She waited. "We're going to stay right here for a while."

He eventually dropped her off at the front door of her father's house, thanked her, and drove off in his car, which, he had explained, was a Sterling, a nonsense car. She guessed that the license plates on the car had been stolen so that he could not be traced. Whoever he was—Augenblick! what a name!—he would not return. She wondered for a moment or two what his name actually had been, where he had worked, and whether any of it, that is, the actual, mattered, now or ever.

She paid the babysitter and then went upstairs to check on Eric.

The ghosts of the house were gathered around her son. The couples who had lived here from one generation to the next, the solitaries, the happy and unhappy, the gay and the straight and the young and the old: she felt them grouped behind her as a community corralled in the room, touching her questioningly as she bent over the crib and watched her boy, her perfection, breathe in and out, his Catalan-American breaths.

She tiptoed into her father's room. He was still sitting up, carefully studying the wallpaper.

"Hey, Daddy," she said.

"Hey, Sugar," he replied, tilting his head in his characteristically odd way. "How did it go? Your date with this Augenblick?"

"Oh, fine," she said, shunning the narrative of what had happened, how she had fought off his information with a little kiss. Her father wouldn't be interested—especially about her mother.

"I didn't like him. I was hoping you wouldn't have sex with him again. I didn't want to listen. He wasn't out of the top drawer."

"More like the middle drawer. But that's all right," Melinda said. "I won't see him again."

"Good," her father said. "I thought he was a fortune-hunter, after your millions." He laughed hoarsely. "Heh heh. He looked very unsuccessful, I must say, with that dyed hair." He tilted his head the other way. "I went to the Gates of Heaven today," he said, "on the bus. The number eight bus."

"How did it look?" she asked. "The gates?"

"Tarnished," he said. "They could use a shine. No one ever seems to do maintenance anymore. The bus was empty. Even though I was the thing riding on it." He tilted his head the other way. "Completely empty, with me at a window seat. That's how I knew I was almost gone. Honey, you should have more friends, better friends. Someone who doesn't make you groan during sex."

It didn't shock her somehow, that he had heard them. "I have friends. Just not here. I'm moving back home," she said. "To my house. Where I live. I can't stay here anymore, Daddy. I can't take care of you anymore. I love you, Daddy, but I can't do it. I'll arrange for somebody to watch you and to cook." She leaned down to kiss the top of his head.

"I know," he said. "Oh, I know, honey. Staying here makes you a child, doesn't it?"

"Yes." She could feel the goddamn tears flooding over her. And she could feel the ghosts of the house gathering around *him*, now, easing his way into the next world that awaited him. And somewhere on the planet, her mother, too, drove toward the horizon, forever. "I'll watch out for you, though. I'll drop in. I'll check on you."

"No, you probably won't," he said. "No one does. But that's all right. That's how it happens. By the way, do you hear that violin? That girl is practicing as if her life depended on it."

Melinda bent her ear to the silence. "Yes," she agreed. "I do hear it. All the time. Morning and night. It never stops."

Nominated by Marianne Boruch, Philip Levine,
Maura Stanton, Jane Hirshfield, DeWitt Henry, Ploughshares

AUDUBON DIPTYCH

by MATT DONOVAN

from THE KENYON REVIEW

I. Wherein the Swallows Instruct Us In Pleasure

Because they daubed with poppy sap the stricken eyes of their
   young
& because each thin body, it was believed, contained a bright red
   stone
that could honey the word-addled tongue, balm the frenzied brain,

they were restorers, the ancients taught.
                                      And were the restored, too,
since year after year farmers observed them, just after the autumn
   frosts,
plummet single file, like a bead of pearls, into lakes where they
   remained

submerged until spring when they'd wing back in dripping columns.
All of which is no less improbable than Audubon's account
of the slate-green birds pouring into a sycamore trunk *like bees*

hurrying into the hive. The thunder of wings in this slow
   inhalation—
for the tree seemed to breathe in bird upon bird—was first matched
by thunder building behind the Silver Hills, & then was paired,
   once

he pressed his ear to the bark, with the delicate clamor & scratch
of each one inching through the hollow. *Those wings,*

he imagined,

by my lantern's light, & until his light possessed them, what use

to see them merely thread the air? What use were the half-done
    sketches
of his flycatcher, grouse, that for-now unworkable clapper rail beak
& hearing, instead of their ravishing wing-frenzied stream, jam jars
    rattling

in a boil? Thus a hired woodsman pries back the bark & allows him
one night to burrow in.

Who wouldn't want this too? To stand within

the tree's eight-foot trunk & gaze upon them teeming in rows?

To reach into, as he did, the crushed-quill mat & pluck them from
    sleep
& kill—soundlessly, with a kind of care—as many as he could carry?
Closing the entrance, Audubon concludes, *we marched towards
    Louisville,*
perfectly elated.

And despite where his story is hard to believe, no one doubts

this joy. For what could have been lacking, that journey home?
    There was
the road's moonlit, moss-webbed oak, seen as if for the first time,

& here in his pockets filled-to-bursting, the slender, still-warm
    forms.

II. RESURRECTION & THE COMMON MERGANSER

Before he could restore even one part—tail-plunge, talon-tips
sunk into catfish flesh & whatever it is that makes his warbler
weightless on the azalea stem—Audubon invariably failed. To make,

as was always his plan, the watercolors' stippled touch return
the quick breaths

of each bird. He tried first with a pigeon slung

against a barn door, but even if he managed its burnt-orange throat,

he could only render it as it was before him: gangly in a one-legged
    splay.
And before he pummeled it to pieces—humbled, irate—he tried
to build a Universal Bird, a manikin of cork & narrow wooden
    stumps

barely reminiscent of wings, let alone a kind of flight. But life,
he believed, could be brushstroked back & he blundered towards
nimbler forms.
                Aesacus, hidden within another story, can no longer watch

river-water pearl on Hesperia's skin, & so pursues her, lust-driven,
through the fields & woods until death reaches for her ankle
in the lithe form of a snake. Only then do his desires change

& when he flings himself, guilt-stricken, headlong from the cliff,
a god, as the gods will rarely do, denies him the privilege of death.
This time, Ovid tells us, the body doesn't change in a whirlwind fit

but rather, as Aesacus plunges down towards the waves, feathers
pierce his skin. Before long he'll become the first merganser,
the same crested fish-diving duck
                        Audubon clips almost daily

from the Mississippi's iced-over banks. Of one he notes
its triangular tongue, the nine-inch bottom-feeder lodged in its gut,
that its legs, were, as usual, the color of sealing wax, & then begins

to rekindle its life through the method by then he'd learned: first,
    impale
with wire the sun-dried wings, its mandible & mottled breast; attach
    it
to a plank with a backdrop grid & mold it to a lifelike pose. Odd,

how in the watercolors for *The Birds of America*, we're missing
the engraver's final work: the river is just a few light-blue strokes
& instead of an intricate tangle of grass, a merganser soars

through an empty page. Aesacus,
                        for a while, isn't finished either,

though he will be soon. Even as he thrashes in his rage & grief,
not quite bird or man, he can feel it, the lure of it beginning

in his beginning-to-be-hollow bones. What else can he do
but unburden himself, give himself over to the body's suppleness,
its impossible glistening, the grace afforded after all?

Nominated by Brigit Kelly, Eamon Grennan, Dana Levin

OLD MACDONALD HAD A FARMER'S MARKET

by BILL MCKIBBEN

from IN CHARACTER

Gᴇɴᴇʀᴀᴛɪᴏɴs ᴏꜰ ᴄᴏʟʟᴇɢᴇ ꜰʀᴇsʜᴍᴇɴ, asked to read *Walden*, have sputtered with indignation when they learned that Henry David went back to Concord for dinner with his family every week or two. He's *cheating*, his grand experiment is a fraud. This outrage is a useful tactic; it prevents them from having to grapple with the most important (and perhaps the most difficult) book in the American canon, one that asks impossibly searching questions about the emptiness of a consumer economy, the vacuity of an information-soaked era. But it also points to something else: Thoreau, our apostle of solitary, individual self-reliance, out in his cabin with his hoe and his beans, the most determinedly asocial man of his time—nonetheless was immersed in his community to a degree few people today can comprehend.

Consider the sheer number of people who happened to drop by the cabin of an obscure eccentric. "I had three chairs in my house; one for solitude, two for friendship, three for society," he writes. Often more visitors came than could sit—sometimes twenty or thirty at a time. "Half-witted men from the almshouse," busybodies who "pried into my cupboard and bed when I was out," a French-Canadian woodchopper, a runaway slave "whom I helped to forward toward the north star," doctors, lawyers, the old and infirm and the timid, the self-styled reformers. It's not that Thoreau was necessarily a cheerful host—there were visitors "who did not know when their visit had terminated, though I went about my business again, answering them from greater and greater remoteness." Instead, it was simply a visiting age—as most of human history has been a visiting age, and every human culture a visiting culture.

Until ours. I doubt if many people reading these words have had a spontaneous visit from a neighbor in the past week—less than a fifth of Americans report visiting regularly with friends and neighbors, and the percentage is declining steadily. The number of close friends that an American claims has dropped steadily for the last fifty years too; three-quarters of us don't know our *next-door neighbors*. Even the people who share our houses are becoming strangers: *The Wall Street Journal* reported recently that "major builders and top architects are walling off space. They're touting one-person 'internet alcoves,' locked-door 'away rooms,' and his-and-her offices on opposite ends of the house." The new floor plans, says the director of research for the National Association of Home Builders, are "good for the dysfunctional family." Or, as another executive put it, these are the perfect homes for "families that don't want anything to do with one another." Compared to these guys, Thoreau with his three-chair cabin was practically Martha Stewart.

Every culture has its pathologies, and ours is self-reliance. From some mix of our frontier past, our *Little House on the Prairie* heritage, our Thoreauvian desire for solitude, and our amazing wealth we've derived a level of independence never seen before on this round earth. We've built an economy where we need no one else; with a credit card, you can harvest the world's bounty from the privacy of your room. And we've built a culture much the same—the dream houses those architects build, needless to say, come with a plasma screen in every room. As long as we can go on earning good money in our own tiny niche, we don't need a helping hand from a soul—save, of course, from the invisible hand that cups us all in its benign grip.

There are a couple of problems with this fine scenario, of course. One is: we're miserable. Reported levels of happiness and life-satisfaction are locked in long-term one-way declines, almost certainly *because* of this lack of connection. Does this sound subjective and airy? Find one of the tens of millions of Americans who don't belong to *anything* and convince them to join a church, a softball league, a bird-watching group. In the next year their mortality—the risk that they will die in the next year—falls by half.

The other trouble is that our self-reliance is actually a reliance on cheap fossil fuel and the economy it's built. Take that away—either because we start to run out of oil, or because global warming forces us to stop using it in current quantities—and our vaunted independence will start to lurch like a Hummer with four flat tires. Just think for a moment about that world and then decide if you want to live on an acre all your own in the outermost ring of suburbs.

The idea of self-reliance is so deep in our psyches, however, that even when we attempt to escape from the unhappy and unsustainable cul-de-sac of our society, we're likely to turn toward yet more "independence." The "back-to-the-land" movement, for instance, often added the words "by myself." Think about how proudly a certain kind of person talks about his "off-the-grid" life—he makes his own energy and grows his own food, he can deal with whatever the world throws at him. One such person may be left-wing in politics (à la Scott and Helen Nearing); another may be conservative. But they are united in their lack of need for the larger world. Not even to school their kids—they'll take care of that as well.

Such folks are admirable, of course—they have a wide variety of skills now missing in most Americans; they're able to amuse themselves; they work hard. But as an ideal, especially an economic ideal, that radical self-reliance strikes me as being almost as empty as the consumer society from which it dissents. Consider, for instance, the idea of growing all your own food. It's clearly better than relying on food from thousands of miles away—from our current industrialized food economy, which figures "it's always summer somewhere" and so orders take-out from that distant field every night of the year. Compared with that, an enormous garden and a root cellar full of all you'll need for the winter is virtue incarnate. But if you believe in many of the (entirely plausible) horror stories about what's to come—peak oil, climate change—then the world ends with you standing shotgun in hand above your vegetable patch, protecting your carrots from the poaching urban horde.

Contrast that with another vision, one taking shape in at least a few places around the country: a matrix of small farmers growing food for their local areas. Farmers' markets are the fastest-growing part of our food economy, with sales showing double-digit growth annually. Partly that's because people want good food (all kinds of people: immigrants and ethnic Americans tend to be the most avid farmers' market shoppers). And partly it's because they want more *company*. One team of sociologists reported recently that shoppers at farmers' markets engaged in ten times more conversations per visit than customers in supermarkets. I spent the past winter eating only from my valley; a little of the food I grew myself, but the idea of my experiment was to see what remained of the agricultural infrastructure that had once supported this place. And the payoff was not only a delicious six months, but also a deep network of new friends, a much stronger sense of the cultural geography of my place.

Or consider energy. Since the 1970s, a particular breed of noble ex-hippie has been building "off-the-grid" homes, often relying on solar panels. This has been important work—they've figured out many of the techniques and technologies that we desperately need to get free of our climate change predicament. But the most exciting new gadget is a home-scale inverter, one that allows you to send the power your rooftop generates down the line instead of down into the basement. Where the isolated system has a stack of batteries, the grid-tied solar panel uses the whole region's electric system as its battery: my electric meter spins merrily backward all afternoon because while the sun shines I'm a utility; then at night I draw from somewhere else. It's a two-way flow, in the same way that the internet allows ideas to bounce in many directions.

You can do the same kind of calculation with almost any commodity. Music doesn't need to come from Nashville or Hollywood on a small disc, for instance. But you don't have to produce it all yourself either. More fun to join with the neighbors, to make music together or to listen to the local stars. A hundred years ago, Iowa had 1,300 opera houses. Radio doesn't need to come from the ClearChannel headquarters in some Texas office park; new low-power FM lets valleys make their own. Even currency can become a joint local project—all it takes is the trust that underwrites any system of money. In hundreds of communities, people are trying to build that trust locally, with money that only works within the region.

Thinking this way won't be easy. We're used to independence as the prime virtue—so used to it that three quarters of American Christians believe the phrase "God helps those who help themselves" comes from the Bible, instead of Ben Franklin. "Love your neighbor as yourself" is harder advice, but sweeter and more sage. We don't need to live on communes (though more and more old people are finding themselves enrolling in "retirement communities" that are gray-haired, upscale versions). But we will, I think, need to figure out how to stop relying on both oil and ourselves, and instead learn the lesson that the other primates and the other human cultures never forgot: we're built to rely on each other.

Nominated by Genie Chipps

ANGEL WITH

BIG BOOK

by **KATHRYN MARIS**

from POETRY REVIEW

The angel's book is blue and dense and God knows the book,
which is nailed to the sky.

The angel is my friend and yet to say he has a good heart
is to be a poor physician,

for his wings are in his dodgy chest, speedy wings that beat
to a bad time.

His wings are all he's put away. His papers sit on rock and bog
and wind and desk,

on every noun in the world, even the flimsy nouns of the mind.

We all have dead friends, but he has more, and his big book
is the chronicle of harm.

Like his heart's flutter and his room's clutter, this book is his burden,
and he has kept me out

using charm and guile and even lies, and I was grateful for my
exclusion,
I was surprised.

To know the angel is to sense that you are gone. But to love him is
to love

what isn't gone

like the world, the word and this angel who is fragile and who claims
no generosity, but is wrong.

Nominated by Josip Novakovich

MY ACCIDENTAL JIHAD

by KRISTA BREMER

from THE SUN

Eᴀʀʟʏ ᴏɴᴇ ᴍᴏʀɴɪɴɢ in September, when our house is pitch-dark and the entire family is still asleep, my husband, Ismail, sits upright at the first sound of his alarm, dresses quickly, and leaves our bedroom. Later, after I've woken up and made my way downstairs for a cup of coffee, I find him standing at the counter, stuffing the last of his breakfast into his mouth, his eye on the clock as if he were competing in a pie-eating contest at the fair. The minute hand clicks forward, and, on cue, Ismail drops the food he's holding. I'm momentarily confused. My husband and I usually sit down together over our first cup of coffee, and he rarely eats breakfast. Then I realize: Ramadan has begun.

For the next month, nothing will touch my husband's mouth between sunup and sundown: Not food. Not water. Not my lips. A chart posted on our refrigerator tells him the precise minute when his fast must begin and end each day. I will find him in front of this chart again this evening, staring at his watch, waiting for it to tell him he may eat.

Ramadan is the ninth month of the lunar calendar, the month during which the Koran was revealed to the Prophet Mohammed through the angel Gabriel. Each year, more than one billion Muslims observe Ramadan by fasting from dawn to dusk. In addition to avoiding food and drink during daylight hours, Muslims are expected to refrain from all other indulgences: sexual relations, gossip, evil thoughts—even looking at "corrupt" images on television, in magazines, or on the Internet. Ramadan is a month of purification, during which Muslims are called upon to make peace with enemies, strengthen ties with family and friends, cleanse themselves of impurities, and refocus their lives on God. It's like a month-long spiritual tuneup.

My husband found fasting easier when he lived in Libya, surrounded by fellow Muslims. Everyone's life changes there during the fast: people work less (at least, those who work outside the home), take long naps during the day, and feast with family and friends late into the night. Now, with a corporate job and an American wife who works full time, my husband has a totally different experience of Ramadan. He spends most of his waking hours at work, just as he does every other month of the year. He still picks up our son from day care and shares cooking and cleaning responsibilities at home. Having no Muslim friends in our Southern college town, he breaks his fast alone, standing at our kitchen counter. Here in the United States, Ramadan feels more like an extreme sport than a spiritual practice. Secretly I've come to think of it as "Ramathon."

I try to be supportive of Ismail's fast, but it's hard. The rules seem unnecessarily harsh to me, an American raised in the seventies by parents who challenged the status quo. The humility required to submit to such a grueling, seemingly illogical exercise is not in my blood. In my family, we don't submit. We question the rules. We debate. And we do things our own way. I resent the fact that Ismail's life is being micromanaged by the chart in the kitchen. Would Allah really hold it against him if he finished his last bite of toast, even if the clock says it's a minute past sunrise? The no-water rule seems especially cruel to me, and I find the prohibition against kissing a little melodramatic. I'm tempted to argue with Ismail that the rules are outdated, but he has a billion Muslims in his corner, whereas I have yet to find another disgruntled American wife who feels qualified to rewrite one of the five pillars of Islam.

People say that for a relationship to work, a couple needs to have a shared passion. My husband and I do have one: food. Years ago, when we first met, we shared other passions, such as travel, long runs on wooded trails, live music, and poetry readings. But now that we have two small kids, those indulgences have fallen by the wayside one by one. No matter how busy our lives get, however, we have to eat. On days when it seems we have nothing in common, when I struggle to recall what brought us together in the first place, one good meal can remind me. Ismail is an amazing cook. I remember in great detail the meal he prepared for me the first night we spent together: the walnuts simmering slowly in the thick, sweet blood-red pomegranate sauce; the chicken that slipped delicately away from the bone, like silk falling from skin. The next morning the scent of coriander ground into strong coffee filled his small apartment as he served me olives and fresh bread for breakfast.

Our love heated up like a sauce on the stove, our lives slowly blending together, the flavors becoming increasingly subtle and complex. I'd watch him prepare a bunch of cilantro on the counter, carefully separating the stalks with patient attention, gently plucking each leaf from its stem. He could toast pine nuts in a pan while carrying on a conversation with me and not burn a single one, magically rescuing them from the heat just as they turned the perfect shade of brown. Using his buttery fingertips, he would separate paper-thin sheets of phyllo dough without tearing any. He always served me first and studied my expression closely as I took a bite, his face lighting up in response to my pleasure. When he took his first taste, his eyes closed halfway, and a low moan of pleasure escaped from his mouth. There in the kitchen, all the evidence was before me: he was patient, attentive, thorough, economical, generous, creative, and sensual. I was ready to bear his children.

But when my husband fasts, our relationship becomes a bland, lukewarm concoction that I find difficult to swallow. I'm not proud of this fact. After all, he isn't the only one in our house with a spiritual practice: I stumble out of bed in the dark most mornings and meditate in the corner of our room with my back to him, trying to find that bottomless truth beyond words. Once in a great while, I'll drag him to church on Sunday. Whenever I suggest we say grace at the table, he reaches willingly for my hand, and words of gratitude flow easily from him. He has never criticized my practices, even when they are wildly inconsistent or contradictory. But Ramadan is not ten minutes of meditation or an hour-long sermon; it's an entire month of deprivation. Ismail's God is the old-fashioned kind, omnipresent and stern, uncompromising with his demands. During Ramadan this God expects him to pray on time, five times a day—and to squeeze in additional prayers of forgiveness as often as he can. My God would never be so demanding. My God is a flamboyant and fickle friend with a biting wit who likes a good party. My God is transgendered and tolerant to a fault; he/she shows up unexpectedly during peak moments, when life feels glorious and synchronous, then disappears for long stretches of time.

But Ramadan leaves little room for dramatic flair. There is no chorus of voices or public celebration—just a quiet and steady submission to Allah in the privacy of one's home. For some Muslims who live in the West, the holiday becomes even more private, since their friends and colleagues are often not even aware of their fast.

During the early days of Ramadan, Ismail deals with his hunger by planning his next meal and puttering around the kitchen. In the last half-hour before the sun sets, he rearranges the food in our refrigerator or wipes down our already-clean counters. At night in bed, as I drift off to sleep, he reviews each ingredient in the baklava he intends to make the following evening. "Do you think I should replace the walnuts with pistachios?" he whispers. In the middle of the workday, when I call his cellphone, I hear the beeping of a cash register in the background. He is wandering the aisles of our local grocery store. "I needed to get out of the office," he says matter-of-factly, as if all men escaped to the grocery store during lunch.

The last hours before he breaks his fast are the most difficult and volatile time of day for him. Coincidentally, they are the same hours at which I return home from work. I open the door and find him collapsed on the couch, pale and exhausted, our children running in circles around the room. Ismail is irritable, and his thoughts trail off in midsentence. I dread seeing him in this state. I count on my husband to speak coherently, to smile on a regular basis, and to enjoy our children. This humorless person on my couch is no fun. Every few days I ask (with what I hope sounds like innocent curiosity) what he's learned from his fast so far. I know this is an unfair question. How would I feel if he poked his head into our bedroom while I was meditating and asked, *How's it going? Emptied your mind yet?*

One balmy Saturday in the middle of Ramadan, we go to hear an outdoor lecture by a Sufi Muslim teacher who is visiting from California. The teacher sits cross-legged under a tree on a colorful pillow while the sun streams down on him through a canopy of leaves. After a long silence, he sweeps his arms in front of him, a beatific expression on his face, and reminds us to notice the beauty that surrounds us. "If you don't," he says, "you're not fasting—you're just going hungry."

I take a sidelong glance at Ismail. He is looking very hungry to me these days. I guess I imagined that during his fast a new radiance would emanate from him. I imagined him moving more slowly, but also more lovingly. I imagined a Middle Eastern Gandhi, sitting with our children in the garden when I got home from work. In short, I imagined that his spiritual practice would look more . . . well, *spiritual*. I didn't imagine the long silences between us or how much his exhaustion would irritate me. I didn't imagine him leaping out of bed in a panic, having slept through his alarm, and running downstairs to swallow chunks of bread and gulp coffee before the sun came up. I didn't imagine his terse replies to my attempts to start a conversation, or his impatience with our children.

I thought I understood the rules of Ramadan: the timetable on the refrigerator, the five daily prayers. But I didn't understand that the real practice is addressing a toddler's temper tantrum or a wife's hostile silence when you haven't eaten or drunk anything in ten hours. I was like the children of Israel in the Bible, who once complained that, despite their dutiful fasting, God *still* wasn't answering their prayers. The children of Israel had it all wrong: God doesn't count calories. The fast itself only sets the stage. God is interested in our behavior and intentions *while* we are hungry. Through his prophet Isaiah, God gave the children of Israel a piece of his mind:

> Behold, in the day of your fast you seek your own pleasure, and oppress all your workers. Behold, you fast only to quarrel and to fight and to hit with a wicked fist. Fasting like yours this day will not make your voice to be heard on high. (Isaiah 58:3–4)

Ismail tells me that in the Middle East, Ramadan is a time of extremes: There are loving gatherings among family and friends at night, and a tremendous public outpouring of charity and generosity to those in need. At the same time, the daytime streets become more dangerous, filled with nicotine and caffeine addicts in withdrawal. People stumble through the morning without their green or black tea, drunk so dark and thick with sugar that it leaves permanent stains even on young people's teeth. Desperate smokers who light up in public risk being ridiculed or even attacked by strangers. The streets reverberate with angry shouts and car horns, and traffic conflicts occasionally escalate into physical violence.

Our home, too, becomes more volatile during Ramadan. Ismail's temper is short; my patience with him runs thin. I accuse him of being grumpy. He accuses me of being unsupportive. I tell him he is failing at Ramadan, as if it were some sort of exam. I didn't ask for

548

this spiritual test, I tell him. As if I could pick and choose which parts of him to take into my life. As if he were served up to me on a plate, and I could primly push aside what I didn't care for—his temper, his doubt, his self-pity—and keep demanding more of his delicious tenderness.

And then there is my husband's unmistakable Ramadan scent. Normally I love the way he smells: the faint scent of soap and laundry detergent mixed with the warm muskiness of his skin. But after a few days of fasting, Ismail begins to smell *different*. Mostly it's his breath. The odor is subtle but distinct and persists no matter how many times he brushes or uses mouthwash. When I get close to him, it's the first thing I notice. I do a Google search for "Ramadan and halitosis" and learn that this is a common side effect of fasting—so common that the Prophet Mohammed himself even had something to say about it: "The smell of the fasting person's breath is sweeter to Allah than that of musk." Allah may delight in this smell, but I don't. I no longer rest my head on Ismail's chest when we lie in bed at night. I begin to avoid eye contact and increase the distance between us when we speak. I no longer kiss him on impulse in the evening. I sleep with my back to him, resentful of this odor, which hangs like an invisible barrier between us.

The purpose of fasting during Ramadan is not simply to suffer hunger, thirst, or desire, but to bring oneself closer to *taqwa*: a state of sincerity, discipline, generosity, and surrender to Allah; the sum total of all Muslim teachings. When, in a moment of frustration, I grumble to my husband about his bad breath, he responds in the spirit of *taqwa*: He listens sympathetically and then apologizes and promises to keep his distance. He offers to sleep on the couch if that would make me more comfortable. He says he wishes I had told him earlier so he could have spared me any discomfort. His humility catches me off guard and makes my resentment absurd.

This month of Ramadan has revealed to me the limits of my compassion. I recall a conversation I had with Ismail in the aftermath of September 11, 2001, when the word *jihad* often appeared in news stories about Muslim extremists who were hellbent on destroying the United States. According to Ismail, the Prophet Mohammed taught that the greatest jihad, or struggle, of our lives is not the one that takes place on a battlefield, but the one that takes place within our hearts—the struggle to increase self-discipline and become a better person. This month of Ramadan has thrown me into my own accidental jihad, forcing me to wrestle with my intolerance and self-absorption. And I have been losing ground in this battle, forgetting my husband's intentions and focusing instead on the petty ways I am inconvenienced by his practice.

Ramadan is meant to break our rigid habits of overindulgence, the ones that slip into our lives as charming guests and then refuse to leave, taking up more and more space and stealing our attention away from God. And it's not just the big habits, the ones that grab us by the throat—alcohol, coffee, cigarettes—but the little ones that take us gently by the hand and lead us stealthily away from the truth. I begin to notice my own compulsions, the small and socially acceptable ones that colonize my day: The way I depend on regular exercise to bolster my mood. The number of times I check my e-mail. The impulse to watch a movie with my husband after our children are in bed, rather than let the silence envelop us both. And the words: all the words in books, in magazines, on the computer; words to distract me from the mundane truth of the moment. I begin to notice how much of my thinking revolves around what I will consume next.

I am plump with my husband's love, overfed by his kindness, yet I still treat our marriage like an all-you-can-eat buffet, returning to him over and over again to fill my plate, as if our vows guaranteed me unlimited nourishment. During Ramadan, when he turns inward and has less to offer me, I feel indignant. I want to make a scene. I want to speak to whoever is in charge, to demand what I think was promised me when I entered this marriage. But now I wonder: Is love an endless feast, or is it what people manage to serve each other when their cupboards are bare?

In the evening, just before sundown, Ismail arranges three dates on a small plate and pours a tall glass of water, just as the Koran instructs him to do, just as the Prophet Mohammed himself did long ago. Then he sits down next to me at the kitchen counter while I thumb through cookbooks, wondering what to make for dinner. He waits dutifully while the phone rings, while our daughter practices scales on the piano, while our son sends a box of Legos crashing onto our wood floor. Then, at the moment the sun sets, he lifts a date to his mouth and closes his eyes.

Nominated by The Sun

SPECIAL MENTION

(The editors also wish to mention the following important works published by small presses last year. Listings are in no particular order.)

NONFICTION

On Writing Rapture—Jeanne Larsen (Arts & Letters)
Reality Hunger: A Manifesto—David Shields (Seneca Review)
Space For Name—Walker Rumble (Massachusetts Review)
My Long-Playing Records—Richard Jespers (Boulevard)
Lincoln Kirstein, the Last Tycoon—Nicholas Jenkins (Raritan)
Free (Market) Verse—Steve Evans (The Baffler)
Sudden Impact—Paul Zimmer (Gettysburg Review)
It Takes A Village to Tell A Story—Yiyun Li (Tin House)
The Lustres—Lia Purpura (Agni)
Visitations—Joy Passanante (Shenandoah)
The Bridge—Mary Gaitskill (Other Voices)
The Museum of Lost Language—Bill Capossere (Rosebud)
Five Positions—Renée K. Nicholson (Gettysburg Review)
Wonder Bread—Melvin Jules Bukiet (American Scholar)
Pursuing The Great Bad Novelist—Laura Sewell Matter (Georgia Review)
Missing—Merilee D. Karr (Creative Nonfiction)
To A Nightingale—Edward Hirsch (Five Points)
Istanbul In Winter—Richard Tillinghast (Southern Review)
"Mem, Mem, Mem"—Paul West (American Scholar)
Cities of Possibility—Barrie Jean Borich (Water-Stone)
Netting The Future—Donna Seaman (Creative Nonfiction)
Miss Hale—Paul Harding (Harvard Review)
My Father Tongue—Carol Paik (Gettysburg Review)

Milosz's Choice—Stephen O'Connor (Agni)

Flotsam, Jetsam—Kelly Grey Carlisle (Subtropics)

Seeing Things—Michelle Herman (Southern Review)

Pym, M., and Me—Sidney Burris (Five Points)

T.S. Eliot and the Rise of the Geezer—Kevin Jackson (Cimarron Review)

Variations on Desire—Siri Hustvedt (Conjunctions)

Catechism—Margaret Gibson (Southern Review)

Size Matters—Debra Spark (Post Road)

The Man From 'Stanbul—Peter Selgin (The Sun)

Paddling the Middle Fork—Jill Christman (Riverteeth)

More Than Air—Claire Davis (Gulf Coast)

Dead of the Night—Patricia Hampl (Ploughshares)

The Gross-Out Factor—Pauline W. Chen (Virginia Quarterly)

Leaving Home for Home—Harry Crews (Georgia Review)

Unplugged Schools—Lowell Monke (Orion)

To Make the Final Unity: Metaphor's Matter and Spirit—Mark Jarman (The Southern Review)

FICTION

Beanball—Ron Carlson (One Story)

Hiroshima—Nam Le (Harvard Review)

Beast—Samantha Hunt (Tin House)

The Seige—Seth Fried (Missouri Review)

Knife, Barn, My Harvey—René Houtrides (Georgia Review)

Quality of Life—Christine Sneed (New England Review)

Bar Joke, Arizona—Sam Allingham (One Story)

Pasadena. 1901—Erin McGraw (The Hopkins Review)

Special—Joyce Carol Oates (Boulevard)

Why The Devil Chose New England for His Work—Jason Brown (Epoch)

Allegiance—Joan Silber (Ploughshares)

Broadax Inc.—Bill Roorbach (Ecotone)

Cohabiting—Enid Harlow (Nimrod)

Mendoza-Burke's Reform—Peter LaSalle (Agni)

Sylvia's Idea—Bradford Morrow (Ontario Review)

Giving Up The Ghost—Nicholas Montemarano (Gettysburg Review)

Evelyn—Ellen Wilbur (Yale Review)

Treasure Hunt—John Michael Cummings (Chattahoochee Review)

Child of God—Jennifer Moses (Glimmer Train)

Beauty, What Can I Bring You?—Diane Williams (sic)

Bridge—Jane Ashley (Bellevue Literary Review)

Shot Girls—Kim Chinquee (Mississippi Review)

Movie Nights In Rangoon—Kenneth Wong (Agni)

Change of Address—Christopher Tilghman (Ploughshares)

Ultimate Thule—Lee Smith (The Southern Review)

Republican—Bret Anthony Johnston (Ploughshares)

The Palmer System—Laurence C. Peacock (Noon)

Sixty-five Million Years—Richard Pausch (NarrativeMagazine.com)

The Great Speckled Bird—Clyde Edgerton (The Southern Review)

Rodney Valen's Second Life—Kent Meyers (Georgia Review)

Niña Pérdida: Love Song for Iris—Melanie Rae Thon (Five Points)

Joe Messinger Is Dreaming—Pinckney Benedict (Appalachian Heritage)

Birding With Lanioturdus—Peter Orner (Conjunctions)

When The Bear Came—Benjamin Percy (American Short Fiction)

I Was In Kilter With Him A Little—Gary Lutz (Noon)

Icebergs—Alistair Morgan (Paris Review)

Bride—Deb Olin Unferth (McSweeney's)

Andrea Is Changing Her Name—Kevin Brockmeier (Zoetrope)

My American Jon—Chimamanda Ngozi Adichie (Conjunctions)

Yuri—Connor Kilpatrick (McSweeney's)

'Sang—R.T. Smith (Arts & Letters)

Elephant—Rick Bass (Tin House)

This Road—Bonnie Nadzam (Callaloo)

He Who Would Have Become "Joshua," 1791—Thomas Glave (Callaloo)

A Good Pine—Chris Offutt (Appalachian Heritage)

Yayi and Those Who Walk on Water: A Fable—Bayo Ojikutu (Other Voices)

Uno—Eileen Pollack (Prairie Schooner)

Dutch Treat—Josip Novakovich (Witness)

Camp Winnesaka—Ethan Rutherford (Faultline)

Ben In Amboy—Alan Cheuse (Witness)

The End of the World In Slow Motion—Ann Pancake (NarrativeMagazine.com)

Roof Topped—Terese Svoboda (Bomb)

September, 1981—Rusty Dolleman (Iowa Review)

Red Winter—Kate Lane (Third Coast)

POETRY

Riddle of Self Worth—Christopher Kennedy (BOA)
Hidden Costs—Bruce Cohen (Poetry)
The Ocracoke Ponies—Jennifer Grotz (New England Review)
The Other Odyssey—Richard Garcia (Barrow Street)
In The Calm—Fady Joudah (Beloit Poetry Journal)
After the Fall—Edward Field (University of Pittsburgh Press)
A Mouthful of Crickets—F. Daniel Rzicznek (Salamander)
Milk Pail Market—Gretchen Primak (Field)
Alex—David Hernandez (Pearl)
Erosion—Bruce Bennett (The Heading Muse)
Eschatology On Interstate 84 at 70 MPH—Oliver De La Paz (Crab Creek Review)
A Rabbit Must Be Walking—Anna Journey (Blackbird)
Conjugated Visits—Diane Kirsten Martin (Field)
Your Words—Fred Marchant (Image)
Don't Come Home—Todd Boss (TriQuarterly)
Interior—Deborah Landau (Cincinnati Review)
Theology—Jane Hirshfield (McSweeney's)
Candlemas, Vermont—G.C. Waldrep (Runes)
Winged Ignatz—Monica Youn (Paris Review)
Thermopylae—Meghan O'Rourke (Yale Review)
Sabbaths 2005—Wendell Berry (Shenandoah)
Now In Our Most Ordinary Voices—Carl Phillips (Boulevard)
St. Ursula's Mirror, 2—Barbara Claire Freeman (New American Writing)
1981—Abraham Sutzkever, Translated by Jacqueline Osherow (Poetry)
To Andrew: At Twenty-Three Months—Joelle Biele (New Delta Review)
Book Three—Kathleen Graber (American Poetry Review)
Ode To the Letter M—Barbara Hamby (TriQuarterly)
Come Back—Andrew Hudgins (Southern Review)
The Dead—Jason Schneiderman (American Poetry Review)
Tendril—Bin Ramke (Tendril)
Kalinin—City of Tver—Andrey Gritsman (Paper Street)
Old-Style Plentiful—John Ashbery (Canary)

PRESSES FEATURED IN THE PUSHCART PRIZE EDITIONS SINCE 1976

Acts
Agni
Ahsahta Press
Ailanthus Press
Alaska Quarterly Review
Alcheringa/Ethnopoetics
Alice James Books
Ambergris
Amelia
American Letters and Commentary
American Literature
American PEN
American Poetry Review
American Scholar
American Short Fiction
The American Voice
Amicus Journal
Amnesty International
Anaesthesia Review
Anhinga Press
Another Chicago Magazine
Antaeus
Antietam Review
Antioch Review
Apalachee Quarterly
Aphra
Aralia Press

The Ark
Art and Understanding
Arts and Letters
Artword Quarterly
Ascensius Press
Ascent
Aspen Leaves
Aspen Poetry Anthology
Assembling
Atlanta Review
Autonomedia
Avocet Press
The Baffler
Bakunin
Bamboo Ridge
Barlenmir House
Barnwood Press
Barrow Street
Bellevue Literary Review
The Bellingham Review
Bellowing Ark
Beloit Poetry Journal
Bennington Review
Bilingual Review
Black American Literature Forum
Blackbird
Black Rooster

Black Scholar
Black Sparrow
Black Warrior Review
Blackwells Press
Bloom
Bloomsbury Review
Blue Cloud Quarterly
Blueline
Blue Unicorn
Blue Wind Press
Bluefish
BOA Editions
Bomb
Bookslinger Editions
Boston Review
Boulevard
Boxspring
Bridge
Bridges
Brown Journal of Arts
Burning Deck Press
Caliban
California Quarterly
Callaloo
Calliope
Calliopea Press
Calyx
The Canary
Canto
Capra Press
Caribbean Writer
Carolina Quarterly
Cedar Rock
Center
Chariton Review
Charnel House
Chattahoochee Review
Chautauqua Literary Journal
Chelsea
Chicago Review
Chouteau Review
Chowder Review
Cimarron Review

Cincinnati Poetry Review
City Lights Books
Cleveland State Univ. Poetry Ctr.
Clown War
CoEvolution Quarterly
Cold Mountain Press
Colorado Review
Columbia: A Magazine of Poetry and
    Prose
Confluence Press
Confrontation
Conjunctions
Connecticut Review
Copper Canyon Press
Cosmic Information Agency
Countermeasures
Counterpoint
Crawl Out Your Window
Crazyhorse
Crescent Review
Cross Cultural Communications
Cross Currents
Crosstown Books
Crowd
Cue
Cumberland Poetry Review
Curbstone Press
Cutbank
Dacotah Territory
Daedalus
Dalkey Archive Press
Decatur House
December
Denver Quarterly
Desperation Press
Dogwood
Domestic Crude
Doubletake
Dragon Gate Inc.
Dreamworks
Dryad Press
Duck Down Press
Durak

East River Anthology
Eastern Washington University Press
Ecotone
Ellis Press
Empty Bowl
Epiphany
Epoch
Ergo!
Evansville Review
Exquisite Corpse
Faultline
Fence
Fiction
Fiction Collective
Fiction International
Field
Fine Madness
Firebrand Books
Firelands Art Review
First Intensity
Five Fingers Review
Five Points Press
Five Trees Press
The Formalist
Fourth Genre
Frontiers: A Journal of Women
    Studies
Fugue
Gallimaufry
Genre
The Georgia Review
Gettysburg Review
Ghost Dance
Gibbs-Smith
Glimmer Train
Goddard Journal
David Godine, Publisher
Graham House Press
Grand Street
Granta
Graywolf Press
Great River Review
Green Mountains Review

Greenfield Review
Greensboro Review
Guardian Press
Gulf Coast
Hanging Loose
Hard Pressed
Harvard Review
Hayden's Ferry Review
Hermitage Press
Heyday
Hills
Hollyridge Press
Holmgangers Press
Holy Cow!
Home Planet News
Hudson Review
Hungry Mind Review
Icarus
Icon
Idaho Review
Iguana Press
Image
In Character
Indiana Review
Indiana Writes
Intermedia
Intro
Invisible City
Inwood Press
Iowa Review
Ironwood
Jam To-day
The Journal
Jubilat
The Kanchenjuga Press
Kansas Quarterly
Kayak
Kelsey Street Press
Kenyon Review
Kestrel
Latitudes Press
Laughing Waters Press
Laurel Poetry Collective

Laurel Review
L'Epervier Press
Liberation
Linquis
Literal Latté
Literary Imagination
The Literary Review
The Little Magazine
Living Hand Press
Living Poets Press
Logbridge-Rhodes
Louisville Review
Lowlands Review
Lucille
Lynx House Press
Lyric
The MacGuffin
Magic Circle Press
Malahat Review
Mānoa
Manroot
Many Mountains Moving
Marlboro Review
Massachusetts Review
McSweeney's
Meridian
Mho & Mho Works
Micah Publications
Michigan Quarterly
Mid-American Review
Milkweed Editions
Milkweed Quarterly
The Minnesota Review
Mississippi Review
Mississippi Valley Review
Missouri Review
Montana Gothic
Montana Review
Montemora
Moon Pony Press
Mount Voices
Mr. Cogito Press
MSS

Mudfish
Mulch Press
Nada Press
National Poetry Review
Nebraska Review
New America
New American Review
New American Writing
The New Criterion
New Delta Review
New Directions
New England Review
New England Review and Bread Loaf
     Quarterly
New Issues
New Letters
New Orleans Review
New Virginia Review
New York Quarterly
New York University Press
Nimrod
9 × 9 Industries
Ninth Letter
Noon
North American Review
North Atlantic Books
North Dakota Quarterly
North Point Press
Northeastern University Press
Northern Lights
Northwest Review
Notre Dame Review
O. ARS
O. Blēk
Obsidian
Obsidian II
Ocho
Oconee Review
October
Ohio Review
Old Crow Review
Ontario Review
Open City

Open Places

Orca Press

Orchises Press

Oregon Humanities

Orion

Other Voices

Oxford American

Oxford Press

Oyez Press

Oyster Boy Review

Painted Bride Quarterly

Painted Hills Review

Palo Alto Review

Paris Press

Paris Review

Parkett

Parnassus: Poetry in Review

Partisan Review

Passages North

Pebble Lake Review

Penca Books

Pentagram

Penumbra Press

Pequod

Persea: An International Review

Perugia Press

Pipedream Press

Pitcairn Press

Pitt Magazine

Pleiades

Ploughshares

Poet and Critic

Poet Lore

Poetry

Poetry Atlanta Press

Poetry East

Poetry Ireland Review

Poetry Northwest

Poetry Now

Post Road

Prairie Schooner

Prescott Street Press

Press

Promise of Learnings

Provincetown Arts

A Public Space

Puerto Del Sol

Quaderni Di Yip

Quarry West

The Quarterly

Quarterly West

Raccoon

Rainbow Press

Raritan: A Quarterly Review

Rattle

Red Cedar Review

Red Clay Books

Red Dust Press

Red Earth Press

Red Hen Press

Release Press

Republic of Letters

Review of Contemporary Fiction

Revista Chicano-Riquena

Rhetoric Review

Rivendell

River Styx

River Teeth

Rowan Tree Press

Runes

Russian *Samizdat*

Salmagundi

San Marcos Press

Sarabande Books

Sea Pen Press and Paper Mill

Seal Press

Seamark Press

Seattle Review

Second Coming Press

Semiotext(e)

Seneca Review

Seven Days

The Seventies Press

Sewanee Review

Shankpainter

Shantih

Shearsman

Sheep Meadow Press

Shenandoah

A Shout In the Street

Sibyl-Child Press

Side Show

Small Moon

Smartish Pace

The Smith

Snake Nation Review

Solo

Solo 2

Some

The Sonora Review

Southern Poetry Review

Southern Review

Southwest Review

Speakeasy

Spectrum

Spillway

The Spirit That Moves Us

St. Andrews Press

Story

Story Quarterly

Streetfare Journal

Stuart Wright, Publisher

Sulfur

The Sun

Sun & Moon Press

Sun Press

Sunstone

Sycamore Review

Tamagwa

Tar River Poetry

Teal Press

Telephone Books

Telescope

Temblor

The Temple

Tendril

Texas Slough

Third Coast

13th Moon

THIS

Thorp Springs Press

Three Rivers Press

Threepenny Review

Thunder City Press

Thunder's Mouth Press

Tia Chucha Press

Tikkun

Tin House

Tombouctou Books

Toothpaste Press

Transatlantic Review

Triplopia

TriQuarterly

Truck Press

Tupelo Press

Turnrow

Undine

Unicorn Press

University of Chicago Press

University of Georgia Press

University of Illinois Press

University of Iowa Press

University of Massachusetts Press

University of North Texas Press

University of Pittsburgh Press

University of Wisconsin Press

University Press of New England

Unmuzzled Ox

Unspeakable Visions of the Individual

Vagabond

Verse

Vignette

Virginia Quarterly Review

Volt

Wampeter Press

Washington Writers Workshop

Water-Stone

Water Table

Wave Books

West Branch

Western Humanities Review

Westigan Review

White Pine Press
Wickwire Press
Willow Springs
Wilmore City
Witness
Word Beat Press
Word-Smith
World Literature Today
Wormwood Review

Writers Forum
Xanadu
Yale Review
Yardbird Reader
Yarrow
Y'Bird
Zeitgeist Press
Zoetrope: All-Story
ZYZZYVA

CONTRIBUTING SMALL PRESSES FOR PUSHCART PRIZE XXXIII

A

Abramelin, Box 337, Brookhaven, NY 11719

Adastra Press, 16 Reservation Rd., Easthampton, MA 01027

Agni, Creative Writing Program, Boston Univ., 236 Bay State Rd., Boston, MA 02215

Ahadada Books, Meikai Univ., 8 Akemi, Urayasu-shi, Chiba-ken, 279-8550, Japan

Akashic Books, 232 Third St., #B404, Brooklyn, NY 11215

Alaska Quarterly Review, 3211 Providence Dr., Anchorage, AK 99508

Alice Blue, 11301 SE 10th St. #78, Vancouver, WA 98664

Alice James Books, 238 Main St., Farmington, ME 04938

Alimentum, P.O. Box 776, New York, NY 10163

Allbook Books, P.O. Box 562, Selden, NY 11784

Alligator Juniper, 220 Grove Ave., Prescott, AZ 86301

American Journal of Nursing, 333 Seventh Ave., Floor 19, New York, NY 10001

American Literary Review, P.O. Box 311307, Denton, TX 76203-1307

American Poetry Review, 117 S. 17th St. (#910) Philadelphia, PA 19103

The American Scholar, 1606 New Hampshire Ave., NW, Washington, DC 20009

American Short Fiction, P.O. Box 301209, Austin, TX 78703

Anhinga Press, P.O. Box 10595, Tallahassee, FL 32302

Another Chicago Magazine, 3709 N. Kenmore, Chicago, IL 60613

The Antioch Review, P.O. Box 148, Yellow Springs, OH 45387

Apple Valley Review, Queen's Postal Outlet, Box 12, Kingston, ON, Canada K7L 3R9

Arctos Press, P.O. Box 401, Sausalito, CA 94966-0401

Argestes, 2941 170th St., South Amana, IA 52334

Arizona Authors Association, 6145 West Echo Lane, Glendale, AZ 85302

Arkansas Review, P.O. Box 1890, State University, AR 72467

Arsenic Lobster, 1830 W. 18th St., Chicago, IL 60608

Asheville Poetry Review, P.O. Box 7086, Asheville, NC 28802

The Ashland Poetry Press, Ashland University, Ashland, OH 44805

Asterius Press, P.O. Box 5122, Seabrook, NJ 08302

Astounding Beauty Ruffian Press, 2155 Elk Creek Rd., Stuart, VA 24171

Atlanta Review, P.O. Box 8248, Atlanta, GA 31106

Aunt Lute Books, P.O. Box 410687, San Francisco, CA 94141

The Aurorean, P. O. Box 187, Farmington, ME 04938

Autumn House Press, 87 Westwood St., Pittsburgh, PA 15211

B

Backwards City Review, P.O. Box 41317, Greensboro, NC 27404

The Backwaters Press, 3502 North 52nd St., Omaha, NE 68104-3506

Ballard Street Poetry Journal, P.O. Box 3560, Worcester, MA 01613

Bamboo Ridge Press, P.O. Box 61781, Honolulu, HI 96839-1781

Barbaric Yawp, Bone World Publishing, 3700 Country Route 24, Russell, NY 13684

The Barefoot Muse, P.O. Box 115, Hainesport, NJ 08036

Barrelhouse Magazine, 3500 Woodridge Ave., Wheaton, MD 20902

Barrow Street, P.O. Box 1831, New York, NY 10156

The Bat City Review, Univ. of Texas, 1 University Station B5000, Austin, TX 78751

Bayou Magazine, Univ. of New Orleans, 2000 Lakeshore Dr., New Orleans, LA 70148

Bear Parade, 228 Montrose Ave. #3, Brooklyn, NY 11206

Bear Star Press, 185 Hollow Oak Dr., Cohasset, CA 95973

Bedbug Press, P.O. Box 39, Brownsville, OR 97327

Bellday Books, Inc., P.O. Box 3687, Pittsburgh, PA 15230

Belle Books, P.O. Box 67, Smyrna, GA 30081

Bellevue Literary Press, NYU School of Medicine, 550 First Ave., New York, NY 10016

Bellingham Review, MS-9053 WWU, Bellingham, WA 98225

Beloit Poetry Journal, P.O. Box 151, Farmington, ME 04938

Big Sky Journal, P.O. Box 1069, Bozeman, MT 59771

Birch Brook Press, P.O. Box 81, Delhi, NY 13753

Birmingham Poetry Review, Univ. of Alabama, Birmingham, AL 35294

BkMk Press, UMKC, 5101 Rockhill Rd., Kansas City, MO 64110

Black Clock, 24700 McBean Pkwy, Valencia, CA 91355

Black Ocean, P.O. Box 990962, Boston, MA 02199

Black Warrior Review, Box 870170, Tuscaloosa, AL 35487-0170

Blackbird, P.O. Box 843082, Richmond, VA 23284

Blaze Vox, 14 Tremaine Ave., Kenmore, NY 14217-2616

Blue Cubicle Press, P.O. Box 250382, Plano, TX 75025

Blue Fifth Review, 267 Lark Meadow Cr., Bluff City, TN 37618

Blue Line Press, 44 Pierrepont Ave., Potsdam, NY 13676-2294

Blue Unicorn, 22 Avon Rd., Kensington, CA 94707

BOA Editions, LTD., 250 No. Goodman St., Ste. 306, Rochester, NY 14607

Boulevard, 7505 Byron Place, #1, Clayton, MO 63105

Boxcar Poetry Review, 401 S. LaFayette Park Pl., #309, Los Angeles, CA 90057

Brain, Child, P.O. Box 714, Lexington, VA 24450

Breath & Shadow, 161 Stovepipe Alley, Monroe, ME 04951

Briar Cliff Review, P.O. Box 2100, Sioux City, IA 51104-0100

Brilliant Corners, English Dept., Lycoming College, Williamsport, PA 17701

The Broadkill Review, 104 Federal St., Milton, DE 19968

Brown Jacket Books, 3760 Latimer Place, Oakland, CA 94609

Bull City Press, 1217 Odyssey Dr., Durham, NC 27713

Burning Bush Publications, P.O. Box 4658, Santa Rosa, CA 95402

C

CAB/NET, 4495 Perry St., Denver, CO 80212

Café Irreal, P.O. Box 87031, Tucson, AZ 85754

Caketrain, Box 82588, Pittsburgh, PA 15218

Callaloo, Texas A&M Univ., 249 Blocker Bldg., College Station, TX 77843-0001

Calyx Inc., P.O. Box B, 216 SW Madison #7, Corvallis, OR 97339-0539

The Caribbean Writer, Univ. of the Virgin Islands, St. Croix, U.S. Virgin Islands 00850

Carve Magazine, P.O. Box 701510, Dallas, TX 75370

Cave Wall Press, PO. Box 29546, Greensboro, NC 27429-9546

CCTE Studies, Tarleton State Univ., Box T-0300, Stephenville, TX 76402

Cellar Roots, Eastern Michigan University, 235-A King Hall, Ypsilanti, MI 48197

Center, University of Missouri-Columbia, 202 Tate Hall, Columbia, MO 65211

Central Avenue Press, 8400 Menaul Blvd. NE, Ste. 211-A, Albuquerque, NM 87112

Cervena Barva Press, P.O. Box 440357, W. Somerville, MA 02144

Cezanne's Carrot, P.O. Box 6037, Santa Fe, NM 87502

Chattahoochee Review, 2101 Womack Rd. Dunwoody, GA 30338

Chautauqua Literary Journal, P.O. Box 2039, York Beach, ME 03910

Chelsea, Box 125, Cooper Station, New York, NY 10276-0125

Chicory Blue Press, Inc., 795 East Street North, Goshen, CT 06756

Chimaera Literary Miscellany, 18760 Cypress Rd., Fort Bragg, CA 95437

Chrysalis Reader, 1745 Gravel Hill Rd., Dillwyn, VA 23936-2343

Cider Press Review, 777 Braddock Lane, Halifax, PA 17032

Cimarron Review, Oklahoma State Univ., 205 Morrill Hall, Stillwater, OK 74078

Cincinnati Review, McMicken Hall, Rm.369, P.O. Box 210069, Cincinnati, OH 45221

Coal City Review, English Dept., Univ. of Kansas, Lawrence, KS 66045

Coal Hill Review, 87   Westwood St., Pittsburgh, PA 15211

Coconut Poetry, 2331 Eastway Rd., Decatur, GA 30033

Cold-drill, English Dept., Boise State Univ., 1910 University Dr., Boise, ID 83725

The Cold River Review, P.O. Box 107, Acworth, NH 03601

Colorado Review, Colorado State University, Fort Collins, CO 80523

Concrete Wolf, P.O. Box 788, Kirkland, WA 98083

Conjunctions, Bard College, Annandale-On-Hudson, NY 12504

Court Green, Columbia College, 600 South Michigan Ave., Chicago, IL 60605

Crab Creek Review, P.O. Box 85088, Seattle, WA 98145

Crazyhorse, English Dept., College of Charleston, 66 George St., Charleston, SC 29424

Creative Nonfiction, 5501 Walnut St., Ste. 202, Pittsburgh, PA 15232

Curbstone Press, 321 Jackson St., Willimantic, CT 06226

Cyco, 25 E. 21st St., New York, NY 10010

D

D-N Publishing, 598 Indian Trail Rd., South #111, Indian Trail, NC 28079

Dalton Publishing, P.O. Box 242, Austin, TX 78767

Dappled Things Magazine, 5850 Cameron Run Terrace, #516, Alexandria, VA 22303

Destructible Heart Press, P.O. Box 257, Albuquerque, NM 87103

Diner, Box 60676, Greendale Station, Worcester, MA 01606

Diode, 421 S. Pine St., Richmond, VA 23220

The Distillery, Motlow State Community College, P.O. Box 8500, Lynchburg, TN 37352

Divine Whine, P.O. Box 23067, St. Louis, MO 63156

DMQ Review, 16393 Bonnie Lane, Los Gatos, CA 95032

Dogwood, English Dept., Fairfield Univ., Fairfield, CT 06824-5195

Doorways Magazine, 1447 E. Poplar St., #1, Stockton, CA 95205

The Dos Passos Review, Longwood Univ., 201 High St., Farmville, VA 23909

Drash: Northwest Mosaic, 8221 30th Ave. NE, Seattle, WA 98115

DuPage Writers Group, 23 Willabay Dr., Unit D, Williams Bay, WI 53191

E

Ecotone, 622 Waynich Blvd. (#102), Wrightsville Beach, NC 28480

Edge Publications, P.O. Box Ocean Park, WA 98640

Eggemoggin Reach Review, 32 Burnt Cove Rd., Stonington, ME 04681

Ekphrasis, P.O. Box 161236, Sacramento, CA 95816

Electric Velocipede, P.O. Box 266, Bettendorf, IA 52722

Eleven Eleven, 1111 8th St., San Francisco, CA 94107

Elimae, 423 Azalea, Duncanville, TX 75137

Elkhound, P.O. Box 1453, Gracie Station, New York, NY 10028

Epiphany, 71 Bedford St., New York, NY 10014

Epoch, 251 Goldwin Smith Hall, Cornell Univ., Ithaca, NY 14853-3201

Esopus, 532 Laguardia Place, #486, New York, NY 10012

Eureka Literary Magazine, Eureka College, 300 E. College Ave., Eureka, IL 61530-1500

The Evansville Review, 1800 Lincoln Ave., Evansville, IN 47722

Event, Douglas College, P.O. Box 2503, New Westminster, BC, V3L 5B2, Canada

EWU Press, 534 E. Spokane Falls Blvd., Ste. 203, Spokane, WA 99202

Exit 13 Magazine, P.O. Box 423, Fanwood, NJ 07023

F

Failbetter, 2022 Grove Ave., Richmond, VA 23220

Faultline, English Dept., University of California, Irvine, CA 92697-2650

Featherproof Books, 2201 W. Iowa St., #3, Chicago, IL 60622

Fiction International, English Dept., San Diego State Univ., San Diego, CA 92182-6020

Field, Oberlin College, 50 N. Professor St., Oberlin, OH 44074

Fifth Wednesday Books, P.O. Box 4033, Lisle, IL 60532

Finishing Line Press, P.O. Box 1626, Georgetown, KY 40324

The First Line, P.O. Box 250382, Plano, TX 75025-0382

Fithian Press, P.O. Box 2790, McKinleyville, CA 95519

5 AM, Box 205, Spring Church, PA 15686

Five Points, Georgia State Univ., P.O. Box 3999, Atlanta, GA 30302-3999

Flame Books Limited, P.O. Box 430, Durham, DN1 1SE, United Kingdom

Flashquake, 1004 Celia Lane, Lexington, KY 40504

Flask Review, 5 Barry St., Randolph, MA 02368

The Florida Review, English Dept., Univ. of Central Florida, Orlando, FL 32816

Flume Press, 400 W. First St., Chico, CA 95929-0830

Foliate Oak, Univ. of Arkansas, Monticello, AR 71656

Fourteen Hills, SF State Univ., 1600 Holloway Ave., San Francisco, CA 94132

Fourth Genre, Michigan State Univ., 285 Bessey Hall, East Lansing, MI 48824

The Fourth River, Chatham Univ., Woodland Rd., Pittsburgh, PA 15232

Free Lunch, P.O. Box 717, Glenview, IL 60025

Free Verse, M233 Marsh Rd., Marshfield, WI 54449

Freshwater, Asnuntuck Community College, 170 Elm St., Enfield, CT 06082

Fugue, English Dept., P.O. Box 441102, Univ. of Idaho, Moscow, ID 83844

G

Gastronomica, Weston Hall, 995 Main St., Williams College, Williamstown, MA 01267

A Gathering of the Tribes, P.O. Box 20693, Tompkins Sq., Sta., New York, NY 10009

Gentle Strength Quarterly, 16161 Ventura Blvd., #406, Encino, CA 91436

The Georgia Review, Univ. of Georgia, Athens, GA 30602-9009

The Gettysburg Review, Gettysburg College, Gettysburg, PA 17325-1491

Ghost Road Press, 5303 E. Evans Ave., #309, Denver, CO 80222

Ghoti Magazine, 1500 Glencoe Rd., Glencoe, MD 21152

Gilbert Magazine, 3460 N. Hackett Ave., Milwaukee, WI 53211-2945

Gival Press, P.O. Box 3812, Arlington, VA 22203

Glimmer Train Press, Inc., 1211 NW Glisan, #207, Portland, OR 97209

Global City Review, City College of NY, Convent Ave. & 138th St., New York, NY 10031

Goose River Press, 3400 Friendship Rd., Waldoboro, ME 04572

Great River Review, Anderson Center, P.O. Box 406, Red Wing, MN 55066

Green Fuse Community Press, 400 Vortex Dr., Bellvue, CO 80512

Green Hills Literary Lantern, Truman Univ., 100 East Normal, Kirksville, MO 63501

Green Mountains Review, Johnson State College, Johnson, VT 05656

The Greensboro Review, UNCG, P.O. Box 26170, Greensboro, NC 27402

Grist, English Dept., Univ. of Tennessee, 301 McClung Tower, Knoxville, TN 37996

GUD Magazine, 205 Swanson Ave., Stratford, CT 06614

Guernica, 403 E. 69th St., Apt. 3D, New York, NY 10021

Guernica Editions, 11 Mount Royal Ave., Toronto (ON), Canada M6H 2S2

Gulf Coast, English Dept., University of Houston, Houston, TX 77204

H

H.O.W. Journal, 112 Franklin St., 4th fl., New York, NY 10013

Hanging Loose Press, 231 Wyckoff St., Brooklyn, NY 11217

Harp-Strings Poetry Journal, Box 640387, Beverly Hills, FL 34464

Harper Palate, Binghamton Univ., P.O. Box 6000, Binghamton, NY 13902-8927

Harvard Review, Lamont Library, Level 5, Harvard Univ., Cambridge, MA 02138

Hawthorne Books, 1221 SW 10th Ave., Ste. 408, Portland, OR 97205

The Healing Muse, Upstate Medical University, 750 E. Adams St., Syracuse, NY 13210

Hearing Eye, Box 1, 99 Torriano Ave., London NW5 2RX, United Kingdom

Heart Lodge, 9707 W. Chatfield Ave., Unit D, Littleton, CO 80128

The Hedgehog Review, Univ. of Virginia, P.O. Box 400816, Charlottesville, VA 22904

Her Circle Ezine, 335 Cherry, Wyandotte, MI 48192

Hidden Oak, 402 So. 25th St., Philadelphia, PA 19146

High Desert Journal, P.O. Box 7647, Bend, OR 97708

Hobart: A Literary Journal, P.O. Box 1658, Ann Arbor, MI 48106

The Hollins Critic, Hollins University, Roanoke, VA 24020

Home Planet Press, P.O. Box 455, High Falls, NY 12440

The Hudson Review, 684 Park Ave., New York, NY 10065

Hunger Mountain, Vermont College, 36 College St., Montpelier, VT 05602

I

Ibbetson Street Press, 25 School St., Somerville, MA 02143

Ice Cube Press, 205 N. Front St., North Liberty, IA 52317-9302

The Iconoclast, 1675 Amazon Rd., Mohegan Lake, NY 10547

Idaho Review, Boise State Univ., 1910 University Dr., Boise, ID 83725

Illuminations, College of Charleston, 66 George St., Charleston, SC 29424

Illya's Honey, P.O. Box 700865, Dallas, TX 75370

Image, 3307 Third Avenue West, Seattle, WA 98119

In Character, 300 Conshohocken State Rd., (#500), W. Conshohocken, PA 19428

In the Grove, P.O. Box 16195, Fresno, CA 93755

Indiana Review, Ballantine 465, 1020 E. Kirkwood Ave., Bloomington, IN 47405

Inglis House Poetry, 2600 Belmont Ave., Philadelphia, PA 19131

Inkwell, Manhattanville College, 2900 Purchase St., Purchase, NY 10577

Interstice, South Texas College, 3201 W. Pecan Blvd., McAllen, TX 78501

The Iowa Review, 308 EPB, Univ. of Iowa, Iowa City, IA 52242

Iris G. Press, 2848 Nolt Rd., Lancaster, PA 17601

Iron Horse Literary Review, Texas Tech Univ., MS 43091, Lubbock, TX 79409

Isotope, English Dept., Utah State Univ., 3200 Old Main Hill, Logan, UT 84322-3200

J

Jabberwock Review, Drawer E, English Dept., Mississippi State, MS 39762

Jawbone Publishing, 1540 W. Happy Valley Circle, Newnan, GA 30263

The Journal, English Dept., Ohio State Univ., 164 W. 17th Ave., Columbus, OH 43210

Journal of New Jersey Poets, County College, 214 Center Grove Rd., Randolph NJ 07869

Journal of Truth and Consequence, 110 Scenic Dr., Hattiesburg, MS 39401

Juked, 110 Westridge Dr., Tallahassee, FL 32304

K

Kaimana, 509 University Ave. #902, Honolulu, HI 96826

Kaleidotrope, P.O. Box 25, Carle Place, NY 11514

Kaleidowhirl, 63 Parker Rd., Greensburg, KY 42743

Karamu, Eastern Illinois Univ., 600 Lincoln Ave., Charleston, IL 61920

Kelsey Review, P.O. Box B, Trenton, NJ 08690-1099

The Kenyon Review, Neff Cottage, 102 W. Wiggin St., Gambier, OH 43022

Keyhole Magazine, 206 Sentinel Dr., Nashville, TN 37209

The King's English, 3114 NE 47th Ave., Portland, OR 97213

Knock, Antioch University, 2326 Sixth Ave., Seattle, WA 98121-1814

Kyoto Journal, 35 Minamigoshomachi, Okazaki, Sakyo-ku, Kyoto 606-8334, Japan

L

Lake Effect, 170 Irvin Kochel Center, 4951 College Dr., Erie, PA 16563-1501

Lamberson Corona Press, P.O. Box 1116, West Babylon, NY 11704

Lamination Colony, 2571 Beckwith Trl SW, Marietta, GA 30068-3114

Leaf Press, Box 416, Lantzville, BC, Canada V0R 2H0

The League of Laboring Poets, 19850 Arrow Hwy, #C10, Covina, CA 91724

Lilies and Cannonballs Review, P.O. Box 702, Bowling Green Station, New York, NY 10274

LIT Magazine, 66 West 12th St., Rm. 506, New York, NY 10011

The Literary Review, Fairleigh Dickinson Univ., 285 Madison Ave., Madison, NJ 07940

Louisiana State University Press, P.O. Box 25053, Baton Rouge, LA 70894-5053

Lunch Hour Stories, 22833 Bothell-Everett Hwy, Ste. 110, Bothell, WA 98021

Lyric Poetry Review, P.O. Box 2494, Bloomington, IN 47402

M

The MacGuffin, Schoolcraft College, 18600 Haggerty Rd., Livonia, MI 48152

Main Channel Voices, P.O. Box 492, Winona, MN 55987

The Malahat Review, P.O. Box 1700, Stn CSC, Victoria BC V8W 2Y2, Canada

Mandorla, Illinois State Univ., Campus Box 4240, Normal, IL 61790-4240

The Manhattan Review, 440 Riverside Dr., #38, New York, NY 10027

Mannequin Envy, 1830 Maple St., Georgetown, TX 78626

Many Mountains Moving Press, 1705 Lombard St., Philadelphia, PA 19146

Margie, Inc., P.O. Box 250, Chesterfield, MO 63006

Marsh Hawk Press, P.O. Box 206, East Rockaway, NY 11518

The Massachusetts Review, 40 Manning Rd., Conway, MA 01341

Mayapple Press, 408 N. Lincoln St., Bay City, MI 48708

McSweeney's, 849 Valencia St., San Francisco, CA 94110

Measure, English Dept., Univ. of Evansville, 1800 Lincoln Ave., Evansville, IN 47722

Melee, P.O. Box 4724, Fayetteville, AR 72701

Memorious, c/o Frank, 12 Laurel St., Cambridge, MA 02139

Meridian, University of Virginia, Charlottesville, VA 22904

Merlin Press, P.O. Box 5602, San Jose, CA 95150

Micah Publications, Inc., 255 Humphrey St., Marblehead, MA 01945

Michigan Quarterly Review, 915 East Washington St., Ann Arbor, MI 48109

Mid-American Review, Bowling Green State Univ., Bowling Green, OH 43403

Mid-List Press, 4324 12th Ave. So., Minneapolis, MN 55407-3218

Mindprints, 800 South College Dr., Santa Maria, CA 93454

Minnesota Review, English Dept., Carnegie Mellon University, Pittsburgh, PA 15213

MiPOesias, 604 Vale St., Bloomington, IL 61701

Mississippi Crow Magazine, 14051 Oakview Lane N, Dayton, MN 55327

Mississippi Review, 118 College Dr., #5037, Hattiesburg, MS 39406-0001

Missouri Review, 357 McReynolds, UMC, Columbia, MO 65211

MO: Writings from the River, 2100 16th Ave. S., Great Falls, MT 59405

Mobius, P.O. Box 671058, Flushing, NY 11367

Momentum Books, L.L.C., 2145 Crooks Rd., Troy, MI 48084

Motes, P.O. Box 6034, Louisville, KY 40206-0034

Mudfish, 184 Franklin St., Gr. Flr., New York, NY 10013

N

Narrative Magazine, 845 Woodmont Ct., Chico, CA 95926

The New Criterion, 900 Broadway, New York, NY 10003

New Delta Review, 15 Allen Hall, Louisiana State Univ., Baton Rouge, LA 70803

New England Review, Middlebury College, Middlebury, VT 05753

New Issues Poetry & Prose, 1903 W. Michigan Ave., Kalamazoo, MI 49008-5463

New Letters, Univ. of Missouri, 5100 Rockhill Rd., Kansas City, MO 64110-2499

New Madrid, English Dept., Murray State Univ., Murray, KY 42071

New Ohio Review, 360 Ellis Hall, Ohio University, Athens, OH 45701

New Orleans Review, Loyola University New Orleans, New Orleans, LA 70118

The New Orphic Review, 706 Mill St., Nelson, B.C. V1L 4S5, Canada

New Renaissance, 26 Heath Rd., Apt. 11, Arlington, MA 02474

New Voices Magazine, 114 West 26th St., Ste. 1004, New York, NY 10001

New Works Review, P.O. Box 54, Friendswood, TX 77549-0054

Ninth Letter, 608 S. Wright St., Urbana, IL 61801

No Record Press, Art Gallery, Ste. 1, 114 Forrest St., Brooklyn, NY 11206

No Tell Motel, 11436 Fairway Dr., Reston, VA 20190

NOO Journal, 261 Belchertown Rd., Apt., B, Amherst, MA 01002

Noon, 1324 Lexington Ave., PMB 298, New York, NY 10128

North American Review, UNI, 1222 West 27th St., Cedar Falls, IA 50614-0516

North Atlantic Review, P.O. Box 154, Old Mission, MI 49673

North Dakota Quarterly, P.O. Box 7209, Univ. of North Dakota, Grand Forks, ND 58202

The North Sea Poetry Scene Press, 33 Woods Lane, Southampton, NY 11968

Northwest Review, 369 PLC, Univ. of Oregon, Eugene, OR 97403

Not Just Air, 5214 8th Road So., #1, Arlington, VA 22204

Not One of Us, 12 Curtis Rd., Natick, MA 01760

Notre Dame Review, 840 Flanner Hall, Notre Dame, IN 46556-5639

November 3 Club, 66 Fairfax Rd., #3, Worcester, MA 01619

Now Culture, 90 Kennedy Rd., Andover, NJ 07821

O

Off the Coast, P.O. Box 205, Bristol, ME 04539

Old Mountain Press, 2542 S. Edgewater Dr., Fayetteville, NC 28303

One Story, P.O. Box 150618, Brooklyn, NY 11215-0618

Ontario Review, 9 Honey Brook Dr., Princeton, NJ 08540

Open Spaces Quarterly, PMB 134, 6327 SW Capital Hwy., Ste. C, Portland, OR 97239

Opium Magazine, P.O. Box 441, Cedar Falls, IA 50613

Orbis, 17 Greenhow Ave., West Kirby, Wirral, Cheshire, CH48 5EL, UK

Orchises Press, P.O. Box 320533, Alexandria, VA 22320

Oregon Literary Review, 3550 SW Pomona St., Portland, OR 97219

Orion, 187 Main St., Great Barrington, MA 01230

Osiris, P.O. Box 297, Deerfield, M 01342

Overtime, P.O. Box 250382, Plano, TX 75025

Oxford American, 201 Donaghey Ave., Main 107, Conway, AR 72035-5001

Oyez Review, Roosevelt University, 430 So. Michigan Ave., Chicago, IL 60605-1394

P

P. R. A. Publishing, P.O. Box 211701, Martinez, GA 30917

The Pacific Review, CSUSB, 5500 University Parkway, San Bernardino, CA 92407-2397

Paddlefish, Mount Marty College, 1105 W. Eighth St., Yankton, SD 57078-3724

Palindrome Publishing, 304 E. Third St., #6, Pella, IA 50219-1979

Panhandler, Univ. of West Florida, 11000 University Pkwy, Pensacola, FL 32514-5750

Paper Street Press, P.O. Box 14786, Pittsburgh, PA 15234

The Paris Review, 62 White St., New York, NY 10013

Parkway Publishers, Inc., P.O. Box 3678, Boone, NC 28607

Parlor, 1400 Montgomery Ave., Rosemont, PA 19010-1699

Parnassus: Poetry in Review, 205 West 89th St., Apt. 8F, New York, NY 10024-1835

Parthenon West Review, 15 Littlefield Terrace, San Francisco, CA 94107

Passages North, Northern Michigan Univ., 1401 Presque Isle Ave., Marquette, MI 49885

Paycock Press, 3819 13th St. N., Arlington, VA 22201

Pearl, 3030 E. Second St., Long Beach, CA 90803

Pebble Lake Review, 15318 Pebble Lake Dr., Houston, TX 77095

PEN American Center, 588 Broadway, Ste. 303, New York, NY 10012

Per Contra, 250 So. 13th St., Apt. 10-B, Philadelphia, PA 19107

Perspectives, 300 Jay St., Brooklyn, NY 11201-2983

Perugia Press, P.O. Box 60364, Florence, MA 01062

Petigru Review, 8 Allegheny Run, Simpsonville, SC 29681

Phantasmagoria, Century College, 3300 Century Ave. No., White Bear Lake, MN 55110

Philadelphia Stories, 2021 S. 11th St., Philadelphia, PA 19148

Phoebe, George Mason University, 4400 University Dr., Fairfax, VA 22030-4444

The Pinch, 467 Patterson Hall, Memphis, TN 38152

Plain Spoke, 6199 Steubenville Rd. SE., Amsterdam, OH 43903

Plain View Press, P.O. Box 42255, Austin, TX 78704

Pleiades Press, Univ. of Central Missouri, Warrensburg, MO 64093-5069

Ploughshares, Emerson College, 120 Boylston St., Boston, MA 02116-4624

PMS, 1530 3rd Aveue South, Birmington, AL 35294-1260

Poems Against War Magazine, 2923 St. Paul St., Apt. 2, Baltimore, MD 21218

Poems & Plays, Middle Tennessee State Univ., Murfreesboro, TN 37132

Poetry, 444 N. Michigan Ave. Chicago, IL 60011

Poet Lore, c/o Writer's Center, 4508 Walsh St., Bethesda, MD 20815

Poetry Center, Cleveland State Univ., 2121 Euclid Ave., Cleveland, OH 44115-2214

Poetry in the Arts, 4917 Ravenswood Dr., #260, San Antonio, TX 78227-4353

Poetry Kanto, Kanto Gakuin Univ., 3-22-1 Kamariya-Minami, Kanazawa-ku, Yokohama 236-8052 Japan

Poetry Midwest, 12345 College Blvd., Overland Park, KS

Poetry Northwest, 4232 SE Hawthorne Blvd., Portland, OR 97215

The Poetry Project Newsletter, 131 East 10th St., New York, NY 10003

Poetry Review, 22 Betterton St., London WC2H 9B+

Poets Wear Prada, 533 Bloomfield St., 2nd floor, Hoboken, NJ 07030

POOL, P.O. Box 49738, Los Angeles, CA 90049

Post Road Magazine, P.O. Box 400951, Cambridge, MA 02470

Potomac Review, Montgomery College, 51 Mannakee St., Rockville, MD 20850

Prairie Schooner, UNL, 201 Andrews Hall, P.O. Box 880334, Lincoln, NE 68588-0334

Presa Press, P.O. Box 792, Rockford, MI 49341

Press 53, P.O. Box 30314, Winston Salem, NC 27130

Prick of the Spindle, 305 Willow Bend Circle, Leesville, LA 71446

Prism International, Univ. British Columbia, Vancouver, BC V6T 1Z1, Canada

Provincetown Arts, 650 Commercial St., Provincetown, MA 02657

A Public Space, 323 Dean St., Brooklyn, NY 11217

Publishing Genius, 1818 E. Lafayette Ave., Baltimore, MD 21213

Pudding House Publications, 81 Shadymere Lane, Columbus, OH 43213

Q

Quarterly West, 255 S. Central Campus Dr., Univ. of Utah, Salt Lake City, UT 84112

The Quirk, 1275 N. Third St., Shreve B507, West Lafayette, IN 47906

R

Radiant Turnstile, 19910 Stuebner Airline Rd., Spring, TX 77379

Rager Media, Inc., 1016 West Abbey Dr., Medina, OH 44256

Ragged Sky Press, 270 Griggs Dr., Princeton, NJ 08540

Rain Mountain Press, 68 East Third St, #16, New York, NY 10003

The Raintown Review, Hunter College, CUNY, 695 Park Ave., New York, NY 10065

Rambler Magazine, P.O. Box 5070, Chapel Hill, NC 27514

Raritan, 31 Mine St., New Brunswick, NJ 08903

Rattle, 12411 Ventura Blvd., Studio City, CA 91604

Raving Dove, Inc., P.O. Box 28, West Linn, OR 97068

RAW ArT Press, 4110 Crestview Dr., Pittsburg, CA 94565

Red Hen Press, P.O. Box 3537, Granada Hills, CA 91394

Redactions: Poetry & Poetics, 24 College St., Apt. 1, Brockport, NY 14420

Redivider, 226 Beacon St., Unit 3, Boston, MA 02116

Relief, 800 Pointe Dr., Crystal Lake, IL 60014

Rhino, P.O. Box 591, Evanston, IL 60204

Rivendell, P.O. Box 9594, Asheville, NC 28815

River City Publishing, 1719 Mulberry St., Montgomery, AL 36106

River Styx, 3547 Olive St., Ste. 107, St. Louis, MO 63103-1014

Roanoke Review, 221 College Lane, Salem, VA 24153-3794

Rock Salt Plum Review, Kandinskystr. 12, 67657 Kaiserslautern, Germany

Roger, Creative Writing Dept., Roger Williams Univ., 1 Old Ferry Rd., Bristol, RI 02809

Rogue Poetry Review, Box 5853, Kansas City, MO 64171-0853
The Rose & Thorn, 3 Diamond Crt., Montebello, NY 10901
RoyalAir Press, 435 S. Ridgewood Ave., Ste. 200, Daytona Beach, FL 32114
The Runestone Journal, P.O. Box 25294, Portland, OR 97298

S

Sacred Fools Press, 215 River Ave., Providence, RI 02908
Sage Hill Press, 4841 5th Ave. N., Grand Forks, ND 58203
Saint Ann's Review, 129 Pierrepont St., Brooklyn, NY 11201
Salamander, English Dept., Suffolk University, 41 Temple St., Boston, MA 02114
Salt Flats Annual, P.O. Box 2381, Layton, UT 84041-9381
Salt Hill, English Dept., Syracuse Univ., Syracuse, NY 13244
Santa Monica Review, Santa Monica College, 1900 Pico Blvd., Santa Monica, CA 90405
Sarabande Books Inc., 2234 Dundee Rd., Ste. 200, Louisville, KY 40205
Schuylkill Valley Journal, 240 Golf Hills Rd., Havertown, PA 19083
Scissor Press, P.O. Box 382, Ludlow, VT 05149
Scope Magazine, 61 Duncairn Gardens, Belfast, Antrim BT15 2GB, Ireland
SCR+II, 90 Kennedy Rd., Andover, NJ 07821
Sea Stories, 21 Eldridge Rd., Jamaica Plain, MA 02130
Sentence, Western Connecticut State Univ., 181 White St., Danbury, CT 06810
The Sewanee Review, 735 University Ave., Sewanee, TN 37383-1000
Shady Lane Press, 9138 Queen Elizabeth Ct, Orlando, FL 32818
Shalla Magazine, 23645 Maple Springs Dr., Diamond Bar, CA 91765
Shenandoah, Mattingly House, Washington & Lee Univ., Lexington, VA 24450
Sideshow Press, 10 Withey Hill Rd., Moosup, CT 06354
Silent Actor, 5 Barry St., Randolph, MA 02368
Silent Voices, P.O. Box 11180, Glendale, CA 91226
Skidrow Penthouse Press, 68 East Third St., #16, New York, NY 10003
Skyline Publications, P.O. Box 295, Stormville, NY 12582
Slipstream, P.O. Box 2071, Niagra Falls, NY 14301
Small Beer Press, 176 Prospect Press, Northampton, MA 01060
Smartish Pace, P.O. Box 22161, Baltimore, MD 21203
Snapshot Press, P.O. Box 132, Waterloo, Liverpool, L22 8WZ, United Kingdom
Song of the San Joaquin Quarterly, P.O. Box 1161, Modesto, CA 95353-1161
Sonora Review, English Dept., University of Arizona, Tucson, AZ 85721
The Southampton Review, Stony Brook Southampton, 239 Montauk Hwy, Southampton, NY 11968
The Southeast Review, English Dept., Florida State Univ., Tallahassee, FL 32306
Southern Illinois University Press, 1915 University Press Dr., Carbondale, IL 62901
Southern Indiana Review, 8600 University Blvd., Evansville, Indiana 47712
Southern Poetry Review, 11935 Abercorn St., Savannah, GA 31419-1997
The Southern Review, Louisiana State Univ., Baton Rouge, LA 70803
Southern Writers Review, P.O. Box 4536, Garden Grove, CA 92842
Southwest Review, Southern Methodist Univ., P.O. Box 750374, Dallas, TX 75275-0374
Sou'wester, Box 1438, Edwardsville, IL 62026
Spoon River Poetry Review, Illinois State Univ., Campus Box 4241, Normal, IL 61790
Spot Write Literary Corporation, P.O. Box 3833, Palos Verdes Peninsula, CA 90274
St. Petersburg Review, Box 2889, Concord, NH 03302
Starving Writers Publishing, 3730 W. Buckingham, Ste. 326, Garland, TX 75042
Steel City Review, 324 Carnegie Pl., Pittsburgh, PA 15208
Stirring, 218 Stevens Dr., Hattiesburg, MS 39401
Stone Canoe, Syracuse Univ., 700 University Ave., Syracuse, NY 13244
Stone River Press, 2468 Southline Rd., Conroe, TX 77384-4332
Story Circle Network, 5802 Wynona Ave., Austin, TX 78756
Story Quarterly, 431 Sheridan Rd., Kenilworth, IL 60043

Storyglossia, 1004 Commercial Ave., #1110, Anacortes, WA 98221

storySouth, 898 Chelsea Ave., Bexley, OH 43209

StringTown Magazine, P.O. Box 1406, Medical Lake, WA 99022-1406

Summerset Hall Press, 416 Commonwealth Ave., Ste. 612, Boston, MA 02215

The Summerset Review, 25 Summerset Dr, Smithtown, NY 11787

The Sun, 107 North Roberson St., Chapel Hill, NC 27516

Sunnyoutside, P.O. Box 911, Buffalo, NY 14207

Swan Scythe Press, 2052 Calaveras Ave., Davis, CA 95616-3021

T

Texas Tech University Press, Lubbock, TX 79409-1037

Third Coast Magazine, English Dept., WMU, Kalamazoo, MI 49008

Third Wednesday, 174 Greenside Up, Ypsilanti, MI 48197

32 Poems Magazine, Texas Tech Univ., Box 43091, Lubbock, TX 79409

3:AM Magazine, 226 Montrose Ave., New York, NY 11206

The Threepenny Review, P.O. Box 9131, Berkeley, CA 94709

Tiferet Journal, 211 Dryden Rd., Bernardsville, NJ 07924

Tiger's Eye Press, P.O. Box 2935, Eugene, OR 97402

Tightrope Books, 17 Greyton Cres., Toronto, Canada M6E 2G1

Timber Creek Review, P.O. Box 16542, Greensboro, NC 27416

Timberline, 6281 Red Bud, Fulton, MO 65251

Tin House, 2601 NW Thurman St., Portland, OR 97210

Titular Journal, 225 Second Ave., #1, San Francisco, CA 94118

To Topos Poetry International Journal, 905 West 25th St., 202A TMHL, Kearny, NE 68847

Toadlily Press, PO Box 2, Chappaqua, NY 10514

TQR Stories, c/o Hansen, 8424 Rising Star Pl. NE, Albuquerque, NM 87122

Traprock Books, 1330 E. 25th Ave., Eugene, OR 97403

Triplopia, 6816 Mt. Vernon Ave., Salisbury, MD 21804

TriQuarterly, Northwestern Univ. Press, 629 Noyes St., Evanston IL 60208

Tuesday: An Art Project, P.O. Box 1074, Arlington, MA 02474

Tupelo Press, P.O. Box 539, Dorset, VT 05251

Turtle Ink Press, 704 Allen St., Syracuse, NY 13210

Two Review, P.O. Box 200639, Anchorage, AK 99520

U

U.S. 1 Poets' Cooperative, U.S. 1 Worksheets, P.O. Box 127, Kingston, NJ 08528

Underground Voices, P.O. Box 931671, Los Angeles, CA 90093

University of Georgia Press, 330 Research Dr., Athens, GA 30602

University of Nebraska Press, 1111 Lincoln Mall, Lincoln, NE 68588

University of Tampa Press, 401 W. Kennedy Blvd., Tampa, FL 33606

Unlikely 2.0, P.O. Box 1277, El Paso, TX 79947

Unsaid, 193 16th St., Apt. 5, Brooklyn, NY 11215

Unsplendid.com, 410 George St., Baltimore, MD 21201

Upstreet, P.O. Box 105, Richmond, MA 01254

Utah State University Press, 7800 Old Main Hill, Logan, UT 84322

V

Valley Voices Mississippi Valley State Univ., Itta Bena, MS 38941-1400

Valparaiso Poetry Review, Valparaiso University, Valparaiso, IN 46383 vanZeno Press, 28 Stonebridge Way, Berlin, CT 06037

Versal, Postbus 3865, 1001 AR Amsterdam, The Netherlands

Vestal Review, 2609 Dartmouth Dr., Vestal, NY 13850

Viking Dog Press, 501 S. Market St., Muncy, PA 17756

The Virginia Quarterly Review, One West Range, P.O. Box 400223, Charlottesville, VA 22904

Virtual Artists Collective, 5710 S. Kimbark #3, Chicago, IL 60637

The Vocabula Review, 5A Holbrook Crt., Rockport, MA 01966

Voice Catcher, 3568 NE US Grant Pl., Portland, OR 97212

Voices Rising, 2008 W. Jackson St., #E-1, Hollywood, FL 33020

Volt, P.O Box 657, Corte Madera, CA 94976

Vox, P.O. Box 4936, University, MS 38677

W

Walter Forest Press, P.O. Box 295, Stormville, NY 12582

The Wapshott Press, P.O. Box 31513, Los Angeles, CA 90031

Washington Writers' Publishing House, P.O. Box 15271, Washington, DC 20003

Water-Stone Review, MS-A1730, 1536 Hewitt Ave., Saint Paul, MN 55104-1284

Wave Books, 1938 Fairview Avenue East, Seattle, WA 98102

Wayne State University Press, 4809 Woodward Ave., Detroit, MI 48201

West Branch, Bucknell Univ., Lewisburg, PA 17837

The Westchester Review, P.O. Box 2464, Scarsdale, NY 10583

Whispering Prairie Press, P.O. Box 8342, Prairie Village, KS 66208

Whistling Shade, P.O. Box 7084, St. Paul, MN 55107

White Pelican Review, P.O. Box 7833, Lakeland, FL 33813

White Pine Press, P.O. Box 236, Buffalo, NY 14201

Wide Array, P.O. Box 20511, Waco, TX 76702

Willow Springs, 501 N. Riverpoint Blvd., Ste. 425, Spokane, WA 99202

Wings Press, 627 E. Guenther, San Antonio, TX 78210

Witness, UNLV, 4505 Maryland Pkwy., Box 455085, Las Vegas, NV 89154-5085

The Worcester Review, 1 Elkman St., Worcester, MA 01607

Wordcraft of Oregon, P.O. Box 3235, La Grande, OR 97850

WordFarm, 2010 Michigan Ave., La Porte, IN 46350

Word'n Woman Press, 130 Worden Ave., Ann Arbor, MI 48103

Words on Walls, 18348 Coral Chase Dr., Boca Raton, FL 33498

The Wordsmith Press, 11462 East Lane, Whitmore Lake, MI 48189

World Audience Inc., 303 Park Ave. S., #1440, New York, NY 10010-3657

World Literature Today, 630 Parrington Oval, Ste. 110, Norman, OK 73019-4033

The Write Side Up, 2347 32nd Ave., San Francisco, CA 94116

Writecorner Press, P.O. Box 140310, Gainesville, FL 32614

Writer's Chronicle, Mail Stop 1E3, George Mason Univ., Fairfax, VA 22030

The Writer's Circle, 680 Kirkwood Dr., Bldg. 1, Sudbury, Ontario, P3E 1X3, Canada

Y

Ye Olde Font Shoppe, P.O. Box 8328, New Haven, CT 06530

Z

Zahir Publishing, 315 S. Coast Hwy. 101, Ste. U8, Encinitas, CA 92024

Zoetrope: All Story, 916 Kearny St., San Francisco, CA 94133

ZYZZYVA, P.O. Box 590069, San Francisco, CA 94159

THE PUSHCART PRIZE FELLOWSHIPS

The Pushcart Prize Fellowships Inc., a 501 (c) (3) nonprofit corporation, is the endowment for The Pushcart Prize. We also make grants to promising new writers. "Members" donated up to $249 each, "Sponsors" gave between $250 and $999. "Benefactors" donated from $1000 to $4,999. "Patrons" donated $5,000 and more. We are very grateful for these donations. Gifts of any amount are welcome. For information write to the Fellowships at PO Box 380, Wainscott, NY 11975.

John Gill
Robert Giron
Doris Grumbach & Sybil Pike
Gwen Head
The Healing Muse
Robin Hemley
Jane Hirshfield
Helen H. Houghton
Joseph Hurka
Janklow & Nesbit Asso.
Edmund Keeley
Thomas E. Kennedy
Sydney Lea

Gerald Locklin
Thomas Lux
Markowitz, Fenelon and Bank
Elizabeth McKenzie
McSweeney's
Joan Murray
Barbara and Warren Phillips
Hilda Raz
Mary Carlton Swope
Julia Wendell
Philip White
Eleanor Wilner
Richard Wyatt & Irene Eilers

MEMBERS

Anonymous (3)
Betty Adcock
Agni
Carolyn Alessio
Dick Allen
Henry H. Alley
Lisa Alvarez
Jan Lee Ande
Ralph Angel
Antietam Review
Ruth Appelhof
Philip and Marjorie Appleman
Linda Aschbrenner
Renee Ashley
Ausable Press
David Baker
Catherine Barnett
Dorothy Barresi
Barrow Street Press
Jill Bart
Ellen Bass
Judith Baumel
Ann Beattie
Madison Smartt Bell
Beloit Poetry Journal
Pinckney Benedict
Karen Bender
Andre Bernard
Christopher Bernard
Wendell Berry
Linda Bierds
Stacy Bierlein
Bitter Oleander Press
Mark Blaeuer
Blue Lights Press
Carol Bly
BOA Editions
Deborah Bogen
Susan Bono
Anthony Brandt

James Breeden
Rosellen Brown
Jane Brox
Andrea Hollander Budy
E. S. Bumas
Richard Burgin
Skylar H. Burris
David Caliguiuri
Kathy Callaway
Janine Canan
Henry Carlile
Fran Castan
Chelsea Associates
Marianne Cherry
Phillis M. Choyke
Suzanne Cleary
Martha Collins
Joan Connor
John Copenhaven
Dan Corrie
Tricia Currans-Sheehan
Jim Daniels
Thadious Davis
Maija Devine
Sharon Dilworth
Edward J. DiMaio
Kent Dixon
John Duncklee
Elaine Edelman
Renee Edison & Don Kaplan
Nancy Edwards
M.D. Elevitch
Failbetter.com
Irvin Faust
Tom Filer
Susan Firer
Nick Flynn
Stakey Flythe Jr.
Peter Fogo
Linda N. Foster

Fugue
Alice Fulton
Eugene K. Garber
Frank X. Gaspar
A Gathering of the Tribes
Reginald Gibbons
Emily Fox Gordon
Philip Graham
Eamon Grennan
Lee Meitzen Grue
Habit of Rainy Nights
Rachel Hadas
Susan Hahn
Meredith Hall
Harp Strings
Jeffrey Harrison
Lois Marie Harrod
Healing Muse
Alex Henderson
Lily Henderson
Daniel Henry
Neva Herington
Lou Hertz
William Heyen
Bob Hicok
R. C. Hildebrandt
Kathleen Hill
Jane Hirshfield
Edward Hoagland
Daniel Hoffman
Doug Holder
Richard Holinger
Rochelle L. Holt
Richard M. Huber
Brigid Hughes
Lynne Hugo
Illya's Honey
Susan Indigo
Mark Irwin
Beverly A. Jackson
Richard Jackson
David Jauss
Marilyn Johnston
Alice Jones
Journal of New Jersey Poets
Robert Kalich
Julia Kasdorf
Miriam Poli Katsikis
Meg Kearney
Celine Keating
Brigit Kelly
John Kistner
Judith Kitchen
Stephen Kopel
Peter Krass
David Kresh
Maxine Kumin

Valerie Laken
Babs Lakey
Maxine Landis
Lane Larson
Dorianne Laux & Joseph Millar
Sydney Lea
Donald Lev
Dana Levin
Gerald Locklin
Rachel Loden
Radomir Luza, Jr.
Annette Lynch
Elzabeth MacKierman
Elizabeth Macklin
Leah Maines
Mark Manalang
Norma Marder
Jack Marshall
Michael Martone
Tara L. Masih
Dan Masterson
Peter Matthiessen
Alice Mattison
Tracy Mayor
Robert McBrearty
Jane McCafferty
Rebecca McClanahan
Bob McCrane
Jo McDougall
Sandy McIntosh
James McKean
Roberta Mendel
Didi Menendez
Barbara Milton
Alexander Mindt
Mississippi Review
Martin Mitchell
Roger Mitchell
Jewell Mogan
Patricia Monaghan
Jim Moore
James Morse
William Mulvihill
Nami Mun
Carol Muske-Dukes
Edward Mycue
Deirdre Neilen
W. Dale Nelson
Jean Nordhaus
Ontario Review Foundation
Daniel Orozco
Other Voices
Pamela Painter
Paris Review
Alan Michael Parker
Ellen Parker
Veronica Patterson

David Pearce
Robert Phillips
Donald Platt
Valerie Polichar
Pool
Jeffrey & Priscilla Potter
Marcia Preston
Eric Puchner
Tony Quagliano
Barbara Quinn
Belle Randall
Martha Rhodes
Nancy Richard
Stacey Richter
Katrina Roberts
Judith R. Robinson
Jessica Roeder
Martin Rosner
Kay Ryan
Sy Safransky
Brian Salchert
James Salter
Sherod Santos
R.A. Sasaki
Valerie Sayers
Alice Schell
Dennis & Loretta Schmitz
Helen Schulman
Philip Schultz
Shenandoah
Peggy Shinner
Vivian Shipley
Joan Silver
Skyline
John E. Smelcer
Raymond J. Smith
Philip St. Clair
Lorraine Standish
Maureen Stanton
Michael Steinberg
Jody Stewart
Barbara Stone
Storyteller Magazine

Bill & Pat Strachan
Julie Suk
Sun Publishing
Sweet Annie Press
Katherine Taylor
Pamela Taylor
Susan Terris
Marcelle Thiébaux
Robert Thomas
Andrew Tonkovich
Juanita Torrence-Thompson
William Trowbridge
Martin Tucker
Victoria Valentine
Tino Villanueva
William & Jeanne Wagner
BJ Ward
Susan Oard Warner
Rosanna Warren
Margareta Waterman
Michael Waters
Sandi Weinberg
Andrew Weinstein
Jason Wesco
West Meadow Press
Susan Wheeler
Dara Wier
Ellen Wilbur
Galen Williams
Marie Sheppard Williams
Eleanor Wilner
Irene K. Wilson
Steven Wingate
Sandra Wisenberg
David Wittman
Wings Press
Robert W. Witt
Margo Wizansky
Matt Yurdana
Christina Zawadiwsky
Sander Zulauf
ZYZZYVA

SUSTAINING MEMBERS

Anonymous
Agni
Carolyn Alessio
Dick Allen
Henry Alley
Jacob Appel
Philip & Marjorie Appleman
Linda Aschbrenner
Renée Ashley
Jim Barnes
Catherine Barnett

Judith Baumel
Ann Beattie
Beloit Poetry Journal
Madison Smartt Bell
Joe David Bellamy
Karen Bender
Laura & Pinckney Benedict
Linda Bierds
Kate Braverman
Rosellen Brown
Richard Burgin

581

CONTRIBUTORS' NOTES

DAN ALBERGOTTI is the author of *The Boatloads* (BOA, 2008), winner of the A. Poulin Jr. Poetry Prize.

KEITH ALTHAUS is the author of *Ladder of Hours* (Ausable Press, 2005) and *Rival Heavens* (Provincetown Arts, 1993). He lives in Truro, Massachusetts.

DAVID BAKER's latest collection of poetry is *Midwest Ecologue* (2005). He is poetry editor of *The Kenyon Review* and a past poetry co-editor of The Pushcart Prize.

JOHN BARTH's fiction has won the National Book Award, the PEN/Malamud Award, and the Lannan Foundation Lifetime Achievement Award. *The Development* is out soon from Houghton Mifflin and includes "Progressive Dinner."

CHARLES BAXTER's *Beyond Plot* is just out from Graywolf. He has written four novels and four story collections. He lives in Minneapolis.

MARVIN BELL is a past poetry co-editor of this series. His essays and poems have appeared in five previous Pushcart Prize volumes.

CIARAN BERRY's first collection of poems, *The Sphere of Birds*, has just been published in the United States and in Ireland. He teaches at New York University.

MARIE BERTINO is an assistant editor at *One Story*. Her fiction has appeared in *North American Review* and *Inkwell*.

BETSY BOYD has published stories in *Shenandoah* and *Verb*. She lives in Baltimore.

KRISTA BREMER is associate publisher of *The Sun*. Her essays have appeared in *Utne Reader*, *Brain, Child*, *Hip Mama* and other publications.

KURT BROWN founded the Aspen Writers' Conference. He is the author of six chapbooks and five poetry collections, including the just published *No Other Paradise*.

ELENA KARINA BYRNE is a visual artist, teacher, editor, poet and Poetry Consultant and Moderator for the *Los Angeles Times* Festival of Books. She has appeared in dozens of journals and her books include *The Flammable Bird* (Zoo Press) and *Masque*, forthcoming from Tupelo

AKHIM YUSEFF CABEY was born and raised in the Bronx. His work has appeared in *Obsidian II*, *Callaloo* and *The Sun*. He is working on a memoir about his childhood.

SHANNON CAIN is the Executive Director of Kore Press. Her stories have been featured in the *Massachusetts Review*, *New England Review* and elsewhere.

PETER CAMPION is the author of the poetry collection *Other People* (University of Chicago Press, 2005). He teaches at Washington College in Maryland.

KATIE CHASE holds an MFA from the Iowa Writers Workshop. "Man and Wife" is her first published story.

ETHAN COEN is the co-director of the movies *Fargo*, *No Country for Old Men* and others. He is the author of the story collection *Gates of Eden*.

JEREMY COLLINS lives in Knoxville, Tennessee and is at work on a memoir about the north Georgia mountains. "Shadow Boxing" is his first publication

JOHN D'AGATA is the author of *Halls of Fame*, *The Next American Essay* and the forthcoming *About A Mountain*.

WILLIAM DeBUYS is the author of six books, including *River of Traps* and, most recently, *The Walk*, from which "Errands in the Forest" is excerpted. He teaches at the College of Santa Fe.

ANTHONY DOERR is the author of three books, *The Shell Collector*, *About Grace*, and *Four Seasons in Rome*. The British magazine *Granta* named Doerr one of the 21 best young American novelists in 2007.

MATT DONOVAN teaches at the College of Santa Fe. He is the author of *Vellum* (Houghton Mifflin, 2007).

JACK DRISCOLL's novel *How Like An Angel* was recently published by the University of Michigan Press, which also re-released his 1987 short story collection *Wanting Only To Be Heard*. His novel *Lucky Man, Lucky Woman* was published by Pushcart Press.

CHRIS FORHAN is the author of *The Actual Moon, The Actual Stars* and *Forgive Us Our Happiness*, winner of the Bakeless Prize. He lives in Auburn, Alabama.

JOHN ROLFE GARDINER lives in Middleburg, Virginia. He has published eight novels and short story collections, most recently *The Magellan House* (Counterpoint).

LOUISE GLÜCK lives in Cambridge, Massachusetts. This is her ninth poem to win a Pushcart Prize. Her most recent book is *The Seven Ages* (Ecco). In 2003 she was named Poet Laureate of the United States.

SARAH GREEN teaches at Emerson and Wheaton colleges. Her poems have appeared in *Passages North*, *Redivider* and *Gettysburg Review*.

HEIDI HART's books include the memoir *Grace Notes* (University of Utah Press, 2004) and a chapbook, *In Ordinary Time*. She is in training to provide harp and vocal music for the dying.

BOB HICOK's most recent book of poetry is *This Clumsy Life* (University of Pittsburgh, 2007) winner of the Bobbit Prize from The Library of Congress. He was a finalist for the National Book Critics Circle Award.

PAUL HOSTOVSKY has published two prize-winning poetry collections. He lives in Medfield, Massachusetts.

LOUIS B. JONES is the author of the novels *Ordinary Money, Particles and Lucka* and *California's Over*. He lives in Nevada City, California.

BEENA KAMLANI's fiction has appear in *Ploughshares* and other journals. She lives in New York and is at work on her first novel.

MARY KINZIE's "The Water-Brooks" is the lead poem in her latest collection of poems and lyrical essays, *California Sorrow* (Knopf). She lives in Evanston, Illinois.

GERRY LaFEMINA is the author of five poetry collections, two books of prose poems and a forthcoming short story gathering, *Proofreading America*. He co-edits *Review Revue*.

JACK LIVINGS was a Stegner Fellow at Stanford. His work has also appeared in *Best American Short Stories* and *Tin House*.

KATHRYN MARIS lives in London where she teaches at Morley College and writes essays and reviews for British and American publications. Her poetry collection is *The Book of Jobs* (Four Way Books)

ANDREW McCUAIG teaches English in Madison, Wisconsin. His fiction has appeared in *Hunger Mountain* and the anthology *Flash Fiction Forward* (Norton, 2005).

BILL McKIBBEN's latest book is *The Bill McKibben Reader*, a collection of essays from various journals. He is the author of a dozen books—the first was *The End of Nature*.

JOSEPH MILLAR grew up in Western Pennsylvania, and after a stop on Philadelphia's Main Line, moved west to San Francisco where he worked for 25 years at a variety of jobs from telephone repairman to commercial fisherman. His first book, *Overtime*, was a finalist for the Oregon Book Award.

BRENDA MILLER has won five Pushcart Prizes. She lives in Bellingham, Washington, and is the author of the forthcoming *Blessing of the Animals* (Eastern Washington University Press).

SUSAN MITCHELL is a past poetry co-editor of this series. Her poems have appear in PPIX and XIII, and she is the author of three poetry collections—*Erotikon* (2000) *Rapture* (1992) and *The Water Inside The Water* (1983).

MICAELA MORRISSETTE is a senior editor at *Conjunctions*. Her reviews have appeared in *Jacket* and *Rain Taxi*. She lives in Brooklyn, New York.

AIMEE NEZHUKUMATATHIL is the author of the poetry collections *Drive-In-Volcano* and *Miracle Fruit*. She is co-winner of the Global Filipino Literary Award and a finalist for the Asian American Literary Award.

EDITH PEARLMAN has published three collections of her stories—*Vaquita* (1996), *Love Among the Greats* (2002) and *How to Fall* (2005). She lives in Brookline Massachusetts.

LYDIA PEELLE's short story collection, *Reasons and Advantages of Breathing*, will be published by Harper Perennial soon. She lives in Nashville.

SUZANNE RIVECCA is a former Wallace Stegner fellow. Her fiction has appeared in *Fence, StoryQuarterly, New England Review* and elsewhere.

MATTHEW ROHRER is the author of *Rise Up* (Wave Books, 2007) and *A Green Light* (Verse Press, 2004), short listed for the 2005 Griffin Poetry Prize. He lives in Brooklyn.

BRANDON R. SCHRAND is the author of *Enders Hotel: A Memoir* (Bison Books), a 2008 Barnes & Noble Discover Great New Writers selection. He lives in Moscow, Idaho.

FLOYD SKLOOT's most recent book is the memoir *The Wink of the Zenith: The Shaping of A Writer's Life* (University of Nebraska Press, 2008). He lives in Portland, Oregon.

TOM SLEIGH is the author of *Space Walk* (Houghton Mifflin, 2007) and a book of essays, *Interview With A Ghost* (Graywolf, 2006). He teaches at Hunter College.

BRUCE SMITH is the author of five books of poems. He teaches in the graduate writing program at Syracuse University.

HARRISON SOLOW, originally from California, now lives in Wales where she teaches writing at the University of Wales. She is currently writing a novel about Wales and a series of poems about Timothy Evans. She is a member of the Welsh Academi.

ELIZABETH SPIRES' sixth collection of poetry, *The Wave-Maker*, is just out from Norton. She is a past poetry co-editor of this series, and lives in Baltimore.

SUSAN STEWART's poem is her first appearance in the Pushcart Prize. She is the author of five books of poems, including *Columbarium* which won the 2003 National Book Critics Circle Award.

ELIZABETH TALLENT teaches at Stanford University. Her work appeared in *Pushcart Prize VI*.

WELLS TOWER's collection of short fiction will be published by Farrar, Straus & Giroux soon. His writing has appeared in *Harper's*, *Paris Review*, *A Public Space* and elsewhere. This is his second Pushcart Prize.

DEREK WALCOTT won the Nobel Prize in 1992. He previously appeared in *Pushcart Prize VI* and *VII*.

DON WATERS' story collection, *Desert Gothic*, won the 2007 Iowa Short Fiction Award. He lives in Santa Fe.

AFAA MICHAEL WEAVER's tenth poetry collection, *The Plum Flower Dance*, is just out from The Pitt Poetry Series. He was named the first elder of Cave Canem.

NAOMI J. WILLIAMS' stories have appeared in ZYZZYVA, *American Short Fiction*, *The Colorado Review* and elsewhere. She lives in Davis, California.

ELEANOR WILNER is a past poetry co-editor of this series. She has published six poetry collections including, most recently, *The Girl with Bees In Her Hair*.

CHRISTIAN WIMAN is editor of *Poetry*. His essay "The Limit" appeared in *Pushcart Prize XXVII*.

ROBERT WRIGLEY lives in Moscow, Idaho. His work has appeared in four previous editions of The Pushcart Prize.

INDEX

The following is a listing in alphabetical order by author's last name of works reprinted in the *Pushcart Prize* editions since 1976.

586

587

593

595

596

599

600

601

603

607

609

612

614

615

616

618